# Eleven Modern Short Novels

# Eleven Modern Short Novels

## Second Edition

EDITED AND WITH COMMENTARIES BY

## Leo Hamalian
## and Edmond L. Volpe

## G. P. Putnam's Sons

**NEW YORK**

**To Kay and Rose**

HAMALIAN AND VOLPE: Eleven Modern Short Novels.

Library of Congress Catalog
Card Number: 77–156879
SBN 399-30004-X
*Second Edition*
*Revised*

Twenty-first Impression

MANUFACTURED IN THE UNITED STATES OF AMERICA

# ACKNOWLEDGMENTS

We wish to express our gratitude to Bernard Garniez, New York University, and Richard Stang, Washington University, St. Louis, for advice and assistance and to Jim Roers, formerly of G. P. Putnam's Sons for patient, genial editorial guidance and to the many students and teachers whose suggestions contributed to the second edition. In addition, our thanks to the persons and publishers listed below for their kind cooperation in granting permission to reprint copyrighted material.

*The Death of Iván Ilých,* by Leo Tolstoy. Translated by Aylmer Maud and published by Oxford University Press. Used with permission of the Publisher.

*Heart of Darkness,* by Joseph Conrad, published by J. M. Dent & Sons, Ltd. Used with permission of the Publisher.

*The Beast in the Jungle,* from *The Better Sort,* by Henry James, copyright 1903 by Charles Scribner's Sons, 1931 by Henry James. Reprinted by permission of the Publisher.

*Abel Sanchez,* by Miguel de Unanumo y Jugo. Translated by Anthony Kerrigan and published by Henry Regnery Company. Used with permission of the Publishers.

*The Pastoral Symphony,* reprinted from *Two Symphonies,* by Andre Gide, by permission of Alfred A. Knopf, Inc., copyright 1931 by Alfred A. Knopf, Inc.

*Mario and the Magician,* reprinted from *Stories of Three Decades,* by Thomas Mann, by permission of Alfred A. Knopf, Inc., copyright 1931, 1936 by Alfred A. Knopf, Inc.

*Old Man,* by William Faulkner, copyright 1939 by Random House, Inc. Reprinted by permission of Random House, Inc.

*The Stranger,* by Albert Camus, used by permission of Alfred A. Knopf, Inc., copyright 1946 by Alfred A. Knopf, Inc. Circulation in Canada by permission of Hamish Hamilton Ltd., publishers of the British edition of *The Stranger.*

*The Man Who Lived Underground* by Richard Wright, first published in *Cross-section: A Collection of New American Writing,* edited by Edwin Seaver. Copyright © 1944 by L. B. Fischer Publishing Corporation, New York. Used by permission of Paul R. Reynolds, Inc.

*Agostino,* from *Five Novels* by Alberto Moravia, copyright 1955 by Valentino Bompiani, published by Farrar, Straus and Cudahy, Inc. and used with permission of the publishers. Circulation in Canada by permission of Martin Secker and Warburg, Ltd.

# PREFACE
# TO THE SECOND EDITION

IN our preface to the first edition of this anthology (*Ten Modern Short Novels*) in 1958, we predicted that basic surveys of literature would be replaced by courses that emphasized complete works instead of snippets and excerpts from many writers. It seems clear, thirteen years later, that this shift in emphasis has been no passing fashion. Teachers of literature have recognized that at the introductory level, exploration in depth of a literary work can make the experience of literature more memorable and probably more meaningful than a broad, superficial exposure.

A collection of short novels by modern masters, we noted, could provide an excellent means of introducing the student to the world of fiction. A student's interest in literature, many of us in teaching have come belatedly to realize, may more readily be awakened if his sensibility is exposed to works that dramatize the problems, the tensions, and the spiritual mood of his own world, and that the transition from the present to the past, rather than the reverse, is more easily made by the young. Also, the bringing together of short novels from a number of countries provided variety as well as substantial, complete literary works that could be subjected to careful and penetrating analysis of theme and form. Sometimes the short story is borne down by the weight of intensive analysis, and the novel may be too long and complex for such analysis by the neophyte. The inescapable characteristics of the short story are its brevity and unity (of time, place, mood), and through the combination of these two qualities, the full and immediate impact it can produce is unique in itself. In general, the novel, with its broader scope of inquiry, its panoply of people, and its more complex design of events, does not achieve such effects. But the novel may aspire to and attain harmonic and heroic dimensions that are not permitted to the short story, an essentially minute form of fiction. The short novel, an intermediate form (generally, from thirteen to forty thousand words), has the capacity to share the advantages of both forms, providing the just balance of concentration and dilution which gives this genre its very special flavor.

The new selections in this volume, we believe, meet the criteria we set for ourselves in 1958. In choosing the original ten short novels, we sought works of high literary quality that explored, sensitively and profoundly, the experience of modern men and women. Soon after the anthology was published, we began to discuss writers and works we might have included had we had more space. That discussion has extended over more than a decade. With frequent questionaires, we brought into our discussion literally hundreds of our colleagues throughout the country who had used the book in high schools, community colleges, or universities. We received countless suggestions for possible inclusion in a new edition. On the basis of our own preference and that of many advisors we were certain that Franz Kafka's *The Metamorphosis* and Richard Wright's *The Man Who Lived Underground* would enhance the collection. We had also concluded, after teaching the anthology many times, that Leonid Andreyev's *The Seven That Were Hanged*, was not as successful in the classroom as were the other selections, probably because its comparatively simple narrative structure could not effectively support its attempt to focus upon the responses of so many characters facing death. Thus *Ten Modern Short Novels* became *Eleven Modern Short Novels*.

Much has changed in our society since the late 1950's, when this book first began to be used in the classroom, but like all great literature, these short novels have enduring interest. We have not yet concluded that exploration of self, that quest for values and meaning which the protagonists of these short novels undertake.

Leo Hamalian
California Institute of the Arts

Edmond L. Volpe
The City College of the
City University of New York

# PREFACE
# TO THE FIRST EDITION

$S$URVEY courses in literature have in recent years undergone a quiet shift in emphasis. The reading of selected snippets from many writers, it has been recognized, encourages the student to learn many titles and the names of many authors without encouraging him to savor the full experience of a complete and extended work of art. An intensive examination of two or three great books has several advantages, and the course in concentrated reading has been nudging the cafeteria-style survey out of college curricula. But the intensive approach also has disadvantages: it is much too limited in scope; it does not offer the student a sufficient variety or range in his reading, and it limits the instructor's presentation of pertinent biographical and historical background, which most students want and need.

The shortcomings of both these approaches may be overcome by an anthology of the short novel. Its use in a literature course permits the combination of intensive reading with a more general survey. The short novel offers a more representative expression of the writer's ideas and his means of shaping them than selected passages could ever do. More complicated than the short story and more compact than the full-length novel, it is becoming increasingly popular with students and teachers of literature alike. Our own experiences with the problems of teaching general literature courses suggested this anthology.

The short novel has never been adequately defined and perhaps never will be, for each author adapts the form to his own purposes.

It might, with as much justification, be called the long story as the short novel. It has the singleness of theme, the limited number of characters, the quality of concentration that characterize the short story. But the modern novel, too, often has these same qualities. A list of characteristics of the short novel could be assembled, but only one of them would really serve to distinguish this form of fiction—length. And the length, too, of the form has never been set within precise limits. Some writers, for instance, describe a thirty thousand word tale as a short novel; others do not. We have, for this collection, established an approximate limit of fifteen thousand to forty thousand words for those works that we call short novels. We recognize that these limits are arbitrary. We are aware, too, that previous anthologists, despite attempts to define the genre, have also had in practice to depend upon length to justify their classification of a given piece of fiction as a short novel.

Our selections are based upon several considerations, the most important of which is literary excellence. We have included only those writers whose works we feel will be of as much literary interest to future readers as they are to present. Reading fiction, we believe, should be an esthetic adventure in self-discovery; it should provoke a new awareness of one's inner and outer world; and if it is to some a form of escape, it ought to be the kind of escape from which one returns enriched and changed.

Guided by these convictions, we have chosen novels that cover a wide range of human experience, including innocence, self-deception, sin, guilt, death, and redemption. The literature of seven countries, England, France, Germany, Italy, Russia, Spain, and the United States is represented by twentieth-century writers whose interests provide a cross-section of the experiences most significant to Western man, and perhaps to all men.

In our comments, which we have elected to place *after* each selection, we have tried to be informative without being overly interpretative. It has been our experience that a lengthy explication by an anthologist not only hampers the instructor but often prevents the student from making his own voyage of discovery. No biographical introduction nor critical explication should allow the reader to arrive at a destination without knowing the joy of traveling.

We have, therefore, tried only to stimulate interest in the writer and in the work by providing important and enlightening biographical information and sufficient critical analysis for an intelligent reading of the story. And we have sought, whenever possible, to reveal the actual experience in the life of the author which stimulated the creative impulse and which he translated into art, because we believe that an appreciation of literature often starts with the recognition that literature *is* life—comprehended, interpreted, artistically rendered.

To the end of each introduction we have appended a short bibliography of criticism and biography, which we hope will lead the student to further reading about the writer and his work.

Whatever we have done in this anthology we have done with the idea that the book is for students rather than for teachers—for we believe that once a student's interest is stimulated by good reading under the guidance of a good teacher, he will eventually develop a devotion to the best in literature.

Leo Hamalian and Edmond L. Volpe
City College of New York

# CONTENTS

# THE DEATH OF IVÁN ILÝCH

## BY LEO TOLSTOY

First published, 1886

# THE DEATH OF IVÁN ILÝCH

## CHAPTER I

**D**URING an interval in the Melvínski trial in the large building of the Law Courts the members and public prosecutor met in Iván Egórovich Shébek's private room, where the conversation turned on the celebrated Krasóvski case. Fëdor Vasílievich warmly maintained that it was not subject to their jurisdiction, Iván Egóro-vich maintained the contrary, while Peter Ivánovich, not having entered into the discussion at the start, took no part in it but looked through the *Gazette* which had just been handed in.

"Gentlemen," he said, "Iván Ilých has died!"

"You don't say so!"

"Here, read it yourself," replied Peter Ivánovich, handing Fëdor Vasílievich the paper still damp from the press. Surrounded by a black border were the words: "Praskóvya Fëdorovna Goloviná, with profound sorrow, informs relatives and friends of the demise of her beloved husband Iván Ilých Golovín, Member of the Court of Justice, which occurred on February the 4th of this year 1882. The funeral will take place on Friday at one o'clock in the afternoon."

Iván Ilých had been a colleague of the gentlemen present and was liked by them all. He had been ill for some weeks with an illness said to be incurable. His post had been kept open for him, but there had been conjectures that in case of his death Alexéev might receive his appointment, and that either Vínnikov or Shtábel would succeed Alexéev. So on receiving the news of Iván Ilých's death the first thought of each of the gentlemen in that private room was of the changes and promotions it might occasion among themselves or their acquaintances.

"I shall be sure to get Shtábel's place or Vínnikov's," thought Fëdor Vasílievich. "I was promised that long ago, and the promotion means an extra eight hundred rubles a year for me besides the allowance."

"Now I must apply for my brother-in-law's transfer from Kalúga," thought Peter Ivánovich. "My wife will be very glad, and then she won't be able to say that I never do anything for her relations."

"I thought he would never leave his bed again," said Peter Ivánovich aloud. "It's very sad."

"But what really was the matter with him?"

"The doctors couldn't say—at least they could, but each of them said something different. When last I saw him I thought he was getting better."

"And I haven't been to see him since the holidays. I always meant to go."

"Had he any property?"

"I think his wife had a little—but something quite trifling."

"We shall have to go to see her, but they live so terribly far away."

"Far away from you, you mean. Everything's far away from your place."

"You see, he never can forgive my living on the other side of the river," said Peter Ivánovich, smiling at Shébek. Then, still talking of the distances between different parts of the city, they returned to the Court.

Besides considerations as to the possible transfers and promotions likely to result from Iván Ilých's death, the mere fact of the death of a near acquaintance aroused, as usual, in all who heard of it the complacent feeling that "it is he who is dead and not I."

Each one thought or felt, "Well, he's dead but I'm alive!" But the more intimate of Iván Ilých's acquaintances, his so-called friends, could not help thinking also that they would now have to fulfill the very tiresome demands of propriety by attending the funeral service and paying a visit of condolence to the widow.

Fëdor Vasílievich and Peter Ivánovich had been his nearest acquaintances. Peter Ivánovich had studied law with Iván Ilých and had considered himself to be under obligations to him.

Having told his wife at dinner-time of Iván Ilých's death, and of his conjecture that it might be possible to get her brother transferred to their circuit, Peter Ivánovich sacrificed his usual nap, put on his evening clothes, and drove to Iván Ilých's house.

At the entrance stood a carriage and two cabs. Leaning against the wall in the hall downstairs near the cloak-stand was a coffin-lid covered with cloth of gold, ornamented with gold cord and tassels, that had been polished up with metal powder. Two ladies in black were taking off their fur cloaks. Peter Ivánovich recognized one of them as Iván Ilých's sister, but the other was a stranger to him. His colleague Schwartz was just coming downstairs, but on seeing Peter Ivánovich enter he stopped and winked at him, as if to say: "Iván Ilých has made a mess of things—not like you and me."

Schwartz's face with his Piccadilly whiskers, and his slim figure in evening dress, had as usual an air of elegant solemnity which contrasted with the playfulness of his character and had a special piquancy here, or so it seemed to Peter Ivánovich.

Peter Ivánovich allowed the ladies to precede him and slowly followed them upstairs. Schwartz did not come down but remained where he was, and Peter Ivánovich understood that he wanted to arrange where they should play bridge that evening. The ladies went upstairs to the widow's room, and Schwartz with seriously compressed lips but a playful look in his eyes, indicated by a twist of his eyebrows the room to the right where the body lay.

Peter Ivánovich, like everyone else on such occasions, entered feeling uncertain what he would have to do. All he knew was that at such times it is always safe to cross oneself. But he was not quite sure whether one should make obeisances while doing so. He therefore adopted a middle course. On entering the room he began crossing himself and made a slight movement resembling a bow. At the same time, as far as the motion of his head and arm allowed, he surveyed the room. Two young men—apparently nephews, one of whom was a high-school pupil—were leaving the room, crossing themselves as they did so. An old woman was standing motionless, and a lady with strangely arched eyebrows was saying something to her in a whisper. A vigorous, resolute Church Reader, in a frock-coat, was reading something in a loud voice with an expression that precluded any contradiction. The butler's assistant, Gerásim, stepping lightly in front of Peter Ivánovich, was strewing something on the floor. Noticing this, Peter Ivánovich was immediately aware of a faint odour of a decomposing body.

The last time he had called on Iván Ilých, Peter Ivánovich had seen Gerásim in the study. Iván Ilých had been particularly fond of him and he was performing the duty of a sick nurse.

Peter Ivánovich continued to make the sign of the cross slightly inclining his head in an intermediate direction between the coffin, the Reader, and the icons on the table in a corner of the room. Afterwards, when it seemed to him that this movement of his arm in crossing himself had gone on too long, he stopped and began to look at the corpse.

The dead man lay, as dead men always lie, in a specially heavy way, his rigid limbs sunk in the soft cushions of the coffin, with the head forever bowed on the pillow. His yellow waxen brow with bald patches over his sunken temples was thrust up in the way peculiar to the dead, the protruding nose seeming to press on the upper lip. He was much changed and had grown even thinner since Peter Ivánovich had last seen him, but, as is always the case with the dead, his face was handsomer and above all more dignified than when he was alive. The expression on the face said that what was necessary had been accomplished, and accomplished rightly. Besides this there was in that expression a reproach and a warning to the living. This warning seemed to Peter Ivánovich out of place, or at least not applicable to him. He felt a certain discomfort and so he hurriedly crossed himself once more and turned and went out of the door—too hurriedly and too regardless of propriety, as he himself was aware.

Schwartz was waiting for him in the adjoining room with legs spread wide apart and both hands toying with his top-hat behind his back. The mere sight of that playful, well-groomed, and elegant figure refreshed Peter Ivánovich. He felt that Schwartz was above all these happenings and would not surrender to any depressing influences. His very look said that this incident of a church service for Iván Ilých could not be a sufficient reason for infringing the order of the session—in other words, that it would certainly not prevent his unwrapping a new pack of cards and shuffling them that evening while a footman placed four fresh candles on the table: in fact, there was no reason for supposing that this incident would hinder their spending the evening agreeably. Indeed he said this in a whisper as Peter Ivánovich passed him, proposing that they should meet for a game at Fëdor Vasílievich's. But apparently Peter Ivánovich was not destined to play bridge that evening. Praskóvya Fëdorovna (a short, fat woman who despite all efforts to the contrary had continued to broaden steadily from her shoulders downwards and who had the same extraordinarily arched eyebrows as the lady who had been standing by the coffin), dressed all in black, her head covered with lace, came out of her own room with some other ladies, conducted them to the room where the dead body lay, and said: "The service will begin immediately. Please go in."

Schwartz, making an indefinite bow, stood still, evidently neither accepting nor declining this invitation. Praskóvya Fëdorovna recognizing Peter Ivánovich, sighed, went close up to him, took his hand, and said: "I know you were a true friend to Iván Ilých . . ." and looked at him awaiting some suitable response. And Peter Ivánovich knew that, just as it had been the right thing to cross himself in that room, so what he had to do here was to press her hand, sigh, and say, "Believe me . . ." So he did all this and as he did it felt that the desired result had been achieved: that both he and she were touched.

"Come with me. I want to speak to you before it begins," said the widow. "Give me your arm."

Peter Ivánovich gave her his arm and they went to the inner rooms, passing Schwartz who winked at Peter Ivánovich compassionately. "That does for our bridge! Don't object if we find another player. Perhaps you can cut in when you do escape," said his playful look.

Peter Ivánovich sighed still more deeply and despondently, and Praskóvya Fëdorovna pressed his arm gratefully. When they reached the drawing-room, upholstered in pink cretonne and lighted by a dim lamp, they sat down at the table—she on a sofa and Peter Ivánovich on a low pouffe, the springs of which yielded spasmodically under his weight. Praskóvya Fëdorovna had been on the point of warning him to take another seat, but felt that such a warning was out of keeping with her present condition and so changed her mind. As he sat down on the pouffe Peter Ivánovich recalled how Iván Ilých had arranged this room and had consulted him regarding this pink cretonne with green leaves. The whole room was full of furniture and knick-knacks, and on her way to the sofa the lace of the widow's black shawl caught on the carved edge of the table. Peter Ivánovich rose to detach it, and the springs of the pouffe, relieved of his weight, rose also and gave him a push. The widow began detaching her shawl herself, and Peter Ivánovich again sat down, suppressing the rebellious springs of the pouffe under him. But the widow had not quite freed herself and Peter Ivánovich got up again, and again the pouffe rebelled and even creaked. When this was all over she took out a clean cambric handkerchief and began to weep. The episode with the shawl and the struggle with the pouffe had cooled Peter Ivánovich's emotions and he sat there with a sullen look on his face. This awkward situation was interrupted by Sokolóv, Iván Ilých's butler, who came to report that the plot in the cemetery that Praskóvya Fëdorovna had chosen would cost two hundred rubles. She stopped weeping and, looking at Peter Ivánovich with the air of a victim, remarked in French that it was very hard for her. Peter Ivánovich made a silent gesture signifying his full conviction that it must indeed be so.

"Please smoke," she said in a magnanimous yet crushed voice, and turned to discuss with Sokolóv the price of the plot for the grave.

Peter Ivánovich while lighting his cigarette heard her inquiring very circumstantially into the price of different plots in the cemetery and finally decide which she would take. When that was done she gave instructions about engaging the choir. Sokolóv then left the room.

"I look after everything myself," she told Peter Ivánovich, shifting the albums that lay on the table; and noticing that the table was endangered by his cigarette-ash, she immediately passed him an ashtray, saying as she did so: "I consider it an affectation to say that my grief prevents my attending to practical affairs. On the contrary, if anything can—I won't say console me, but—distract me, it is seeing to everything concerning him." She again took out her handkerchief as if preparing to cry, but suddenly, as if mastering her feeling, she shook herself and began to speak calmly. "But there is something I want to talk to you about."

Peter Ivánovich bowed, keeping control of the springs of the pouffe, which immediately began quivering under him.

"He suffered terribly the last few days."

"Did he?" said Peter Ivánovich.

"Oh, terribly! He screamed unceasingly, not for minutes but for hours. For the last three days he screamed incessantly. It was unendurable. I cannot understand how I bore it; you could hear him three rooms off. Oh, what I have suffered!"

"Is it possible that he was conscious all that time?" asked Peter Ivánovich.

"Yes," she whispered. "To the last moment. He took leave of us a quarter of an hour before he died, and asked us to take Volódya away."

The thought of the sufferings of this man he had known so intimately, first as a merry little boy, then as a school-mate, and later as a grown-up colleague, suddenly struck Peter Ivánovich with horror, despite an unpleasant consciousness of his own and this woman's dissimulation. He again saw that brow, and that nose pressing down on the lip, and felt afraid for himself.

"Three days of frightful suffering and then death! Why, that might suddenly, at any time, happen to me," he thought, and for a moment felt terrified. But—he did not himself know how—the customary reflection at once occurred to him that this had happened to Iván Ilých and not to him, and that it should not and could not happen to him, and that to think that it could would be yielding to depression which he ought not to do, as Schwartz's expression plainly showed. After which reflection Peter Ivánovich felt reassured, and began to ask with interest about the details of Iván Ilých's death, as though death was an accident natural to Iván Ilých but certainly not to himself.

After many details of the really dreadful physical sufferings Iván Ilých had endured (which details he learnt only from the effect those sufferings had produced on Praskóvya Fëdorovna's nerves) the widow apparently found it necessary to get to business.

"Oh, Peter Ivánovich, how hard it is! How terribly, terribly hard!" and she again began to weep.

Peter Ivánovich sighed and waited for her to finish blowing her nose. When she had done so he said, "Believe me . . ." and she again began talking and brought out what was evidently her chief concern with him—namely, to question him as to how she could obtain a grant of money from the government on the occasion of her husband's death. She made it appear that she was asking Peter Ivánovich's advice about her pension, but he soon saw that she already knew about that to the minutest detail, more even than he did himself. She knew how much could be got out of the government in consequence of her husband's death, but wanted to find out whether she could not possibly extract something more. Peter Ivánovich tried to think of some means of doing so, but after reflecting for a while and, out of propriety, condemning the government for its niggardliness, he said he thought that nothing more could be got. Then she sighed and evidently began to devise means of getting rid of her visitor. Noticing this, he put out his cigarette, rose, pressed her hand, and went out into the anteroom.

In the dining-room where the clock stood that Iván Ilých had liked so much and had bought at an antique shop, Peter Ivánovich met a priest and a few acquaintances who had come to attend the service, and he recognized Iván Ilých's daughter, a handsome young woman. She was in black and her slim figure appeared slimmer than ever. She had a gloomy, determined, almost angry expression, and bowed to Peter Ivánovich as though he were in some way to blame. Behind her, with the same offended look, stood a wealthy young man, an examining magistrate, whom Peter Ivánovich also knew and who was her fiancé, as he had heard. He bowed mournfully to them and was about to pass into the death-chamber, when from under the stairs appeared the figure of Iván Ilých's schoolboy son, who was extremely like his father. He seemed a little Iván Ilých, such as Peter Ivánovich remembered when they studied law together. His tear-stained eyes had in them the look that is seen in the eyes of boys of thirteen or fourteen who are not pure-minded. When he saw Peter Ivánovich he scowled morosely and shame-facedly. Peter Ivánovich nodded to him and entered the death-chamber. The service began: candles, groans, incense, tears, and sobs. Peter Ivánovich stood looking gloomily down at his feet. He did not look once at the dead man, did not yield to any depressing influence, and was one of the first to leave the room. There was no one in the anteroom, but Gerásim darted out of the dead man's room, rummaged with his strong hands among the fur coats to find Peter Ivánovich's and helped him on with it.

"Well, friend Gerásim," said Peter Ivánovich, so as to say something. "It's a sad affair, isn't it?"

"It's God's will. We shall all come to it some day," said Gerásim, displaying his teeth—the even, white teeth of a healthy peasant—and, like a man in the thick of urgent work, he briskly opened the front door, called the coachman, helped Peter Ivánovich into the sledge, and sprang back to the porch as if in readiness for what he had to do next.

Peter Ivánovich found the fresh air particularly pleasant after the smell of incense, the dead body, and carbolic acid.

"Where to, sir?" asked the coachman.

"It's not too late even now. . . . I'll call round on Fëdor Vasílievich."

He accordingly drove there and found them just finishing the first rubber, so that it was quite convenient for him to cut in.

## CHAPTER II

Iván Ilých's life had been most simple and most ordinary and therefore most terrible.

He had been a member of the Court of Justice, and died at the age of forty-five. His father had been an official who after serving in various ministries and departments in Petersburg had made the sort of career which brings men to positions from which by reason of their long service they cannot be dismissed, though they are obviously unfit to hold any responsible position, and for whom therefore posts are specially created, which though fictitious carry salaries of from six to ten thousand rubles that are not fictitious, and in receipt of which they live on to a great age.

Such was the Privy Councillor and superfluous member of various superfluous institutions, Ilyá Epímovich Golovín.

He had three sons, of whom Iván Ilých was the second. The eldest son was following in his father's footsteps only in another department, and was already approaching that stage in the service at which a similar sinecure would be reached. The third son was a failure. He had ruined his prospects in a number of positions and was now serving in the railway department. His father and brothers, and still more their wives, not merely disliked meeting him, but avoided remembering his existence unless compelled to do so. His sister had married Baron Greff, a Petersburg official of her father's type. Iván Ilých was *le phénix de la famille* as people said. He was neither as cold and formal as his elder brother nor as wild as the younger, but was a happy mean between them—an intelligent, polished, lively and agreeable man. He had studied with his younger brother at the School of Law, but the latter had failed to complete the course and was expelled when he was in the fifth class. Iván Ilých finished the course well. Even when he was at the School of Law he was just what he remained for the rest of his life: a capable, cheerful, good-natured, and sociable man, though strict in the fulfilment of what he considered to be his duty: and he considered his duty to be what was so considered by those in authority. Neither as a boy nor as a man was he a toady, but from early youth was by nature attracted to people of high station as a fly is drawn to the light, assimilating their ways and views of life and establishing friendly relations with them. All the enthusiasms of childhood and youth passed without leaving much trace on him; he succumbed to sensuality, to vanity, and latterly among the highest classes to liberalism, but always within limits which his instinct unfailingly indicated to him as correct.

At school he had done things which had formerly seemed to him very horrid and made him feel disgusted with himself when he did them; but when later on he saw that such actions were done by people of good position and that they did not regard them as wrong, he was able not exactly to regard them as right, but to forget about them entirely or not be at all troubled at remembering them.

Having graduated from the School of Law and qualified for the tenth rank of the civil service, and having received money from his father for his equipment, Iván Ilých ordered himself clothes at Scharmer's, the fashionable tailor, hung a medallion inscribed *respice finen* on his watch-chain, took leave of his professor and the prince who was patron of the school, had a farewell dinner with his comrades at Donon's first-class restaurant, and with his new and fashionable portmanteau, linen, clothes, shaving and other toilet appliances, and a travelling rug, all purchased at the best shops, he set off for one of the provinces where, through his father's influence, he had been attached to the Governor as an official for special service.

In the province Iván Ilých soon arranged as easy and agreeable a position for himself as he had had at the School of Law. He performed his official tasks, made his career, and at the same time amused himself pleasantly and decorously. Occasionally he paid official visits to country districts, where he behaved with dignity both to his superiors and inferiors, and performed the duties entrusted to him, which related chiefly to the sectarians, with an exactness and incorruptible honesty of which he could not but feel proud.

In official matters, despite his youth and taste for frivolous gaiety, he was exceedingly reserved, punctilious, and even severe; but in society he was often amusing and witty, and always good-natured, correct in his manner, and *bon enfant*, as the governor and his wife—with whom he was like one of the family—used to say of him.

In the provinces he had an affair with a lady who made advances to the elegant young lawyer, and there was also a milliner; and there were carousals with aides-de-camp who visited the district, and after-supper visits to a certain outlying street of doubtful reputation; and there was too some obsequiousness to his chief and even to his chief's wife, but all this was done with such a tone of good breeding that no hard names could be applied to it. It all came under the heading of the French saying: "*Il faut que jeunesse se passe.*" [1] It was all done with clean hands, in clean linen, with French phrases, and above all among people of the best society and consequently with the approval of people of rank.

So Iván Ilých served for five years and then came a change in his official life. The new and reformed judicial institutions were introduced, and new men were needed. Iván Ilých became such a new man. He was offered the post of Examining Magistrate, and he accepted it though the post was in another province and obliged him to give up the connexions he had formed and to make new ones. His friends met to give him a send-off; they had a group-photograph

[1] Youth must have its fling.

taken and presented him with a silver cigarette-case, and he set off to his new post.

As examining magistrate Iván Ilých was just as *comme il faut* and decorous a man, inspiring general respect and capable of separating his official duties from his private life, as he had been when acting as an official on special service. His duties now as examining magistrate were far more interesting and attractive than before. In his former position it had been pleasant to wear an undress uniform made by Scharmer, and to pass through the crowd of petitioners and officials who were timorously awaiting an audience with the governor, and who envied him as with free and easy gait he went straight into his chief's private room to have a cup of tea and a cigarette with him. But not many people had then been directly dependent on him—only police officials and the sectarians when he went on special missions—and he liked to treat them politely, almost as comrades, as if he were letting them feel that he who had the power to crush them was treating them in this simple, friendly way. There were then but few such people. But now, as an examining magistrate, Iván Ilých felt that everyone without exception, even the most important and self-satisfied, was in his power, and that he need only write a few words on a sheet of paper with a certain heading, and this or that important, self-satisfied person would be brought before him in the role of an accused person or a witness, and if he did not choose to allow him to sit down, would have to stand before him and answer his questions. Iván Ilých never abused his power; he tried on the contrary to soften its expression, but the consciousness of it and of the possibility of softening its effect, supplied the chief interest and attraction of his office. In his work itself, especially in his examinations, he very soon acquired a method of eliminating all considerations irrelevant to the legal aspect of the case, and reducing even the most complicated case to a form in which it would be presented on paper only in its externals, completely excluding his personal opinion of the matter, while above all observing every prescribed formality. The work was new and Iván Ilých was one of the first men to apply the new Code of 1864.[2]

On taking up the post of examining magistrate in a new town, he made new acquaintances and connexions, placed himself on a new footing, and assumed a somewhat different tone. He took up an attitude of rather dignified aloofness towards the provincial authori-

[2] The emancipation of the serfs in 1861 was followed by a thorough all-round reform of judicial proceedings.—A.M.

ties, but picked out the best circle of legal gentlemen and wealthy gentry living in the town and assumed a tone of slight dissatisfaction with the government, of moderate liberalism, and of enlightened citizenship. At the same time, without at all altering the elegance of his toilet, he ceased shaving his chin and allowed his beard to grow as it pleased.

Iván Ilých settled down very pleasantly in this new town. The society there, which inclined towards opposition to the Governor, was friendly, his salary was larger, and he began to play *vint* [a form of bridge], which he found added not a little to the pleasure of life, for he had a capacity for cards, played good-humouredly, and calculated rapidly and astutely, so that he usually won.

After living there for two years he met his future wife, Praskóvya Fëdorovna Míkhel, who was the most attractive, clever, and brilliant girl of the set in which he moved, and among other amusements and relaxations from his labours as examining magistrate, Iván Ilých established light and playful relations with her.

While he had been an official on special service he had been accustomed to dance, but now as an examining magistrate it was exceptional for him to do so. If he danced now, he did it as if to show that though he served under the reformed order of things, and had reached the fifth official rank, yet when it came to dancing he could do it better than most people. So at the end of an evening he sometimes danced with Praskóvya Fëdorovna, and it was chiefly during these dances that he captivated her. She fell in love with him. Iván Ilých had at first no definite intention of marrying, but when the girl fell in love with him he said to himself: "Really, why shouldn't I marry?"

Praskóvya Fëdorovna came of a good family, was not bad looking, and had some little property. Iván Ilých might have aspired to a more brilliant match, but even this was good. He had his salary, and she, he hoped, would have an equal income. She was well connected, and was a sweet, pretty, and thoroughly correct young woman. To say that Iván Ilých married because he fell in love with Praskóvya Fëdorovna and found that she sympathized with his views of life would be as incorrect as to say that he married because his social circle approved of the match. He was swayed by both these considerations: the marriage gave him personal satisfaction, and at the same time it was considered the right thing by the most highly placed of his associates.

So Iván Ilých got married.

The preparations for marriage and the beginning of married life, with its conjugal caresses, the new furniture, new crockery, and new linen, were very pleasant until his wife became pregnant—so that Iván Ilých had begun to think that marriage would not impair the easy, agreeable, gay and always decorous character of his life, approved of by society and regarded by himself as natural, but would even improve it. But from the first months of his wife's pregnancy, something new, unpleasant, depressing, and unseemly, and from which there was no way of escape, unexpectedly showed itself.

His wife, without any reason—*de gaieté de cœur* as Iván Ilých expressed it to himself—began to disturb the pleasure and propriety of their life. She began to be jealous without any cause, expected him to devote his whole attention to her, found fault with everything, and made coarse and ill-mannered scenes.

At first Iván Ilých hoped to escape from the unpleasantness of this state of affairs by the same easy and decorous relation to life that had served him heretofore: he tried to ignore his wife's disagreeable moods, continued to live in his usual easy and pleasant way, invited friends to his house for a game of cards, and also tried going out to his club or spending his evenings with friends. But one day his wife began upbraiding him so vigorously, using such coarse words, and continued to abuse him every time he did not fulfil her demands, so resolutely and with such evident determination not to give way till he submitted—that is, till he stayed at home and was bored just as she was—that he became alarmed. He now realized that matrimony —at any rate with Praskóvya Fëdorovna—was not always conducive to the pleasures and amenities of life but on the contrary often infringed both comfort and propriety, and that he must therefore entrench himself against such infringement. And Iván Ilých began to seek for means of doing so. His official duties were the one thing that imposed upon Praskóvya Fëdorovna, and by means of his official work and the duties attached to it he began struggling with his wife to secure his own independence.

With the birth of their child, the attempts to feed it and the various failures in doing so, and with the real and imaginary illnesses of mother and child, in which Iván Ilých's sympathy was demanded but about which he understood nothing, the need of securing for himself an existence outside his family life became still more imperative.

As his wife grew more irritable and exacting and Iván Ilých transferred the centre of gravity of his life more and more to his official work, so did he grow to like his work better and became more ambitious than before.

Very soon, within a year of his wedding, Iván Ilých had realized that marriage, though it may add some comforts to life, is in fact a very intricate and difficult affair towards which in order to perform one's duty, that is, to lead a decorous life approved of by society, one must adopt a definite attitude just as towards one's official duties.

And Iván Ilých evolved such an attitude towards married life. He only required of it those conveniences—dinner at home, housewife, and bed—which it could give him, and above all that propriety of external forms required by public opinion. For the rest he looked for light-hearted pleasure and propriety, and was very thankful when he found them, but if he met with antagonism and querulousness he at once retired into his separate fenced-off world of official duties, where he found satisfaction.

Iván Ilých was esteemed a good official, and after three years was made Assistant Public Prosecutor. His new duties, their importance, the possibility of indicting and imprisoning anyone he chose, the publicity his speeches received, and the success he had in all these things, made his work still more attractive.

More children came. His wife became more and more querulous and ill-tempered, but the attitude Iván Ilých had adopted towards his home life rendered him almost impervious to her grumbling.

After seven years' service in that town he was transferred to another province as Public Prosecutor. They moved, but were short of money and his wife did not like the place they moved to. Though the salary was higher the cost of living was greater, besides which two of their children died and family life became still more unpleasant for him.

Praskóvya Fëdorovna blamed her husband for every inconvenience they encountered in their new home. Most of the conversations between husband and wife, especially as to the children's education, led to topics which recalled former disputes, and those disputes were apt to flare up again at any moment. There remained only those rare periods of amorousness which still came to them at times but did not last long. These were islets at which they anchored for a while and then again set out upon that ocean of veiled hostility which showed itself in their aloofness from one another. This aloofness might have grieved Iván Ilých had he considered that it ought not to exist, but he now regarded the position as normal, and even made it the goal at which he aimed in family life. His aim was to free himself more and more from those unpleasantnesses and to give them a semblance of harmlessness and propriety. He attained this by spending less and less time with his family, and when obliged to be at home he tried to safeguard his position by the presence of outsiders. The chief thing however was that he had his official duties. The whole interest of his life now centred in the official world and that interest absorbed him. The consciousness of his power, being able to ruin anybody he wished to ruin, the importance, even the external dignity of his entry into court, or meetings with his subordinates, his success with superiors and inferiors, and above all his masterly handling of cases, of which he was conscious—all this gave him pleasure and filled his life, together with chats with his colleagues, dinners, and bridge. So that on the whole Iván Ilých's life continued to flow as he considered it should do—pleasantly and properly.

So things continued for another seven years. His eldest daughter was already sixteen, another child had died, and only one son was left, a schoolboy and a subject of dissension. Iván Ilých wanted to put him in the School of Law, but to spite him Praskóvya Fëdorovna entered him at the High School. The daughter had been educated at home and had turned out well: the boy did not learn badly either.

## CHAPTER III

So Iván Ilých lived for seventeen years after his marriage. He was already a Public Prosecutor of long standing, and had declined several proposed transfers while awaiting a more desirable post, when an unanticipated and unpleasant occurrence quite upset the peaceful course of his life. He was expecting to be offered the post of presiding judge in a University town, but Happe somehow came to the front and obtained the appointment instead. Iván Ilých became irritable, reproached Happe, and quarrelled both with him and with his immediate superiors—who became colder to him and again passed him over when other appointments were made.

This was in 1880, the hardest year of Iván Ilých's life. It was then that it became evident on the one hand that his salary was insufficient for them to live on, and on the other that he had been forgotten, and not only this, but that what was for him the greatest and most cruel

injustice appeared to others a quite ordinary occurrence. Even his
father did not consider it his duty to help him. Iván Ilých felt himself abandoned by everyone, and that they regarded his position with
a salary of 3,500 rubles [about $2,000] as quite normal and even
fortunate. He alone knew that with the consciousness of the injustices done him, with his wife's incessant nagging, and with the
debts he had contracted by living beyond his means, his position was
far from normal.

In order to save money that summer he obtained leave of absence
and went with his wife to live in the country at her brother's place.

In the country, without his work, he experienced *ennui* for the
first time in his life, and not only *ennui* but intolerable depression,
and he decided that it was impossible to go on living like that, and
that it was necessary to take energetic measures.

Having passed a sleepless night pacing up and down the veranda,
he decided to go to Petersburg and bestir himself, in order to punish
those who had failed to appreciate him and to get transferred to
another ministry.

Next day, despite many protests from his wife and her brother, he
started for Petersburg with the sole object of obtaining a post with a
salary of five thousand rubles a year. He was no longer bent on any
particular department, or tendency, or kind of activity. All he now
wanted was an appointment to another post with a salary of five
thousand rubles, either in the administration, in the banks, with the
railways, in one of the Empress Márya's Institutions, or even in the
customs—but it had to carry with it a salary of five thousand rubles
and be in a ministry other than that in which they had failed to
appreciate him.

And this quest of Iván Ilých's was crowned with remarkable and
unexpected success. At Kursk an acquaintance of his, F. I. Ilýin, got
into the first-class carriage, sat down beside Iván Ilých, and told him
of a telegram just received by the Governor of Kursk announcing that
a change was about to take place in the ministry: Peter Ivánovich
was to be superseded by Iván Semënovich.

The proposed change, apart from its significance for Russia, had a
special significance for Iván Ilých, because by bringing forward a new
man, Peter Petróvich, and consequently his friend Zachár Ivánovich,
it was highly favourable for Iván Ilých, since Zachár Ivánovich was a
friend and colleague of his.

In Moscow this news was confirmed, and on reaching Petersburg

Iván Ilých found Zachár Ivánovich and received a definite promise of an appointment in his former Department of Justice.

A week later he telegraphed to his wife: "Zachár in Miller's place. I shall receive appointment on presentation of report."

Thanks to this change of personnel, Iván Ilých had unexpectedly obtained an appointment in his former ministry which placed him two stages above his former colleagues besides giving him five thousand rubles salary and three thousand five hundred rubles for expenses connected with his removal. All his ill humour towards his former enemies and the whole department vanished, and Iván Ilých was completely happy.

He returned to the country more cheerful and contented than he had been for a long time. Praskóvya Fëdorovna also cheered up and a truce was arranged between them. Iván Ilých told of how he had been fêted by everybody in Petersburg, how all those who had been his enemies were put to shame and now fawned on him, how envious they were of his appointment, and how much everybody in Petersburg had liked him.

Praskóvya Fëdorovna listened to all this and appeared to believe it. She did not contradict anything, but only made plans for their life in the town to which they were going. Iván Ilých saw with delight that these plans were his plans, that he and his wife agreed, and that, after a stumble, his life was regaining its due and natural character of pleasant lightheartedness and decorum.

Iván Ilých had come back for a short time only, for he had to take up his new duties on the 10th of September. Moreover, he needed time to settle into the new place, to move all his belongings from the province, and to buy and order many additional things: in a word, to make such arrangements as he had resolved on, which were almost exactly what Praskóvya Fëdorovna too had decided on.

Now that everything had happened so fortunately, and that he and his wife were at one in their aims and moreover saw so little of one another, they got on together better than they had done since the first years of marriage. Iván Ilých had thought of taking his family away with him at once, but the insistence of his wife's brother and her sister-in-law, who had suddenly become particularly amiable and friendly to him and his family, induced him to depart alone.

So he departed, and the cheerful state of mind induced by his success and by the harmony between his wife and himself, the one intensifying the other, did not leave him. He found a delightful house, just the thing both he and his wife had dreamt of. Spacious, lofty reception rooms in the old style, a convenient and dignified study, rooms for his wife and daughter, a study for his son—it might have been specially built for them. Iván Ilých himself superintended the arrangements, chose the wall-papers, supplemented the furniture (preferably with antiques which he considered particularly *comme il faut*), and supervised the upholstering. Everything progressed and progressed and approached the ideal he had set himself: even when things were only half completed they exceeded his expectations. He saw what a refined and elegant character, free from vulgarity, it would all have when it was ready. On falling asleep he pictured to himself how the reception-room would look. Looking at the yet unfinished drawing-room he could see the fireplace, the screen, the what-not, the little chairs dotted here and there, the dishes and plates on the walls, and the bronzes, as they would be when everything was in place. He was pleased by the thought of how his wife and daughter, who shared his taste in this matter, would be impressed by it. They were certainly not expecting as much. He had been particularly successful in finding, and buying cheaply, antiques which gave a particularly aristocratic character to the whole place. But in his letters he intentionally understated everything in order to be able to surprise them. All this so absorbed him that his new duties—though he liked his official work—interested him less than he had expected. Sometimes he even had moments of absent-mindedness during the Court Sessions, and would consider whether he should have straight or curved cornices for his curtains. He was so interested in it all that he often did things himself, rearranging the furniture, or rehanging the curtains. Once when mounting a step-ladder to show the upholsterer, who did not understand, how he wanted the hangings draped, he made a false step and slipped, but being a strong and agile man he clung on and only knocked his side against the knob of the window frame. The bruised place was painful but the pain soon passed, and he felt particularly bright and well just then. He wrote: "I feel fifteen years younger." He thought he would have everything ready by September, but it dragged on till mid-October. But the result was charming not only in his eyes but to everyone who saw it.

In reality it was just what is usually seen in the houses of people of moderate means who want to appear rich, and therefore succeed only in resembling others like themselves: there were damasks, dark wood, plants, rugs, and dull and polished bronzes—all the things people of a certain class have in order to resemble other people of that class. His house was so like the others that it would never have been noticed, but to him it all seemed to be quite exceptional. He was very happy when he met his family at the station and brought them to the newly furnished house all lit up, where a footman in a white tie opened the door into the hall decorated with plants, and when they went on into the drawing-room and the study uttering exclamations of delight. He conducted them everywhere, drank in their praises eagerly, and beamed with pleasure. At tea that evening, when Praskóvya Fëdorovna among other things asked him about his fall, he laughed, and showed them how he had gone flying and had frightened the upholsterer.

"It's a good thing I'm a bit of an athlete. Another man might have been killed, but I merely knocked myself, just here; it hurts when it's touched, but it's passing off already—it's only a bruise."

So they began living in their new home—in which, as always happens, when they got thoroughly settled in they found they were just one room short—and with the increased income, which as always was just a little (some five hundred rubles) too little, but it was all very nice.

Things went particularly well at first, before everything was finally arranged and while something had still to be done: this thing bought, that thing ordered, another thing moved, and something else adjusted. Though there were some disputes between husband and wife, they were both so well satisfied and had so much to do that it all passed off without any serious quarrels. When nothing was left to arrange it became rather dull and something seemed to be lacking, but they were then making acquaintances, forming habits, and life was growing fuller.

Iván Ilých spent his mornings at the law court and came home to dinner, and at first he was generally in a good humour, though he occasionally became irritable just on account of his house. (Every spot on the tablecloth or the upholstery, and every broken window-blind string, irritated him. He had devoted so much trouble to arranging it all that every disturbance of it distressed him.) But on the whole his life ran its course as he believed life should do: easily, pleasantly, and decorously.

He got up at nine, drank his coffee, read the paper, and then put on his undress uniform and went to the law courts. There the harness in which he worked had already been stretched to fit him and he donned it without a hitch: petitioners, inquiries at the chancery, the chancery itself, and the sittings public and administrative. In all this the thing was to exclude everything fresh and vital, which always disturbs the regular course of official business, and to admit only official relations with people, and then only on official grounds. A man would come, for instance, wanting some information. Iván Ilých, as one in whose sphere the matter did not lie, would have nothing to do with him: but if the man had some business with him in his official capacity, something that could be expressed on officially stamped paper, he would do everything, positively everything he could within the limits of such relations, and in doing so would maintain the semblance of friendly human relations, that is, would observe the courtesies of life. As soon as the official relations ended, so did everything else. Iván Ilých possessed this capacity to separate his real life from the official side of affairs and not mix the two, in the highest degree, and by long practice and natural aptitude had brought it to such a pitch that sometimes, in the manner of a virtuoso, he would even allow himself to let the human and official relations mingle. He let himself do this just because he felt that he could at any time he chose resume the strictly official attitude again and drop the human relation. And he did it all easily, pleasantly, correctly, and even artistically. In the intervals between the sessions he smoked, drank tea, chatted a little about politics, a little about general topics, a little about cards, but most of all about official appointments. Tired, but with the feelings of a virtuoso—one of the first violins who has played his part in an orchestra with precision —he would return home to find that his wife and daughter had been out paying calls, or had a visitor, and that his son had been to school, had done his homework with his tutor, and was duly learning what is taught at High Schools. Everything was as it should be. After dinner, if they had no visitors, Iván Ilých sometimes read a book that was being much discussed at the time, and in the evening settled down to work, that is, read official papers, compared the depositions of witnesses, and noted paragraphs of the Code applying to them. This was neither dull nor amusing. It was dull when he might have been playing bridge, but if no bridge was available it was at any rate better than doing nothing or sitting with his wife. Iván Ilých's chief pleasure was giving little dinners to which he invited men and women of good social position, and just as his drawing-room resembled all other drawing-rooms so did his enjoyable little parties resemble all other such parties.

Once they even gave a dance. Iván Ilých enjoyed it and everything went off well, except that it led to a violent quarrel with his wife about the cakes and sweets. Praskóvya Fëdorovna had made her own plans, but Iván Ilých insisted on getting everything from an expensive confectioner and ordered too many cakes, and the quarrel occurred because some of those cakes were left over and the confectioner's bill came to forty-five rubles. It was a great and disagreeable quarrel. Praskóvya Fëdorovna called him "a fool and an imbecile," and he clutched at his head and made angry allusions to divorce.

But the dance itself had been enjoyable. The best people were there, and Iván Ilých had danced with Princess Trúfonova, a sister of the distinguished founder of the Society "Bear my Burden."

The pleasures connected with his work were pleasures of ambition; his social pleasures were those of vanity; but Iván Ilých's greatest pleasure was playing bridge. He acknowledged that whatever disagreeable incident happened in his life, the pleasure that beamed like a ray of light above everything else was to sit down to bridge with good players, not noisy partners, and of course to four-handed bridge (with five players it was annoying to have to stand out, though one pretended not to mind), to play a clever and serious game (when the cards allowed it) and then to have supper and drink a glass of wine. After a game of bridge, especially if he had won a little (to win a large sum was unpleasant), Iván Ilých went to bed in specially good humour.

So they lived. They formed a circle of acquaintances among the best people and were visited by people of importance and by young folk. In their views as to their acquaintances, husband, wife and daughter were entirely agreed, and tacitly and unanimously kept at arm's length and shook off the various shabby friends and relations who, with much show of affection, gushed into the drawing-room with its Japanese plates on the walls. Soon these shabby friends ceased to obtrude themselves and only the best people remained in the Golovíns' set.

Young men made up to Lisa, and Petríshchev, an examining magistrate and Dmítri Ivánovich Petríshchev's son and sole heir, began to be so attentive to her that Iván Ilých had already spoken to Praskóvya Fëdorovna about it, and considered whether they should not arrange a party for them, or get up some private theatricals.

So they lived, and all went well, without change, and life flowed pleasantly.

## CHAPTER IV

They were all in good health. It could not be called ill health of Iván Ilých sometimes said that he had a queer taste in his mouth and felt some discomfort in his left side.

But this discomfort increased and, though not exactly painful, grew into a sense of pressure in his side accompanied by ill humour. And his irritability became worse and worse and began to mar the agreeable, easy, and correct life that had established itself in the Golovín family. Quarrels between husband and wife became more and more frequent, and soon the ease and amenity disappeared and even the decorum was barely maintained. Scenes again became frequent, and very few of those islets remained on which husband and wife could meet without an explosion. Praskóvya Fëdorovna now had good reason to say that her husband's temper was trying. With characteristic exaggeration she said he had always had a dreadful temper, and that it had needed all her good nature to put up with it for twenty years. It was true that now the quarrels were started by him. His bursts of temper always came just before dinner, often just as he began to eat his soup. Sometimes he noticed that a plate or dish was chipped, or the food was not right, or his son put his elbow on the table, or his daughter's hair was not done as he liked it, and for all this he blamed Praskóvya Fëdorovna. At first she retorted and said disagreeable things to him, but once or twice he fell into such a rage at the beginning of dinner that she realized it was due to some physical derangement brought on by taking food, and so she restrained herself and did not answer, but only hurried to get the dinner over. She regarded this self-restraint as highly praiseworthy. Having come to the conclusion that her husband had a dreadful temper and made her life miserable, she began to feel sorry for herself, and the more she pitied herself the more she hated her husband. She began to wish he would die; yet she did not want him to die because then his salary would cease. And this irritated her against him still more. She considered herself dreadfully unhappy just because not even his death could save her, and though she concealed her exasperation, that hidden exasperation of hers increased his irritation also.

After one scene in which Iván Ilých had been particularly unfair and after which he had said in explanation that he certainly was irritable but that it was due to his not being well, she said that if he was ill it should be attended to, and insisted on his going to see a celebrated doctor.

He went. Everything took place as he had expected and as it always does. There was the usual waiting and the important air assumed by the doctor, with which he was so familiar (resembling that which he himself assumed in court), and the sounding and listening, and the questions which called for answers that were forgone conclusions and were evidently unnecessary, and the look of importance which implied that "if only you put yourself in our hands we will arrange everything—we know indubitably how it has to be done, always in the same way for everybody alike." It was all just as it was in the law courts. The doctor put on just the same air towards him as he himself put on towards an accused person.

The doctor said that so-and-so indicated that there was so-and-so inside the patient, but if the investigation of so-and-so did not confirm this, then he must assume that and that. If he assumed that and that, then . . . and so on. To Iván Ilých only one question was important: was his case serious or not? But the doctor ignored that inappropriate question. From his point of view it was not the one under consideration, the real question was to decide between a floating kidney, chronic catarrh, or appendicitis. It was not a question of Iván Ilých's life or death, but one between a floating kidney and appendicitis. And that question the doctor solved brilliantly, as it seemed to Iván Ilých, in favour of the appendix, with the reservation that should an examination of the urine give fresh indications the matter would be reconsidered. All this was just what Iván Ilých had himself brilliantly accomplished a thousand times in dealing with men on trial. The doctor summed up just as brilliantly, looking over his spectacles triumphantly and even gaily at the accused. From the doctor's summing up Iván Ilých concluded that things were bad, but that for the doctor, and perhaps for everybody else, it was a matter of indifference, though for him it was bad. And this conclusion struck him painfully, arousing in him a great feeling of pity for himself and of bitterness towards the doctor's indifference to a matter of such importance.

He said nothing of this, but rose, placed the doctor's fee on the table, and remarked with a sigh: "We sick people probably often put inappropriate questions. But tell me, in general, is this complaint dangerous, or not? . . ."

The doctor looked at him sternly over his spectacles with one eye, as if to say: "Prisoner, if you will not keep to the questions put to you, I shall be obliged to have you removed from the court."

"I have already told you what I consider necessary and proper. The analysis may show something more." And the doctor bowed.

Iván Ilých went out slowly, seated himself disconsolately in his sledge, and drove home. All the way home he was going over what the doctor had said, trying to translate those complicated, obscure, scientific phrases into plain language and find in them an answer to the question: "Is my condition bad? Is it very bad? Or is there as yet nothing much wrong?" And it seemed to him that the meaning of what the doctor had said was that it was very bad. Everything in the streets seemed depressing. The cabmen, the houses, the passers-by, and the shops, were dismal. His ache, this dull gnawing ache that never ceased for a moment, seemed to have acquired a new and more serious significance from the doctor's dubious remarks. Iván Ilých now watched it with a new and oppressive feeling.

He reached home and began to tell his wife about it. She listened, but in the middle of his account his daughter came in with her hat on, ready to go out with her mother. She sat down reluctantly to listen to this tedious story, but could not stand it long, and her mother too did not hear him to the end.

"Well, I am very glad," she said. "Mind now to take your medicine regularly. Give me the prescription and I'll send Gerásim to the chemist's." And she went to get ready to go out.

While she was in the room Iván Ilých had hardly taken time to breathe, but he sighed deeply when she left it.

"Well," he thought, "perhaps it isn't so bad after all."

He began taking his medicine and following the doctor's directions, which had been altered after the examination of the urine. But then it happened that there was a contradiction between the indications drawn from the examination of the urine and the symptoms that showed themselves. It turned out that what was happening differed from what the doctor had told him, and that he had either forgotten, or blundered, or hidden something from him. He could not, however, be blamed for that, and Iván Ilých still obeyed his orders implicitly and at first derived some comfort from doing so.

From the time of his visit to the doctor, Iván Ilých's chief occupation was the exact fulfilment of the doctor's instructions regarding hygiene and the taking of medicine, and the observation of his pain and his excretions. His chief interests came to be people's ailments and people's health. When sickness, deaths, or recoveries, were mentioned in his presence, especially when the illness resembled his own, he listened with agitation which he tried to hide, asked questions, and applied what he heard to his own case.

The pain did not grow less, but Iván Ilých made efforts to force himself to think that he was better. And he could do this so long as nothing agitated him. But as soon as he had any unpleasantness with his wife, any lack of success in his official work, or held bad cards at bridge, he was at once acutely sensible of his disease. He had formerly borne such mischances, hoping soon to adjust what was wrong, to master it and attain success, or make a grand slam. But now every mischance upset him and plunged him into despair. He would say to himself: "There now, just as I was beginning to get better and the medicine had begun to take effect, comes this accursed misfortune, or unpleasantness . . ." And he was furious with the mishap, or with the people who were causing the unpleasantness and killing him, for he felt that this fury was killing him but could not restrain it. One would have thought that it should have been clear to him that this exasperation with circumstances and people aggravated his illness, and that he ought therefore to ignore unpleasant occurrences. But he drew the very opposite conclusion: he said that he needed peace, and he watched for everything that might disturb it and became irritable at the slightest infringement of it. His condition was rendered worse by the fact that he read medical books and consulted doctors. The progress of his disease was so gradual that he could deceive himself when comparing one day with another—the difference was so slight. But when he consulted the doctors it seemed to him that he was getting worse, and even very rapidly. Yet despite this he was continually consulting them.

That month he went to see another celebrity, who told him almost the same as the first had done but put his questions rather differently, and the interview with this celebrity only increased Iván Ilých's doubts and fears. A friend of a friend of his, a very good doctor, diagnosed his illness again quite differently from the others, and though he predicted recovery, his questions and suppositions bewildered Iván Ilých still more and increased his doubts. A homoeopathist diagnosed the disease in yet another way, and prescribed medicine which Iván Ilých took secretly for a week. But after a week, not feeling any improvement and having lost confidence both in the former doctor's treatment and in this one's, he became still more despondent. One day a lady acquaintance mentioned a cure effected by a wonder-working icon. Iván Ilých caught himself listening attentively and beginning to believe that it had occurred. This incident alarmed him. "Has my mind really weakened to such an extent?" he asked himself. "Nonsense! It's all rubbish. I mustn't give way to nervous fears but having chosen a doctor must keep strictly to his treatment. That is what I will do. Now it's all settled. I won't think about it, but will follow the treatment seriously till summer, and then we shall see. From now there must be no more of this wavering!" This was easy to say but impossible to carry out. The pain in his side oppressed him and seemed to grow worse and more incessant, while the taste in his mouth grew stranger and stranger. It seemed to him that his breath had a disgusting smell, and he was conscious of a loss of appetite and strength. There was no deceiving himself: something terrible, new, and more important than anything before in his life, was taking place within him of which he alone was aware. Those about him did not understand or would not understand it, but thought everything in the world was going on as usual. That tormented Iván Ilých more than anything. He saw that his household, especially his wife and daughter who were in a perfect whirl of visiting, did not understand anything of it and were annoyed that he was so depressed and so exacting, as if he were to blame for it. Though they tried to disguise it he saw that he was an obstacle in their path, and that his wife had adopted a definite line in regard to his illness and kept to it regardless of anything he said or did. Her attitude was this: "You know," she would say to her friends, "Iván Ilých can't do as other people do, and keep to the treatment prescribed for him. One day he'll take his drops and keep strictly to his diet and go to bed in good time, but the next day unless I watch him he'll suddenly forget his medicine, eat sturgeon—which is forbidden—and sit up playing cards till one o'clock in the morning."

"Oh, come, when was that?" Iván Ilých would ask in vexation. "Only once at Peter Ivánovich's."

"And yesterday with Shébek."

"Well, even if I hadn't stayed up, this pain would have kept me awake."

"Be that as it may you'll never get well like that, but will always make us wretched."

Praskóvya Fëdorovna's attitude to Iván Ilých's illness, as she expressed it both to others and to him, was that it was his own fault and was another of the annoyances he caused her. Iván Ilých felt that this opinion escaped her involuntarily—but that did not make it easier for him.

At the law courts too, Iván Ilých noticed, or thought he noticed, a strange attitude towards himself. It sometimes seemed to him that people were watching him inquisitively as a man whose place might soon be vacant. Then again, his friends would suddenly begin to chaff him in a friendly way about his low spirits, as if the awful, horrible, and unheard-of thing that was going on within him, incessantly gnawing at him and irresistibly drawing him away, was a very agreeable subject for jests. Schwartz in particular irritated him by his jocularity, vivacity, and *savoir-faire*, which reminded him of what he himself had been ten years ago.

Friends came to make up a set and they sat down to cards. They dealt, bending the new cards to soften them, and he sorted the diamonds in his hand and found he had seven. His partner said "No trumps" and supported him with two diamonds. What more could be wished for? It ought to be jolly and lively. They would make a grand slam. But suddenly Iván Ilých was conscious of that gnawing pain, that taste in his mouth, and it seemed ridiculous that in such circumstances he should be pleased to make a grand slam.

He looked at his partner Mikháil Mikháylovich, who rapped the table with his strong hand and instead of snatching up the tricks pushed the cards courteously and indulgently towards Iván Ilých that he might have the pleasure of gathering them up without the trouble of stretching out his hand for them. "Does he think I am too weak to stretch out my arm?" thought Iván Ilých, and forgetting what he was doing he over-trumped his partner, missing the grand slam by three tricks. And what was most awful of all was that he saw how upset Mikháil Mikháylovich was about it but did not himself care. And it was dreadful to realize why he did not care.

They all saw that he was suffering, and said: "We can stop if you are tired. Take a rest." Lie down? No, he was not at all tired, and he finished the rubber. All were gloomy and silent. Iván Ilých felt that he had diffused this gloom over them and could not dispel it. They had supper and went away, and Iván Ilých was left alone with the consciousness that his life was poisoned and was poisoning the lives of others, and that this poison did not weaken but penetrated more and more deeply into his whole being.

With this consciousness, and with physical pain besides the terror, he must go to bed, often to lie awake the greater part of the night.

Next morning he had to get up again, dress, go to the law courts, speak, and write; or if he did not go out, spend at home those twenty-four hours a day each of which was a torture. And he had to live thus all alone on the brink of an abyss, with no one who understood or pitied him.

## CHAPTER V

So one month passed and then another. Just before the New Year his brother-in-law came to town and stayed at their house. Iván Ilých was at the law courts and Praskóvya Fëdorovna had gone shopping. When Iván Ilých came home and entered his study he found his brother-in-law there—a healthy, florid man—unpacking his portmanteau himself. He raised his head on hearing Iván Ilých's footsteps and looked up at him for a moment without a word. That stare told Iván Ilých everything. His brother-in-law opened his mouth to utter an exclamation of surprise but checked himself, and that action confirmed it all.

"I have changed, eh?"

"Yes, there is a change."

And after that, try as he would to get his brother-in-law to return to the subject of his looks, the latter would say nothing about it. Praskóvya Fëdorovna came home and her brother went out to her. Iván Ilých locked the door and began to examine himself in the glass, first full face, then in profile. He took up a portrait of himself taken with his wife, and compared it with what he saw in the glass. The change in him was immense. Then he bared his arms to the elbow, looked at them, drew the sleeves down again, sat down on an ottoman, and grew blacker than night.

"No, no, this won't do!" he said to himself, and jumped up, went to the table, took up some law papers and began to read them, but could not continue. He unlocked the door and went into the reception-room. The door leading to the drawing-room was shut. He approached it on tiptoe and listened.

"No, you are exaggerating!" Praskóvya Fëdorovna was saying.

"Exaggerating! Don't you see it? Why, he's a dead man! Look at his eyes—there's no light in them. But what is it that is wrong with him?"

"No one knows. Nikoláevich [that was another doctor] said something, but I don't know what. And Leshchetítsky [this was the celebrated specialist] said quite the contrary . . ."

Iván Ilých walked away, went to his own room, lay down, and began musing: "The kidney, a floating kidney." He recalled all the doctors had told him of how it detached itself and swayed about. And by an effort of imagination he tried to catch that kidney and arrest it and support it. So little was needed for this, it seemed to him. "No, I'll go to see Peter Ivánovich again." [That was the friend whose friend was a doctor.] He rang, ordered the carriage, and got ready to go.

"Where are you going, Jean?" asked his wife, with a specially sad and exceptionally kind look.

This exceptionally kind look irritated him. He looked morosely at her.

"I must go to see Peter Ivánovich."

He went to see Peter Ivánovich, and together they went to see his friend, the doctor. He was in, and Iván Ilých had a long talk with him.

Reviewing the anatomical and physiological details of what in the doctor's opinion was going on inside him, he understood it all.

There was something, a small thing, in the vermiform appendix. It might all come right. Only stimulate the energy of one organ and check the activity of another, then absorption would take place and everything would come right. He got home rather late for dinner, ate his dinner, and conversed cheerfully, but could not for a long time bring himself to go back to work in his room. At last, however, he went to his study and did what was necessary, but the consciousness that he had put something aside—an important, intimate matter which he would revert to when his work was done—never left him. When he had finished his work he remembered that this intimate matter was the thought of his vermiform appendix. But he did not give himself up to it, and went to the drawing-room for tea. There were callers there, including the examining magistrate who was a desirable match for his daughter, and they were conversing, playing the piano and singing. Iván Ilých, as Praskóvya Fëdorovna remarked, spent that evening more cheerfully than usual, but he never for a moment forgot that he had postponed the important matter of the appendix. At eleven o'clock he said good-night and went to his bedroom. Since his illness he had slept alone in a small room next to his study. He undressed and took up a novel by Zola, but instead of reading it he fell into thought, and in his imagination that desired improvement in the vermiform appendix occurred. There was the absorption and evacuation and the re-establishment of normal activity. "Yes, that's it!" he said to himself. "One need only assist nature, that's all." He remembered his medicine, rose, took it, and lay down on his back watching for the beneficent action of the medicine and for it to lessen the pain. "I need only take it regularly and avoid all injurious influences. I am already feeling better, much better." He began touching his side: it was not painful to the touch. "There, I really don't feel it. It's much better already." He put out the light and turned on his side . . . "The appendix is getting better, absorption is occurring." Suddenly he felt the old, familiar, dull, gnawing pain, stubborn and serious. There was the same familiar loathsome taste in his mouth. His heart sank and he felt dazed. "My God! My God!" he muttered. "Again, again! And it will never cease." And suddenly the matter presented itself in a quite different aspect. "Vermiform appendix! Kidney!" he said to himself. "It's not a question of appendix or kidney, but of life and . . . death. Yes, life was there and now it is going, going and I cannot stop it. Yes. Why deceive myself? Isn't it obvious to everyone but me that I'm dying, and that it's only a question of weeks, days . . . it may happen this moment. There was light and now there is darkness. I was here and now I'm going there! Where?" A chill came over him, his breathing ceased, and he felt only the throbbing of his heart.

"When I am not, what will there be? There will be nothing. Then where shall I be when I am no more? Can this be dying? No, I don't want to!" He jumped up and tried to light the candle, felt for it with trembling hands, dropped candle and candlestick on the floor, and fell back on his pillow.

"What's the use? It makes no difference," he said to himself, staring with wide-open eyes into the darkness. "Death. Yes, death. And none of them know or wish to know it, and they have no pity for me. Now they are playing." (He heard through the door the distant sound of a song and its accompaniment.) "It's all the same to them, but they will die too! Fools! I first, and they later, but it will be the same for them. And now they are merry . . . the beasts!"

Anger choked him and he was agonizingly, unbearably miserable. "It is impossible that all men have been doomed to suffer this awful horror!" He raised himself.

"Something must be wrong. I must calm myself—must think it all over from the beginning." And he again began thinking. "Yes, the beginning of my illness: I knocked my side, but I was still quite well that day and the next. It hurt a little, then rather more. I saw the doctors, then followed despondency and anguish, more doctors, and I drew nearer to the abyss. My strength grew less and I kept coming nearer and nearer, and now I have wasted away and there is no light in my eyes. I think of the appendix—but this is death! I think of mending the appendix, and all the while here is death! Can it really be death?" Again terror seized him and he gasped for breath. He leant down and began feeling for the matches, pressing with his elbow on the stand beside the bed. It was in his way and hurt him, he grew furious with it, pressed on it still harder, and upset it. Breathless and in despair he fell on his back, expecting death to come immediately.

Meanwhile the visitors were leaving. Praskóvya Fëdorovna was seeing them off. She heard something fall and came in.

"What has happened?"

"Nothing. I knocked it over accidentally."

She went out and returned with a candle. He lay there panting heavily, like a man who has run a thousand yards, and stared upwards at her with a fixed look.

"What is it, Jean?"

"No . . . o . . . thing. I upset it." ("Why speak of it? She won't understand," he thought.)

And in truth she did not understand. She picked up the stand, lit his candle, and hurried away to see another visitor off. When she came back he still lay on his back, looking upwards.

"What is it? Do you feel worse?"

"Yes."

She shook her head and sat down.

"Do you know, Jean, I think we must ask Leshchetítsky to come and see you here."

This meant calling in the famous specialist, regardless of expense. He smiled malignantly and said "No." She remained a little longer and then went up to him and kissed his forehead.

While she was kissing him he hated her from the bottom of his soul and with difficulty refrained from pushing her away.

"Good-night. Please God you'll sleep."

"Yes."

## CHAPTER VI

Iván Ilých saw that he was dying, and he was in continual despair.

In the depth of his heart he knew he was dying, but not only was he not accustomed to the thought, he simply did not and could not grasp it.

The syllogism he had learnt from Kiezewetter's Logic: "Caius is a man, men are mortal, therefore Caius is mortal," had always seemed to him correct as applied to Caius, but certainly not as applied to himself. That Caius—man in the abstract—was mortal, was perfectly correct, but he was not Caius, not an abstract man, but a creature quite, quite separate from all others. He had been little Ványa, with a mamma and a papa, with Mitya and Volódya, with the toys, a coachman and a nurse, afterwards with Kátenka and with all the joys, griefs, and delights of childhood, boyhood, and youth. What did Caius know of the smell of that striped leather ball Ványa had been so fond of? Had Caius kissed his mother's hand like that, and did the silk of her dress rustle so for Caius? Had he rioted like that at school when the pastry was bad? Had Caius been in love like that? Could Caius preside at a session as he did? "Caius really was mortal, and it was right for him to die; but for me, little Ványa, Iván Ilých, with all my thoughts and emotions, it's altogether a different matter. It cannot be that I ought to die. That would be too terrible."

Such was his feeling.

"If I had to die like Caius I should have known it was so. An inner voice would have told me so, but there was nothing of the sort in me and I and all my friends felt that our case was quite different from that of Caius. And now here it is!" he said to himself. "It can't be. It's impossible! But here it is. How is this? How is one to understand it?"

He could not understand it, and tried to drive this false, incorrect, morbid thought away and to replace it by other proper and healthy thoughts. But that thought, and not the thought only but the reality itself, seemed to come and confront him.

And to replace that thought he called up a succession of others, hoping to find in them some support. He tried to get back into the former current of thoughts that had once screened the thought of death from him. But strange to say, all that had formerly shut off, hidden, and destroyed, his consciousness of death, no longer had that effect. Iván Ilých now spent most of his time in attempting to re-establish that old current. He would say to himself: "I will take up my duties again—after all I used to live by them." And banishing all doubts he would go to the law courts, enter into conversation with his colleagues, and sit carelessly as was his wont, scanning the crowd with a thoughtful look and leaning both his emaciated arms on the arms of his oak chair; bending over as usual to a colleague and drawing his papers nearer he would interchange whispers with him, and then suddenly raising his eyes and sitting erect would pronounce certain words and open the proceedings. But suddenly in the midst of those proceedings the pain in his side, regardless of the stage the proceedings had reached, would begin its own gnawing work. Iván Ilých would turn his attention to it and try to drive the thought of it away, but without success. *It* would come and stand before him and look at him, and he would be petrified and the light would die out of his eyes, and he would again begin asking himself whether *It* alone was true. And his colleagues and subordinates would see with surprise and distress that he, the brilliant and subtle judge, was becoming confused and making mistakes. He would shake himself, try to pull himself together, manage somehow to bring the sitting to a close, and return home with the sorrowful consciousness that his judicial labours could not as formerly hide from him what he wanted them to hide, and could not deliver him from *It*. And what was worst of all was that *It* drew his attention to itself not in order to make him take some action but only that he should look at *It*, look it straight in the face: look at it and without doing anything, suffer inexpressibly.

And to save himself from this condition Iván Ilých looked for con-solations—new screens—and new screens were found and for a while seemed to save him, but then they immediately fell to pieces or rather became transparent, as if *It* penetrated them and nothing could veil *It*.

In these latter days he would go into the drawing-room he had arranged—that drawing-room where he had fallen and for the sake of which (how bitterly ridiculous it seemed) he had sacrificed his life—for he knew that his illness originated with that knock. He would enter and see that something had scratched the polished table. He would look for the cause of this and find that it was the bronze ornamentation of an album, that had got bent. He would take up the expensive album which he had lovingly arranged, and feel vexed with his daughter and her friends for their untidiness—for the album was torn here and there and some of the photographs turned upside down. He would put it carefully in order and bend the ornamentation back into position. Then it would occur to him to place all those things in another corner of the room, near the plants. He would call the footman, but his daughter or wife would come to help him. They would not agree, and his wife would contradict him, and he would dispute and grow angry. But that was all right, for then he did not think about It. It was invisible.

But then, when he was moving something himself, his wife would say: "Let the servants do it. You will hurt yourself again." And suddenly It would flash through the screen and he would see it. It was just a flash, and he hoped it would disappear, but he would involuntarily pay attention to his side. "It sits there as before, gnawing just the same!" And he could no longer forget It, but could distinctly see it looking at him from behind the flowers. "What is it all for?"

"It really is so I lost my life over that curtain as I might have done when storming a fort. It that possible? How terrible and how stupid. It can't be true! It can't, but it is."

He would go to his study, lie down, and again be alone with It: face to face with It. And nothing could be done with It except to look at it and shudder.

## CHAPTER VII

How it happened it is impossible to say because it came about step by step, unnoticed, but in the third month of Iván Ilých's illness, his wife, his daughter, his son, his acquaintances, the doctors, the servants, and above all he himself, were aware that the whole interest he had for other people was whether he would soon vacate his place, and at last release the living from the discomfort caused by his presence and be himself released from his sufferings.

He slept less and less. He was given opium and hypodermic injections of morphine, but this did not relieve him. The dull depression he experienced in a somnolent condition at first gave him a little relief, but only as something new, afterwards it became as distressing as the pain itself or even more so.

Special foods were prepared for him by the doctors' orders, but all those foods became increasingly distasteful and disgusting to him.

For his excretions also special arrangements had to be made, and this was a torment to him every time—a torment from the uncleanliness, the unseemliness, and the smell, and from knowing that another person had to take part in it.

But just through this most unpleasant matter Iván Ilých obtained comfort. Gerásim, the butler's young assistant, always came in to carry the things out. Gerásim was a clean, fresh peasant lad, grown stout on town food and always cheerful and bright. At first the sight of him, in his clean Russian peasant costume, engaged on that disgusting task embarrassed Iván Ilých.

Once when he got up from the commode too weak to draw up his trousers, he dropped into a soft armchair and looked with horror at his bare, enfeebled thighs with the muscles so sharply marked on them.

Gerásim with a firm light tread, his heavy boots emitting a pleasant smell of tar and fresh winter air, came in wearing a clean Hessian apron, the sleeves of his print shirt tucked up over his strong bare young arms; and refraining from looking at his sick master out of consideration for his feelings, and restraining the joy of life that beamed from his face, went up to the commode.

"Gerásim!" said Iván Ilých in a weak voice.

Gerásim started, evidently afraid he might have committed some blunder, and with a rapid movement turned his fresh, kind, simple young face which just showed the first downy signs of a beard.

"Yes, sir?"

"That must be very unpleasant for you. You must forgive me. I am helpless."

"Oh, why, sir," and Gerásim's eyes beamed and he showed his glistening white teeth, "what's a little trouble? It's a case of illness with you, sir."

And his deft strong hands did their accustomed task, and he went out of the room stepping lightly. Five minutes later he as lightly returned.

Iván Ilých was still sitting in the same position in the armchair.

"Gerásim," he said when the latter had replaced the freshly-washed utensil. "Please come here and help me." Gerásim went up to him. "Lift me up. It is hard for me to get up, and I have sent Dmítri away."

Gerásim went up to him, grasped his master with his strong arms deftly but gently, in the same way that he stepped—lifted him, supported him with one hand, and with the other drew up his trousers

and would have set him down again, but Iván Ilých asked to be led
to the sofa. Gerásim, without an effort and without apparent pressure, led him, almost lifting him, to the sofa and placed him on it.

"Thank you. How easily and well you do it all!"

Gerásim smiled again and turned to leave the room. But Iván
Ilých felt his presence such a comfort that he did not want to let him
go.

"One thing more, please move up that chair. No, the other one—
under my feet. It is easier for me when my feet are raised."

Gerásim brought the chair, set it down gently in place, and raised
Iván Ilých's legs on to it. It seemed to Iván Ilých that he felt better
while Gerásim was holding up his legs.

"It's better when my legs are higher," he said. "Place that cushion
under them."

Gerásim did so. He again lifted the legs and placed them, and
again Iván Ilých felt better while Gerásim held his legs. When he
set them down Iván Ilých fancied he felt worse.

"Gerásim," he said. "Are you busy now?"

"Not at all, sir," said Gerásim, who had learnt from the townsfolk
how to speak to gentlefolk.

"What have you still to do?"

"What have I to do? I've done everything except chopping the
logs for to-morrow."

"Then hold my legs up a bit higher, can you?"

"Of course I can. Why not?" And Gerásim raised his master's
legs higher and Iván Ilých thought that in that position he did not
feel any pain at all.

"And how about the logs?"

"Don't trouble about that, sir. There's plenty of time."

Iván Ilých told Gerásim to sit down and hold his legs, and began
to talk to him. And strange to say it seemed to him that he felt better
while Gerásim held his legs up.

After that Iván Ilých would sometimes call Gerásim and get him to
hold his legs on his shoulders, and he liked talking to him. Gerásim
did it all easily, willingly, simply, and with a good nature that touched
Iván Ilých. Health, strength, and vitality in other people were
offensive to him, but Gerásim's strength and vitality did not mortify
but soothed him.

What tormented Iván Ilých most was the deception, the lie, which
for some reason they all accepted, that he was not dying but was
simply ill, and that he only need keep quiet and undergo a treatment

and then something very good would result. He however knew that do what they would nothing would come of it, only still more agonizing suffering and death. This deception tortured him—their not wishing to admit what they all knew and what he knew, but wanting to lie to him concerning his terrible condition, and wishing and forcing him to participate in that lie. Those lies—lies enacted over him on the eve of his death and destined to degrade this awful, solemn act to the level of their visitings, their curtains, their sturgeon for dinner—were a terrible agony for Iván Ilých. And strangely enough, many times when they were going through their antics over him he had been within a hairbreadth of calling out to them: "Stop lying! You know and I know that I am dying. Then at least stop lying about it!" But he had never had the spirit to do it. The awful, terrible act of his dying was, he could see, reduced by those about him to the level of a casual, unpleasant, and almost indecorous incident (as if someone entered a drawing-room diffusing an unpleasant odour) and this was done by that very decorum which he had served all his life long. He saw that no one felt for him, because no one even wished to grasp his position. Only Gerásim recognized it and pitied him. And so Iván Ilých felt at ease only with him. He felt comforted when Gerásim supported his legs (sometimes all night long) and refused to go to bed, saying: "Don't you worry, Iván Ilých. I'll get sleep enough later on," or when he suddenly became familiar and exclaimed: "If you weren't sick it would be another matter, but as it is, why should I grudge a little trouble?" Gerásim alone did not lie; everything showed that he alone understood the facts of the case and did not consider it necessary to disguise them, but simply felt sorry for his emaciated and enfeebled master. Once when Iván Ilých was sending him away he even said straight out: "We shall all of us die, so why should I grudge a little trouble?"—expressing the fact that he did not think his work burdensome, because he was doing it for a dying man and hoped someone would do the same for him when his time came.

Apart from this lying, or because of it, what most tormented Iván Ilých was that no one pitied him as he wished to be pitied. At certain moments after prolonged suffering he wished most of all (though he would have been ashamed to confess it) for someone to pity him as a sick child is pitied. He longed to be petted and comforted. He knew he was an important functionary, that he had a beard turning grey, and that therefore what he longed for was impossible, but still he longed for it. And in Gerásim's attitude towards him there was something akin to what he wished for, and so that attitude comforted him. Iván Ilých wanted to weep, wanted to be petted and cried over, and then his colleague Shébek would come, and instead of weeping and being petted, Iván Ilých would assume a serious, severe, and profound air, and by force of habit would express his opinion on a decision of the Court of Cassation and would stubbornly insist on that view. This falsity around him and within him did more than anything else to poison his last days.

## CHAPTER VIII

It was morning. He knew it was morning because Gerásim had gone, and Peter the footman had come and put out the candles, drawn back one of the curtains, and begun quietly to tidy up. Whether it was morning or evening, Friday or Sunday, made no difference, it was all just the same: the gnawing, unmitigated, agonizing pain, never ceasing for an instant, the consciousness of life inexorably waning but not yet extinguished, that approach of that ever dreaded and hateful Death which was the only reality, and always the same falsity. What were days, weeks, hours, in such a case?

"Will you have some tea, sir?"

"He wants things to be regular, and wishes the gentlefolk to drink tea in the morning," thought Iván Ilých, and only said "No".

"Wouldn't you like to move onto the sofa, sir?"

"He wants to tidy up the room, and I'm in the way. I am uncleanliness and disorder," he thought, and said only:

"No, leave me alone."

The man went on bustling about. Iván Ilých stretched out his hand. Peter came up, ready to help.

"What is it, sir?"

"My watch."

Peter took the watch which was close at hand and gave it to his master.

"Half-past eight. Are they up?"

"No sir, except Vladímir Ivánich" (the son) "who has gone to school. Praskóvya Fëdorovna ordered me to wake her if you asked for her. Shall I do so?"

"No, there's no need to." "Perhaps I'd better have some tea," he thought, and added aloud: "Yes, bring me some tea."

Peter went to the door but Iván Ilých dreaded being left alone. "How can I keep him here? Oh yes, my medicine." "Peter, give me my medicine." "Why not? Perhaps it may still do me some good." He took a spoonful and swallowed it. "No, it won't help. It's all tomfoolery, all deception," he decided as soon as he became aware of the familiar, sickly, hopeless taste. "No, I can't believe in it any longer. But the pain, why this pain? If it would only cease just for a moment!" And he moaned. Peter turned towards him. "It's all right. Go and fetch me some tea."

Peter went out. Left alone Iván Ilých groaned not so much with pain, terrible though that was, as from mental anguish. Always and for ever the same, always these endless days and nights. If only it would come quicker! If only *what* would come quicker? Death, darkness? . . . No, no! Anything rather than death!

When Peter returned with the tea on a tray, Iván Ilých stared at him for a time in perplexity, not realizing who and what he was. Peter was disconcerted by that look and his embarrassment brought Iván Ilých to himself.

"Oh, tea! All right, put it down. Only help me to wash and put on a clean shirt."

And Iván Ilých began to wash. With pauses for rest, he washed his hands and then his face, cleaned his teeth, brushed his hair, and looked in the glass. He was terrified by what he saw, especially by the limp way in which his hair clung to his pallid forehead.

While his shirt was being changed he knew that he would be still more frightened at the sight of his body, so he avoided looking at it. Finally he was ready. He drew on a dressing-gown, wrapped himself in a plaid, and sat down in the armchair to take his tea. For a moment he felt refreshed, but as soon as he began to drink the tea he was again aware of the same taste, and the pain also returned. He finished it with an effort, and then lay down stretching out his legs, and dismissed Peter.

Always the same. Now a spark of hope flashes up, then a sea of despair rages, and always pain; always pain, always despair, and always the same. When alone he had a dreadful and distressing desire to call someone, but he knew beforehand that with others present it would be still worse. "Another dose of morphine—to lose consciousness. I will tell him, the doctor, that he must think of something else. It's impossible, impossible, to go on like this."

An hour and another pass like that. But now there is a ring at the door bell. Perhaps it's the doctor? It is. He comes in fresh, hearty, plump, and cheerful, with that look on his face that seems to say: "There now, you're in a panic about something, but we'll arrange it all for you directly!" The doctor knows this expression is out of place here, but he has put it on once for all and can't take it off—like a man who has put on a frock-coat in the morning to pay a round of calls.

The doctor rubs his hands vigorously and reassuringly.

"Brr! How cold it is! There's such a sharp frost; just let me warm myself!" he says, as if it were only a matter of waiting till he was warm, and then he would put everything right.

"Well now, how are you?"

Iván Ilých feels that the doctor would like to say: "Well, how are our affairs?" but that even he feels that this would not do, and says instead: "What sort of a night have you had?"

Iván Ilých looks at him as much as to say: "Are you really never ashamed of lying?" But the doctor does not wish to understand this question, and Iván Ilých says: "Just as terrible as ever. The pain never leaves me and never subsides. If only something . . ."

"Yes, you sick people are always like that. . . . There, now I think I am warm enough. Even Praskóvya Fëdorovna, who is so particular, could find no fault with my temperature. Well, now I can say good-morning," and the doctor presses his patient's hand.

Then, dropping his former playfulness, he begins with a most serious face to examine the patient, feeling his pulse and taking his temperature, and then begins the sounding and auscultation.

Iván Ilých knows quite well and definitely that all this is nonsense and pure deception, but when the doctor, getting down on his knee, leans over him, putting his ear first higher then lower, and performs various gymnastic movements over him with a significant expression on his face, Iván Ilých submits to it all as he used to submit to the speeches of the lawyers, though he knew very well that they were all lying and why they were lying.

The doctor, kneeling on the sofa, is still sounding him when Praskóvya Fëdorovna's silk dress rustles at the door and she is heard scolding Peter for not having let her know of the doctor's arrival.

She comes in, kisses her husband, and at once proceeds to prove that she has been up a long time already, and only owing to a misunderstanding failed to be there when the doctor arrived.

Iván Ilých looks at her, scans her all over, sets against her the whiteness and plumpness and cleanness of her hands and neck, the gloss of her hair, and the sparkle of her vivacious eyes. He hates her with his whole soul. And the thrill of hatred he feels for her makes him suffer from her touch.

Her attitude towards him and his disease is still the same. Just as the doctor had adopted a certain relation to his patient which he could not abandon, so had she formed one towards him—that he was not doing something he ought to do and was himself to blame, and that she reproached him lovingly for this—and she could not now change that attitude.

"You see he doesn't listen to me and doesn't take his medicine at the proper time. And above all he lies in a position that is no doubt bad for him—with his legs up."

She described how he made Gerásim hold his legs up.

The doctor smiled with a contemptuous affability that said: "What's to be done? These sick people do have foolish fancies of that kind, but we must forgive them."

When the examination was over the doctor looked at his watch, and then Praskóvya Fëdorovna announced to Iván Ilých that it was of course as he pleased, but she had sent to-day for a celebrated specialist who would examine him and have a consultation with Michael Danílovich (their regular doctor).

"Please don't raise any objections. I am doing this for my own sake," she said ironically, letting it be felt that she was doing it all for his sake and only said this to leave him no right to refuse. He remained silent, knitting his brows. He felt that he was so surrounded and involved in a mesh of falsity that it was hard to unravel anything.

Everything she did for him was entirely for her own sake, and she told him she was doing for herself what she actually was doing for herself, as if that was so incredible that he must understand the opposite.

At half-past eleven the celebrated specialist arrived. Again the sounding began and the significant conversations in his presence and in another room, about the kidneys and the appendix, and the questions and answers, with such an air of importance that again, instead of the real question of life and death which now alone confronted him, the question arose of the kidney and appendix which were not behaving as they ought to and would now be attacked by Michael Danílovich and the specialist and forced to amend their ways.

The celebrated specialist took leave of him with a serious though not hopeless look, and in reply to the timid question Iván Ilých, with

eyes glistening with fear and hope, put to him as to whether there
was a chance of recovery, said that he could not vouch for it but
there was a possibility. The look of hope with which Iván Ilých
watched the doctor out was so pathetic that Praskóvya Fëdorovna,
seeing it, even wept as she left the room to hand the doctor his fee.

The gleam of hope kindled by the doctor's encouragement did not
last long. The same room, the same pictures, curtains, wall-paper,
medicine bottles, were all there, and the same aching suffering body,
and Iván Ilých began to moan. They gave him a subcutaneous in-
jection and he sank into oblivion.

It was twilight when he came to. They brought him his dinner and
he swallowed some beef tea with difficulty, and then everything was
the same again and night was coming on.

After dinner, at seven o'clock, Praskóvya Fëdorovna came into the
room in evening dress, her full bosom pushed up by her corset, and
with traces of powder on her face. She had reminded him in the
morning that they were going to the theatre. Sarah Bernhardt was
visiting the town and they had a box, which he had insisted on their
taking. Now he had forgotten about it and her toilet offended him,
but he concealed his vexation when he remembered that he had himself insisted on their securing a box and going because it would be an
instructive and aesthetic pleasure for the children.

Praskóvya Fëdorovna came in, self-satisfied but yet with a rather
guilty air. She sat down and asked how he was but, as he saw, only
for the sake of asking and not in order to learn about it, knowing that
there was nothing to learn—and then went on to what she really
wanted to say: that she would not on any account have gone but that
the box had been taken and Helen and their daughter were going,
as well as Petríshchev (the examining magistrate, their daughter's
fiancé) and that it was out of the question to let them go alone; but
that she would have much preferred to sit with him for a while; and
he must be sure to follow the doctor's orders while she was away.

"Oh, and Fëdor Petróvich" (the fiancé) "would like to come in.
May he? And Lisa?"

"All right."

Their daughter came in in full evening dress, her fresh young
flesh exposed (making a show of that very flesh which in his own
case caused so much suffering), strong, healthy, evidently in love,
and impatient with illness, suffering, and death, because they inter-
fered with her happiness.

Fëdor Petróvich came in too, in evening dress, his hair curled *à la Capoul*, a tight stiff collar round his long sinewy neck, an enormous white shirt-front and narrow black trousers tightly stretched over his strong thighs. He had one white glove tightly drawn on, and was holding his opera hat in his hand.

Following him the schoolboy crept in unnoticed, in a new uniform, poor little fellow, and wearing gloves. Terribly dark shadows showed under his eyes, the meaning of which Iván Ilých knew well.

His son had always seemed pathetic to him, and now it was dreadful to see the boy's frightened look of pity. It seemed to Iván Ilých that Vásya was the only one besides Gerásim who understood and pitied him.

They all sat down and again asked how he was. A silence followed. Lisa asked her mother about the opera-glasses, and there was an altercation between mother and daughter as to who had taken them and where they had been put. This occasioned some unpleasantness.

Fëdor Petróvich inquired of Iván Ilých whether he had ever seen Sarah Bernhardt. Iván Ilých did not at first catch the question, but then replied: "No, have you seen her before?"

"Yes, in *Adrienne Lecouvreur*."

Praskóvya Fëdorovna mentioned some roles in which Sarah Bernhardt was particularly good. Her daughter disagreed. Conversation sprang up as to the elegance and realism of her acting—the sort of conversation that is always repeated and is always the same.

In the midst of the conversation Fëdor Petróvich glanced at Iván Ilých and became silent. The others also looked at him and grew silent. Iván Ilých was staring with glittering eyes straight before him, evidently indignant with them. This had to be rectified, but it was impossible to do so. The silence had to be broken, but for a time no one dared to break it and they all became afraid that the conventional deception would suddenly become obvious and the truth become plain to all. Lisa was the first to pluck up courage and break that silence, but by trying to hide what everybody was feeling, she betrayed it.

"Well, if we are going it's time to start," she said, looking at her watch, a present from her father, and with a faint and significant smile at Fëdor Petróvich relating to something known only to them. She got up with a rustle of her dress.

They all rose, said good-night, and went away.

When they had gone it seemed to Iván Ilých that he felt better;

the falsity had gone with them. But the pain remained—that same pain and that same fear that made everything monotonously alike, nothing harder and nothing easier. Everything was worse.

Again minute followed minute and hour followed hour. Everything remained the same and there was no cessation. And the inevitable end of it all became more and more terrible.

"Yes, send Gerásim here," he replied to a question Peter asked.

## CHAPTER IX

His wife returned late at night. She came in on tiptoe, but he heard her, opened his eyes, and made haste to close them again. She wished to send Gerásim away and to sit with him herself, but he opened his eyes and said: "No, go away."

"Are you in great pain?"

"Always the same."

"Take some opium."

He agreed and took some. She went away.

Till about three in the morning he was in a state of stupefied misery. It seemed to him that he and his pain were being thrust into a narrow, deep black sack, but though they were pushed further and further in they could not be pushed to the bottom. And this, terrible enough in itself, was accompanied by suffering. He was frightened yet wanted to fall through the sack, he struggled but yet co-operated. And suddenly he broke through, fell, and regained consciousness. Gerásim was sitting at the foot of the bed dozing quietly and patiently, while he himself lay with his emaciated stockinged legs resting on Gerásim's shoulders; the same shaded candle was there and the same unceasing pain.

"Go away, Gerásim," he whispered.

"It's all right, sir. I'll stay a while."

"No. Go away."

He removed his legs from Gerásim's shoulders, turned sideways onto his arm, and felt sorry for himself. He only waited till Gerásim had gone into the next room and then restrained himself no longer but wept like a child. He wept on account of his helplessness, his terrible loneliness, the cruelty of man, the cruelty of God, and the absence of God.

"Why hast Thou done all this? Why hast Thou brought me here? Why, why dost Thou torment me so terribly?"

He did not expect an answer and yet wept because there was no answer and could be none. The pain again grew more acute, but he did not stir and did not call. He said to himself: "Go on! Strike me! But what is it for? What have I done to Thee? What is it for?"

Then he grew quiet and not only ceased weeping but even held his breath and became all attention. It was as though he were listening not to an audible voice but to the voice of his soul, to the current of thoughts arising within him.

"What is it you want?" was the first clear conception capable of expression in words, that he heard.

"What do you want? What do you want?" he repeated to himself.

"What do I want? To live and not to suffer," he answered.

And again he listened with such concentrated attention that even his pain did not distract him.

"To live? How?" asked his inner voice.

"Why, to live as I used to—well and pleasantly."

"As you lived before, well and pleasantly?" the voice repeated.

And in imagination he began to recall the best moments of his pleasant life. But strange to say none of these best moments of his pleasant life now seemed at all what they had then seemed—none of them except the first recollections of childhood. There, in childhood, there had been something really pleasant with which it would be possible to live if it could return. But the child who had experienced that happiness existed no longer, it was like a reminiscence of somebody else.

As soon as the period began which had produced the present Iván Ilých, all that had then seemed joys now melted before his sight and turned into something trivial and often nasty.

And the further he departed from childhood and the nearer he came to the present the more worthless and doubtful were the joys. This began with the School of Law. A little that was really good was still found there—there was light-heartedness, friendship, and hope. But in the upper classes there had already been fewer of such good moments. Then during the first years of his official career, when he was in the service of the Governor, some pleasant moments again occurred: they were the memories of love for a woman. Then all became confused and there was still less of what was good; later on again there was still less that was good, and the further he went the less there was. His marriage, a mere accident, then the disenchantment that followed it, his wife's bad breath and the sensuality and hypocrisy: then that deadly official life and those preoccupations about money, a year of it, and two, and ten, and twenty, and always the same thing. And the longer it lasted the more deadly it became. "It is as if I had been going downhill while I imagined I was going up. And that is really what it was. I was going up in public opinion, but to the same extent life was ebbing away from me. And now it is all done and there is only death."

"Then what does it mean? Why? It can't be that life is so senseless and horrible. But if it really has been so horrible and senseless, why must I die and die in agony? There is something wrong!"

"Maybe I did not live as I ought to have done," it suddenly occurred to him. "But how could that be, when I did everything properly?" he replied, and immediately dismissed from his mind this, the sole solution of all the riddles of life and death, as something quite impossible.

"Then what do you want now? To live? Live how? Live as you lived in the law courts when the usher proclaimed "The judge is coming!" The judge is coming, the judge!" he repeated to himself. "Here he is, the judge. But I am not guilty!" he exclaimed angrily. "What is it for?" And he ceased crying, but turning his face to the wall continued to ponder on the same question: Why, and for what purpose, is there all this horror? But however much he pondered he found no answer. And whenever the thought occurred to him, as it often did, that it all resulted from his not having lived as he ought to have done, he at once recalled the correctness of his whole life and dismissed so strange an idea.

## CHAPTER X

Another fortnight passed. Iván Ilých now no longer left his sofa. He would not lie in bed but lay on the sofa, facing the wall nearly all the time. He suffered ever the same unceasing agonies and in his loneliness pondered always on the same insoluble question: "What is this? Can it be that it is Death?" And the inner voice answered: "Yes, it is Death."

"Why these sufferings?" And the voice answered, "For no reason—they just are so." Beyond and besides this there was nothing.

From the very beginning of his illness, ever since he had first been to see the doctor, Iván Ilých's life had been divided between two contrary and alternating moods: now it was despair and the expectation of this uncomprehended and terrible death, and now hope and an intently interested observation of the functioning of his organs. Now before his eyes there was only a kidney or an intestine that temporarily evaded its duty, and now only that incomprehensible and dreadful death from which it was impossible to escape.

These two states of mind had alternated from the very beginning of his illness, but the further it progressed the more doubtful and fantastic became the conception of the kidney, and the more real the sense of impending death.

He had but to call to mind what he had been three months before and what he was now, to call to mind with what regularity he had been going downhill, for every possibility of hope to be shattered.

Latterly during that loneliness in which he found himself as he lay facing the back of the sofa, a loneliness in the midst of a populous town and surrounded by numerous acquaintances and relations but that yet could not have been more complete anywhere—either at the bottom of the sea or under the earth—during that terrible loneliness Iván Ilých had lived only in memories of the past. Pictures of his past rose before him one after another. They always began with what was nearest in time and then went back to what was most remote—to his childhood—and rested there. If he thought of the stewed prunes that had been offered him that day, his mind went back to the raw shrivelled French plums of his childhood, their peculiar flavour and the flow of saliva when he sucked their stones, and along with the memory of that taste came a whole series of memories of those days: his nurse, his brother, and their toys. "No, I mustn't think of that. . . . It is too painful," Iván Ilých said to himself, and brought himself back to the present—to the button on the back of the sofa and the creases in its morocco. "Morocco is expensive, but it does not wear well: there had been a quarrel about it. It was a different kind of quarrel and a different kind of morocco that time when we tore father's portfolio and were punished, and mamma brought us some tarts. . . ." And again his thoughts dwelt on his childhood, and again it was painful and he tried to banish them and fix his mind on something else.

Then again together with that chain of memories another series passed through his mind—of how his illness had progressed and grown worse. There also the further back he looked the more life there had been. There had been more of what was good in life and more of life itself. The two merged together. "Just as the pain went on getting worse and worse so my life grew worse and worse," he thought. "There is one bright spot there at the back, at the beginning of life, and afterwards all becomes blacker and blacker and proceeds more and more rapidly—in inverse ratio to the square of the distance from death," thought Iván Ilých. And the example of a stone falling downwards with increasing velocity entered his mind. Life, a series of increasing sufferings, flies further and further towards its end— the most terrible suffering. "I am flying. . . ." He shuddered, shifted himself, and tried to resist, but was already aware that resistance was impossible, and again with eyes weary of gazing but unable to cease seeing what was before them, he stared at the back of the sofa and waited—awaiting that dreadful fall and shock and destruction.

"Resistance is impossible!" he said to himself. "If I could only understand what it is all for! But that too is impossible. An explanation would be possible if it could be said that I have not lived as I ought to. But it is impossible to say that," and he remembered all the legality, correctitude, and propriety of his life. "That at any rate can certainly not be admitted," he thought, and his lips smiled ironically as if someone could see that smile and be taken in by it. "There is no explanation! Agony, death. . . . What for?"

## CHAPTER XI

Another two weeks went by in this way and during that fortnight an event occurred that Iván Ilých and his wife had desired. Petríshchev formally proposed. It happened in the evening. The next day Praskóvya Fëdorovna came into her husband's room considering how best to inform him of it, but that very night there had been a fresh change for the worse in his condition. She found him still lying on the sofa but in a different position. He lay on his back, groaning and staring fixedly straight in front of him.

She began to remind him of his medicines, but he turned his eyes towards her with such a look that she did not finish what she was saying; so great an animosity, to her in particular, did that look express.

"For Christ's sake, let me die in peace!" he said.

She would have gone away, but just then their daughter came in and went up to say good morning. He looked at her as he had done at his wife, and in reply to her inquiry about his health said dryly that he would soon free them all of himself. They were both silent and after sitting with him for a while went away.

"Is it our fault?" Lisa said to her mother. "It's as if we were to blame! I am sorry for papa, but why should we be tortured?"

The doctor came at his usual time. Iván Ilých answered "Yes" and "No", never taking his angry eyes from him, and at last said: "You know you can do nothing for me, so leave me alone."

"We can ease your sufferings."

"You can't even do that. Let me be."

The doctor went into the drawing-room and told Praskóvya Fëdorovna that the case was very serious and that the only resource left was opium to allay her husband's sufferings, which must be terrible.

It was true, as the doctor said, that Iván Ilých's physical sufferings were terrible, but worse than the physical sufferings were his mental sufferings which were his chief torture.

His mental sufferings were due to the fact that that night, as he looked at Gerásim's sleepy, good-natured face with its prominent cheek-bones, the question suddenly occurred to him: "What if my whole life has really been wrong?"

It occurred to him that what had appeared perfectly impossible before, namely that he had not spent his life as he should have done, might after all be true. It occurred to him that his scarcely perceptible attempts to struggle against what was considered good by the most highly placed people, those scarcely noticeable impulses which he had immediately suppressed, might have been the real thing, and all the rest false. And his professional duties and the whole arrangement of his life and of his family, and all his social and official interests, might all have been false. He tried to defend all those things to himself and suddenly felt the weakness of what he was defending. There was nothing to defend.

"But if that is so," he said to himself, "and I am leaving this life with the consciousness that I have lost all that was given me and it is impossible to rectify it—what then?"

He lay on his back and began to pass his life in review in quite a new way. In the morning when he saw first his footman, then his wife, then his daughter, and then the doctor, their every word and movement confirmed to him the awful truth that had been revealed to him during the night. In them he saw himself—all that for which he had lived—and saw clearly that it was not real at all, but a terrible and huge deception which had hidden both life and death. This consciousness intensified his physical suffering tenfold. He groaned and tossed about, and pulled at his clothing which choked and stifled him. And he hated them on that account.

He was given a large dose of opium and became unconscious, but at noon his sufferings began again. He drove everybody away and tossed from side to side.

His wife came to him and said:

"Jean, my dear, do this for me. It can't do any harm and often helps. Healthy people often do it."

He opened his eyes wide.

"What? Take communion? Why? It's unnecessary! However. . . ." She began to cry.

"Yes, do, my dear. I'll send for our priest. He is such a nice man."

"All right. Very well," he muttered.

When the priest came and heard his confession, Iván Ilých was softened and seemed to feel a relief from his doubts and consequently from his sufferings, and for a moment there came a ray of hope. He again began to think of the vermiform appendix and the possibility of correcting it. He received the sacrament with tears in his eyes.

When they laid him down again afterwards he felt a moment's ease, and the hope that he might live awoke in him again. He began to think of the operation that had been suggested to him. "To live! I want to live!" he said to himself.

His wife came in to congratulate him after his communion, and when uttering the usual conventional words she added:

"You feel better, don't you?"

Without looking at her he said "Yes".

Her dress, her figure, the expression of her face, the tone of her voice, all revealed the same thing. "This is wrong, it is not as it should be. All you have lived for and still live for is falsehood and deception, hiding life and death from you." And as soon as he admitted that thought, his hatred and his agonizing physical suffering again sprang up, and with that suffering a consciousness of the unavoidable, approaching end. And to this was added a new sensation of grinding shooting pain and a feeling of suffocation.

The expression of his face when he uttered that "yes" was dreadful. Having uttered it, he looked her straight in the eyes, turned on his face with a rapidity extraordinary in his weak state and shouted:

"Go away! Go away and leave me alone!"

## CHAPTER XII

From that moment the screaming began that continued for three days, and was so terrible that one could not hear it through two closed doors without horror. At the moment he answered his wife he realized that he was lost, that there was no return, that the end had come, the very end, and his doubts were still unsolved and remained doubts.

"Oh! Oh! Oh!" he cried in various intonations. He had begun by screaming "I won't!" and continued screaming on the letter "o".

For three whole days, during which time did not exist for him, he struggled in that black sack into which he was being thrust by an invisible, resistless force. He struggled as a man condemned to death struggles in the hands of the executioner, knowing that he cannot save himself. And every moment he felt that despite all his efforts he was drawing nearer and nearer to what terrified him. He felt that his agony was due to his being thrust into that black hole and still more to his not being able to get right into it. He was hindered from getting into it by his conviction that his life had been a good one. That very justification of his life held him fast and prevented his moving forward, and it caused him most torment of all.

Suddenly some force struck him in the chest and side, making it still harder to breathe, and he fell through the hole and there at the bottom was a light. What had happened to him was like the sensation one sometimes experiences in a railway carriage when one thinks one is going backwards while one is really going forwards and suddenly becomes aware of the real direction.

"Yes, it was all not the right thing," he said to himself, "but that's no matter. It can be done. But what *is* the right thing?" he asked himself, and suddenly grew quiet.

This occurred at the end of the third day, two hours before his death. Just then his schoolboy son had crept softly in and gone up to the bedside. The dying man was still screaming desperately and waving his arms. His hand fell on the boy's head, and the boy caught it, pressed it to his lips, and began to cry.

At that very moment Iván Ilých fell through and caught sight of the light, and it was revealed to him that though his life had not been what it should have been, this could still be rectified. He asked himself, "What *is* the right thing?" and grew still, listening. Then he felt that someone was kissing his hand. He opened his eyes, looked at his son, and felt sorry for him. His wife came up to him and he glanced at her. She was gazing at him open-mouthed, with undried tears on her nose and cheek and a despairing look on her face. He felt sorry for her too.

"Yes, I am making them wretched," he thought. "They are sorry, but it will be better for them when I die." He wished to say this but had not the strength to utter it. "Besides, why speak? I must act," he thought. With a look at his wife he indicated his son and said: "Take him away . . . sorry for him . . . sorry for you too. . . ." He tried to add, "forgive me," but said "forego" and waved his hand, knowing that He whose understanding mattered would understand.

And suddenly it grew clear to him that what had been oppressing him and would not leave him was all dropping away at once from two sides, from ten sides, and from all sides. He was sorry for them, he must act so as not to hurt them: release them and free himself from these sufferings. "How good and how simple!" he thought. "And the pain?" he asked himself. "What has become of it? Where are you, pain?"

He turned his attention to it.

"Yes, here it is. Well, what of it? Let the pain be."

"And death . . . where is it?"

He sought his former accustomed fear of death and did not find it. "Where is it? What death?" There was no fear because there was no death.

In place of death there was light.

"So that's what it is!" he suddenly exclaimed aloud. "What joy!"

To him all this happened in a single instant, and the meaning of that instant did not change. For those present his agony continued for another two hours. Something rattled in his throat, his emaciated body twitched, then the gasping and rattle became less and less frequent.

"It is finished!" said someone near him.

He heard these words and repeated them in his soul.

"Death is finished," he said to himself. "It is no more!"

He drew in a breath, stopped in the midst of a sigh, stretched out, and died.

[*Translated by* Aylmer Maude]

# NOW THAT YOU'VE READ TOLSTOY'S
# THE DEATH OF IVÁN ILÝCH:

One difficulty in discussing Tolstoy is that so much is known about him. There are biographies, studies, and family recollections of the full life and remarkable career this unusual man crowded into his eighty-two years. In addition, we have his own memoirs, confessions, tracts, and autobiographical fiction. Yet among all these volumes, many imposing in length, none is more revealing of the essential tensions and tendencies of his nature than the short novel *The Death of Iván Ilých*. This terrifying travelogue of the soul's dark journey stands as Tolstoy's best expression of the spiritual crisis that was to shape his life and work. To grasp the implications of *Iván Ilých* and the crisis which inspired it, one needs to follow Tolstoy's development as a man and as an artist.

Born Lvev Nikolayevich Tolstoy in 1828 on the family estate of Yasnaya Polyana (Bright Glade) to wealthy, aristocratic parents, he was orphaned early in childhood. He was educated first by private tutors, then at the Universities of Kazan and Petersburg. An indifferent student, he took a degree at neither but at both cities, his connections enabled him to enter aristocratic society, and soon he was engaged in the fashionable diversions of his set. He was small and in appearance unprepossessing. "I knew very well that I was not good looking," he wrote. "There were moments when I was overcome with despair: I imagined that there could be no happiness on earth for one with such a broad nose, such thick lips and such small grey eyes as mine; and I asked God to perform a miracle, and make me handsome, and all I then had . . . I would have given for a handsome face." He dressed smartly, hoping that modishness would make up for his misfortune. The introspective young man did not know that his homely face revealed an inner strength which was remarkably appealing, nor that his ugliness could not conceal a charm of manner.

In 1851, at the age of twenty-three, Tolstoy joined his brother Nikolai in the Czar's mounted artillery. His behaviour under arms was typical of most young Russian nobles: he rode, fought, drank, gambled, and chased after women, all with great gusto. His appetites were prodigious and his vigor unbelievable. Following a night of debauchery, he would suffer pangs of remorse; nevertheless, he faithfully repeated the performance at the next opportunity. On one occasion, he contracted syphilis, and on another, a gambling debt so huge that he had to sell a house to pay it off. But the five years of military service in the Caucasus proved valuable, too, for Tolstoy acquired the intimate knowledge of war (he was cited for "distinguished bravery and courage" in the Crimean War) he needed for his great novel War and Peace, and he also found time to produce his first literature: Tales of Sebastopol; Childhood, Boyhood, and Youth; The Snowstorm, and The Two Hussars. "If God will but grant long life to Tolstoy," wrote his compatriot Ivan Turgenev, "I think he will surprise us all."

When the peace was signed in 1856, he surrendered his commission and returned to Petersburg, where at first his growing fame brought him a warm welcome. But he did not like the people he met there, nor did they like him. They found him irritable, impatient, and arrogant; he found them insincere, effete, and materialistic.

Disgusted and dissatisfied with modern society, Tolstoy might have been driven to damaging dissipations had there not at that time arisen a wave of liberalism in Russia, with the emancipation of the serfs as the key issue. He went back to Yasnaya Polyana and proposed to his serfs a plan for their freedom. Suspecting a catch, they turned down the proposal. Undaunted, Tolstoy travelled through Western Europe to study methods of educating the peasants. Upon his return, he started a radically "progressive" school for the children of his serfs, working with and teaching its students (among whom was Ivan Vassilievich Yegorov, later the family coachman and possibly the prototype of the faithful retainer in Iván Ilých). Apparently education did not absorb Tolstoy's energy completely, for he had a tumultuous affair with the wife of one of his serfs. He purged himself of this passion by writing a powerful story about it called The Devil.

In 1862, disappointed with the educational experiment and tired of sowing his oats, Tolstoy married Sophia Andreyevna Behrs, the daughter of a physician who owned the neighboring estate. Of the first stages of this union, he wrote, "I have lived thirty-four years without knowing that one could love so much and be so happy." He soon settled into an active and contented life. He rode and shot on his estate, expanded his holdings, supervised his fruitful acres, helped to rear his children, and sought to ameliorate the lot of the poor. About the only thing that distinguished him from the familiar liberal-minded landed aristocrat was his artistic production, spanned by The Cossacks (1863) and Anna Karenina (1878), but marked by the more popular War and Peace (1867-69). Although each of these novels contains tragedy of varying degrees, there is little in them to contradict the impression, attested to by his biographer Alymer Maude and his friend Maxim Gorky, that Tolstoy's life was interesting, full, and happy.

Yet something very strange began to happen as he approached the middle span of years, often a dangerous one for men. Youth is past, and old age, with the chilling prospect of death, is ahead. And now the fear of death—not as the mere end of consciousness, but as an active force waiting to drag him into an evil darkness—came to Tolstoy, really settled inside his being. His anguished thoughts he set down in that remarkable document A *Confession*, published in 1884, two years before *The Death of Iván Ilých*:

Suddenly my life stopped. I had no more desires. I knew there was nothing to desire. The truth is that life was absurd. I had arrived at an abyss and I saw that before me there was only death. I, a happy, healthy man, felt that I could no longer live. . . . My mental condition presented itself to me in this way: my life is a stupid and spiteful joke someone has played on me.

According to the critic Isaiah Berlin, Tolstoy himself was the joker as well as the victim. There was a hopeless and tragic discrepancy between his mind and his heart. His mind was in fact a critical machine. It broke up the surface of human life, explored the foundations of men's motives, exposed their hidden desires, and saw life in all its multitudinous variety, on all its levels. It was protean, diverse, disparate. It distinguished but never unified. And here, says Mr. Berlin, is the irony. For Tolstoy desired above all to see the world as a unity. He longed in his heart to find again (when still a boy, he lost his belief in God) some central single organizing principle: he wished for something to relate all this diverse experience, for something which would give him an explanation of the purpose of life and the nature of good and evil.

Obsessed by these riddles, Tolstoy viewed them through the lens of logic. "If I exist," he wrote, "there must be some cause of it, and a cause of causes. And the first cause of all is what men call God." But men seldom live by head alone, and Tolstoy spent the rest of his life searching for a solution that would satisfy the heart and that would banish the instinctive terror of death.

The search began in the Russian Church, but where or even whether it ended no one can say with certainty. His moral nature was revolted by the church's theological condemnation of other faiths and its apology for war, and the solutions which other doctrines offered, his critical mind destroyed. He began to draw near to the believers among the poor and unlettered, and the more he looked into their simple ways, the more convinced he became that they possessed a faith which filled their lives with real purpose. Since that faith seemed to grow out of the Gospels, he learned enough Greek to study the early translations of the New Testament. Though he rejected the dogma of the divinity of Christ and the superstitions of the peasants, Tolstoy was influenced by simple christian ideals when he came to formulate his own faith after years of soul-searching and meditation.

How was one to live? Tolstoy's answer may be summarized as follows: one should judge things by what the peasants like or dislike and by what the Gospels declared to be good. One should not live by the head but by the heart. We are part of a universe that cannot be understood through accumulated knowledge or observation, which make us cleverer but not wiser. Only through intuition can we learn to accept things as they are and not to resist them. We should be like that simple creature, Gerásim, who attends Iván Ilých. We must learn to renounce the pleasures of life, to turn the other cheek, to suffer, and to be merciful. We must learn to put aside selfishness, smugness, and frivolity.

For Tolstoy, to believe was to act, and he devoted his next years to the practice of his principles. He became a vegetarian and teetotaler, made his own boots, worked with his peasants at chopping wood and ploughing land, and occasionally came home smelling of manure. His children were growing up, and for the sake of their education, he moved to Moscow for the winters. A visit to the slums of that city appalled him and he decided that to possess wealth was to share in a constantly repeated crime. But when he moved to rid himself of everything he owned on the principle that wealth corrupted, his wife, who did not wish to answer the riddles of the universe, tried to have him declared incompetent.

But by this time, cults of followers had sprung up at home and abroad. His influence as a spiritual leader and his prestige as a writer, augmented by *The Kretuzer Sonata* (1889) and a number of tracts and plays, had assumed such magnitude that even the Czarist government, which detested his doctrines (as do the Soviets now), dared not interfere with his activities. In 1891, he gave his wife the copyright of all his works written before 1881 and *Iván Ilých*, but everything written after that date became free to all. He divided his property among his family and lived on the charities of his wife or son. In 1892, despite his reluctance to use money, he conducted effective famine relief in central Russia, and in 1899, completed *Resurrection* in order to raise funds which would help the Dukhobors (the peasant sectarians who, following his principle, refused military service) to emigrate to Canada.

In "Non-Acting," an essay written in 1893 opposing Emile Zola's proposition that work was the only answer to the pangs, disasters, and sorrows of life, Tolstoy denounces work. Modern world labor, he asserts, is usually in the service of something pernicious and is generally accepted because, like opium, it stopped thought and stifled conscience.

Two forces, said Tolstoy, rule mankind: the force of routine, of keeping on the same path, and the force of reason and love drawing men to light. Work was in the service of routine. As an admirer of Lao Tsze and the Tao, he also believed that a great part of men's unhappiness arose from their inability to stay quietly in their own chambers. Until men could practice *non-acting*, they would not be relieved from their personal calamities. This conception lies at the root of Tolstoy's doctrine of passive resistance and non-violence. The power of the state lies in the physical power of its servants. At the end of *The Kingdom of God Is Within You*, after describing the flogging of a peasant by a contingent of soldiers, he says:

All power therefore depends on those who with their own hands execute the deeds of violence—that is, on the soldiers and the police.

Here we encounter another one of the Tolstoy paradoxes. John Henry Raleigh, writing in *Novel: A Forum of Fiction*, puts the paradox this way: though everything finally depends upon the human body and though physical passivity is a simple concept to understand, the last thing men can do is to cease what they are doing. The wheel of Necessity binds them, body and soul, from the beginning, "and the bondage, while initiated by the circumstances of birth . . . successively broadens out as the individual life goes on. It comes under the aegis of the state and finally under the dominion of history itself. At each stage each individual is thrust into an on-going mechanism, each time entering into a web of events over which he has no control and can only react in a stimulus-response fashion."

Thus, *The Death of Iván Ilých* up to a point reminds us of *The Metamorphosis* of Franz Kafka: individual man is a puny creature and mankind itself, for all its power and force, can only make things happen within the framework which the past has bequeathed. Thus, man is a slave to history, and the thing that Tolstoy most prized, "the unique configuration of a single personality, disappears into the faceless anonymity of mass-history."

But reason, the jailor of mankind, could also deliver man from present tyrannies and advance him into a freer future. Reason itself, twin-bladed, was the greatest of the paradoxes. At the same time that reason possessed all we know of history, it was also overpowering in so far as it could deal with the multiplicity of factors that formed history. It could for the present and for the future be the herald of freedom and the dissolver of the tyrannies of the past and the irrationalities of human life. And the only freedom for man lay in his own single individual consciousness. In some sense, a single ego could cancel or revoke the miasmic mass of the past that weighed or loomed, in Marx's phrase, like an alp or succubus in the brain of the living. The key is to be found in his *Last Diaries*:

I remember very vividly that I am conscious of myself in exactly the same way now, at eighty-one, as I was conscious of myself, my "I" at five or six years of age . . . and consciousness is everything (this is good).

During his last ten years, he wrote only short pieces. When the grow-ing friction between himself and his wife became unbearable and when his followers pressed him to carry out his principles to completion, he noted in his journal: "I have a terrible desire to go away." Two years later, he wrote, "My soul seeks rest and solitude with all its force, seeks to live in harmony with my conscience . . . to escape the screaming discords which exist between my life as it is and my faith."

Finally, on October 28, 1910, determined to seclude himself in a monastery, Tolstoy left home with his youngest daughter, Alexandra, on the celebrated journey which ended in disaster. The aged traveler became ill on the train and had to stop at a place called Astapovo. Within a day, the world knew of his condition, and for the next week, his family, his disciples, newspapermen, priests, and police crowded into the provincial town where the great man lay dying amid a blaze of publicity. He knew he was dying at last, but at last he was unafraid, convinced that the Self did not cease with the death of the body. "This is the end," he muttered, "and it doesn't matter." In his deathbed delirium, he called out, "To escape! Oh, to escape!" On the morning of November 7, he "drew in a breath, stopped in the midst of a sigh, stretched out and died." As he had requested, he was buried in an unmarked grave at Yasnaya Polyana (today maintained as a museum by the Soviets) in a grove of trees hal-lowed to him by a childhood memory.

No writer during his lifetime had ever reached so many readers as Tolstoy. *The Death of Iván Ilých* is perhaps less popular but no less powerful than some of the longer novels. Judged by many as his most successful artistic work of the period of his conversion, its effect on publi-cation was great, in Europe at large as well as in Russia. It impressed the French public in particular, and apparently created a sensation among the middle-class readers in the French provinces, a class which could take art or leave it alone.

The story depicts the author's own spiritual struggle, but it goes far beyond mere autobiography. It is Tolstoy's projection, his nightmare vision, of what he might have become had he continued to live the worldly life which he repudiated as corrupt at the core. Iván suffers from cancer of both body and spirit. If he is saved at the end, it is only because the shocks that flesh and spirit are heir to have removed the scales from his eyes and prepared him for the ultimate grace. But Iván's belated enlightenment, we are reminded, is his tragedy more than his salvation.

Although Tolstoy's religious ardor swells up strongly at times, it is always kept in rein by his artistry. The picture of Iván Ilých is so full of intimate, minute details and passionate personality that it becomes re-markably individual. Yet at the same time, as his name, the counterpart of our John Doe, suggests, the picture is also representative. Iván Ilých stands for the ordinary bourgeois man living in a society which knows the price of everything and the value of nothing. Such people, Tolstoy intimates, may have no enemies, but their friends do not care for them. Ilých is the prototype of modern secular man whom the reader may recognize in Camus' Mersault or Conrad's Kurtz: all three lack or have lost the values which could have given meaning to their wasted lives.

The people who surround Iván Ilých we also recognize. They spring to life in Tolstoy's marvelous observations of them, of how they move, how they speak, how they think, how they act. Sometimes this relentless realism is so ruthless and merciless as to be almost inquisitorial. On the other hand, there is the compassion, the feeling for man's fate, which allows this brutal power to issue in a serene, tender, beautiful climax. In this fine work of imagination, almost excessive in its realism, clarity, and starkness of design, Tolstoy has shown us what agony and what affirmation may lie behind the laconic and common report, "died of cancer."

## FOR FURTHER INFORMATION:

Isaiah Berlin. *The Hedgehog and The Fox*. Weidenfeld and Nicholson: London, 1953.

John Boyley. *Tolstoy and the Novel*. *Viking Press: New York, 1967.*

Janko Lavrin. *Tolstoy: An Approach*. Methuen and Co. Ltd.: London, 1944.

Alymer Maude. *Leo Tolstoy and His Works*. Methuen and Co. Ltd.: London, 1930.

John Henry Raleigh. "Tolstoy and the Ways of History," *Novel: A Forum of Fiction*, II, No. 1 (Fall, 1968), 55-68.

Ernest Simmons. *Leo Tolstoy*. Little, Brown and Co.: Boston, 1946.

Alexander Tolstoy. *Tolstoy: A Life of My Father*. Harper & Bros.: New York, 1953.

Henri Troyat. *Tolstoy*. Doubleday: New York, 1967.

# HEART OF DARKNESS

## BY JOSEPH CONRAD

First published, 1899

# HEART OF DARKNESS

## CHAPTER I

THE *Nellie*, a cruising yawl, swung to her anchor without a flutter of the sails, and was at rest. The flood had made, the wind was nearly calm, and being bound down the river, the only thing for it was to come to and wait for the turn of the tide.

The sea-reach of the Thames stretched before us like the beginning of an interminable waterway. In the offing the sea and the sky were welded together without a joint, and in the luminous space the tanned sails of the barges drifting up with the tide seemed to stand still in red clusters of canvas sharply peaked, with gleams of varnished spirits. A haze rested on the low shores that ran out to sea in vanishing flatness. The air was dark above Gravesend, and farther back still seemed condensed into a mournful gloom, brooding motionless over the biggest, and the greatest, town on earth.

The Director of Companies was our captain and our host. We four affectionately watched his back as he stood in the bows looking to seaward. On the whole river there was nothing that looked half so nautical. He resembled a pilot, which to a seaman is trustworthiness personified. It was difficult to realize his work was not out there in the luminous estuary, but behind him, within the brooding gloom.

Between us there was, as I have already said somewhere, the bond of the sea. Besides holding our hearts together through long periods of separation, it had the effect of making us tolerant of each other's yarns—and even convictions. The lawyer—the best of old fellows—had, because of his many years and many virtues, the only cushion on deck, and was lying on the only rug. The accountant had brought out already a box of dominoes, and was toying architecturally with the bones. Marlow sat cross-legged right aft, leaning against the mizzenmast. He had sunken cheeks, a yellow complexion, a straight back, an ascetic aspect, and, with his arms dropped, the palms of hands outwards, resembled an idol. The director, satisfied the anchor had good hold, made his way aft and sat down amongst us. We exchanged a few words lazily. Afterwards there was silence on board the yacht. For some reason or other we did not begin that game of dominoes. We felt meditative, and fit for nothing but placid staring. The day was ending in a serenity of still and exquisite brilliance. The water shone pacifically; the sky, without a speck, was a benign immensity of unstained light; the very mist on the Essex marshes was like a gauzy and radiant fabric, hung from the wooded rises inland, and draping the low shores in diaphanous folds. Only the gloom to the west, brooding over the upper reaches, became more somber every minute, as if angered by the approach of the sun.

And at last, in its curved and imperceptible fall, the sun sank low, and from glowing white changed to a dull red without rays and without heat, as if about to go out suddenly, stricken to death by the touch of that gloom brooding over a crowd of men.

Forthwith a change came over the waters, and the serenity became less brilliant but more profound. The old river in its broad reach rested unruffled at the decline of day, after ages of good service done to the race that peopled its banks, spread out in the tranquil dignity of a waterway leading to the uttermost ends of the earth. We looked at the venerable stream not in the vivid flush of a short day that comes and departs forever, but in the august light of abiding memories. And indeed nothing is easier for a man who has, as the phrase goes, "followed the sea" with reverence and affection, than to evoke the great spirit of the past upon the lower reaches of the Thames. The tidal current runs to and fro in its unceasing service, crowded with memories of men and ships it had borne to the rest of home or to the battles of the sea. It had known and served all the men of whom the nation is proud, from Sir Francis Drake to Sir John Franklin, knights all, titled and untitled—the great knights-errant of the sea. It had borne all the ships whose names are like jewels flashing in the night of time, from the *Golden Hind* returning with her round flanks full of treasure, to be visited by the Queen's Highness and thus pass out of the gigantic tale, to the *Erebus* and *Terror*, bound on other conquests—and that never returned. It had known the ships and the men. They had sailed from Deptford, from Greenwich, from

Erith—the adventurers and the settlers; kings' ships and the ships of men on 'Change; captains, admirals, the dark "interlopers" of the Eastern trade, and the commissioned "generals" of East India fleets. Hunters for gold or pursuers of fame, they all had gone out on that stream, bearing the sword, and often the torch, messengers of the might within the land, bearers of a spark from the sacred fire. What greatness had not floated on the ebb of that river into the mystery of an unknown earth! . . . The dreams of men, the seed of common-wealths, the germs of empires.

The sun set; the dusk fell on the stream, and lights began to appear along the shore. The Chapman lighthouse, a three-legged thing erect on a mud-flat, shone strongly. Lights of ships moved in the fairway—a great stir of lights going up and going down. And farther west on the upper reaches the place of the monstrous town was still marked ominously on the sky, a brooding gloom in sunshine, a lurid glare under the stars.

"And this also," said Marlow suddenly, "has been one of the dark places of the earth."

He was the only man of us who still "followed the sea." The worse that could be said of him was that he did not represent his class. He was a seaman, but he was a wanderer, too, while most seamen lead, if one may so express it, a sedentary life. Their minds are of the stay-at-home order, and their home is always with them—the ship; and so is their country—the sea. One ship is very much like another, and the sea is always the same. In the immutability of their surroundings the foreign shores, the foreign faces, the changing immensity of life, glide past, veiled not by a sense of mystery but by a slightly disdainful ignorance; for there is nothing mysterious to a seaman unless it be the sea itself, which is the mistress of his existence and as inscrutable as destiny. For the rest, after his hours of work, a casual stroll or a casual spree on shore suffices to unfold for him the secret of a whole continent, and generally he finds the secret not worth knowing. The yarns of seamen have a direct simplicity, the whole meaning of which lies within the shell of a cracked nut. But Marlow was not typical (if his propensity to spin yarns be excepted), and to him the meaning of an episode was not inside like a kernel but outside, enveloping the tale which brought it out only as a glow brings out a haze, in the likeness of one of these misty halos that sometimes are made visible by the spectral illumination of moonshine.

His remark did not seem at all surprising. It was just like Marlow.

It was accepted in silence. No one took the trouble to grunt even; and presently he said, very slow:

"I was thinking of very old times, when the Romans first came here, nineteen hundred years ago—the other day. . . . Light came out of this river since—you say knights? Yes; but it is like a running blaze on a plain, like a flash of lightning in the clouds. We live in the flicker—may it last as long as the old earth keeps rolling! But darkness was here yesterday. Imagine the feelings of a commander of a fine—what d'ye call 'em?—trireme in the Mediterranean, ordered suddenly to the north; run overland across the Gauls in a hurry; put in charge of one of these craft the legionaries—a wonderful lot of handy men they must have been, too—used to build, apparently by the hundred, in a month or two, if we may believe what we read. Imagine him here—the very end of the world, a sea the color of lead, a sky the color of smoke, a kind of ship about as rigid as a concertina —and going up this river with stores, or orders, or what you like. Sandbanks, marshes, forests, savages—precious little to eat fit for a civilized man, nothing but Thames water to drink. No Falernian wine here, no going ashore. Here and there a military camp lost in a wilderness, like a needle in a bundle of hay—cold, fog, tempests, disease, exile, and death—death skulking in the air, in the water, in the bush. They must have been dying like flies here. Oh, yes—he did it. Did it very well, too, no doubt, and without thinking much about it either, except afterwards to brag of what he had gone through in his time, perhaps. They were men enough to face the darkness. And perhaps he was cheered by keeping his eyes on a chance of promotion to the fleet at Ravenna by and by, if he had good friends in Rome and survived the awful climate. Or think of a decent young citizen in a toga—perhaps too much dice, you know —coming out here in the train of some prefect, or tax-gatherer, or trader even, to mend his fortunes. Land in a swamp, march through the woods, and in some inland post feel the savagery, the utter savagery, had closed round him—all that mysterious life of the wilderness that stirs in the forest, in the jungles, in the hearts of wild men. There's no initiation either into such mysteries. He has to live in the midst of the incomprehensible, which is also detestable. And it has a fascination, too, that goes to work upon him. The fascination of the abomination—you know imagine the growing regrets, the longing to escape, the powerless disgust, the surrender, the hate."

He paused.

"Mind," he began again, lifting one arm from the elbow, the palm of the hand outwards, so that, with his legs folded before him, he had the pose of a Buddha preaching in European clothes and without a lotus flower—"Mind, none of us would feel exactly like this. What saves us is efficiency—the devotion to efficiency. But these chaps were not much account, really. They were no colonists; their administration was merely a squeeze, and nothing more, I suspect. They were conquerors, and for that you want only brute force—nothing to boast of, when you have it, since your strength is just an accident arising from the weakness of others. They grabbed what they could get for the sake of what was to be got. It was just robbery with violence, aggravated murder on a great scale, and men going at it blind—as is very proper for those who tackle a darkness. The conquest of the earth, which mostly means the taking it away from those who have a different complexion or slightly flatter noses than ourselves, is not a pretty thing when you look into it too much. What redeems it is the idea only. An idea at the back of it; not a sentimental pretence but an idea; and an unselfish belief in the idea—something you can set up, and bow down before, and offer a sacrifice to. . . ."

He broke off. Flames glided in the river, small green flames, red flames, white flames, pursuing, overtaking, joining, crossing each other—then separating slowly or hastily. The traffic of the great city went on in the deepening night upon the sleepless river. We looked on, waiting patiently—there was nothing else to do till the end of the flood; but it was only after a long silence, when he said, in a hesitating voice, "I suppose you fellows remember I did once turn fresh-water sailor for a bit," that we knew we were fated, before the ebb began to run, to hear about one of Marlow's inconclusive experiences.

"I don't want to bother you much with what happened to me personally," he began, showing in this remark the weakness of many tellers of tales who seem so often unaware of what their audience would best like to hear; "yet to understand the effect of it on me you ought to know how I got out there, what I saw, how I went up that river to the place where I first met the poor chap. It was the farthest point of navigation and the culminating point of my experience. It seemed somehow to throw a kind of light on everything about me—and into my thoughts. It was somber enough, too—and pitiful—not extraordinary in any way—not very clear either. No, not very clear. And yet it seemed to throw a kind of light.

"I had then, as you remember, just returned to London after a lot of Indian Ocean, Pacific, China Seas—a regular dose of the East

—six years or so, and I was loafing about, hindering you fellows in your work and invading your homes, just as though I had got a heavenly mission to civilize you. It was very fine for a time, but after a bit I did get tired of resting. Then I began to look for a ship—I should think the hardest work on earth. But the ships wouldn't even look at me. And I got tired of that game, too.

"Now when I was a little chap I had a passion for maps. I would look for hours at South America, or Africa, or Australia, and lose myself in all the glories of exploration. At that time there were many blank spaces on the earth, and when I saw one that looked particularly inviting on a map (but they all look that) I would put my finger on it and say, 'When I grow up I will go there.' The North Pole was one of these places, I remember. Well, I haven't been there yet, and shall not try now. The glamor's off. Other places were scattered about the Equator, and in every sort of latitude all over the two hemispheres. I have been in some of them, and . . . well, we won't talk about that. But there was one yet—the biggest, the most blank, so to speak—that I had a hankering after.

"True, by this time it was not a blank space any more. It had got filled since my boyhood with rivers and lakes and names. It had ceased to be a blank space of delightful mystery—a white patch for a boy to dream gloriously over. It had become a place of darkness. But there was in it one river especially, a mighty big river, that you could see on the map, resembling an immense snake uncoiled, with its head in the sea, its body at rest curving afar over a vast country, and its tail lost in the depths of the land. And as I looked at the map of it in a shop window, it fascinated me as a snake would a bird—a silly little bird. Then I remembered there was a big concern, a company for trade on that river. Dash it all! I thought to myself, they can't trade without using some kind of craft on that lot of fresh water—steamboats! Why shouldn't I try to get charge of one? I went on along Fleet Street, but could not shake off the idea. The snake had charmed me.

"You understand it was a continental concern, that trading society; but I have a lot of relations living on the continent, because it's cheap and not so nasty as it looks, they say.

"I am sorry to own I began to worry them. This was already a fresh departure for me. I was not used to get things that way, you know. I always went my own road and on my own legs where I had a mind to go. I wouldn't have believed it of myself; but, then—you see—I felt somehow I must get there by hook or by crook. So I

worried them. The men said 'My dear fellow,' and did nothing. Then
—would you believe it?—I tried the women. I, Charlie Marlow, set
the women to work—to get a job. Heavens! Well, you see, the notion
drove me. I had an aunt, a dear enthusiastic soul. She wrote: 'It
will be delightful. I am ready to do anything, anything for you. It
is a glorious idea. I know the wife of a very high personage in the
administration, ánd also a man who has lots of influence with,' etc.,
etc. She was determined to make no end of fuss to get me appointed
skipper of a river steamboat, if such was my fancy.

"I got my appointment—of course; and I got it very quick. It
appears the company had received news that one of their captains
had been killed in a scuffle with the natives. This was my chance,
and it made me the more anxious to go. It was only months and
months afterwards, when I made the attempt to recover what was left
of the body, that I heard the original quarrel arose from a misunderstanding about some hens. Yes, two black hens. Fresleven—that was
the fellow's name, a Dane—thought himself wronged somehow in
the bargain, so he went ashore and started to hammer the chief of
the village with a stick. Oh, it didn't surprise me in the least to hear
this, and at the same time to be told that Fresleven was the gentlest,
quietest creature that ever walked on two legs. No doubt he was; but
he had been a couple of years already out there engaged in the noble
cause, you know, and he probably felt the need at last of asserting
his self-respect in some way. Therefore he whacked the old nigger
mercilessly, while a big crowd of his people watched him, thunderstruck, till some man—I was told the chief's son—in desperation at
hearing the old chap yell, made a tentative jab with a spear at the
white man—and of course it went quite easy between the shoulder
blades. Then the whole population cleared into the forest, expecting
all kinds of calamities to happen, while, on the other hand, the
steamer Fresleven commanded left also in a bad panic, in charge
of the engineer, I believe. Afterwards nobody seemed to trouble
much about Fresleven's remains, till I got out and stepped into his
shoes. I couldn't let it rest, though; but when an opportunity offered
at last to meet my predecessor, the grass growing through his ribs
was tall enough to hide his bones. They were all there. The supernatural being had not been touched after he fell. And the village was
deserted, the huts gaped black, rotting, all askew within the fallen
enclosures. A calamity had come to it, sure enough. The people had
vanished. Mad terror had scattered them, men, women, and children,
through the bush, and they had never returned. What became of

the hens I don't know either. I should think the cause of progress got them, anyhow. However, through this glorious affair I got my appointment, before I had fairly begun to hope for it.

"I flew around like mad to get ready, and before forty-eight hours I was crossing the Channel to show myself to my employers, and sign the contract. In a very few hours I arrived in a city that always makes me think of a whited sepulcher. Prejudice no doubt. I had no difficulty in finding the company's offices. It was the biggest thing in the town, and everybody I met was full of it. They were going to run an oversea empire, and make no end of coin by trade.

"A narrow and deserted street in deep shadow, high houses, innumerable windows with venetian blinds, a dead silence, grass sprouting between the stones, imposing carriage archways right and left, immense double doors standing ponderously ajar. I slipped through one of these cracks, went up a swept and ungarnished staircase, as arid as a desert, and opened the first door I came to. Two women, one fat and the other slim, sat on straw-bottomed chairs, knitting black wool. The slim one got up and walked straight at me—still knitting with downcast eyes—and only just as I began to think of getting out of her way, as you would for a somnambulist, stood still, and looked up. Her dress was as plain as an umbrella-cover, and she turned round without a word and preceded me into a waiting room. I gave my name, and looked about. Deal table in the middle, plain chairs all round the walls, on one end a large shining map, marked with all the colors of a rainbow. There was a vast amount of red—good to see at any time, because one knows that some real work is done in there, a deuce of a lot of blue, a little green, smears of orange, and, on the East Coast, a purple patch, to show where the jolly pioneers of progress drink the jolly lager beer. However, I wasn't going into any of these. I was going into the yellow. Dead in the center. And the river was there—fascinating—deadly—like a snake. Ough! A door opened, a white-haired secretarial head, but wearing a compassionate expression, appeared, and a skinny forefinger beckoned me into the sanctuary. Its light was dim, and a heavy writing desk squatted in the middle. From behind that structure came out an impression of pale plumpness in a frock coat. The great man himself. He was five feet six, I should judge, and had his grip on the handle-end of ever so many millions. He shook hands, I fancy, murmured vaguely, was satisfied with my French. *Bon voyage.*

"In about forty-five seconds I found myself again in the waiting room with the compassionate secretary, who, full of desolation and

sympathy, made me sign some document. I believe I undertook
amongst other things not to disclose any trade secrets. Well, I am
not going to.

"I began to feel slightly uneasy. You know I am not used to such
ceremonies, and there was something ominous in the atmosphere. It
was just as though I had been let into some conspiracy—I don't
know—something not quite right; and I was glad to get out. In
the outer room the two women knitted black wool feverishly. People
were arriving, and the younger one was walking back and forth introducing them. The old one sat on her chair. Her flat cloth slippers
were propped up on a foot-warmer, and a cat reposed on her lap.
She wore a starched white affair on her head, had a wart on one *switch*
cheek, and silver-rimmed spectacles hung on the tip of her nose.
She glanced at me above the glasses. The swift and indifferent pla-
cidity of that look troubled me. Two youths with foolish and cheery
countenances were being piloted over, and she threw at them the
same quick glance of unconcerned wisdom. She seemed to know all
about them and about me, too. An eerie feeling came over me. She
seemed uncanny and fateful. Often far away there I thought of
these two, guarding the door of darkness, knitting black wool as for
a warm pall, one introducing, introducing continuously to the unknown, the other scrutinizing the cheery and foolish faces with unconcerned old eyes. *Ave!* Old knitter of black wool. *Morituri te
salutant.* Not many of those she looked at ever saw her again—not
half, by a long way.

"There was yet a visit to the doctor. 'A simple formality,' assured
me the secretary, with an air of taking an immense part in all my
sorrows. Accordingly a young chap wearing his hat over the left
eyebrow, some clerk I suppose—there must have been clerks in the
business, though the house was as still as a house in a city of the
dead—came from somewhere upstairs, and led me forth. He was
shabby and careless, with inkstains on the sleeves of his jacket, and
his cravat was large and billowy, under a chin shaped like the toe
of an old boot. It was a little too early for the doctor, so I proposed a drink, and thereupon he developed a vein of joviality. As
we sat over our vermouths he glorified the company's business, and
by and by I expressed casually my surprise at him not going out there.
He became very cool and collected all at once. 'I am not such a fool
as I look, quoth Plato to his disciples,' he said sententiously, emptied
his glass with great resolution, and we rose.

"The old doctor felt my pulse, evidently thinking of something else the while. 'Good, good for there,' he mumbled, and then with a certain eagerness asked me whether I would let him measure my head. Rather surprised, I said 'yes,' when he produced a thing like calipers and got the dimensions back and front and every way, taking notes carefully. He was an unshaven little man in a threadbare coat like a gaberdine, with his feet in slippers, and I thought him a harmless fool. 'I always ask leave, in the interests of science, to measure the crania of those going out there,' he said. 'And when they come back, too?' I asked. 'Oh, I never see them,' he remarked; 'and, moreover, the changes take place inside, you know.' He smiled, as if at some quiet joke. 'So you are going out there. Famous. Interesting, too.' He gave me a searching glance, and made another note. 'Ever any madness in your family?' he asked, in a matter-of-fact tone. I felt very annoyed. 'Is that question in the interests of science, too?' 'It would be,' he said, without taking notice of my irritation, 'interesting for science to watch the mental changes of individuals, on the spot, but . . .' 'Are you an alienist?' I interrupted. 'Every doctor should be—a little,' answered that original, imperturbably. 'I have a little theory which you messieurs who go out there must help me to prove. This is my share in the advantages my country shall reap from the possession of such a magnificent dependency. The mere wealth I leave to others. Pardon my questions, but you are the first Englishman coming under my observation. . . .' I hastened to assure him I was not in the least typical. 'If I were,' said I, 'I wouldn't be talking like this with you.' 'What you say is rather profound, and probably erroneous,' he said, with a laugh. 'Avoid irritation more than exposure to the sun. Adieu. How do you English say, eh? Good-by. Ah! Good-by. Adieu. In the tropics one must before everything keep calm.' . . . He lifted a warning forefinger. . . . '*Du calme, du calme. Adieu.*'

"One thing more remained to do—say good-by to my excellent aunt. I found her triumphant. I had a cup of tea—the last decent cup of tea for many days—and in a room that most soothingly looked just as you would expect a lady's drawing room to look, we had a long quiet chat by the fireside. In the course of these confidences it became quite plain to me I had been represented to the wife of the high dignitary, and goodness knows to how many more people besides, as an exceptional and gifted creature—a piece of good fortune for the company—a man you don't get hold of every day. Good heavens! and I was going to take charge of a two-penny-half-penny river steamboat with a penny whistle attached! It appeared, however, I was also one of the Workers, with a capital—you know. Something like an emissary of light, something like a lower sort of apostle. There had been a lot of such rot let loose in print and talk just about that time, and the excellent woman, living right in the rush of all that humbug, got carried off her feet. She talked about 'weaning those ignorant millions from their horrid ways,' till, upon my word, she made me quite uncomfortable. I ventured to hint that the company was run for profit.

" 'You forget, dear Charlie, that the laborer is worthy of his hire,' she said, brightly. It's queer how out of touch with truth women are. They live in a world of their own, and there had never been anything like it, and never can be. It is too beautiful altogether, and if they were to set it up it would go to pieces before the first sunset. Some confounded fact we men have been living contentedly with ever since the day of creation would start up and knock the whole thing over.

"After this I got embraced, told to wear flannel, be sure to write often, and so on—and I left. In the street—I don't know why—a queer feeling came to me that I was an impostor. Odd thing that I, who used to clear out for any part of the world at twenty-four hours' notice, with less thought than most men give to the crossing of a street, had a moment—I won't say of hesitation, but of startled pause, before this commonplace affair. The best way I can explain it to you is by saying that, for a second or two, I felt as though, instead of going to the center of a continent, I were about to set off for the center of the earth.

"I left in a French steamer, and she called in every blamed port they have out there, for, as far as I could see, the sole purpose of landing soldiers and customhouse officers. I watched the coast. Watching a coast as it slips by the ship is like thinking about an enigma. There it is before you—smiling, frowning, inviting, grand, mean, insipid, or savage, and always mute with an air of whispering, Come and find out. This one was almost featureless, as if still in the making, with an aspect of monotonous grimness. The edge of a colossal jungle, so dark-green as to be almost black, fringed with white surf, ran straight, like a ruled line, far, far away along a blue sea whose glitter was blurred by a creeping mist. The sun was fierce, the land seemed to glisten and drip with steam. Here and there grayish-whitish specks showed up clustered inside the white surf, with a flag flying above them perhaps. Settlements some centuries old, and still no bigger than pinheads on the untouched expanse of their background. We pounded along, stopped, landed soldiers; went on, landed customhouse clerks to levy toll in what looked like a God-forsaken wilderness, with a tin shed and a flagpole lost in it; landed more soldiers—to take care of the customhouse clerks, presumably. Some, I heard, got drowned in the surf; but whether they did or not, nobody seemed particularly to care. They were just flung out there, and on we went. Every day the coast looked the same, as though we had not moved; but we passed various places—trading places—with names like Gran' Bassam, Little Popo; names that seemed to belong to some sordid farce acted in front of a sinister back-cloth. The idle-ness of a passenger, my isolation amongst all these men with whom I had no point of contact, the oily and languid sea, the uniform somberness of the coast, seemed to keep me away from the truth of things, within the toil of a mournful and senseless delusion. The voice of the surf heard now and then was a positive pleasure, like the speech of a brother. It was something natural, that had its reason, that had a meaning. Now and then a boat from the shore gave one a momentary contact with reality. It was paddled by black fellows. You could see from afar the white of their eyeballs glistening. They shouted, sang; their bodies streamed with perspiration; they had faces like grotesque masks—these chaps; but they had bone, muscle, a wild vitality, an intense energy of movement, that was as natural and true as the surf along their coast. They wanted no excuse for being there. They were a great comfort to look at. For a time I would feel I belonged still to a world of straightforward facts; but the feeling would not last long. Something would turn up to scare it away. Once, I remember, we came upon a man-of-war anchored off the coast. There wasn't even a shed there, and she was shelling the bush. It ap-pears the French had one of their wars going on thereabouts. Her en-sign dropped limp like a rag; the muzzles of the long six-inch guns stuck out all over the low hull; the greasy, slimy swell swung her up lazily and let her down, swaying her thin masts. In the empty immen-sity of earth, sky, and water, there she was, incomprehensible, firing into a continent. Pop, would go one of the six-inch guns; a small flame would dart and vanish, a little white smoke would disappear, a tiny projectile would give a feeble screech—and nothing happened. Nothing could happen. There was a touch of insanity in the pro-ceeding, a sense of lugubrious drollery in the sight; and it was not dissipated by somebody on board assuring me earnestly there was a camp of natives—he called them enemies!—hidden out of sight somewhere.

"We gave her her letters (I heard the men in that lonely ship were dying of fever at the rate of three a day) and went on. We called at some more places with farcical names, where the merry dance of death and trade goes on in a still and earthly atmosphere as of an overheated catacomb; all along the formless coast bordered by dangerous surf, as if Nature herself had tried to ward off intruders; in and out of rivers, streams of death in life, whose banks were rotting into mud, whose waters, thickened into slime, invaded the contorted mangroves, that seemed to writhe at us in the extremity of an impotent despair. Nowhere did we stop long enough to get a particularized impression, but the general sense of vague and oppressive wonder grew upon me. It was like a weary pilgrimage amongst hints for nightmares.

"It was upward of thirty days before I saw the mouth of the big river. We anchored off the seat of the government. But my work would not begin till some two hundred miles farther on. So as soon as I could I made a start for a place thirty miles higher up.

"I had my passage on a little seagoing steamer. Her captain was a Swede, and knowing me for a seaman, invited me on the bridge. He was a young man, lean, fair, and morose, with lanky hair and a shuffling gait. As we left the miserable little wharf, he tossed his head contemptuously at the shore. 'Been living there?' he asked. I said, 'Yes.' 'Fine lot these government chaps—are they not?' he went on, speaking English with great precision and considerable bitterness. 'It is funny what some people will do for a few francs a month. I wonder what becomes of that kind when it goes up country?' I said to him I expected to see that soon. 'So-o-o!' he exclaimed. He shuffled athwart, keeping one eye ahead vigilantly. 'Don't be too sure,' he continued. 'The other day I took up a man who hanged himself on the road. He was a Swede, too.' 'Hanged himself! Why, in God's name?' I cried. He kept on looking out watchfully. 'Who knows? The sun too much for him, or the country perhaps.'

"At last we opened a reach. A rock cliff appeared, mounds of turned-up earth by the shore, houses on a hill, others with iron roofs, amongst a waste of excavations, or hanging to the declivity. A continuous noise of the rapids above hovered over this scene of inhabited devastation. A lot of people, mostly black and naked, moved about like ants. A jetty projected into the river. A blinding sunlight drowned all this at times in a sudden recrudescence of glare. 'There's your company's station,' said the Swede, pointing to three wooden barrack-like structures on the rocky slope. 'I will send your things up. Four boxes did you say? So. Farewell.'

"I came upon a boiler wallowing in the grass, then found a path leading up the hill. It turned aside for the boulders, and also for an undersized railway truck lying there on its back with its wheels in the air. One was off. The thing looked as dead as the carcass of some animal. I came upon more pieces of decaying machinery, a stack of rusty rails. To the left a clump of trees made a shady spot, where dark things seemed to stir feebly. I blinked, the path was steep. A horn tooted to the right, and I saw the black people run. A heavy and dull detonation shook the ground, a puff of smoke came out of the cliff, and that was all. No change appeared on the face of the rock. They were building a railway. The cliff was not in the way or anything, but this objectless blasting was all the work going on.

"A slight clinking behind me made me turn my head. Six black men advanced in a file, toiling up the path. They walked erect and slow, balancing small baskets full of earth on their heads, and the clink kept time with their footsteps. Black rags were wound round their loins, and the short ends behind waggled to and fro like tails. I could see every rib, the joints of their limbs were like knots in a rope; each had an iron collar on his neck, and all were connected together with a chain whose bights swung between them, rhythmically clinking. Another report from the cliff made me think suddenly of that ship of war I had seen firing into a continent. It was the same kind of ominous voice; but these men could by no stretch of imagination be called enemies. They were called criminals, and the outraged law, like the bursting shells, had come to them, an insoluble mystery from the sea. All their meager breasts panted together, the violently dilated nostrils quivered, the eyes stared stonily uphill. They passed me within six inches, without a glance, with that complete, deathlike indifference of unhappy savages. Behind this raw matter one of the reclaimed, the product of the new forces at work, strolled despondently, carrying a rifle by its middle. He had a uniform jacket with one button off, and seeing a white man on the path, hoisted his weapon to his shoulder with alacrity. This was simple prudence, white men being so much alike at a distance that he could not tell who I might be. He was speedily reassured, and with a large, white, rascally grin, and a glance at his charge, seemed to take me into partnership in his exalted trust. After all, I also was a part of the great cause of these high and just proceedings.

"Instead of going up, I turned and descended to the left. My idea was to let that chain gang get out of sight before I climbed the hill. You know I am not particularly tender; I've had to strike and to fend off. I've had to resist and to attack sometimes—that's only one way of resisting—without counting the exact cost, according to the demands of such sort of life as I had blundered into. I've seen the devil of violence, and the devil of greed, and the devil of hot desire; but, by all the stars! these were strong, lusty, red-eyed devils, that swayed and drove men—men, I tell you. But as I stood on this hillside, I foresaw that in the blinding sunshine of that land I would become acquainted with a flabby, pretending, weak-eyed devil of a rapacious and pitiless folly. How insidious he could be, too, I was only to find out several months later and a thousand miles farther. For a moment I stood appalled, as though by a warning. Finally I descended the hill, obliquely, towards the trees I had seen.

"I avoided a vast artificial hole somebody had been digging on the slope, the purpose of which I found it impossible to divine. It wasn't a quarry or a sandpit, anyhow. It was just a hole. It might have been connected with the philanthropic desire of giving the criminals something to do. I don't know. Then I nearly fell into a very narrow ravine, almost no more than a scar in the hillside. I discovered that a lot of imported drainage pipes for the settlement had been tumbled in there. There wasn't one that was not broken. It was a wanton smashup. At last I got under the trees. My purpose was to stroll into the shade for a moment; but no sooner within than it seemed to me I had stepped into the gloomy circle of some inferno. The rapids were near, and an uninterrupted, uniform, head-long, rushing noise filled the mournful stillness of the grove, where not a breath stirred, not a leaf moved, with a mysterious sound—as though the tearing pace of the launched earth had suddenly become audible.

"Black shapes crouched, lay, sat between the trees leaning against the trunks, clinging to the earth, half coming out, half effaced within the dim light, in all the attitudes of pain, abandonment, and despair. Another mine on the cliff went off, followed by a slight shudder of the soil under my feet. The work was going on. The work! And this was the place where some of the helpers had withdrawn to die.

"They were dying slowly—it was very clear. They were not enemies, they were not criminals, they were nothing earthly now, nothing but black shadows of disease and starvation, lying confusedly in the greenish gloom. Brought from all the recesses of the coast in all the legality of time contracts, lost in uncongenial surroundings, fed on unfamiliar food, they sickened, became inefficient, and were then allowed to crawl away and rest. These moribund shapes were free as air—and nearly as thin. I began to distinguish the gleam of the eyes under the trees. Then, glancing down, I saw a face near my hand. The black bones reclined at full length with one shoulder against the tree, and slowly the eyelids rose and the sunken eyes looked up at me, enormous and vacant, a kind of blind, white flicker in the depths of the orbs, which died out slowly. The man seemed young—almost a boy—but you know with them it's hard to tell. I found nothing else to do but to offer him one of my good Swede's ship's biscuits I had in my pocket. The fingers closed slowly on it and held—there was no other movement and no other glance. He had tied a bit of white worsted round his neck—Why? Where did he get it? Was it a badge—an ornament—a charm—a propitiatory act? Was there any idea at all connected with it? It looked startling round his black neck, this bit of white thread from beyond the seas.

"Near the same tree two more bundles of acute angles sat with their legs drawn up. One, with his chin propped on his knees, stared at nothing, in an intolerable and appalling manner: his brother phantom rested its forehead, as if overcome with a great weariness; and all about others were scattered in every pose of contorted collapse, as in some picture of a massacre or a pestilence. While I stood horror-struck, one of these creatures rose to his hands and knees, and went off on all fours towards the river to drink. He lapped out of his hand, then sat up in the sunlight, crossing his shins in front of him, and after a time let his wooly head fall on his breastbone.

"I didn't want any more loitering in the shade, and I made haste towards the station. When near the buildings I met a white man, in such an unexpected elegance of getup that in the first moment I took him for a sort of vision. I saw a high starched collar, white cuffs, a light alpaca jacket, snowy trousers, a clear necktie, and varnished boots. No hat. Hair parted, brushed, oiled, under a green-lined parasol held in a big white hand. He was amazing, and had a penholder behind his ear.

"I shook hands with this miracle, and I learned he was the company's chief accountant, and that all the bookkeeping was done at this station. He had come out for a moment, he said, 'to get a breath of fresh air.' The expression sounded wonderfully odd, with its suggestion of sedentary desk life. I wouldn't have mentioned the fellow to you at all, only it was from his lips that I first heard the name of the man who is so indissolubly connected with the memories of that time. Moreover, I respected the fellow. Yes; I respected his collars, his vast cuffs, his brushed hair. His appearance was certainly that of a hairdresser's dummy; but in the great demoralization of the land he kept up his appearance. That's backbone. His starched collars and got-up shirt fronts were achievements of character. He had been out nearly three years and, later, I could not help asking him how he managed to sport such linen. He had just the faintest blush, and said modestly, 'I've been teaching one of the native women about the station. It was difficult. She had a distaste for the work.' Thus this man had truly accomplished something. And he was devoted to his books, which were in apple-pie order.

"Everything else in the station was in a muddle—heads, things, buildings. Strings of dusty niggers with splay feet arrived and departed; a stream of manufactured goods, rubbishy cottons, beads, and brass wire set into the depths of darkness, and in return came a precious trickle of ivory.

"I had to wait in the station for ten days—an eternity. I lived in a hut in the yard, but to be out of the chaos I would sometimes get into the accountant's office. It was built of horizontal planks, and so badly put together that, as he bent over his high desk, he was barred from neck to heels with narrow strips of sunlight. There was no need to open the big shutter to see. It was hot there, too; big flies buzzed fiendishly, and did not sting, but stabbed. I sat generally on the floor, while, of faultless appearance (and even slightly scented), perching on a high stool, he wrote, he wrote. Sometimes he stood up for exercise. When a truckle bed with a sick man (some invalid agent from upcountry) was put in there, he exhibited a gentle annoyance. 'The groans of this sick person,' he said, 'distract my attention. And without that it is extremely difficult to guard against clerical errors in this climate.'

"One day he remarked, without lifting his head, 'In the interior you will no doubt meet Mr. Kurtz.' On my asking who Mr. Kurtz was, he said he was a first-class agent; and seeing my disappointment at this information, he added slowly, laying down his pen, 'He is a very remarkable person.' Further questions elicited from him that Mr. Kurtz was at present in charge of a trading post, a very important one, in the true ivory-country, at 'the very bottom of there. Sends in as much ivory as all the others put together. . . .' He began to write again. The sick man was too ill to groan. The flies buzzed in a great peace.

"Suddenly there was a growing murmur of voices and a great tramping of feet. A caravan had come in. A violent babble of uncouth sounds burst out on the other side of the planks. All the carriers were speaking together, and in the midst of the uproar the lamentable voice of the chief agent was heard 'giving it up' tearfully for the twentieth time that day. . . . He rose slowly. 'What a frightful row,' he said. He crossed the room gently to look at the sick man, and returning, said to me, 'He does not hear.' 'What! Dead?' I asked, startled. 'No, not yet,' he answered, with great composure. Then, alluding with a toss of the head to the tumult in the station yard, 'When one has got to make correct entries, one comes to hate those savages—hate them to the death.' He remained thoughtful for a moment. 'When you see Mr. Kurtz,' he went on, 'tell him from me that everything here'—he glanced at the desk— 'is very satisfactory. I don't like to write to him—with those messengers of ours you never know who may get hold of your letter—at that Central Station.' He stared at me for a moment with his mild, bulging eyes. 'Oh, he will go far, very far,' he began again. 'He will be a somebody in the administration before long. They, above—the council in Europe, you know—mean him to be.'

"He turned to his work. The noise outside had ceased, and presently in going out I stopped at the door. In the steady buzz of flies the homeward-bound agent was lying flushed and insensible; the other, bent over his books, was making correct entries of perfectly correct transactions; and fifty feet below the doorstep I could see the still treetops of the grove of death.

"Next day I left that station at last, with a caravan of sixty men, for a two-hundred-mile tramp.

"No use telling you much about that. Paths, paths, everywhere; a stamped-in network of paths spreading over the empty land, through long grass, through burnt grass, through thickets, down and up chilly ravines, up and down stony hills ablaze with heat; and a solitude, a solitude, nobody, not a hut. The population had cleared out a long time ago. Well, if a lot of mysterious niggers armed with all kinds of fearful weapons suddenly took to traveling on the road between Deal and Gravesend, catching the yokels right and left to carry heavy loads for them, I fancy every farm and cottage thereabouts would get empty very soon. Only here the dwellings were gone, too. Still I passed through several abandoned villages. There's something pathetically childish in the ruins of grass walls. Day after day, with the stamp and shuffle of sixty pair of bare feet behind me, each pair under a sixty-lb. load. Camp, cook, sleep, strike camp, march. Now and then a carrier dead in harness, at rest in the long grass near the path, with an empty water gourd and his long staff lying by his side. A great silence around and above. Perhaps on some quiet night the tremor of far-off drums, sinking, swelling, a tremor vast, faint; a sound weird, appealing, suggestive, and wild—and perhaps with as profound a meaning as the sound of bells in a Christian country. Once a white man in an unbuttoned uniform, camping on the path with an armed escort of lank Zanzibaris, very hospitable and festive—not to say drunk. Was looking after the up-keep of the road he declared. Can't say I saw any road or any upkeep, unless the body of a middle-aged Negro, with a bullethole in the forehead, upon which I absolutely stumbled three miles farther on, may be considered as a permanent improvement. I had a white companion, too, not a bad chap, but rather too fleshy and with the exasperating habit of fainting on the hot hillsides, miles away from the least bit of shade and water. Annoying, you know, to hold your own coat like a parasol over a man's head while he is coming to. I couldn't help asking him once what he meant by coming there at all. 'To make money, of course. What do you think?' he said, scornfully. Then he got fever, and had to be carried in a hammock slung under a pole. As he weighed 224 pounds I had no end of rows with the carriers. They jibbed, ran away, sneaked off with their loads in the night—quite a mutiny. So, one evening, I made a speech in English with gestures, not one of which was lost to the sixty pairs of eyes before me, and the next morning I started the hammock off in front all right. An hour afterwards I came upon the whole concern wrecked in a bush—man, hammock, groans, blankets, horrors. The heavy pole had skinned his poor nose. He was very anxious for me to kill somebody, but there wasn't the shadow of a carrier near. I remember the old doctor, 'It would be interesting for science to watch the mental changes of individuals, on the spot.' I felt I was becoming scientifically interesting. However, all that is to no purpose. On the fifteenth day I came in sight of the big river again, and hobbled into the Central Station. It was on a back water surrounded by scrub and forest, with a pretty border of smelly mud on one side, and on the three others enclosed by a crazy fence of rushes. A neglected gap was all the gate it had, and the first glance at the place was enough to let you see the flabby devil was running that show. White men with long staves in their hands appeared languidly from amongst the buildings, strolling up to take a look at me, and then retired out of sight somewhere. One of them, a stout, excitable chap with black mustaches, informed me with great volubility and many digressions, as soon as I told him who I was, that my steamer was at the bottom of the river. I was thunderstruck. What, how, why? Oh, it was 'all right.' The 'manager himself' was there. All quite correct. 'Everybody had behaved splendidly! splendidly!'—'you must,' he said in agitation, 'go and see the general manager at once. He is waiting!'

"I did not see the real significance of that wreck at once. I fancy I see it now, but I am not sure—not at all. Certainly the affair was too stupid—when I think of it—to be altogether natural. Still . . . But at the moment it presented itself simply as a confounded nuisance. The steamer was sunk. They had started two days before in a sudden hurry up the river with the manager on board, in charge of some volunteer skipper, and before they had been out three hours they tore the bottom out of her on stones, and she sank near the south bank. I asked myself what I was to do there, now my boat was lost. As a matter of fact, I had plenty to do in fishing my command out of the river. I had to set about it the very next day. That, and the repairs when I brought the pieces to the station, took some months.

"My first interview with the manager was curious. He did not ask me to sit down after my twenty-mile walk that morning. He was commonplace in complexion, in feature, in manners, and in voice. He was of middle size and of ordinary build. His eyes, of the usual blue, were perhaps remarkably cold, and he certainly could make his glance fall on one as trenchant and heavy as an axe. But even at these times the rest of his person seemed to disclaim the intention. Otherwise there was only an indefinable, faint expression of his lips, something stealthy—a smile—not a smile—I remember it, but I can't explain. It was unconscious, this smile was, though just after he had said something it got intensified for an instant. It came at the end of his speeches like a seal applied on the words to make the meaning of the commonest phrase appear absolutely inscrutable. He was a common trader, from his youth up employed in these parts— nothing more. He was obeyed, yet he inspired neither love nor fear, nor even respect. He inspired uneasiness. That was it! Uneasiness. Not a definite mistrust—just uneasiness—nothing more. You have no idea how effective such a . . . a . . . faculty can be. He had no genius for organizing, for initiative, or for order even. That was evident in such things as the deplorable state of the station. He had no learning, and no intelligence. His position had come to him— why? Perhaps because he was never ill. . . . He had served three terms of three years out there. . . . Because triumphant health in the general rout of constitutions is a kind of power in itself. When he went home on leave he rioted on a large scale—pompously. Jack ashore—with a difference—in externals only. This one could gather from his casual talk. He originated nothing, he could keep the routine going—that's all. But he was great. He was great by this little thing that it was impossible to tell what could control such a man. He never gave that secret away. Perhaps there was nothing within him. Such a suspicion made one pause—for out there there were no external checks. Once when various tropical diseases had laid low almost every 'agent' in the station, he was heard to say, 'Men who come out here should have no entrails.' He sealed the utterance with that smile of his, as though it had been a door opening into a darkness he had in his keeping. You fancied you had seen things— but the seal was on. When annoyed at mealtimes by the constant quarrels of the white men about precedence, he ordered an immense round table to be made, for which a special house had to be built. This was the station's messroom. Where he sat was the first place— the rest were nowhere. One felt this to be his unalterable conviction. He was neither civil nor uncivil. He was quiet. He allowed his 'boy'—an overfed young Negro from the coast—to treat the white men, under his very eyes, with provoking insolence.

"He began to speak as soon as he saw me. I had been very long on the road. He could not wait. Had to start without me. The up-river stations had to be relieved. There had been so many delays already that he did not know who was dead and who was alive, and how they got on—and so on, and so on. He paid no attention to my explanations, and, playing with a stick of sealing wax, repeated several times that the situation was 'very grave, very grave.' There were rumors that a very important station was in jeopardy, and its chief, Mr. Kurtz, was ill. Hoped it was not true. Mr. Kurtz was . . . I felt weary and irritable. Hang Kurtz, I thought. I interrupted him by saying I had heard of Mr. Kurtz on the coast. 'Ah! So they talk of him down there, he murmured to himself. Then he began again, assuring me Mr. Kurtz was the best agent he had, an exceptional man, of the greatest importance to the company; therefore I could understand his anxiety. He was, he said, 'very, very uneasy.' Certainly he fidgeted on his chair a good deal, exclaimed, 'Ah, Mr. Kurtz!' broke the stick of sealing wax and seemed dumbfounded by the accident. Next thing he wanted to know 'how long it would take to' . . . I interrupted him again. Being hungry, you know, and kept on my feet, too, I was getting savage. 'How could I tell?' I said. 'I hadn't even seen the wreck yet—some months, no doubt.' All this talk seemed to me so futile. 'Some months,' he said. 'Well, let us say three months before we can make a start. Yes. That ought to do the affair.' I flung out of his hut (he lived all alone in a clay hut with a sort of veranda) muttering to myself my opinion of him. He was a chattering idiot. Afterwards I took it back when it was borne in upon me startlingly with what extreme nicety he had estimated the time requisite for the 'affair.'

"I went to work the next day, turning, so to speak, my back on that station. In that way only it seemed to me I could keep my hold on the redeeming facts of life. Still, one must look about sometimes; and then I saw this station, these men strolling aimlessly about in the sunshine of the yard. I asked myself sometimes what it all meant. They wandered here and there with their absurd long staves in their hands, like a lot of faithless pilgrims bewitched inside a rotten fence. The word 'ivory' rang in the air, was whispered, was sighed. You would think they were praying to it. A taint of imbecile rapacity blew through it all, like a whiff from some corpse. By Jove! I've never seen anything so unreal in my life. And outside, the silent wilderness surrounding this cleared speck on the earth struck me as something great and invincible, like evil or truth, waiting patiently for the passing away of this fantastic invasion.

"Oh, these months! Well, never mind. Various things happened. One evening a grass shed full of calico, cotton prints, beads, and I don't know what else, burst into a blaze so suddenly that you would have thought the earth had opened to let an avenging fire consume all that trash. I was smoking my pipe quietly by my dismantled steamer, and saw them all cutting capers in the light, with their arms lifted high, when the stout man with mustaches came tearing down to the river, a tin pail in his hand, assured me that everybody was 'behaving splendidly, splendidly,' dipped about a quart of water and tore back again. I noticed there was a hole in the bottom of his pail.

"I strolled up. There was no hurry. You see the thing had gone off like a box of matches. It had been hopeless from the very first. The flame had leaped high, driven everybody back, lighted up everything —and collapsed. The shed was already a heap of embers glowing fiercely. A nigger was being beaten near by. They said he had caused the fire in some way; be that as it may, he was screeching most horribly. I saw him, later, for several days, sitting in a bit of shade looking very sick and trying to recover himself; afterwards he arose and went out—and the wilderness without a sound took him into its bosom again. As I approached the glow from the dark I found myself at the back of two men, talking. I heard the name of Kurtz pronounced, then the words, 'take advantage of this unfortunate accident.' One of the men was the manager. I wished him a good evening. 'Did you ever see anything like it—eh? It is incredible,' he said, and walked off. The other man remained. He was a first-class agent, young, gentlemanly, a bit reserved, with a forked little beard and a hooked nose. He was standoffish with the other agents, and they on their side said he was the manager's spy upon them. As to me, I had hardly ever spoken to him before. We got into talk, and by and by we strolled away from the hissing ruins. Then he asked me to his room, which was in the main building of the station. He struck a match, and I perceived that this young aristocrat had not only a silver-mounted dressing case but also a whole candle all to himself. Just at that time the manager was the only man supposed to have any right to candles. Native mats covered the clay walls; a collection of spears, assagais, shields, knives was hung up in trophies. The business intrusted to this fellow was the making of bricks—so I had been informed; but there wasn't a fragment of a brick anywhere in the station, and he had been there more than a year—waiting. It seems he could not make bricks without something, I don't know what—straw maybe. Anyways, it could not be found there, and as it was not likely to be sent from Europe, it did not appear clear to me what he was waiting for. An act of special creation perhaps. However, they were all waiting—all the sixteen or twenty pilgrims of them—for something; and upon my word it did not seem an uncongenial occupation, from the way they took it, though the only thing that ever came to them was disease—as far as I could see. They beguiled the time by backbiting and intriguing against each other in a foolish kind of way. There was an air of plotting about that station, but nothing came of it, of course. It was as unreal as everything else—as the philanthropic pretense of the whole concern, as their talk, as their government, as their show of work. The only real feeling was a desire to get appointed to a trading post where ivory was to be had, so that they could earn percentages. They intrigued and slandered and hated each other only on that account, but as to effectually lifting a little finger—oh, no. By heavens! There is something after all in the world allowing one man to steal a horse while another must not look at a halter. Steal a horse straight out.

Very well. He has done it. Perhaps he can ride. But there is a way of looking at a halter that would provoke the most charitable of saints into a kick.

"I had no idea why he wanted to be sociable, but as we chatted in there it suddenly occurred to me the fellow was trying to get at something—in fact, pumping me. He alluded constantly to Europe, to the people I was supposed to know there—putting leading questions as to my acquaintances in the sepulchral city, and so on. His little eyes glittered like mica discs—with curiosity—though he tried to keep up a bit of superciliousness. At first I was astonished, but very soon I became awfully curious to see what he would find out from me. I couldn't possibly imagine what I had in me to make it worth his while. It was very pretty to see how he baffled himself, for in truth my body was full only of chills, and my head had nothing in it but that wretched steamboat business. It was evident he took me for a perfectly shameless prevaricator. At last he got angry, and, to conceal a movement of furious annoyance, he yawned. I rose. Then I noticed a small sketch in oils, on a panel, representing a woman, draped and blindfolded, carrying a lighted torch. The background was somber—almost black. The movement of the woman was stately, and the effect of the torchlight on the face was sinister.

"It arrested me, and he stood by civilly, holding an empty half-pint champagne bottle (medical comforts) with the candle stuck in it. To my question he said Mr. Kurtz had painted this—in this very station more than a year ago—while waiting for means to go to his trading post. 'Tell me, pray,' said I, 'who is this Mr. Kurtz?'

" 'The chief of the Inner Station,' he answered in a short tone, looking away. 'Much obliged,' I said, laughing. 'And you are the brickmaker of the Central Station. Everyone knows that.' He was silent for a while. 'He is a prodigy,' he said at last. 'He is an emissary of pity, and science, and progress, and devil knows what else. We want,' he began to declaim suddenly, 'for the guidance of the cause intrusted to us by Europe, so to speak, higher intelligence, wide sympathies, a singleness of purpose.' 'Who says that?' I asked. 'Lots of them,' he replied. 'Some even write that; and so *he* comes here, a special being, as you ought to know.' 'Why ought I to know?' I interrupted, really surprised. He paid no attention. 'Yes. Today he is chief of the best station, next year he will be assistant manager, two years more and . . . but I daresay you know what he will be in two years' time. You are of the new gang—the gang of virtue. The same people who sent him specially also recommended you. Oh, don't say no. I've my own eyes to trust.' Light dawned upon me. My dear aunt's influential acquaintances were producing an unexpected effect upon that young man. I nearly burst into a laugh. 'Do you read the company's confidential correspondence?' I asked. He hadn't a word to say. It was great fun. 'When Mr. Kurtz,' I continued, severely, 'is general manager, you won't have the opportunity.'

"He blew the candle out suddenly, and we went outside. The moon had risen. Black figures strolled about listlessly, pouring water on the glow, whence proceeded a sound of hissing; steam ascended in the moonlight, the beaten nigger groaned somewhere. 'What a row the brute makes!' said the indefatigable man with the mustaches, appearing near us. 'Serve him right. Transgression—punishment— bang! Pitiless, pitiless. That's the only way. This will prevent all conflagrations for the future. I was just telling the manager . . .' He noticed my companion, and became crestfallen all at once. 'Not in bed yet,' he said, with a kind of servile heartiness; it's so natural. Ha! Danger—agitation.' He vanished. I went on to the river side, and the other followed me. I heard a scathing murmur at my ear, 'Heap of muffs—go to.' The pilgrims could be seen in knots gesticulating, discussing. Several had still their staves in their hands. I truly believe they took these sticks to bed with them. Beyond the fence the forest stood up spectrally in the moonlight, and through the dim stir, through the faint sounds of that lamentable courtyard, the silence of the land went home to one's very heart—its mystery, its greatness, the amazing reality of its concealed life. The hurt nigger moaned feebly somewhere near by, and then fetched a deep sigh that made me mend my pace away from there. I felt a hand introducing itself under my arm. 'My dear sir,' said the fellow, 'I don't want to be misunderstood, and especially by you, who will see Mr. Kurtz long before I can have that pleasure. I wouldn't like him to get a false idea of my disposition. . . .'

"I let him run on, this papier mâché Mephistopheles, and it seemed to me that if I tried I could poke my forefinger through him, and would find nothing inside but a little loose dirt, maybe. He, don't you see, had been planning to be assistant manager by and by under the present man, and I could see that the coming of that Kurtz had upset them both not a little. He talked precipitately, and I did not try to stop him. I had my shoulders against the wreck of my steamer, hauled up on the slope like a carcass of some big river animal. The smell of mud, of primeval mud, by Jove! was in my nostrils, the high stillness of primeval forest was before my eyes;

there were shiny patches on the black creek. The moon had spread over everything a thin layer of silver—over the rank grass, over the mud, upon the wall of matted vegetation standing higher than the wall of a temple, over the great river I could see through a somber gap glittering, glittering, as it flowed broadly by without a murmur. All this was great, expectant, mute, while the man jabbered about himself. I wondered whether the stillness on the face of the immensity looking at us two were meant as an appeal or as a menace. What were we who had strayed in here? Could we handle that dumb thing, or would it handle us? I felt how big, how confoundedly big, was that thing that couldn't talk, and perhaps was deaf as well. What was in there? I could see a little ivory coming out from there, and I had heard Mr. Kurtz was in there. I had heard enough about it, too —God knows! Yet somehow it didn't bring any image with it—no more than if I had been told an angel or a fiend was in there. I believed it in the same way one of you might believe there are inhabitants in the planet Mars. I knew once a Scotch sailmaker who was certain, dead sure, there were people in Mars. If you asked him for some idea how they looked and behaved, he would get shy and mutter something about 'walking on all fours.' If you as much as smiled, he would—though a man of sixty—offer to fight you. I would not have gone so far as to fight for Kurtz, but I went for him near enough to a lie. You know I hate, detest, and can't bear a lie, not because I am straighter than the rest of us, but simply because it appalls me. There is a taint of death, a flavor of mortality in lies— which is exactly what I hate and detest in the world—what I want to forget. It makes me miserable and sick, like biting something rotten would do. Temperament, I suppose. Well, I went near enough to it by letting the young fool there believe anything he liked to imagine as to my influence in Europe. I became in an instant as much of a pretense as the rest of the bewitched pilgrims. This simply because I had a notion it somehow would be of help to that Kurtz whom at the time I did not see—you understand. He was just a word for me. I did not see the man in the name any more than you do. Do you see him? Do you see the story? Do you see anything? It seems to me I am trying to tell you a dream—making a vain attempt, because no relation of a dream can convey the dream-sensation, that commingling of absurdity, surprise, and bewilderment in a tremor of struggling revolt, that notion of being captured by the incredible which is of the very essence of dreams. . . ."

He was silent for a while.

". . . No, it is impossible; it is impossible to convey the life-sensation of any given epoch of one's existence—that which makes its truth, its meaning—its subtle and penetrating essence. It is impossible. We live, as we dream—alone. . . ."

He paused again as if reflecting, then added:

"Of course in this you fellows see more than I could then. You see me, whom you know. . . ."

It had become so pitch dark that we listeners could hardly see one another. For a long time already he, sitting apart, had been no more to us than a voice. There was not a word from anybody. The others might have been asleep, but I was awake. I listened, I listened on the watch for the sentence, for the word, that would give me the clue to the faint uneasiness inspired by this narrative that seemed to shape itself without human lips in the heavy night air of the river.

". . . Yes—I let him run on," Marlow began again, "and think what he pleased about the powers that were behind me. I did! And there was nothing behind me! There was nothing but that wretched, old, mangled steamboat I was leaning against, while he talked fluently about 'the necessity for every man to get on.' 'And when one comes out here, you conceive, it is not to gaze at the moon.' Mr. Kurtz was a 'universal genius,' but even a genius would find it easier to work with 'adequate tools—intelligent men.' He did not make bricks—why, there was a physical impossibility in the way—as I was well aware; and if he did secretarial work for the manager, it was because 'no sensible man rejects wantonly the confidence of his superiors.' Did I see it? I saw it. What more did I want? What I really wanted was rivets, by heaven! Rivets. To get on with the work—to stop the hole. Rivets I wanted. There were cases of them down at the coast—cases—piled up—burst—split! You kicked a loose rivet at every second step in that station yard on the hillside. Rivets had rolled into the grove of death. You could fill your pockets with rivets for the trouble of stooping down—and there wasn't one rivet to be found where it was wanted. We had plates that would do, but nothing to fasten them with. And every week the messenger, a lone Negro, letter bag on shoulder and staff in hand, left our station for the coast. And several times a week a coast caravan came in with trade goods—ghastly glazed calico that made you shudder only to look at it, glass beads, value about a penny a quart, confounded spotted cotton handkerchiefs. And no rivets. Three carriers could have brought all that was wanted to set that steamboat afloat.

He was becoming confidential now, but I fancy my unresponsive attitude must have exasperated him at last, for he judged it necessary to inform me he feared neither God nor devil, let alone any mere man. I said I could see that very well, but what I wanted was a certain quantity of rivets—and rivets were what really Mr. Kurtz wanted, if he had only known it. Now letters went to the coast every week. . . . 'My dear sir,' he cried, 'I write from dictation.' I demanded rivets. There was a way—for an intelligent man. He changed his manner; became very cold, and suddenly began to talk about a hippopotamus; wondered whether sleeping on board the steamer (I stuck to my salvage night and day) I wasn't disturbed. There was an old hippo that had the bad habit of getting out on the bank and roaming at night over the station grounds. The pilgrims used to turn out in a body and empty every rifle they could lay hands on at him. Some even had sat up o' nights for him. All this energy was wasted, though. 'That animal has a charmed life,' he said; 'but you can say this only of brutes in this country. No man—you apprehend me?—no man here bears a charmed life.' He stood there for a moment in the moonlight with his delicate hooked nose set a little askew, and his mica eyes glittering without a wink, then, with a curt good night, he strode off. I could see he was disturbed and considerably puzzled, which made me feel more hopeful than I had been for days. It was a great comfort to turn from that chap to my influential friend, the battered, twisted, ruined, tinpot steamboat. I clambered on board. She rang under my feet like an empty Huntley and Palmer biscuit tin kicked along a gutter; she was nothing so solid in make, and rather less pretty in shape, but I had expended enough hard work on her to make me love her. No influential friend would have served me better. She had given me a chance to come out a bit—to find out what I could do. No, I don't like work. I had rather laze about and think of all the fine things that can be done. I don't like work—no man does—but I like what is in the work, the chance to find yourself. Your own reality—for yourself, not for others—what no other man can ever know. They can only see the mere show, and never can tell what it really means.

"I was not surprised to see somebody sitting aft, on the deck, with his legs dangling over the mud. You see I rather chummed with the few mechanics there were in that station, whom the other pilgrims naturally despised—on account of their imperfect manners, I suppose. This was the foreman—a boilermaker by trade—a good worker. He was a lank, bony, yellow-faced man, with big intense eyes. His aspect was worried, and his head was as bald as the palm of my hand; but his hair in falling seemed to have stuck to his chin, and had prospered in the new locality, for his beard hung down to his waist. He was a widower with six young children (he had left them in charge of a sister of his to come out there), and the passion of his life was pigeon flying. He was an enthusiast and a connoisseur. He would rave about pigeons. After work hours he used sometimes to come over from his hut for a talk about his children and his pigeons; at work, when he had to crawl in the mud under the bottom of the steamboat, he would tie up that beard of his in a kind of white serviette he brought for the purpose. It had loops to go over his ears. In the evening he could be seen squatted on the bank rinsing that wrapper in the creek with great care, then spreading it solemnly on a bush to dry.

"I slapped him on the back and shouted 'We shall have rivets!' He scrambled to his feet exclaiming 'No! Rivets!' as though he couldn't believe his ears. Then in a low voice, 'You . . . eh?' I don't know why we behaved like lunatics. I put my finger to the side of my nose and nodded mysteriously. 'Good for you!' he cried, snapped his fingers above his head, lifting one foot. I tried a jig. We capered on the iron deck. A frightful clatter came out of that hulk, and the virgin forest on the other bank of the creek sent it back in a thundering roll upon the sleeping station. It must have made some of the pilgrims sit up in their hovels. A dark figure obscured the lighted doorway of the manager's hut, vanished, then, a second or so after, the doorway itself vanished, too. We stopped, and the silence driven away by the stamping of our feet flowed back again from the recesses of the land. The great wall of vegetation, an exuberant and entangled mass of trunks, branches, leaves, boughs, festoons, motionless in the moonlight, was like a rioting invasion of soundless life, a rolling wave of plants, piled up, crested, ready to topple over the creek, to sweep every little man of us out of his little existence. And it moved not. A deadened burst of mighty splashes and snorts reached us from afar, as though an ichthyosaurus had been taking a bath of glitter in the great river. 'After all,' said the boilermaker in a reasonable tone, 'why shouldn't we get the rivets?' Why not, indeed! I did not know of any reason why we shouldn't. 'They'll come in three weeks,' I said, confidently.

"But they didn't. Instead of rivets there came an invasion, an infliction, a visitation. It came in sections during the next three weeks, each section headed by a donkey carrying a white man in new clothes and tan shoes, bowing from that elevation right and left to the impressed pilgrims. A quarrelsome band of footsore sulky niggers trod on the heels of the donkey; a lot of tents, campstools, tin boxes, white cases, brown bales would be shot down in the court-yard, and the air of mystery would deepen a little over the muddle of the station. Five such instalments came, with their absurd air of disorderly flight with the loot of innumerable outfit shops and provision stores, that, one would think, they were lugging, after a raid, into the wilderness for equitable division. It was an inextricable mess of things decent in themselves but that human folly made look like spoils of thieving.

"This devoted band called itself the Eldorado Exploring Expedi-tion, and I believe they were sworn to secrecy. Their talk, however, was the talk of sordid buccaneers: it was reckless without hardihood, greedy without audacity, and cruel without courage; there was not an atom of foresight or of serious intention in the whole batch of them, and they did not seem aware these things are wanted for the work of the world. To tear treasure out of the bowels of the land was their desire, with no more moral purpose at the back of it than there is in burglars breaking into a safe. Who paid the expenses of the noble enterprise I don't know; but the uncle of our manager was leader of that lot.

"In exterior he resembled a butcher in a poor neighborhood, and his eyes had a look of sleepy cunning. He carried his fat paunch with ostentation on his short legs, and during the time his gang infested the station spoke to no one but his nephew. You could see these two roaming about all day long with their heads close together in an everlasting confab.

"I had given up worrying myself about the rivets. One's capacity for that kind of folly is more limited than you would suppose. I said Hang!—and let things slide. I had plenty of time for meditation, and now and then I would give some thought to Kurtz. I wasn't very interested in him. No. Still, I was curious to see whether this man, who had come out equipped with moral ideas of some sort, would climb to the top after all and how he would set about his work when there."

## CHAPTER II

"One evening as I was lying flat on the deck of my steamboat, I heard voices approaching—and there were the nephew and the uncle strolling along the bank. I laid my head on my arm again, and had nearly lost myself in a doze, when somebody said in my ear, as it were: 'I am as harmless as a little child, but I don't like to be dictated to. Am I the manager—or am I not? I was ordered to send him there. It's incredible.' . . . I became aware that the two were standing on the shore alongside the forepart of the steamboat, just below my head. I did not move; it did not occur to me to move: I was sleepy. 'It *is* unpleasant,' grunted the uncle. 'He has asked the administration to be sent there,' said the other, 'with the idea of showing what he could do; and I was instructed accordingly. Look at the influence that man must have. Is it not frightful?' They both agreed it was frightful, then made several bizarre remarks: 'Make rain and fine weather—one man—the council—by the nose'—bits of absurd sentences that got the better of my drowsiness, so that I had pretty near the whole of my wits about me when the uncle said, 'The climate may do away with this difficulty for you. Is he alone there?' 'Yes,' answered the manager; 'he sent his assistant down the river with a note to me in these terms: "Clear this poor devil out of the country, and don't bother sending more of that sort. I had rather be alone than have the kind of men you can dispose of with me." It was more than a year ago. Can you imagine such impudence!' 'Anything since then?' asked the other, hoarsely. 'Ivory,' jerked the nephew; 'lots of it—prime sort—lots—most annoying, from him.' 'And with that?' questioned the heavy rumble. 'Invoice,' was the reply fired out, so to speak. Then silence. They had been talking about Kurtz.

"I was broad awake by this time, but, lying perfectly at ease, remained still, having no inducement to change my position. 'How did that ivory come all this way?' growled the elder man, who seemed very vexed. The other explained that it had come with a fleet of canoes in charge of an English half-caste clerk Kurtz had with him; that Kurtz had apparently intended to return himself, the station being by that time bare of goods and stores, but after coming three hundred miles, had suddenly decided to go back, which he started to do alone in a small dugout with four paddlers, leaving the half-caste to continue down the river with the ivory. The two fellows there seemed astounded at anybody attempting such a thing. They were at a loss for an adequate motive. As to me, I seemed to see Kurtz for the first time. It was a distinct glimpse: the dugout, four paddling savages, and the lone white man turning his back suddenly on the headquarters, on relief, on thoughts of home—perhaps; setting his face towards the depths of the wilderness, towards his empty and desolate station. I did not know the motive. Perhaps he was just simply a fine fellow who stuck to his work for its own sake. His name, you understand, had not been pronounced once. He was 'that man.' The half-caste, who, as far as I could see, had conducted a difficult trip with great prudence and pluck, was invariably alluded to as 'that scoundrel.' The 'scoundrel' had reported that the 'man' had been very ill—had recovered imperfectly. . . . The two below me moved away then a few paces, and strolled back and forth at some little distance. I heard: 'Military post—doctor—two hundred miles— quite alone now—unavoidable delays—nine months—no news— strange rumors.' They approached again, just as the manager was saying, 'No one, as far as I know, unless a species of wandering trader—a pestilential fellow, snapping ivory from the natives.' Who was it they were talking about now? I gathered in snatches that this was some man supposed to be in Kurtz's district, and of whom the manager did not approve. 'We will not be free from unfair compe- tition till one of these fellows is hanged for an example,' he said. 'Certainly,' grunted the other; 'get him hanged! Why not? Anything —anything can be done in this country. That's what I say; nobody here, you understand, *here*, can endanger your position. And why? You stand the climate—you outlast them all. The danger is in Europe; but there before I left I took care to—' They moved off and whispered, then their voices rose again. 'The extraordinary series of delays is not my fault. I did my best.' The fat man sighed. 'Very sad.' 'And the pestiferous absurdity of his talk,' continued the other; 'he bothered me enough when he was here. "Each station should be like a beacon on the road towards better things, a center for trade of course, but also for humanizing, improving, instructing." Con- ceive you—that ass! And he wants to be manager! No, it's—' Here he got choked by excessive indignation, and I lifted my head the least bit. I was surprised to see how near they were—right under me. I could have spat upon their hats. They were looking on the ground, absorbed in thought. The manager was switching his leg with a slender twig; his sagacious relative lifted his head. 'You have been well since you came out this time?' he asked. The other gave a start. 'Who? I? Oh! Like a charm—like a charm. But the rest— oh, my goodness! All sick. They die so quick, too, that I haven't the time to send them out of the country—it's incredible!' 'H'm. Just so,' grunted the uncle. 'Ah! my boy, trust to this—I say, trust to this.' I saw him extend his short flipper of an arm for a gesture that took in the forest, the creek, the mud, the river—seemed to beckon with a dishonoring flourish before the sunlit face of the land a treacherous appeal to the lurking death, to the hidden evil, to the profound darkness of its heart. It was so startling that I leaped to my feet and looked back at the edge of the forest, as though I had expected an answer of some sort to that black display of confidence. You know the foolish notions that come to one sometimes. The high stillness confronted these two figures with its ominous patience, waiting for the passing away of a fantastic invasion.

"They swore aloud together—out of sheer fright, I believe—then pretending not to know anything of my existence, turned back to the station. The sun was low; and leaning forward side by side, they seemed to be tugging painfully uphill their two ridiculous shadows of unequal length, that trailed behind them slowly over the tall grass without bending a single blade.

"In a few days the Eldorado Expedition went into the patient wilderness, that closed upon it as the sea closes over a diver. Long afterwards the news came that all the donkeys were dead. I know nothing as to the fate of the less valuable animals. They, no doubt, like the rest of us, found what they deserved. I did not inquire. I was then rather excited at the prospect of meeting Kurtz very soon. When I say very soon I mean it comparatively. It was just two months from the day we left the creek when we came to the bank below Kurtz's station.

"Going up that river was like traveling back to the earliest beginnings of the world, when vegetation rioted on the earth and the big trees were kings. An empty stream, a great silence, an impenetrable forest. The air was warm, thick, heavy, sluggish. There was no joy in the brilliance of sunshine. The long stretches of the waterway ran on, deserted, into the gloom of overshadowed distances. On silvery sandbanks hippos and alligators sunned themselves side by side. The broadening waters flowed through a mob of wooded islands; you lost your way on that river as you would in a desert, and butted all day long against shoals, trying to find the channel, till you thought yourself bewitched and cut off forever from everything you had known once—somewhere—far away—in another existence perhaps. There were moments when one's past came back to one, as it will sometimes when you have not a moment to spare to yourself; but it came in the shape of an unrestful and noisy dream, remembered with wonder amongst the overwhelming realities of this strange world of plants, and water, and silence. And this stillness of life did not in the least resemble a peace. It was the stillness of an implacable force brooding over an inscrutable intention. It looked at you with a vengeful aspect. I got used to it afterwards; I did not see it any more; I had no time. I had to keep guessing at the channel; I had to discern, mostly by inspiration, the signs of hidden banks; I watched for sunken stones; I was learning to clap my teeth smartly before my heart flew out, when I shaved by a fluke some infernal sly old snag that would have ripped the life out of the tin-pot steamboat and drowned all the pilgrims; I had to keep a lookout for the signs of dead wood we could cut up in the night for next day's steaming. When you have to attend to things of that sort, to the mere incidents of the surface, the reality—the reality, I tell you—fades. The inner truth is hidden—luckily, luckily. But I felt it all the same; I felt often its mysterious stillness watching me at my monkey tricks, just as it watches you fellows performing on your respective tightropes for—what is it? a half crown a tumble—"

"Try to be civil, Marlow," growled a voice, and I knew there was at least one listener awake besides myself.

"I beg your pardon. I forgot the heartache which makes up the rest of the price. And indeed what does the price matter, if the trick be well done? You do your tricks very well. And I didn't do badly either, since I managed not to sink that steamboat on my first trip. It's a wonder to me yet. Imagine a blindfolded man set to drive a van over a bad road. I sweated and shivered over that business considerably, I can tell you. After all, for a seaman, to scrape the bottom of the thing that's supposed to float all the time under his care is the unpardonable sin. No one may know of it, but you never forget the thump—eh? A blow on the very heart. You remember it, you dream of it, you wake up at night and think of it—years after—and go hot and cold all over. I don't pretend to say that steamboat floated all the time. More than once she had to wade for a bit, with twenty cannibals splashing around and pushing. We had enlisted some of these chaps on the way for a crew. Fine fellows—cannibals—in their place. They were men one could work with, and I am grateful to them. And, after all, they did not eat each other before my face: they had brought along a provision of hippo meat which went rotten, and made the mystery of the wilderness stink in my nostrils. Phoo! I can sniff it now. I had the manager on board and three or four pilgrims with their staves—all complete. Sometimes we came upon a station close by the bank, clinging to the skirts of the unknown, and the white men rushing out of a tumble-down hovel, with great gestures of joy and surprise and welcome, seemed very strange—had the appearance of being held there captive by a spell. The word ivory would ring in the air for a while—and on we went again into the silence, along empty reaches, round the still bends, between the high walls of our winding way, reverberating in hollow claps the ponderous beat of the stern wheel. Trees, trees, millions of trees, massive, immense, running up high; and at their foot, hugging the bank against the stream, crept the little begrimed steamboat, like a sluggish beetle crawling on the floor of a lofty portico. It made you feel very small, very lost, and yet it was not altogether depressing, that feeling. After all, if you were small, the grimy beetle crawled on—which was just what you wanted it to do. Where the pilgrims imagined it crawled to I don't know. To some place where they expected to get something, I bet! For me it crawled towards Kurtz—exclusively; but when the steam pipes started leaking we crawled very slow. The reaches opened before us and closed behind, as if the forest had stepped leisurely across the water to bar the way for our return. We penetrated deeper and deeper into the heart of darkness. It was very quiet there. At night sometimes the roll of drums behind the curtain of trees would run up the river and remain sustained faintly, as if hovering in the air high over our heads, till the first break of day. Whether it meant war, peace, or prayer we could not tell. The dawns were heralded by the descent of a chill stillness; the woodcutters slept, their fires burned low; the snapping of a twig would make you start. We were wanderers on prehistoric earth, on an earth that wore the aspect of an unknown planet. We could have fancied ourselves the first of men taking possession of an accursed inheritance, to be subdued at the cost of profound anguish and of excessive toil. But suddenly, as we struggled round a bend, there would be a glimpse of rush walls, of peaked grass roofs, a burst of yells, a whirl of black limbs, a mass of hands clapping, of feet stamping, of bodies swaying, of eyes rolling, under the droop of heavy and motionless foliage. The steamer toiled along slowly on the edge of a black and incomprehensible frenzy. The prehistoric man was cursing us, praying to us, welcoming us—who could tell? We were cut off from the comprehension of our surroundings; we glided past like phantoms, wondering and secretly appalled, as sane men would be before an enthusiastic outbreak in a madhouse. We could not understand because we were too far and could not remember, because we were traveling in the night of first ages, of those ages that are gone, leaving hardly a sign—and no memories.

"The earth seemed unearthly. We are accustomed to look upon the shackled form of a conquered monster, but there—there you could look at a thing monstrous and free. It was unearthly, and the

men were— No, they were not inhuman. Well, you know, that was
the worst of it—this suspicion of their not being inhuman. It would
come slowly to one. They howled and leaped, and spun, and made
horrid faces; but what thrilled you was just the thought of their
humanity—like yours—the thought of your remote kinship with this
wild and passionate uproar. Ugly. Yes, it was ugly enough; but if
you were man enough you would admit to yourself that there was
in you just the faintest trace of a response to the terrible frankness
of that noise, a dim suspicion of there being a meaning in it which
you—you so remote from the night of first ages—could comprehend. And why not? The mind of man is capable of anything—because everything is in it, all the past as well as all the future. What
was there after all? Joy, fear, sorrow, devotion, valor, rage—who can
tell?—but truth—truth stripped of its cloak of time. Let the fool
gape and shudder—the man knows, and can look on without a wink.
But he must at least be as much of a man as these on the shore. He
must meet that truth with his own true stuff—with his own inborn
strength. Principles won't do. Acquisitions, clothes, pretty rags—rags
that would fly off at the first good shake. No; you want a deliberate
belief. An appeal to me in this fiendish row—is there? Very well;
I hear; I admit, but I have a voice, too, and for good or evil mine
is the speech that cannot be silenced. Of course, a fool, what with
sheer fright and fine sentiments, is always safe. Who's that grunting?
You wonder I didn't go ashore for a howl and a dance? Well, no—
I didn't. Fine sentiments, you say? Fine sentiments, be hanged! I
had no time. I had to mess about with white lead and strips of
woolen blanket helping to put bandages on those leaky steam pipes—
I tell you. I had to watch the steering, and circumvent those snags,
and get the tin-pot along by hook or by crook. There was surface
truth enough in these things to save a wiser man. And between whiles
I had to look after the savage who was fireman. He was an improved
specimen; he could fire up a vertical boiler. He was there below me,
and, upon my word, to look at him was as edifying as seeing a dog
in a parody of breeches and a feather hat, walking on his hind legs.
A few months of training had done for that really fine chap. He
squinted at the steam gauge and at the water gauge with an evident
effort of intrepidity—and he had filed teeth, too, the poor devil, and
the wool of his pate shaved into queer patterns, and three ornamental
scars on each of his cheeks. He ought to have been clapping his hands
and stamping his feet on the bank, instead of which he was hard at
work, a thrall to strange witchcraft, full of improving knowledge.

He was useful because he had been instructed; and what he knew was this—that should the water in that transparent thing disappear, the evil spirit inside the boiler would get angry through the greatness of his thirst, and take a terrible vengeance. So he sweated and fired up and watched the glass fearfully (with an impromptu charm, made of rags, tied to his arm, and a piece of polished bone, as big as a watch, stuck flatways through his lower lip), while the wooded banks slipped past us slowly, the short noise was left behind, the interminable miles of silence—and we crept on, towards Kurtz. But the snags were thick, the water was treacherous and shallow, the boiler seemed indeed to have a sulky devil in it, and thus neither that fireman nor I had any time to peer into our creepy thoughts.

"Some fifty miles below the Inner Station we came upon a hut of reeds, an inclined and melancholy pole, with the unrecognizable tatters of what had been a flag of some sort flying from it, and a neatly stacked wood pile. This was unexpected. We came to the bank, and on the stack of firewood found a flat piece of board with some faded pencil writing on it. When deciphered it said: 'Wood for you. Hurry up. Approach cautiously.' There was a signature, but it was illegible—not Kurtz—a much longer word. Hurry up. Where? Up the river? 'Approach cautiously.' We had not done so. But the warning could not have been meant for the place where it could be only found after approach. Something was wrong above. But what— and how much? That was the question. We commented adversely upon the imbecility of that telegraphic style. The bush around said nothing, and would not let us look very far, either. A torn curtain of red twill hung in the doorway of the hut, and flapped sadly in our faces. The dwelling was dismantled; but we could see a white man had lived there not very long ago. There remained a rude table —a plank on two posts; a heap of rubbish reposed in a dark corner, and by the door I picked up a book. It had lost its covers, and the pages had been thumbed into a state of extremely dirty softness; but the back had been lovingly stitched afresh with white cotton thread, which looked clean yet. It was an extraordinary find. Its title was, *An Inquiry into Some Points of Seamanship*, by a man Tower, Towson—some such name—Master in his Majesty's Navy. The matter looked dreary reading enough, with illustrative diagrams and repulsive tables of figures, and the copy was sixty years old. I handled this amazing antiquity with the greatest possible tenderness, lest it should dissolve in my hands. Within, Towson or Towser was inquiring earnestly into the breaking strain of ships' chains and tackle, and other such matters. Not a very enthralling book; but at the first glance you could see there a singleness of intention, an honest concern for the right way of going to work, which made these humble pages, thought out so many years ago, luminous with another than a professional light. The simple old sailor, with his talk of chains and purchases, made me forget the jungle and the pilgrims in a delicious sensation of having come upon something unmistakably real. Such a book being there was wonderful enough; but still more astounding were the notes penciled in the margin, and plainly referring to the text. I couldn't believe my eyes! They were in cipher! Yes, it looked like cipher. Fancy a man lugging with him a book of that description into this nowhere and studying it—and making notes—in cipher at that! It was an extravagant mystery.

"I had been dimly aware for some time of a worrying noise, and when I lifted my eyes I saw the wood pile was gone, and the manager, aided by all the pilgrims, was shouting at me from the river side. I slipped the book into my pocket. I assure you to leave off reading was like tearing myself away from the shelter of an old and solid friendship.

"I started the lame engine ahead. 'It must be this miserable trader—this intruder,' exclaimed the manager, looking back malevolently at the place we had left. 'He must be English,' I said. 'It will not save him from getting into trouble if he is not careful,' muttered the manager darkly. I observed with assumed innocence that no man was safe from trouble in this world.

"The current was more rapid now, the steamer seemed at her last gasp, the stern wheel flopped languidly, and I caught myself listening on tiptoe for the next beat of the boat, for in sober truth I expected the wretched thing to give up every moment. It was like watching the last flickers of a life. But still we crawled. Sometimes I would pick out a tree a little way ahead to measure our progress towards Kurtz by, but I lost it invariably before we got abreast. To keep the eyes so long on one thing was too much for human patience. The manager displayed a beautiful resignation. I fretted and fumed and took to arguing with myself whether or no I would talk openly with Kurtz; but before I could come to any conclusion it occurred to me that my speech or my silence, indeed any action of mine, would be a mere futility. What did it matter what anyone knew or ignored? What did it matter who was manager? One gets sometimes such a flash of insight. The essentials of this affair lay deep under the surface, beyond my reach, and beyond my power of meddling.

"Towards the evening of the second day we judged ourselves about eight miles from Kurtz's station. I wanted to push on; but the manager looked grave, and told me the navigation up there was so dangerous that it would be advisable, the sun being very low already, to wait where we were till next morning. Moreover, he pointed out that if the warning to approach cautiously were to be followed, we must approach in daylight—not at dusk, or in the dark. This was sensible enough. Eight miles meant nearly three hours' steaming for us, and I could also see suspicious ripples at the upper end of the reach. Nevertheless, I was annoyed beyond expression at the delay, and most unreasonably, too, since one night more could not matter much after so many months. As we had plenty of wood, and caution was the word, I brought up in the middle of the stream. The reach was narrow, straight, with high sides like a railway cutting. The dusk came gliding into it long before the sun had set. The current ran smooth and swift, but a dumb immobility sat on the banks. The living trees, lashed together by the creepers and every living bush of the undergrowth, might have been changed into stone, even to the slenderest twig, to the lightest leaf. It was not sleep—it seemed unnatural, like a state of trance. Not the faintest sound of any kind could be heard. You looked on amazed, and began to suspect yourself of being deaf—then the night came suddenly, and struck you blind as well. About three in the morning some large fish leaped, and the loud splash made me jump as though a gun had been fired. When the sun rose there was a white fog, very warm and clammy, and more blinding than the night. It did not shift or drive; it was just there, standing all round you like something solid. At eight or nine, perhaps, it lifted as a shutter lifts. We had a glimpse of the towering multitude of trees, of the immense matted jungle, with the blazing little ball of the sun hanging over it—all perfectly still —and then the white shutter came down again, smoothly, as if sliding in greased grooves. I ordered the chain, which we had begun to heave in, to be paid out again. Before it stopped running with a muffled rattle, a cry, a very loud cry, as of infinite desolation, soared slowly in the opaque air. It ceased. A complaining clamor, modulated in savage discords, filled our ears. The sheer unexpectedness of it made my hair stir under my cap. I don't know how it struck the others: to me it seemed as though the mist itself had screamed, so suddenly, and apparently from all sides at once, did this tumultuous and mournful uproar arise. It culminated in a hurried outbreak of almost intolerably excessive shrieking, which stopped short, leaving us stiffened in a variety of silly attitudes, and obstinately listening to the nearly as appalling and excessive silence. 'Good God! What is the meaning—' stammered at my elbow one of the pilgrims, a little fat man, with sandy hair and red whiskers, who wore side-spring boots, and pink pajamas tucked into his socks. Two others remained openmouthed a whole minute, then dashed into the little cabin, to rush out incontinently and stand darting scared glances, with Winchesters at 'ready' in their hands. What we could see was just the steamer we were on, her outlines blurred as though she had been on the point of dissolving, and a misty strip of water, perhaps two feet broad, around her—and that was all. The rest of the world was nowhere, as far as our eyes and ears were concerned. Just nowhere. Gone, disappeared; swept off without leaving a whisper or a shadow behind.

"I went forward, and ordered the chain to be hauled in short, so as to be ready to trip the anchor and move the steamboat at once if necessary. 'Will they attack?' whispered an awed voice. 'We will be all butchered in this fog,' murmured another. The faces twitched with the strain, the hands trembled slightly, the eyes forgot to wink. It was very curious to see the contrast of expressions of the white men and of the black fellows of our crew, who were as much strangers to that part of the river as we, though their homes were only eight hundred miles away. The whites, of course greatly discomposed, had besides a curious look of being painfully shocked by such an outrageous row. The others had an alert, naturally interested expression; but their faces were essentially quiet, even those of the one or two who grinned as they hauled at the chain. Several exchanged short, grunting phrases, which seemed to settle the matter to their satisfaction. Their headman, a young, broad-chested black, severely draped in dark-blue fringed cloths, with fierce nostrils and his hair all done up artfully in oily ringlets, stood near me. 'Aha!' I said, just for good fellowship's sake. 'Catch 'im,' he snapped, with a bloodshot widening of his eyes and a flash of sharp teeth—'catch 'im. Give 'im to us.' 'To you, eh?' I asked; 'what would you do with them?' 'Eat 'im!' he said, curtly, and, leaning his elbow on the rail, looked out into the fog in a dignified and profoundly pensive attitude. I would no doubt have been properly horrified, had it not occurred to me that he and his chaps must be very hungry: that they must have been growing increasingly hungry for at least this month past. They had been engaged for six months (I don't think a single one of them had any clear idea of time, as we at the end of countless ages have. They still belonged to the beginnings of time—had no inherited experience to teach them as it were), and of course, as long as there was a piece of paper written over in accordance with some farcical law or other made down the river, it didn't enter anybody's head to trouble how they would live. Certainly they had brought with them some rotten hippo meat, which couldn't have lasted very long, anyway, even if the pilgrims hadn't, in the midst of a shocking hullabaloo, thrown a considerable quantity of it overboard. It looked like a high-handed proceeding; but it was really a case of legitimate self-defense. You can't breathe dead hippo waking, sleeping, and eating, and at the same time keep your precarious grip on existence. Besides that, they had given them every week three pieces of brass wire, each about nine inches long; and the theory was they were to buy their provisions with that currency in river-side villages. You can see how *that* worked. There were either no villages, or the people were hostile, or the director, who like the rest of us fed out of tins, with an occasional old he-goat thrown in, didn't want to stop the steamer for some more or less recondite reasons. So, unless they swallowed the wire itself, or made loops of it to snare the fishes with, I don't see what good their extravagant salary could be to them. I must say it was paid with a regularity worthy of a large and honorable trading company. For the rest, the only thing to eat—though it didn't look eatable in the least—I saw in their possession was a few lumps of some stuff like half-cooked dough, of a dirty lavender color, they kept wrapped in leaves, and now and then swallowed a piece of, but so small that it seemed done more for the looks of the thing than for any serious purpose of sustenance. Why in the name of all the gnawing devils of hunger they didn't go for us—they were thirty to five—and have a good tuck in for once, amazes me now when I think of it. They were big powerful men, with not much capacity to weigh the consequences, with courage, with strength, even yet, though their skins were no longer glossy and their muscles no longer hard. And I saw that something restraining, one of those human secrets that baffle probability, had come into play there. I looked at them with a swift quickening of interest—not because it occurred to me I might be eaten by them before very long, though I own to you that just then I perceived—in a new light, as it were—how unwholesome the pilgrims looked, and I hoped, yes, I positively hoped, that my aspect was not so—what shall I say?—so—unappetizing: a touch of fantastic vanity which fitted well with the dream-sensation that pervaded all my days at that time. Perhaps I had a little fever, too. One can't live with one's finger everlastingly on one's pulse. I had often 'a little fever,' or a little touch of other things—the playful paw-strokes of the wilderness, the preliminary trifling before the more serious onslaught which came in due course. Yes; I looked at them as you would on any human being, with a curiosity of their impulses, motives, capacities, weaknesses, when brought to the test of an inexorable physical necessity. Restraint! What possible restraint? Was it superstition, disgust, patience, fear—or some kind of primitive honor? No fear can stand up to hunger, no patience can wear it out, disgust simply does not exist where hunger is; and as to superstition, beliefs, and what you may call principles, they are less than chaff in a breeze. Don't you know the devilry of lingering starvation, its exasperating torment, its black thoughts, its somber and brooding ferocity? Well, I do. It takes a man all his inborn strength to fight hunger properly. It's really easier to face bereavement, dishonor, and the perdition of one's soul—than this kind of prolonged hunger. Sad, but true. And these chaps, too, had no earthly reason for any kind of scruple. Restraint! I would just as soon have expected restraint from a hyena prowling amongst the corpses of a battle-field. But there was the fact facing me—the fact dazzling, to be seen, like the foam on the depths of the sea, like a ripple on an unfathomable enigma, a mystery greater—when I thought of it—than the curious, inexplicable note of desperate grief in this savage clamor that had swept by us on the river bank, behind the blind whiteness of the fog.

"Two pilgrims were quarreling in hurried whispers as to which bank. 'Left.' 'No, no; how can you? Right, right, of course.' 'It is very serious,' said the manager's voice behind me; 'I would be desolated if anything should happen to Mr. Kurtz before we came up.' I looked at him, and had not the slightest doubt he was sincere. He was just the kind of man who would wish to preserve appearances. That was his restraint. But when he muttered something about going on at once, I did not even take the trouble to answer him. I knew, and he knew, that it was impossible. Were we to let go our hold of the bottom, we would be absolutely in the air—in space. We wouldn't be able to tell where we were going to—whether up- or down-stream, or across—till we fetched against one bank or the other, and then we wouldn't know at first which it was. Of course I made no move. I had no mind for a smashup. You couldn't imagine a more deadly place for a shipwreck. Whether drowned at once or not, we were sure to perish speedily in one way or another. 'I authorize you to take all the risks,' he said, after a short silence. 'I refuse to take any,' I said, shortly; which was just the answer he expected, though its tone might have surprised him. 'Well, I must defer to your judgment. You are captain,' he said, with marked civility. I turned my shoulder to him in sign of my appreciation, and looked into the fog. How long would it last? It was the most hopeless lookout. The approach to this Kurtz grubbing for ivory in the wretched bush was beset by as many dangers as though he had been an enchanted princess sleeping in a fabulous castle. 'Will they attack, do you think?' asked the manager, in a confidential tone.

"I did not think they would attack, for several obvious reasons. The thick fog was one. If they left the bank in their canoes they would get lost in it, as we would be if we attempted to move. Still, I had also judged the jungle of both banks quite impenetrable— and yet eyes were in it, eyes that had seen us. The riverside bushes were certainly very thick; but the undergrowth behind was evidently penetrable. However, during the short lift I had seen no canoes any-where in the reach—certainly not abreast of the steamer. But what made the idea of attack inconceivable to me was the nature of the noise—of the cries we had heard. They had not the fierce character boding of immediate hostile intention. Unexpected, wild, and violent as they had been, they had given me an irresistible impression of sorrow. The glimpse of the steamboat had for some reason filled those savages with unrestrained grief. The danger, if any, I ex-pounded, was from our proximity to a great human passion let loose. Even extreme grief may ultimately vent itself in violence—but more generally takes the form of apathy. . . .

"You should have seen the pilgrims stare! They had no heart to grin, or even to revile me: but I believe they thought me gone mad —with fright, maybe. I delivered a regular lecture. My dear boys, it was no good bothering. Keep a lookout? Well, you may guess I watched the fog for the signs of lifting as a cat watches a mouse; but for anything else our eyes were of no more use to us than if we had been buried miles deep in a heap of cotton-wool. It felt like it, too —choking, warm, stifling. Besides, all I said, though it sounded extravagant, was absolutely true to fact. What we afterwards alluded to as an attack was really an attempt at repulse. The action was very far from being aggressive—it was not even defensive, in the usual sense: it was undertaken under the stress of desperation, and in its essence was purely protective.

"It developed itself, I should say, two hours after the fog lifted, and its commencement was at a spot, roughly speaking, about a mile and a half below Kurtz's station. We had just floundered and flopped round a bend, when I saw an islet, a mere grassy hummock of bright green, in the middle of the stream. It was the only thing of the kind; but as we opened the reach more, I perceived it was the head of a long sandbank, or rather of a chain of shallow patches stretching down the middle of the river. They were discolored, just awash, and the whole lot was seen just under the water, exactly as a man's backbone is seen running down the middle of his back under the skin. Now, as far as I did see, I could go to the right or to the left of this. I didn't know either channel, of course. The banks looked pretty well alike, the depth appeared the same; but as I had been informed the station was on the west side, I naturally headed for the western passage.

"No sooner had we fairly entered it than I became aware it was much narrower than I had supposed. To the left of us there was the long uninterrupted shoal, and to the right a high, steep bank heavily overgrown with bushes. Above the bush the trees stood in serried ranks. The twigs overhung the current thickly, and from distance to distance a large limb of some tree projected rigidly over the stream. It was then well on in the afternoon, the face of the forest was gloomy, and a broad strip of shadow had already fallen on the water. In this shadow we steamed up—very slowly, as you may imagine. I sheered her well inshore—the water being deepest near the bank, as the sounding pole informed me.

"One of my hungry and forbearing friends was sounding in the bows just below me. This steamboat was exactly like a decked scow. On the deck, there were two little teakwood houses, with doors and windows. The boiler was in the fore-end, and the machinery right astern. Over the whole there was a light roof, supported on stanchions. The funnel projected through that roof, and in front of the funnel a small cabin built of light planks served for a pilot house. It contained a couch, two campstools, a loaded Martini-Henry leaning in one corner, a tiny table, and the steering wheel. It had a wide door in front and a broad shutter at each side. All these were always thrown open, of course. I spent my days perched up there on the extreme fore-end of that roof, before the door. At night I slept, or tried to, on the couch. An athletic black belonging to some coast tribe, and educated by my poor predecessor, was the helmsman. He sported a pair of brass earrings, wore a blue cloth wrapper from the waist to the ankles, and thought all the world of himself. He was the most unstable kind of fool I had ever seen. He steered with no end of swagger while you were by; but if he lost sight of you, he became instantly the prey of an abject funk, and would let that cripple of a steamboat get the upper hand of him in a minute.

"I was looking down at the sounding pole, and feeling much annoyed to see at each try a little more of it stick out of that river, when I saw my poleman give up the business suddenly, and stretch himself flat on the deck, without even taking the trouble to haul his pole in. He kept hold on it though, and it trailed in the water. At the same time the fireman, whom I could also see below me, sat down abruptly before his furnace and ducked his head. I was amazed. Then I had to look at the river mighty quick, because there was a snag in the fairway. Sticks, little sticks, were flying about—thick: they were whizzing before my nose, dropping below me, striking behind me against my pilot house. All this time the river, the shore, the woods, were very quiet—perfectly quiet. I could only hear the heavy splashing thump of the stern wheel and the patter of these things. We cleared the snag clumsily. Arrows, by Jove! We were being shot at! I stepped in quickly to close the shutter on the land side. That fool helmsman, his hands on the spokes, was lifting his knees high, stamping his feet, champing his mouth, like a reined-in horse. Confound him! And we were staggering within ten feet of the bank. I had to lean right out to swing the heavy shutter, and I saw a face amongst the leaves on the level with my own, looking at me very fierce and steady; and then suddenly, as though a veil had been removed from my eyes, I made out, deep in the tangled gloom, naked breasts, arms, legs, glaring eyes—the bush was swarming with human limbs in movement, glistening, of bronze color. The twigs shook, swayed, and rustled, the arrows flew out of them, and then the shutter came to. 'Steer her straight,' I said to the helmsman. He held his head rigid, face forward; but his eyes rolled, he kept on, lifting and setting down his feet gently, his mouth foamed a little. 'Keep quiet!' I said in a fury. I might just as well have ordered a tree not to sway in the wind. I darted out. Below me there was a great scuffle of feet on the iron deck; confused exclamations; a voice screamed, 'Can you turn back?' I caught sight of a V-shaped ripple on the water ahead. What? Another snag! A fusillade burst out under my feet. The pilgrims had opened with their Winchesters, and were simply squirting lead into that bush. A deuce of a lot of smoke came up and drove slowly forward. I swore at it. Now I couldn't see the ripple or the snag either. I stood in the doorway, peering, and the arrows came in swarms. They might have been poisoned, but they looked as though they wouldn't kill a cat. The bush began to howl. Our woodcutters raised a warlike whoop; the report of a rifle just at my back deafened me. I glanced over my shoulder, and the pilot house was yet full of noise and smoke when I made a dash at the wheel. The fool nigger had dropped everything, to throw the shutter open and let off that Martini-Henry. He stood before the wide opening, glaring, and I yelled at him to come back, while I straightened the sudden twist out of that steamboat. There was no room to turn even if I had wanted to, the snag was some-where very near ahead in that confounded smoke, there was no time to lose, so I just crowded her into the bank—right into the bank, where I knew the water was deep.

"We tore slowly along the overhanging bushes in a whirl of broken twigs and flying leaves. The fusillade below stopped short, as I had foreseen it would when the squirts got empty. I threw my head back to a glinting whizz that traversed the pilot house, in at one shutter-hole and out at the other. Looking past that mad helmsman, who was shaking the empty rifle and yelling at the shore, I saw vague forms of men running bent double, leaping, gliding, distinct, in-complete, evanescent. Something big appeared in the air before the shutter, the rifle went overboard, and the man stepped back swiftly, looked at me over his shoulder in an extraordinary, profound, familiar manner, and fell upon my feet. The side of his head hit the wheel twice, and the end of what appeared a long cane clattered round and knocked over a little campstool. It looked as though after wrenching that thing from somebody ashore he had lost his balance in the effort. The thin smoke had blown away, we were clear of the snag, and looking ahead I could see that in another hundred yards or so I would be free to sheer off, away from the bank; but my feet felt so very warm and wet that I had to look down. The man had rolled on his back and stared straight up at me; both his hands clutched that cane. It was the shaft of a spear that, either thrown or lunged through the opening, had caught him in the side just below the ribs; the blade had gone in out of sight, after making a frightful gash; my shoes were full; a pool of blood lay very still, gleaming dark-red under the wheel; his eyes shone with an amazing luster. The fusillade burst out again. He looked at me anxiously, gripping the spear like something precious, with an air of being afraid I would try to take it away from him. I had to make an effort to free my eyes from his gaze and attend to the steering. With one hand I felt above my head for the line of the steam whistle, and jerked out screech after screech hurriedly. The tumult of angry and warlike yells was checked instantly, and then from the depths of the woods went out such a tremulous and prolonged wail of mournful fear and utter despair as may be imagined to follow the flight of the last hope from the earth. There was a great commotion in the bush; the shower of arrows stopped, a few dropping shots rang out sharply—then silence, in which the languid beat of the stern wheel came plainly to my ears. I put the helm hard a-starboard at the moment when the pilgrim in pink pajamas, very hot and agitated, appeared in the doorway. 'The manager sends me—' he began in an official tone, and stopped short. 'Good God!' he said, glaring at the wounded man.

"We two whites stood over him, and his lustrous and inquiring glance enveloped us both. I declare it looked as though he would presently put to us some question in an understandable language; but he died without uttering a sound, without moving a limb, without twitching a muscle. Only in the very last moment, as though in response to some sign we could not see, to some whisper we could not hear, he frowned heavily, and that frown gave to his black death mask an inconceivably somber, brooding, and menacing expression. The luster of inquiring glance faded swiftly into vacant glassiness. 'Can you steer?' I asked the agent eagerly. He looked very dubious; but I made a grab at his arm, and he understood at once I meant him to steer whether or no. To tell you the truth, I was morbidly anxious to change my shoes and socks. 'He is dead,' murmured the fellow, immensely impressed. 'No doubt about it,' said I, tugging like mad at the shoelaces. 'And by the way, I suppose Mr. Kurtz is dead as well by this time.'

"For the moment that was the dominant thought. There was a sense of extreme disappointment, as though I had found out I had been striving after something altogether without a substance. I couldn't have been more disgusted if I had traveled all this way for the sole purpose of talking with Mr. Kurtz. Talking with . . . I flung one shoe overboard, and became aware that that was exactly what I had been looking forward to—a talk with Kurtz. I made the strange discovery that I had never imagined him as doing, you know, but as discoursing. I didn't say to myself, 'Now I will never see him,' or 'Now I will never shake him by the hand,' but, 'now I will never hear him.' The man presented himself as a voice. Not of course that I did not connect him with some sort of action. Hadn't I been told in all the tones of jealousy and admiration that he had collected, bartered, swindled, or stolen more ivory than all the other agents together? That was not the point. The point was in his being a gifted creature, and that of all his gifts the one that stood out pre-eminently, that carried with it a sense of real presence, was his ability to talk, his words—the gift of expression, the bewildering, the illuminating, the most exalted and the most contemptible, the pulsating stream of light, or the deceitful flow from the heart of an impenetrable darkness.

"The other shoe went flying unto the devil-god of that river. I thought, by Jove! it's all over. We are too late; he has vanished—the gift has vanished, by means of some spear, arrow, or club. I will never hear that chap speak after all, and my sorrow had a startling extravagance of emotion, even such as I had noticed in the howling sorrow of these savages in the bush. I couldn't have felt more of lonely desolation somehow, had I been robbed of a belief or had missed my destiny in life. . . . Why do you sigh in this beastly way, somebody? Absurd? Well, absurd. Good Lord! mustn't a man ever—Here, give me some tobacco." . . .

There was a pause of profound stillness, then a match flared, and Marlow's lean face appeared, worn, hollow, with downward folds and dropped eyelids, with an aspect of concentrated attention; and as he took vigorous draws at his pipe, it seemed to retreat and advance out of the night in the regular flicker of the tiny flame. The match went out.

"Absurd!" he cried. "This is the worst of trying to tell. . . . Here you all are, each moored with two good addresses, like a hulk with two anchors, a butcher round one corner, a policeman round another, excellent appetites, and temperature normal—you hear—normal from year's end to year's end. And you say, Absurd! Absurd be—exploded! Absurd! My dear boys, what can you expect from a man who out of sheer nervousness had just flung overboard a pair of new shoes! Now I think of it, it is amazing I did not shed tears. I am, upon the whole, proud of my fortitude. I was cut to the quick at the idea of having lost the inestimable privilege of listening to the gifted Kurtz. Of course I was wrong. The privilege was waiting for me. Oh, yes, I heard more than enough. And I was right, too. A voice. He was very little more than a voice. And I heard—him—it—this voice—other voices—all of them were so little more than voices—and the memory of that time itself lingers around me, impalpable, like a dying vibration of one immense jabber, silly, atrocious, sordid, savage, or simply mean, without any kind of sense. Voices, voices—even the girl herself—now—"

He was silent for a long time.

"I laid the ghost of his gifts at last with a lie," he began, suddenly. "Girl! What? Did I mention a girl? Oh, she is out of it—completely. They—the women I mean—are out of it—should be out of it. We must help them to stay in that beautiful world of their own, lest ours gets worse. Oh, she had to be out of it. You should have heard the disinterred body of Mr. Kurtz saying, 'My Intended.' You would have perceived directly then how completely she was out of it. And the lofty frontal bone of Mr. Kurtz! They say the hair goes on growing sometimes, but this—ah—specimen, was impressively bald. The wilderness had patted him on the head, and, behold, it was like a ball—an ivory ball; it had caressed him, and—lo!—he had withered; it had taken him, loved him, embraced him, got into his veins, consumed his flesh, and sealed his soul to its own by the inconceivable ceremonies of some devilish initiation. He was its spoiled and pampered favorite. Ivory? I should think so. Heaps of it, stacks of it. The old mud shanty was bursting with it. You would think there was not a single tusk left either above or below the ground in the whole country. 'Mostly fossil,' the manager had remarked, disparagingly. It was no more fossil than I am; but they call it fossil when it is dug up. It appears these niggers do bury the tusks sometimes—but evidently they couldn't bury this parcel deep enough to save the gifted Mr. Kurtz from his fate. We filled the steamboat with it, and had to pile a lot on the deck. Thus he could see and enjoy as long as he could see, because the appreciation of his favor had remained with him to the last. You should have heard him say, 'My ivory.' Oh yes, I heard him. 'My Intended, my ivory, my station, my river, my—' everything belonged to him. It made me hold my breath in expectation of hearing the wilderness burst into a prodigious peal of laughter that would shake the fixed stars in their places. Everything belonged to him—but that was a trifle. The thing was to know what he belonged to, how many powers of darkness claimed him for their own. That was the reflection that made you creepy all over. It was impossible—it was not good for one either—trying to imagine. He had taken a high seat amongst the devils of the land—I mean literally. You can't understand. How could you?—with solid pavement under your feet, surrounded by kind neighbors ready to cheer you or to fall on you, stepping delicately between the butcher and the policeman, in the holy terror of scandal and gallows and lunatic asylums—how can you imagine what particular region of the first ages a man's untrammeled feet may take him into by the way of solitude—utter solitude without a policeman—by the way of silence

—utter silence, where no warning voice of a kind neighbor can be heard whispering of public opinion? These little things make all the great difference. When they are gone you must fall back upon your own innate strength, upon your own capacity for faithfulness. Of course you may be too much of a fool to go wrong—too dull even to know you are being assaulted by the powers of darkness. I take it, no fool ever made a bargain for his soul with the devil: the fool is too much of a fool, or the devil too much of a devil—I don't know which. Or you may be such a thunderingly exalted creature as to be altogether deaf and blind to anything but heavenly sights and sounds. Then the earth for you is only a standing place—and whether to be like this is your loss or your gain I won't pretend to say. But most of us are neither one nor the other. The earth for us is a place to live in, where we must put up with sights, with sounds, with smells, too, by Jove!—breathe dead hippo, so to speak, and not be contaminated. And there, don't you see? Your strength comes in, the faith in your ability for the digging of unostentatious holes to bury the stuff in—your power of devotion, not to yourself, but to an obscure, back-breaking business. And that's difficult enough. Mind, I am not trying to excuse or even explain—I am trying to account to myself for—for—Mr. Kurtz—for the shade of Mr. Kurtz. This initiated wraith from the back of Nowhere honored me with its amazing confidence before it vanished altogether. This was because it could speak English to me. The original Kurtz had been educated partly in England, and—as he was good enough to say himself—his sympathies were in the right place. His mother was half-English, his father was half-French. All Europe contributed to the making of Kurtz; and by and by I learned that, most appropriately, the International Society for the Suppression of Savage Customs had intrusted him with the making of a report, for its future guidance. And he had written it, too. I've seen it. I've read it. It was eloquent, vibrating with eloquence, but too high-strung, I think. Seventeen pages of close writing he had found time for! But this must have been before his—let us say—nerves, went wrong, and caused him to preside at certain midnight dances ending with unspeakable rites, which—as far as I reluctantly gathered from what I heard at various times— were offered up to him—do you understand?—to Mr. Kurtz himself. But it was a beautiful piece of writing. The opening paragraph, however, in the light of later information, strikes me now as ominous. He began with the argument that we whites, from the point of development we had arrived at, 'must necessarily appear to them [savages] in the nature of supernatural beings—we approach them with the might as of a deity,' and so on, and so on. 'By the simple exercise of our will we can exert a power for good practically unbounded,' etc., etc. From that point he soared and took me with him. The peroration was magnificent, though difficult to remember, you know. It gave me the notion of an exotic Immensity ruled by an august Benevolence. It made me tingle with enthusiasm. This was the unbounded power of eloquence—of words—of burning noble words. There were no practical hints to interrupt the magic current of phrases, unless a kind of note at the foot of the last page, scrawled evidently much later, in an unsteady hand, may be regarded as the exposition of a method. It was very simple, and at the end of that moving appeal to every altruistic sentiment it blazed at you, luminous and terrifying, like a flash of lightning in a serene sky: 'Exterminate all the brutes!' The curious part was that he had apparently forgotten all about that valuable postscriptum, because, later on, when he in a sense came to himself, he repeatedly entreated me to take good care of 'my pamphlet' (he called it), as it was sure to have in the future a good influence upon his career. I had full information about all these things, and, besides, as it turned out, I was to have the care of his memory. I've done enough for it to give me the indisputable right to lay it, if I choose, for an everlasting rest in the dust bin of progress, amongst all the sweepings and, figuratively speaking, all the dead cats of civilization. But then, you see, I can't choose. He won't be forgotten. Whatever he was, he was not common. He had the power to charm or frighten rudimentary souls into an aggravated witch dance in his honor; he could also fill the small souls of the pilgrims with bitter misgivings: he had one devoted friend at least, and he had conquered one soul in the world that was neither rudimentary nor tainted with self-seeking. No; I can't forget him, though I am not prepared to affirm the fellow was exactly worth the life we lost in getting to him. I missed my late helmsman awfully—I missed him even while his body was still lying in the pilot house. Perhaps you will think it passing strange this regret for a savage who was no more account than a grain of sand in a black Sahara. Well, don't you see, he had done something, he had steered; for months I had him at my back—a help—an instrument. It was a kind of partnership. He steered for me—I had to look after him, I worried about his deficiencies, and thus a subtle bond had been created, of which I only became aware when it was suddenly broken. And the intimate profundity of that look he gave me when he

received his hurt remains to this day in my memory—like a claim of distant kinship affirmed in a supreme moment.

"Poor fool! If he had only left that shutter alone. He had no restraint—just like Kurtz—a tree swayed by the wind. As soon as I had put on a dry pair of slippers, I dragged him out, after first jerking the spear out of his side, which operation I confess I performed with my eyes shut tight. His heels leaped together over the little doorstep; his shoulders were pressed to my breast; I hugged him from behind desperately. Oh! he was heavy, heavy; heavier than any man on earth, I should imagine. Then without more ado I tipped him overboard. The current snatched him as though he had been a wisp of grass, and I saw the body roll over twice before I lost sight of it forever. All the pilgrims and the manager were then congregated on the awning deck about the pilot house, chattering at each other like a flock of excited magpies, and there was a scandalized murmur at my heartless promptitude. What they wanted to keep that body hanging about for I can't guess. Embalm it, maybe. But I had also heard another, and a very ominous, murmur on the deck below. My friends the woodcutters were likewise scandalized, and with a better show of reason—though I admit that the reason itself was quite inadmissible. Oh, quite! I had made up my mind that if my late helmsman was to be eaten, the fishes alone should have him. He had been a very second-rate helmsman while alive, but now he was dead he might have become a first-class temptation, and possibly cause some startling trouble. Besides, I was anxious to take the wheel, the man in pink pajamas showing himself a hopeless duffer at the business.

"This I did directly the simple funeral was over. We were going half-speed, keeping right in the middle of the stream, and I listened to the talk about me. They had given up Kurtz, they had given up the station; Kurtz was dead, and the station had been burnt—and so on—and so on. The red-haired pilgrim was beside himself with the thought that at least this poor Kurtz had been properly avenged. 'Say! We must have made a glorious slaughter of them in the bush. Eh? What do you think? Say?' He positively danced, the bloodthirsty little gingery beggar. And he had nearly fainted when he saw the wounded man! I could not help saying, 'You made a glorious lot of smoke, anyhow.' I had seen, from the way the tops of the bushes rustled and flew, that almost all the shots had gone too high. You can't hit anything unless you take aim and fire from the shoulder; but these chaps fired from the hip with their eyes shut. The retreat, I maintained—and I was right—was caused by the screeching of the steam whistle. Upon this they forgot Kurtz, and began to howl at me with indignant protests.

"The manager stood by the wheel murmuring confidentially about the necessity of getting well away down the river before dark at all events, when I saw in the distance a clearing on the river side and the outlines of some sort of building. 'What's this?' I asked. He clapped his hands in wonder. 'That station!' he cried. I edged in at once, still going half-speed.

"Through my glasses I saw the slope of a hill interspersed with rare trees and perfectly free from undergrowth. A long decaying building on the summit was half buried in the high grass; the large holes in the peaked roof gaped black from afar; the jungle and the woods made a background. There was no enclosure or fence of any kind; but there had been one apparently, for near the house half-a-dozen slim posts remained in a row, roughly trimmed, and with their upper ends ornamented with round carved balls. The rails, or whatever there had been between, had disappeared. Of course the forest surrounded all that. The river bank was clear, and on the water side I saw a white man under a hat like a cart wheel beckoning persistently with his whole arm. Examining the edge of the forest above and below, I was almost certain I could see movements—human forms gliding here and there. I steamed past prudently, then stopped the engines and let her drift down. The man on the shore began to shout, urging us to land. 'We have been attacked,' screamed the manager. 'I know—I know. It's all right,' yelled back the other, as cheerful as you please. 'Come along. It's all right. I am glad.'

"His aspect reminded me of something I had seen—something funny I had seen somewhere. As I maneuvered to get alongside, I was asking myself, 'What does this fellow look like?' Suddenly I got it. He looked like a harlequin. His clothes had been made of some stuff that was brown holland probably, but it was covered with patches all over, with bright patches, blue, red, and yellow—patches on the back, patches on the front, patches on elbows, on knees; colored binding around his jacket, scarlet edging at the bottom of his trousers; and the sunshine made him look extremely gay and wonderfully neat withal, because you could see how beautifully all this patching had been done. A beardless, boyish face, very fair, no features to speak of, nose peeling, little blue eyes, smiles and frowns chasing each other over that open countenance like sunshine and shadow on a wind-swept plain. 'Look out, captain!' he cried; 'there's a snag lodged in here last night.' What! Another snag? I confess I swore shamefully. I had nearly holed my cripple, to finish off that charming trip. The harlequin on the bank turned his little pug nose up to me. 'You English?' he asked, all smiles. 'Are you?' I shouted from the wheel. The smiles vanished, and he shook his head as if sorry for my disappointment. Then he brightened up. 'Never mind!' he cried, encouragingly. 'Are we in time?' I asked. 'He is up there,' he replied, with a toss of the head up the hill, and becoming gloomy all of a sudden. His face was like the autumn sky, overcast one moment and bright the next.

"When the manager, escorted by the pilgrims, all of them armed to the teeth, had gone to the house this chap came on board. 'I say, I don't like this. These natives are in the bush,' I said. He assured me earnestly it was all right. 'They are simple people,' he added; 'well, I am glad you came. It took me all my time to keep them off.' 'But you said it was all right,' I cried. 'Oh, they meant no harm,' he said; and as I stared he corrected himself, 'Not exactly.' Then vivaciously, 'My faith, your pilot house wants a clean-up!' In the next breath he advised me to keep enough steam on the boiler to blow the whistle in case of any trouble. 'One good screech will do more for you than all your rifles. They are simple people,' he repeated. He rattled away at such a rate he quite overwhelmed me. He seemed to be trying to make up for lots of silence, and actually hinted, laughing, that such was the case. 'Don't you talk with Mr. Kurtz?' I said. 'You don't talk with that man—you listen to him,' he exclaimed with severe exaltation. 'But now—' He waved his arm, and in the twinkling of an eye was in the uttermost depths of despondency. In a moment he came up again with a jump, possessed himself of both my hands, shook them continuously, while he gabbled: 'Brother sailor . . . honor . . . pleasure . . . delight . . . introduce myself . . . Russian . . . son of an arch-priest . . . Government of Tambov . . . What? Tobacco! English tobacco; the excellent English tobacco! Now, that's brotherly. Smoke? Where's a sailor that does not smoke?'

"The pipe soothed him, and gradually I made out he had run away from school, had gone to sea in a Russian ship; ran away again; served some time in English ships; was now reconciled with the arch-priest. He made a point of that. 'But when one is young one must see things, gather experience, ideas; enlarge the mind.' 'Here!' I interrupted. 'You can never tell! Here I met Mr. Kurtz,' he said, youthfully solemn and reproachful. I held my tongue after that. It appears he had persuaded a Dutch trading house on the coast to fit him out with stores and goods, and had started for the interior with a light heart, and no more idea of what would happen to him than a baby. He had been wandering about that river for nearly two years alone, cut off from everybody and everything. 'I am not so young as I look. I am twenty-five,' he said. 'At first old Van Shuyten would tell me to go to the devil,' he narrated with keen enjoyment; 'but I stuck to him, and talked and talked, till at last he got afraid I would talk the hind leg off his favorite dog, so he gave me some cheap things and a few guns, and told me he hoped he would never see my face again. Good old Dutchman, Van Shuyten. I've sent him one small lot of ivory a year ago, so that he can't call me a little thief when I get back. I hope he got it. And for the rest I don't care. I had some wood stacked for you. That was my old house. Did you see?'

"I gave him Towson's book. He made as though he would kiss me, but restrained himself. 'The only book I had left, and I thought I had lost it,' he said, looking at it ecstatically. 'So many accidents happen to a man going about alone, you know. Canoes get upset sometimes—and sometimes you've got to clear out so quick when the people get angry.' He thumbed the pages. 'You made notes in Russian?' I asked. He nodded. 'I thought they were written in cipher,' I said. He laughed, then became serious. 'I had lots of trouble to keep these people off,' he said. 'Did they want to kill you?' I asked. 'Oh, no!' he cried, and checked himself. 'Why did they attack us?' I pursued. He hesitated, then said shamefacedly, 'They don't want him to go.' 'Don't they?' I said, curiously. He nodded a nod full of mystery and wisdom. 'I tell you,' he cried, 'this man has enlarged my mind.' He opened his arms wide, staring at me with his little blue eyes that were perfectly round."

## CHAPTER III

"I looked at him, lost in astonishment. There he was before me, in motley, as though he had absconded from a troupe of mimes, enthusiastic, fabulous. His very existence was improbable, inexplicable, and altogether bewildering. He was an insoluble problem. It was inconceivable how he had existed, how he had succeeded in getting so far, how he had managed to remain—why he did not instantly disappear. 'I went a little farther,' he said, 'then still a little farther—till I had gone so far that I don't know how I'll ever get back. Never mind. Plenty time. I can manage. You take Kurtz away quick—quick—I tell you.' The glamor of youth enveloped his particolored rags, his destitution, his loneliness, the essential desolation of his futile wanderings. For months—for years—his life hadn't been worth a day's purchase; and there he was gallantly, thoughtlessly alive, to all appearance indestructible solely by the virtue of his few years and of his unreflecting audacity. I was seduced into something like admiration—like envy. Glamor urged him on, glamor kept him unscathed. He surely wanted nothing from the wilderness but space to breathe in and to push on through. His need was to exist, and to move onwards at the greatest possible risk, and with a maximum of privation. If the absolutely pure, uncalculating, unpractical spirit of adventure had ever ruled a human being, it ruled this be-patched youth. I almost envied him the possession of this modest and clear flame. It seemed to have consumed all thought of self so completely, that even while he was talking to you, you forget that it was he—the man before your eyes—who had gone through these things. I did not envy him his devotion to Kurtz, though. He had not meditated over it. It came to him, and he accepted it with a sort of eager fatalism. I must say that to me it appeared about the most dangerous thing in every way he had come upon so far.

"They had come together unavoidably, like two ships becalmed near each other, and lay rubbing sides at last. I suppose Kurtz wanted an audience, because on a certain occasion, when encamped in the forest, they had talked all night, or more probably Kurtz had talked. 'We talked of everything,' he said, quite transported at the recollection. 'I forgot there was such a thing as sleep. The night did not seem to last an hour. Everything! Everything! . . . Of love, too.' 'Ah, he talked to you of love!' I said, much amused. 'It isn't what you think,' he cried, almost passionately. 'It was in general. He made me see things—things.'

"He threw his arms up. We were on deck at the time, and the headman of my woodcutters, lounging near by, turned upon him his heavy and glittering eyes. I looked around, and I don't know why, but I assure you that never, never before, did this land, this river, this jungle, the very arch of this blazing sky, appear to me so hopeless and so dark, so impenetrable to human thought, so pitiless to human weakness. 'And, ever since, you have been with him, of course?' I said.

"On the contrary. It appears their intercourse had been very much broken by various causes. He had, as he informed me proudly, managed to nurse Kurtz through two illnesses (he alluded to it as you would to some risky feat), but as a rule Kurtz wandered alone, far in the depths of the forest. 'Very often coming to this station, I had to wait days and days before he would turn up,' he said. 'Ah, it was worth waiting for!—sometimes.' 'What was he doing? Exploring or what?' I asked. 'Oh, yes, of course'; he had discovered lots of villages, a lake, too—he did not know exactly in what direction; it was dangerous to inquire too much—but mostly his expeditions had been for ivory. 'But he had no goods to trade with by that time,' I objected. 'There's a good lot of cartridges left even yet,' he answered, looking away. 'To speak plainly, he raided the country,' I said. He nodded. 'Not alone, surely!' He muttered something about the villages round that lake. 'Kurtz got the tribe to follow him, did he?' I suggested. He fidgeted a little. 'They adored him,' he said. The tone of these words was so extraordinary that I looked at him searchingly. It was curious to see his mingled eagerness and reluctance to speak of Kurtz. The man filled his life, occupied his thoughts, swayed his emotions. 'What can you expect?' he burst out; 'he came to them with thunder and lightning, you know—and they had never seen anything like it—and very terrible. He could be very terrible. You can't judge Mr. Kurtz as you would an ordinary man. No, no, no! Now—just to give you an idea—I don't mind telling you, he wanted to shoot me, too, one day—but I don't judge him.' 'Shoot you!' I cried. 'What for?' 'Well, I had a small lot of ivory the chief of that village near my house gave me. You see I used to shoot game for them. Well, he wanted it, and wouldn't hear reason. He declared he would shoot me unless I gave him the ivory and then cleared out of the country, because he could do so, and had a fancy for it, and there was nothing on earth to prevent him killing whom he jolly well pleased. And it was true, too. I gave him the ivory. What did I care! But I didn't clear out. No, no. I couldn't leave him. I had to be careful, of course, till we got friendly again for a time. He had his second illness then. Afterwards I had to keep out of the way; but I didn't mind. He was living for the most part in those villages on the lake. When he came down to the river, sometimes he would take to me, and sometimes it was better for me to be careful. This man suffered too much. He hated all this, and somehow he couldn't get away. When I had a chance I begged him to try and leave while there was time; I offered to go back with him. And he would say yes, and then he would remain; go off on another ivory hunt; disappear for weeks; forget himself amongst these people—forget himself—you know.' 'Why! he's mad,' I said. He protested indignantly. Mr. Kurtz couldn't be mad. If I had heard him talk, only two days ago, I wouldn't dare hint at such a thing. . . . I had taken up my binoculars while we talked, and was looking at the shore, sweeping the limit of the forest at each side and at the back of the house. The consciousness of there being people in that bush, so silent, so quiet—as silent and quiet as the ruined house on the hill—made me uneasy. There was no sign on the face of nature of this amazing tale that was not so much told as suggested to me in desolate exclamations, completed by shrugs, in interrupted phrases, in hints ending in deep sighs. The woods were unmoved, like a mask—heavy, like the closed door of a prison—they looked with their air of hidden knowledge, of patient expectation, of unapproachable silence. The Russian was explaining to me that it was only lately that Mr. Kurtz had come down to the river, bringing along with him all the fighting men of that lake tribe. He had been absent for several months— getting himself adored, I suppose—and had come down unexpectedly, with the intention to all appearances of making a raid either across the river or downstream. Evidently the appetite for more ivory had got the better of the—what shall I say?—less material aspirations. However he had got much worse suddenly. 'I heard he was lying helpless, and so I came up—took my chance,' said the Russian. 'Oh, he is bad, very bad.' I directed my glass to the house. There were no signs of life, but there was the ruined roof, the long mud wall peeping above the grass, with three little square window holes, no two of the same size; all this brought within reach of my hand, as it were. And then I made a brusque movement, and one of the remaining posts of that vanished fence leaped up in the field of my glass. You remember I told you I had been struck at the distance by certain attempts at ornamentation, rather remarkable in the ruinous aspect of the place. Now I had suddenly a nearer view, and its first result was to make me throw my head back as if before a blow. Then I went carefully from post to post with my glass, and I saw my mistake. These round knobs were not ornamental but symbolic; they were expressive and puzzling, striking and disturbing— food for thought and also for the vultures if there had been any looking down from the sky; but at all events for such ants as were industrious enough to ascend the pole. They would have been even more impressive, those heads on the stakes, if their faces had not been turned to the house. Only one, the first I had made out, was facing my way. I was not so shocked as you may think. The start back I had given was really nothing but a movement of surprise. I had expected to see a knob of wood there, you know. I returned deliberately to the first I had seen—and there it was, black, dried, sunken, with closed eyelids, a head that seemed to sleep at the top of that pole, and, with the shrunken dry lips showing a narrow white line of the teeth, was smiling, too, smiling continuously at some endless and jocose dream of that eternal slumber.

"I am not disclosing any trade secrets. In fact, the manager said afterwards that Mr. Kurtz's methods had ruined the district. I have no opinion on that point, but I want you clearly to understand that there was nothing exactly profitable in these heads being there. They only showed that Mr. Kurtz lacked restraint in the gratification of his various lusts, . . . there was something wanting in him—some small matter which, when the pressing need arose, could not be found under his magnificent eloquence. Whether he knew of this deficiency himself I can't say. I think the knowledge came to him at last—only at the very last. But the wilderness had found him out early, and had taken on him a terrible vengeance for the fantastic invasion. I think it had whispered to him things about himself which he did not know, things of which he had no conception till he took counsel with this great solitude—and the whisper had proved irresistibly fascinating. It echoed loudly within him because he was hollow at the core. . . . I put down the glass, and the head that had appeared near enough to be spoken to seemed at once to have leaped away from me into inaccessible distance.

"The admirer of Mr. Kurtz was a bit crestfallen. In a hurried, indistinct voice he began to assure me he had not dared to take these—say, symbols—down. He was not afraid of the natives; they would not stir till Mr. Kurtz gave the word. His ascendancy was extraordinary. The camps of these people surrounded the place, and the chiefs came every day to see him. They would crawl. . . . 'I don't want to know anything of the ceremonies used when approaching Mr. Kurtz,' I shouted. Curious, this feeling that came over me that such details would be more intolerable than those heads drying on the stakes under Mr. Kurtz's windows. After all, that was only a savage sight, while I seemed at one bound to have been transported into some lightless region of subtle horrors, where pure, uncomplicated savagery was a positive relief, being something that had a right to exist—obviously—in the sunshine. The young man looked at me with surprise. I suppose it did not occur to him that Mr. Kurtz was no idol of mine. He forgot I hadn't heard any of these splendid monologues on, what was it? On love, justice, conduct of life—or whatnot. If it had come to crawling before Mr. Kurtz, he crawled as much as the veriest savage of them all. I had no idea of the conditions, he said: these heads were the heads of rebels. I shocked him excessively by laughing. Rebels! What would be the next definition I was to hear? There had been enemies, criminals, workers—and these were rebels. Those rebellious heads looked very subdued to me on their sticks. 'You don't know how such a life tries a man like Kurtz,' cried Kurtz's last disciple. 'Well, and you?' I said. 'I! I! I am a simple man. I have no great thoughts. I want nothing from anybody. How can you compare me to? . . .' His feelings were too much for speech, and suddenly he broke down. 'I don't understand,' he groaned. 'I've been doing my best to keep him alive, and that's enough. I had no hand in all this. I have no abilities. There hasn't been a drop of medicine or a mouthful of invalid food for months here. He was shamefully abandoned. A man like this, with such ideas. Shamefully! Shamefully! I—I—haven't slept for the last ten nights. . . .'

"His voice lost itself in the calm of the evening. The long shadows of the forest had slipped downhill while we talked, had gone far beyond the ruined hovel, beyond the symbolic row of stakes. All this was in the gloom, while we down there were yet in the sunshine, and the stretch of the river abreast of the clearing glittered in a still and dazzling splendor, with a murky and overshadowed bend above and below. Not a living soul was seen on the shore. The bushes did not rustle.

"Suddenly round the corner of the house a group of men appeared, as though they had come up from the ground. They waded waist-deep in the grass, in a compact body, bearing an improvised stretcher in their midst. Instantly, in the emptiness of the landscape a cry arose whose shrillness pierced the still air like a sharp arrow flying straight to the very heart of the land; and, as if by enchantment, streams of human beings—of naked human beings—with spears in their hands, with bows, with shields, with wild glances and savage movements, were poured into the clearing by the dark-faced and pensive forest. The bushes shook, the grass swayed for a time, and then everything stood still in attentive immobility.

" 'Now, if he does not say the right thing to them we are all done for,' said the Russian at my elbow. The knot of men with the stretcher had stopped, too, halfway to the steamer, as if petrified. I saw the man on the stretcher sit up, lank and with an uplifted arm, above the shoulders of the bearers. 'Let us hope that the man who can talk so well of love in general will find some particular reason to spare us this time,' I said. I resented bitterly the absurd danger of our situation, as if to be at the mercy of that atrocious phantom had been a dishonoring necessity. I could not hear a sound, but through my glasses I saw the thin arm extended commandingly, the lower jaw moving, the eyes of that apparition shining darkly far in its bony head that nodded with grotesque jerks. Kurtz—Kurtz—that means short in German—don't it? * Well, the name was as true as everything else in his life—and death. He looked at least seven feet long. His covering had fallen off, and his body emerged from it pitiful and appalling as from a winding sheet. I could see the cage of his ribs all astir, the bones of his arm waving. It was as though an animated image of death carved out of old ivory had been shaking its hand with menaces at a motionless crowd of men made of dark and glittering bronze. I saw him open his mouth wide—it gave him a weirdly voracious aspect, as though he had wanted to swallow all the air, all the earth, all the men before him. A deep voice reached me faintly. He must have been shouting. He fell back suddenly. The stretcher shook as the bearers staggered forward again, and almost at the same time I noticed that the crowd of savages was vanishing without any perceptible movement of retreat, as if the forest that had ejected these beings so suddenly had drawn them in again as the breath is drawn in a long aspiration.

"Some of the pilgrims behind the stretcher carried his arms—two shotguns, a heavy rifle, and a light revolver carbine—the thunderbolts of that pitiful Jupiter. The manager bent over him murmuring as he walked beside his head. They laid him down in one of the little cabins—just a room for a bedplace and a campstool or two, you know. We had brought his belated correspondence, and a lot of torn envelopes and open letters littered his bed. His hand roamed feebly amongst these papers. I was struck by the fire of his eyes and the composed languor of his expression. It was not so much the exhaustion of disease. He did not seem in pain. This shadow looked satiated and calm, as though for the moment it had had its fill of all the emotions.

"He rustled one of the letters, and looking straight in my face said, 'I am glad.' Somebody had been writing to him about me. These special recommendations were turning up again. The volume

* The true-life model of Kurtz was a Belgian named Georges-Antoine Klein.

of tone he emitted without effort, almost without the trouble of moving his lips, amazed me. A voice! a voice! It was grave, profound, vibrating, while the man did not seem capable of a whisper. However, he had enough strength in him—factitious no doubt—to very nearly make an end of us, as you shall hear directly.

"The manager appeared silently in the doorway; I stepped out at once and he drew the curtain after me. The Russian, eyed curiously by the pilgrims, was staring at the shore. I followed the direction of his glance.

"Dark human shapes could be made out in the distance, flitting indistinctly against the gloomy border of the forest, and near the river two bronze figures, leaning on tall spears, stood in the sunlight under fantastic headdresses of spotted skins, warlike and still in statuesque repose. And from right to left along the lighted shore moved a wild and gorgeous apparition of a woman.

"She walked with measured steps, draped in striped and fringed cloths, treading the earth proudly, with a slight jingle and flash of barbarous ornaments. She carried her head high; her hair was done in the shape of a helmet; she had brass leggings to the knee, brass wire gauntlets to the elbow, a crimson spot on her tawny cheek, innumerable necklaces of glass beads on her neck; bizarre things, charms, gifts of witch men, that hung about her, glittered and trembled at every step. She must have had the value of several elephant tusks upon her. She was savage and superb, wild-eyed and magnificent; there was something ominous and stately in her deliberate progress. And in the hush that had fallen suddenly upon the whole sorrowful land, the immense wilderness, the colossal body of the fecund and mysterious life seemed to look at her, pensive, as though it had been looking at the image of its own tenebrous and passionate soul.

"She came abreast of the steamer, stood still, and faced us. Her long shadow fell to the water's edge. Her face had a tragic and fierce aspect of wild sorrow and of dumb pain mingled with the fear of some struggling, half-shaped resolve. She stood looking at us without a stir, and like the wilderness itself, with an air of brooding over an inscrutable purpose. A whole minute passed, and then she made a step forward. There was a low jingle, a glint of yellow metal, a sway of fringed draperies, and she stopped as if her heart had failed her. The young fellow by my side growled. The pilgrims murmured at my back. She looked at us all as if her life had depended upon the unswerving steadiness of her glance. Suddenly she opened her bared arms and threw them up rigid above her head, as though in an uncontrollable desire to touch the sky, and at the same time the swift shadows darted out on the earth, swept around on the river, gathering the steamer into a shadowy embrace. A formidable silence hung over the scene.

"She turned away slowly, walked on, following the bank, and passed into the bushes to the left. Once only her eyes gleamed back at us in the dusk of the thickets before she disappeared.

"'If she offered to come aboard I really think I would have tried to shoot her,' said the man of patches, nervously. 'I had been risking my life every day for the last fortnight to keep her out of the house. She got in one day and kicked up a row about those miserable rags I picked up in the storeroom to mend my clothes with. I wasn't decent. At least it must have been that, for she talked like a fury to Kurtz for an hour, pointing at me now and then. I don't understand the dialect of this tribe. Luckily for me, I fancy Kurtz felt too ill that day to care, or there would have been mischief. I don't understand. . . . No—it's too much for me. Ah, well, it's all over now.'

"At this moment I heard Kurtz's deep voice behind the curtain: 'Save me!—save the ivory, you mean. Don't tell me. Save *me!* Why, I've had to save you. You are interrupting my plans now. Sick! Sick! Not so sick as you would like to believe. Never mind. I'll carry my ideas out yet—I will return. I'll show you what can be done. You with your little peddling notions—you are interfering with me. I will return. I . . .'

"The manager came out. He did me the honor to take me under the arm and lead me aside. 'He is very low, very low,' he said. He considered it necessary to sigh, but neglected to be consistently sorrowful. 'We have done all we could for him—haven't we? But there is no disguising the fact, Mr. Kurtz has done more harm than good to the Company. He did not see the time was not ripe for vigorous action. Cautiously, cautiously—that's my principle. We must be cautious yet. The district is closed to us for a time. Deplorable! Upon the whole, the trade will suffer. I don't deny there is a remarkable quantity of ivory—mostly fossil. We must save it, at all events—but look how precarious the position is—and why? Because the method is unsound.' 'Do you,' said I, looking at the shore, 'call it "unsound method?"' 'Without doubt,' he exclaimed, hotly. 'Don't you?' . . .

"'No method at all,' I murmured after a while. 'Exactly,' he exulted. 'I anticipated this. Shows a complete want of judgment. It is my duty to point it out in the proper quarter.' 'Oh,' said I, 'that fellow—what's his name?—the brickmaker, will make a readable report for you.' He appeared confounded for a moment. It seemed to me I had never breathed an atmosphere so vile, and I turned mentally to Kurtz for relief—positively for relief. 'Nevertheless I think Mr. Kurtz is a remarkable man,' I said with emphasis. He started, dropped on me a cold heavy glance, said very quietly, 'he *was*,' and turned his back on me. My hour of favor was over; I found myself lumped along with Kurtz as a partisan of methods for which the time was not ripe: I was unsound! Ah! but it was something to have at least a choice of nightmares.

"I had turned to the wilderness really, not to Mr. Kurtz, who, I was ready to admit, was as good as buried. And for a moment it seemed to me as if I also were buried in a vast grave full of unspeakable secrets. I felt an intolerable weight oppressing my breast, the smell of the damp earth, the unseen presence of victorious corruption, the darkness of an impenetrable night. . . . The Russian tapped me on the shoulder. I heard him mumbling and stammering something about 'brother seaman—couldn't conceal—knowledge of matters that would affect Mr. Kurtz's reputation.' I waited. For him evidently Mr. Kurtz was not in his grave; I suspect that for him Mr. Kurtz was one of the immortals. 'Well!' said I at last, 'speak out. As it happens, I am Mr. Kurtz's friend—in a way.'

"He stated with a good deal of formality that had we not been 'of the same profession,' he would have kept the matter to himself without regard to consequences. 'He suspected there was an active ill will towards him on the part of these white men that—' 'You are right,' I said, remembering a certain conversation I had overheard. 'The manager thinks you ought to be hanged.' He showed a concern at this intelligence which amused me at first. 'I had better get out of the way quietly,' he said, earnestly. 'I can do no more for Kurtz now, and they would soon find some excuse. What's to stop them? There's a military post three hundred miles from here.' 'Well, upon my word,' said I, 'perhaps you had better go if you have any friends amongst the savages near by.' 'Plenty,' he said. 'They are simple people—and I want nothing, you know.' He stood biting his lip, then: 'I don't want any harm to happen to these whites here, but of course I was thinking of Mr. Kurtz's reputation—but you are a brother seaman and—' 'All right,' said I, after a time. 'Mr. Kurtz's reputation is safe with me.' I did not know how truly I spoke.

"He informed me, lowering his voice, that it was Kurtz who had ordered the attack to be made on the steamer. 'He hated sometimes the idea of being taken away—and then again . . . But I don't understand these matters. I am a simple man. He thought it would scare you away—that you would give it up, thinking him dead. I could not stop him. Oh, I had an awful time of it this last month.' 'Very well,' I said. 'He is all right now.' 'Ye-e-es,' he muttered, not very convinced apparently. 'Thanks,' said I; 'I shall keep my eyes open.' 'But quiet—eh?' he urged, anxiously. 'It would be awful for his reputation if anybody here—' I promised a complete discretion with great gravity. 'I have a canoe and three black fellows waiting not very far. I am off. Could you give me a few Martini-Henry cartridges?' I could, and did, with proper secrecy. He helped himself, with a wink at me, to a handful of my tobacco. 'Between sailors—you know—good English tobacco.' At the door of the pilot house he turned round—'I say, haven't you a pair of shoes you could spare?' He raised one leg. 'Look.' The soles were tied with knotted strings sandalwise under his bare feet. I rooted out an old pair, at which he looked with admiration before tucking it under his left arm. One of his pockets (bright red) was bulging with cartridges, from the other (dark blue) peeped 'Towson's Inquiry,' etc., etc. He seemed to think himself excellently well equipped for a renewed encounter with the wilderness. 'Ah! I'll never, never meet such a man again. You ought to have heard him recite poetry—his own, too, it was, he told me. Poetry!' He rolled his eyes at the recollection of these delights. 'Oh, he enlarged my mind!' 'Goodby,' said I. He shook hands and vanished in the night. Sometimes I ask myself whether I had ever really seen him —whether it was possible to meet such a phenomenon! . . .

"When I woke up shortly after midnight his warning came to my mind with its hint of danger that seemed, in the starred darkness, real enough to make me get up for the purpose of having a look round. On the hill a big fire burned, illuminating fitfully a crooked corner of the station house. One of the agents with a picket of a few of our blacks, armed for the purpose, was keeping guard over the ivory; but deep within the forest, red gleams that wavered, that seemed to sink and rise from the ground amongst confused columnar shapes of intense blackness, showed the exact position of the camp where Mr. Kurtz's adorers were keeping their uneasy vigil. The monotonous beating of a big drum filled the air with muffled shocks and a lingering vibration. A steady droning sound of many men chanting each to himself some weird incantation came out from the black, flat wall of the woods as the humming of bees comes out of a hive, and had a strange narcotic effect upon my half-awake senses. I believe I dozed off leaning over the rail, till an abrupt burst of yells, an overwhelming outbreak of a pent-up and mysterious frenzy, woke me up in a bewildered wonder. It was cut short all at once, and the low droning went on with an effect of audible and soothing silence. I glanced casually into the little cabin. A light was burning within, but Mr. Kurtz was not there.

"I think I would have raised an outcry if I had believed my eyes. But I didn't believe them at first—the thing seemed so impossible. The fact is I was completely unnerved by a sheer blank fright, pure abstract terror, unconnected with any distinct shape of physical danger. What made this emotion so overpowering was—how shall I define it?—the moral shock I received, as if something altogether monstrous, intolerable to thought and odious to the soul, had been thrust upon me unexpectedly. This lasted of course the merest fraction of a second, and then the usual sense of commonplace, deadly danger, the possibility of a sudden onslaught and massacre, or something of the kind, which I saw impending, was positively welcome and composing. It pacified me, in fact, so much, that I did not raise an alarm.

"There was an agent buttoned up inside an ulster and sleeping on a chair on deck within three feet of me. The yells had not awakened him; he snored very slightly; I left him to his slumbers and leaped ashore. I did not betray Mr. Kurtz—it was ordered I should never betray him—it was written I should be loyal to the nightmare of my choice. I was anxious to deal with this shadow by myself alone—and to this day I don't know why I was so jealous of sharing with anyone the peculiar blackness of that experience.

"As soon as I got on the bank I saw a trail—a broad trail through the grass. I remembered the exultation with which I said to myself, 'He can't walk—he is crawling on all fours—I've got him.' The grass was wet with dew. I strode rapidly with clenched fists. I fancy I had some vague notion of falling upon him and giving him a drubbing. I don't know. I had some imbecile thoughts. The knitting old woman with the cat obtruded herself upon my memory as a most improper person to be sitting at the other end of such an affair. I saw a row of pilgrims squirting lead in the air out of Winchesters held to the hip. I thought I would never get back to the steamer, and imagined myself living alone and unarmed in the woods to an advanced age. Such silly things—you know. And I remember I confounded the beat of the drum with the beating of my heart, and was pleased at its calm regularity.

"I kept to the track though—then stopped to listen. The night was very clear; a dark blue space, sparkling with dew and starlight, in which black things stood very still. I thought I could see a kind of motion ahead of me. I was strangely cocksure of everything that night. I actually left the track and ran in a wide semicircle (I truly believe chuckling to myself) so as to get in front of that stir, of that motion I had seen—if indeed I had seen anything. I was circumventing Kurtz as though it had been a boyish game.

"I came upon him, and, if he had not heard me coming, I would have fallen over him, too, but he got up in time. He rose, unsteady, long, pale, indistinct, like a vapor exhaled by the earth, and swayed slightly, misty and silent before me; while at my back the fires loomed between the trees, and the murmur of many voices issued from the *hell* forest. I had cut him off cleverly; but when actually confronting him I seemed to come to my senses, I saw the danger in its right proportion. It was by no means over yet. Suppose he began to shout? Though he could hardly stand, there was still plenty of vigor in his voice. 'Go away—hide yourself,' he said, in that profound tone. It was very awful. I glanced back. We were within thirty yards from the nearest fire. A black figure stood up, strode on long black legs, waving long black arms, across the glow. It had horns—antelope *devil* horns, I think—on its head. Some sorcerer, some witch man, no doubt: it looked fiend-like enough. 'Do you know what you are doing?' I whispered. 'Perfectly,' he answered, raising his voice for that single word: it sounded to me far off and yet loud, like a hail through a speaking trumpet. If he makes a row we are lost, I thought to myself. This clearly was not a case for fisticuffs, even apart from the very natural aversion I had to beat that Shadow—this wandering and tormented thing. 'You will be lost,' I said—'utterly lost.' One gets sometimes such a flash of inspiration, you know. I did say the right thing, though indeed he could not have been more irretrievably lost than he was at this very moment, when the foundations of our intimacy were being laid—to endure—to endure—even to the end—even beyond.

"'I had immense plans,' he muttered irresolutely. 'Yes,' said I; 'but if you try to shout I'll smash your head with— There was not a stick or a stone near. 'I will throttle you for good,' I corrected myself. 'I was on the threshold of great things,' he pleaded, in a voice of longing, with a wistfulness of tone that made my blood run cold. 'And now for this stupid scoundrel—' 'Your success in Europe is assured in any case,' I affirmed, steadily. I did not want to have the throttling of him, you understand—and indeed it would have been very little use for any practical purpose. I tried to break the spell—the heavy, mute spell of the wilderness—that seemed to draw him to its pitiless breast by the awakening of forgotten and brutal instincts, by the memory of gratified and monstrous passions. This alone, I was convinced, had driven him out to the edge of the forest, to the bush, towards the gleam of fires, the throb of drums, the drone of weird incantations; this alone had beguiled his unlawful soul beyond the bounds of permitted aspirations. And, don't you see, the terror of the position was not in being knocked on the head—though I had a very lively sense of that danger, too—but in this, that I had to deal with a being to whom I could not appeal in the name of anything high or low. I had, even like the niggers, to invoke him—himself—his own exalted and incredible degradation. There was nothing either above or below him, and I knew it. He had kicked himself loose of the earth. Confound the man! he had kicked the very earth to pieces. He was alone, and I before him did not know whether I stood on the ground or floated in the air. I've been telling you what we said—repeating the phrases we pronounced—but what's the good? They were common everyday words—the familiar, vague sounds exchanged on every waking day of life. But what of that? They had behind them, to my mind, the terrific suggestiveness of words heard in dreams, of phrases spoken in nightmares. Soul! If anybody had ever struggled with a soul, I am the man. And I wasn't arguing with a lunatic either. Believe me or not, his intelligence was perfectly clear—concentrated, it is true, upon himself with horrible intensity, yet clear; and therein was my only chance—barring, of course, the killing him there and then, which wasn't so good, on account of unavoidable noise. But his soul was mad. Being alone in the wilderness, it had looked within itself, and, by heavens! I tell you, it had gone mad. I had—for my sins, I suppose—to go through the ordeal of looking into myself. No eloquence could have been so withering to one's belief in mankind as his final burst of sincerity. He struggled with himself, too. I saw it, I heard it. I saw the inconceivable mystery of a soul that knew no restraint, no faith, and no fear, yet struggling blindly with itself. I kept my head pretty well; but when I had him at last stretched on the couch, I wiped my forehead, while my legs shook under me as though I had carried half a ton on my back down that hill. And yet I had only supported him, his bony arm clasped round my neck—and he was not much heavier than a child.

"When next day we left at noon, the crowd, of whose presence behind the curtain of trees I had been acutely conscious all the time, flowed out of the woods again, filled the clearing, covered the slope with a mass of naked, breathing, quivering, bronze bodies. I steamed up a bit, then swung downstream, and two thousand eyes followed the evolutions of the splashing, thumping, fierce river-demon beating the water with its terrible tail and breathing black smoke into the air. In front of the first rank, along the river, three men, plastered with bright red earth from head to foot, strutted to and fro restlessly. When we came abreast again, they faced the river, stamped their feet, nodded their horned heads, swayed their scarlet bodies; they shook towards the fierce river-demon a bunch of black feathers, a mangy skin with a pendent tail—something that looked like a dried gourd; they shouted periodically together strings of amazing words that resembled no sounds of human language; and the deep murmurs of the crowd, interrupted suddenly, were like the response of some satanic litany.

"We had carried Kurtz into the pilot house: there was more air there. Lying on the couch, he stared through the open shutter. There was an eddy in the mass of human bodies, and the woman with helmeted head and tawny cheeks rushed out to the very brink of the stream. She put out her hands, shouted something, and all that wild mob took up the shout in a roaring chorus of articulated, rapid, breathless utterance.

" 'Do you understand this?' I asked.

"He kept on looking out past me with fiery, longing eyes, with a mingled expression of wistfulness and hate. He made no answer, but I saw a smile, a smile of indefinable meaning, appear on his colorless lips that a moment after twitched convulsively. 'Do I not?' he said slowly, gasping, as if the words had been torn out of him by a supernatural power.

"I pulled the string of the whistle, and I did this because I saw the pilgrims on deck getting out their rifles with an air of anticipating a jolly lark. At the sudden screech there was a movement of abject terror through that wedged mass of bodies. 'Don't! Don't you frighten them away,' cried someone on deck disconsolately. I pulled the string time after time. They broke and ran, they leaped, they crouched, they swerved, they dodged the flying terror of the sound. The three red chaps had fallen flat, face down on the shore, as though they had been shot dead. Only the barbarous and superb woman did not so much as flinch, and stretched tragically her bare arms after us over the somber and glittering river.

"And then that imbecile crowd down on the deck started their little fun, and I could see nothing more for smoke.

"The brown current ran swiftly out of the heart of darkness, bearing us down towards the sea with twice the speed of our upward progress; and Kurtz's life was running swiftly, too, ebbing, ebbing out of his heart into the sea of inexorable time. The manager was very placid, he had no vital anxieties now, he took us both in with a comprehensive and satisfied glance: the 'affair' had come off as well as could be wished. I saw the time approaching when I would be left alone of the party of 'unsound method.' The pilgrims looked upon me with disfavor. I was, so to speak, numbered with the dead. It is strange how I accepted this unforeseen partnership, this choice of nightmares forced upon me in the tenebrous land invaded by these mean and greedy phantoms.

"Kurtz discoursed. A voice! a voice! It rang deep to the very last. It survived his strength to hide in the magnificent folds of eloquence the barren darkness of his heart. Oh, he struggled! he struggled! The wastes of his weary brain were haunted by shadowy images now— images of wealth and fame revolving obsequiously round his unextinguishable gift of noble and lofty expression. My Intended, my station, my career, my ideas—these were the subjects for the occasional utterances of elevated sentiments. The shade of the original Kurtz frequented the bedside of the hollow sham, whose fate it was to be buried presently in the mold of primeval earth. But both the diabolic love and the unearthly hate of the mysteries it had penetrated fought for the possession of that soul satiated with primitive emotions, avid of lying fame, of sham distinction, of all the appearances of success and power.

"Sometimes he was contemptibly childish. He desired to have kings meet him at railway stations on his return from some ghastly Nowhere, where he intended to accomplish great things. 'You show them you have in you something that is really profitable, and then there will be no limits to the recognition of your ability,' he would say. 'Of course you must take care of the motives—right motives— always.' The long reaches that were like one and the same reach, monotonous bends that were exactly alike, slipped past the steamer with their multitude of secular trees looking patiently after this grimy fragment of another world, the forerunner of change, of conquest, of trade, of massacres, of blessings. I looked ahead—piloting. 'Close the shutter,' said Kurtz suddenly one day; 'I can't bear to look at this.' I did so. There was a silence. 'Oh, but I will wring your heart yet! he cried at the invisible wilderness.

"We broke down—as I had expected—and had to lie-up for repairs at the head of an island. This delay was the first thing that shook Kurtz's confidence. One morning he gave me a packet of papers and a photograph—the lot tied together with a shoestring. 'Keep this for me,' he said. 'This noxious fool' (meaning the manager) 'is capable of prying into my boxes when I am not looking.' In the afternoon I saw him. He was lying on his back with closed eyes, and I withdrew quietly, but I heard him mutter, 'Live rightly, die, die. . . .' I listened. There was nothing more. Was he rehearsing some speech in his sleep, or was it a fragment of a phrase from some newspaper article? He had been writing for the papers and meant to do so again, 'for the furthering of my ideas. It's a duty.'

"His was an impenetrable darkness. I looked at him as you peer down at a man who is lying at the bottom of a precipice where the sun never shines. But I had not much time to give him, because I was helping the engine driver to take to pieces the leaky cylinders, to straighten a bent connecting rod, and in other such matters. I lived in an infernal mess of rust, filings, nuts, bolts, spanners, hammers, ratchet drills—things I abominate, because I don't get on with them. I tended the little forge we fortunately had aboard; I toiled wearily in a wretched scrapheap—unless I had the shakes too bad to stand.

"One evening coming in with a candle I was startled to hear him say a little tremulously, 'I am lying here in the dark waiting for death.' The light was within a foot of his eyes. I forced myself to murmur, 'Oh, nonsense!' and stood over him as if transfixed.

"Anything approaching the change that came over his features I have never seen before, and hope never to see again. Oh, I wasn't touched. I was fascinated. It was as though a veil had been rent. I saw on that ivory face the expression of somber pride, of ruthless power, of craven terror—of an intense and hopeless despair. Did he live his life again in every detail of desire, temptation, and surrender during that supreme moment of complete knowledge? He cried in a whisper at some image, at some vision—he cried out twice, a cry that was no more than a breath: 'The horror! The horror!' *understands*

"I blew the candle out and left the cabin. The pilgrims were dining in the messroom, and I took my place opposite the manager, who lifted his eyes to give me a questioning glance, which I successfully ignored. He leaned back, serene, with that peculiar smile of his sealing the unexpressed depths of his meanness. A continuous shower of small flies streamed upon the lamp, upon the cloth, upon our hands and faces. Suddenly the manager's boy put his insolent black head in the doorway, and said in a tone of scathing contempt—

" 'Mistah Kurtz—he dead.'

"All the pilgrims rushed out to see. I remained, and went on with my dinner. I believe I was considered brutally callous. However, I did not eat much. There was a lamp in there—light, don't you know—and outside it was so beastly, beastly dark. I went no more near the remarkable man who had pronounced a judgment upon the adventures of his soul on this earth. The voice was gone. What else had been there? But I am of course aware that next day the pilgrims buried something in a muddy hole.

"And then they very nearly buried me.

"However, as you see, I did not go to join Kurtz there and then. I did not. I remained to dream the nightmare out to the end, and to show my loyalty to Kurtz once more. Destiny. My destiny! Droll thing life is—that mysterious arrangement of merciless logic for a futile purpose. The most you can hope from it is some knowledge of yourself—that comes too late—a crop of unextinguishable regrets. I have wrestled with death. It is the most unexciting contest you can imagine. It takes place in an impalpable grayness, with nothing underfoot, with nothing around, without spectators, without clamor, without glory, without the great desire of victory, without the great fear of defeat, in a sickly atmosphere of tepid skepticism, without much belief in your own right, and still less in that of your adversary. If such is the form of ultimate wisdom, then life is a greater riddle than some of us think it to be. I was within a hair's-breadth of the last opportunity for pronouncement, and I found with humiliation that probably I would have nothing to say. This is the reason why I affirm that Kurtz was a remarkable man. He had something to say. He said it. Since I had peeped over the edge myself, I understand better the meaning of his stare, that could not see the flame of the candle, but was wide enough to embrace the whole universe, piercing enough to penetrate all the hearts that beat in the darkness. He had summed up—he had judged. 'The horror!' He was a remarkable man. After all, this was the expression of some sort of belief; it had candor, it had conviction, it had a vibrating note of revolt in its whisper, it had the appalling face of a glimpsed truth—the strange commingling of desire and hate. And it is not my own extremity I remember best —a vision of grayness without form filled with physical pain, and a careless contempt for the evanescence of all things—even of this pain itself. No! It is his extremity that I seem to have lived through. True, he had made that last stride, he had stepped over the edge, while I had been permitted to draw back my hesitating foot. And perhaps in this is the whole difference; perhaps all the wisdom, and all truth, and all sincerity, are just compressed into that inappreciable moment of time in which we step over the threshold of the invisible. Perhaps! I like to think my summing-up would not have been a word of careless contempt. Better his cry—much better. It was an affirmation, a moral victory paid for by innumerable defeats, by abominable terrors, by abominable satisfactions. But it was a victory! That is why I have remained loyal to Kurtz to the last, and even beyond, when a long time after I heard once more, not his own voice, but the echo of his magnificent eloquence thrown to me from a soul as translucently pure as a cliff of crystal.

"No, they did not bury me, though there is a period of time which I remember mistily, with a shuddering wonder, like a passage through some inconceivable world that had no hope in it and no desire. I found myself back in the sepulchral city resenting the sight of people hurrying through the streets to filch a little money from each other, to devour their infamous cookery, to gulp their unwholesome beer, to dream their insignificant and silly dreams. They trespassed upon my thoughts. They were intruders whose knowledge of life was to me an irritating pretense, because I felt so sure they could not possibly know the things I knew. Their bearing, which was simply the bearing of commonplace individuals going about their business in the assurance of perfect safety, was offensive to me like the outrageous flauntings of folly in the face of a danger it is unable to comprehend. I had no particular desire to enlighten them, but I had some difficulty in restraining myself from laughing in their faces, so full of stupid importance. I daresay I was not very well at that time. I tottered about the streets—there were various affairs to settle—grinning bitterly at perfectly respectable persons. I admit my behavior was inexcusable, but then my temperature was seldom normal in these days. My dear aunt's endeavors to 'nurse up my strength' seemed altogether beside the mark. It was not my strength that wanted nursing, it was my imagination that wanted soothing. I kept the bundle of papers given me by Kurtz, not knowing exactly what to do with it. His mother had died lately, watched over, as I was told, by his Intended. A clean-shaved man, with an official manner and wearing gold-rimmed spectacles, called on me one day and made inquiries, at first circuitous, afterwards suavely pressing, about what he was pleased to denominate certain 'documents.' I was not surprised, because I had had two rows with the manager on the subject out there. I had refused to give up the smallest scrap out of that package, and I took the same attitude with the spectacled man. He became darkly menacing at last, and with much heat argued that the company had the right to every bit of information about its 'territories.' And said he, 'Mr. Kurtz's knowledge of unexplored regions must have been necessarily extensive and peculiar—owing to his great abilities and to the deplorable circumstances in which he had been placed: therefore—' I assured him Mr. Kurtz's knowledge, however extensive, did not bear upon the problem of commerce or administration. He invoked then the name of science. 'It would be an incalculable loss if,' etc., etc. I offered him the report on the 'Suppression of Savage Customs,' with the postscriptum torn off. He took it up eagerly, but ended by sniffing at it with an air of contempt. 'This is not what we had a right to expect,' he remarked. 'Expect nothing else,' I said. 'There are only private letters.' He withdrew upon some threat of legal proceedings, and I saw him no more; but another fellow, calling himself Kurtz's cousin, appeared two days later, and was anxious to hear all the details about his dear relative's last moments. Incidentally he gave me to understand that Kurtz had been essentially a great musician. 'There was the making of an immense success,' said the man, who was an organist, I believe, with lank gray hair flowing over a greasy coat collar. I had no reason to doubt his statement; and to this day I am unable to say what was Kurtz's profession, whether he ever had any—which was the greatest of his talents. I had taken him for a painter who wrote for the papers, or else for a journalist who could paint—but even the cousin (who took snuff during the interview) could not tell me what he had been—exactly. He was a universal genius—on that point I agreed with the old chap, who thereupon blew his nose noisily into a large cotton handkerchief and withdrew in senile agitation, bearing off some family letters and memoranda without importance. Ultimately a journalist anxious to know something of the fate of his 'dear colleague' turned up. This visitor informed me Kurtz's proper sphere ought to have been politics 'on the popular side.' He had furry straight eyebrows, bristly hair cropped short, an eyeglass on a broad ribbon, and, becoming expansive, confessed his opinion that Kurtz really couldn't write a bit—'but heavens! how that man could talk. He electrified large meetings. He had faith—don't you see?—he had the faith. He could get himself to believe anything —anything. He would have been a splendid leader of an extreme party.' 'What party?' I asked. 'Any party,' answered the other. 'He was an—an—extremist.' Did I not think so? I assented. Did I know, he asked, with a sudden flash of curiosity, 'what it was that had induced him to go out there?' 'Yes,' said I, and forthwith handed him the famous report for publication, if he thought fit. He glanced through it hurriedly, mumbling all the time, judged 'it would do,' and took himself off with this plunder.

"Thus I was left at last with a slim packet of letters and the girl's portrait. She struck me as beautiful—I mean she had a beautiful expression. I know that the sunlight can be made to lie, too, yet one felt that no manipulation of light and pose could have conveyed the delicate shade of truthfulness upon those features. She seemed ready to listen without mental reservation, without suspicion, without a thought for herself. I concluded I would go and give her back her portrait and those letters myself. Curiosity? Yes; and also some other feeling perhaps. All that had been Kurtz's had passed out of my hands: his soul, his body, his station, his plans, his ivory, his career. There remained only his memory and his Intended—and I wanted to give that up, too, to the past, in a way—to surrender personally all that remained of him with me to that oblivion which is the last word of our common fate. I don't defend myself. I had no clear perception of what it was I really wanted. Perhaps it was an impulse of unconscious loyalty, or the fulfilment of one of these ironic necessities that lurk in the facts of human existence. I don't know. I can't tell. But I went.

"I thought his memory was like the other memories of the dead that accumulate in every man's life—a vague impress on the brain of shadows that had fallen on it in their swift and final passage; but before the high and ponderous door, between the tall houses of a street as still and decorous as a well-kept alley in a cemetery, I had a vision of him on the stretcher, opening his mouth voraciously, as if to devour all the earth with all its mankind. He lived then before me; he lived as much as he had ever lived—a shadow insatiable of splendid appearances, of frightful realities; a shadow darker than the shadow of the night, and draped nobly in the folds of a gorgeous eloquence. The vision seemed to enter the house with me—the stretcher, the phantom-bearers, the wild crowd of obedient worshipers, the gloom of the forests, the glitter of the reach between the murky bends, the beat of the drum, regular and muffled like the beating of a heart—the heart of a conquering darkness. It was a moment of triumph for the wilderness, an invading and vengeful rush which, it seemed to me, I would have to keep back alone for the salvation of another soul. And the memory of what I had heard him say afar there, with the horned shapes stirring at my back, in the glow of fires, within the patient woods, those broken phrases came back to me, were heard again in their ominous and terrifying simplicity. I remembered his abject pleading, his abject threats, the colossal scale of his vile desires, the meanness, the torment, the tempestuous anguish of his soul. And later on I seemed to see his collected languid manner, when he said one day, 'This lot of ivory now is really mine. The company did not pay for it. I collected it myself at a very great personal risk. I am afraid they will try to claim it as theirs though. H'm. It is a difficult case. What do you think I ought to do—resist? Eh? I want no more than justice. . . .' He wanted no more than justice—no more than justice. I rang the bell before a mahogany door on the first floor, and while I waited he seemed to stare at me out of the glassy panel—stare with that wide and immense stare embracing, condemning, loathing all the universe. I seemed to hear the whispered cry, 'The horror! The horror!'

"The dusk was falling. I had to wait in a lofty drawing room with three long windows from floor to ceiling that were like three luminous and bedraped columns. The bent gilt legs and backs of the furniture shone in indistinct curves. The tall marble fireplace had a cold and monumental whiteness. A grand piano stood massively in a corner; with dark gleams on the flat surfaces like a somber and polished sarcophagus. A high door opened—closed. I rose.

"She came forward, all in black, with a pale head, floating towards me in the dusk. She was in mourning. It was more than a year since his death, more than a year since the news came; she seemed as though she would remember and mourn forever. She took both my hands in hers and murmured, 'I had heard you were coming.' I noticed she was not very young—I mean not girlish. She had a mature capacity for fidelity, for belief, for suffering. The room seemed to have grown darker, as if all the sad light of the cloudy evening had taken refuge on her forehead. This fair hair, this pale visage, this pure brow, seemed surrounded by an ashy halo from which the dark eyes looked out at me. Their glance was guileless, profound, confident, and trustful. She carried her sorrowful head as though she were proud of that sorrow, as though she would say, I—I alone know how to mourn for him as he deserves. But while we were still shaking hands, such a look of awful desolation came upon her face that I perceived she was one of those creatures that are not the playthings of Time. For her he had died only yesterday. And, by Jove! the impression was so powerful that for me, too, he seemed to have died only yesterday—nay, this very minute. I saw her and him in the same instant of time—his death and her sorrow—I saw her sorrow in the very moment of his death. Do you understand? I saw them together—I heard them together. She had said, with a deep catch of the breath, 'I have survived' while my strained ears seemed to hear distinctly, mingled with her tone of despairing regret, the summing-up whisper of his eternal condemnation. I asked myself what I was doing there, with a sensation of panic in my heart as though I had blundered into a place of cruel and absurd mysteries not fit for a human being to behold. She motioned me to a chair. We sat down. I laid the packet gently on the little table, and she put her hand over it. . . . 'You knew him well,' she murmured, after a moment of mourning silence.

" 'Intimacy grows quickly out there,' I said. 'I knew him as well as it is possible for one man to know another.'

" 'And you admired him,' she said. 'It was impossible to know him and not to admire him. Was it?'

" 'He was a remarkable man,' I said, unsteadily. Then before the appealing fixity of her gaze, that seemed to watch for more words on my lips, I went on, 'It was impossible not to—'

" 'Love him,' she finished eagerly, silencing me into an appalled dumbness. 'How true! how true! But when you think that no one knew him so well as I! I had all his noble confidence. I knew him best.'

" 'You knew him best,' I repeated. And perhaps she did. But with every word spoken the room was growing darker, and only her forehead, smooth and white, remained illumined by the unextinguishable light of belief and love.

" 'You were his friend,' she went on. 'His friend,' she repeated, a little louder. 'You must have been, if he had given you this, and sent you to me. I feel I can speak to you—and oh! I must speak. I want you—you who have heard his last words—to know I have been worthy of him. . . . It is not pride. . . . Yes! I am proud to know I understood him better than anyone on earth—he told me so himself. And since his mother died I have had no one—no one—to—to—'

"I listened. The darkness deepened. I was not even sure whether he had given me the right bundle. I rather suspect he wanted me to take care of another batch of his papers which, after his death, I saw the manager examining under the lamp. And the girl talked, easing her pain in the certitude of my sympathy; she talked as thirsty men drink. I had heard that her engagement with Kurtz had been disapproved by her people. He wasn't rich enough or something. And indeed I don't know whether he had not been a pauper all his life. He had given me some reason to infer that it was his impatience of comparative poverty that drove him out there.

"'. . . Who was not his friend who had heard him speak once?' she was saying. 'He drew men towards him by what was best in them.' She looked at me with intensity. 'It is the gift of the great,' she went on, and the sound of her low voice seemed to have the accompaniment of all the other sounds, full of mystery, desolation, and sorrow, I had ever heard—the ripple of the river, the soughing of the trees swayed by the wind, the murmurs of the crowds, the faint ring of incomprehensible words cried from afar, the whisper of a voice speaking from beyond the threshold of an eternal darkness. 'But you have heard him! You know!' she cried.

"'Yes, I know,' I said with something like despair in my heart, but bowing my head before the faith that was in her, before that great and saving illusion that shone with an unearthly glow in the darkness, in the triumphant darkness from which I could not have defended her—from which I could not even defend myself.

"'What a loss to me—to us!'—she corrected herself with beautiful generosity; then added in a murmur, 'To the world.' By the last gleams of twilight I could see the glitter of her eyes, full of tears—of tears that would not fall.

"'I have been very happy—very fortunate—very proud,' she went on. 'Too fortunate. Too happy for a little while. And now I am unhappy for—for life.'

"She stood up; her fair hair seemed to catch all the remaining light in a glimmer of gold. I rose, too.

"'And of all this,' she went on, mournfully, 'of all his promise, and of all his greatness, of his generous mind, of his noble heart, nothing remains—nothing but a memory. You and I—'

"'We shall always remember him,' I said, hastily.

"'No!' she cried. 'It is impossible that all this should be lost—that such a life should be sacrificed to leave nothing—but sorrow. You know what vast plans he had. I knew of them, too—I could not perhaps understand—but others knew of them. Something must remain. His words, at least, have not died.'

" 'His words will remain,' I said.

" 'And his example,' she whispered to herself. 'Men looked up to him—his goodness shone in every act. His example—'

" 'True,' I said, 'his example, too. Yes, his example. I forgot that.'

" 'But I do not. I cannot—I cannot believe—not yet. I cannot believe that I shall never see him again, that nobody will see him again, never, never, never.'

"She put out her arms as if after a retreating figure, stretching them black and with clasped pale hands across the fading and narrow sheen of the window. Never see him! I saw him clearly enough then. I shall see this eloquent phantom as long as I live, and I shall see her, too, a tragic and familiar Shade, resembling in this gesture another one, tragic also, and bedecked with powerless charms, stretching bare brown arms over the glitter of the infernal stream, the stream of darkness. She said suddenly very low, 'He died as he lived.'

" 'His end,' said I, with dull anger stirring in me, 'was in every way worthy of his life.'

" 'And I was not with him,' she murmured. My anger subsided before a feeling of infinite pity.

" 'Everything that could be done—' I mumbled.

" 'Ah, but I believed in him more than anyone on earth—more than his own mother, more than—himself. He needed me! Me! I would have treasured every sigh, every word, every sign, every glance.'

"I felt like a chill grip on my chest. 'Don't,' I said, in a muffled voice.

" 'Forgive me. I—I have mourned so long in silence—in silence. . . . You were with him—to the last? I think of his loneliness. Nobody near to understand him as I would have understood. Perhaps no one to hear. . . .'

" 'To the very end,' I said, shakily. 'I heard his very last words. . . .' I stopped in a fright.

" 'Repeat them,' she murmured in a heartbroken tone. 'I want—I want—something—something—to—to live with.'

"I was on the point of crying at her, 'Don't you hear them?' The dusk was repeating them in a persistent whisper all around us, in a whisper that seemed to swell menacingly like the first whisper of a rising wind. 'The horror! the horror!'

" 'His last word—to live with,' she insisted. 'Don't you understand I loved him—I loved him—I loved him!'

"I pulled myself together and spoke slowly.

" 'The last word he pronounced was—your name.'

"I heard a light sigh and then my heart stood still, stopped dead short by an exulting and terrible cry, by the cry of inconceivable triumph and of unspeakable pain. 'I knew it—I was sure!' . . . She knew. She was sure. I heard her weeping; she had hidden her face in her hands. It seemed to me that the house would collapse before I could escape, that the heavens would fall upon my head. But nothing happened. The heavens do not fall for such a trifle. Would they have fallen, I wonder, if I had rendered Kurtz that justice which was his due? Hadn't he said he wanted only justice? But I couldn't. I could not tell her. It would have been too dark—too dark altogether. . . ."

Marlow ceased, and sat apart, indistinct and silent, in the pose of a meditating Buddha. Nobody moved for a time. "We have lost the first of the ebb," said the director, suddenly. I raised my head. The offing was barred by a black bank of clouds, and the tranquil waterway leading to the uttermost ends of the earth flowed somber under an overcast sky—seemed to lead into the heart of an immense darkness.

# NOW THAT YOU'VE READ CONRAD'S
# HEART OF DARKNESS:

There are interesting similarities between the life and work of Joseph Conrad and of his friend Henry James. They were born fourteen years apart, and died within eight years of each other. Each was a descendant of an illustrious family, and each inherited his father's intellectual and literary predisposition. Both received highly individualized educations, and after becoming voluntary exiles from their native lands, both became British subjects. Their mature work requires the reader to focus attention not upon mere story but upon the manner of presentation, which is not always simple and clear but sometimes deliberately complex. In place of formal, direct descriptions of people, there is a gradual unfolding by means of suggestive touches, outer action being minimized in favor of psychological analysis of character.

There are, also, illuminating points of contrast. While James led a quiet, unspectacular existence, Conrad pursued adventure on tropical seas and strange rivers surrounded by dark forests. James had the ability to make the familiar exciting, Conrad the exciting familiar: one extracted drama from life in the cultivated, sophisticated spheres of society, the other searched the hearts of men of action and the holds of rough ships. James concentrated on the subtleties of complex people, Conrad on the complexities of simple people. Finally, James fitted beautifully into the English scene, whereas Conrad, though he yearned to be regarded as an Englishman, remained in personality and attitude no less than in speech the unusual combination of Polish patrician and seaman who became a great writer of the English language.

How he became a writer at all is itself a tale as romantic as any he ever imagined. Born in 1857 in southern Poland, then, as now, under Russian rule, he was christened Jozef Teodor Konrad Nalęca Korzeniowski. In his father, Apollo Korzeniowski, burned two passions: one for liberty and the other for letters, both of which he passed on to his son. At the age of nine, Conrad was reading his father's poetry and translations of Shakespeare and Victor Hugo (whose *Toilers of the Sea* gave him a foretaste of the sailor's life). The father's revolutionary activities led to his arrest and exile to Russia in 1862 with his family. After three winters of hardship and suffering, his wife died, and in 1866 the boy was sent to live with his uncle in the Polish Ukraine. Conrad's sense of struggle with dark and terrible forces, afterwards heightened by his experiences at sea, probably derived from the dread and hatred Russia inspired in him at this time (his Russophobia, clear in *Under Western Eyes*, was so great that he even denied merit to Dostoyevsky).

The following year, Conrad was re-united with his father, who had been granted amnesty, and they lived in Galicia and then Cracow. There in 1869, the father died, leaving the twelve-year-old schoolboy under the guardianship of an uncle. The boy found temporary release from his bereavement in books: "I don't know what would have become of me if I had not been a reading boy," he wrote later in *A Personal Record*. "I suppose that in a futile childish way, I would have gone crazy." This early loss of both parents gave him an insight into the meaning of loneliness, a sense of human isolation which was to haunt his great efforts of the imagination.

It was during the year 1872 that the fifteen-year-old youth, born in a country with no seacoast, announced his determination to go to sea. His uncle, unaware that the boy had been harboring the desire for some time and nourishing it by avid reading, opposed him at first. But when he saw that it was something more than a childish fancy, he relented, and at the age of seventeen, Conrad left home for Marseilles and the sea. During the first stages of his apprenticeship, he displayed what has been called a "pleasing fund of that joyous recklessness which is amiable in youth." He sailed locally, ran guns for the Carlists (adventures recalled in *The Mirror of the Sea* and *The Arrow of Gold*), got into debt, had an affair with a mysterious lady and, according to recent evidence, attempted suicide.

His first impulse to study English came as he gazed across the Mediterranean one morning and heard someone's clear English speech ring in his ears. Because he liked the sound of an English voice and the cut of an English jib, Conrad joined the British merchant service, taking a berth on a coastal bark working between Lowestoft and Newcastle. From the sailors he began to learn English. "My teachers," he said, "were coast men, with steady eyes, mighty limbs and gentle voice; men of very few words, which at least were never bare of meaning." In mastering his adopted language, Conrad was aided by London newspapers and a one-volume Shakespeare bought in 1878 with his first English pay.

For the next fifteen years, he lived and labored on British ships that plied to all corners of the earth, gradually rising by a fierce exercise of will from common sailor to mate and then to master by the age of twenty-nine. Both at sea and ashore, he was something of a dandy. His checked trousers, his spade-shaped beard, his exquisite, accented conversation, as if he were tasting his words before pronouncing them, and the monocle through which he could scrutinize a face as a watchmaker looks into the works of a watch earned him the nickname of "The Count."

During a voyage to Borneo, he met a Dutch half-caste who had gone native. His impressions of this derelict inspired Conrad, in 1889, to begin his first novel, *Almayer's Folly*. While pursuing his memories of the tropical scenes, he was suddenly and unaccountably seized by the notion to command a Congo riverboat. Years before, he had vowed to explore the heart of Africa:

> It was in 1868, when nine years old or thereabouts, that while looking at a map of Africa . . . and putting my finger on the blank space then representing the unsolved mystery of the continent, I said to myself, "When I grow up, I shall go *there*." And of course I thought no more about it . . . till an opportunity offered to go there.

Conrad's mood and situation (he was unemployed), his visit to the office of the company which offered him the opportunity, his dismal expedition to the Kinchassa station, the delay while he waited for his ship to be repaired, his encounter with the dying agent, and his horror at the spectacle of Belgian exploitation were later to provide the raw material for Marlow's unforgettable account in *Heart of Darkness*. Later when he spoke about the Congo, he was to say that he never really recovered from the moral and physical shock of the experience.

When refused the command of the repaired ship, Conrad returned to Leopoldville in a native canoe and thence to London. The immediate result of this episode was a protracted illness which permanently impaired his health. But this illness, by immobilizing him for a long period, forced him to look into himself, to think over the many experiences crammed into his thirty-three years. The latent novelist in Conrad had been awakened, but the Congo experience was to shape the course of the next years and above all his views about the evils of colonialism. Three years later, after struggling with it "line by line" for five years, he was able to publish *Almayer's Folly*. He never again sailed as a seaman.

Despite his poverty, illness, and years, he dedicated himself remorselessly to his new vocation. In 1896, appeared *An Outcast of the Islands*. Like his first novel, to which it is a prologue, it is a study of progressive moral disintegration and reveals Conrad's profound interest in racial differences, in ironic twists of circumstance, and in the processes of despair. Three weeks after its publication, Conrad married Miss Jessie George, the twenty-two-year-old daughter of a London bookseller. In its earlier stage, their life together was beset by material cares, for while his books brought Conrad a reputation with discerning critics, they brought him little income. After living in Brittany and Essex for a time, the family (there was now a son) settled in a quiet corner of Kent. Isolated in his cottage, where he could sniff the sea, Conrad sometimes became despondent about his writing and thought of becoming a pearl fisherman or a Suez pilot. But encouraged by friends like John Galsworthy, Henry James, H. G. Wells, George Gissing, and Stephen Crane, his genius unfolded in a steady succession of books and he gradually gained wider recognition. *The Nigger of the Narcissus* (1897) dissects the influence of a dying black sailor upon the men who sail with him from Bombay. Jim Wait's final protest against his fate ("The horror . . .") foreshadows the death of Kurtz in *Heart of Darkness*. In 1900, came his classic *Lord Jim*, a prolonged analysis of self-betrayal and redemption which points toward his later studies in a similar spirit.

In *Lord Jim*, Marlow, that reluctant cynic of *Heart of Darkness*, makes his bow. Chronicler and chorus at once, he is a means of bringing the story closer to the reader. He produces evidence, detective-like, as he picks it up from observation or scraps of conversation. The reader is the jury, and in that role, hears the evidence and passes judgment. If this complex technique makes the plot harder to follow, it also lends the illusion of real life. This method is especially effective in *Nostromo* (1904), a cunningly constructed romance of men who are lured to adventure and death by the spirit of silver, and in *Chance* (1914), whose huge success marked the turning point of his career. His last half-dozen novels, written at the height of his slowly achieved but finally great reputation, are, excepting *Victory* (1915), less readable than the earlier works, upon which his fame rests most firmly today.

Once he had settled on his career, Conrad did little traveling, but he did visit the United States once, in 1923, to see his publisher. He was lavishly feted, but remained the reserved Polish aristocrat turned Englishman. Conrad continued to write, and was working on a Napoleonic novel until shortly before his death the following year of a stroke in Bishopsbourne, Kent.

Of the English writers of their time, perhaps only he and Thomas Hardy spoke with the authentic voice of tragedy. But Conrad's vision of life is not so unrelentingly melancholy as Hardy's. To Hardy, man is the plaything of the gods, a puny creature at the mercy of hostile or indifferent forces threatening his existence. Conrad, too, shows us a sombre universe, friendly to man only insofar as it has afforded conditions under which human values may develop. The universe gives no indication of being itself committed to those values; on the contrary, man faces the "immense indifference of things." In the words of Bertrand Russell, Conrad thought of "civilized and morally tolerable human life as a dangerous walk on a thin crust of barely cooled lava which at any moment might break and let the unwary sink into fiery depths." For most of Conrad's heroes, the walk is more than merely dangerous: they die (even in victory) or come to grief, or if successful, pay too dearly for their success.

But to Conrad—and this distinguishes his outlook from Hardy's—the fault is not in their stars, but in themselves. The tragedy of his heroes is triggered by some flaw of character for which Conrad seems to hold them responsible. If the stars cannot be changed, then we can be, by learning how to control the unruly heart. He believed firmly in the need for discipline from within (he despised indiscipline and hated externally imposed discipline). Only through such inner discipline, Conrad was convinced, could man snatch at least a spiritual victory from the brink of defeat. Without such discipline, he would sink into the "fiery depths." This philosophy is expressed most completely in the harrowing story, *Heart of Darkness* (1902). With one other story, "An Outpost of Progress" (1896), it was all the spoil that Conrad brought out of the center of Africa.

Six days after the first installment appeared in *Blackwood's Magazine*, he wrote to his friend Cunninghame Graham, "There are two more installments in which the idea is so wrapped up in secondary notions that you—even you!—may miss it." As this statement suggests, the essence of the story is elusive, its meaning suspected rather than seen. The narrative at first glance seems to be dominated by the spell of the primeval African landscape. However, the wilderness remains inscrutable to Marlow and he is unable to shed light on its darkness. Another "secondary notion" is the idea of progress, which Conrad regarded with considerable scepticism (expressed in "An Outpost"). According to his friend Edward Garnett, "the sinister voice of the Congo with its murmuring undertone of human fatuity, baseness, and greed swept away all the generous illusions of his youth . . ." In the heart of the immense darkness, Marlow, like Conrad, gazes upon the tragedy of colonial greed, the ends to which men will go to exploit their fellow human beings. The odor of imbecile European rapacity blows to his nose like the whiff of the decaying corpses in the jungle. In one searing image—a white man standing ankle-deep in black man's blood—Conrad conveys his full feeling.

But Conrad was so much interested in exploitation as in the exploiter. The something—or nothing—that lies at the innermost core of man when all the outer layers have been peeled away is what fascinated Conrad. For him, neither colonialism nor the Congo could match the spectacle of the soul stripped naked by its surroundings. Such a soul is Kurtz. Armed with ideals, this representative of European man comes to the African waste with the intention of making every station a beacon in the darkness. But driven by his isolation and loneliness among the savages, he loses his inner discipline. He permits the ivory to dominate his body and soul, just as the silver of Sulaco victimizes men in *Nostromo*. The jungle darkness merges with his undisciplined heart, and he is left, like the stuff for which he sells himself, hollow at the core. His magnificently idealistic report contrasts ironically with his conduct.

But before the finish, this ruin of a once noble nature has a final pronouncement to croak. Summoning his failing powers before he goes over the edge, Kurtz passes judgment on the darkness inside and outside of man. This judgment, from the very depths of his being, expresses a suddenly perceived certainty, and to Marlow, takes on the face of glimpsed truth. Kurtz sees what life is like, and once we see what life is like, we win a victory over it even in defeat.

Seen from this angle, the summing up in *Heart of Darkness* ("The horror! The horror!") leads on a straight line to the conclusion of Camus' *The Stranger*.

There is, then, an existential quality latent in much of Conrad's work, especially in the vision of those tortured figures who struggle to create meaning in an essentially meaningless universe. Sartre describes the grey insane stuff of contingency in *La Nausee*, in which all human gestures are equally and willfully imposed, but Conrad before him had taken a similar view of the cosmos: man creates his own meanings, and these man-made systems of values collide and capsize each other. Each man in the end is alone (Jim, Heyst, Kurtz, Marlow) groping his way through a hostile faceless landscape of absurdity, king in his own brain, clown in the grip of circumstance. The Russian is cognate with Kurtz: the tragedy is equally comedy, for it involves no relation to any absolute. The royal arrogance of Kurtz is as meaningless as motley. Conrad's is the art of the grotesque: love, honor, murder, are equally ridiculous because equally unavailing.

There is no escaping the darkness of Conrad's universe if the reader has the courage to plumb it to the core.

In its exactness and economy of expression, the story presents Conrad at the peak of his power. The colorful early writing, with its adjectives that run in floods before and after nouns and its rich rhetoric and exuberance, gives way to a leaner, more symbolic manner, with "sinister resonance, a tonality of its own, a continued vibration that hangs in the air and dwells on the ear after the last note has been struck."

## FOR FURTHER INFORMATION:

Jocelyn Baines. *Joseph Conrad*. McGraw-Hill: New York, 1960.

*Joseph Conrad's Diary of His Journey up the Valley of the Congo in 1890*, With an Introduction and Notes by Richard Curle. Privately printed: London, 1926.

Albert Guerard. *Conrad the Novelist*. Harvard University Press: Cambridge, 1958.

Frederick R. Karl. *A Reader's Guide to Joseph Conrad*. Farrar, Straus & Giroux: New York, 1960 (Rev. ed. 1969).

Bernard Meyer, *Joseph Conrad: A Psychoanalytic Biography*. Princeton University Press: Princeton, 1967.

Zdzisław Najder. *Conrad's Polish Background: Letters to and From Polish Friends*. Oxford University Press: London, 1964.

# THE BEAST IN THE JUNGLE

## BY HENRY JAMES

First published, 1901

# THE BEAST IN THE JUNGLE

## CHAPTER I

**W**HAT determined the speech that startled him in the course of their encounter scarcely matters, being probably but some words spoken by himself quite without intention—spoken as they lingered and slowly moved together after their renewal of acquaintance. He had been conveyed by friends an hour or two before to the house at which she was staying; the party of visitors at the other house, of whom he was one, and thanks to whom it was his theory, as always, that he was lost in the crowd, had been invited over to luncheon. There had been after luncheon much dispersal, all in the interest of the original motive, a view of Weatherend itself and the fine things, intrinsic features, pictures, heirlooms, treasures of all the arts, that made the place almost famous; and the great rooms were so numerous that guests could wander at their will, hang back from the principal group and in cases where they took such matters with the last seriousness give themselves up to mysterious appreciations and measurements. There were persons to be observed, singly or in couples, bending toward objects in out-of-the-way corners with their hands on their knees and their heads nodding quite as with the emphasis of an excited sense of smell. When they were two they either mingled their sounds of ecstasy or melted into silences of even deeper import, so that there were aspects of the occasion that gave it for Marcher much the air of the "look round," previous to a sale highly advertised, that excites or quenches, as may be, the dream of acquisition. The dream of acquisition at Weatherend would have had to be wild indeed, and John Marcher found himself, among such suggestions, disconcerted almost equally by the presence of those who knew too much and by that of those who knew nothing. The great rooms caused so much poetry and history to press upon him that he needed some straying apart to feel in a proper relation with them, though this impulse was not, as happened, like the gloating of some of his companions, to be compared to the movements of a dog sniffing a cupboard. It had an issue promptly enough in a direction that was not to have been calculated.

It led, briefly, in the course of the October afternoon, to his closer meeting with May Bartram, whose face, a reminder, yet not quite a remembrance, as they sat much separated at a very long table, had begun merely by troubling him rather pleasantly. It affected him as the sequel of something of which he had lost the beginning. He knew it, and for the time quite welcomed it, as a continuation, but didn't know what it continued, which was an interest or an amusement the greater as he was also somehow aware—yet without a direct sign from her—that the young woman herself hadn't lost the thread. She hadn't lost it, but she wouldn't give it back to him, he saw, without some putting forth of his hand for it; and he not only saw that, but saw several things more, things odd enough in the light of the fact that at the moment some accident of grouping brought them face to face he was still merely fumbling with the idea that any contact between them in the past would have had no importance. If it had had no importance he scarcely knew why his actual impression of her should so seem to have so much; the answer to which, however, was that in such a life as they all appeared to be leading for the moment one could but take things as they came. He was satisfied, without in the least being able to say why, that this young lady might roughly have ranked in the house as a poor relation; satisfied also that she was not there on a brief visit, but was more or less a part of the establishment—almost a working, a remunerated part. Didn't she enjoy at periods a protection that she paid for by helping, among other services, to show the place and explain it, deal with the tiresome people, answer questions about the dates of the building, the styles of the furniture, the authorship of the pictures, the favourite haunts of the ghost? It wasn't that she looked as if you could have given her shillings—it was impossible to look less so. Yet when she finally drifted toward him, distinctly handsome, though ever so much older—older than when he had seen her before—it might have been as an effect of her guessing that he had, within the couple of hours, devoted more imagination to her

than to all the others put together, and had thereby penetrated to
a kind of truth that the others were too stupid for. She *was* there on
harder terms than any one; she was there as a consequence of things
suffered, one way and another, in the interval of years; and she remembered him very much as she was remembered—only a good
deal better.

By the time they at last thus came to speech they were alone in
one of the rooms—remarkable for a fine portrait over the chimney-
place—out of which their friends had passed, and the charm of it
was that even before they had spoken they had practically arranged
with each other to stay behind for talk. The charm, happily, was
in other things too—partly in there being scarce a spot at Weatherend without something to stay behind for. It was in the way the
autumn day looked into the high windows as it waned; the way the
red light, breaking at the close from under a low sombre sky, reached
out in a long shaft and played over old wainscots, old tapestry, old
gold, old colour. It was most of all perhaps in the way she came to
him as if, since she had been turned on to deal with the simpler
sort, he might, should he choose to keep the whole thing down,
just take her mild attention for a part of her general business. As
soon as he heard her voice, however, the gap was filled up and the
missing link supplied; the slight irony he divined in her attitude lost
its advantage. He almost jumped at it to get there before her. "I
met you years and years ago in Rome. I remember all about it."
She confessed to disappointment—she had been so sure he didn't;
and to prove how well he did he began to pour forth the particular
recollections that popped up as he called for them. Her face and
her voice, all at his service now, worked the miracle—the impression
operating like the torch of a lamplighter who touches into flame, one
by one, a long row of gas-jets. Marcher flattered himself the illumination was brilliant, yet he was really still more pleased on her showing
him, with amusement, that in his haste to make everything right
he had got most things rather wrong. It hadn't been at Rome—it
had been at Naples; and it hadn't been eight years before—it had
been more nearly ten. She hadn't been, either, with her uncle and
aunt, but with her mother and her brother; in addition to which it
was not with the Pembles *he* had been, but with the Boyers, coming
down in their company from Rome—a point on which she insisted,
a little to his confusion, and as to which she had her evidence in
hand. The Boyers she had known, but didn't know the Pembles,
though she had heard of them, and it was the people he was with

who had made them acquainted. The incident of the thunderstorm that had raged round them with such violence as to drive them for refuge into an excavation—this incident had not occurred at the Palace of the Cæsars, but at Pompeii, on an occasion when they had been present there at an important find.

He accepted her amendments, he enjoyed her corrections, though the moral of them was, she pointed out, that he *really* didn't remember the least thing about her; and he only felt it as a drawback that when all was made strictly historic there didn't appear much of anything left. They lingered together still, she neglecting her office—for from the moment he was so clever she had no proper right to him—and both neglecting the house, just waiting as to see if a memory or two more wouldn't again breathe on them. It hadn't taken them many minutes, after all, to put down on the table, like the cards of a pack, those that constituted their respective hands; only what came out was that the pack was unfortunately not perfect—that the past, invoked, invited, encouraged, could give them, naturally, no more than it had. It had made them anciently meet—her at twenty, him at twenty-five; but nothing was so strange, they seemed to say to each other, as that, while so occupied, it hadn't done a little more for them. They looked at each other as with the feeling of an occasion missed; the present would have been so much better if the other, in the far distance, in the foreign land, hadn't been so stupidly meagre. There weren't apparently, all counted, more than a dozen little old things that had succeeded in coming to pass between them; trivialities of youth, simplicities of freshness, stupidities of ignorance, small possible germs, but too deeply buried—too deeply (didn't it seem?) to sprout after so many years. Marcher could only feel he ought to have rendered her some service—saved her from a capsized boat in the Bay or at least recovered her dressing-bag, filched from her cab in the streets of Naples by a lazzarone with a stiletto. Or it would have been nice if he could have been taken with fever all alone at his hotel, and she could have come to look after him, to write to his people, to drive him out in convalescence. *Then* they would be in possession of the something or other that their actual show seemed to lack. It yet somehow presented itself, this show, as too good to be spoiled; so that they were reduced for a few minutes more to wondering a little helplessly why—since they seemed to know a certain number of the same people—their reunion had been so long averted. They didn't use that name for it, but their delay from minute to minute to join the others was a kind of confession that they didn't quite want it to be a failure. Their attempted supposition of reasons for their not having met but showed how little they knew of each other. There came in fact a moment when Marcher felt a positive pang. It was vain to pretend she was an old friend, for all the communities were wanting, in spite of which it was as an old friend that he saw she would have suited him. He had new ones enough—was surrounded with them for instance on the stage of the other house; as a new one he probably wouldn't have so much as noticed her. He would have liked to invent something, get her to make-believe with him that some passage of a romantic or critical kind *had* originally occurred. He was really almost reaching out in imagination—as against time—for something that would do, and saying to himself that if it didn't come this sketch of a fresh start would show for quite awkwardly bungled. They would separate, and now for no second or no third chance. They would have tried and not succeeded. Then it was, just at the turn, as he afterwards made it out to himself, that, everything else failing, she herself decided to take up the case and, as it were, save the situation. He felt as soon as she spoke that she had been consciously keeping back what she said and hoping to get on without it; a scruple in her that immensely touched him when, by the end of three or four minutes more, he was able to measure it. What she brought out, at any rate, quite cleared the air and supplied the link—the link it was so odd he should frivolously have managed to lose.

"You know you told me something I've never forgotten and that again and again has made me think of you since; it was that tremendously hot day when we went to Sorrento, across the bay, for the breeze. What I allude to was what you said to me, on the way back, as we sat under the awning of the boat enjoying the cool. Have you forgotten?"

He had forgotten and was even more surprised than ashamed. But the great thing was that he saw in this no vulgar reminder of any "sweet" speech. The vanity of women had long memories, but she was making no claim on him of a compliment or a mistake. With another woman, a totally different one, he might have feared the recall possibly even of some imbecile "offer." So, in having to say that he had indeed forgotten, he was conscious rather of a loss than of a gain; he already saw an interest in the matter of her mention. "I try to think—but I give it up. Yet I remember the Sorrento day."

"I'm not very sure you do," May Bartram after a moment said; "and I'm not very sure I ought to want you to. It's dreadful to bring a person back at any time to what he was ten years before. If you've lived away from it," she smiled, "so much the better."

"Ah if *you* haven't why should I?" he asked.

"Lived away, you mean, from what I myself was?"

"From what *I* was. I was of course an ass," Marcher went on; "but I would rather know from you just the sort of ass I was than—from the moment you have something in your mind—not know anything."

Still, however, she hesitated. "But if you've completely ceased to be that sort—?"

"Why I can then all the more bear to know. Besides, perhaps I haven't."

"Perhaps. Yet if you haven't," she added, "I should suppose you'd remember. Not indeed that *I* in the least connect with my impression the invidious name you use. If I had only thought you foolish," she explained, "the thing I speak of wouldn't so have remained with me. It was about yourself." She waited as if it might come to him; but as, only meeting her eyes in wonder, he gave no sign, she burnt her ships. "Has it ever happened?"

Then it was that, while he continued to stare, a light broke for him and the blood slowly came to his face, which began to burn with recognition. "Do you mean I told you—?" But he faltered, lest what came to him shouldn't be right, lest he should only give himself away.

"It was something about yourself that it was natural one shouldn't forget—that is if one remembered you at all. That's why I ask you," she smiled, "if the thing you then spoke of has ever come to pass?"

Oh then he saw, but he was lost in wonder and found himself embarrassed. This, he also saw, made her sorry for him, as if her allusion had been a mistake. It took him but a moment, however, to feel it hadn't been, much as it had been a surprise. After the first little shock of it her knowledge on the contrary began, even if rather strangely, to taste sweet to him. She was the only other person in the world then who would have it, and she had had it all these years, while the fact of his having so breathed his secret had unaccountably faded from him. No wonder they couldn't have met as if nothing had happened. "I judge," he finally said, "that I know what you mean. Only I had strangely enough lost any sense of having taken you so far into my confidence."

"Is it because you've taken so many others as well?"

"I've taken nobody. Not a creature since then."

"So that I'm the only person who knows?"

"The only person in the world."

"Well," she quickly replied, "I myself have never spoken. I've never, never repeated of you what you told me." She looked at him so that he perfectly believed her. Their eyes met over it in such a way that he was without a doubt. "And I never will."

She spoke with an earnestness that, as if almost excessive, put him at ease about her possible derision. Somehow the whole question was a new luxury to him—that is from the moment she was in possession. If she didn't take the sarcastic view she clearly took the sympathetic, and that was what he had had, in all the long time, from no one whomsoever. What he felt was that he couldn't at present have begun to tell her, and yet could profit perhaps exquisitely by the accident of having done so of old. "Please don't then. We're just right as it is."

"Oh I am," she laughed, "if you are!" To which she added: "Then you do still feel in the same way?"

It was impossible he shouldn't take to himself that she was really interested, though it all kept coming as perfect surprise. He had thought of himself so long as abominably alone, and lo he wasn't alone a bit. He hadn't been, it appeared, for an hour—since those moments on the Sorrento boat. It was *she* who had been, he seemed to see as he looked at her—she who had been made so by the graceless fact of his lapse of fidelity. To tell her what he had told her—what had it been but to ask something of her? something that she had given, in her charity, without his having, by a remembrance, by a return of the spirit, failing another encounter, so much as thanked her. What he had asked of her had been simply at first not to laugh at him. She had beautifully not done so for ten years, and she was not doing so now. So he had endless gratitude to make up. Only for that he must see just how he had figured to her. "What, exactly, was the account I gave—?"

"Of the way you did feel? Well, it was very simple. You said you had had from your earliest time, as the deepest thing within you, the sense of being kept for something rare and strange, possibly prodigious and terrible, that was sooner or later to happen to you, that you had in your bones the foreboding and the conviction of, and that would perhaps overwhelm you."

"Do you call that very simple?" John Marcher asked.

She thought a moment. "It was perhaps because I seemed, as you spoke, to understand it."

"You do understand it?" he eagerly asked.

Again she kept her kind eyes on him. "You still have the belief?"

"Oh!" he exclaimed helplessly. There was too much to say.

"Whatever it's to be," she clearly made out, "it hasn't yet come."

He shook his head in complete surrender now. "It hasn't yet come. Only, you know, it isn't anything I'm to *do*, to achieve in the world, to be distinguished or admired for. I'm not such an ass as *that*. It would be much better, no doubt, if I were."

"It's to be something you're merely to suffer?"

"Well, say to wait for—to have to meet, to face, to see suddenly break out in my life; possibly destroying all further consciousness, possibly annihilating me; possibly, on the other hand, only altering everything, striking at the root of all my world and leaving me to the consequences, however they shape themselves."

She took this in, but the light in her eyes continued for him not to be that of mockery. "Isn't what you describe perhaps but the expectation—or at any rate the sense of danger, familiar to so many people—of falling in love?"

John Marcher wondered. "Did you ask me that before?"

"No—I wasn't so free-and-easy then. But it's what strikes me now."

"Of course," he said after a moment, "it strikes you. Of course it strikes *me*. Of course what's in store for me may be no more than that. The only thing is," he went on, "that I think if it had been that I should by this time know."

"Do you mean because you've *been* in love?" And then as he but looked at her in silence: "You've been in love, and it hasn't meant such a cataclysm, hasn't proved the great affair?"

"Here I am, you see. It hasn't been overwhelming."

"Then it hasn't been love," said May Bartram.

"Well, I at least thought it was. I took it for that—I've taken it till now. It was agreeable, it was delightful, it was miserable," he explained. "But it wasn't strange. It wasn't what *my* affair's to be."

"You want something all to yourself—something that nobody else knows or *has* known?"

"It isn't a question of what I 'want'—God knows I don't want anything. It's only a question of the apprehension that haunts me —that I live with day by day."

He said this so lucidly and consistently that he could see it further impose itself. If she hadn't been interested before she'd have been interested now. "Is it a sense of coming violence?"

Evidently now too again he liked to talk of it. "I don't think of it as—when it does come—necessarily violent. I only think of it as natural and as of course above all unmistakeable. I think of it simply as *the* thing. *The* thing will of itself appear natural."

"Then how will it appear strange?"

Marcher bethought himself. "It won't —to *me*."

"To whom then?"

"Well," he replied, smiling at last, "say to you."

"Oh then I'm to be present?"

"Why you *are* present—since you know."

"I see." She turned it over. "But I mean at the catastrophe."

At this, for a minute, their lightness gave way to their gravity; it was as if the long look they exchanged held them together. "It will only depend on yourself—if you'll watch with me."

"Are you afraid?" she asked.

"Don't leave me *now*," he went on.

"Are you afraid?" she repeated.

"Do you think me simply out of my mind?" he pursued instead of answering. "Do I merely strike you as a harmless lunatic?"

"No," said May Bartram. "I understand you. I believe you."

"You mean you feel how my obsession—poor old thing!—may correspond to some possible reality?"

"To some possible reality."

"Then you *will* watch with me?"

She hesitated, then for the third time put her question. "Are you afraid?"

"Did I tell you I was—at Naples?"

"No, you said nothing about it."

"Then I don't know. And I should *like* to know," said John Marcher. "You'll tell me yourself whether you think so. If you'll watch with me you'll see."

"Very good then." They had been moving by this time across the room, and at the door, before passing out, they paused as for the full wind-up of their understanding. "I'll watch with you," said May Bartram.

## CHAPTER II

The fact that she "knew"—knew and yet neither chaffed him nor betrayed him—had in a short time begun to constitute between them a goodly bond, which became more marked when, within the year that followed their afternoon at Weatherend, the opportunities for meeting multiplied. The event that thus promoted these occasions was the death of the ancient lady her great-aunt, under whose wing, since losing her mother, she had to such an extent found shelter, and who, though but the widowed mother of the new successor to the property, had succeeded—thanks to a high tone and a high temper—in not forfeiting the supreme position at the great house. The deposition of this personage arrived but with her death, which, followed by many changes, made in particular a difference for the young woman in whom Marcher's expert attention had recognised from the first a dependent with a pride that might ache though it didn't bristle. Nothing for a long time had made him easier than the thought that the aching must have been much soothed by Miss Bartram's now finding herself able to set up a small home in London. She had acquired property, to an amount that made that luxury just possible, under her aunt's extremely complicated will, and when the whole matter began to be straightened out, which indeed took time, she let him know that the happy issue was at last in view. He had seen her again before that day, both because she had more than once accompanied the ancient lady to town and because he had paid another visit to the friends who so conveniently made of Weatherend one of the charms of their own hospitality. These friends had taken him back there; he had achieved there again with Miss Bartram some quiet detachment; and he had in London succeeded in persuading her to more than one brief absence from her aunt. They went together, on these latter occasions, to the National Gallery and the South Kensington Museum, where, among vivid reminders, they talked of Italy at large—not now attempting to recover, as at first, the taste of their youth and their ignorance. That recovery, the first day at Weatherend, had served its purpose well, had given them quite enough; so that they were, to Marcher's sense, no longer hovering about the head waters of their stream, but had felt their boat pushed sharply off and down the current.

They were literally afloat together; for our gentleman this was marked, quite as marked as that the fortunate cause of it was just the buried treasure of her knowledge. He had with his own hands dug up this little hoard, brought to light—that is, to within reach of the dim day constituted by their discretions and privacies—the object of value the hiding-place of which he had, after putting it into the ground himself, so strangely, so long forgotten. The rare luck of his having again just stumbled on the spot made him indifferent to any other question; he would doubtless have devoted more time to the odd accident of his lapse of memory if he hadn't been moved to devote so much to the sweetness, the comfort, as he felt, for the future, that this accident itself had helped to keep fresh. It had never entered into his plan that any one should "know," and mainly for the reason that it wasn't in him to tell any one. That would have been impossible, for nothing but the amusement of a cold world would have waited on it. Since, however, a mysterious fate had opened his mouth betimes, in spite of him, he would count that a compensation and profit by it to the utmost. That the right person *should* know tempered the asperity of his secret more even than his shyness had permitted him to imagine; and May Bartram was clearly right, because—well, because there she was. Her knowledge simply settled it; he would have been sure enough by this time had she been wrong. There was that in his situation, no doubt, that disposed him too much to see her as a mere confidant, taking all her light for him from the fact—the fact only—of her interest in his predicament; from her mercy, sympathy, seriousness, her consent not to regard him as the funniest of the funny. Aware, in fine, that her price for him was just in her giving him this constant sense of his being admirably spared, he was careful to remember that she had also a life of her own, with things that might happen to *her*, things that in friendship one should likewise take account of. Something fairly remarkable came to pass with him, for that matter, in this connexion —something represented by a certain passage of his consciousness, in the suddenest way, from one extreme to the other.

He had thought himself, so long as nobody knew, the most disinterested person in the world, carrying his concentrated burden, his perpetual suspense, ever so quietly, holding his tongue about it, giving others no glimpse of it nor of its effect upon his life, asking of them no allowance and only making on his side all those that were asked. He hadn't disturbed people with the queerness of their having to know a haunted man, though he had had moments of rather special temptation on hearing them say they were forsooth "unsettled." If they were as unsettled as he was—he who had never been settled for an hour in his life—they would know what it meant. Yet it wasn't, all the same, for him to make them, and he listened to them civilly enough. This was why he had such good—though possibly such rather colourless—manners; this was why, above all, he could regard himself, in a greedy world, as decently—as in fact perhaps even a little sublimely—unselfish. Our point is accordingly that he valued this character quite sufficiently to measure his present danger of letting it lapse, against which he promised himself to be much on his guard. He was quite ready, none the less, to be selfish just a little, since surely no more charming occasion for it had come to him. "Just a little," in a word, was just as much as Miss Bartram, taking one day with another, would let him. He never would be in the least coercive, and would keep well before him the lines on which consideration for her—the very highest—ought to proceed. He would thoroughly establish the heads under which her affairs, her requirements, her peculiarities—he went so far as to give them the latitude of that name—would come into their intercourse. All this naturally was a sign of how much he took the intercourse itself for granted. There was nothing more to be done about *that*. It simply existed; had sprung into being with her first penetrating question to him in the autumn light there at Weatherend. The real form it should have taken on the basis that stood out large was the form of their marrying. But the devil in this was that the very basis itself put marrying out of the question. His conviction, his apprehension, his obsession, in short, wasn't a privilege he could invite a woman to share; and that consequence of it was precisely what was the matter with him. Something or other lay in wait for him, amid the twists and the turns of the months and the years, like a crouching beast in the jungle. It signified little whether the crouching beast were destined to slay him or to be slain. The definite point was the inevitable spring of the creature; and the definite lesson from that was that a man of feeling didn't cause himself to be accompanied by a lady on a tiger-hunt. Such was the image under which he had ended by figuring his life.

They had at first, none the less, in the scattered hours spent together, made no allusion to that view of it; which was a sign he was handsomely alert to give that he didn't expect, that he in fact didn't care, always to be talking about it. Such a feature in one's outlook was really like a hump on one's back. The difference it made every minute of the day existed quite independently of discussion. One discussed of course *like* a hunchback, for there was always, if nothing else, the hunchback face. That remained, and she was watching him; but people watched best, as a general thing, in silence, so that such would be predominantly the manner of their vigil. Yet he didn't want, at the same time, to be tense and solemn; tense and solemn was what he imagined he too much showed for with other people. The thing to be, with the one person who knew, was easy and natural—to make the reference rather than be seeming to avoid it, to avoid it rather than be seeming to make it, and to keep it, in any case, familiar, facetious even, rather than pedantic and portentous. Some such sonsideration as the latter was doubtless in his mind for instance when he wrote pleasantly to Miss Bartram that perhaps the great thing he had so long felt as in the lap of the gods was no more than this circumstance, which touched him so nearly, of her acquiring a house in London. It was the first allusion they had yet again made, needing any other hitherto so little; but when she replied, after having given him the news, that she was by no means satisfied with such a trifle as the climax to so special a suspense, she almost set him wondering if she hadn't even a larger conception of singularity for him than he had for himself. He was at all events destined to become aware little by little, as time went by, that she was all the while looking at his life, judging it, measuring it, in the light of the thing she knew, which grew to be at last, with the consecration of the years, never mentioned between them save as "the real truth" about him. That had always been his own form of reference to it, but she adopted the form so quietly that, looking back at the end of a period, he knew there was no moment at which it was traceable that she had, as he might say, got inside his idea, or exchanged the attitude of beautifully indulging for that of still more beautifully believing him.

It was always open to him to accuse her of seeing him but as the most harmless of maniacs, and this, in the long run—since it covered so much ground—was his easiest description of their friendship. He had a screw loose for her, but she liked him in spite of it and was practically, against the rest of the world, his kind wise keeper, unremunerated but fairly amused and, in the absence of other near ties, not disreputably occupied. The rest of the world of course thought him queer, but she, she only, knew how, and above all why, queer; which was precisely what enabled her to dispose the concealing veil in the right folds. She took his gaiety from him—since it had to pass with them for gaiety—as she took everything else; but she certainly so far justified by her unerring touch his finer sense of the degree to which he had ended by convincing her. *She* at least never spoke of the secret of his life except as "the real truth about you," and she had in fact a wonderful way of making it seem, as such, the secret of her own life too. That was in fine how he so constantly felt her as allowing for him; he couldn't on the whole call it anything else. He allowed for himself, but she, exactly, allowed still more;

partly because, better placed for a sight of the matter, she traced his unhappy perversion through reaches of its course into which he could scarce follow it. He knew how he felt, but, besides knowing that, she knew how he *looked* as well; he knew each of the things of importance he was insidiously kept from doing, but she could add up the amount they made, understand how much, with a lighter weight on his spirit, he might have done, and thereby establish how, clever as he was, he fell short. Above all she was in the secret of the difference between the forms he went through—those of his little office under Government, those of caring for his modest patrimony, for his library, for his garden in the country, for the people in London whose invitations he accepted and repaid—and the detachment that reigned beneath them and that made of all behaviour, all that could in the least be called behaviour, a long act of dissimulation. What it had come to was that he wore a mask painted with the social simper, out of the eye-holes of which there looked eyes of an expression not in the least matching the other features. This the stupid world, even after years, had never more than half-discovered. It was only May Bartram who had, and she achieved, by an art indescribable, the feat of at once—or perhaps it was only alternately—meeting the eyes from in front and mingling her own vision, as from over his shoulder, with their peep through the apertures.

So while they grew older together she did watch with him, and so she let this association give shape and colour to her own existence. Beneath *her* forms as well detachment had learned to sit, and behaviour had become for her, in the social sense, a false account of herself. There was but one account of her that would have been true all the while and that she could give straight to nobody, least of all to John Marcher. Her whole attitude was a virtual statement, but the perception of that only seemed called to take its place for him as one of the many things necessarily crowded out of his consciousness. If she had moreover, like himself, to make sacrifices to their real truth, it was to be granted that her compensation might have affected her as more prompt and more natural. They had long periods, in this London time, during which, when they were together, a stranger might have listened to them without in the least pricking up his ears; on the other hand the real truth was equally liable at any moment to rise to the surface, and the auditor would then have wondered indeed what they were talking about. They had from an early hour made up their mind that society was, luckily, unintelligent, and the margin allowed them by this had fairly become one of their commonplaces. Yet there were still moments when the situation turned almost fresh—usually under the effect of some expression drawn from herself. Her expressions doubtless repeated themselves, but her intervals were generous. "What saves us, you know, is that we answer so completely to so usual an appearance: that of the man and woman whose friendship has become such a daily habit—or almost—as to be at last indispensable." That for instance was a remark she had frequently enough had occasion to make, though she had given it at different times different developments. What we are especially concerned with is the turn it happened to take from her one afternoon when he had come to see her in honour of her birthday. This anniversary had fallen on a Sunday, at a season of thick fog and general outward gloom; but he had brought her his customary offering, having known her now long enough to have established a hundred small traditions. It was one of his proofs to himself, the present he made her on her birthday, that he hadn't sunk into real selfishness. It was mostly nothing more than a small trinket, but it was always fine of its kind, and he was regularly careful to pay for it more than he thought he could afford. "Our habit saves you at least, don't you see? because it makes you, after all, for the vulgar, indistinguishable from other men. What's the most inveterate mark of men in general? Why, the capacity to spend endless time with dull women—to spend it I won't say without being bored, but without minding that they are, without being driven off at a tangent by it; which comes to the same thing. I'm your dull woman, a part of the daily bread for which you pray at church. That covers your tracks more than anything."

"And what covers yours?" asked Marcher, whom his dull woman could mostly to this extent amuse. "I see of course what you mean by your saving me, in this way and that, so far as other people are concerned—I've seen it all along. Only what is it that saves *you*? I often think, you know, of that."

She looked as if she sometimes thought of that too, but rather in a different way. "Where other people, you mean, are concerned?"

"Well, you're really so in with me, you know—as a sort of result of my being so in with yourself. I mean of my having such an immense regard for you, being so tremendously mindful of all you've done for me. I sometimes ask myself if it's quite fair. Fair I mean to have so involved and—since one may say it—interested you. I almost feel as if you hadn't really had time to do anything else."

"Anything else but be interested?" she asked. "Ah what else does one ever want to be? If I've been 'watching' with you, as we long ago agreed I was to do, watching's always in itself an absorption."

"Oh certainly," John Marcher said, "if you hadn't had your curiosity—! Only doesn't it sometimes come to you as time goes on that your curiosity isn't being particularly repaid?"

May Bartram had a pause. "Do you ask that, by any chance, because you feel at all that yours isn't? I mean because you have to wait so long."

Oh he understood what she meant! "For the thing to happen that never does happen? For the beast to jump out? No, I'm just where I was about it. It isn't a matter as to which I can *choose*, I can decide for a change. It isn't one as to which there *can* be a change. It's in the lap of the gods. One's in the hands of one's law—there one is. As to the form the law will take, the way it will operate, that's its own affair."

"Yes," Miss Bartram replied; "of course one's fate's coming, of course it *has* come in its own form and its own way, all the while. Only, you know, the form and the way in your case were to have been—well, something so exceptional and, as one may say, so particularly *your* own."

Something in this made him look at her with suspicion. "You say 'were to *have* been,' as if in your heart you had begun to doubt."

"Oh!" she vaguely protested.

"As if you believe," he went on, "that nothing will now take place."

She shook her head slowly but rather inscrutably. "You're far from my thought."

He continued to look at her. "What then is the matter with you?"

"Well," she said after another wait, "the matter with me is simply that I'm more sure than ever my curiosity, as you call it, will be but too well repaid."

They were frankly grave now; he had got up from his seat, had turned once more about the little drawing-room to which, year after year, he brought his inevitable topic; in which he had, as he might have said, tasted their intimate community with every sauce, where every object was as familiar to him as the things of his own house and the very carpets were worn with his fitful walk very much as the desks in old counting-houses are worn by the elbows of generations of clerks. The generations of his nervous moods had been at work there, and the place was the written history of his whole middle life. Under the impression of what his friend had just said he knew himself, for some reason, more aware of these things; which made him, after a moment, stop again before her. "Is it possibly that you've grown afraid?"

"Afraid?" He thought, as she repeated the word, that his question had made her, a little, change colour; so that, lest he should have touched on a truth, he explained very kindly: "You remember that that was what you asked *me* long ago—that first day at Weatherend."

"Oh yes, and you told me you didn't know—that I was to see for myself. We've said little about it since, even in so long a time."

"Precisely," Marcher interposed—"quite as if it were too delicate a matter for us to make free with. Quite as if we might find, on pressure, that I *am* afraid. For then," he said, "we shouldn't, should we? quite know what to do."

She had for the time no answer to this question. "There have been days when I thought you were. Only, of course," she added, "there have been days when we have thought almost anything."

"Everything. Oh!" Marcher softly groaned as with a gasp, half-spent, at the face, more uncovered just then than it had been for a long while, of the imagination always with them. It had always had its incalculable moments of glaring out, quite as with the very eyes of the very Beast, and, used as he was to them, they could still draw from him the tribute of a sigh that rose from the depths of his being. All they had thought, first and last, rolled over him; the past seemed to have been reduced to mere barren speculation. This in fact was what the place had just struck him as so full of—the simplification of everything but the state of suspense. That remained only by seeming to hang in the void surrounding it. Even his original fear, if fear it had been, had lost itself in the desert. "I judge, however," he continued, "that you see I'm not afraid now."

"What I see, as I make it out, is that you've achieved something almost unprecedented in the way of getting used to danger. Living with it so long and so closely you've lost your sense of it; you know it's there, but you're indifferent, and you cease even, as of old, to have to whistle in the dark. Considering what the danger is," May Bartram wound up, "I'm bound to say I don't think your attitude could well be surpassed."

John Marcher faintly smiled. "It's heroic?"

"Certainly—call it that."

It was what he would have liked indeed to call it. "I *am* then a man of courage?"

"That's what you were to show me."

He still, however, wondered. "But doesn't the man of courage know what he's afraid of—or *not* afraid of? I don't know *that,* you see. I don't focus it. I can't name it. I only know I'm exposed."

"Yes, but exposed—how shall I say?—so directly. So intimately. That's surely enough."

"Enough to make you feel then—as what we may call the end and the upshot of our watch—that I'm not afraid?"

"You're not afraid. But it isn't," she said, "the end of our watch. That is it isn't the end of yours. You've everything still to see."

"Then why haven't *you?*" he asked. He had had, all along, today, the sense of her keeping something back, and he still had it. As this was his first impression of that it quite made a date. The case was the more marked as she didn't at first answer; which in turn made him go on. "You know something I don't." Then his voice, for that of a man of courage, trembled a little. "You know what's to happen." Her silence, with the face she showed, was almost a confession—it made him sure. "You know, and you're afraid to tell me. It's so bad that you're afraid I'll find out."

All this might be true, for she did look as if, unexpectedly to her, he had crossed some mystic line that she had secretly drawn round her. Yet she might, after all, not have worried; and the real climax was that he himself, at all events, needn't. "You'll never find out."

## CHAPTER III

It was all to have made, none the less, as I have said, a date; which came out in the fact that again and again, even after long intervals, other things that passed between them wore in relation to this hour but the character of recalls and results. Its immediate effect had been indeed rather to lighten insistence—almost to provoke a reaction; as if their topic had dropped by its own weight and as if moreover, for that matter, Marcher had been visited by one of his occasional warnings against egotism. He had kept up, he felt, and very decently on the whole, his consciousness of the importance of not being selfish, and it was true that he had never sinned in that direction without promptly enough trying to press the scales the other way. He often repaired his fault, the season permitting, by inviting his friend to accompany him to the opera; and it not in-

frequently thus happened that, to show he didn't wish her to have
but one sort of food for her mind, he was the cause of her appearing
there with him a dozen nights in the month. It even happened that,
seeing her home at such times, he occasionally went in with her to
finish, as he called it, the evening, and, the better to make his point,
sat down to the frugal but always careful little supper that awaited
his pleasure. His point was made, he thought, by his not eternally
insisting with her on himself; made for instance, at such hours, when
it befell that, her piano at hand and each of them familiar with it,
they went over passages of the opera together. It chanced to be on
one of these occasions, however, that he reminded her of not having
answered a certain question he had put to her during the talk that
had taken place between them on her last birthday. "What is it that
saves *you*?"—saved her, he meant, from that appearance of variation
from the usual human type. If he had practically escaped remark, as
she pretended, by doing, in the most important particular, what
most men do—find the answer to life in patching up an alliance of
a sort with a woman no better than himself—how had she escaped
it, and how could the alliance, such as it was, since they must suppose
it had been more or less noticed, have failed to make her rather
positively talked about?

"I never said," May Bartram replied, "that it hadn't made me a
good deal talked about."

"Ah well then you're not 'saved.'"

"It hasn't been a question for me. If you've had your woman I've
had," she said, "my man."

"And you mean that makes you all right?"

Oh it was always as if there were so much to say! "I don't know
why it shouldn't make me—humanly, which is what we're speaking
of—as right as it makes you."

"I see," Marcher returned. "'Humanly,' no doubt, as showing
that you're living for something. Not, that is, just for me and my
secret."

May Bartram smiled. "I don't pretend it exactly shows that I'm
not living for you. It's my intimacy with you that's in question."

He laughed as he saw what she meant. "Yes, but since, as you say,
I'm only, so far as people make out, ordinary, you're—aren't you?—
no more than ordinary either. You help me to pass for a man like
another. So if I *am*, as I understand you, you're not compromised. Is
that it?"

She had another of her waits, but she spoke clearly enough. "That's it. It's all that concerns me—to help you to pass for a man like another."

He was careful to acknowledge the remark handsomely. "How kind, how beautiful, you are to me! How shall I ever repay you?"

She had her last grave pause, as if there might be a choice of ways. But she chose. "By going on as you are."

It was into this going on as he was that they relapsed, and really for so long a time that the day inevitably came for a further sounding of their depths. These depths, constantly bridged over by a structure firm enough in spite of its lightness and of its occasional oscillation in the somewhat vertiginous air, invited on occasion, in the interest of their nerves, a dropping of the plummet and a measurement of the abyss. A difference had been made moreover, once for all, by the fact that she had all the while not appeared to feel the need of rebutting his charge of an idea within her that she didn't dare to express—a charge uttered just before one of the fullest of their later discussions ended. It had come up for him then that she "knew" something and that what she knew was bad—too bad to tell him. When he had spoken of it as visibly so bad that she was afraid he might find it out, her reply had left the matter too equivocal to be let alone and yet, for Marcher's special sensibility, almost too formidable again to touch. He circled about it at a distance that alternately narrowed and widened and that still wasn't much affected by the consciousness in him that there was nothing she could "know," after all, any better than he did. She had no source of knowledge he hadn't equally—except of course that she might have finer nerves. That was what women had where they were interested; they made out things, where people were concerned, that the people often couldn't have made out for themselves. Their nerves, their sensibility, their imagination, were conductors and revealers, and the beauty of May Bartram was in particular that she had given herself so to his case. He felt in these days what, oddly enough, he had never felt before, the growth of a dread of losing her by some catastrophe—some catastrophe that yet wouldn't at all be *the* catastrophe: partly because she had almost of a sudden begun to strike him as more useful to him than ever yet, and partly by reason of an appearance of uncertainty in her health, coincident and equally new. It was characteristic of the inner detachment he had hitherto so successfully cultivated and to which our whole account of him is a reference, it was characteristic that his complications, such as they were, had never yet seemed so as at this crisis to thicken about him, even to the point of making him ask himself if he were, by any chance, of a truth, within sight or sound, within touch or reach, within the immediate jurisdiction, of the thing that waited.

When the day came, as come it had to, that his friend confessed to him her fear of a deep disorder in her blood, he felt somehow the shadow of a change and the chill of a shock. He immediately began to imagine aggravations and disasters, and above all to think of her peril as the direct menace for himself of personal privation. This indeed gave him one of those partial recoveries of equanimity that were agreeable to him—it showed him that what was still first in his mind was the loss she herself might suffer. "What if she should have to die before knowing, before seeing—?" It would have been brutal, in the early stages of her trouble, to put that question to her; but it had immediately sounded for him to his own concern, and the possibility was what most made him sorry for her. If she did "know," moreover, in the sense of her having had some—what should he think?—mystical irresistible light, this would make the matter not better, but worse, inasmuch as her original adoption of his own curiosity had quite become the basis of her life. She had been living to see what would *be* to be seen, and it would quite lacerate her to have to give up before the accomplishment of the vision. These reflexions, as I say, quickened his generosity; yet, make them as he might, he saw himself, with the lapse of the period, more and more disconcerted. It lapsed for him with a strange steady sweep, and the oddest oddity was that it gave him, independently of the threat of much inconvenience, almost the only positive surprise his career, if career it could be called, had yet offered him. She kept the house as she had never done; he had to go to her to see her—she could meet him nowhere now, though there was scarce a corner of their loved old London in which she hadn't in the past, at one time or another, done so; and he found her always seated by her fire in the deep old-fashioned chair she was less and less able to leave. He had been struck one day, after an absence exceeding his usual measure, with her suddenly looking much older to him than he had ever thought of her being; then he recognised that the suddenness was all on his side—he had just simply and suddenly noticed. She looked older because inevitably, after so many years, she *was* old, or almost; which was of course true in still greater measure of her companion. If she was old, or almost, John Marcher assuredly was, and yet it was her showing of the lesson, not his own, that brought the truth home to him. His surprises began here; when once they had begun they multiplied; they came rather with a rush: it was as if, in the oddest way in the world, they had all been kept back, sown in a thick cluster, for the late afternoon of life, the time at which for people in general the unexpected has died out.

One of them was that he should have caught himself—for he *had* so done—*really* wondering if the great accident would take form now as nothing more than his being condemned to see this charming woman, this admirable friend, pass away from him. He had never so unreservedly qualified her as while confronted in thought with such a possibility; in spite of which there was small doubt for him that as an answer to his long riddle the mere effacement of even so fine a feature of his situation would be an abject anti-climax. It would represent, as connected with his past attitude, a drop of dignity under the shadow of which his existence could only become the most grotesque of failures. He had been far from holding it a failure—long as he had waited for the appearance that was to make it a success. He had waited for quite another thing, not for such a thing as that. The breath of his good faith came short, however, as he recognised how long he had waited, or how long at least his companion had. That she, at all events, might be recorded as having waited in vain—this affected him sharply, and all the more because of his at first having done little more than amuse himself with the idea. It grew more grave as the gravity of her condition grew, and the state of mind it produced in him, which he himself ended by watching as if it had been some definite disfigurement of his outer person, may pass for another of his surprises. This conjoined itself still with another, the really stupefying consciousness of a question that he would have allowed to shape itself had he dared. What did everything mean—what, that is, did *she* mean, she and her vain waiting and her probable death and the soundless admonition of it all—unless that, at this time of day, it was simply, it was overwhelmingly too late? He had never at any stage of his queer consciousness admitted the whisper of such a correction; he had never till within these last few months been so false to his conviction as not to hold that what was to come to him had time, whether *he* struck himself as having it or not. That at last, at last, he certainly hadn't it, to speak of, or had it but in the scantiest measure—such, soon enough, as things went with him, became the inference with which his old obsession had to reckon: and this it was not helped to do by the more and more confirmed appearance that the great vagueness casting the long shadow in which he had lived had, to attest itself, almost no margin left. Since it was in Time that he was to have met his fate, so it was in Time that his fate was to have acted; and as he waked up to the sense of no longer being young,. which was exactly the sense of being stale, just as that, in turn, was the sense of being weak, he waked up to another matter beside. It all hung together; they were subject, he and the great vagueness, to an equal and indivisible law. When the possibilities themselves had accordingly turned stale, when the secret of the gods had grown faint, had perhaps even quite evaporated, that, and that only, was failure. It wouldn't have been failure to be bankrupt, dishonoured, pilloried, hanged; it was failure not to be anything. And so, in the dark valley into which his path had taken its unlooked-for twist, he wondered not a little as he groped. He didn't care what awful crash might overtake him, with what ignominy or what monstrosity he might yet be associated—since he wasn't after all too utterly old to suffer—if it would only be decently proportionate to the posture he had kept, all his life, in the threatened presence of it. He had but one desire left—that he shouldn't have been "sold."

## CHAPTER IV

Then it was that, one afternoon, while the spring of the year was young and new she met all in her own way his frankest betrayal of these alarms. He had gone in late to see her, but evening hadn't settled and she was presented to him in that long fresh light of waning April days which affects us often with a sadness sharper than the greyest hours of autumn. The week had been warm, the spring was supposed to have begun early, and May Bartram sat, for the first time in the year, without a fire; a fact that, to Marcher's sense, gave the scene of which she formed part a smooth and ultimate look, an air of knowing, in its immaculate order and cold meaningless cheer, that it would never see a fire again. Her own aspect—he could scarce have said why—intensified this note. Almost as white as wax, with the marks and signs in her face as numerous and as fine as if they had been etched by a needle, with soft white draperies relieved by a faded green scarf on the delicate tone of which the years had further refined, she was the picture of a serene and exquisite but impenetrable sphinx, whose head, or indeed all whose person, might have been powdered with silver. She was a sphinx, yet with her white petals and green fronds she might have been a lily too—only an artificial lily, wonderfully imitated and constantly kept, without dust or stain, though not exempt from a slight droop and a complexity of faint creases, under some clear glass bell. The perfection of household care, of high polish and finish, always reigned in her rooms, but they now looked most as if everything had been wound up, tucked in, put away, so that she might sit with folded hands and with nothing more to do. She was "out of it," to Marcher's vision; her work was over; she communicated with him as across some gulf or from some island of rest that she had already reached, and it made him feel strangely abandoned. Was it—or rather wasn't it—that if for so long she had been watching with him the answer to their question must have swum into her ken and taken on its name, so that her occupation was verily gone? He had as much as charged her with this in saying to her, many months before, that she even then knew something she was keeping from him. It was a point he had never since ventured to press, vaguely fearing as he did that it might become a difference, perhaps a disagreement, between them. He had in this later time turned nervous, which was what he in all the other years had never been; and the oddity was that his nervousness should have waited till he had begun to doubt, should have held off so long as he was sure. There was something, it seemed to him, that the wrong word would bring down on his head, something that would so at least ease off his tension. But he wanted not to speak the wrong word; that would make everything ugly. He wanted the knowledge he lacked to drop on him, if drop it could, by its own august weight. If she was to forsake him it was surely for her to take leave. This was why he didn't directly ask her again what she knew; but it was also why, approaching the matter from another side, he said to her in the course of his visit: "What do you regard as the very worst that at this time of day *can* happen to me?"

He had asked her that in the past often enough; they had, with the odd irregular rhythm of their intensities and avoidances, exchanged ideas about it and then had seen the ideas washed away by cool intervals, washed like figures traced in sea-sand. It had ever been the mark of their talk that the oldest allusions in it required but a little dismissal and reaction to come out again, sounding for the hour as new. She could thus at present meet his enquiry quite freshly and patiently. "Oh yes, I've repeatedly thought, only it always seemed to me of old that I couldn't quite make up my mind. I thought of dreadful things, between which it was difficult to choose; and so must you have done."

"Rather! I feel now as if I had scarce done anything else. I appear to myself to have spent my life in thinking of nothing *but* dreadful things. A great many of them I've at different times named to you, but there were others I couldn't name."

"They were too, too dreadful?"

"Too, too dreadful—some of them."

She looked at him a minute, and there came to him as he met it an inconsequent sense that her eyes, when one got their full clearness, were still as beautiful as they had been in youth, only beautiful with a strange cold light—a light that somehow was a part of the effect, if it wasn't rather a part of the cause, of the pale hard sweetness of the season and the hour. "And yet," she said at last, "there are horrors we've mentioned."

It deepened the strangeness to see her, as such a figure in such a picture, talk of "horrors," but she was to do in a few minutes something stranger yet—though even of this he was to take the full measure but afterwards—and the note of it already trembled. It was, for the matter of that, one of the signs that her eyes were having again the high flicker of their prime. He had to admit, however, what she said. "Oh yes, there were times when we did go far." He caught himself in the act of speaking as if it all were over. Well, he wished it were; and the consummation depended for him clearly more and more on his friend.

But she had now a soft smile. "Oh far—!"

It was oddly ironic. "Do you mean you're prepared to go further?"

She was frail and ancient and charming as she continued to look at him, yet it was rather as if she had lost the thread. "Do you consider that we went far?"

"Why I thought it the point you were just making—that we *had* looked most things in the face."

"Including each other?" She still smiled. "But you're quite right. We've had together great imaginations, often great fears; but some of them have been unspoken."

"Then the worst—we haven't faced that. I *could* face it, I believe, if I knew what you think it. I feel," he explained, "as if I had lost my power to conceive such things." And he wondered if he looked as blank as he sounded. "It's spent."

"Then why do you assume," she asked, "that mine isn't?"

"Because you've given me signs to the contrary. It isn't a question for you of conceiving, imagining, comparing. It isn't a question now of choosing." At last he came out with it. "You know something I don't. You've shown me that before."

These last words had affected her, he made out in a moment, exceedingly, and she spoke with firmness. "I've shown you, my dear, nothing."

He shook his head. "You can't hide it."

"Oh, oh!" May Bartram sounded over what she couldn't hide. It was almost a smothered groan.

"You admitted it months ago, when I spoke of it to you as of something you were afraid I should find out. Your answer was that I couldn't, that I wouldn't, and I don't pretend I have. But you had something therefore in mind, and I now see how it must have been, how it still is, the possibility that, of all possibilities, has settled itself for you as the worst. This," he went on, "is why I appeal to you. I'm only afraid of ignorance to-day—I'm not afraid of knowledge." And then as for a while she said nothing: "What makes me sure is that I see in your face and feel here, in this air and amid these appearances, that you're out of it. You've done. You've had your experience. You leave me to my fate."

Well, she listened, motionless and white in her chair, as on a decision to be made, so that her manner was fairly an avowal, though still, with a small fine inner stiffness, an imperfect surrender. "It *would* be the worst," she finally let herself say. "I mean the thing I've never said."

It hushed him a moment. "More monstrous than all the monstrosities we've named?"

"More monstrous. Isn't that what you sufficiently express," she asked, "in calling it the worst?"

Marcher thought. "Assuredly—if you mean, as I do, something that includes all the loss and all the shame that are thinkable."

"It would if it *should* happen," said May Bartram. "What we're speaking of, remember, is only my idea."

"It's your belief," Marcher returned. "That's enough for me. I feel your beliefs are right. Therefore if, having this one, you give me no more light on it, you abandon me."

"No, no!" she repeated. "I'm with you—don't you see?—still." And as to make it more vivid to him she rose from her chair—a movement she seldom risked in these days—and showed herself, all draped and all soft, in her fairness and slimness. "I haven't forsaken you."

It was really, in its effort against weakness, a generous assurance, and had the success of the impulse not, happily, been great, it would have touched him to pain more than to pleasure. But the cold charm in her eyes had spread, as she hovered before him, to all the rest of her person, so that it was for the minute almost a recovery of youth. He couldn't pity her for that; he could only take her as she showed —as capable even yet of helping him. It was as if, at the same time, her light might at any instant go out; wherefore he must make the most of it. There passed before him with intensity the three or four things he wanted most to know; but the question that came of itself to his lips really covered the others. "Then tell me if I shall consciously suffer."

She promptly shook her head. "Never!"

It confirmed the authority he imputed to her, and it produced on him an extraordinary effect. "Well, what's better than that? Do you call that the worst?"

"You think nothing is better?" she asked.

She seemed to mean something so special that he again sharply wondered, though still with the dawn of a prospect of relief. "Why not, if one doesn't *know*?" After which, as their eyes, over his question, met in a silence, the dawn deepened and something to his purpose came prodigiously out of her very face. His own, as he took it in, suddenly flushed to the forehead, and he gasped with the force of a perception to which, on the instant, everything fitted. The sound of his gasp filled the air; then he became articulate. "I see—if I don't suffer!"

In her own look, however, was doubt. "You see what?"

"Why what you mean—what you've always meant."

She again shook her head. "What I mean isn't what I've always meant. It's different."

"It's something new?"

She hung back from it a little. "Something new. It's not what you think. I see what you think."

His divination drew breath then; only her correction might be wrong. "It isn't that I *am* a blockhead?" he asked between faintness and grimness. "It isn't that it's all a mistake?"

"A mistake?" she pityingly echoed. *That* possibility, for her, he saw, would be monstrous; and if she guaranteed him the immunity from pain it would accordingly not be what she had in mind. "Oh no," she declared; it's nothing of that sort. You've been right."

Yet he couldn't help asking himself if she weren't, thus pressed, speaking but to save him. It seemed to him he should be most in a hole if his history should prove all a platitude. "Are you telling me the truth, so that I shan't have been a bigger idiot than I can bear to know? I *haven't* lived with a vain imagination, in the most besotted illusion? I haven't waited but to see the door shut in my face?"

She shook her head again. "However the case stands *that* isn't the truth. Whatever the reality, it *is* a reality. The door isn't shut. The door's open," said May Bartram.

"Then something's to come?"

She waited once again, always with her cold sweet eyes on him. "It's never too late." She had, with her gliding step, diminished the distance between them, and she stood nearer to him, close to him, a minute, as if still charged with the unspoken. Her movement might have been for some finer emphasis of what she was at once hesitating and deciding to say. He had been standing by the chimney-piece, fireless and sparely adorned, a small perfect old French clock and two morsels of rosy Dresden constituting all its furniture; and her hand grasped the shelf while she kept him waiting, grasped it a little as for support and encouragement. She only kept him waiting, however; that is he only waited. It had become suddenly, from her movement and attitude, beautiful and vivid to him that she had something more to give him; her wasted face delicately shone with it—it glittered almost as with the white lustre of silver in her expression. She was right, incontestably, for what he saw in her face was the truth, and strangely, without consequence, while their talk of it as dreadful was still in the air, she appeared to present it as inordinately soft. This, prompting bewilderment, made him but gape the more gratefully for her revelation, so that they continued for some minutes silent, her face shining at him, her contact imponderably pressing, and his stare all kind but all expectant. The end, none the less, was that what he had expected failed to come to him. Something else took place instead, which seemed to consist at first in the mere closing of her eyes. She gave way at the same instant to a slow fine shudder, and though he remained staring—though he stared in fact but the harder—turned off and regained her chair. It was the end of what she had been intending, but it left him thinking only of that.

"Well, you don't say—?"

She had touched in her passage a bell near the chimney and had sunk back strangely pale. "I'm afraid I'm too ill."

"Too ill to tell me?" It sprang up sharp to him, and almost to his lips, the fear she might die without giving him light. He checked himself in time from so expressing his question, but she answered as if she had heard the words.

"Don't you know—now?"

" 'Now'—?" She had spoken as if some difference had been made within the moment. But her maid, quickly obedient to her bell, was already with them. "I know nothing." And he was afterwards to say to himself that he must have spoken with odious impatience, such an impatience as to show that, supremely disconcerted, he washed his hands of the whole question.

"Oh!" said May Bartram.

"Are you in pain?" he asked as the woman went to her.

"No," said May Bartram.

Her maid, who had put an arm round her as if to take her to her room, fixed on him eyes that appealingly contradicted her; in spite of which, however, he showed once more his mystification. "What then has happened?"

She was once more, with her companion's help, on her feet, and, feeling withdrawal imposed on him, he had blankly found his hat and gloves and had reached the door. Yet he waited for her answer. "What *was* to," she said.

## CHAPTER V

He came back the next day, but she was then unable to see him, and as it was literally the first time this had occurred in the long stretch of their acquaintance he turned away, defeated and sore, almost angry—or feeling at least that such a break in their custom was really the beginning of the end—and wandered alone with his thoughts, especially with the one he was least able to keep down. She was dying and he would lose her; she was dying and his life would end. He stopped in the Park, into which he had passed, and stared before him at his recurrent doubt. Away from her the doubt pressed again; in her presence he had believed her, but as he felt his forlornness he threw himself into the explanation that, nearest at hand, had most of a miserable warmth for him and least of a cold torment. She had deceived him to save him—to put him off with something in which he should be able to rest. What could the thing that was to happen to him be, after all, but just this thing that had begun to happen? Her dying, her death, his consequent solitude—*that* was what he had figured as the Beast in the Jungle, that was what had been in the lap of the gods. He had had her word for it as he left her—what else on earth could she have meant? It wasn't a thing of a monstrous order; not a fate rare and distinguished; not a stroke of fortune that overwhelmed and immortalised; it had only the stamp of the common doom. But poor Marcher at this hour judged the common doom sufficient. It would serve his turn, and even as the consummation of infinite waiting he would bend his pride to accept it. He sat down on a bench in the twilight. He hadn't been a fool. Something had *been*, as she had said, to come. Before he rose indeed it had quite struck him that the final fact really matched with the long avenue through which he had had to reach it. As sharing his suspense and as giving herself all, giving her life, to bring it to an end, she had come with him every step of the way. He had lived by her aid, and to leave her behind would be cruelly, damnably to miss her. What could be more overwhelming than that?

Well, he was to know within the week, for though she kept him a while at bay, left him restless and wretched during a series of days on each of which he asked about her only again to have to turn away, she ended his trial by receiving him where she had always received him. Yet she had been brought out at some hazard into the presence of so many of the things that were, consciously, vainly, half their past, and there was scant service left in the gentleness of her mere desire, all too visible, to check his obsession and wind up his long trouble. That was clearly what she wanted, the one thing more for her own peace while she could still put out her hand. He was so affected by her state that, once seated by her chair, he was moved to let everything go; it was she herself therefore who brought him back, took up again, before she dismissed him, her last word of the other time. She showed how she wished to leave their business in order. "I'm not sure you understood. You've nothing to wait for more. It *has* come."

Oh how he looked at her! "Really?"

"Really."

"The thing that, as you said, *was* to?"

"The thing that we began in our youth to watch for."

Face to face with her once more he believed her; it was a claim to which he had so abjectly little to oppose. "You mean that it has come as a positive definite occurrence, with a name and a date?"

"Positive. Definite. I don't know about the 'name,' but oh with a date!"

He found himself again too helplessly at sea. "But come in the night—come and passed me by?"

May Bartram had her strange faint smile. "Oh no, it hasn't passed you by!"

"But if I haven't been aware of it and it hasn't touched me—?"

"Ah your not being aware of it"—and she seemed to hesitate an instant to deal with this—"your not being aware of it is the strangeness *in* the strangeness. It's the wonder *of* the wonder." She spoke as with the softness almost of a sick child, yet now at last, at the end of all, with the perfect straightness of a sibyl. She visibly knew that she knew, and the effect on him was of something co-ordinate, in its high character, with the law that had ruled him. It was the true voice of the law; so on her lips would the law itself have sounded. "It *has* touched you," she went on. "It has done its office. It has made you all its own."

"So utterly without my knowing it?"

"So utterly without your knowing it." His hand, as he leaned to her, was on the arm of her chair, and, dimly smiling always now, she placed her own on it. "It's enough if *I* know it."

"Oh!" he confusedly breathed, as she herself of late so often had done.

"What I long ago said is true. You'll never know now, and I think you ought to be content. You've *had* it," said May Bartram.

"But had what?"

"Why what was to have marked you out. The proof of your law. It has acted. I'm too glad," she then bravely added, "to have been able to see what it's *not*."

He continued to attach his eyes to her, and with the sense that it was all beyond him, and that *she* was too, he would still have sharply challenged her hadn't he so felt it an abuse of her weakness to do more than take devoutly what she gave him, take it hushed as to a revelation. If he did speak, it was out of the fore-knowledge of his loneliness to come. "If you're glad of what it's 'not' it might then have been worse?"

She turned her eyes away, she looked straight before her; with which after a moment: "Well, you know our fears."

He wondered. "It's something then we never feared?"

On this slowly she turned to him. "Did we ever dream, with all our dreams, that we should sit and talk of it thus?"

He tried for a little to make out that they had; but it was as if their dreams, numberless enough, were in solution in some thick cold mist through which thought lost itself. "It might have been that we couldn't talk?"

"Well"—she did her best for him—"not from this side. This, you see," she said, "is the *other* side."

"I think," poor Marcher returned, "that all sides are the same to me." Then, however, as she gently shook her head in correction: "We mightn't, as it were, have got across—?"

"To where we are—no. We're *here*"—she made her weak emphasis.

"And much good does it do us!" was her friend's frank comment.

"It does us the good it can. It does us the good that *it* isn't here. It's past. It's behind," said May Bartram. "Before—" but her voice dropped.

He had got up, not to tire her, but it was hard to combat his yearning. She after all told him nothing but that his light had failed—which he knew well enough without her. "Before—?" he blankly echoed.

"Before, you see, it was always to *come*. That kept it present."

"Oh I don't care what comes now! Besides," Marcher added, "it seems to me I liked it better present, as you say, than I can like it absent with *your* absence."

"Oh mine!"—and her pale hands made light of it.

"With the absence of everything." He had a dreadful sense of standing there before her for—so far as anything but this proved, this bottomless drop was concerned—the last time of their life. It rested on him with a weight he felt he could scarce bear, and this weight it apparently was that still pressed out what remained in him of speakable protest. "I believe you; but I can't begin to pretend I understand. *Nothing*, for me, is past; nothing *will* pass till I pass myself, which I pray my stars may be as soon as possible. Say, however," he added, "that I've eaten my cake, as you contend, to the last crumb—how can the thing I've never felt at all be the thing I was marked out to feel?"

She met him perhaps less directly, but she met him unperturbed. "You take your 'feelings' for granted. You were to suffer your fate. That was not necessarily to know it."

"How in the world—when what is such knowledge but suffering?"

She looked up at him a while in silence. "No—you don't understand."

"I suffer," said John Marcher.

"Don't, don't!"

"How can I help at least *that?*"

"*Don't!*" May Bartram repeated.

She spoke it in a tone so special, in spite of her weakness, that he stared an instant—stared as if some light, hitherto hidden, had shimmered across his vision. Darkness again closed over it, but the gleam had already become for him an idea. "Because I haven't the right—?"

"Don't *know*—when you needn't," she mercifully urged. "You needn't—for we shouldn't."

"Shouldn't?" If he could but know what she meant!

"No—it's too much."

"Too much?" he still asked but, with a mystification that was the next moment of a sudden to give way. Her words, if they meant something, affected him in this light—the light also of her wasted face—as meaning *all*, and the sense of what knowledge had been for herself came over him with a rush which broke through into a question. "Is it of that then you're dying?"

She but watched him, gravely at first, as to see, with this, where he was, and she might have seen something or feared something that moved her sympathy. "I would live for you still—if I could." Her eyes closed for a little, as if, withdrawn into herself, she were for a last time trying. "But I can't!" she said as she raised them again to take leave of him.

She couldn't indeed, as but too promptly and sharply appeared, and he had no vision of her after this that was anything but darkness and doom. They had parted for ever in that strange talk; access to her chamber of pain, rigidly guarded, was almost wholly forbidden him; he was feeling now moreover, in the face of doctors, nurses, the two or three relatives attracted doubtless by the presumption of what she had to "leave," how few were the rights, as they were called in such cases, that he had to put forward, and how odd it might even seem that their intimacy shouldn't have given him more of them. The stupidest fourth cousin had more, even though she had been nothing in such a person's life. She had been a feature of features in *his*, for what else was it to have been so indispensable? Strange beyond saying were the ways of existence, baffling for him the anomaly of his lack, as he felt it to be, of producible claim. A woman might have been, as it were, everything to him, and it might yet present him in no connexion that any one seemed held to recognise. If this was the case in these closing weeks it was the case more sharply on the occasion of the last offices rendered, in the great grey London cemetery, to what had been mortal, to what had been precious, in his friend. The concourse at her grave was not numerous, but he saw himself treated as scarce more nearly concerned with it than if there had been a thousand others. He was in short from this moment face to face with the fact that he was to profit extraordinarily little by the interest May Bartram had taken in him. He couldn't quite have said what he expected, but he hadn't surely expected this approach to a double privation. Not only had her interest failed him, but he seemed to feel himself unattended— and for a reason he couldn't seize—by the distinction, the dignity, the propriety, if nothing else, of the man markedly bereaved. It was as if in the view of society he had not *been* markedly bereaved, as if there still failed some sign or proof of it, and as if none the less his character could never be affirmed nor the deficiency ever made up. There were moments as the weeks went by when he would have liked, by some almost aggressive act, to take his stand on the intimacy of his loss, in order that it *might* be questioned and his retort, to the relief of his spirit, so recorded; but the moments of an irritation more helpless followed fast on these, the moments during which, turning things over with a good conscience but with a bare horizon, he found himself wondering if he oughtn't to have begun, so to speak, further back.

He found himself wondering indeed at many things, and this last speculation had others to keep it company. What could he have done, after all, in her lifetime, without giving them both, as it were, away? He couldn't have made known she was watching him, for that would have published the superstition of the Beast. This was what closed his mouth now—now that the Jungle had been threshed to vacancy and that the Beast had stolen away. It sounded too foolish and too flat; the difference for him in this particular, the extinction in his life of the element of suspense, was such as in fact to surprise him. He could scarce have said what the effect resembled; the abrupt cessation, the positive prohibition, of music perhaps, more than anything else, in some place all adjusted and all accustomed to sonority and to attention. If he could at any rate have conceived lifting the veil from his image at some moment of the past (what had he done, after all, if not lift it to *her?*) so to do this to-day, to talk to people at large of the Jungle cleared and confide to them that he now felt it as safe, would have been not only to see them listen as to a goodwife's tale, but really to hear himself tell one. What it presently came to in truth was that poor Marcher waded through his beaten grass, where no life stirred, where no breath sounded, where no evil eye seemed to gleam from a possible lair, very much as if vaguely looking for the Beast, and still more as if acutely missing it. He walked about in an existence that had grown strangely more spacious and, stopping fitfully in places where the undergrowth of life struck him as closer, asked himself yearningly, wondered secretly and sorely, if it would have lurked here or there. It would have at all events *sprung;* what was at least complete was his belief in the truth itself of the assurance given him. The change from his old sense to his new was absolute and final: what was to happen *had* so absolutely and finally happened that he was as little able to know a fear for his future as to know a hope; so absent in short was any question of anything still to come. He was to live entirely with the other question, that of his unidentified past, that of his having to see his fortune impenetrably muffled and masked.

The torment of this vision became then his occupation; he couldn't perhaps have consented to live but for the possibility of guessing. She had told him, his friend, not to guess; she had forbidden him, so far as he might, to know, and she had even in a sort denied the power in him to learn: which were so many things, precisely, to deprive him of rest. It wasn't that he wanted, he argued for fairness, that anything past and done should repeat itself; it was only that he shouldn't, as an anticlimax, have been taken sleeping so sound as not to be able to win back by an effort of thought the lost stuff of consciousness. He declared to himself at moments that he would either win it back or have done with consciousness for ever; he made this idea his one motive in fine, made it so much his passion that none other, to compare with it, seemed ever to have touched him. The lost stuff of consciousness became thus for him as a strayed or stolen child to an unappeasable father; he hunted it up and down very much as if he were knocking at doors and enquiring of the police. This was the spirit in which, inevitably, he set himself to travel; he started on a journey that was to be as long as he could make it; it danced before him that, as the other side of the globe couldn't possibly have less to say to him, it might, by a possibility of suggestion, have more. Before he quitted London, however, he made a pilgrimage to May Bartram's grave, took his way to it through the endless avenues of the grim suburban metropolis, sought it out in the wilderness of tombs, and, though he had come but for the renewal of the act of farewell, found himself, when he had at last stood by it, beguiled into long intensities. He stood for an hour, powerless to turn away and yet powerless to penetrate the darkness of death; fixing with his eyes her inscribed name and date, beating his forehead against the fact of the secret they kept, drawing his breath, while he waited, as if some sense would in pity of him rise from the stones. He kneeled on the stones, however, in vain; they kept what they concealed; and if the face of the tomb did become a face for him it was because her two names became a pair of eyes that didn't know him. He gave them a last long look, but no palest light broke.

## CHAPTER VI

He stayed away, after this, for a year; he visited the depths of Asia, spending himself on scenes of romantic interest, of superlative sanctity; but what was present to him everywhere was that for a man who had known what *he* had known the world was vulgar and vain. The state of mind in which he had lived for so many years shone out to him, in reflexion, as a light that coloured and refined, a light beside which the glow of the East was garish cheap and thin. The terrible truth was that he had lost—with everything else—a distinction as well; the things he saw couldn't help being common when he had become common to look at them. He was simply now one of them himself—he was in the dust, without a peg for the sense of difference; and there were hours when, before the temples of gods and the sepulchres of kings, his spirit turned for nobleness of association to the barely discriminated slab in the London suburb. That had become for him, and more intensely with time and distance, his one witness of a past glory. It was all that was left to him for proof or pride, yet the past glories of Pharaohs were nothing to him as he thought of it. Small wonder then that he came back to it on the morrow of his return. He was drawn there this time as irresistibly as the other, yet with a confidence, almost, that was doubtless the effect of the many months that had elapsed. He had lived, in spite of himself, into his change of feeling, and in wandering over the earth had wandered, as might be said, from the circumference to the centre of his desert. He had settled to his safety and accepted perforce his extinction; figuring to himself, with some colour, in the likeness of certain little old men he remembered to have seen, of whom, all meagre and wizened as they might look, it was related that they had in their time fought twenty duels or been loved by ten princesses. They indeed had been wondrous for others while he was but wondrous for himself; which, however, was exactly the cause of his haste to renew the wonder by getting back, as he might put it, into his own presence. That had quickened his steps and checked his delay. If his visit was prompt it was because he had been separated so long from the part of himself that alone he now valued.

It's accordingly not false to say that he reached his goal with a certain elation and stood there again with a certain assurance. The creature beneath the sod *knew* of his rare experience, so that, strangely now, the place had lost for him its mere blankness of expression. It met him in mildness—not, as before, in mockery; it wore for him the air of conscious greeting that we find, after absence, in things that have closely belonged to us and which seem to confess of themselves to the connexion. The plot of ground, the graven tablet, the tended flowers affected him so as belonging to him that he resembled for the hour a contented landlord reviewing a piece of property. Whatever had happened—well, had happened. He had not come back this time with the vanity of that question, his former worrying "what, *what?*" now practically so spent. Yet he would none the less never again so cut himself off from the spot; he would come back to it every month, for if he did nothing else by its aid he at least held up his head. It thus grew for him, in the oddest way, a positive resource; he carried out his idea of periodical returns, which took their place at last among the most inveterate of his habits. What it all amounted to, oddly enough, was that in his finally so simplified world this garden of death gave him the few square feet of earth on which he could still most live. It was as if, being nothing anywhere else for any one, nothing even for himself, he were just everything here, and if not for a crowd of witnesses or indeed for any witness but John Marcher, then by clear right of the register that he could scan like an open page. The open page was the tomb of his friend, and *there* were the facts of the past, there the truth of his life, there the backward reaches in which he could lose himself. He did this from time to time with such effect that he seemed to wander through the old years with his hand in the arm of a companion who was, in the most extraordinary manner, his other, his younger self; and to wander, which was more extraordinary yet, round and round a third presence—not wandering she, but stationary, still, whose eyes, turning with his revolution, never ceased to follow him, and whose seat was his point, so to speak, of orientation. Thus in short he settled to live—feeding all on the sense that he once *had* lived, and dependent on it not alone for a support but for an identity.

It sufficed him in its way for months and the year elapsed; it would doubtless even have carried him further but for an accident, superficially slight, which moved him, quite in another direction, with a force beyond any of his impressions of Egypt or of India. It was a thing of the merest chance—the turn, as he afterwards felt, of a hair, though he was indeed to live to believe that if light hadn't come to him in this particular fashion it would still have come in another. He was to live to believe this, I say, though he was not to live, I may not less definitely mention, to do much else. We allow him at any rate the benefit of the conviction, struggling up for him at the end, that, whatever might have happened or not happened, he would have come round of himself to the light. The incident of an autumn day had put the match to the train laid from of old by his misery. With the light before him he knew that even of late his ache had only been smothered. It was strangely drugged, but it throbbed; at the touch it began to bleed. And the touch, in the event, was the face of a fellow mortal. This face, one grey afternoon when the leaves were thick in the alleys, looked into Marcher's own, at the cemetery, with an expression like the cut of a blade. He felt it, that is, so deep down that he winced at the steady thrust. The person who so mutely assaulted him was a figure he had noticed, on reaching his own goal, absorbed by a grave a short distance away, a grave apparently fresh, so that the emotion of the visitor would probably match it for frankness. This fact alone forbade further attention, though during the time he stayed he remained vaguely conscious of his neighbour, a middle-aged man appparently, in mourning, whose bowed back, among the clustered monuments and mortuary yews, was constantly presented. Marcher's theory that these were elements in contact with which he himself revived, had suffered, on this occasion, it may be granted, a marked, an excessive check. The autumn day was dire for him as none had recently been, and he rested with a heaviness he had not yet known on the low stone table that bore May Bartram's name. He rested without power to move, as if some spring in him, some spell vouchsafed, had suddenly been broken for ever. If he could have done that moment as he wanted he would simply have stretched himself on the slab that was ready to take him, treating it as a place prepared to receive his last sleep. What in all the wide world had he now to keep awake for? He stared before him with the question, and it was then that, as one of the cemetery walks passed near him, he caught the shock of the face.

His neighbour at the other grave had withdrawn, as he himself, with force enough in him, would have done by now, and was advancing along the path on his way to one of the gates. This brought him close, and his pace was slow, so that—and all the more as there was a kind of hunger in his look—the two men were for a minute directly confronted. Marcher knew him at once for one of the deeply stricken—a perception so sharp that nothing else in the picture comparatively lived, neither his dress, his age, nor his presumable character and class; nothing lived but the deep ravage of the features he showed. He *showed* them—that was the point; he was moved, as he passed, by some impulse that was either a signal for sympathy or, more possibly, a challenge to an opposed sorrow. He might already have been aware of our friend, might at some previous hour have noticed in him the smooth habit of the scene, with which the state of his own senses so scantly consorted, and might thereby have been stirred as by an overt discord. What Marcher was at all events conscious of was in the first place that the image of scarred passion presented to him was conscious too—of something that profaned the air; and in the second that, roused, startled, shocked, he was yet the next moment looking after it, as it went, with envy. The most extraordinary thing that had happened to him—though he had given that name to other matters as well—took place, after his immediate vague stare, as a consequence of this impression. The stranger passed, but the raw glare of his grief remained, making our friend wonder in pity what wrong, what wound it expressed, what injury not to be healed. What had the man *had*, to make him by the loss of it so bleed and yet live?

Something—and this reached him with a pang—that *he*, John Marcher, hadn't; the proof of which was precisely John Marcher's arid end. No passion had ever touched him, for this was what passion meant; he had survived and maundered and pined, but where had been *his* deep ravage? The extraordinary thing we speak of was the sudden rush of the result of this question. The sight that had just met his eyes named to him, as in letters of quick flame, something

he had utterly, insanely missed, and what he had missed made these
things a train of fire, made them mark themselves in an anguish of
inward throbs. He had seen *outside* of his life, not learned it within,
the way a woman was mourned when she had been loved for herself:
such was the force of his conviction of the meaning of the stranger's
face, which still flared for him as a smoky torch. It hadn't come to
him, the knowledge, on the wings of experience; it had brushed him,
jostled him, upset him, with the disrespect of chance, the insolence
of accident. Now that the illumination had begun, however, it blazed
to the zenith, and what he presently stood there gazing at was the
sounded void of his life. He gazed, he drew breath, in pain; he turned
in his dismay, and, turning, he had before him in sharper incision
than ever the open page of his story. The name on the table smote
him as the passage of his neighbour had done, and what it said to
him, full in the face, was that *she* was what he had missed. This was
the awful thought, the answer to all the past, the vision at the dread
clearness of which he grew as cold as the stone beneath him. Everything fell together, confessed, explained, overwhelmed; leaving him
most of all stupefied at the blindness he had cherished. The fate
he had been marked for he had met with a vengeance—he had
emptied the cup to the lees; he had been the man of his time, *the*
man, to whom nothing on earth was to have happened. That was the
rare stroke—that was his visitation. So he saw it, as we say, in pale
horror, while the pieces fitted and fitted. So *she* had seen it while he
didn't, and so she served at this hour to drive the truth home. It
was the truth, vivid and monstrous, that all the while he had waited
the wait was itself his portion. This the companion of his vigil had
at a given moment made out, and she had then offered him the
chance to baffle his doom. One's doom, however, was never baffled,
and on the day she told him his own had come down she had seen
him but stupidly stare at the escape she offered him.

The escape would have been to love her; then, *then* he would
have lived. *She* had lived—who could say now with what passion?—
since she had loved him for himself; whereas he had never thought
of her (ah how it hugely glared at him!) but in the chill of his egotism
and the light of her use. Her spoken words came back to him—the
chain stretched and stretched. The Beast had lurked indeed, and the
Beast, at its hour, had sprung; it had sprung in that twilight of the
cold April when, pale, ill, wasted, but all beautiful, and perhaps
even then recoverable, she had risen from her chair to stand before
him and let him imaginably guess. It had sprung as he didn't guess;

it had sprung as she hopelessly turned from him, and the mark, by
the time he left her, had fallen where it *was* to fall. He had justified
his fear and achieved his fate; he had failed, with the last exactitude,
of all he was to fail of; and a moan now rose to his lips as he remembered she had prayed he mightn't know. This horror of waking—*this*
was knowledge, knowledge under the breath of which the very tears
in his eyes seemed to freeze. Through them, none the less, he tried
to fix it and hold it; he kept it there before him so that he might
feel the pain. That at least, belated and bitter, had something of the
taste of life. But the bitterness suddenly sickened him, and it was
as if, horribly, he saw, in the truth, in the cruelty of his image, what
had been appointed and done. He saw the Jungle of his life and
saw the lurking Beast; then, while he looked, perceived it, as by a
stir of the air, rise, huge and hideous, for the leap that was to settle
him. His eyes darkened—it was close; and, instinctively turning, in
his hallucination, to avoid it, he flung himself, face down, on the
tomb.

# NOW THAT YOU'VE READ JAMES'
# THE BEAST IN THE JUNGLE:

In *The Beast in the Jungle* Henry James put his skill as a story-teller to
a supreme test: to write a story about a man whose sole distinction is to
be the one person to whom nothing has happened. Most literary heroes
are people to whom everything and anything happens; they are mainly
interesting because of what happens to them. But James's hero, John
Marcher, keeps free from all human entanglements, experiences no
passions, accomplishes nothing of note, does not even work for a living.
And yet about such a person James was able to write a fascinating,
exciting fantasy, a story charged with mystery and filled with suspense.
By 1901, when he wrote this short novel, he had been writing fiction for
nearly forty years and been nurturing his genius with a devotion that, in
some ways, cut him off from the usual human attachments. His biography

is the record of a developing consciousness, of an active inner life rather than of a career of participation in the affairs of the world.

He was born (1843) in New York City, the son of a philosopher, Henry James Sr., and the younger brother of the future psychologist and philosopher, William James. In a home frequented by famous writers and thinkers, presided over by a voluble, individualistic father and entertained by an articulate and brilliant elder brother, Henry, the second of five children, was a quiet but keenly observant child. And it is the image of the child grown into a man, standing apart, participating only through understanding and feeling, watching, reacting, analyzing that is evoked by a reading of James's fiction.

The future writer was provided with the opportunity for many varied experiences during his youth. Henry James Sr. believed in the educational value of European travel and took his family on extended tours of England and the Continent, employing governesses for his children and later enrolling his elder boys in French and Swiss schools. An injury to his back kept young Henry out of the Civil War and he entered Harvard Law School, following his elder brother to Cambridge. William, in the medical school, enjoyed his studies, but Henry was bored by law courses. He had begun to write, secretly, and after a year he left Harvard to devote himself to writing. In 1864 his first short story was published anonymously, and he began to publish critical reviews. He crossed the Atlantic again in 1869 and traveled slowly throughout Europe, preparing himself for a writing career by deliberately storing impressions for use in his future fiction and by studying the art of contemporary writers, particularly the French. Not until 1874, when he was in his thirties, did he feel ready to begin writing his first novel, *Roderick Hudson*. Though he loved Italy and France, James felt at home in London, and there he settled, living the life of a dignified, literary bachelor, accepting numerous invitations to dinner, meeting the famous writers of Victorian England, and describing in stories the English mothers who tried to capture eligible bachelors for their daughters (James, determined to devote himself exclusively to his art, stayed free of their clutches).

The novelist found in Europe what the young mid-nineteenth-century America could not offer: a culture centuries old, traditions, a formal society in which a code of manners rigidly controlled the conduct of its members. One part of his being responded to this highly civilized world, but another part remained loyal to the world which had produced the people of charm, naïveté, sincerity, and moral integrity whom he had loved and admired as a youth. Straddling the old world and the new, James recognized the drama inherent in the meeting of the two cultures. In his first short novel, *Daisy Miller* (1879), he brought a sincere, charming young American girl into contact with European society. Daisy, the heroine, loses the social battle but wins the moral victory. She was the first of a large number of Jamesian heroes and heroines to tangle with the rigid, corrupt old-world society and retain their moral integrity. *Daisy Miller* made James internationally famous, and though none of his other fiction attained the same kind of popular success, his reputation among critics and writers continued to grow as his list of publications lengthened. In 1896 he bought a house in a small English town, Rye, and settled there. He continued to write novels and stories, returned to America several times, and when, in 1914, the war broke out, plunged into war relief work, putting aside two novels which he had started. He could not erase from his memory the sufferings of the soldiers he visited in the hospitals, nor the stories of atrocities in Belgium. He was unable to understand why the United States did not enter the war immediately, and, partly as a protest and partly as a token of admiration and gratitude, he became a British citizen. He died in February, 1916, a few weeks after he had been honored by the British government with one of its highest awards, the Order of Merit.

When, in 1895, James first conceived the idea for *The Beast in the Jungle*, he noted in his notebook that the story would require skillful handling. For six years he let the idea germinate and then after he had completed a novel, *The Ambassadors*, in which a middle-aged American in Europe suddenly realizes that he has not lived fully and advises a young friend to "Live all you can," James was ready to handle the idea of a wasted life and to create John Marcher, a man too absorbed in himself to live.

With the obverse of this theme of the opportunity to live being wasted, the novelist had worked many times before and was to work again. It is, in fact, one of the dominant motifs of his novels, particularly of the great international novels—*The Portrait of a Lady* (1881), *The Wings of the Dove* (1902), *The Ambassadors* (1903), *The Golden Bowl* (1904). In these tales the hero or heroine at the outset is a sensitive, perceptive, dynamic person whose potentialities in the traditionless, barren American society have remained undeveloped. The adventures of these Americans in Europe are records of their developing social, esthetic, and intellectual awareness and their moral triumph over the evils inherent in the European society.

John Marcher's temperament is the antithesis of such personalities. They eagerly embrace the experiences of life; he shies away from all commitments. They are the kind of people to whom things will happen; John Marcher is not. James needed all the technical skill he had been developing for so many years to bring this negative personality to life and to make out of so wasted an existence an exciting story.

With no external action to depict, James had to delve deeply into the mind of John Marcher, and for such a revelation of inner life the novelist was well prepared. Early in his career he had decided that his province in fiction should be man's consciousness, that his tales should record what happened in man's inner world. This decision, which he set down in an article about a French writer, Pierre Loti, was an important one for the development of the novel. James opened new fictional paths for future novelists Virginia Woolf and James Joyce, for example, whose works would deal almost exclusively with man's inner existence.

To lay bare the secret, complicated inner sphere of human thought and feeling, James required new story-telling techniques, and these he had developed by 1901, when he wrote *The Beast in the Jungle*. He had borrowed, for example, Nathaniel Hawthorne's allegorical use of the symbol to portray an emotional or moral state and adapted it so skillfully that he could now use the symbol of the beast in the jungle to mirror John Marcher's entire life. (Joseph Conrad, who called James "The Master," used this technique effectively in *Heart of Darkness*.) James made the poetic image a part of the novelist's art. He also adapted many stage techniques, the product of his five years as a playwright, to the novel form. In *The Awkward Age* (1899) he developed his story with a minimum of description and comment, relying as a dramatist does (and as Miguel de Unamuno did some years later in *Abel Sanchez*) almost entirely on dialogue. *The Beast in the Jungle*, however, is more representative of James's final story-telling methods, with its skillful exposition and analysis leading up to or following pivotal dramatic scenes. Each of the six chapters in this short novel is centered about a single scene. The expository sections of the chapter prepare the reader for the big scene, consisting almost wholly of dialogue charged with meaning and action that moves the story forward.

With this kind of technique James transformed the sprawling, nineteenth-century English language novel into a carefully constructed work of art. The effectiveness of any novel, and particularly of the short novel, is due, to a great extent, to its structural unity. *The Beast in the Jungle* is an excellent example of the careful craftsmanship which characterizes James's fiction. The tone, the mood of impending disaster is sustained throughout the story, developing gradually in intensity until Marcher's nightmarish horror of a lurking beast ready to spring and destroy becomes a reality for the reader. Nothing that is not essential to presenting Marcher's plight, that does not lead directly to the revelation scene in the graveyard is included. Everything that we need to know, the time that elapses, the activities of John and May throughout the years, their relationship with the rest of the world, is sketched in so lightly that we perceive these details only as necessary background to the major scenes.

But of most importance to the success of *The Beast in the Jungle* is the style that James had developed to record his subtle thoughts and observations. It is not an easy style for readers used to journalistic fiction, but though the sentences are structurally complicated, the vocabulary is not difficult and the images and phrasing are always precise and perfect. James's style requires of the reader nothing more than what every good writer deserves: full and complete concentration. The style makes real the intangible inner life of the human being by capturing in its flow, its intricacy, its nuances, the complexity and subtlety of man's inner existence. By means of his style James draws the reader so deep into John Marcher's mind and into his private jungle that when the beast springs, it springs not only upon the hero but also upon the reader.

## FOR FURTHER INFORMATION:

Oscar Cargill. *The Novels of Henry James.* Macmillan: New York, 1961.

Frederick C. Crews. *The Tragedy of Manners: Moral Drama in The Later Novels of Henry James.* Yale University Press: New Haven, 1957.

F. W. Dupee. *Henry James.* William Sloan Associates: New York, 1951.

Leon Edel. *Henry James: The Untried Years 1843-1870; The Conquest of London 1870-1881; The Middle Years 1882-1895; The Treacherous Years 1895-1901.* Lippincott: Philadelphia, 1953-1969.

Henry James. *The Notebooks of Henry James.* Edited by F. O. Matthiessen and Kenneth B. Murdock. Oxford University Press: New York, 1947.

F. O. Matthiessen. *Henry James: The Major Phase.* Oxford University Press: New York, 1944.

Samuel G. Putt. *Henry James: A Reader's Guide.* Cornell University Press: Ithaca, 1966.

# THE METAMORPHOSIS

## BY FRANZ KAFKA

First published, 1915

# THE METAMORPHOSIS

I

**A**S Gregor Samsa awoke one morning from a troubled dream, he found himself changed in his bed to some monstrous kind of vermin.

He lay on his back, which was as hard as armor plate, and, raising his head a little, he could see the arch of his great, brown belly, divided by bowed corrugations. The bedcover was slipping helplessly off the summit of the curve, and Gregor's legs, pitiably thin compared with their former size, fluttered helplessly before his eyes.

"What has happened?" he thought. It was no dream. His room, a real man's room—though rather small—lay quiet within its four familiar walls. Over the table, where a collection of cloth samples was scattered—Samsa was a commercial traveler—hung the picture that he had recently cut from an illustrated paper and had put in a pretty gilded frame. This picture showed a lady sitting very upright, wearing a small fur hat and a fur boa; she offered to the gaze a heavy muff into which her arm was thrust up to the elbow.

Gregor looked toward the window; rain could be heard falling on the panes; the foggy weather made him sad. "How would it be if I go to sleep again for awhile and forget all this stupidity?" he thought; but it was absolutely impossible, for he was used to sleeping on the right side and in his present plight he could not get into that position. However hard he tried to throw himself violently on his side, he always turned over on his back with a little swinging movement. He tried a hundred times, closing his eyes so that he should not see the trembling of his legs, and he did not give up until he felt in his side a slight but deep pain, never before experienced.

"God!" he thought, "What a job I've chosen. Traveling day in, day out. A much more worrying occupation than working in the office! And apart from business itself, this plague of traveling: the anxieties of changing trains, the irregular, inferior meals, the ever changing faces, never to be seen again, people with whom one has no chance to be friendly. To hell with it all!" He felt a little itch above his stomach and wriggled nearer to the bedpost, dragging himself slowly on his back so that he might more easily raise his head; and he saw, just where he was itching, a few little white points, whose purpose he could not guess at; he tried to scratch the place with one of his feet but he had to draw it back quickly, for the contact made him shudder coldly.

He turned to his former position. He said to himself: "Nothing is more degrading than always to have to rise so early. A man must have his sleep. Other travelers can live like harem women. When I return to the hotel in the morning to enter my orders, I find these gentlemen still at breakfast. I'd like to see what my boss would say if I tried it; I should be sacked immediately. Who knows if that wouldn't be a good thing, after all! If I didn't hold back because of my parents, I would have given notice long ago; I would have gone to the boss and I wouldn't have minced matters. He would have fallen from his desk. That's a funny thing; to sit on a desk so as to speak to one's employees from such a height, especially when one is hard of hearing and people must come close! Still, all hope is not lost; once I have got together the money my parents owe him—that will be in about five or six years—I shall certainly do it. Then I'll take the big step! Meanwhile, I must get up, for my train goes at five."

He looked at the alarm clock which was ticking on the chest. "My God!" he thought; it was half-past six; quarter to seven was not far off. Hadn't the alarm gone? From the bed it could be seen that the little hand was set at four, right enough; the alarm had sounded. But had he been able to sleep calmly through that furniture-shattering din? Calmly, no; his sleep had not been calm; but he had slept only the sounder for that. What should he do now?

The next train went at seven; to catch it he must hurry madly, and his collection of samples was not packed; besides, he himself did not feel at all rested nor inclined to move. And even if he did catch the train, his employer's anger was inevitable, since the firm's errand boy would have been waiting at the five o'clock train and would have notified the firm of his lapse. He was just a toady to his boss, a stupid and servile boy. Supposing Gregor pretended to be ill? But that would be very tiresome, and suspicious, too, for during the four years he had been with the firm he had never had the slightest illness. The manager would come with the Health Insurance doctor; he would reproach his parents for their son's idleness and would cut short any objections by giving the doctor's arguments that no people are sick, only idle. And would he be so far wrong, in such a case? Gregor felt in very good fettle, apart from his unnecessary need for more sleep after such a long night; he even had an unusually keen appetite.

Just as he was quickly turning these thoughts over in his mind without being able to decide to leave the bed—while the alarm clock struck a quarter to seven—he heard a cautious knock on his door, close by his bed's head.

"Gregor," someone called—it was his mother—"it is a quarter to seven. Didn't you want to catch the train?"

What a soft voice! Gregor trembled as he heard his own voice reply. It was unmistakably his former voice, but with it could be heard, as if from below, a painful whining, which only allowed the words their real shape for a moment, immediately to confuse their sound so that one wondered if one had really heard aright. Gregor would have liked to answer fully and to give an explanation but, in these circumstances, he contented himself by saying, "Yes, yes, thank you, mother. I am just getting up." No doubt the door prevented her from judging the change in Gregor's voice, for the explanation reassured his mother, who went away, shuffling in her slippers. But because of this little dialogue the other members of the family had become aware that, contrary to custom, Gregor was still in the house, and his father started to knock on one of the side doors, softly, but with his fists.

"Gregor, Gregor," he cried, "what is the matter?" And, after a moment, in a warning tone, "Gregor! Gregor!"

At the other side door, the young man's sister softly called, "Gregor, aren't you well? Do you need anything?"

"I am getting ready," said Gregor, answering both sides and forcing himself to pronounce carefully and to separate each word with a long pause, to keep a natural voice.

His father went back to breakfast, but the sister still whispered, "Gregor, open the door, I beg you." But Gregor had no intention of answering this request; on the contrary, he complimented himself on having learned the habit of always locking his door, as if in a hotel.

He would get up quietly, without being bothered by anyone; he would dress, and, above all, he would have breakfast; then would come the time to reflect, for he felt it was not in bed that a reasonable solution could be found. He recalled how often an unusual position adopted in bed had resulted in slight pains which proved imaginary as soon as he arose, and Gregor was curious to see his present hallucination gradually dissolve. As for the change in his voice, his private opinion was that it was the prelude to some serious quinsy, the occupational malady of travelers.

He had no difficulty in turning back the coverlet; he needed only to blow himself up a little, and it fell of its own accord. But beyond that he was impeded by his tremendous girth. To get up, he needed arms and hands; but he had only numerous little legs, in perpetual vibration, over which he had no control. Before he could bend one leg, he first had to stretch it out; and when at last he had performed the desired movement, all the other legs worked uncontrollably, in intensely painful agitation. "I must not stay uselessly in bed," said Gregor to himself.

To get his body out of bed, he first tried moving the hind part. But unfortunately this hind part, which he had not yet seen, and of which he could form no very precise idea, went so slowly it proved to be very difficult to move; he summoned all his strength to throw himself forward but, ill-calculating his course, he hurled himself violently against one of the bedposts, and the searing pain he felt showed that the lower part of his body was without doubt the most sensitive.

He then tried to start with the fore part of his body and cautiously turned his head toward the side of the bed. In this he succeeded quite easily, and the rest of his body, despite its weight and size, followed the direction of his head. But when his head left the bed and was hanging in mid-air, he was afraid to continue any further; if he were to fall in this position, it would be a miracle if he did not crack his head; and this was no moment to lose his senses— better to stay in bed.

But when, panting after his efforts, he again found himself stretched out just as before, when he saw his little legs struggling more wildly than ever, despairing of finding any means of bringing peace and order into this chaotic procedure, he once again realized that he absolutely could not stay in bed and that it was perfectly reasonable to sacrifice everything to the slightest chance of getting out. At the same time he did not forget that cool and wise reflection would be far better than desperate resolutions. Ordinarily, at such moments he turned his eyes to the window to gain encouragement and hope. But this day the fog prevented him from seeing the other side of the street; the window gave him neither confidence nor strength. "Seven o'clock already," he said as he listened once more to the sound of the alarm clock. "Seven o'clock already, and the fog has got no thinner!" He lay back again for a moment, breathing weakly, as though, in the complete silence, he could calmly await the return to his normal self.

Then he said, "Before a quarter past it is absolutely essential for me to be up. In any case, someone will be sent from the office to ask for me before then, for the place opens at seven." And he began to rock on his back in order to get his whole body out of bed in one movement. In this manner he would be able to protect his head by raising it sharply as he fell. His back seemed to be hard; nothing would be risked by falling on it to the floor; his only fear was that the noise of his fall, which must surely resound through the whole house, might arouse terror, or, at the very least, uneasiness. However, that would have to be risked.

When Gregor had half his body out of bed—the new method seemed more like a game than a task, for he had only to swing himself on his back—he began to think how easily he could have got up if only he had had a little assistance. Two strong people—he thought of his father and the servant girl—would have been quite enough; they would have needed only to pass their arms under his round back, raise it from the bed, quickly lean forward with their burden, and then wait carefully till he had completed the operation of settling himself on the ground, where he hoped his feet would at last find a way of working together. But even if the doors had not been closed, would it have been wise for him to call for help? At this idea, despite his misery, he could not repress a smile.

Now he had progressed so far that, by sharply accentuating his swinging movement, he felt he was nearly losing his balance; he would have to make a serious decision, for in five minutes it would be a quarter to eight—but suddenly there was a knock at the front door. "Someone from the office," he said to himself, and he felt his blood run cold, while his little legs quickened their saraband. For a moment all was quiet.

"They're not going to the door," thought Gregor, in an excess of absurd hope. But of course the maid, with a firm tread, went to the door and opened it. Gregor needed to hear only the caller's first words of greeting to know immediately who it was—the manager himself. Why was Gregor, particularly, condemned to work for a firm where the worst was suspected at the slightest inadvertence of the employees? Were the employees, without exception, all scoundrels? Was there among their number not one devoted, faithful servant, who, if it did so happen that by chance he missed a few hours work one morning, might have found himself so numbed with remorse that he just could not leave his bed? Would it not have been enough to send some apprentice to put things right—if, in any case, it was necessary to make inquiries at all—instead of the manager himself having to come, in order to let the whole innocent family know that the clearing-up of so suspicious an affair could only be entrusted to a person of his importance? These thoughts so irritated Gregor that he swung himself out of bed with all his might. This made a loud thud, but not the terrible crash that he had feared. The carpet somewhat softened the blow, and Gregor's back was more elastic than he had thought, and so his act was not accompanied by any din. Only his head had been slightly hurt. Gregor had not raised it enough, and it had been knocked in the fall. He turned over a little to rub it on the carpet, in pain and anger.

"Something fell in there just then," cried the manager, in the room on the left. Gregor tried to imagine his employer's face if such a mishap had occurred to him; for such a thing was possible, he had to admit. But, as if in brutal reply, the manager began pacing up and down in the next room, making his patent-leather boots creak.

And in the other room on the right, Gregor's sister whispered to warn her brother, "Gregor, the manager is here."

"I know," said Gregor to himself, but he dared not raise his voice enough for his sister to hear.

"Gregor," said his father in the room on the left, "the manager has come to find out why you didn't catch the early train. We don't know what to say. He wants to speak to you personally. So please open the door. I'm sure he will be kind enough to excuse the untidiness of your room."

"Good morning, good morning, Mr. Samsa," interrupted the manager, cordial and brisk.

"He is not well," said his mother to the manager, while his father went on shouting through the door. "Believe me, he is not well, sir. How else could Gregor have missed the train? The boy thinks of nothing but his work! It makes me upset to see how he never goes out after supper; do you know he's just spent a whole week here and been at home every evening! He sits down with us at the table and stays there, quietly reading the paper or studying his timetables. His greatest indulgence is to do a little fretwork. Just lately he made a small picture frame. It was finished in two or three evenings, and you'd be surprised how pretty it is; it is hanging up in his room. As soon as Gregor opens his door, you will be able to see it. I am so glad you came, sir, because without you we would never have got Gregor to open his door, he is so obstinate; and surely he must be ill, even though he denied it this morning."

"I am just coming," said Gregor slowly and carefully, but he continued to lie still, so as not to miss a word of the conversation.

"I can offer no other suggestion," declared the manager. "Let us only hope it is nothing serious. However, we businessmen must often—fortunately or not, as you will—get on with our jobs and ignore our little indispositions."

"Well, can the manager come in now?" asked his father impatiently, rapping on the door again.

"No," said Gregor. In the room on the left there was a painful silence; in that on the right the sister began to sob.

Why did she not go to the others? Possibly she had only just got out of bed and was not yet dressed. And why did she weep? Because he did not get up to let the manager in, because he risked losing his position, and because the boss would once more worry his parents about their old debts? These were misplaced troubles! Gregor was still there and had not the slightest intention of letting his family down. At this very moment he was stretched out on the carpet, and nobody seeing him in this state could seriously have demanded that he should let the manager enter his room. But it was not on account of this slight impoliteness—for which in normal times he could easily have made his excuses later—that Gregor would be dismissed. And he thought it would be more reasonable, just now, to leave him alone rather than to upset him with tears and speeches. But it was just this uncertainty which was making the others uneasy and which excused their behavior.

"Herr Samsa," now cried the manager, raising his voice, "what is the matter? You barricade yourself in your room, you don't answer yes or no, you needlessly upset your parents, and you neglect your professional duties in an unheard-of manner. I am speaking in the name of your employer and of your parents, and I beg you seriously to give us a satisfactory explanation immediately. I am astonished, astonished! I took you for a quiet, reasonable young man, and here you suddenly give yourself airs, behaving in an absolutely fantastic manner! The head of the firm, speaking to me this morning in your absence, suggested an explanation which I rejected; he mentioned the samples which were entrusted to you a while ago. I gave him my word of honor that this had nothing to do with the affair, but now that I have been witness to your obstinacy, I can assure you, Herr Samsa, that it deprives me of any wish to defend you. Your job is by no means safe! I had intended to tell you this in private but, since you oblige me to waste my time here for nothing, I see no reason for keeping quiet before your parents. I'd have you know that lately your work has been far from satisfactory; we realize, of course, that the time of the year is not propitious for big business, but you must understand, Herr Samsa, that a period with no business at all should not and can not be tolerated!"

Gregor was beside himself; in his anxiety he forgot everything else. "But, sir," he cried, "I will open the door immediately. I will open it. I felt a little ill; a slight giddiness prevented me from getting up. I am still in bed. But I feel better already. I am just getting up. Only a moment's patience. I am not quite so well as I thought. But I am all right, really. How can it be that illness should take one so quickly? Only yesterday I felt quite well, my parents can tell you; and then last evening I had a slight symptom. They must have noticed it. Why didn't I let them know at the office! But then, one always thinks one will be able to get rid of an illness without staying at home. Please, sir, spare my parents. The complaints you made just now are really without foundation. No one has even suggested them before. Perhaps you have not seen the last orders I sent in. I will leave on the eight o'clock train; these few moments of rest have done me a great deal of good. Please don't stay, sir, I shall be at the office immediately; and please inform the director of what has happened and put in a good word for me."

And while Gregor hastily cried these words, scarcely realizing what he said, he had, with an ease due to his previous exertions, approached the chest of drawers, against which he now tried to raise himself. He wanted to open the door; he wanted to be seen and to speak with the manager. He was curious to know what impression he would make on these people who were so imperiously demanding his presence. If he frightened them, that would be reassuring, for he would stop being cross-questioned and be left in peace. If they took everything quietly then he, too, need not be alarmed. And if he hurried he might still catch the eight o'clock train. The chest was polished, and Gregor slipped on it several times but, by a supreme effort, he managed to get upright. He paid no attention to the pains in his stomach, though they were hurting him. He let himself drop forward onto the top of a near-by chair and clung there with his little legs. Then, finding himself master of his body, he stayed very quiet in order to listen to what the manager had to say.

"Did you understand a word of what he said?" the manager asked the parents. "Is he trying to make fools of us?"

"Good heavens," cried the mother, already in tears. "Perhaps he is seriously ill, and here we are torturing him all this while! Grete! Grete!" she called.

"Mother!" cried the daughter from the other side. They were separated by Gregor's room.

"Fetch a doctor immediately. Gregor is ill. A doctor, quickly! Did you hear him speak?"

"It was an animal's voice," said the manager; after the cries of the women, his voice seemed curiously gentle.

"Anna, Anna!" shouted the father through the hall into the kitchen, clapping his hands. "Get a locksmith, quick!" And already the two young girls—how could his sister have dressed so soon?—ran along the corridor with rustling skirts and opened the front door. No one heard the door close; no doubt it had been left open, as is the custom in houses to which a great misfortune has come.

However, Gregor had become calmer. Doubtless they had not understood his words, though they had seemed clear enough to him, clearer, indeed, than the first time; perhaps his ears were becoming more accustomed to the sounds. But at least they were obliged to realize that his case was not normal, and they were ready, now, to help him. The assurance and resourcefulness with which the first steps had been taken comforted him considerably. He felt himself integrated into human society once again, and, without differentiating between them, he hoped for great and surprising things from the locksmith and the doctor. To clear his throat for the decisive conversation which he would have to hold soon, he coughed a little, but as quietly as possible, for he feared that even his cough might not sound human. Meanwhile, in the next room, it had become quiet. Perhaps his parents were sitting at table in a secret conference with the manager; perhaps everyone was leaning against the door, listening.

Gregor made his way slowly toward it with the chair; then he abandoned the chair and flung himself at the door, holding himself erect against the woodwork—for the bottoms of his feet secreted a sticky substance—and he rested a moment from his efforts. After this, he tried to turn the key in the lock with his mouth. Unfortunately, it seemed he had no proper teeth. How could he take hold of the key? In compensation, instead of teeth he possessed a pair of very strong mandibles and succeeded in seizing the key in the lock, regardless of the pain this caused him; a brownish liquid flowed out of his mouth, spread over the lock, and dropped to the floor.

"Listen!" said the manager in the next room. "He is just turning the key."

This was valuable encouragement for Gregor; he would have liked his father, his mother, everybody, to start calling to him, "Courage, Gregor, go on, push hard!" And, with the idea that everyone was following his efforts with passionate attention, he clutched the key with all the power of his jaws until he was nearly unconscious. Following the progress of the turning key, he twisted himself around the lock, hanging on by his mouth, and, clinging to the key, pressed it down again, whenever it slipped, with all the weight of his body. The clear click of the lock as it snapped back awoke Gregor from his momentary coma.

"I have dispensed with the locksmith," he thought, and sighed and leaned his head against the handle to open one panel of the double doors completely.

This method, the only possible one, prevented the others from seeing him for some time, even with the door open. Still erect, he had to grope his way round the door with great caution in order not to spoil his entry by falling flat on his back; so he was concentrating toward this end, with all his attention absorbed by the maneuver, when he heard the manager utter a sonorous, "Oh!" such as the roaring of the wind produces, and saw him—he was just by the door—press his hand over his open mouth and slowly stagger back as if some invisible and intensely powerful force were driving him from the spot. His mother—who, despite the presence of the manager, was standing by with her hair in curlers, still disordered by sleep—began to look at the father, clasping her hands; then she made two steps toward Gregor and fell backward into the family circle in the midst of a confusion of skirts which spread around her, while her face, falling on her breast, was concealed from sight. The father clenched his fists with a menacing air, as if to beat Gregor back into his room; then he looked around the dining room in perplexity, covered his eyes with his hand, and wept with great sobs which shook his powerful chest.

Gregor did not enter the room; he stood against the closed half of the double doors, allowing only a part of his body to be seen, while, above, he turned his head to one side to see what would happen. Meanwhile, it had grown much lighter; on either side of the street a part of the long, dark building opposite could clearly be seen—it was a hospital, with regular windows startlingly pitting its façade; it was still raining, but in great separate drops which fell to the ground, one by one. The breakfast crockery was spread all over the table, for breakfast was the most important meal of the day for Gregor's father; he would prolong it for hours while he read various newspapers. On the wall hung a photograph of Gregor in lieutenant's uniform, taken while he was in military service; he was smiling; his hand lay on the hilt of his sword. By his expression, he seemed happy to be alive; by his gesture, he appeared to command respect for his rank. The living-room door was ajar, and, as the front door was also open, the balcony and the first steps of the stairway could just be seen.

"Now," said Gregor, and he realized that he was the only one to have kept calm, "now I will get dressed, collect my samples, and go. Will you, will you let me go? Surely you can now see, sir, that I am not obstinate, that I do mean to work; commercial traveling is tiresome, I admit, but without it I cannot live. Where are you going, sir? To the office? Yes? Will you give them a faithful account of what has happened? After all, anyone might find for a moment that they were incapable of resuming their work, but that's just a good opportunity to review the work they have been doing, and to bear in mind that, once the obstacle is removed, they will be able to return with twice the heart. I owe so much to the director, as you know very well. I have my parents and my sister to consider. I am in an awkward position, but I shall return to work. Only, please do not make things more difficult for me; they are hard enough as it is. Take my part at the office. I know only too well they don't like travelers. They think we earn our money too easily, that we lead too grand a life. I realize that the present situation doesn't encourage the removal of this prejudice; but you, sir, the manager, can judge the circumstances better than the rest of the staff, better than the director himself—though this is between ourselves—for in his executive capacity he is often easily misled by an employee's prejudice. You know quite well that the traveler, who is hardly ever in the office the whole year round, is often the victim of scandal, of a chance, undeserved complaint against which he is powerless to defend himself, for he does not even know that he is being accused; he only learns of it as he returns, exhausted, at the end of his trip, when the sad consequences of an affair, whose circumstances he can no longer recall, painfully confront him. Please, sir, don't leave me without a word to show that you think all this at least a little reasonable."

But, at Gregor's first words, the manager had turned away and only glanced back, with snarling lips, over his trembling shoulder. During Gregor's speech, he had not stood still for a moment; instead, he had retreated furtively, step by step, toward the door—always keeping Gregor in sight—as if some secret law forbade him to leave the room. He had already reached the hall and, as he took the very last step out of the living room, one would have thought the floor was burning his shoes, so sharply did he spring. Then he stretched his hand toward the balustrade, as if some unearthly deliverance awaited him at the foot of the stairs.

Gregor realized that, if he were to keep his job, on no account must the manager be allowed to leave in this condition. Unfortunately, his parents did not realize the position very clearly; they had for so long held the idea that Gregor was settled in the firm for life and were so taken up with their present troubles that they had little thought for such a contingency. But Gregor had more foresight. The manager must be stopped, calmed, convinced, and finally won over. The future of Gregor and of his family depended on it! If only his sister were there! She had understood, she had actually begun to weep while Gregor still lay quietly on his back. And the manager, who liked women, would have listened to her; he would have let himself be guided by her; she would have closed the door and would have proved to him, in the hall, how unreasonable his terror was. But she was not there; Gregor himself must manage this affair. And without even considering whether he would ever be able to return to work, nor whether his speech had been understood, he let go of the doorpost to glide through the opening and overtake the manager (who was clutching the balustrade with both hands in a ridiculous manner), vainly sought for a foothold, and, uttering a cry, he fell, with his frail little legs crumpled beneath him.

Suddenly, for the first time that whole morning, he experienced a feeling of physical well-being; his feet were on firm ground; he noticed with joy that his legs obeyed him wonderfully and were even eager to carry him wherever he might wish. But while, under the nervous influence of his need for haste, he hesitated on the spot, not far from his mother, he saw her suddenly jump, fainting though she seemed to be, and throw her arms about with outspread fingers, crying, "Help, for God's sake, help!" She turned her head, the better to see Gregor; then, in flagrant contradiction, she began to retreat madly, having forgotten that behind her stood the table, still laden with breakfast things. She staggered against it and sat down suddenly, like one distraught, regardless of the fact that, at her elbow, the overturned coffeepot was making a pool of coffee on the carpet.

"Mother, mother," whispered Gregor, looking up at her. The manager had quite gone out of his mind. Seeing the coffee spilling, Gregor could not prevent himself from snapping his jaws several times in the air, as if he were eating. Thereupon his mother again began to shriek and quickly jumped up from the table and fell into the arms of the father, who had rushed up behind her. But Gregor had no time to bother about them. The manager was already on the stairs; with his chin on the balustrade, he was looking back for the last time.

Gregor summoned all his courage to try to bring him back; the manager must have suspected something of the sort, for he leaped several steps at a single bound and disappeared with a cry of "Huh!" which resounded in the hollow of the stair well. This flight had the unfortunate effect of causing Gregor's father—who till now had remained master of himself—to lose his head completely; instead of running after the manager, or at least not interfering with Gregor in his pursuit, he seized in his right hand the manager's walking stick, which had been left behind on a chair with his overcoat and hat, took up in his left a newspaper from the table, and began stamping his feet and brandishing the newspaper and the cane to drive Gregor back into his room. Gregor's prayers were unavailing, were not even understood; he had turned to his father a supplicating head, but, meek though he showed himself, his father merely stamped all the louder. In the dining room, despite the cold, the mother had opened the window wide and was leaning out as far as possible, pressing her face in her hands. A great rush of air swept the space between the room and the stairway; the curtains billowed, the papers rustled, and a few sheets flew over the carpet. But the father pursued Gregor pitilessly, whistling and whooping like a savage, and Gregor, who was not used to walking backward, progressed but slowly.

Had he been able to turn around, he could have reached his room quickly, but he feared to make his father impatient by the slowness of his turning and feared also that at any moment he might receive a mortal blow on his head or on his back from this menacing stick. Soon Gregor had no choice; for he realized with terror that when he was going backward he was not master of his direction and, still fearfully watching the attitude of his father out of the corner of his eye, he began his turning movement as quickly as possible, which was really only very slowly. Perhaps his father realized his good intention for, instead of hindering this move, he guided him from a little distance away, helping Gregor with the tip of the stick. If only he had left off that insupportable whistling! Gregor was completely losing his head. He had nearly completed his turn when, bewildered by the din, he mistook his direction and began to go back to his former position. When at last, to his great joy, he found himself facing the half-opened double doors, he discovered that his body was too big to pass through without hurt. Naturally, it never occurred to his father, in his present state, to open the other half of the double doors in order to allow Gregor to pass. He was dominated by the one fixed idea that Gregor should be made to return to his room as quickly as possible. He would never have entertained the long-winded performance which Gregor would have needed to rear up and pass inside. Gregor heard him storming behind him, no doubt to urge him through as though there were no obstacle in his path; the hubbub no longer sounded like the voice of one single father. Now was no time to play, and Gregor—come what may—hurled himself into the doorway. There he lay, jammed in a slanting position, his body raised up on one side and his flank crushed by the door jamb, whose white paint was now covered with horrible brown stains. He was caught fast and could not free himself unaided; on one side his little legs fluttered in the air, on the other they were painfully pressed under his body; then his father gave him a tremendous blow from behind with the stick. Despite the pain, this was almost a relief; he was lifted bodily into the middle of the room and fell, bleeding thickly. The door was slammed by a thrust of the stick, and then, at last, all was still.

## II

It was dusk when Gregor awoke from his heavy, deathlike sleep. Even had he not been disturbed, he would doubtless soon have awakened, for he felt he had had his fill of rest and sleep; however, he seemed to have been awakened by the cautious, furtive noise of a key turning in the lock of the hall door. The reflection of the electric tramway lay dimly here and there about the ceiling and on the upper parts of the furniture, but below, where Gregor was, it was dark. Slowly he dragged himself toward the door to ascertain what had happened and fumbled around clumsily with his feelers, whose use he was at last learning to appreciate. His left side seemed to him to be one long, irritating scar, and he limped about on his double set of legs. One of his legs had been seriously injured during the morning's events—it was a miracle that only one should be hurt—and it dragged lifelessly behind.

When he reached the door, he realized what had attracted him: the smell of food. For there was a bowl of sweetened milk in which floated little pieces of bread. He could have laughed with delight, his appetite had grown so since morning; he thrust his head up to the eyes in the milk. But he drew it back quickly; his painful left side gave him some difficulty, for he could only eat by convulsing his whole body and snorting; also, he could not bear the smell of milk, which once had been his favorite drink and which his sister had no doubt prepared for this special reason. He turned from the bowl in disgust and dragged himself to the middle of the room.

The gas was lit in the dining room; he could see it through the cracks of the door. Now was the time when, ordinarily, his father would read aloud to his family from the evening paper, but this time Gregor heard nothing. Perhaps this traditional reading, which his sister always retailed to him in her conversation and in her letters, had not lapsed entirely from the customs of the household. But everywhere was still, and yet surely someone was in the room.

"What a quiet life my family has led," thought Gregor, staring before him in the darkness, and he felt very proud, for it was to him that his parents and his sister owed so placid a life in so nice a flat. What would happen now, if this peace, this satisfaction, this well-being should end in terror and disaster? In order to dissipate such gloomy thoughts, Gregor began to take a little exercise and crawled back and forth over the floor.

Once during the evening he saw the door on the left open slightly, and once it was the door on the right; someone had wished to enter but had found the task too risky. Gregor resolved to stop by the dining-room door and to entice the hesitant visitor as best he might or at least to see who it was; but the door never opened again, and

Gregor waited in vain. That morning, when the door had been locked, everyone had tried to invade his room; but now that they had succeeded in opening it no one came to see him; they had even locked his doors on the outside.

Not till late was the light extinguished, and Gregor could guess that his parents and his sister had been waiting till then, for he heard them all go off on tiptoe. Now no one would come to him till the morning, and so he would have the necessary time to reflect on the ordering of his new life; but his great room, in which he was obliged to remain flat on his stomach on the floor, frightened him in a way that he could not understand—for he had lived in it for the past five years—and, with a half-involuntary action of which he was a little ashamed, he hastily slid under the couch; he soon found that here his back was a little crushed and he could not raise his head; he only regretted that his body was too large to go entirely under the couch.

He spent the whole night there, sometimes in a half-sleep from which the pangs of hunger would wake him with a start, sometimes ruminating on his misfortune and his vague hopes, always concluding that his duty was to remain docile and to try to make things bearable for his family, whatever unpleasantness the situation might impose upon them.

Early in the morning he had a chance to test the strength of his new resolutions; it was still almost dark; his sister, already half dressed, opened the hall door and looked in curiously. She did not see Gregor at once but when she perceived him under the sofa—"Heavens, he must be somewhere; he can't have flown away!"—she was overcome by an unmanageable terror and rushed off, slamming the door. Then, repenting her gesture, she opened it again and entered on tiptoe, as if it were the room of a stranger or one seriously ill. Gregor stretched his head out from the side of the sofa and watched her. Would she notice that he had left the milk, and not from lack of appetite? Would she bring him something which suited his taste better? If she did not do so of her own accord, he would rather have died of hunger than draw her attention to these things, despite his overwhelming desire to rush out of his hiding place, to throw himself at his sister's feet, and to beg for something to eat. But suddenly the sister saw the full bowl in astonishment. A little milk had been spilled around it; using a piece of paper, she took up the bowl without touching it and carried it off to the kitchen. Gregor waited anxiously to see what she would bring him in its place and racked his brains to guess. But he had never realized to what lengths his sister's kindness would go. In order to discover her brother's likes, she brought a whole choice of eatables spread on an old newspaper. There were half-rotted stumps of vegetables, the bones of yesterday's dinner covered with a thick white sauce, a few currents and raisins, some almonds, some cheese that Gregor, a few days before, had declared uneatable, a stale loaf, a piece of salted bread and butter, and another without salt. Besides this she brought back the bowl which had become so important to Gregor. This time it was filled with water, and, guessing that her brother would not like to eat before her, she very kindly retired, closing and locking the door to show him that he might eat in peace. Now that his meal was ready, Gregor felt all his legs trembling. His wounds seemed cured, for he felt not the slightest hindrance, and he was astonished to remember that when he had been human and had cut his finger slightly only a few months ago, it had pained him for several days after.

"Have I become less sensitive?" he wondered; but already he had begun sucking at the cheese, which had suddenly and imperiously attracted him above all the other food. Gluttonously he swallowed in turn the cheese, the vegetables, and the sauce, his eyes moist with satisfaction; as to the fresh things, he wanted none of them; their smell repelled him, and, in order to eat, he separated them from the others.

When he had finished and was idly making up his mind to return to his place, his sister slowly began to turn the key in the lock to give him the signal for retreat. He was very frightened, though he was half asleep, and hurried to reach the sofa. It needed great determination to remain beneath it during the time, however short, that his sister was in the room; his heavy meal had so swollen his body that he could scarcely breathe in his retreat. Between two fits of suffocation he saw, with his eyes filled with tears, that his sister, intending no harm, was sweeping up the remains of his meal with the very things that he had not touched, as if he needed them no more; she put the refuse into a bucket, which she covered with a wooden lid and hastily carried away. Hardly had she turned the handle before Gregor struggled out from his hiding place to expand his body to its proper size.

So he was fed each day; in the morning, before his parents and the maid were awake, and in the afternoon, when lunch was over and while his parents were taking their nap and the maid had been provided with some task or other by his sister. Certainly they did not wish Gregor to die of hunger but perhaps they preferred to know nothing about his meals except by hearsay—they could not have borne to see him—perhaps, also, in order to diminish their disgust, his sister was taking pains to spare them the slightest trouble. He must realize that they, too, had their share of misfortune.

Gregor never learned what excuses they had made to rid themselves of the doctor and the locksmith, for, as no one attempted to understand him, no one, not even his sister, imagined that he could understand them. He had to be content, when she came into his room, to listen to her invoking the saints between her sighs. It was only much later, when Grete had become somewhat accustomed to the new situation—to which she never really became reconciled—that Gregor would occasionally overhear an expression which showed some kindness or allowed him to guess at such a meaning. When he had eaten all the food off the newspaper she would say, "He liked what I brought today"; at other times, when he had no appetite—and lately this had become more frequent—she would say, almost sadly, "Now he has left it all."

But even if he could learn no news directly, Gregor overheard a good deal of what was said in the dining room; as soon as he heard anyone speak, he would hurry to the most propitious door and press his whole body close against it. At first, especially, there was little conversation which did not bear more or less directly on his predicament. For two whole days, the mealtimes were given over to deliberating on the new attitude which must be maintained toward Gregor; even between meals they spoke mostly on the same theme, for now at least two members of the household always remained at home, each one fearing to remain alone and, particularly, to leave Gregor unwatched.

It was not very clear how much the maid knew of what had happened, but, on the very first day, she had fallen on her knees and begged his mother to let her go; and a quarter of an hour later she had left the house in tearful gratitude, as if her release were the greatest evidence of the kindness she had met with in the house; and of her own accord she took a long and boring oath never to reveal the secret to anyone. Now his sister and his mother had to look after the cooking; this entailed little trouble, for the appetite of the Samsa family had gone. Occasionally Gregor would hear one member of the family vainly exhorting another to eat. The reply was always the same: "Thank you, I have had enough," or some such phrase. Perhaps, also, they did not drink. Often his sister would ask her father if he would like some beer; she would cheerfully offer to fetch it, or, faced with her father's silence, she would say, to remove any scruples on his part, that the landlady could go for it, but her father would always reply with a loud, "No!" and nothing more would be said.

In the course of the very first day, the father had clearly explained their precise financial situation to his wife and daughter. From time to time he would get up from the table and hunt for some paper or account book in his Wertheim safe, which he had saved from the crash when his business had failed five years before. He could be heard opening the complicated locks of the safe and closing it again after he had taken out what he sought. Ever since he became a prisoner, nothing had given Gregor such pleasure as these financial explanations. He had always imagined that his father had been unable to save a penny from the ruins of his business; in any case, his father had never said anything to undeceive him, and Gregor had never questioned him on the matter; he had done all he could to help his family to forget as quickly as possible the disaster which had plunged them into such despair.

He had set to work with splendid ardor; in less than no time, from being a junior clerk he had been promoted to the position of traveler, with all the benefits of such a post; and his successes were suddenly transformed into hard cash which could be spread on the table before the surprised and delighted eyes of his family. Those were happy times—they had never since recovered such a sense of delight, though Gregor now earned enough to feed the whole Samsa family. Everyone had grown accustomed to it, his family as much as himself; they took the money gratefully, he gave it willingly, but the act was accompanied by no remarkable effusiveness. Only his sister had remained particularly affectionate toward Gregor, and it was his secret plan to have her enter the conservatory next year regardless of the considerable cost of such an enterprise, which he would try to meet in some way; for, unlike him, Grete was very fond of music and wished to take up the study of the violin. This matter of the conservatory recurred often in the brief conversations between Gregor and his sister, whenever Gregor had a few days to spend with his family; they hardly ever spoke of it except as a dream impossible to realize; his parents did not much like the innocent allusions to the subject, but Gregor thought very seriously of it and had promised himself that he would solemnly announce his plan next Christmas Eve.

It was ideas of this kind, ideas completely unsuited to his present situation, which now passed constantly through Gregor's mind while he held himself pressed erect against the door, listening. He would get so tired that he could no longer hear anything; then he would let himself go and allow his head to fall against the door; but he would draw it back immediately, for the slightest noise was noticed in the dining room and would be followed by an interval of silence.

"What can he be doing now?" his father would say after a moment's pause, turning, no doubt, toward the door; the interrupted conversation would only gradually be resumed.

His father was often obliged to repeat his explanations in order to recall forgotten details or to make them understood by his wife, who did not always grasp them the first time. Gregor thus learned, by what the father said, that, despite all their misfortunes, his parents had been able to save a certain amount from their former property—little enough, it is true, but it had been augmented, to some extent, by interest. Also, they had not spent all the money that Gregor, keeping only a few shillings for himself, had handed over to his family each week, enabling them to gather together a little capital. Behind his door, Gregor nodded his head in approval; he was so happy at this unexpected foresight and thrift. Doubtless, with these savings his father could have more rapidly paid off the debt he had contracted to Gregor's employer, which would have brought nearer the date of Gregor's release; but under the circumstances it was much better that his father had acted as he had.

Unfortunately this money was not quite sufficient to enable the family to live on its interest; it would last a year, perhaps two, but no more. It was a sum which must not be touched, which must be kept for a case of urgent necessity. As for money on which to live, that would have to be earned. Now, despite his good health, the father was nevertheless an old man who had ceased to work five years before and who could not be expected to entertain any foolish hopes of getting employment; during these five years of retirement—his first holiday in a life entirely devoted to work and unsuccess—he had become very fat and moved with great difficulty. And the old mother would not be able to earn much, suffering as she did from asthma, for even now it was an effort for her to get about the house; she passed a good deal of her time each day lying on the sofa, panting and wheezing under the open window. And was the breadwinner to be the sister, who was still but a child, seventeen years old, so suited to the life she had led till then, nicely dressed, getting plenty of sleep, helping in the house, taking part in a few harmless little entertainments, and playing her violin? Whenever the conversation fell on this topic, Gregor left the door and lay on the leather sofa, whose coolness was so soothing to his body, burning as it was with anxiety and shame.

Often he lay all night, sleepless, and hearing no sound for hours on end save the creak of the leather as he turned. Or, uncomplainingly, he would push his armchair toward the window, crawl up on it, and, propped on the seat, he would lean against the window, not so much to enjoy the view as to recall the sense of release he once used to feel whenever he looked across the pavements; for now he was daily becoming more shortsighted, he could not even make out the hospital opposite, which he had cursed when he was human because he could see it all too clearly; and had he not known so well that he was living in Charlottenstrasse, a quiet but entirely urban street, he might have thought his window gave out on a desert, where the gray of the sky and the gray of the earth merged indistinguishably together. His attentive sister had only to see the armchair by the window twice to understand; from then on, each time she tidied the room she would push the armchair to the window, and would always leave its lower half open.

If only Gregor had been able to speak to his sister, to thank her for all she was doing for him, he could have borne her services easier; but as it was, they pained and embarrassed him. Grete naturally tried to hide any appearance of blame or trouble regarding the situation, and as time went on she played her part even better, but she could not prevent her brother from realizing his predicament more and more clearly. Each time she entered his room, it was terrible for Gregor. Hardly had she entered, when, despite the pains she always took to spare the others the sight of its interior, she would not even take time to shut the door but would run to the window, open it hastily with a single push, as if to escape imminent suffocation, and would stand there for a minute, however cold it might be, breathing deeply. Twice a day she terrified Gregor with this rush and clatter; he shrank trembling under the couch the whole time; he knew his sister would have spared him this had she been able to stand being in the room with him with the window shut.

One day—it must have been a month after Gregor's change, and his sister had no grounds for astonishment at his appearance—she came a little earlier than usual and found him looking out of the window, motionless and in such a position as to inspire terror. If she had not liked to enter, that would not have surprised Gregor, for his position prevented her from opening the window. But not only would she not enter; she sprang back, slammed the door, and locked it; a stranger might have thought that Gregor was lying in wait for his sister, to attack her. Naturally he hid himself under the couch immediately, but he had to wait till midday for Grete's return, and, when she did come, she appeared unusually troubled. He realized that his appearance was still disgusting to the poor girl, that it would always be so, and that she must fiercely resist her own impulse to flee the moment she caught sight of the tiniest part of Gregor's body protruding from under the sofa. To spare her this sight, he took a sheet on his back, dragged it to the sofa—a task which occupied some hours—and spread it in such a way that his sister could see nothing under the sofa, even if she stooped. Had she found this precaution unnecessary, she would have taken the sheet away, for she guessed that Gregor did not so completely shut himself away for pleasure; but she left the sheet where it lay, and Gregor, prudently parting the curtain with his head to see what impression this new arrangement had made upon his sister, thought he detected a look of gratitude in her face.

During the first fortnight his parents had not been able to bring themselves to enter his room, and he often heard them praising the zeal of his sister, whom they had regarded, so far, as a useless young girl and of whom they had often complained. But now, both his father and mother would wait quite frequently outside Gregor's door while his sister was tidying the room, and scarcely had she come out again before they would make her tell them in detail exactly how she had found the room, what Gregor had eaten, and, in detail, what he was doing at that moment; they would ask her, too, if there were the slightest signs of improvement. His mother seemed impatient to see Gregor, but the father and sister restrained her with argument to which she listened very attentively and with which she wholly agreed. Later, however, they had to use force, and when his mother began to cry, "Let me go to Gregor! My poor boy! Don't you understand that I must see him!" Gregor thought that perhaps it would be as well if his mother did come in, not every day, of course, but perhaps once a week; she would understand things better than his sister, who was but a child, for all her courage, and had perhaps taken on such a difficult task out of childish lightheartedness.

Gregor's wish to see his mother was soon realized. Gregor avoided showing himself at the window during the day, out of consideration to his parents; but his restricted walks around the floor did not fully compensate him for this self-denial, nor could he bear to lie still for long, even during the night; he took no more pleasure in eating, and it soon became his habit to distract himself by walking—around the room, back and forth along the walls, and across the ceiling, on which he would hang; it was quite a different matter from walking across the floor. His breathing became freer, a light, swinging motion went through his body, and he felt so elated that now and then, to his own surprise, he would let himself go and fall to the floor. But by now, knowing better how to manage his body, he succeeded in rendering these falls harmless. His sister soon noticed his new pastime, for he left sticky marks here and there in his track, and Grete took it into her head to help him in his walks by removing all the furniture likely to be a hindrance, particularly the chest and the desk. Unfortunately, she was not strong enough to manage this on her own and dared not ask the help of her father; as for the maid, she certainly would have refused, for if this sixteen-year-old child had worked bravely since the former cook had left, it was on condition that she could stay continually barricaded in the kitchen, whose doors she would only open on special demand. So there was nothing else for it; Grete would have to enlist the mother's help one day when the father was away.

The mother gladly consented, but her exclamations of joy were hushed before Gregor's door. The sister first made sure that everything was in order in the room; then she allowed the mother to enter. In his great haste, Gregor had pulled the sheet down further than usual, and the many folds in which it fell gave the scene the air of a still life. This time he refrained from peeping under the sheet to spy on his mother but he was delighted to have her near.

"You may come in; he is not in sight," said his sister; and, taking her mother by the hand, she led her into the room. Then Gregor heard the two frail women struggling to remove the heavy old chest; the sister undertook the hardest part of the task, despite the warnings of her mother, who feared she might do herself some harm. It took a long time. They had been struggling with the chest for four hours when the mother declared that it might be best to leave it where it was, that it was too heavy for them, that they would not finish moving it before the father returned, and that, with the chest in the middle of the room, Gregor would be considerably impeded in his movements, and, finally, who knew whether he might not be displeased by the removal of his furniture?

The mother thought he would be; the sight of the bare walls

struck cold at her heart; might Gregor not feel the same, having long grown so accustomed to the furniture, and would he not feel forsaken in his empty room? "Isn't it a fact," said the mother in a low voice—she had spoken in whispers ever since she entered the room, so that Gregor whose hiding place she had not yet discovered, might not overhear, not so much what she was saying—for she was persuaded that he could not understand—but the very sound of her voice. "Isn't it a fact that when we remove the furniture, we seem to imply that we are giving up all hope of seeing him cured and are wickedly leaving him to his fate? I think it would be better to keep the room just as it was before, so that Gregor will find nothing changed when he comes back to us and will be able the more easily to forget what has happened meanwhile."

Hearing his mother's words, Gregor realized how these two monotonous months, in the course of which nobody had addressed a word to him, must have affected his mind; he could not otherwise explain his desire for an empty room. Did he really wish to allow this warm, comfortable room with its genial furniture to be transformed into a cavern in which, in rapid and complete forgetfulness of his human past, he might exercise his right to crawl all over the walls? It seemed he was already so near to forgetting; and it had required nothing less than his mother's voice, which he had not heard for so long, to rouse him. Nothing should be removed, everything must stay as it is, he could not bear to forego the good influence of his furniture, and, if it prevented him from indulging his crazy impulses, then so much the better.

Unfortunately, his sister was not of this opinion; she had become accustomed to assume authority over her parents where Gregor was concerned—this was not without cause—and now the mother's remarks were enough to make her decide to remove not only the desk and the chest—which till now had been their only aim—but all the other furniture as well, except the indispensable sofa. This was not the result of mere childish bravado, nor the outcome of that new feeling of self-confidence which she had just acquired so unexpectedly and painfully. No, she really believed that Gregor had need of plenty of room for exercise and that, as far as she could see, he never used the furniture. Perhaps, also, the romantic character of girls of her age was partly responsible for her decision, a sentiment which strove to satisfy itself on every possible occasion and which now drove her to dramatize her brother's situation to such an extent that she could devote herself to Gregor even more passionately than hitherto;

for in a room over whose bare walls Gregor reigned alone, no one but Grete dare enter and stay.

She did not allow herself to be turned from her resolve by her mother, made irresolute by the oppressive atmosphere of the room, and who did not hesitate now to remove the chest as best she could. Gregor could bear to see the chest removed, at a pinch, but the desk must stay. And hardly had the women left the room, panting as they pushed the chest, than Gregor put out his head to examine the possibilities of making a prudent and tactful appearance. But unfortunately it was his mother who returned first, while Grete, in the side room, her arms around the chest, was rocking it from side to side without being able to settle it in position. The mother was not used to the sight of Gregor; it might give her a serious shock. Terrified, he hastened to retreat to the other end of the sofa, but he could not prevent the sheet from fluttering slightly, which immediately attracted his mother's attention. She stopped short, stood stockstill for a moment, then hurried back to Grete.

Gregor assured himself that nothing extraordinary was happening —they were merely removing a few pieces of furniture—but the coming and going of the women, their little cries, the scraping of the furniture over the floor, seemed to combine in such an excruciating din that, however much he withdrew his head, contracted his legs, and pressed himself to the ground, he had to admit that he could not bear this torture much longer. They were emptying his room, taking away from him all that he loved; they had already removed the chest in which he kept his saw and his fretwork outfit; now they were shifting his desk, which had stood so solid and fast to the floor all the time it was in use, that desk on which he had written his lessons while he was at the commercial school, at the secondary school, even at the preparatory school. However, he could no longer keep pace with their intentions, for so absent minded had he become he had almost forgotten their existence, now that fatigue had quieted them and the clatter of their weary feet could no longer be heard.

So he came out—the women were only leaning against the desk in the next room, recovering their breath—and he found himself so bewildered that he changed his direction four times; he really could not decide what he should first salvage—when suddenly he caught sight of the picture of the woman in furs which assumed tremendous importance on the bare wall; he hastily climbed up and pressed himself against the glass, which stuck to his burning belly and refreshed him delightfully. This picture, at least, which Gregor entirely covered, should not be snatched away from him by anyone. He turned his head toward the dining-room door to observe the women as they returned.

They had had but a short rest and were already coming back; Grete's arm was round her mother's waist, supporting her.

"Well, what shall we take now?" said Grete, and she looked around. Her eyes met those of Gregor on the wall. If she succeeded in keeping her presence of mind, it was only for her mother's sake, toward whom she leaned her head to prevent her from seeing anything and said, a little too quickly and with a trembling voice, "Come, wouldn't it be better to go back to the living room for a minute?" The girl's intention was clear to Gregor: she wished to put her mother in a safe place and then to drive him from the wall. Well, let her try! He lay over his picture, and he would not let it go. He would rather leap into his sister's face.

But Grete had merely disquieted her mother; now she turned, saw the gigantic brown stain spread over the wallpaper and, before she realized that it was Gregor she was seeing, she cried, "O God! O God!" in a screaming, raucous voice, fell on the sofa with outspread arms in a gesture of complete renunciation, and gave no further sign of life. "You, Gregor!" cried the sister, raising her fist and piercing Gregor with a look. It was the first word she had addressed to him directly ever since his metamorphosis. Then she ran to get some smelling salts from the dining room to rouse her mother from her swoon. Gregor decided to help—there was still time to save the picture—alas, he found he had stuck fast to the glass and had to make a violent effort to detach himself; then he hurried into the dining room as if able to give his sister some good advice, but he was obliged to content himself with remaining passively behind her while she rummaged among the bottles, and he frightened her so terribly when she turned around that a bottle fell and broke on the floor, a splinter wounded Gregor in the face, and a corrosive medicine flowed round his feet; then Grete hastily grabbed up all the bottles she could carry and rushed in to her mother, slamming the door behind her with her foot. Now Gregor was shut out from his mother, who perhaps was nearly dead through his fault; he dared not open the door lest he drive away his sister, who must stay by his mother; so there was nothing to do but wait, and, gnawed by remorse and distress, he began to wander over the walls, the furniture, and the ceilings so rapidly that everything began to spin around him, till in despair he fell heavily on to the middle of the huge table.

A moment passed; Gregor lay stretched there; around all was still; perhaps that was a good sign. But suddenly he heard a knock. The maid was naturally barricaded in her kitchen; Grete herself must go to the door. His father had returned.

"What has happened?" were his first words; no doubt Grete's expression had explained everything.

The girl replied in a stifled voice—probably she leaned her face against her father's breast—"Mother fainted, but she is better now. Gregor has got out."

"I was waiting for that," said the father, "I told you all along, but you women will never listen."

Gregor realized by these words that his father had misunderstood Grete's brief explanation and imagined that his son had broken loose in some reprehensible way. There was no time to explain. Gregor had to find some way of pacifying his father, so he quickly crawled to the door of his room and pressed himself against it for his father to see, as he came in, how he had every intention of returning to his own room immediately and that it was not at all necessary to drive him back with violence; one had only to open the door and he would quickly withdraw.

But his father was in no mood to notice these fine points. As he entered he cried, "Ah!" in a tone at once of joy and anger; Gregor turned his head away from the door and lifted it toward his father. He was astonished. He had never imagined his father as he stood before him now; it is true that for some time now he had neglected to keep himself acquainted with the events of the house, preferring to devote himself to his new mode of existence, and he had therefore been unaware of a certain change of character in his family. And yet—and yet, was that really his father? Was it really the same man who once had lain wearily in bed when Gregor had been leaving on his journeys, who met him, on his return, in his nightshirt, seated in an armchair out of which he could not even lift himself, throwing his arms high to show how pleased he was? Was this that same old man who, on the rare walks which the family would take together, two or three Sundays a year and on special holidays, would hobble between Gregor and his mother, while they walked slower and slower for him, as he, covered with an old coat, carefully set his stick before him and prudently worked his way forward; and yet, despite their slowness, he would be obliged to stop, whenever he wished to say anything, and call his escort back to him? How up-standing he had become since then!

Now he was wearing a blue uniform with gold buttons, without a single crease, just as you see the employees of banking houses wearing; above the big, stiff collar his double chin spread its power-ful folds; under his bristly eyebrows the watchful expression of his black eyes glittered young and purposefully; his white hair, ordi-narily untidy, had been carefully brushed till it shone. He threw on to the sofa his cap, ornamented with the gilded monogram of some bank, making it describe the arc of a circle across the room, and, with his hands in his trouser pockets, the long flaps of his coat turned back, he walked toward Gregor with a menacing air. He himself did not know what he was going to do; however, he raised his feet very high, and Gregor, astonished at the enormous size of the soles of his boots, took care to remain still, for he knew that, from the first day of his metamorphosis, his father had held the view that the greatest severity was the only attitude to take up toward Gregor. Then he began to beat a retreat before his father's approach, halting when the other stopped and beginning again at his father's slightest move. In this way they walked several times round the room without any decisive result; it did not even take on the appearance of a pursuit, so slow was their pace.

Gregor was provisionally keeping to the floor; he feared that if his father saw him climbing about the walls or rushing across the ceiling, he might take this maneuver for some refinement of bad behavior. However, he had to admit that he could not go on much longer in this way; in the little time his father needed to take a step, Gregor had to make a whole series of gymnastic movements and, as he had never had good lungs, he now began to pant and wheeze; he tried to recover his breath quickly in order to gather all his strength for a supreme effort, scarcely daring to open his eyes, so stupefied that he could think of no other way to safety than by pursuing his present course; he had already forgotten that the walls were at his disposal, and the carefully carved furniture, all covered with festoons of plush and lace as it was. Suddenly something flew sharply by him, fell to the ground, and rolled away. It was an apple, carelessly thrown; a second one flew by. Paralyzed with terror, Gregor stayed still. It was useless to continue his course, now that his father had decided to bombard him. He had emptied the bowls of fruit on the sideboard, filled his pockets, and now threw apple after apple, without waiting to take aim.

These little red apples rolled about the floor as if electrified, knocking against each other. One lightly-thrown apple struck Gregor's back and fell off without doing any harm, but the next one literally pierced his flesh. He tried to drag himself a little further away, as if a change of position could relieve the shattering agony he suddenly felt, but he seemed to be nailed fast to the spot and stretched his body helplessly, not knowing what to do. With his last, hopeless glance, he saw his door opened suddenly, and, in front of his sister, who was shouting at the top of her voice, his mother came running in, in her petticoat, for his sister had partly undressed her that she might breathe easier in her swoon. And his mother, who ran to the father, losing her skirts one by one, stumbled forward, thrust herself against her husband, embraced him, pressed him to her, and, with her hands clasped at the back of his neck—already Gregor could see no more—begged him to spare Gregor's life.

## III

The apple which no one dared draw from Gregor's back remained embedded in his flesh as a palpable memory, and the grave wound which he now had borne for a month seemed to have reminded his father that Gregor, despite his sad and terrible change, remained none the less a member of the family and must not be treated as an enemy; on the contrary, duty demanded that disgust should be overcome and Gregor be given all possible help.

His wound had made him lose, irremediably, no doubt, much of his agility; now, merely to cross his room required a long, long time, as if he were an aged invalid; his walks across the walls could no longer be considered. But this aggravation of his state was largely compensated for, in his opinion, by the fact that now, every evening, the dining-room door was left open; for two hours he would wait for this. Lying in the darkness of his room, invisible to the diners, he could observe the whole family gathered round the table in the lamp-light, and he could, by common consent, listen to all they had to say—it was much better than before.

It must be admitted that they no longer held those lively conversations of which, in former times, he had always thought with such sadness as he crept into his damp bed in some little hotel room. Most of the time, now, they discussed nothing in particular after dinner. The father would soon settle himself to doze in his arm-chair; the mother and daughter would bid each other be silent; the mother, leaning forward in the light, would sew at some fine needle-work for a lingerie shop, and the sister, who had obtained a job as a shop assistant, would study shorthand or French in the hope of improving her position. Now and then the father would wake up and, as if he did not know that he had been asleep, would say to his wife, "How late you are sewing tonight!" and would fall off to sleep again, while the mother and sister would exchange a tired smile.

By some capricious obstinacy, the father always refused to take off his uniform, even at home; his dressing gown hung unused in the wardrobe, and he slept in his armchair in full livery, as if to keep himself always ready to carry out some order; even in his own home he seemed to await his superior's voice. Moreover, the uniform had not been new when it was issued to him, and now each day it be-came more shabby, despite the care which the two women devoted to it; and Gregor often spent the evening staring dully at this coat, so spotted and stained, whose polished buttons always shone so brightly, and in which the old man slept, uncomfortably but peacefully.

As soon as the clock struck ten, the mother, in a low voice, tried to rouse her husband and to encourage him to go to bed, as it was impossible to get proper sleep in such a position, and he must sleep normally before returning to work at six the next morning. But, with the obstinacy which had characterized him ever since he had obtained his position at the bank, he would stay at the table al-though he regularly dropped off to sleep, and thus it would become more and more difficult to induce him to change his armchair for the bed. The mother and sister might insist with their little warn-ings; he stayed there just the same, slowly nodding his head, his eyes shut tight, and would not get up. The mother might shake him by the wrist, might whisper endearments in his ear; the daughter might abandon her work to assist her mother, but all in vain. The old man would merely sink deeper in his chair. At last the two women would have to take him under the arms to make him open his eyes; then he would look at each in turn and say, "What a life! Is this the hard-earned rest of my old days?" and, leaning on the two women, he would rise painfully, as if he were a tremendous weight, and would allow himself to be led to the door by his wife and daughter; then he would wave them off and continue alone, while the mother and sister, the one quickly throwing down her pen, the other her needle, would run after him to help.

Who in the overworked and overtired family had time to attend to Gregor, except for his most pressing needs? The household budget was ever more and more reduced; at last the maid was dismissed. In her place, a gigantic charwoman with bony features and white hair, which stood up all around her head, came, morning and evening, to do the harder work. The rest was done by the mother, over and above her interminable mending and darning. It even happened that they were obliged to sell various family trinkets which formerly had been worn proudly by the mother and sister at ceremonies and festivals, as Gregor discovered one evening when he heard them discussing the price they hoped to get. But their most persistent complaints were about this flat, which was so much larger than they needed and which had now become too expensive for the family purse; they could not leave, they said, for they could not imagine how Gregor could be moved. Alas, Gregor understood that it was not really he who was the chief obstacle to this removal, for he might easily have been transported in a large wooden box pierced with a few air holes. No, what particularly prevented the family from changing their residence was their own despair, the idea that they had been stricken by such a misfortune as had never before occurred in the family or within the circle of their acquaintances.

Of all the deprivations which the world imposes on poor people, not one had been spared them; the father took his day-time meals with the lesser employees of the bank, the mother was killing herself mending the linen of strangers, the sister ran here and there behind her counter at the customers' bidding; but the family had energy for nothing further. It seemed to poor Gregor that his wound reopened whenever his mother and sister, returning from putting the father to bed, would leave their work in disorder and bring their chairs nearer to each other, till they were sitting almost cheek to cheek; then the mother would say, pointing to Gregor's room, "Close the door, Grete," and he would once more be left in darkness, while, outside, the two women mingled their tears or, worse, sat at the table staring with dry eyes.

These days and nights brought Gregor no sleep. From time to time he thought of taking the family affairs in hand, as he once had done, the very next time the door was opened; at the end of a long perspective of time he dimly saw in his mind his employer and the manager, the clerks and apprentices, the porter with his narrow ideas, two or three acquaintances from other offices, a provincial barmaid—a fleeting but dear memory—and a cashier in a hat shop, whom he had pursued earnestly but too slowly; they passed through his mind in confusion, mingled with unknown and unforgotten faces; but none of them could bring help to him or his family; nothing was to be gained from them. He was pleased to be able to dismiss them from his mind but now he no longer cared what happened to his family; on the contrary, he only felt enraged because they neglected to tidy his room and, though nothing imaginable could excite his appetite, he began making involved plans for a raid on the larder, with a view to taking such food as he had a right to, even if he was not hungry. Nowadays his sister no longer tried to guess what might please him; she made a hasty appearance twice a day, in the morning and in the afternoon, before going to her shop, and pushed a few scraps of food into the room with her foot; in the evening, without even bothering to see whether he had touched his meal or whether he had left it entirely—and this was usually the case—she would sweep up the remains with a whisk of the broom.

As for tidying up the room, which Grete now did in the evenings, it could not have been done in a more hasty manner. Great patches of dirt streaked the wall, little heaps of dust and ordure lay here and there about the floor. At first Gregor would place himself in the filthiest places whenever his sister appeared, so that this might seem a reproach to her. But he could have stayed there for weeks, and still Grete would not have altered her conduct; she saw the dirt as well as he but she had finally decided to take no further trouble. This did not prevent her from taking even more jealous care than ever to insure that no other member of the family should presume on her right to the tidying of the room.

Once the mother undertook to give Gregor's room a great cleaning which required several buckets of water, and this deluge deeply upset poor Gregor, crouched under his sofa in bitter immobility—but the mother's punishment soon came. Hardly had the sister, coming home in the evening, noticed the difference in Gregor's room, than, feeling deeply offended, she ran crying and screaming into the dining room, despite the appeal of her mother, who raised her hands in supplication; the father, who was quietly seated at table, leaped up, astonished but powerless to pacify her. Then he, too, became agitated; shouting, he began to attack the mother, on the one hand, for not leaving the care and cleaning of Gregor's room to the girl and, on the other hand, he forbade his daughter ever again to dare to clean it; the mother tried to draw the old man, quivering with anger as he was, into the bedroom; the daughter, shaken with sobs, was banging on the table with her little fists, while Gregor loudly hissed with rage to think that no one had the decency or consideration to close the door and thus spare him the sight of all this trouble and uproar.

But even if the sister, tired out by her work in the shop, could not bother to look after Gregor as carefully as hitherto, she could still have arranged that he should not be neglected without necessarily calling on the aid of her mother, for there was always the charwoman. This old woman, whose bony frame had helped her out of worse trouble during her long life, could not really be said to feel any disgust with Gregor. Though she was not inquisitive, she had opened his door one day and had stood with her hands folded over her stomach, astonished at the sight of Gregor, who began to trot here and there in his alarm, though she had no thought of chasing him. From that day, morning and evening, the old woman never lost an opportunity of opening the door a little to peer into the room.

At first she would call Gregor to make him come out, crying in a familiar tone, "Come on, you old cockroach!" or, "Hey, look at the old cockroach!" To such invitations Gregor would not respond; instead he remained motionless beneath his sofa as if the door had not been opened. If they had only ordered the charwoman to clean his room out each day instead of allowing her to go on teasing and upsetting him! Early one morning, when heavy rain—perhaps a sign of approaching spring—beat on the roofs, Gregor was so annoyed by the old woman as she began to bait him again that he suddenly turned on her, in a somewhat cumbersome and uncertain manner, it must be admitted, but with every intention of attacking her. She was not at all frightened of him; there was a chair by the door; she took it up and brandished it, opening wide her mouth with the obvious intention of not closing it until she had brought the chair down with a crash on Gregor's back. "Ah, is that all?" she asked, seeing him return to his former position, and she quietly put the chair back in its place.

Nowadays Gregor hardly ate at all. When, by some chance, he passed by his scraps, he would amuse himself by taking a piece of food in his mouth and keeping it there for hours, usually spitting it out in the end. At first he had thought that his loss of appetite was due to the misery into which the state of his room had plunged him; no doubt this was a mistake, for he had soon become reconciled to the squalor of his surroundings. His family had got into the habit of piling into his room whatever could not be accommodated else-where, and this meant a great deal, now that one of the rooms had been let to three lodgers. They were very earnest and serious men; all three had thick beards—as Gregor saw one day when he was peering through a crack in the door—and they were fanatically tidy; they insisted on order, not only in their own room, but also, now that they were living here, throughout the whole household, and especially in the kitchen.

They had brought with them all that they needed, and this ren-dered superfluous a great many things about the house which could neither be sold nor thrown away, and which were now all stacked in Gregor's room, as were the ash bucket and the rubbish bin. Every-thing that seemed for the moment useless would be dumped in Gregor's room by the charwoman, who was always in a breathless hurry to get through her work; he would just have time to see a hand brandishing some unwanted utensil, and then the door would slam again. Perhaps the old woman intended to return and find the objects she so carelessly relegated here when she needed them and had time to search; or perhaps she meant to throw them all away some day, but in actual fact they stayed in the room, on the very spot where they had first fallen, so that Gregor was obliged to pick his way among the rubbish to make a place for himself—a game for which his taste began to grow, in spite of the appalling misery and fatigue which followed these peregrinations, leaving him para-lyzed for hours. As the lodgers sometimes dined at home in the living room, the door of this room would be shut on certain eve-nings; however, Gregor no longer attached any importance to this; for some while, now, he had ceased to profit by those evenings when the family would open the door and he would remain shrinking in the darkest corner of his room, where the family could not see him.

One day the woman forgot to close the dining-room door, and it was still ajar when the lodgers came in and lit the gas. They sat down at table in the places that previously had been occupied by the father, the mother, and Gregor; each unfolded his napkin and took up his knife and fork. Soon the mother appeared in the door-way with a plate of meat; the sister followed her, carrying a dish of potatoes. When their meal had been set before them, the lodgers leaned over to examine it, and the one who was seated in the mid-dle and who appeared to have some authority over the others, cut a piece of meat as it lay on the dish to ascertain whether it was tender or whether he should send it back to the kitchen. He seemed satisfied, however, and the two women, who had been anxiously watching, gave each other a smile of relief.

The family itself lived in the kitchen. However, the father, before going into the kitchen, always came into the dining room and bowed once with his cap in his hand, then made his way around the table. The boarders rose together and murmured something in their beards. Once they were alone, they began to eat in silence. It seemed curious to Gregor that he could hear the gnashing of their teeth above all the clatter of cutlery; it was as if they wanted to prove to him that one must have real teeth in order to eat properly, and that the best mandibles in the world were but an unsatisfactory substitute. "I am hungry," thought Gregor sadly, "but not for these things. How these lodgers can eat! And in the meantime I might die, for all they care."

He could not remember hearing his sister play since the arrival of the lodgers; but this evening the sound of the violin came from the kitchen. The lodgers had just finished their meal; the middle one had brought a newspaper and had given a page to each of the others; now they all three read, leaning back in their chairs and smoking. The sound of the violin attracted their attention, and they rose and walked on tiptoe toward the hall door, where they halted and remained very close together.

Apparently they had been heard in the kitchen, for the father cried, "Does the violin upset you gentlemen? We'll stop it immediately."

"On the contrary," said the man in the middle. "Would Fräulein Samsa not like to come in and play to us here in the dining room, where it is much nicer and more comfortable?"

"Oh, thank you," said the father, as if he were the violinist.

The gentlemen walked back across the room and waited. Soon the father came in with the music stand, the mother with the sheets of music, and the sister with the violin. The sister calmly prepared to play; her parents, who had never before let their rooms, were exaggeratedly polite to the boarders and were afraid to seem presumptuous by sitting in their own chairs; the father leaned against the door, his right hand thrust between two buttons of his livery coat; but one of the gentlemen offered the mother a chair, in which she finally sat, not daring to move from her corner throughout the performance.

The girl now began to play, while her father and mother, from either side, watched the movement of her hands. Attracted by the music, Gregor had crawled forward a little and had thrust his head into the room. He was no longer astonished that nowadays he had entirely lost that consideration for others, that anxiety to cause no trouble that once had been his pride. Yet never had he more reason to remain hidden, for now, because of the dirt that lay about his room, flying up at the slightest movement, he was always covered with dust and fluff, with ends of cotton and hairs, and with morsels of stale food, which stuck to his back or to his feet and which he trailed after him wherever he went; his apathy had grown too great for him to bother any more about cleaning himself several times a day by lying on his back and rubbing himself on the carpet, as once he used to do. And this filthy state did not prevent him from crawling over the spotless floor without a moment's shame.

So far, no one had noticed him. The family was too absorbed by the music of the violin, and the lodgers, who had first stood with their hands in their pockets, very close to the music stand—which disturbed the sister a great deal as she was obliged to see their image dancing amid the notes—had at last retired toward the window, where they stood speaking together half aloud, with lowered heads, under the anxious gaze of the father, who was watching attentively. It had become only too evident that they had been deceived in their hopes of hearing some beautiful violin piece, or at least some amusing little tune; it seemed that what the girl was playing bored them and that now they only tolerated her out of politeness. By the way in which they puffed the smoke of their cigars, by the energy with which they blew it toward the ceiling through the mouth or the nose, one could guess how fidgety they were becoming. And the sister was playing so nicely. Her face leaning to one side, her glance followed the score carefully and sadly. Gregor crawled forward a little more and put his head as near as possible to the floor to meet her gaze. Could it be that he was only an animal, when music moved him so? It seemed to him to open a way toward that unknown nourishment he so longed for. He resolved to creep up to his sister and to pull at her dress, to make her understand that she must come with him, for no one here would appreciate her music as much as he. He would never let her out of his room—at least, while he lived—for once, his horrible shape would serve him some useful purpose; he would be at all doors at once, repulsing intruders with his raucous breath; but his sister would not be forced to stay there; she must live with him of her own accord; she would sit by him on the sofa, hearing what he had to say; then he would tell her in confidence that he had firmly intended to send her to the Conservatory and had planned to let everyone know last Christmas—was Christmas really past?—without listening to any objections, had his misfortune not overtaken him too soon. His sister, moved by this explanation, would surely burst into tears, and Gregor, climbing up on her shoulder, would kiss her neck; this would be all the easier, for she had worn neither collar nor ribbon ever since she had been working in the shop.

"Herr Samsa," cried the middle lodger, and he pointed at Gregor, who slowly came into the room. The violin was suddenly silenced, the middle lodger turned to his friends, grinning and shaking his head, then once more he stared at Gregor. The father seemed to consider it more urgent to reassure the lodgers than to drive his son from the room, though the lodgers did not seem to be at all upset by the spectacle; in fact, Gregor seemed to amuse them more highly than did the violin. The father hurried forward and, with outstretched arms, tried to drive them into their room, hiding Gregor from them with his body. Now they began to be really upset, but it is not known whether this was on account of the father's action or because they had been living with such a monstrous neighbor as Gregor without being made aware of it. They demanded explanations, waving their arms in the air; and, fidgeting nervously with their beards, they retreated toward their own door. Meanwhile the sister had recovered from the distress that the sudden interruption of her music had caused her; after remaining a moment completely at a loss, with the violin and the bow hanging from her helpless hands, following the score with her eyes as if she were still playing, she suddenly came back to life, laid the violin in her mother's lap—the mother sat suffocating in her chair, her lungs working violently—and rushed into the next room, toward which the lodgers were rapidly retreating before Herr Samsa's onslaught. One could see how quickly, under Grete's practised hand, pillows and covers were set in order on the beds. The lodgers had not yet reached the room when their beds were already prepared, and Grete had slipped out. The father seemed so possessed by his strange fury that he had quite forgotten the respect due to lodgers.

He drove them to the door of the room, where the middle lodger suddenly came to a stop, stamping thunderously on the floor. "I wish to inform you," said this man, raising his hand and looking around for the two women, "that in view of the disgusting circumstances which govern this family and this house"—and here he spat quickly on the carpet—"I hereby immediately give up my room. Naturally, you will not get a penny for the time I have been living here; on the contrary, I am considering whether I should not claim compensation from you, damages which should easily be awarded in any court of law; it is a matter about which I shall inquire, believe me." He was silent and stared into space, as if awaiting something. Accordingly, his two friends also spoke up: "We, too, give our notice." Thereupon the gentleman in the middle seized the door handle, and they went inside. The door closed with a crash.

The father stumbled toward his chair, put his trembling hands upon the arms, and let himself drop into it; he looked exactly as if he were settling himself for his customary evening nap, but the way his head drooped heavily from side to side showed that he was thinking of something other than sleep. All this time Gregor had stayed still on the spot where he had surprised the lodgers. He felt completely paralyzed with bewilderment at the checking of his plans— perhaps, also, with weakness due to his prolonged fasting. He feared that the whole household would fall upon him immediately; he foresaw the precise moment when this catastrophe would happen, and now he waited. Even the violin did not frighten him as it fell with a clatter from the trembling fingers of his mother, who until now had held it in her lap.

"My dear parents," said his sister, who beat with her hand on the table by way of introduction. "Things cannot go on like this. Even if you do not realize it, I can see it quite clearly. I will not mention my brother's name when I speak of this monster here; I merely want to say: we must find some means of getting rid of it. We have done all that is humanly possible to care for it, to put up with it; I believe that nobody could reproach us in the least."

"She's a thousand times right," said the father. But the mother who had not yet recovered her breath, coughed helplessly behind her hand, her eyes haggard.

The sister hurried toward her mother and held her forehead. Grete's words seemed to have made up the father's mind, for now he sat up in his armchair and fidgeted with his cap among the dishes on the table, from which the lodgers' meal had not yet been cleared; from time to time he stared at Gregor.

"We must find a way of getting rid of it," repeated the sister, now speaking only to her father, for her mother, shaken by her coughing, could hear nothing. "It will bring you both to the grave. I can see it coming. When people have to work all day, as we must, we cannot bear this eternal torture each time we come home at night. I can stand it no longer." And she wept so bitterly that her tears fell on her mother's face, who wiped them off with a mechanical movement of her hand.

"But what can we do, child?" said the father in a pitiful voice. It was surprising to see how well he understood his daughter.

The sister merely shrugged her shoulders as a sign of the perplexity which, during her tears, had replaced her former assurance.

"If he could only understand us," said the father in a half-questioning tone, but the sister, through her tears, made a violent gesture with her hand as a sign that this was not to be thought of.

"If only he could understand us," repeated the father—and he shut his eyes as he spoke, as if to show that he agreed with the sister that such a thing was quite impossible. "If only he could understand us, perhaps there would be some way of coming to an agreement. But as it is . . ."

"It must go!" cried the sister. "That's the only way out. You must get the idea out of your head that this is Gregor. We have believed that for too long, and that is the cause of all our unhappiness. How could it be Gregor? If it were really he, he would long ago have realized that he could not live with human beings and would have gone off on his own accord. I haven't a brother any longer, but we can go on living and can honor his memory. In his place we have this monster that pursues us and drives away our lodgers; perhaps it wants the whole flat to itself, to drive us out into the streets. Look, father, look!" she suddenly screamed, "it's beginning again!" And in an access of terror, which Gregor could not understand, she let go her mother so suddenly that she bounced in the seat of the armchair; it seemed as if the sister would rather sacrifice her mother than stay near Gregor; she hastily took refuge behind her father, who was very upset by her behavior and now stood up, spreading his arms to protect her.

But Gregor had no thought of frightening anyone, least of all his sister. He had merely started to turn around in order to go back to his room; but it must be realized that this looked very alarming, for his weakness obliged him to assist his difficult turning movement with his head, which he raised and lowered many times, clutching at the carpet with his mandibles. At last he ceased and stared at the family. It seemed they realized his good intentions. They were watching him in mute sadness. The mother lay in her armchair, her outstretched legs pressed tightly together, her eyes nearly closed with fatigue; the father and sister were sitting side by side, and the girl's arm was round her father's neck.

"Now, perhaps, they will let me turn," thought Gregor, and he once more set about his task. He could not repress a sigh of weariness; he was obliged to rest from time to time. However, no one hurried him; they left him entirely alone. When he had completed his turn, he immediately beat a retreat, crawling straight ahead. He was astonished at the distance which separated him from his room; he did not realize that this was due merely to his weak state and that a little before he could have covered the distance without noticing it. His family did not disturb him by a single cry, a single exclamation; but this he did not even notice, so necessary was it to concentrate all his will on getting back to his room. It was only when he had at long last reached his door that he thought of turning his head, not completely, because his neck had become very stiff, but sufficiently to reassure himself that nothing had changed behind him; only his sister was now standing up. His last look was toward his mother, who, by this time, was fast asleep.

Hardly was he in his room before the door was slammed, locked, and double bolted. So sudden was the crash that Gregor's legs gave way. It was his sister who had rushed to the door. She had stood up so as to be ready immediately and at the right moment had run forward so lightly that he had not heard her come; as she turned the key in the lock, she cried to her parents, "At last!"

"What now?" asked Gregor, looking around himself in the darkness. He soon discovered that he could not move. This did not surprise him in the least; it seemed to him much more remarkable that such frail legs had hitherto been able to bear his weight. Now he experienced a feeling of relative comfort. True, his whole body ached, but it seemed that these aches became less and less until finally they disappeared. Even the rotted apple embedded in his back hardly hurt him now; no more did the inflammation of the surrounding parts, covered with fine dust, cause him any further discomfort. He thought of his family in tender solicitude. He realized that he must go, and his opinion on this point was even more firm, if possible, than that of his sister. He lay in this state of peaceful and empty meditation till the clock struck the third morning hour. He saw the landscape grow lighter through the window; then, against his will, his head fell forward and his last feeble breath streamed from his nostrils.

When the charwoman arrived early in the morning—and though she had often been forbidden to do so, she always slammed the door so loudly in her vigor and haste that once she was in the house it was impossible to get any sleep—she did not at first notice anything unusual as she paid her customary morning visit to Gregor. She imagined that he was deliberately lying motionless in order to play the role of an "injured party," as she herself would say—she deemed him capable of such refinements; as she had a long broom in her hand, she tried to tickle him from the doorway. Meeting with little success, she grew angry; she gave him one or two hard pushes, and it was only when his body moved unresistingly before her thrusts that she became curious. She quickly realized what had happened, opened her eyes wide, and whistled in astonishment, but she did not stay in the room; she ran to the bedroom, opened the door, and loudly shouted into the darkness, "Come and look! He's stone dead! He's lying there, absolutely dead as a doornail!"

Herr and Frau Samsa sat up in their bed and tried to calm each other; the old woman had frightened them so much and they did not realize the sense of her message immediately. But now they hastily scrambled out of bed, Herr Samsa on one side, his wife on the other; Herr Samsa put the coverlet over his shoulders, Frau Samsa ran out, clad only in her nightdress; and it was thus that they rushed into Gregor's room. Meanwhile, the dining-room door was opened—Grete had been sleeping there since the arrival of the lodgers—she was fully dressed, as if she had not slept all night, and the pallor of her face seemed to bear witness to her sleeplessness.

"Dead?" said Frau Samsa, staring at the charwoman with a questioning look, though she could see as much for herself without further examination.

"I should say so," said the charwoman, and she pushed Gregor to one side with her broom, to support her statement. Frau Samsa made a movement as if to hold back the broom, but she did not complete her gesture.

"Well," said Herr Samsa, "we can thank God for that!" He crossed himself and signed the three women to do likewise.

Grete, whose eyes had never left the corpse, said, "Look how thin he was! It was such a long time since he had eaten anything. His meals used to come out of the room just as they were taken in." And, indeed, Gregor's body was quite flat and dry; this could be seen more easily now that he was no longer supported on his legs and there was nothing to deceive one's sight.

"Come with us a moment, Grete!" said Frau Samsa with a sad smile, and Grete followed her parents into their bedroom, not without turning often to gaze at the corpse. The charwoman closed the door and opened the French windows. Despite the early hour, the fresh morning air had a certain warmth. It was already the end of March.

The three lodgers came out of their room and gazed around in astonishment for their breakfast; they had been forgotten. "Where is our breakfast?" the middle lodger petulantly demanded of the old woman. But she merely laid her finger to her mouth and signed them, with a mute and urgent gesture, to follow her into Gregor's room. So they entered and stood around Gregor's corpse, with their hands in the pockets of their rather shabby coats, in the middle of the room already bright with sunlight.

Then the bedroom door opened and Herr Samsa appeared in his uniform with his wife on one arm, his daughter on the other. All seemed to have been weeping, and from time to time Grete pressed her face against her father's arm.

"Leave my house immediately!" said Herr Samsa, and he pointed to the door, while the women still clung to his arms.

Somewhat disconcerted, the middle lodger said with a timid smile, "Whatever do you mean?"

The two others clasped their hands behind their backs and kept on rubbing their palms together, as if they were expecting some great dispute which could only end in triumph for them.

"I mean exactly what I say!" answered Herr Samsa and, in line with the two women, he marched straight at the lodger. The latter, however, stood quietly in his place, his eyes fixed on the floor, as if reconsidering what he should do.

"Well, then, we will go," he said at last, raising his eyes to Herr Samsa as if searching, in a sudden access of humility, for some slight approval of his resolution.

Herr Samsa merely nodded several times, opening his eyes very wide. Thereupon the lodger walked away with big strides and soon reached the anteroom; his two friends, who for some while had ceased wringing their hands, now bounded after him, as if afraid Herr Samsa might reach the door before them and separate them from their leader. Once they had gained the hall, they took down their hats from the pegs, grabbed their sticks from the umbrella stand, bowed silently, and left the flat.

With a suspicion which, it appears, was quite unjustified, Herr Samsa ran out onto the landing after them with the women and leaned over the balustrade to watch the three men as they slowly, but steadily, descended the interminable stairway, disappearing once as they reached a certain point on each floor, and then, after a few seconds, coming into view again. As they went farther down the staircase, so the Samsa family's interest diminished, and when they had been met and passed by a butcher's boy who came proudly up the stairs with his basket on his head, Herr Samsa and the women quickly left the landing and went indoors again with an air of relief.

They decided to spend the whole day resting; perhaps they might take a walk in the country; they had earned a respite and needed it urgently. And so they sat down to the table to write three letters of excuse: Herr Samsa to the manager of the Bank, Frau Samsa to her employer, and Grete to the head of her department at the shop. The charwoman came in while they were writing and announced that her work was done and that she was going. The three writers at first merely nodded their heads, without raising their eyes, but, as the old woman did not leave, they eventually laid down their pens and looked crossly at her.

"Well?" asked Herr Samsa. The charwoman was standing in the doorway, smiling as if she had some very good news to tell them but which she would not impart till she had been begged to. The little ostrich feather which stood upright on her hat and which had always annoyed Herr Samsa so much ever since the old woman had entered their service, now waved lightly in all directions.

"Well, what is it?" asked Frau Samsa, toward whom the old woman had always shown so much more respect than to the others.

"Well . . ." she replied, and she laughed so much she could hardly speak for some while. "Well, you needn't worry about getting rid of that thing in there, I have fixed it already."

Frau Samsa and Grete leaned over the table as if to resume their letter-writting; Herr Samsa, noticing that the woman was about to launch forth into a detailed explanation, cut her short with a peremptory gesture of his outstretched hand. Then, prevented from speaking, she suddenly remembered that she was in a great hurry and, crying, "Goodbye, everyone," in a peevish tone, she half turned and was gone in a flash, savagely slamming the door behind her.

"This evening we must sack her," declared Herr Samsa; but neither his wife nor his daughter answered; the old woman had not been able to disturb their newly won tranquillity. They arose, went to the window, and stood there, with their arms around each other; Herr Samsa, turning toward them in his armchair, stared at them for a moment in silence. Then he cried, "Come, come, it's all past history now; you can start paying a little attention to me." The women immediately hurried to him, kissed him, and sat down to finish their letters.

Then they all left the apartment together, a thing they had been unable to do for many months past, and they boarded a tram which would take them some way into the country. There were no other passengers in the compartment, which was warm and bright in the sun. Casually leaning back in their seats, they began to discuss their future. On careful reflection, they decided that things were not nearly so bad as they might have been, for—and this was a point they had not hitherto realized—they had all three found really interesting occupations which looked even more promising in the future. They decided to effect what really should be the greatest improvement as soon as possible. That was to move from the flat they occupied at present. They would take a smaller, cheaper flat, but one more practical, and especially in a better neighborhood than the present one, which Gregor had chosen. Hearing their daughter speak in more and more lively tones, Herr and Frau Samsa noticed almost together that, during this affair, Grete had blossomed into a fine strapping girl, despite the make-up which made her cheeks look pale. They became calmer; almost unconsciously they exchanged glances; it occurred to both of them that it would soon be time for her to find a husband. And it seemed to them that their daughter's gestures were a confirmation of these new dreams of theirs, an encouragement for their good intentions, when, at the end of the journey, the girl rose before them and stretched her young body.

[1916, Translator unknown]

# NOW THAT YOU'VE READ KAFKA'S THE METAMORPHOSIS:

An intensely European writer, Franz Kafka has exerted a greater hold on the American imagination than on the European. Probably this is no paradox at all. Within their own lifetime, most Europeans were once sentenced to live in his kind of walled-in world, a world of trial without discernible error, punishment without crime, and freedom only in fantasies. They knew the inside of these walls so existentially that they were disinclined to experience them again vicariously. When fiction comes as close to reality as Kafka's often does, it becomes as it were *too* realistic, *too* faithful, *too* authentic. It loses its mythopoetic quality. It drops all pretense of distance. It ceases to be fiction and becomes instead a painful recreation, a terrifying documentary of the actual.

Kafka became a vogue among intellectuals in America not long after the end of World War II, but those special states of mind conveyed in his fiction did not become familiar to the common reader until the fifties, that age of anxiety when events of the McCarthy era began to overtake that fiction. Masochistically we consumed Kafka. And now, more than ever before, with the dread of nameless threats embedded in everyday life, the sense of aloneness and emptiness, of the precariousness of a person's very being, of Authority shaking itself and arising again from a sick bed in rage, the ghost of Kafka challenges our premises anew. His name has given our language an adjective that describes the metaphysic of much modern America: countless quietly desperate Josephs and Josephines afflicted by all sorts of insecurity, by the threat of dehumanization, by unattainable or indefinable spiritual longings. We feel inexplicably trapped. We are afraid that no one will prevent a uniformed psychopath from pulling the lever on the machine that spells DOOM, we tremble before the prospect that we may be lost forever in the blizzards of disbelief, we suspect that the quester, like K. in *The Castle* may never reach his destination. We are fascinated by the unfolding of what may be the script for the climax of our own greatest drama. If the future that we are promised by some ecologists should ever materialize, then subsequent generations of readers will regard Kafka as bedtime entertainment, but at this moment in history, it would be fatuous indeed even of the most confirmed disciple of progress and democracy not to admit that Kafka's hallucinations may be turning into our realities. We have the direct feeling of being addressed by Kafka because behind all of his questions there arises ominously the great problem of freedom which we thought we had answered once and for all.

It is, then, the experience with the negative elements of our age that Kafka expresses in a variety of forms and it is probably this negative quality in his work that led Communist critics of the forties to accuse him of weakness and middle-class neurosis. But like all cunning craftsmen, Kafka made his weakness his strength. "A writer sheds his sickness in books—repeats and presents again his emotions to be master of them," wrote D. H. Lawrence, a contemporary of Kafka with a more positive bent. Certainly no one has ever mirrored the anxieties of a man victimized not only by his society but by existence itself with greater frankness, wit, imagination, and, in the end, acceptance, than the gangling, sadfaced Jewish lawyer who listened to workers' insurance claims by day and wrote his original fictions by night in a modest apartment adjoining the famed cathedral of the Old Town in Prague. The art he fashioned out of anxiety and despair enables his countrymen to endure, to hold fast to the knowledge that the human spirit can survive the cruellest encroachment and deprivations devisable. As Thomas Mann said of Dostoevski, "They all swear by the name of the great invalid, thanks to whose madness they no longer need to be mad."

Prague provided the cultural milieu which both spiritually starved and stimulated Kafka into creating his factual fables of our times. It was a city where tradition and innovation blended, where four ethnic strains—the German, the Czech, the Jewish, and the Austrian—converged in a continuous flux which should have been a rich soil on which Kafka's imagination could flourish. But curiously enough this milieu left little impression on his art. Kafka's response to his native city is on the surface only (certain Prague landmarks can be identified in his fiction; e.g., the cathedral adjoining his flat appears in *The Trial*), and the alleged sophistication and warmth of Prague's literary circles of that time never seem to have penetrated the frozen sea within the artist. The ax that broke that barrier was forged in the shadows of his private dreams, in the tension created by his white-hot imaginative preoccupation weighed against his disbelief and his detachment, in the struggle of his aesthetic commitment with his social isolation. In these terms, almost all of his work is autobiography, even auto-analysis, an account of the consciousness striving for some real contact with the world which a yet deeper impulse insists upon denying.

It was Kafka's loyalty to this challenge that kept him in a state of endless creative conflict ("neurotic anxiety," some psychologists would say, reminding us of a Kafka aphorism: "For the last time, psychology!"). Out of that unceasing conflict came three novels, all unfinished (*The Trial*, 1925; *The Castle*, 1926; and *America*, 1927), three short novels (*The Metamorphosis*, 1915; *The Burrow*, c. 1923; and *Investigations of a Dog*, 1924), a number of remarkable short stories, prose fragments, and fables; an incomplete play; a collection of very revealing letters, and a diary containing not only his daily ruminations but also a scattering of aphorisms which sound like commentaries on his own fiction ("In the fight between you and world back the world"; "One of the first signs of the beginning of understanding is the wish to die"; "He who seeks does not find, but he who does not seek will be found.") Nothing will explain the mystery of the artist's creativity, but a brief summary of Kafka's career may cast some light on the conditions that produced the conflicts responsible for the creative.

Kafka was born in July 1883, the first among six children. Like Thomas Mann (eight years his senior), he was the son of a wealthy merchant, but whereas Mann's father had gracefully inherited his position, Kafka's had to rise from humble beginnings in a society that despised the Jew and regarded him as vermin to be confined in a corner of the city. Hence, his success by sheer strength of will turned him into a hardened advocate of external authority.

Young Kafka attended the Starpmestle Gymnasium, then reputed to be the best German academy in Prague, and after some hesitation decided to study law at the University of Prague. Upon obtaining his doctorate in 1906, he took a post with the Assicurazioni Generali (1907), which he left a year later to work for an insurance company in the accidents claims division. Although this semi-governmental position enabled him to keep his afternoons free, the sterility of the morning's activities prevented him from pursuing his literary intentions with full energy. Yet Kafka derived a great amount of his knowledge of the world and life, as well as his skeptical pessimism, from his experience in the bureaucratic office and from his contact with workmen suffering under injustice. Whole chapters of *The Trial* and *The Castle* and scenes in "The Penal Colony" contain the elements of absurdity and calmly-accepted cruelty which Kafka found himself surrounded by every morning.

Brief summer vacations gave Kafka the opportunity to travel in Europe with his friends, most often with Max Brod, who was to become his "official" biographer. And even in Prague, where he struggled to maintain a regimen of work, sleep, and writing, he associated with other intellectuals of his time—the theologian Martin Buber, the novelist Franz Werfel, Professor Friedl Pick, the writer Oscar Baum and members of the Bar-Kochba circle. In 1909, two sections from "Description of a Struggle" were published in Franz Blei's journal *Hyperion*, probably Kafka's first appearance in print. In 1910 he began to keep the diary that gives us the mirror-writing of his soul's struggle. Approaching the age of 30, Kafka felt himself now ready to write. By 1913, he was working on three stories, "The Judgement," "The Metamorphosis," and "The Boy Who Was Never More Heard Of," the first sketch of the work published posthumously as *America*. During the summer of that year, while on vacation in Germany, he met Felice Bauer ("F.B."), "the girl from Berlin."

For the next five years, Kafka vacillated between the desire to marry F.B. (or at least maintain the love relationship) and the need to devote his energies to his literary aspirations. He could not do both and he decided to resign himself to isolation in order to preserve his creative self. He left his job for the same reason. When he was afflicted with tuberculosis in September 1917, he felt a great sense of relief: it was God or some force beyond himself, he reasoned, not himself, that made him incapable of living, incapable of love, friendship, and profession.

Despite failing health in 1914, Kafka was making trips to northern Germany and embarked upon "The Penal Colony" and *The Trial*. Both the story and the novel may be interpreted on many levels—the political, the psychological, the theological, and even the autobiographical (see Kafka's aphorism linking celibacy and suicide)—but essentially both of them begin with a crisis in the life of a man who suddenly recognizes the abyss of absurdity yawning before him (some critics have pushed hard the superficial parallels between *The Trial* and *The Stranger*). In "The Penal Colony," the explorer who comes to the island of the execution machine, and in *The Trial*, Joseph K. (whose family name is Karl), must infuse meaning into an existence which may be inherently meaningless. Fixated on this question, Joseph K. falls metaphorically as well as literally "under arrest." Is he criminally guilty or is he guiltlessly guilty, a victim of his own existence who must suffer, like Iván Ilých, punishment without ostensible crime? Two years later, when World War I, the most senseless of conflicts, was to begin, many people must have shared the mood of Kafka's novel.

Like Thomas Mann, Kafka did not participate in the war. His position as a civil servant granted him exemption from the draft and he was able to travel in Hungary and stay for a time in Marienbad with F.B. During this period, he wrote that surreal masterpiece, "A Country Doctor," a story about a physician who answers a call in the night and ends up lost in a blizzard; finished "The Bucket-Rider," a story that reflects, among other things, the fuel shortage that afflicted Prague; began "The Great Wall of China," and wrote the famous letter to his father which he never posted.

After his first attack of tuberculosis in 1917, Kafka took sick leave from his job and launched himself into the study of Hebrew and the philosophy of Soren Kierkegaard (*Sickness Unto Death*; *In Fear and Trembling*). Three years later his condition required treatment in Merano and confinement the following winter to a sanatorium in the Tatra Mountains. About this time he had an affair with Milena Jesenska, his Czech translator, which is described in *Letters to Milena*, an extraordinary document—touching, horrifying, brilliant, sickening, heartbreaking, and infinitely convoluted. Again Kafka was to deny love for the labor of love: "What I have to do, I can only do alone. Become clear about the ultimate things; the Western Jew is not clear about them and therefore has no right to marry." At the same time that he was courting Milena, he was engaged in writing a never quite finished novel, *The Castle* (first translated in 1930). The hero, a land surveyor called K., is summoned to a village that is overlooked and overlorded by "the Castle," where he is to get his instructions. The entire novel consists of K.'s attempts to enter this mystifying edifice and get his instructions. It is a typical, stupendous Kafkan theme of the conspiracy against the most simple human achievement. After his letters to Milena, one reads *The Castle* with fresh insight, since so many lines, notions, situations, flash the reader back to the letters. And possibly Kafka in writing that enigmatic novel came close to the ultimate clarity that he despaired of attaining in the letters: that ultimate clarity is unknowable and unreachable no matter how determined the quest for certainty.

Kafka, who had written in his diary that the only one who could wholly understand him was God, discovered at the end of his life that this was not necessarily true. In 1923, he met and fell in love with Dora Dymant, who was to remain his faithful companion until his death. While living with her in Berlin, he produced some of his finest stories: "The Burrow," "Josephine the Singer," "Investigations of a Dog," and "A Hunger Artist," a story reminiscent of "The Metamorphosis," with the horror and the violence muted, and the Jewish humor about the son who refuses to eat exploited effectively. In 1924, Kafka returned to Prague with Max Brod to seek the hand of Dora Dymant from her father, who refused to give his consent to the match. Dying and disconsolate, accompanied by Dora, Kafka moved from clinic to sanatorium, and on June 3, 1924, at a sanatorium in Kierling, not far from the Vienna Woods, he went into a coma from which he never recovered. He is buried in the Lowy corner of the cemetery behind the Straschnitz synagogue, where the names of his sisters are carved into the brick wall of a memorial to the victims of the Nazi concentration camps.

The kind of transformation that Samsa undergoes in *The Metamorphosis* is not an invention of Kafka. The partial or complete transformation of animals into men or men into animals has a long literary tradition. In Homer, the men of Odysseus are turned into swine, and in Apulieus the protagonist becomes a jackass who retains comprehension. Such metamorphoses are intended to be a stage prior to moral elevation or an episode in a chain of larger events; that is, the metamorphosis is not the beginning, middle, and the end. In the work of writers from Aesop to Orwell, from Swift to Capek, creatures represent classes of human beings, and the aim of these writers is quite different from Kafka's. In such works, the fantastical transformation follows a clearcut line of logic and represents what it in itself is not: the story becomes an allegory and the message could, if necessary, be stated in discursive language with little loss of purpose. Hence, its terms of reference may be abstractions of one kind or another—retribution, hubris, the overthrow of the bourgeoisie, political injustice or tyranny.

When we examine the nature of Kafka's images, however, we are reminded of Albert Camus' remark that Kafka offers the reader everything yet confirms nothing. Dream and reality fuse in a way that obscures (though Kafka's style is never obscure, always clear and simple and direct in the German) any neat allegorical point or pattern. In reference specific and concrete, his images of transformation express his intensely personal response to the world, yet their substance has shadows which suggest what is going on beyond the circle of the private imagination. His images partake of the reality which they render intelligible.

In Dostoevski's *Notes from Underground*, there is a passage that may have been a starting point for Kafka. The narrator of *Notes* at one point encounters an officer who "takes him by the shoulders and without any explanation, without a word, moves him to one side and passes on, as though he did not exist." He knows to the officer he is now nothing, a mere object, a "curious insect"; he becomes very clearly aware that in their midst he is nothing but a "nasty disgusting fly—more intelligent, more highly developed, more refined in feeling than any of them, of course—but a fly that was continually making way for everyone, insulted and injured by everyone." This furthermost point at which he finds himself for a moment is the same world without exit, enlarged to the dimensions of an endless nightmare, in which Gregor Samsa will flounder.

Kafka first tried out the image of metamorphosis (for an instant as in *Notes*) in a story called "Wedding Preparations in the Country" (1907). A commercial traveller, one Eduard Raban, is leaving Prague for a vacation during which he is to marry his fiancée Betty. In the train, Raban rolls anxiously through the night, speaking his interior thoughts:

> As I lie in bed I assume the shape of a big beetle, a stag beetle or a cockchafer, I think. The form of a large beetle, yes. Then I would pretend that it was a matter of hibernating, and I would press my little legs to my bulging belly.

When Raban finally arrives at the village, we are told no more, for the story ends exactly where *The Castle* would open. From the evidence of this fragment, we may assume that the marriage would have taken place and also that the story would not have tapped the deepest layers of Kafka's unconscious. This penetration was to be reserved for *The Metamorphosis* some five years later. The opening lines are intended to make us "suffer like the death of someone we love more than ourselves" (Kafka to Oskar Pollak), but what horrifies and fascinates us at once is that no one within the story regards the happenings as "impossible"; it is a nasty business to be sure, but in various ways the people around Samsa, seemingly sane and simple, adjust themselves to the situation. Even Samsa himself comes to terms with the undeniable urges which compel his body to carry on a life that has become questionable to itself. The final horror is that he must atone for a crime the gravity and even the name of which he cannot know. We suspect the "crime" is related to his father—has Gregor transformed himself without first asking permission and therefore displeasing the father, the symbol of authority?

A similar mood pervades the letter written three years later and beginning: "Dearest Father, you asked me recently why I maintain that I am afraid of you." For accepting the despotism of his father, Kafka denounces himself as a "crawling, furtive creature" destined to be "pushed down into the filth." He confesses the wish "to crawl to a clean little spot on the earth where the sun sometimes shines and one can warm oneself a little." The letter was never sent—otherwise Kafka might have heard his father roar once again his favorite threat, "I'll tear you apart like a fish." If it seems strange that Kafka at the age of 37 should still have regarded himself as vermin in the eyes of his father, it is fortunate for literature at least that he did not succeed in auto-analysing his *Angst* away.

In this letter and in the other Kafka stories of transformation— "Investigations of a Dog," "The Burrow," "The Giant Mole," "Josephine the Singer," "A Report to the Academy," we have what Philip Rahv calls "the nuclear fable to which Kafka returns again and again, varying and complicating its structure with astonishing resourcefulness." The real terror and truth of this fable depends upon the possibility of a unique, unpredictable, intelligent human individual being thrust suddenly into a vast, anonymous, automatic world where the only active decision still required of him is, in the words of Hannah Arendt, "to abandon his individuality, the still individually sensed pain and trouble of living, and acquiesce in a dazed, tranquilized, functional type of behavior." Reducing the individual self to insignificance and powerlessness removes the possibility of conflict (and pain?), but it also brings about a kind of psychic dislocation that manifests itself in the loss or confusion of identity. Unmoored, the mind bends to the shape that corresponds to its reading of the role imposed upon it from without.

Thus, in the phantasmagoria of Kafka's imagination, the human ego is repeatedly shorn of its power and identity. Men become mice or lice, always submissive, always cringing, always insecure and uncertain, always in fear and trembling. They become brutes with brains, who can know neither the insensate condition of the brute nor the pleasures of the intelligence. Fear and guilt invade the will and reduce it to a peculiar *stasis* in which the individual ego perishes yet lives to know its own death.

Kafka had the superhuman courage to precede us to the limits of despair. "Beyond these furthermost limits there remains only vast, empty stupefaction, definitive total-don't understand." As Nathalie Sarraute says, "To remain at the point where he left off, or to attempt to go on from there, are equally impossible. Those who live in a world of human beings can only retrace their steps."

## FOR FURTHER INFORMATION:

Dorrit Cohn. "Kafka's Eternal Present: Narrative Tense in 'Ein Landarzt'' and Other First Person Stories," *Publications of the Modern Language Association*, LXXXIII (1968), 144-50.

Martin Greenberg. *The Terror of Art: Kafka and Modern Literature*. Basic Books: New York, 1968.

Charles Neider. *The Frozen Sea*. Russell and Russell: New York, 1962 (1948).

Heinrich Politzer. *Franz Kafka: Parable and Paradox*. Cornell University Press: Ithaca, 1966 (1962).

Walter Herbert Sokel. *Franz Kafka*. Columbia University Press: New York, 1966.

Mark Spilka. *Dickens and Kafka*. Indiana University Press: Bloomington, 1963.

Herbert Tauber. *Franz Kafka*. Kennikat: Port Washington, N.Y., 1968 (1948).

Alexander Taylor. "The Waking: the theme of Kafka's 'Metamorphosis'," *Studies in Short Fiction*, II (1964), 337-342.

## ABEL SANCHEZ

### BY MIGUEL DE UNAMUNO Y JUGO

First published, 1917

# ABEL SANCHEZ

## The History of a Passion

Following the death of Joaquín Monegro there was found among his papers a kind of memoir of the dark passion which had devoured his life. Fragments taken from this *Confession* (which was the title he gave his journal) are inserted in the following narrative. These fragments serve as a commentary, by Joaquín Monegro himself, on his affliction; they are put in italics.

The *Confession* was addressed to his daughter.

**N**EITHER Abel Sanchez nor Joaquín Monegro could remember a time when they had not known each other. They had known each other since before childhood—since earliest infancy, in fact; for their nursemaids often met and brought the two infants together even before the children knew how to talk. They had each learned about each other as they learned about themselves. Thus had they grown up, friends from birth, and treated almost as brothers in their upbringing.

In their walks, in their games, in their mutual friendships it was Joaquín, the more willful of the two, who seemed to initiate and dominate everything. Still, Abel, who appeared always to yield, always did as he pleased. The truth was that he found not obeying more important than commanding. The two almost never quarreled. "As far as I'm concerned, it's whatever you want. . . ." Abel would say to Joaquín, who would become exasperated; for by this "whatever you want . . ." Abel managed to show his disdain of the argument.

"You never say no!" Joaquín would burst out.

"What's the use?"

"Well, now," Joaquín began one day when they were with some comrades who were preparing to take a walk, "this fellow"—pointing at Abel—"doesn't want to go to the pine grove."

"Me?" yelled Abel. "Who said I don't want to? Of course I want to. It's really up to you. Yes! Yes! Let's go there!"

"No! It's not whatever I want. I've told you that before. It's not whatever I want. The fact is that you don't want to go!"

"I do, I tell you!"

"In that case I don't want to."

"Then I don't either."

"That's not fair"; by now Joaquín was screaming. To the other boys he yelled: "Either go with him or come with me!"

And they all went with Abel, leaving Joaquín to himself.

When Joaquín went to comment, in his *Confession,* on this event of their infancy, he wrote:

Already Abel was, unconsciously, the congenial one, and I the antipathetic one, without my knowing why this was so any better than he did. I was left alone. Ever since childhood my friends left me to myself.

All during their secondary school studies, which they pursued together, Joaquín was the incubator and hatcher, hotly in pursuit of prizes. Joaquín was first in the classroom; Abel was first outside class, in the patio of the Institute, and among his comrades, in the street, in the country, and whenever they played hooky. It was Abel who made everyone laugh with his natural cleverness; he was especially applauded for his caricature of the professors. "Joaquín is much more diligent, but Abel is quicker . . . if he were only to study. . . ." And this prevailing judgment on the part of his classmates, of which Joaquín was aware, served to poison his heart further. He was soon tempted to neglect his studies and strive to excel over Abel in his own field; but he managed to tell himself: "Bah! What do they know. . . ." And in the end he remained faithful to his own nature. Besides, however much he attempted to surpass the other in natural facility or grace, he was unsuccessful. His jokes were not greeted with laughter, and he was considered fundamentally serious and was thought to be basically cold. "You're really macabre," Frederico Cuadrado would say to him, "those jokes of yours would do well at a wake."

The two of them finished their schooling. Abel embarked on an artist's career and began the study of painting; Joaquín entered medical school. They saw each other frequently and spoke of the progress each was making in his respective studies. Often Joaquín would endeavor to prove to Abel that medicine, too, was an art, a fine art even, to which poetic inspiration was native. On other occasions, however, Joaquín denigrated the fine arts, enervators of the will, and extolled science, which "elevated, fortified and expanded the spirit with Truth."

"The truth is that medicine is not actually a science," from Abel. "It is more like an art, a professional practice based on the sciences."

"But I don't intend to dedicate myself to ministering the sick."

"A very honorable and practical ministry. . . ."

"Yes, but not for me," interrupted Joaquín. "It may be altogether as honorable and practical as you like, but I detest such honorableness and practicality. Making money by taking a pulse, looking at tongues, and writing some kind of prescription is for others. I aspire to something higher."

"Higher?"

"Yes. I hope to open new pathways. I expect to devote myself to scientific investigation. The glory of medicine belongs to those who discover the secret of some disease, not to those who apply the discovery with greater or lesser luck."

"It's a pleasure to see you in this idealistic frame of mind."

"Oh, do you suppose that only you people, the artists, the painters, dream of glory?"

"Wait now, no one said that I dream of any such thing. . . ."

"No? In that case why have you taken up painting?"

"Because, if one is successful, it's a profession which promises. . . ."

"What does it promise?"

"Well, now, it promises . . . money."

"Throw that bone to some other dog, Abel. I've known you ever since we were born, almost. You can't tell that to me. I know you."

"And have I ever tried to deceive you?"

"No, but you deceive without trying. Despite your air of not caring about anything, of acting as if life were a game, you're really terribly ambitious."

"Ambitious, me?"

"Yes, ambitious for glory, fame, renown. . . . You always were, you have been since birth, even though you conceal it."

"Wait a bit, Joaquín, and tell me something. Did I ever dispute your prizes with you? Weren't you always first in your class, the 'most promising'?"

"Yes, but the little cock of the walk, the one everybody humored, was you. . . ."

"And what could I do about that?"

"Do you want me to believe that you weren't seeking that kind of popularity?"

"Now, if *you* had sought it. . . ."

"If I had sought it? I despise the masses!"

"All right, all right. Spare me the speech and the nonsense, and save yourself the bother, too. It would be better if you talked about your girl friend again."

"My girl friend?"

"Well, your little cousin, then, whom you'd like to make your girl friend."

Joaquín was, in fact, attempting to storm the heart of his cousin Helena and was displaying all the ardor of his intense and jealous nature in the amorous engagement. And he unburdened himself— the inevitable and salubrious unburdening of the embattled lover— to his confidant and friend, Abel.

How his cousin Helena made him suffer!

"Each time I see her I understand her less," he would complain to Abel. "That girl is like a sphinx to me."

"You know what Oscar Wilde said: every woman is a sphinx without a secret."

"Well, Helena seems to have one. She must be in love with some-one else, even though the other doesn't know it. I'm certain she's in love with someone else."

"Why do you think so?"

"Otherwise I can't explain her attitude toward me."

"You mean that because she doesn't want to love you, want you as a lover . . . for as a cousin she probably loves you. . . ."

"Don't make fun of me!"

"Well then, because she doesn't want you for a lover, or more exactly, for a husband, she must be in love with someone else? Nice logic!"

"I understand what I'm saying."

"Yes, and I understand you, too."

"You?"

"Don't you claim to be the one who understands *me* best? Why is it surprising if I claim to understand you? We met at the same time."

"In any case, I'm telling you that this woman is driving me mad. She'll drive me too far. She's playing with me. If she had said no from the beginning, it would have been all right; but to keep me in suspense, telling me that she'll see, that she'll think it over. . . . These things can't be thought over, coquette that she is!"

"She's probably studying you."

"Studying me? Her? What is there about me to study? What *could* she study?"

"Joaquín, Joaquín, you're underestimating yourself and underestimating her. Or do you think that she has only to see you, and hear you, know that you love her, in order to surrender herself to you?"

"Oh, I know, I've always aroused antipathy. . . ."

"Come, now, don't get yourself into that state. . . ."

"It's just that this woman is playing with me. And it's not honorable to play this way with a man who is sincere, loyal and aboveboard. . . . If you could only see how beautiful she is! And the colder and more disdainful she grows, the more beautiful she becomes! There are times when I don't know if I love her more or hate her more. . . . Would you like me to introduce you to her . . . ?"

"Well, if you . . ."

"Good, I'll introduce you."

"And if she wants . . ."

"What?"

"I'll paint her portrait."

"That's wonderful!"

But that night Joaquín slept badly, envisioning the portrait and haunted by the idea that Abel Sanchez, the guileless charmer, the one who was humored in everything, was going to paint Helena's portrait.

What would come of it? Would Helena, too, like all their mutual friends, find Abel the more endearing? He thought of calling off the introduction, but, since he had already promised. . . .

## CHAPTER II

"What did you think of my cousin?" Joaquín asked Abel the day after the two had been introduced. Abel had broached the matter of the portrait to Helena, and she had received the proposal with extreme satisfaction.

"Well now, do you want the truth?"

"The truth at all times, Abel. If we told each other the truth always, this world would be Paradise."

"Yes, and if each one told himself the truth. . . ."

"Well, the truth then!"

"The truth is that your cousin and future sweetheart, perhaps wife, Helena, seems to me a peacock. . . . I mean a female peacock. . . . You understand what I mean . . . ?"

"Yes, I understand you."

"Since I don't know how to express myself well except with a brush. . . ."

"And so you'll paint this peacock, this female peacock, as it spreads its train, the tail feathers decorated with eyes, the little head piece. . . ."

"As a model, she's excellent! Really excellent, my friend! What eyes! What a mouth! A mouth both full and formed . . . eyes which do not quite look at you . . . and what a neck! Above all, what color, what complexion! If you will not be offended. . . ."

"Offended?"

"I will tell you that she has the color of a wild Indian, or, better still, of an untamed animal. There is something of the panther about her, in the best sense, and she is so totally indifferent to it all, so cold."

"So cold!"

"Anyway, old man, I expect to paint you a stupendous portrait."

"Paint me a portrait? You mean paint *her* a portrait."

"No, the portrait shall be for you, even if it is of her."

"No! The portrait will be for her."

"Well, then, for the two of you. Who knows. . . . Perhaps it will join you together."

"Ah! Why, of course, since from being a portrait painter you take on the role of. . . ."

"Whatever you want, Joaquín, a go-between if you like, as long as you stop suffering as you have. It's painful for me to see you in that state."

The painting sessions began, the three of them assembling for the occasion. Helena would take her seat, solemn and cold, in an attitude of disdain, like a goddess borne along by destiny. "May I talk?" she asked on the first day, and Abel answered her: "Yes, you can talk and move about; it's better for me, in fact, if you do move about and talk, for in that way the features take on life. . . . This will not be a photograph, and besides I don't want you like a statue." And so she talked and talked, but without moving very much, careful of her posture. What did she talk of? The two men were not aware. Because both of them devoured her with their eyes; they saw her, but they did not hear. . . .

And she talked and talked, considering it a sign of good manners not to remain silent; and, whenever possible, she taunted Joaquín.

"Are you having any luck getting patients, little cousin?" she would ask.

"Do you really care about that?"

"Of course I care about it. You think I don't. . . . Imagine . . ."

"No, I can't imagine."

"Since you interest yourself so much in me, I couldn't do less than interest myself in your affairs. And besides, who knows. . . ."

"Who knows what?"

"All right, let's leave the subject," Abel interrupted. "You both don't do anything but scold."

"It's natural," Helena said, "between relatives. . . . And besides, they say that's the way it begins."

"What begins?" Joaquín asked.

"That's something you must know, since you began it."

"What I'm going to do now is finish!"

"Well, there are various ways of finishing something, cousin."

"And various ways of beginning."

"No doubt. Tell me, Abel, do I disarrange myself with this *badinage?*"

"No, no, on the contrary. This *badinage,* as you call it, adds some expression to your look and gesture. But . . ."

Within two days Abel and Helena were addressing each other familiarly; on the third day, Joaquín, who had wanted it this way, missed the painting session.

"Let me see how it looks now," Helena said getting up to stand before the portrait.

"What do you think?"

"I'm not an expert and besides I'm not the one to judge whether or not it's like me."

"What? Don't you have a mirror? Haven't you looked at yourself in it?"

"Yes, but . . ."

"But what . . . ?"

"Oh, I don't know. . . ."

"Don't you see that you're quite stunning?"

"Don't be a flatterer."

"Well then, we'll ask Joaquín."

"Don't speak of him to me, if you please. What a bore!"

"Well, it's of him that I must speak to you."

"Then I'm going. . . ."

"No, listen! What you're doing to that boy is very bad."

"Oh! So now you're going to plead his case for him? Is this business about the portrait simply an excuse?"

"Look, Helena, it isn't right for you to act this way, playing with your cousin. He's something, after all, something . . ."

"Yes, he's insufferable!"

"No, he's engrossed in himself, he's proud, stubborn, full of his own importance, but he's also good, honorable in every respect, intelligent; a brilliant future in his profession is ahead of him; he loves you passionately. . . ."

"And if in spite of all that I don't love him . . . ?"

"Then in that case you should discourage him."

"And haven't I discouraged him enough? I'm tired of telling him that I think he's a good fellow, but for that very reason, because he does strike me as a good fellow, a good cousin, a good 'coz'—and I'm not using the word nastily—I really don't want him for a suitor and for everything that comes later."

"But he says. . . ."

"If he has told you anything else, Abel, he hasn't told you the truth. Can I send him on his way or forbid him from speaking to me since he is, after all, my cousin. Cousin! What a joke!"

"Don't be so mocking."

"The fact is I can't. . . ."

"Moreover, he suspects something else. He insists on making himself believe that since you don't want to love him, you are secretly enamored of someone else. . . ."

"Has he told you that?"

"Yes, he has told me just that."

Helena bit her lips, blushed, and was silent for a moment.

"Yes, he told me that," Abel repeated, letting his right hand rest on the maulstick which he held against the canvas; he was gazing steadily at Helena, as if he wanted to find a meaning in some feature of her face.

"Well, if he insists. . . ."

"What . . . ?"

"He'll succeed in having me fall in love with someone else. . . ."

Abel painted no more that afternoon. And the two became lovers.

## CHAPTER III

Abel's portrait of Helena was a tremendous success. There was always someone standing before the show window where it was exhibited. "Another great painter among us," it was said. And Helena made a point of passing near the place where her portrait was hanging in order to hear the comments, and she strolled through the streets of the city like an immortal portrait imbued with life, like a work of art with a full train. Had she been born perhaps for just this?

Joaquín scarcely slept.

"She's worse than ever," he told Abel. "She's really playing with me now. She'll be my death."

"Naturally. She's become a professional beauty. . . ."

"Yes, you've immortalized her. Another Gioconda!"

"And still, you, as a doctor, can do more, you can lengthen her life. . . ."

"Or shorten it."

"Don't act so tragic."

"What am I going to do, Abel, what am I going to do . . . ?"

"Learn to have patience. . . ."

"And then, she has told me certain things from which I gather you told her of my feeling that she is in love with somebody else. . . ."

"It was in order to help your cause. . . ."

"To help my cause . . . Abel, Abel, you're working with her . . . the two of you are deceiving me. . . ."

"Deceiving you? In what way? Has she promised you anything?"

"And you, has she promised *you* anything?"

"Is she your mistress, perhaps?"

"Is she already *yours* then?"

Abel kept quiet, and changed color.

"You see," exclaimed Joaquín, trembling and beginning to stammer, "you see?"

"See what?"

"Will you deny it now? Are you brazen faced enough to deny it to me?"

"Well, Joaquín, we have been friends since before we knew each other, almost brothers. . . ."

"And a brother is to be treacherously stabbed, is that it?"

"Don't get so furious. Show some patience. . . ."

"Patience? And what has my life been if not a continuous show of patience, continuous suffering? . . . You, the most attractive, the most pampered, the constant victor, the artist . . . And I . . ."

Tears sprang from his eyes and cut short his words.

"And what was I to do, Joaquín, what did you want me to do?"

"Not to have courted her, since it was I who loved her!"

"But it was she, Joaquín, it was she. . . ."

"And naturally it is you, the fortunate one, the artist, the favorite of fortune, you who women court. Well now you have her. . . ."

"She has me, you mean."

"Yes, the female peacock, the professional beauty, the Gioconda, now she has you. . . . You will be her painter. . . . You will paint her in every posture and every light, clothed and unclothed. . . ."

"Joaquín!"

"And so you will immortalize her. She will live as long as your paintings live. Or rather, not *live*—for Helena doesn't live; but endure, and will endure like marble, the marble of which she is made. For she is made of stone, cold and hard like you. A mass of flesh!"

"Don't get into such a rage."

"Oh, I shouldn't get into a rage, you think, I shouldn't be enraged? This is an infamous piece of work you've accomplished, a low, vile trick."

He felt weak and disheartened, however, and grew quiet, as if words with which to match the violence of his passion failed him.

"But stop and consider," Abel said in his most dulcet voice, which was also his most terrible. "Was I going to make her love you, if she doesn't want to love you? She doesn't think of you as her. . . ."

"No, of course not, I'm not attractive to any woman; I was born already condemned."

"I swear to you, Joaquín. . . ."

"Don't bother with oaths."

"I swear to you that if it were up to me alone, Helena would be your beloved now, and tomorrow she would be your wife. If I were able to give her up to you. . . ."

"You'd trade her to me for a mess of potage, is that it?"

"Trade her, no! I would give her up freely and would be more than happy in seeing you both happy, but. . . ."

"I know, she does not love me, and she does love you, isn't that it?"

"That's true."

"She rejects me, who wanted her, and wants you, who rejected her."

"Exactly. Although you won't believe me, it's I who was seduced."

"Oh, what a way of putting on airs! You nauseate me!"

"Airs?"

"Yes. To play the role of the one seduced is worse than playing the seducer. Poor victim! Women fight over you. . . ."

"Don't exasperate me, Joaquín. . . ."

"You? Exasperate *you*? I tell you this is a vile trick, a piece of infamy, a crime. . . . We are through with each other forever!"

But then later, changing his tone, and with fathomless sorrow in his voice:

"Have compassion on me, Abel, have compassion. Don't you see that everyone looks at me askance, that everyone is opposed to me. . . . You are young, fortunate, indulged; there are more than enough women for you. . . . Let me have Helena; you can be sure I won't be able to love another. . . . Let me have Helena. . . ."

"But I already yield her to you. . . ."

"Make her listen to me; make her acknowledge me; make her understand that I am dying for her, that without her I can't live. . . ."

"You don't know her. . . ."

"Yes, I know you both! But, for God's sake, swear to me that you will not marry her. . . ."

"Who spoke of marriage?"

"Ah, then all this is only to make me jealous? It's true that she is nothing but a coquette . . . worse than a coquette, a . . ."

"Be quiet!" roared Abel.

His voice had been such that Joaquín remained silent, staring at him.

"It's impossible, Joaquín; one cannot deal with you. You are impossible."

And Abel turned and walked away.

*I passed a horrible night*—Joaquín wrote in the *Confession* he left behind—*tossing from one side of the bed to the other, biting the pillow spasmodically, and getting up to drink water from the washstand pitcher. I ran a fever. From time to time I drowsed off into bitter dreams. I thought of killing both of them, and I made mental calculations—as if it were a matter of a drama or novel I was creating —planning the details of my bloody vengeance, and I composed imaginary dialogues with the two of them. It seemed to me that Helena had only wanted to affront me, nothing more; that she had made love to Abel to slight me, but that in reality—pure mass of flesh before a mirror that she was—she could not love anybody. And I desired her more than ever and more furiously than before. During one of the interminable half-waking, half-sleeping spells of that night I dreamt that I possessed her beside the cold and inert body of Abel. That night was a tempest of evil desires, of rage, of vile appetites, of futile wrath. With daylight and the weariness of so much suffering, reason returned to me and I understood that I had no right whatsoever to Helena. But I began to hate Abel with all my soul, and, at the same time, to plan the concealment of this loathing, which I would cultivate and tend deep down in my soul's entrails. Loathing, did I say? I did not yet want to give it a name. Nor did I care to understand that I had been born predestined to bear the weight of hatred upon me and its seed within me. That night I was born into my life's hell.*

## CHAPTER IV

"Helena," Abel addressed her, "the incident with Joaquín disturbs my sleep. . . ."

"The incident? Why should it?"

"I wonder what will happen when I tell him we plan to be married. . . . Still, he seems to have quieted down and more or less resigned himself to our relationship. . . ."

"He's a fine example of resignation!"

"The truth is that what we did wasn't altogether well done."

"What? You, too? Are women supposed to be like animals, to be handed round and loaned out and rented and sold?"

"No, but . . ."

"But, what?"

"Well, it was he who introduced me to you, so I could paint your portrait, and I took advantage. . . ."

"And that was well done! Was I, by any chance, engaged to him? And even if I had been! Every one must go his own way."

"Yes, but . . ."

"But what? Are you sorry after all? Well, as far as I'm concerned. . . . Even if you were to leave me now, now that I'm promised to you and everyone knows that you will ask permission to marry me one of these days, even then I wouldn't want Joaquín. No! I'd want him less than ever. I would have more than enough suitors, more of them than fingers on my hand, like this,"—and here she raised her two long hands with their tapering fingers, those hands which Abel had painted with so much love, and she shook her fingers so that they fluttered.

Abel seized her two hands in his own strong ones, carried them to his mouth, and kissed them at great length. And then her mouth. . . .

"Be quiet, Abel!"

"You're right, Helena, we must not undermine our happiness by thinking of what poor Joaquín feels and suffers on account of it. . . ."

"Poor Joaquín? He's nothing but an envious wretch!"

"Still, Helena, there are states of envy. . . ."

"Let him go to the devil!"

After a pause filled with black silence:

"Well, we'll invite him to the wedding. . . ."

"Helena!"

"What harm would there be in that? He's my cousin, and your first friend; we owe to him the fact that we know each other. And if you don't invite him, I will. He won't go? So much the better! He will go? Better than ever!"


## CHAPTER V

When Abel told Joaquín of his impending marriage, the latter said:

"It had to be. Each to his own."

"Now, you must understand. . . ."

"Yes, I understand; don't think me demented or mad; I understand; it's all right; I hope you will be happy. . . . I can never be so again. . . ."

"But, Joaquín, for God's sake, in the name of everything you love most. . . ."

"That's enough. Let's not speak of it any further. Make Helena happy, and may she make you happy, too. . . . I have already forgiven you. . . ."

"Have you truly?"

"Yes, truly. I want to forgive you. I will try to make my own life."

"Then I will venture to invite you to the wedding, in my name . . ."

"And in hers too? . . ."

"In hers too."

"I understand. I will go in order to heighten your happiness. I'll go."

As a wedding gift, Joaquín sent Abel a brace of magnificent damascened pistols, worthy of an artist.

"They're for you to shoot yourself in the head with, when you grow weary of me," Helena told her future husband.

"What are you talking about, woman? What an idea!"

"Who knows his intentions . . . ? He spends his life plotting."

*In the days following the day when he told me they were to be married,—Joaquín wrote in his Confession—I felt as if my soul had frozen. And the icy cold pressed upon my heart, as if flames of ice were suffocating me. I had trouble breathing. My hatred for Helena, and even more, for Abel—and hatred it was, a cold hatred whose roots choked my heart—had become like a petrified growth, as hard as stone. Yet, it was not so much a poisonous plant as it was an iceberg which blocked up my soul; or rather, my soul itself was congealed in hatred. The ice of it was so crystalline that I could see into and through it with complete clarity. I was perfectly well aware that they were right, absolutely right, and that I had no right whatever to Helena; that one ought not, can not, force a woman's love; that since they loved each other, they should be united. And still, confusedly I felt that it had been I who had brought them, not only together, but to the point of love; that they had come together because they both wished to spurn me; that Helena's decision was largely determined by an urge to see me suffer and rage, to make me set my teeth on edge, to humiliate me before Abel; on his part I sensed a supreme egotism which never allowed him to take notice of the suffering of others. Ingenuously, he simply did not pay any attention to the existence of others. The rest of us were, at most, models for his paintings. He did not even hate, so full of himself was he.*

I attended the wedding, my soul frost-bitten with hatred, my heart coated with bitter ice, and seized with the apprehension, the mortal terror, that when I heard their "I do," the ice would crack, and my heart would break, and I would die then and there, or turn into an idiot. I went to the wedding as one goes to one's death. And what happened was more mortal than death itself; it was worse, much worse than dying. I wish I might have died instead.

She was completely beautiful. When she greeted me I felt as if an icy sword was plunged into the ice which froze my heart; it was her insolent smile of compassion which cut through me. "Thank you," she said; "poor Joaquín." I understood. As for Abel, I do not know whether he even really saw me. "I understand your sacrifice," he said, merely to say something. "No, no," I hastened to say, "there is none involved; I told you I would come and I came; you see how reasonable I am; I could not have failed my eternal friend, my brother." My attitude must have seemed interesting to him, though scarcely very picturesque. I was like the Comendador in Don Juan, a guest made of stone.

As the fatal moment drew near I began to count the seconds. "In a very short time," I told myself, "everything is over for me." I believe my heart stopped. Clearly and distinctly I heard each "Yes," his and hers. She looked at me as she uttered the word. And I grew colder than ever, not through any sudden clutching at my heart or any palpitation, but rather as if what I heard did not concern me. This very fact filled me with an infernal terror and fear of myself. I felt myself to be worse than a monster; I felt as if I did not exist, as if I were nothing more than a piece of ice, and as if this would be true forever. I went so far as to touch my skin, to pinch myself, to take my pulse. "Am I really alive? Am I myself?" I asked myself.

I do not wish to recall everything that happened that day. They took leave of me and started out on their honeymoon voyage. I sank myself in my books, in my studies, in my practice, for I was beginning to have one. The mental clarity which resulted from this irreparable blow, the discovery within myself that there is no soul, moved me to seek in study, not consolation—consolation I neither needed nor wanted—but instead the basis for an immense ambition. I must henceforth crush with the fame of my name the fame, already growing, of Abel. My scientific discoveries, a work of art in their own way, of true poetry, must put his paintings in the shade. Helena *must one day come to realize that it was I, the medical man, the antipathetic one, who could surround her with an aureole of glory, and not he, not this painter. I plunged headlong into my studies. I even went so far as to believe I might forget the newly-wedded pair! I wished to turn science into a narcotic, at the same time that I used it as a stimulant.*

## CHAPTER VI

A short while after the couple returned from their honeymoon, Abel fell gravely ill, and Joaquín was summoned to examine and attend him.

"I am very worried, Joaquín," Helena told him; "he was delirious all night; in his delirium he called for you constantly."

Joaquín examined his friend with every care and attention, and then, looking fixedly at his cousin, he told her:

"It's a serious matter, but I think I will be able to save him. It's I for whom there is no salvation."

"Yes, save him for me," she exclaimed. "And you know that . . ."

"Yes, I know!" And Joaquín took his leave.

Helena hurried to her husband's bedside, and laid her hand on her husband's forehead. He was burning with fever, and Helena began to tremble. "Joaquín, Joaquín," Abel called out in his delirium, "forgive us, forgive me!"

"Be quiet," Helena exclaimed, bending almost to his ear, "be quiet; he's come to see you and says he will cure you, that he will make you well. . . . He says you should be quiet. . . ."

"He'll cure me? . . ." the sick man repeated mechanically.

When Joaquín arrived at his house he, too, was feverish, with a kind of icy fever. "And if he should die? . . ." he thought to himself. He threw himself on the bed fully dressed, and began to imagine what would happen if Abel were to die: Helena's mourning, his own meetings and conversation with the widow, her remorse, her discovery of his true character and of his burning desire to revenge the wrong done him, of his violent need of her, of her falling into his arms at last in the realization that her other life, her treason, had been only a nightmare, the bad dream of a coquette; she would know that she had always loved him, Joaquín, and no other. "But he will not die," he told himself. "I will not let him die, I must not let him, my honor is at stake, and . . . I need to have him live! He must live!"

And as he said "he must live!" his soul trembled, just as the foliage of an oak trembles in the upheaval of a storm.

*They were atrocious days, those days of Abel's sickness*—Joaquín wrote in the *Confession—days of incredible torture. It was in my power to let him die without anyone suspecting, without leaving any tell-tale evidence behind. In the course of my practice I have known strange cases of mysterious death which later I have seen illuminated in the tragic light of subsequent events, as, by the remarriage of the widow, or like developments. I struggled then, as I had never struggled with myself before, against that foul dragon which has poisoned and darkened my life. My honor as a doctor was at stake, my honor as a man, and my mental well-being, my sanity itself was involved. I understood that I struggled in the clutches of madness; I saw the spectre of insanity and felt its shadow across my heart. But in the end, I conquered. I saved Abel from death. I never worked more fortunately, more accurately. My excess of unhappiness allowed me to be most happy and correct in my diagnosis.*

"Your . . . husband is completely out of danger," Joaquín reported to Helena one day.

"Thank you, Joaquín, thank you." She grasped him by the hand; and he permitted his hand to rest in her two hands. "You don't know how much we owe you. . . ."

"And you don't know how much I owe you both. . . ."

"For God's sake, don't act that way . . . , now that we owe you so much, let's not go back to that other again. . . ."

"No, I am not returning to anything else. I owe you a good deal. This illness of Abel's has taught me much, really a great deal. . . ."

"Ah, you look on it as one more case?"

"No, no, Helena; it's I who am the case!"

"But, I don't understand you."

"Nor do I, completely. And yet, I can tell you that in these days of fighting to save your husband. . . ."

"Say 'Abel,' call him by his name!"

"Very well; fighting for his life, then, I studied my own sickness along with his, and decided . . . to marry!"

"Ah! But do you have the girl?"

"No, not yet, but I will find her. I need a home. I will look for a wife. Or, do you think, Helena, that I will not find a woman to love me?"

"Of course you will find her, of course you will!"

"A woman who will love me, I mean."

"Yes, I understand, a woman who will love you, yes!"

"Because as far as a good match is concerned. . . ."

"Yes, there is no question but that you are a good match . . . young, not poor, a good career ahead of you, beginning to make a name, good and kind. . . ."

"Good . . . yes, and unappealing, isn't that so?"

"No, no, not at all; you're not lacking appeal."

"Oh, Helena, Helena, where shall I find another woman?"

". . . who will love you?"

"No, who will simply not deceive me, who will tell me the truth, who will not mock me, Helena, who will not mock me! . . . Who may marry me from desperation, perhaps, merely because I will support her, but who will tell me. . . ."

"You were quite right when you said you were ill, Joaquín. You should marry!"

"And do you think, Helena, that there is anyone, man or woman, who might love me?"

"There is no one who cannot find someone to love him."

"And will I love my wife? Will I be able to love her? Tell me."

"Why, nothing would be more likely. . . ."

"Because, really, Helena, the worst is not to be unloved, or to lack the faculty to be loved; the worst is not to be able to love."

"That's what Don Mateo, the parish priest, says about the devil, that he cannot love."

"And the devil is right here on earth, Helena."

"Be quiet; don't say such things."

"It's worse for me to say them to myself."

"Then be quiet altogether!"


## CHAPTER VII

For his own salvation, and in the need to assuage his passion, Joaquín devoted himself to searching for a woman, for the arms of a wife where he might take refuge from the hatred he felt, a lap where he might hide his head, like a child afraid of the dark, afraid to look at the hellish eyes of the ice-dragon.

Then, the poor unfortunate woman named Antonia!

Antonia had been born to be a mother; she was all tenderness and compassion. With superb instinct, she divined the invalid in Joaquín, a man sick of soul, possessed; and, without knowing why, she fell in love with his misfortune. The cold, curt words of the doctor who had no faith in the goodness of others exercised a mysterious attraction for her.

Antonia was the only daughter of a widow who was being treated by Joaquín. "Will my mother come through this crisis?" she asked Joaquín.

"It's a very difficult case, very difficult. The poor little woman is very tired, very run down; she must have suffered a good deal. . . . Her heart is very weak. . . ."

"Save her, Don Joaquín, save her! If I could, I would give my life for hers."

"That cannot be done. Besides, who knows? Your own life, Antonia, may be more needed than hers. . . ."

"My life? For what? For whom?"

"Who knows! . . ."

The death of the poor widow occurred inevitably.

"It could not have been otherwise, Antonia," Joaquín told her. "Science is powerless."

"Yes, God wished it so."

"God?"

"Ah!" exclaimed Antonia, her eyes fastening on the dry, steely-eyed face of Joaquín; "you don't believe in God?"

"I? . . . I don't know! . . ."

The sharp twinge of pity which the unfortunate orphan felt for the doctor momentarily made her forget the death of her mother.

"If I did not believe in Him, what would I do now?"

"Life finds answers for everything, Antonia."

"Death finds more! And now . . . so much alone . . . without anyone . . ."

"That's so, solitude can be terrible. But you have the memory of your holy mother, and a life to devote to commending her to God. . . . There is a solitude much more terrible!"

"What is it?"

"The solitude of a person whom all despise, whom everyone mocks. . . . The solitude of a person to whom no one will tell the truth."

"And what truth is it that you want to be told?"

"Would you tell me the truth, now, at this moment, over the still-warm body of your mother? Would you swear to tell me the truth?"

"Yes, I would tell you the truth."

"Good . . . I am an antipathetic person, isn't that so?"

"No; that is not so!"

"The truth, Antonia . . ."

"No; it isn't so."

"Well, then, what am I? . . ."

"You? You are an unfortunate, a man who suffers. . . ."

The ice in Joaquín began to melt and tears came to his eyes. Once again he trembled to the roots of his soul.

It was not very long afterwards that Joaquín and the recent orphan became engaged, planning to marry as soon as her year of mourning was over.

*My poor little wife*—Joaquín was to write years later in his *Confession*—*she struggled to love me and cure me, to overcome the repugnance that I must have aroused in her. She never told me this, she never even let it be understood. But, could I have failed to arouse repugnance in her especially when I revealed to her the leprosy of my soul, the gangrene of my hatred? She married me as she would have married a leper—I have no doubt of this at all—from motives of pity, a divine pity, and from a Christian spirit of abnegation and self-sacrifice, in order to save my soul, and thereby save her own. She married me out of the heroism of saintliness. And she was a saint! . . . But she did not cure me of Helena, and she did not cure me of Abel. Her saintliness was for me just one more source of remorse.*

*Her gentleness irritated me. There were times when—God forgive me!—I would have wished her wicked, hot-tempered, disdainful.*

## CHAPTER VIII

Meanwhile Abel's fame as an artist continued to spread. He had become one of the most renowned painters of the entire nation, and his name was making itself known across the border. And this growing fame affected Joaquín like the desolation of a hailstorm. "Yes, he is a very *scientific* painter; he is a master of technique; he knows a good deal, a good deal; he is exceedingly clever"; thus spoke Joaquín of his friend, in words that somehow hissed. It was a way of seeming to praise him, by denigrating him.

Because, in truth, it was Joaquín who presumed to be the artist;

a true poet in his profession, a diagnostician of genius, creative, intuitive; he even dreamed of abandoning his clientele in order to dedicate himself to pure science, to theoretical pathology, to research. But, then, he was earning so much! . . .

And yet, it was not profit—he wrote in his posthumous Confession—which most prevented me from devoting myself to scientific investigation. On the one hand, I was drawn to it by a desire to become renowned, to build a great scientific reputation which would overshadow Abel's artistic fame and thereby humiliate Helena, revenging myself on them both, and on everybody else as well—it was my wildest hope. On the other hand, this same murky passion, this extravagant grudge and hatred, deprived me of all serenity of soul. No, I did not have the will to study, the pure and tranquil spirit which was necessary. My practice distracted me, moreover.

My practice distracted me, and yet there were times when I trembled, thinking that my state of inner distraction prevented me from paying the strict attention required by the ills of my poor patients.

Then occurred a case which shook me to my foundations. I was attending a poor woman, who was rather dangerously, but still not desperately, ill. Abel had made a portrait of her; a magnificent portrait, one of his best, one of those which have remained as definitive among his works. And it was this painting which was this first thing that came into my sight—and into my hate—as soon as I entered the sick woman's home. In the portrait she was alive, more alive than in her bed of suffering flesh and bone. And the portrait seemed to say to me: Look, he has given me life forever! Let's see if you can prolong this other, earthly life of mine! At the bedside of the poor invalid, as I listened to her heart and took her pulse, I was obsessed by the other woman, the painted one. I was stupefied, completely stupefied, and as a result the poor woman died on me; or rather, I let her die, in my stupefaction, in my criminal distraction. I was convulsed with horror at myself, my miserable self.

A few days after the woman's death, I found it necessary to go to her house to visit still another sick member of the family, and I entered firmly resolved not to look at the portrait. But it was useless, for the portrait looked at me, regardless of whether or not I looked at it, and it drew my gaze perforce. As I took my leave, the recently bereaved husband accompanied me to the door. We paused at the foot of the portrait, and I, as if I had been impelled by some irresistible and fatal force, exclaimed:

"A *magnificent portrait! It is one of the greatest things Abel has done.*"

"*Yes,*" answered the widower, "*it is the greatest consolation left me now. I gaze at it for hours. It seems to speak to me.*"

"Oh yes, yes," I added, "*Abel is a stupendous artist!*"

As I went out, I said to myself: "*I let her die, and he resurrected her!*"

Joaquín suffered a great deal whenever one of his patients died, especially if they were children; the deaths of certain others, however, left him almost entirely unaffected. "Why should such a one want to live . . . ?" he would ask himself about someone. "I would actually be doing him a favor to let him die. . . ."

His powers of observation as a psychologist had grown sharper as his spirit languished, and he was quick to intuit the most hidden moral lacerations. He perceived, behind all the falsity of convention, how husbands foresaw the death of their wives without any sorrow whatever—when they did not consciously desire it—, and how wives longed to be free of their husbands, longed even to take other husbands already chosen beforehand. In the same year in which a patient named Alvarez died, his widow married Menéndez, the dead man's dear friend, and Joaquín said to himself: "That death was really quite strange. . . . Only now do I see it all clearly. . . . Humanity is absolutely vile! And that lady is a 'charitable' lady, one of the most 'honorable' ladies. . . ."

"Doctor," one of his patients said to him once, "for God's sake, will you kill me? Kill me without telling me anything, for I cannot go on. . . . Give me something which will make me sleep forever. . . ."

"And why should I not do what this man wants me to do," Joaquín asked himself, "if he lives only to suffer? It makes me grieve! What a filthy world!"

His patients were not infrequently mirrors for him.

One day a poor woman of the neighborhood came to see him; she was wasted by her years and work, and her husband, after 25 years of marriage, had formed a liaison with a miserable adventuress. The rejected woman had come to tell the doctor her troubles.

"Ay, Don Joaquín! Let us see if you, who are said to know so much, can give me a remedy to cure my poor husband of the philter which this loose woman has given him."

"But what philter, my good woman?"

"He is going to go and live with her; he is leaving me, after twenty-five years. . . ."

"It would have been even stranger if he had left you when you were a newly-married pair, while you were still young and even. . . ."

"Oh, no sir, no! The fact is that she has given him some kind of love potion which has turned his head. Otherwise, it just could not be . . . it could not be. . . ."

"A love potion," murmured Joaquín, "a love potion? . . ."

"Yes, Don Joaquín; yes, a love potion. . . . And you, who have so much knowledge, let me have some sort of remedy against it."

"Ah, my good woman, the ancients have already searched in vain to find a liquor which would rejuvenate. . . ."

And when the poor woman went away in desolation, Joaquín said to himself: "But doesn't this unfortunate woman look at herself in the mirror? Doesn't she see the ravages of years of hard work? These village people attribute everything to potions or jealousies. . . . For instance, they don't find work. . . . Jealousy is to blame. . . . Some scheme doesn't come out right. . . . Jealousy. The person who attributes all his disasters to the envy of others is in reality an envious person. Aren't we all? Haven't I perhaps been given a potion?"

During the next few days he was obsessed with the idea of a philter, a potion. At length he said to himself: "That is the original sin!"

## CHAPTER IX

Joaquín married Antonia in his search for shelter; the poor woman guessed at her mission from the first, the role she was to play in her husband's heart, as a shield and a source of consolation. She was taking a sick man for a husband, a man who was perhaps an incurable spiritual invalid; her duty would be that of a nurse. And she accepted her destiny with a heart full of compassion, full of love for the misfortune of the person who was joining his life with hers.

Antonia felt that between her and her Joaquín there was an invisible wall, a crystalline and transparent wall of ice. That man could not belong to his wife, for he did not belong to himself, he was not master of himself, but was, instead, both alienated and possessed. Even in the most intimate transports of conjugal relations, an invisible shadow of prophetic melancholy fell between them. Her

husband's kisses seemed to her stolen kisses, when they were not the
kisses of madness.

Joaquín avoided speaking of his cousin Helena in front of his
wife, and Antonia, who noticed this self-conscious avoidance at once,
did not fail to bring her into the conversation at every turn.

This was at the beginning, for a little later she avoided mentioning her any more.

One day Joaquín was called to Abel's house in his capacity of
doctor. There he learned that Helena was already bearing the fruit
of her marriage to Abel, while Antonia showed no signs of such
fruition. The unhappy doctor was assaulted by a shameful suggestion
which arose to humiliate him; some devil was taunting him. "Do
you only see? He is even more of a man than you are! He, who
through his art resurrects and immortalizes those you allow to die
because of your dullness, he is to have a child, he is to bring into
the world a new being, a work of his own, created in flesh, and blood,
and bone, while you . . . You probably are not even capable of . . .
He is more of a man than you!"

He arrived at the shelter of his own home downcast and brooding.

"Have you come from Abel's house?" his wife asked.

"Yes. How did you happen to know?"

"It's in your face. That house is your torment. You should not
go there. . . ."

"And what should I do?"

"Excuse yourself from going! Your health and peace of mind come
first . . ."

"These are only apprehensions of yours. . . ."

"No, Joaquín, don't try to conceal it from me . . ."—and she was
unable to continue, the tears drowning her voice.

The unfortunate Antonia sank to the ground. Her sobs seemed
torn from her body by the roots.

"What is the matter, woman, what is all this? . . ."

"Only tell me, Joaquín, what afflicts you. Confide in me, confess
yourself to me. . . ."

"I have nothing to accuse myself for . . ."

"Come, will you tell me the truth, Joaquín, the truth?"

For a moment, he hesitated, seeming to struggle with an invisible
enemy, with his Guardian Devil, and then, his voice animated with
a sudden, desperate resolution, he almost cried out:

"Yes, I will tell you the truth, the entire truth!"

"You love Helena. You're still in love with Helena."

"No, I am not! I am not! I was, but I am no longer."

"Well then? . . ."

"Then what?"

"What is this torture in which you live? Why is that house, Helena's house, the source of your misery? That house does not let you live in peace. It's Helena. . . ."

"Helena, no! It's Abel!"

"Are you jealous of Abel?"

"Yes, I am jealous of him! I hate him, I hate him, I hate him"—and Joaquín made his hands into fists as he spoke through clenched teeth.

"If you are jealous of Abel . . . then you must love Helena."

"No, I don't love her. If she belonged to someone else, I should not be jealous of that person. No, I don't love Helena. I despise her, I despise that peacock of a woman, that professional beauty, the fashionable painter's model, Abel's mistress. . . ."

"For God's sake, Joaquín, for God's sake! . . ."

"Yes, his mistress . . . his legitimized mistress. Do you think that the benediction of a priest changes an affair into a marriage?"

"Listen, Joaquín, we're married just as they are. . . ."

"As they are, not at all, Antonia, not at all! They got married only to demean me, to humiliate and denigrate me; they married to mock me; they married to hurt me."

The poor man burst into sobs which choked him, cutting off his breathing. He seemed to die.

"Antonia . . . , Antonia . . ." he whispered in a little smothered voice.

"My poor child!" she exclaimed, embracing him.

She reached up and took his head in her lap as if he were a sick child, caressing him while she said:

"Calm yourself, my Joaquín, calm yourself . . . I am here, your wife is here, all yours and only yours. And now that I know all our secrets, I am yours more than before and I love you more than ever. . . . Forget them . . . scorn them. . . . It would have been all the worse if such a woman had loved you."

"Yes, but it's he, Antonia, it's he. . . ."

"Forget him!"

"I cannot forget him. . . . He pursues me. . . . His fame, his renown follow me everywhere. . . ."

"If you work, you will have fame and renown, for you are not any less than he. Leave your practice, we don't need it. We can go to

Renada, to the house which belonged to my parents, and there you can devote yourself to what you like best, to science, to making discoveries of the sort that will earn you notice. . . . I will help you in every way I can. . . . I will see that you are not distracted . . . , and you will be more than he. . . ."

"I can not, Antonia, I can not. His successes take away my sleep and would not allow me to work in peace. . . . The vision of his awesome paintings would come between my eye and the microscope and would prevent my seeing anything others have not seen. . . . I can not. . . . I can not. . . ."

Then, lowering his voice like a child, stammering almost, as if stunned by his fall into the abyss of humiliation, he sobbed:

"And they are going to have a child, Antonia. . . ."

"We will have one also," she whispered in his ear, covering it with a kiss; "the Holy Virgin will not deny me, for I ask her every day. . . . Or the holy water of Lourdes . . ."

"Do you, too, believe in potions, Antonia?"

"I believe in God!"

" 'I believe in God,' " Joaquín repeated when he was alone—alone with the other presence, with his obsession. "What does it mean, to believe in God? Where is God? I shall have to find Him!"

## CHAPTER X

When Abel had his child—Joaquín wrote in his Confession—I felt hate fester in me. He had invited me to attend Helena in her labor, but I had excused myself by saying that I did not attend deliveries, which was true, and that I would not be able to maintain my sangfroid, the necessary cold-bloodedness—benumbed-bloodedness, I should have said—where my cousin was concerned, should she fall into danger. And yet, my own devil suggested the ferocious temptation: attend her and smother the child surreptitiously. I was able to overcome myself and suppress this revolting thought.

This new triumph of Abel's, of Abel the man and not the artist only—for the child was a beauty, a masterpiece of health and vigor, a little angel, as everyone said—bound me all the more to Antonia, from whom I was expecting a child of my own. I longed to make of my wife, I needed to make of this poor victim of my blind rage—the real victim even more than I was myself—I needed to make of *her, to make her be, the mother of my children, flesh of my flesh, heart of my heart, entrails of my entrails which were tortured by the devil. She would be the mother of my children and for that reason superior to the mothers of the children of others. She, unhappy woman, had chosen me, the antipathetic, the despised, the affronted one; she had taken up what another woman had refused with disdain and scorn. And she even spoke well of them to me!*

*Abel's child, little Abelin—for they gave it the same name as the father, as if to continue his lineage and fame—the young Abel, who would with the passage of time be the instrument of my revenge, was a marvel of a child. I needed to have one like him, but even more beautiful.*

## CHAPTER XI

"What are you working on these days?" Joaquín asked Abel one day. The doctor had come to Abel's house to see the child, and had afterwards gone on to visit the painter in his study.

"Well, next I shall paint a historical piece, actually a scene from the Old Testament; at the moment, I am doing research for it. . . ."

"How is that? Looking for models from that epoch?"

"No; reading the Bible and commentaries on it."

"I am well advised when I say that you are a scientific painter. . . ."

"And you, an artistic doctor, isn't that so?"

"Worse than a scientific artist, you're a literary one! Beware of making literature with your brush!"

"Thanks for the advice."

"And what will the subject of your painting be?"

"The death of Abel at the hands of Cain, the first fratricide."

Joaquín turned whiter than ever; gazing fixedly at his first friend he asked in a half-suppressed voice:

"How did you happen to think of that?"

"Very simply," Abel answered without perceiving his friend's meaning; "it was the suggestiveness of the name. Since my name is Abel. . . . I had made two nude studies. . . ."

"Nude of body. . . ."

"Even of soul. . . ."

"You mean to paint their souls?"

"Of course! The soul of Cain, the soul of envy. And the soul of Abel. . . ."

"What is he the soul of?"

"I wish I knew. I'm trying to find out, but I can't put my finger on the right expression. I want to paint him before his death, thrown to the ground and fatally wounded by his brother. I've got *Genesis* here, and I'm reading Lord Byron's *Cain;* do you know the book?"

"Byron's *Cain* I don't know. What have you gotten from the Bible?"

"Very little. . . . You'll see," and, taking up the book, he read: "'And Adam knew Eve his wife: who conceived and brought forth Cain, saying: I have gotten a man through God. And again she brought forth his brother Abel. And Abel was a shepherd, and Cain a husbandman. And it came to pass after many days, that Cain offered, of the fruits of the earth, gifts to the Lord. Abel also offered of the firstlings of his flock, and of their fat: and the Lord had respect to Abel, and to his offerings. But to Cain and his offerings he had no respect. . . .'"

"And why was that?" interrupted Joaquín. "Why did God look with respect on the offering of Abel and look with disfavor on Cain and his offering? . . ."

"It isn't explained here. . . ."

"And haven't you asked yourself the question before setting out to paint your picture?"

"Not yet. . . . Perhaps because God already saw in Cain the future killer of his brother, the invidious. . . ."

"If he was invidious it was because God had made him invidious, and had given him a philter. Go on with the reading."

"'And Cain was exceedingly angry, and his countenance fell. And the Lord said to him: Why art thou angry? And why is thy countenance fallen? If thou do well, shalt thou not receive? But if ill, shall not sin forthwith be present at the door? But the lust thereof shall be under thee, and thou shalt have dominion over it. . . .'"

"Instead, sin dominated him," interrupted Joaquín again, "because God had abandoned him. Go on."

"'And Cain said to Abel his brother: Let us go forth abroad. And when they were in the field, Cain rose up against his brother Abel, and slew him. And the Lord said to Cain. . . .'"

"That's enough! Don't read any more. I'm not interested in what Jehovah told Cain after there was no help for the matter."

Joaquín rested his elbows on the table, his face between the palms of his hands. He fixed a sharp, frozen stare on Abel, who became alarmed at he knew not what. And then Joaquín said:

"Have you never heard of the joke they play on children who learn Sacred History?"

"No."

"Well, they ask them, 'Who killed Cain?'; and the children, completely confused, answer: 'His brother Abel.' "

"I never heard that."

"You have heard it now. And tell me, since you are going to paint this Biblical scene—and how like the Bible it is!—hasn't it occurred to you that if Cain had not killed Abel, it would have been Abel who would have ended by killing Cain?"

"How can you think of such a thing?"

"Abel's sheep were acceptable to God, and Abel the shepherd found grace in the eyes of the Lord, but neither the fruits of the earth offered up by Cain, the husbandman, nor Cain himself found favor with God. His favorite was Abel. The God-forsaken was Cain. . . ."

"And what fault was that of Abel's?"

"Ah, you think, do you, that the fortunate, the favored, are not to blame? The truth is that they are to blame for not concealing—and not concealing it as a shameful thing, which it is—every gratuitous favor, every privilege not earned on proper merit; for not concealing this grace instead of making an ostentatious show of it. For I have no doubt but that Abel flaunted his favor under the snouts of Cain's beasts, or that he taunted him with the smoke of the sheep he offered to God. Those who believe themselves to be of the company of the just tend to be supremely arrogant people bent on crushing others under the ostentation of their 'justice.' As some-one once said, there is no worse canaille than 'honorable' peo-ple. . . ."

"And are you sure," asked the painter, who had become apprehen-sive over the serious aspect the conversation had assumed, "are you sure that Abel boasted of his good fortune?"

"I have no doubt of it, or of the fact that he showed no respect for his elder brother; I do not suppose, either, that he asked the Lord to show his elder brother some favor too. And I know some-thing else; and that is that Abel's successors, the Abelites, have invented Hell as a place for the Cainites, because, if there were no such place, the Abelites would find all their glory insipid. Their pleasure is to see others suffer while they themselves stay free of suffering."

"Joaquín, Joaquín, how very sick you are!"

"You're right. And no one can doctor themselves. . . . Let me have this Cain of Lord Byron's, I want to read it."

"Take it."

"And tell me, doesn't your wife supply you with any inspiration for this painting? Doesn't she provide you with any ideas?"

"My wife? . . . There was no woman in this tragedy."

"There is in every tragedy, Abel."

"Perhaps Eve. . . ."

"Perhaps. . . . Perhaps the woman who gave them both the same milk; or potion. . . ."

## CHAPTER XII

Joaquín read Lord Byron's Cain. And later he wrote in his Confession:

The effect made upon me by reading that book was dreadful. I felt the need to give vent to my feelings, and so I took some notes, which I still have and which are now here before me. And I wonder now if I took them down merely to unburden myself? No, I undoubtedly thought to make use of them some day in writing a great book. Vanity consumes us. We make a spectacle of our most intimate and vile disabilities. I can imagine the existence of a man who would want to have a pestiferous tumor such as no one has ever had before, solely in order to vaunt it about, and to call attention to the struggle he was waging against it. This very Confession, for instance, isn't it something more than a mere unburdening of soul?

I have sometimes thought of tearing it up, so as to free myself from it. But would that free me? No! It is better to make a spectacle than to consume oneself. After all is said and done, life itself is no more than a spectacle.

The reading of Byron's Cain penetrated me to the core. How right Cain was to blame his parents for having taken the fruits of the tree of science instead of those of the tree of life! For me, at any rate, science has not done more than exacerbate the wound.

Would that I had never lived! I say with Cain. Why was I

created? Why must I live? What I do not understand is why Cain did not choose suicide. That would have been the most noble beginning for the human race. But then, why didn't Adam and Eve kill themselves after the fall and before they gave birth to children? Ah, perhaps because Jehovah would have created other such beings as they, another Cain and another Abel? Isn't this same tragedy perhaps repeated in other worlds, up there among the stars?

Perhaps the tragedy has been performed elsewhere, the first-night performance on earth not having quite sufficed. Was it opening night, after all?

When I read how Lucifer declared to Cain that he, Cain, was immortal, at that moment I began to wonder fearfully if I, too, and my hatred with me, were immortal. Must I have a soul; I asked myself, is my hatred the soul? And I came to think finally that it could not be otherwise, that such a hatred could not be the property of the body. That which I could not find in others with a scalpel I now found in myself. A corruptible organism could not hate as I did. Lucifer had aspired to be God, and I, ever since I was very young, had I not aspired to reduce everyone else to nothing? But how could I have been so unfortunate, unless I was made that way by the creator of all misfortune?

It required no effort for Abel to take care of his sheep, just as it required no effort for the other Abel to paint his pictures; for me, on the contrary, a very great effort was needed to diagnose the ills of my patients.

Cain complained that Adah, his own beloved Adah, his wife and his sister, did not understand the mind which overwhelmed him. But my Adah, my poor Adah understood my mind well enough. In all truth, she was a Christian. But then, I did not, in the end, find any sympathy either.

Until I read and re-read the Byronic Cain, I, who had seen so many men die, had not thought of death, had not discovered it. I began to wonder if I would die with my hate, if my hate would die with me, or outlast me; I wondered if hate outlived the haters, if it were something material, transmissable; I speculated as to whether hatred were not the soul, the quintessence of the soul. And I began to believe in Hell, and in Death as a being, as the Devil, as hatred made flesh, as the God of the soul. Everything that science did not explain, the terrible poem of that great hater Lord Byron made clear to me.

My Adah, too, would taunt me gently when I did not work, when

*I could not work. And Lucifer stood between my Adah and myself.
Walk not with this spirit!* my Adah cried. *Poor Antonia! And she
begged me to save her too from the spirit. My poor Adah did not
go so far as to hate these influences as much as I did. But then, did
I go so far as truly to love my Antonia? Ah, if only I had been
capable of loving her I would have been saved. She was for me
another instrument of my vengeance. I wanted her as the mother of
a son or a daughter who would revenge me. Although I did think,
quite naïvely, that once I became a father, I would be cured of all
this. Still, hadn't I gotten married simply to produce hateful beings
like myself, to transmit my hatred, to immortalize it?*

*The scene between Cain and Lucifer in the Abyss of Space
remained engraved in my soul as if it had been burned in. I saw my
science in the light of my sin and the wretchedness of giving life in
order to propagate death. And I saw clearly that this immortal
hatred constituted my soul. This hatred, I thought, must have
preceded my birth and would survive after my death. I was shaken
with horror to think of living always so as to abhor always. This was
Hell. And I had so scoffed at belief in it! It was a literal Hell!*

*When I read how Adah spoke to Cain of his son, of Enoch, I
thought of the son, or the daughter I would surely have; I thought
of you, my daughter, my redemption and my consolation; I thought
of how you would come one day to save me. And as I read of what
Cain said to his own sleeping, innocent son, who knew not that he
was naked, I wondered if it had not been a crime in me to have
engendered you, my poor daughter! Do you forgive me for having
created you? As I read what Adah said to her Cain, I remembered
my own years in paradise, when I was not yet on the hunt for
rewards, when I did not dream of surpassing all the others. No, my
daughter, no; I did not offer up my studies to God with a pure heart;
I did not seek truth and knowledge, but instead sought prizes, and
fame, and the chance to be more than he was.*

*He, Abel, loved his art and cultivated it with a purity of purpose,
and never strove to impose on me. No, it was not he who took away
my peace. And yet I had gone so far, demented as I was, as to think
of overturning Abel's altar! The truth was I had thought only of
myself.*

*The narrative of Abel's death as it is given us by that terrible poet
of the Devil blinded me. As I read I felt everything grow dark, and
I think I suffered a fainting spell, and a kind of nausea. And from
that day on, thanks to the impious Byron, I began to believe.*

## CHAPTER XIII

Antonia presented Joaquín with a daughter. "A daughter," he told himself; "and *he* has a son!" But he soon recovered from this new trick of his demon. And he began to love his daughter with all the force of his passion, and, through her, her mother as well. "She shall be my avenger," he said to himself at first, without knowing what it was she was to avenge him for; but later: "She shall be my salvation, my purification."

*I began to keep this record,* he wrote in the *Confession, a little later, for my daughter's sake, so that once I was dead, she might know her poor father, and feel for him, and love him. As I watched her sleeping in her cradle, innocently dreaming, I thought how in order to bring her up and educate her in purity I should have to purify myself of my passion, cleanse myself of the leprosy of my soul. And I decided to make certain she should love, love everyone, and love them in particular. There, upon the innocence of her dreams, I swore to free myself from my infernal chains. I vowed to be the chief herald of Abel's greatness.*

Abel Sanchez completed his historical canvas and entered it in a large exhibition. There it received widespread acclaim and was hailed as a true masterpiece; inevitably, he was awarded the medal of honor.

Joaquín went often to the exhibition hall to view the painting and to look into it, as into a looking-glass, at the painted Cain, and to watch then the eyes of the people, to see if they looked at him after looking at the other figure.

*I was tortured by the suspicion,* he wrote in the *Confession, that Abel had thought of me when he was painting his Cain, that he had sounded all the depths in the conversation we had held at his house at the time he first told me of his intention to paint his subject and when he had read the passages from Genesis—when I had so completely forgotten him and so completely bared my sickened soul as I thought only of myself. But no, there was not in Abel's Cain the least resemblance to me; he had not thought of me in the painting; he had not attempted to attack me, to denigrate me, nor had Helena apparently influenced him against me. It sufficed them to savor the future triumph, the triumph they were anticipating. They did not even think of me now!*

*And this idea that they did not even think of me, did not even hate me, tortured mé more than the other idea had. To be hated by* him, *with a hatred such as mine for him, would have been something after all, and could have been my salvation.*

And so Joaquín surpassed himself, or simply plumbed himself deeper, and conceived the idea of giving a banquet to celebrate Abel's triumph. He, Joaquín, Abel's everlasting friend, his "friend from before they knew each other," would arrange a banquet for the painter.

Joaquín had a certain fame as an orator. At the Academy of Medicine and Sciences it was he who overawed the others with his cold and cutting manner of address, usually over-precise and sarcastic. His speeches had the effect of a stream of cold water poured upon the enthusiasms of the newcomers; they were dour lessons in pessimistic skepticism. His usual thesis was that nothing was known for certain in medicine, that everything was hypothetical and a constant raveling and unraveling, that distrust was the most justified emotion. For these reasons, when it became known that it was Joaquín who was giving the banquet, most people joyously made ready for an inevitably double-edged address, a pitiless dissection—in the guise of a panegyric—on the subject of scientific, documentary painting; at best, it would be a sarcastic encomium. A malevolent anticipation titillated the hearts of all those who had ever heard Joaquín speak of Abel's painting. And they warned the latter of his peril.

"You are mistaken," Abel told them. "I know Joaquín and do not believe him capable of such a thing. I know something of what is going on within him, but he is possessed of a profound artistic sense, and whatever he says will probably be well worth hearing. I should like next to paint a portrait of him."

"A portrait?"

"Yes, you don't know him as I do. His is a fiery, turbulent soul."

"A colder man. . . ."

"On the outside. In any case, fire burns, as they say. For my purposes, he couldn't be better, a face made on purpose. . . ."

This opinion of Abel's reached the ears of his subject, who once more sank into the sea of speculation. "What must he really think of me?" he asked himself. "Does he really think me to be a 'fiery, turbulent soul'? Or does he in reality see that I am a victim of a whim of fate?"

At this time he went so far as to do something for which he was later deeply ashamed. It happened that a maid entered his service who had formerly served in Abel's house, and he made overtures to her, confidentially importuning her—without compromising himself —for the sole purpose of ascertaining what she might have heard about him in the other house.

"Come now, is it possible you never heard them speak of me?"

"They said nothing, sir, absolutely nothing."

"Didn't they ever speak of me?"

"Well, talk they did, just talk; but they said nothing."

"Nothing, never anything?"

"I didn't hear them speak very much. At table, while I served them, they spoke very little, and only of those small things usually spoken of at the table. About his paintings. . . ."

"I understand. But nothing, never anything about me?"

"I don't remember anything."

As he left the maid he was seized with a profound self-aversion. "I'm making an idiot of myself," he said to himself. "What must this girl think of me!" He was so humiliated by his action that he contrived the girl's dismissal on some small pretext. "But suppose she goes back now into Abel's service," he asked himself then, "and tells him all this?" So that he was on the point of asking his wife to summon her back. But he dared not. And thereafter he shuddered at the thought of meeting her in the street.

## CHAPTER XIV

The day of the banquet arrived. Joaquín had not slept on the night before.

"I am going to the battle, Antonia," he told his wife as he left the house.

"May God light your way and guide you, Joaquín."

"I should like to see the little girl, our poor little Joaquinita. . . ."

"Yes, come and see her . . . she's sleeping. . . ."

"Poor little thing! She doesn't yet know the Devil exists! But I swear to you, Antonia, I shall learn to tear him from me. I will tear him out, I will strangle him, and I will throw him at the feet of Abel. . . . I would give her a kiss if I weren't afraid of waking her. . . ."

"No, no! Kiss her."

The father bent over and kissed the sleeping child, who smiled in her dreams as she felt herself kissed.

"You see, Joaquín, she blesses you too."

"Goodbye, my wife!" And he kissed her, with a very long kiss.

Antonia was left behind to pray before the statue of the Virgin Mary.

A malicious undercurrent of expectation ran through the conversation at the banquet table. Joaquín, seated on Abel's right, was very pale; he scarcely ate or spoke. Abel himself began to feel some trepidation.

As the dessert was served, some of the diners began to hiss as a call for silence, and a hush fell, in which someone said: "Let him speak." Joaquín stood up. He began to talk in a muffled, trembling voice; but soon it cleared and began to vibrate with a new accent. His voice filled the silence, and nothing else was to be heard. The surprise was general. A more ardent, more impassioned eulogy had scarcely ever been heard, or one more filled with admiration and affection for both the artist and his work. Many felt tears springing to their eyes as Joaquín evoked the days of his common infancy with Abel, when neither of them yet dreamed of what they would one day become.

"No one has known him more intimately than I," he said; "I believe I know you," addressing Abel, "better than I know myself, with more purity, because looking into one's own heart one tends to see only the dust from which one has been created. It is in others that we see the best part of ourselves, a part which we can love; and thus, our admiration. He has accomplished in his art what I should like to have accomplished in mine; for this reason, he is one of my models; his glory is a spur to my work and is a consolation for the glory which I have not been able to gain. He belongs to us all; above all he is mine, and I, enriched by his work, try to make this work as much mine as he made it his by the act of creation. Thus am I able to be a satisfied subject of my mediocrity. . . ."

From time to time his voice cried out. His audience was under his spell, obscurely aware of the titanic battle between this soul and its demon.

"And behold the face of Cain"—Joaquín let the fiery words form like single drops—"the tragic Cain, the roving husbandman, the first to found cities, the father of industry, envy and community life. Behold his face! See with what affection, with what compassion, with what love the unfortunate is painted. Wretched Cain! Our Abel

Sanchez *admires* Cain just as Milton admired Satan, he is enamored of his Cain just as Milton was of his Satan, for to admire is to love and to love is to pity. Our Abel has sensed all the misery, all the unmerited misfortune of the one who killed the first Abel, and who, according to Biblical legend, brought death into the world. Our Abel makes us understand Cain's guilt, for guilt there was, and he makes us pity him and love him. . . . This painting is an act of love!"

When Joaquín finished speaking, there was a heavy silence, until a salvo of applause thundered out. Abel stood up then; pale, shaking, hesitatingly, with tears in his eyes, he addressed his friend:

"What you have said, Joaquín, is worth more, has greater value, much greater, than my painting, than all the paintings I have made, than those that I shall ever make. . . . Your words are a work of art, and of the heart. I did not know what I had accomplished until I heard you. You, and not I, have made my painting, you alone!"

The two eternal friends embraced amid their own tears and the clamorous applause and cheers of the assemblage, which had risen to its feet.

In the middle of the embrace his demon whispered to Joaquín: "If you could only crush him in your arms! . . ."

"Stupendous," they were saying. "What an orator! What a great speech! Who would have thought . . . ? It's a shame that there were no reporters present!"

"Prodigious!" said one man, "I don't expect to hear another such speech again."

"Chills ran through me as I listened," said another.

"Just see how pale he is!"

Such was the case, in truth. Joaquín, as he resumed his seat following his success, felt overcome, overborne by a wave of sadness. No, his demon was not yet dead. His address had been a success the like of which he had never before enjoyed, nor would likely enjoy again, and now the idea came to him of devoting himself to speaking as a means of gaining a fame which would obscure the fame of his friend in painting.

"Did you see how Abel wept?" one man asked as he came out.

"The truth is that this address by Joaquín is worth all the paintings of the other. The speech made the painting. It will be necessary to call it The Painting of the Speech. Take away the speech, and what's left of the painting! Nothing, despite the first prize."

When Joaquín arrived home, Antonia came out to open the door and to embrace him:

"I already know, they've already told me. Yes, yes! You're better than he, much better. He must know that if his painting is to have value it will be because of your speech."

"It's true, Antonia, it's true, but . . ."

"But what? Do you still . . ."

"Still! I don't wish to tell you the things my demon whispered while Abel and I embraced. . . ."

"No, don't tell me!"

She closed his mouth with a long, warm, humid kiss, as her eyes grew moist with tears.

"Let's see if you can draw the demon out of me this way, Antonia; let's see if you can suck him out."

"Should I absorb him then, so that he stays in me?" the poor woman asked, trying to laugh.

"Yes, draw him in, for he can't harm you; in you he will die, he will drown in your blood as in holy water. . . ."

At his home, Abel found himself alone with Helena. She said:

"I've been told all about Joaquín's oration. He's had to swallow your triumph . . . he's had to swallow it! . . ."

"Don't talk that way; you didn't hear him."

"It's just as if I had."

"His words came from the heart. I was deeply moved. I must tell you that even I did not know what I had painted until I heard his exposition."

"Don't trust him . . . don't trust him . . . when he eulogizes you like that, it must be for some reason. . . ."

"Might he not have said what he felt?"

"You know he is dying with envy of you. . . ."

"Be quiet!"

"Dying, yes, almost dead, with envy of you. . . ."

"Be quiet, woman, be quiet!"

"No; and it's not jealousy, for he no longer loves me, if he ever did . . . it's envy . . . envy. . . ."

"Be quiet!" roared Abel.

"All right, I'll be quiet, but you shall see. . . ."

"I've already seen and heard, and that's enough. Be quiet, now!"

## CHAPTER XV

And yet, that heroic act did not restore poor Joaquín.

*I began to feel remorse,* he wrote in his *Confession, of having said what I had, of not having let my evil passion pour forth and thus gotten free of it, of not having broken with him artistically, denouncing the falsity and affectation of his art, his imitation, his cold, calculated technique, his lack of emotion. I was sorry for not having destroyed his fame. By so doing I would have freed myself, told the truth, and reduced his prestige to its true scale. Who knows but that Cain, the Biblical Cain, who killed the other Abel, began to love his victim as soon as he saw him dead. And it was at this juncture that I began really to believe: among the effects of that address were the elements of my conversion.*

The conversion alluded to by Joaquín in his *Confession* proceeded from the fact that his wife Antonia, seeing her husband was not cured,—fearing that he was perhaps incurable,—induced him to seek help in prayer, and in the religion of his fathers, the religion which was hers, the religion which would be their daughter's.

"You should first go to Confession."

"But I haven't been to church for years."

"All the same. . . ."

"But I don't believe in these things. . . ."

"You believe you don't. But the priest has explained to me how it is that you men of science believe you don't believe, and all the same believe. I know that the things your mother taught you, the things I shall teach our daughter . . ."

"All right, all right, leave me alone!"

"No, I will not. Go and confess yourself, I beg you."

"And what will the people who know my ideas say?"

"Oh, is that it? Is it out of social considerations. . . ."

However, Joaquín's heart was touched, and he asked himself if he really did not believe; moreover, he wanted to see if the Church could cure him, even if he did not believe. And he began to frequent the services, almost too conspicuously, as if by way of challenge to those who knew his irreligious convictions; finally, he sought out a confessor. And, once in the confessional, his soul was loosed.

"I hate him, Father, I hate him with all my heart, and if I did not believe as I do, or as I want to believe, I would kill him. . . ."

"But that, my son, that is not necessarily hatred. It is more like envy."

"All hatred is envy, Father, all hatred is envy."

"You should change it into noble emulation, into a desire to succeed in your profession, and in the service of God, to do the best you can accomplish. . . ."

"I cannot, I cannot, I cannot work. His fame and glory do not allow me."

"You must make an effort . . . it is for this purpose that man is free. . . ."

"I do not believe in free will, Father. I am a doctor."

"Still. . . ."

"What did I do that God should make me this way, rancorous, envious, evil? What bad blood did my father bequeath me?"

"My son . . . my son. . . ."

"No, I do not believe in human liberty, and whoever can not believe in liberty is surely not free. And I am not! To be free is to believe oneself free!"

"It is evil of one to doubt God."

"Is it evil to doubt, Father?"

"I don't mean to say that, but simply that your evil passion comes from your doubting God. . . ."

"Is it evil, then, to doubt God? I ask you again."

"Yes, it is evil."

"Then I doubt God because he made me evil. Just as he made Cain evil, God made me doubt. . . ."

"He made you free."

"Yes, free to be evil."

"And to be good!"

"Ah, why was I born, Father?"

"Ask rather to what end. . . ."

## CHAPTER XVI

Abel had painted a Virgin with the Child in arms: the painting was in actuality a portrait of Helena, and the child, Abelito. It had been well received, was reproduced and, before a splendid photograph of it, Joaquín prayed the most holy Virgin, asking her to protect and save him.

But while he prayed, susurrating in a low voice, as if to hear himself, he fought to stifle another voice more profound, which welled from deep within him saying: "If he would only die! If he would only leave her free for you!"

"So," Abel hailed him one day, "you have become a reactionary."

"I have?"

"Yes, they tell me you have given yourself up to the church and go to Mass every day. Since you never did believe either in God or the Devil,—and it can scarcely be a matter of having made a conversion just like that—well, then, you must have turned reactionary!"

"What does it all matter to you?"

"I'm not calling you to account, you understand. But, well now . . . do you really believe?"

"I need to believe."

"That's something else again. I mean do you really believe?"

"As I've already told you, I need to believe. Don't ask me again."

"For my part, art is enough. Art is my religion."

"Still, you have painted Virgins. . . ."

"Yes, Helena."

"Who is not precisely a virgin. . . ."

"For me, it's as if she were. She is the mother of my child. . . ."

"Only that?"

"And every mother is a virgin by virtue of being a mother."

"You're entering the realms of theology!"

"I don't know about that, but I hate stupid conservatism and prudery, which is something born merely of envy, it seems to me, and it surprises me to find signs of it in you. I had faith in your being able to withstand the mediocrity of the vulgar, and I am surprised to see you wearing their uniform."

"What do you mean, Abel? Come, explain yourself."

"It's clear enough. Common, vulgar spirits are never distinguished, and, unable to bear the fact that others are, they attempt to impose upon others more fortunate the uniform of dogma—which is a kind of dull fatigue uniform—so that the uncommon may appear undistinguished. The origin of all orthodoxy, in religion as in art, is envy, have no doubt of it. If we were all to dress as we pleased, there would be one among us who would think up some striking mode of dress which would accentuate his natural elegance; if it were a man who did this, women would naturally be attracted to him; and yet if a vulgar, common individual were to do the same thing, he would merely look ridiculous. It is for this reason that the vulgar, that is to say, the envious, have invented a kind of uniform, a manner of dressing themselves like puppets, which comes to be the fashion—for fashion, too, is another matter of orthodoxy. Don't deceive yourself, Joaquín, those ideas which are called dangerous, daring, impious, are merely those that never suggest themselves to the poor routine intelligences, the people who don't have even a grain of personal initiative or originality, but do have 'common sense'—and vulgarity. Imagination is what they most hate,—especially since the fact is that they don't have any."

"Even though this is the case," Joaquín exclaimed, "don't those we call the vulgar, the common, the mediocre have the right to defend themselves?"

"On another occasion, at my house, you remember, you defended Cain, the envious; then, later, in that unforgettable speech which I shall repeat till I die, in that speech—to which I owe a good deal of my reputation—you showed us, at least you showed me, Cain's soul. But Cain was scarcely a mediocrity, a vulgarian, a common man. . . ."

"But he was the father of all the envious."

"Yes, but of another kind of envy, not the envy of the bigots. . . . Cain's envy was something grandiose; the envy of the fanatical inquisitor is picayune and miserably small. And it shocks me to see you on the side of the inquisitors."

"Can this man read my thoughts, then?" Joaquín asked himself as he took leave of Abel. "He doesn't seem to notice what I suffer, and still. . . . He talks and thinks in the same way he paints, without knowing what he says or paints. He works unconsciously, no matter how much I try to see in him the thoughtful technician. . . ."

## CHAPTER XVII

Joaquín became aware that Abel was involved with one of his former models; this information corroborated his suspicion that Abel had not married Helena from motives of love. "They married," Joaquín told himself, "to humiliate me." And he added: "And Helena doesn't love him, nor is she capable of loving him . . . she doesn't love anyone, she's incapable of affection; she's no more than a beautiful shell of vanity. . . . She married from vanity and disdain for me, and from vanity or caprice she is capable of betraying her husband

. . . even with the man she didn't want as husband." A spark glowed among the embers of recollections, a live coal which he had thought extinguished under his ice-cold hatred: it was his old love for Helena. Yes, in spite of everything he was still enamored of this female peacock, this coquette, this artist's model to her husband. Antonia was very much superior to her, without any doubt, but the other was the other. Then, there was revenge . . . and revenge was so sweet! So warming to a frozen heart!

In a few days he went to Abel's house, carefully choosing an hour when Abel himself would be out. He found his cousin Helena alone with her child, Helena before whose image made divine he had vainly sought protection and salvation.

"Abel has told me," Helena said to him now, "that you've taken up going to church. Is it because Antonia has dragged you there, or do you go there to escape Antonia?"

"What do you mean?"

"You husbands tend to become holy men either while tracking down a wife, or escaping her. . . ."

"There are those who escape their wives, but not precisely to go to church."

"Oh?"

"Yes. But your husband, who has borne this tale to you, doesn't seem to know something else, which is that the church is not the only place where I pray. . . ."

"Naturally not! Every devout man should say prayers at home."

"And I do. And my chief prayer is to the Virgin, to ask her for protection and salvation."

"That strikes me as very sensible."

"And do you know before whose image I ask this?"

"Not unless you are to tell me. . . ."

"Before the painting made by your husband. . . ."

Helena turned away abruptly, her face deeply flushed, toward the child sleeping in a corner of the parlor. The suddenness of the attack had disconcerted her. Composing herself, however, she said:

"This is an act of impiety on your part, Joaquín, and proves that your new devotion is no more than a farce, and perhaps something worse. . . ."

"I swear to you, Helena. . . ."

"The second commandment,—don't take His holy name in vain."

"Therefore I truly swear to you, Helena, that my conversion was sincere; I mean that I have wanted to believe, I have wanted to defend myself with faith against a passion that devours me. . . ."

"Yes, I know your passion. . . ."

"No, you don't know it!"

"*I know it*. It is that you cannot endure Abel's existence."

"Why can't I endure him?"

"That is something only you may know. You have never been able to endure him, not even before you introduced him to me."

"That's untrue, utterly untrue!"

"It's the truth! The utter truth!"

"Why should I not be able to endure him?"

"Because he is becoming well known, because he has a reputation. . . . Don't you have a good practice? Don't you make a good living?"

"Listen, Helena, I am going to tell you the truth, all of it! I am not satisfied with what I have. I wanted to become famous, to find something new in science, to link my name to some scientific discovery. . . ."

"Well, then, apply yourself to it, for it's not talent you lack."

"Apply myself . . . apply myself. . . . Yes, I could have applied myself, Helena, if I had been able to offer up the triumph at your feet. . . ."

"And why not at Antonia's feet?"

"Please, let's not speak of her."

"Ah, have you come for this, then! Have you waited until my Abel"—and she emphasized the *my*—"was gone, so that you could come for this?"

"Your Abel . . . your Abel . . . a precious lot of attention your Abel is paying you!"

"Oh? Do you also play the role of informer, tattletale, gossip?"

"Your Abel has other models beside you."

"What of it?" Helena exclaimed, bridling. "And what if he does have them? It's a sign that he knows how to win them! Or, are you jealous of him for that too? Is it because you haven't any recourse but to content yourself with . . . your Antonia? Ah, and because he has shown that he knew how to find himself another, have you thought of coming here today to find yourself another too? And do you come to me like this, to bring me these tales? Aren't you ashamed? Get away from me, get out! The sight of you makes me sick."

"O my God! Stop, Helena, you're killing me . . . you're killing me!"

"Go, go to church, you hypocrite, you envious hypocrite; go and let your wife take care of you and cure you, for you are very sick."

"Helena, Helena, only you can cure me! In the name of all you love most, remember you are condemning a man and losing him forever!"

"Ah, and in order to save you, you would have me lose another man, my own?"

"You won't lose him; you've already lost him. He's not interested in any part of you. He's incapable of loving you. I, I am the one who loves you, with all my soul, with a love that you can't conceive."

Helena stood up, went over to the child and, awakening him, took him in her arms; then she turned around to Joaquín and said: "Get out! This child, the son of Abel, orders you from his house. Get out!"

## CHAPTER XVIII

Joaquín worsened. Wrath at having laid bare his heart before Helena and despair at the manner in which she had rejected him finally withered his soul. He succeeded in mastering himself for a time and he sought consolation in his wife and daughter. But his home life grew more somber, and he more bitter.

At this time he had a maid in his house who was very devout, who managed to attend Mass every day, and who passed every moment which domestic service permitted her shut up in her room saying her prayers. She went about with her eyes lowered and fixed on the ground, and she responded to everything with the greatest meekness, in a somewhat sniveling voice. Joaquín could not bear her, and was constantly scolding her without any pretext whatever. She habitually replied: "The master is right."

"What do you mean, I'm right?" Joaquín burst out on one occasion. "I'm not right at all!"

"Very well, sir, please do not be angered. You're not right then."

"Is that all?"

"I don't understand, sir."

"What do you mean, you don't understand, you prude, you hypocrite! Why don't you defend yourself? Why don't you answer back? Why don't you rebel?"

"Rebel? I, sir? God and the Blessed Virgin keep me from any rebellion, sir."

"What more can you want," interposed Antonia, "if she admits her own shortcomings?"

"She doesn't admit them at all. She is steeped in arrogance!"

"In arrogance, I, sir?"

"You see? The hypocrite is proud of not admitting anything. She is simply using me, at my expense, to do exercises in humility and patience. She uses my fits of temper as a kind of hair shirt to bring out in her the virtue of patience. At my expense, mind you! No, it shall not be; not at my expense. She can't use me as an instrument to pile up good marks in heaven! That's real hypocrisy for you!"

The poor little maid wept, as she prayed between her teeth.

"But, it's really true that she is humble. . . . Why should she rebel? If she *had* rebelled, you would have been even more irritated."

"No! It's a gross breach of faith to use the foibles of someone else as a means of exercising one's own virtue. Let her reply to me, let her be insolent, let her be a human being . . . and not just a servant. . . ."

"In which case, Joaquín, you would be much more annoyed."

"No, what really irritates me most are all these pretensions to greater perfection."

"You are mistaken, sir," said the maid without lifting her eyes from the ground; "I don't think I am better than anyone."

"You don't, eh? Well I do! And whoever doesn't think himself better than another is a fool. You probably think yourself the greatest woman sinner of all time, isn't that it? Come on now, answer me!"

"These things cannot be asked, sir."

"Come now, answer me, for they say that St. Louis Gonzaga believed himself the greatest sinner among men, and you, answer me yes or no, don't you think you're the greatest sinner among women?"

"The sins of other women are not on my soul, sir."

"Idiot! Worse than idiot! Get out of here!"

"God forgive you, as I do, sir!"

"For what? Come back and tell me. For what? What will God have to forgive me for? Come on, tell me!"

"Very well. For your sake, ma'am, I am sorry to go, but I shall leave this house."

"That's the way you should have begun. . . ." Joaquín concluded.

Later, alone with his wife, he said to her:

"Won't this innocent hypocrite go around now saying that I am mad? Antonia, am I not, perhaps, mad? Tell me, am I mad, or not?"

"For God's sake, Joaquín, don't become. . . ."

"Yes, yes, I believe I am mad. . . . Send me away. All this will put an end to me."

"You must put an end to *it*."

## CHAPTER XIX

Joaquín now lavished all his ardor upon his daughter, in raising her, in educating her, in keeping her free of the world's immoralities.

"It's just as well she is the only one," he would say to his wife. "It's just as well that we didn't have another."

"Wouldn't you have liked a son?"

"No, no, a daughter is better; it's easier to isolate a girl from this vile world. Besides, if there had been two, jealousies would have developed between them. . . ."

"Oh, no!"

"Oh, yes! Affection cannot be divided equally between several: what is given one is taken away from another. Each one demands everything for himself, and for himself alone. No, no, I shouldn't want to see myself in God's plight. . . ."

"What is that, now?"

"The one of having so many children. Isn't it said that we are all children of God?"

"Don't say these things, Joaquín. . . ."

"There are well people so that there may be infirm. . . . One has only to look at the way illness is distributed!"

Joaquín did not want his daughter to have anything to do with people. He brought a private teacher to the house, and he himself, in moments of leisure, gave her instruction.

Joaquina, the poor girl, saw in her father an invalid, a sick man, a patient rather than a doctor. Meanwhile, from him she received a somber view of the world and of life.

"I tell you," Joaquín continued the argument with his wife, "that she is enough, alone, so that we need not divide our affections. . . ."

"They say that the more it is divided, the more it grows. . . ."

"Don't believe it. You remember poor Ramirez, the solicitor? His father had two sons and two daughters and very few resources. In their house they ate aperitifs and soup, but never an entree. Only the father, Ramirez senior, ate a main course; from time to time, he would share a little with one of the sons and one of the daughters, but never with the others. When they 'celebrated,' on special occasions, they were served two entrees to be divided among the family, plus one for him, since, as master of the house, he had to be distinguished in some way. The hierarchy had to be preserved. And at night, as he retired to sleep, Ramirez senior would kiss one of his sons and one of his daughters, but not the remaining two."

"How awful! Why did he do that?"

"How do I know? . . . Perhaps the two favorites looked more attractive. . . ."

"It sounds like the case of Carvajal, who can't bear his youngest daughter. . . ."

"That's because the last child was born six years after the other and at a time when he was low in funds. She was just one more burden, an unexpected one. That's why they call her The Intruder."

"Good God, how horrible!"

"Such is life, Antonia, a seed-bed of horrors. And let us thank God that we don't have to distribute our affection."

"Don't say that!"

"I'll say no more."

And he made her be quiet too.

## CHAPTER XX

Abel's son was studying medicine and his father made a habit of keeping Joaquín informed on the progress of the boy's studies. Joaquín himself spoke to the boy a few times and gradually grew attached to him, or simply "fond" of him, as he thought at the time.

"How does it happen that you prepare him for medicine instead of for painting?" Joaquín asked the father.

"I am not preparing him, he is preparing himself. He doesn't feel any vocation toward art. . . ."

"I see, and to study medicine one needs, of course, no 'vocation.' . . ."

"I didn't say that. You always take everything the worst way. He not only does not feel any vocation toward art, but he is not even curious about it. He scarcely stops to see what I am painting; nor does he inform himself about it."

"Perhaps it's better that way. . . ."

"Why do you say that?"

"Because if he had devoted himself to painting he would neces-sarily become a better or a worse painter than you. If worse, it would not do, nor could he have endured it, to be called, not merely Abel Sanchez, the younger, but Abel Sanchez the Bad, or Sanchez the Bad, or Abel the Bad. . . ."

"And if he were better than I?"

"Then it would be you who could not endure it."

" 'The thief thinks that everyone else is a thief.' "

"Oh, that's it. Turn on me with an insult. No artist can tolerate the fame of another, especially if it is a son or brother. Better the fame of a stranger. That one of the same blood should triumph . . . never! How explain it? . . . You do well to train him for medicine."

"In any case, he will earn more."

"Do you mean to imply that you don't make a good income from painting?"

"I make something."

"Yes, and have fame besides."

"Fame? For whatever that's worth . . . as long as it lasts."

"Money doesn't last either."

"It's a little more substantial."

"Don't be a fraud, Abel, and pretend to despise fame."

"I assure you that what concerns me now is to leave my son a fortune."

"You will leave him a name."

"There is no market quotation on a name."

"On yours, there is!"

"On my signature, but it's only . . . Sanchez! And he might very well decide to sign himself Abel S. Puig, or some such thing. Let him be Marquis of the house of Sanchez. The Abel takes away the sting from the Sanchez. And Abel Sanchez sounds well enough."

## CHAPTER XXI

In flight from himself, and, so as to suppress in his sick and melan-choly consciousness that ever-present image of Abel which haunted him, Joaquín began to frequent a nightly gathering at his club. The light conversation would serve as a narcotic, and he hoped he might even be intoxicated by it. Do not some men give themselves up to drink so to drown the passion which devastates them, and to allow their frustrated love to flow away with the wine? And so he would give himself up to the talk in the club, listening rather more than taking an active part, so as to drown his passion.

Only, the remedy turned out to be worse than the ill.

He always went prepared to keep himself in restraint, to laugh and joke, to gossip pleasantly, to appear as a kind of disinterested spectator of life, generous as only a professed skeptic can be, heedful of the fact that to understand is to forgive, prepared never to allow the cancer of hatred which consumed his will to show through. But the evil escaped through his lips, in his words, when he least expected it, and the odor of wickedness was perceived by all. He would return home exasperated with himself, reproaching himself for cowardice and his lack of self-control, and would resolve to return no more to the club gatherings. "I will not go again," he would tell himself, "I must not. All this only worsens the matter, aggravates it. The ambient there is poisonous, the air is filled with suppressed evils and passions. No, I shall not return there. What I need is solitude, solitude. Blessed solitude!"

And yet he would go back.

He would go back because he was unable to endure his solitude. For in solitude he never managed to be alone, the other one was always present. The other one! He went so far as to catch himself in a dialogue with him, supplying the other's words for him. The other, in these solitary dialogues, these monologues in dialogues, spoke to him without rancor of any kind, of indifferent matters, even sometimes of pleasant things. "My God, why doesn't he hate me?" Joaquín came to ask himself. "Why doesn't he hate me?"

One day he even found himself on the point of addressing God, of asking Him in a diabolic speech to infiltrate some hatred into Abel's heart, hatred toward himself, Joaquín. Another time he burst out: "Oh, if he only envied me . . . if he only envied me." And this idea, which flashed lividly across the black clouds of his bitter spirit, brought him a relaxing joy, a joy which caused him to tremble in the marrow of his shivering soul. "To be envied! . . . Only to be envied! . . ."

"But," he asked himself, "doesn't all this simply prove that I hate myself, that I envy myself?" He went to the door, locked it with a key, looked about him and, certain that he was alone, fell to his knees. In a voice scalded by tears he murmured: "Lord, you have told me to love my neighbor as myself, and I cannot love him at all, for I don't love myself, I don't know how to love myself, I cannot love myself. What have you done with me, Lord?"

He went then and got his Bible, and opened it to where it reads: "And Jehovah said to Cain: Where is thy brother Abel?" Slowly he closed the book, murmuring: "And where am I?"

At this moment he heard sounds outside, and he hastened to open the door. "Papa! Papa!" his daughter was joyfully shouting, as she came in. Her fresh, young voice seemed to bring him back into the light. He kissed the girl and then, grazing her ear with his lips he told her in a low voice, so that no one else might hear: "Pray for your father, my daughter."

"Father, Father!" cried the girl, throwing her arms about his neck.

He hid his head in the girl's shoulder and burst into tears.

"What is the matter, Papa, are you sick?"

"Yes, I am sick. . . . But you mustn't ask any more."


## CHAPTER XXII

And he returned to the club. It was useless to fight against going back. Every day he invented another pretext for going. And the mill of conversation continued to grind.

One of the figures there was Federico Cuadrado, an implacable man, who, when he heard anyone speak well of another would ask: "Against whom is that eulogy directed?"

"I can't be fooled," he would say in his small, cold, cutting voice. "When someone is vigorously praised, the speaker always has someone else in mind whom he is trying to debase with this eulogy, a second someone who is a rival to the praised party. This is true when it's not a matter of deliberately trying to vent one's scorn on the person mentioned. . . . You can be sure that no one eulogizes with good intentions."

"Wait a minute," interjected León Gómez, who took a great delight in making the cynic talk; "there's Don Leovigildo, now, whom no one has ever heard say a word against another. . . ."

"Well," a provincial deputy put in, "the fact is Don Leovigildo is a politician, and politicians must remain on good terms with everybody. What do you say, Federico?"

"I say that Don Leovigildo will die without having spoken badly or thought well of any man. . . . He would not give, perhaps, the slightest little push to send another sprawling, even if no one were to see it, because he not only fears the penal code, but also hell. But if the other person falls and breaks his crown, he will feel delight to his very marrow. And, in order to enjoy his pleasure in the broken skull, he will be the first to go and offer his sympathy and condolences."

"I don't know how it is possible to live with such sentiments," interposed Joaquín.

"What sentiments?" Federico caught him up. "Don Leovigildo's, mine, or yours?"

"No one has mentioned me in this conversation!"; Joaquín spoke with acid displeasure.

"I do, now, my good fellow, for we all know each other here. . . ."

Joaquín felt himself turn pale. The phrase "My good fellow," which Federico, inspired by his guardian devil, lightly bestowed upon anyone into whom he got his hooks, had pierced Joaquín in his innermost will.

"I can't understand why you have such an aversion for Don Leovigildo," blurted Joaquín, who was sorry as soon as he had spoken, for he felt he was poking a sputtering, dangerous fire.

"Aversion? Aversion, I? For Don Leovigildo?"

"Yes. . . . I don't know what harm he could have done you."

"In the first place, my good fellow, it is not necessary for someone to harm you for you to take a dislike to him. When you have a dislike for someone, an 'aversion,' it becomes easy to invent some harmful or malevolent action, that is to say, to imagine that the harm has been done one. . . . In the second place, I don't have any greater 'aversion' for Don Leovigildo than I have for anyone else whomsoever. He's a man, and that's enough. Moreover, he's an 'honorable' man!"

"Just as you are a professional misanthrope. . . ." began the provincial deputy.

"Man is the rottenest and most indecent vermin there is; I've said so a thousand times. And the 'honorable' man is the worst of the lot."

"Come on now," said León Gómez; and then, addressing the deputy: "What do you say to that, you who were talking the other day about honorable politicians, referring to Don Leovigildo?"

"An honorable politician," Federico burst out. "Oh, no, not that! That's completely impossible!"

"Why?" exclaimed three voices at once.

"Why, you ask? Because he himself has belied it in his own words. He had the audacity in the course of a speech he was delivering to call himself honorable. And it is not honorable to declare oneself so. The Gospel says that Christ our Lord. . . ."

"Don't mention Christ, I beg you!" Joaquín interrupted him.

"What, does Christ hurt you too, my good fellow?"

There was a short silence, sombre and cold.

"Christ our Lord," reiterated Federico, "said that he should not be called good, for only God is good. And yet there are Christian swine who dare to call themselves honorable."

"*Honorable* is not exactly the same as *good*," interpolated Don Vicente, the magistrate.

"Ah, now you have said it yourself, Don Vicente. Thank the Lord for the opportunity to hear a sentence like that, both reasonable and just, from a magistrate!"

"So that one must not confess oneself to be honorable, is that it?" asked Joaquín. "But how about confessing oneself a rogue?"

"That isn't necessary."

"What Señor Cuadrado wants," said Don Vicente, the magistrate, "is for men to confess themselves scoundrels, and continue on in their normal course, isn't that it?"

"Bravo!" exclaimed the provincial deputy.

"I shall tell you, my good fellow," answered Federico, considering his reply. "You must certainly know what constitutes the excellence of the sacrament of confession in our most wise mother the Church. . . ."

"Some other barbarity, now," interrupted the magistrate.

"Barbarity not at all, but a very wise institution. Confession allows more graceful, more tranquil sinning, since one knows that one's sins will be forgiven. Isn't that so, Joaquín?"

"Yet, if one does not repent. . . ."

"Oh, yes, my good fellow, yes, one must repent, and then again sin and once again repent, knowing while one is sinning that one will repent, and knowing when one repents that one will sin again, so that finally one is both sinning and repenting at the same time. Isn't that true?"

"Man is a mystery," said León Gómez.

"There is no need for inanities!" replied Federico.

"Why is that inane?"

"Any 'philosophical' maxim, stated just like that, any off-hand

maxim, any solemn, general statement, put in the form of an aphorism, results in an inanity."

"And philosophy, then?"

"There is no other philosophy than what we are doing here right
now. . . ."

"You mean flaying our fellow men?"

"Exactly. Man is best when flayed."

After the club gathering, Federico approached Joaquín to ask
if he were going home, for he would have liked to accompany him
for a short distance; but when Joaquín told him he was not going
home, but simply going on a visit close by, Federico said:

"I understand. The business about the visit is simply a blind.
What you want is to be left alone. I understand."

"How do you understand it?"

"One is never better off than when one is alone. But, when solitude weighs on you, call upon me. You will find no one who will
better distract you from your burdens."

"What about your own?" Joaquín blurted out.

"Bah! Who cares about them?" . . .

Whereupon they parted company.

## CHAPTER XXIII

There roamed about the city a poor needy man, an Aragonese,
father of five children, who earned a living as best he could, as a
scribe or at whatever turned up. The poor man frequently appealed to
friends—if such men as he can indeed be said to have any—petition-
ing them under a thousand pretexts for the advance of two or three
five-peseta notes. The saddest aspect of the whole thing was that he
sometimes sent around one of his children, or even his wife, who
appeared at the homes of acquaintances bearing little begging
letters. Joaquín had occasionally helped him, especially when he had
sent for him as a doctor to treat someone in his family. For Joaquín
found a singular satisfaction in helping the poor man; he saw in
him a victim of human badness.

One time Joaquín asked Abel about him.

"Yes, I know him," the latter said. "I even gave him work for a
while. But he's an idler, a vagrant. With the excuse that he is drowning his sorrows, he doesn't let a day go by without showing up at

the cafe, even though at home the stove can't be lit. Nor will he be without his little package of cigarettes. He wants to turn his troubles into smoke."

"That isn't the whole story, Abel. It would be necessary to examine the case from within. . . ."

"Listen, don't be absurd. Something I can't tolerate is that line about 'I'll return this loan as soon as I can. . . .' Let him ask for alms and be done with it! It would be more open and noble. The last time, he asked me for fifteen pesetas and I gave him five, but told him: 'Not to be paid back!' He's a loafer!"

"How can you blame him? . . ."

"Come now, here we go again: 'Whose fault is it?' "

"Exactly! Whose fault *is* it?"

"All right, then. Let's forget it. If you want to help him, please do so; I won't stand in the way. I'm sure that I myself will, if he asks me again, give him what he wants."

"I knew that without your telling me, for underneath it all you are. . . ."

"Let's not go 'underneath it all'. I am a painter and I don't paint the person underneath. Even more, I'm convinced that all men wear outside everything that they are inside."

"Well, then, for you, a man is no more than a painter's model. . . ."

"Does that seem a small matter to you? For you, he is no more than a sick man, a patient. You're the one who goes about looking into men, auscultating them, listening in. . . ."

"Yes, it's a piddling business. . . ."

"How so?"

"And then, when one is habituated to looking into people, one ends by looking into oneself, auscultating oneself, listening in. . . ."

"There's an advantage in that. I've had enough when I look at myself in the mirror. . . ."

"Have you ever really looked at yourself in the mirror?"

"Naturally! You must know that I've painted a self portrait."

"A masterpiece, no doubt. . . ."

"Well now, it's not altogether bad. . . . And you, have you examined yourself thoroughly?"

The day following this conversation Joaquín left the club with Federico because he wanted to ask the latter if he knew the poor man who roamed about begging in a shameful fashion. "And tell me the truth, now, for we're alone. None of your ferocious statements."

"Well look; he's a poor devil who should be in jail, where he would at least eat better than he does and where he would live more calmly."

"But what has he done?"

"No; he hasn't done anything; he should have; and that's why I say he should be in jail."

"What is it he should have done?"

"Killed his brother."

"Now you're starting up again!"

"I shall explain it to you. This poor man is, as you know, from the province of Aragon, and there, in his native region, absolute liberty in disposing of property still exists. He had the misfortune to be the first born son and legitimate heir, and then he had the misfortune to fall in love with a poor girl, comely and honorable though she was to all appearances. The father opposed their relationship with all his might, threatening to disinherit him if he went so far as to marry the girl. And our man, blind with love, first compromised the girl seriously, thinking thus to convince the father, and ended by marrying her and leaving home. He stayed on in the town, working as best he might at the home of his in-laws, hoping to soften his father. And the latter, a good Aragonese, grew more and more unyielding; and died disinheriting the poor devil and leaving his estate to the second son; and a rather fair-sized estate it was, too. When his in-laws died a little while later, the poor man appealed to his brother for help and work; and his brother denied him; and, so as not to kill this false brother—which is what his natural anger urged him to do—he has come here to live from alms and caging. This, then, is the story; as you see, very edifying."

"So very edifying!"

"Had he killed his brother, that species of Jacob, it would have been an evil; and not killing him, an evil too. . . . Perhaps a worse one."

"Don't say that, Federico."

"It's true, for he not only lives wretchedly and shamefully, a parasite, but he lives hating his brother."

"And if he had killed him?"

"Then he would have been cured of his hatred, and today, repentant of his crime, he would be honoring his brother's memory. Action liberates one and dissipates poisoned sentiment, and it is poisoned sentiment which sickens the soul. Believe me, Joaquín, for I know it very well."

Joaquín looked at him deliberately:

"And you?" he thrust out.

"I? You wouldn't want to know things that don't concern you, would you, my boy? Let it be enough for you to know that all my cynicism is defensive. I am not the son of the man everyone takes to be my father; I am the child of an adultery, and there is no one in this world whom I hate worse than my own father, my illegitimate father, who was the executioner of the other one, the father who out of cowardice and baseness gave me his name, this indecent name which I bear."

"Still, the father is not the one who begets, but the one who raises the offspring. . . ."

"The truth is that this other father, the one you think has raised me, did no such thing, but instead weaned me on the venom of hatred which he bears my natural father, who engendered me and forced him to marry my mother."

## CHAPTER XXIV

The course of study pursued by Abelín, Abel's son, came to an end, and the father called on Joaquín to see if he would take on his son to practice with him as his assistant. Joaquín accepted the boy.

*I accepted him,*—Joaquín wrote later in the *Confession* dedicated to his daughter—*from a strange mixture of curiosity, abhorence of his father, and affection for the boy (who at that time seemed to me to be a mediocrity) coupled with a desire to free myself by this means from my evil passion. At the same time, deeper down in my heart, my demon whispered that the failure of the son would negate the pre-eminence of the father. So that on the one hand, I wanted to redeem myself of my hatred for the father by my affection for the son, and, on the other, I took a secret delight in anticipating that though Abel Sanchez triumphed in painting, another Abel Sanchez of his own blood would fail in medicine. I never would have been able at that time to imagine how deep a love I would come to feel for the son of the man who embittered and darkened the life of my spirit.*

And thus it came to pass that Joaquín and the son of Abel felt drawn to each other. Abelín was quick-witted and he avidly followed the precepts of Joaquín, whom he addressed as "maestro." His teacher proposed to make a good doctor of him, entrusting him with the wealth of his clinical experience. "I will lead him," he told himself, "to make the discoveries which this misbegotten restlessness of spirit has prevented me from making."

"Maestro," Abelín addressed him one day, "why don't you assemble all the scattered observations, all the random notes you have shown me, and write a book? It would be enormously interesting and highly instructive. There are scatterings of genius throughout the material, and extraordinary scientific wisdom."

"The truth is, son (it was thus he habitually addressed him), that I can't. I simply cannot. . . . I don't have the taste for it, I don't have the will, the courage, the serenity, the I-don't-know-what . . ."

"It would merely be a question of getting started. . . ."

"Yes, son, of course; it would merely be a question of getting started, but as many times as I've thought of it I've never come to the point of decision. To set myself to write a book . . . here in Spain . . . on medicine . . . ! No, it's not worth the effort. It would fall in the void. . . ."

"No, your work would not, I am sure of it."

"What I should have done is precisely what you must do: abandon this insufferable clientele and dedicate yourself to pure research, to true science, to physiology, histology, pathology, and not to the paying sick. You, who have some little means—your father's paintings must assure you of some—devote yourself to that."

"You may well be right, sir; but this does not alter the fact that you ought to publish your memoirs as a diagnostician."

"Look! If you want, we will arrange something. I will give you my notes, all of them. I will amplify them orally, I will answer all your questions. And you will publish the book. Does that appeal to you?"

"Wonderful! It would be wonderful. I have taken notes, ever since I have been assisting here, of everything I have heard and learned."

"Very well, my son, very well." And he embraced the boy with deep feeling.

Later, Joaquín said to himself: "This boy shall be my handiwork! Mine, and not his father's. In the end he will venerate me and understand that I am more worthy than his father, that there is more art in my practice of medicine than in his father's painting. And then, I will take him away from Abel, yes, I will take him away from him. He took Helena away from me, and I will take away his son from him. Abelín will become my son, and who knows? . . . perhaps he will finally renounce his father, when he finally knows him and finds out what he did to me."

## CHAPTER XXV

"But tell me," Joaquín asked his disciple one day, "how did you really come to study medicine?"

"I am not sure. . . ."

"Because it would have been most natural for you to have been attracted to painting. Young men usually feel called upon to practice their fathers' professions; from a spirit of emulation . . . the very ambient . . ."

"Painting never did interest me."

"Your father told me . . ."

"My father's painting even less."

"What do you mean by that?"

"I don't feel it, and I don't know whether he does either. . . ."

"That's a large statement. Would you explain? . . ."

"There is no one to hear what I say, and you, sir, you are like a second father to me . . . a second . . . Well, then. . . . Besides, you are his oldest friend, before you had either one reached the age of reason, and you are almost like brothers. . . ."

"Yes, yes, that's true enough. Abel and I are like brothers. . . . Go on."

"Well, then, today I would like to open my heart to you."

"Do so. Whatever you tell me will never be known."

"Yes, the truth is that I doubt that my father has any feeling for what he paints—or for anything else. He paints like a machine. He has a natural gift for it. But feeling? . . ."

"This is what I have always believed."

"Why, it was you, according to everyone, who contributed the largest impetus to his fame with that famous address which is still spoken of."

"How else could I have spoken?"

"That is what I say to myself. In any case, I think that my father feels neither painting nor anything else. He is made of cork."

"I wouldn't say that, son."

"Yes, cork. He lives only for his own glory. All that talk about his despising fame is a farce, pure farce. On the contrary, he seeks only applause. And he is an egotist, a perfect egotist. He doesn't love anyone else."

"Well, now . . . no one else . . . that's pretty strong."

"It's true, no one else. I don't even know how he came to marry my mother. I doubt that it was for love."

Joaquín turned pale.

"I know," the youth continued, "that he has had entanglements and affairs with some of his models. But they have been a matter of caprice and a little bit of showing off. He doesn't really care for anyone."

"But it seems to me that you are the one who should. . . ."

"He has never paid any attention to me. He has supported me, has paid for my education and studies, he has not stinted nor does he now stint me with respect to money. And still, I scarcely exist as far as he is concerned. Whenever I have asked him something, in regard to history, art, technique, painting, his travels, or anything else, he has said to me: 'Leave me alone, leave me in peace.' Once he said: 'Learn it yourself! Learn it, as I did! There are the books.' How different that is from you!"

"It might be that he didn't know, my son. Parents sometimes act unjustly towards their children simply because they do not want to admit they are more ignorant or slow than the youngsters."

"No, it wasn't that. . . . And there is something worse."

"Worse? What could it be?"

"Yes, worse. He has never reprimanded me, no matter what I may have done. Although I am not, nor ever have been, either dissolute or wild, still everyone who is young has his slips and falls. Nevertheless, he has never inquired into them and, even if he knew about them, has said nothing."

"That shows respect for your integrity, confidence in you. . . . It is probably the most generous and noble way to bring up a son, and demonstrates faith. . . ."

"No, it is nothing like that, in this case. It is simply indifference."

"Don't exaggerate, it isn't indifference. . . . What could he say to you that your conscience wouldn't already have told you? A father can't be a judge."

"But he can be comrade, an adviser, a friend or teacher like you."

"And yet there are things which decorum forbids mentioning between father and son."

"It is only natural that you, his greatest and oldest friend, almost his brother, should defend him even though. . . ."

"Even though what?"

"May I tell you everything?"

"Yes, tell everything."

"Well then, I have never heard him speak otherwise than well of you, too well, but . . ."

"But what?"

"That's just it. He speaks too well of you."

"What do you mean by speaking too well?"

"For instance, before I came to know you, I thought of you as someone completely different than you are."

"Explain yourself."

"For my father you are a kind of tragic being, with a soul tortured by profound passions. 'If one might only paint the soul of Joaquín,' he has often said. He speaks as if there were a secret operating between you and him. . . ."

"These are merely suspicions of yours. . . ."

"No, they are not."

"And your mother?"

"Ah, my mother . . ."

## CHAPTER XXVI

"Listen, Joaquín," Antonia said to her husband one day, "it seems to me that one of these fine days our daughter will leave us, or be taken away from us. . . ."

"Joaquina? Where to?"

"To the convent!"

"Impossible!"

"On the contrary, highly possible. You have simply been engrossed in your own affairs, and now you are taken up with this son of Abel's, whom you seem to have adopted. . . . Anyone would say you were more fond of him than of your own daughter. . . ."

"The point is that I am trying to save him, to redeem him from his antecedents. . . ."

"No, what you are really trying to do is to take revenge. How vengeful you are! You neither forgive nor forget! I fear that God will punish you, will punish us. . . ."

"Oh, and is that the reason Joaquina wants to enter a convent?"

"I didn't say that."

"But I do, and that's the same thing. Is she going because she is jealous of Abelin? Is she afraid that I will grow to love him more than I do her? Because if that's the reason. . . ."

"That is not the reason."

"What, then?"

"I don't know. . . . She says she has a vocation, that God calls her there. . . ."

"God? God? Her confessor, more likely. Who is he?"

"Father Echevarria."

"The one who was my confessor?"

"The same."

Joaquín seemed crestfallen. He began to muse. On the following day he called his wife aside and told her:

"I believe I have uncovered the motives for Joaquina's impulse to enter the cloister, or rather, the motives for Father Echevarria's inducing her to become a nun. Do you remember how I sought help and refuge in the church against that wretched obsession which takes possession of my whole soul, against that spitefulness which through the years grows older—harder and more stubborn, and do you remember how, despite all my efforts, I did not succeed in my purpose. No, Father Echevarria did not give me any help, he could not. For that evil there is no remedy but one, only one."

He was silent for a moment, as if expecting a question from his wife, and, as she kept quiet, he went on:

"For that evil there is no remedy but death. Who knows? . . . I was almost born with him, and perhaps I shall die with him. Well then, this little priestling, who could not help me nor convert me, is now, without a doubt, pushing my daughter, your daughter, our daughter, toward the convent, so that there she may pray for me, so that she may save me by sacrificing herself. . . ."

"But it is not a sacrifice, . . . she says it is her vocation. . . ."

"That's not true, Antonia; it's a lie. Most of those who become nuns, do so to escape work, to lead a poor, but easy life, a mystic *siesta.* Either that, or they are running away from home. Our daughter is running away from home, from us."

"It must be from you. . . ."

"Yes, she is running away from me. She has guessed my secret!"

"And now that you have formed this attachment for that. . . ."

"Do you mean to tell me that she is running away from him too?"

"From your capriciousness, your new caprice. . . ."

"Caprice? Caprice, you say? I am anything but capricious, Antonia. I take everything seriously, everything, do you understand?"

"Yes, too seriously," added the woman dissolving into tears.

"Come now, don't cry, Antonia, my little saint, my good angel, and forgive me if I have said anything. . . ."

"What you say isn't the worst, it's what you don't say."

"Listen, for God's sake, Antonia, for God's sake, see to it that our daughter doesn't leave us. If she goes into a convent, it will kill me; yes, it will kill me, it will simply kill me. Make her stay here, and I will do whatever she wants . . . if she wants me to send Abelin away, to dismiss him, I will do it. . . ."

"I remember when you said you were glad we had only the one daughter, because that way we did not have to divide our affections or spread them. . . ."

"But I don't divide them!"

"Something worse then. . . ."

"Antonia, our daughter wants to sacrifice herself for my sake, and she doesn't know that if she enters a convent she will leave me in despair. This house is her convent!"

## CHAPTER XXVII

Two days later Joaquín took counsel in his study with his wife and daughter.

"Papa, it's God's desire!" Joaquina said to him resolutely, gazing at him squarely.

"It isn't God who wants it, but that little priestling of yours," her father replied. "How does a kid like you know what God wants? When have you communicated with Him?"

"I go to Communion every week, Father."

"And you think the attacks of dizziness which come from your fasting stomach are revelations from God?"

"A fasting heart breeds worse delusions."

"This decision cannot stand. God doesn't want it, He can't. I tell you He can't want it!"

"I don't know what God wants, but you, Father, know what He doesn't want, is that it? You may know a good deal about things of the body, but about things of God, of the soul. . . ."

"Of the soul, is it? So you think I know nothing of the soul?"

"Perhaps you know something it would be better not to know."

"Are you accusing me?"

"No. It is you, Father, who accuse yourself."

"You see, Antonia, do you see, didn't I tell you?"

"And what did he tell you, Mama?"

"Nothing, my child, nothing. Suspicions and imaginings of your father. . . ."

"Well, then," exclaimed Joaquín, like a man who has come to a decision, "you are entering a convent in order to save me, isn't that true?"

"Perhaps you are not too far from the truth."

"And what is it you want to save me from?"

"I am not sure."

"Would I know? . . . From what, from whom?"

"From whom, Father, from whom? Why, from the devil or from yourself."

"And what do you know about it?"

"For God's sake, Joaquín, for God's sake. . . ." Antonia's voice was tearful; she was frightened by her husband's tone and appearance.

"Leave us, leave us alone, she and I. This does not concern you!"

"How can it not concern me? . . . She is my daughter. . . ."

"She's mine, you mean! She's a Monegro, and I'm a Monegro. Leave us. You don't understand, you couldn't understand these things. . . ."

"Father, if you continue to treat mother in this way in front of me, I am leaving. Don't cry, Mother."

"But do you believe, my daughter . . . ?"

"What I believe, and know, is that I am as much his daughter as yours."

"As much?"

"Perhaps more."

"Don't talk like that, for God's sake," the mother burst out, in tears, "if you go on I will leave the room."

"That would be best," added the daughter. "Alone, we would better be able to see each other's face, or rather souls, we Monegros."

The mother stopped to kiss her daughter before leaving the room.

"Well now," began the father coldly, as soon as he found himself alone with his daughter, "to save me from what or whom are you going to a convent?"

"From whom or from what I don't know, Father; I know only that you must be saved. I don't know either what is wrong in this house, between you and my mother, I don't know what is wrong with you, but there is certainly something wrong. . . ."

"Did the little priestling tell you that?"

"No, the little priestling did not tell me that; he hasn't had to tell me; no one has told me, I have simply breathed it in since I was born. Here in this house we live as if in spiritual darkness!"

"Nonsense! That's something you've read in a book!"

"Just as you have read other things in your books. Or do you really believe that only those books which deal with the insides of the body, those books of yours with the ugly illustrations, are the ones to teach the truth?"

"Very well. And this spiritual darkness which you talk about, what is it?"

"You should know better than I, Father. In any case, don't deny that something is taking place here, that a sadness hangs over us like a black cloud and penetrates everywhere, that you are never satisfied and are suffering, as if you bore a great weight on your back. . . ."

"Yes; original sin," said Joaquín maliciously.

"Truer than you think," answered his daughter. "You haven't yet expiated it."

"I was baptized. . . ."

"That doesn't make any difference."

"And as a remedy for all this you propose to stick yourself in a nunnery, is that it? Well, the first thing to have done would have been to find out what the cause was. . . ."

"God forbid that I should judge you and my mother."

"But you don't object to condemning me?"

"Condemn you?"

"Yes, condemn me; your going off in this fashion is a condemnation. . . ."

"What if I went off with a husband? If I left you for a man? . . ."

"It depends on the man."

There was a brief silence.

"The truth is, my daughter, I am not well," Joaquín resumed. "I do suffer, I have been suffering nearly all my life. There is a good deal of truth in what you have guessed. Nevertheless, your decision to become a nun is the finishing blow, it exacerbates and heightens my pain. Have compassion on your father, your bedeviled father. . . ."

"It's from compassion. . . ."

"No, it's from egotism. You're running away. You see me suffer and you run away. It's egotism, indifference, lack of affection which leads you to the cloister. Suppose that I had a contagious and long-lasting disease, leprosy for example, would you leave me to go off to the convent and pray God to cure me? . . . Come now, answer, would you leave me?"

"No, I wouldn't leave you; I'm your only child, after all."

"Well imagine that I am a leper. Stay and cure me. I'll place myself in your care, and do what you order."

"If that's the way it is. . . ."

The father rose and gazed an instant at his daughter through his tears before he embraced her. Then, holding her in his arms he whispered in her ear:

"Do you want to cure me, my daughter?"

"Yes, Papa."

"Then marry Abelin."

"What!" exclaimed the girl, detaching herself from her father and staring into his face.

"Does it surprise you?" stammered the father, surprised in his turn.

"Me, marry Abelin, the son of your enemy? . . ."

"Who called him that?"

"Your silence through past years"

"Well, that's the reason—because he is the son of the man you call my enemy."

"I don't know what there is between you, I don't want to know, but lately . . . seeing how you grew attached to his son, I became frightened, I feared . . . I don't know what. To me your affection for Abelin seemed monstrous, something infernal. . . ."

"No, my daughter, it was not that. In him I sought redemption. And believe me, if you succeed in bringing him into my house, if you make him my son, it will be as if the sun were at last to shine in my soul. . . ."

"But do you, my father, want me to court him, to solicit him?"

"I don't say that."

"Well, then? . . ."

"If he . . ."

"Ah, so you already had it planned between the two of you, without consulting me?"

"No, I hadn't thought it out, I, your father, your poor father, I . . ."

"You grieve me, Father."

"I grieve myself. And now I am responsible for everything. Weren't you thinking of sacrificing yourself for me?"

"That's true, yes, I will sacrifice myself for you. Ask whatever you like of me!"

The father went to kiss her, but she, breaking away from him, exclaimed:

"No, not now! When you deserve it. Or do you want me, too, to quiet you with kisses?"

"Where did you hear that, Daughter?"

"Walls have ears."

"And accusing tongues!"

## CHAPTER XXVIII

"Ah, to be you, Don Joaquín," said the poor disinherited Aragonese father of five to Joaquín one day, after he had succeeded in extracting some money from his benefactor.

"You want to be me! I don't understand."

"Yes, I would give everything to be you, Don Joaquín."

"What is this 'everything' you would give, now?"

"Everything I can give, everything I have."

"And what is that?"

"My life!"

"Your life to be me!" To himself Joaquín added: "I would give my own to be someone else entirely!"

"Yes, my life in order to be you."

"This is something I can't very well understand, my friend. I can't understand anyone's being disposed to give up their life to be someone else. To be someone else is to cease to be oneself, to cease to be the person one is."

"Doubtless so."

"Which is the same as ceasing to exist."

"Doubtless."

"And with no guarantee of becoming another . . ."

"Doubtless. What I mean to say, Don Joaquín, is that I would cease to exist, with a very good will, or more clearly, that I would put a bullet in my head or throw myself in the river, if I could be sure that my family, who keep me tied to this miserable life, who don't allow me to take my life, would find a father in you. Don't you understand now?"

"Yes I do understand. So that . . ."

". . . a wretched bit of attachment I have to this life! I would be very glad to give up being myself and to kill off my memories, if it were not for my family. Although, in truth, there is something else which restrains me, too."

"What?"

"The fear that my memories, my story, my history might accompany me beyond death. Ah, to be you!"

"And suppose motives just like your own, my friend, keep me alive?"

"Impossible, you're rich."

"Rich . . . rich . . ."

"A rich man never has cause for complaint. You lack nothing. A wife, daughter, a good practice, reputation . . . what more could you want? You weren't disinherited by your father; you weren't put out of your house to beg by your brother. You weren't obliged to become a beggar! Ah, to be you, Don Joaquín!"

When Don Joaquín found himself alone later he said to himself: "Ah, to be me! That man actually envies me, he envies *me!* And I, who would I like to be?"

## CHAPTER XXIX

A few days later Abelín and Joaquina were betrothed. And, in the *Confession*, dedicated to his daughter, Joaquín not long afterwards wrote:

*It is scarcely possible, my daughter, to explain to you how I brought Abel, your present husband, to the point of proposing to you. I had to make him think you were in love with him or at least wanted him to be in love with you; I had to do this without the slightest hint of the talk you and I had held when your mother told me you wanted to enter a convent for my sake. I saw my salvation in this marriage. Only by linking your fate with that of young Abel, the son of the man who had poisoned the fountain of my life, only by mixing our two blood lines could there be any hope for my salvation.*

*And yet, it occurred to me that perhaps your children, my grandchildren, the children of his children, his grandchildren, the heirs to our blood, might some day find themselves warring within them-*

*selves, bearing hatred in their seed. Still, I thought, isn't hatred toward oneself, toward one's very blood brother, the only remedy against hating others? The Scripture says that Esau and Jacob were already fighting in the womb of Rebecca. Who knows but that some day you will conceive twins, one with my blood and the other with his and that they will hate each other and fight, beginning in your womb, before coming out into the air and into consciousness. This is the human tragedy, and like Job, every man is a child of contradictions.*

*And I have trembled to think that I had perhaps joined you together, not for a union of your blood, but instead to separate the two lines even more and perpetuate a hatred. Forgive me! . . . I am prey to a certain delirium.*

*But it is not only my blood and his that are involved; there is also Helena's. . . . The blood of Helena! This is what most disturbs me: the blood which flowers in her cheeks, her forehead, her lips, that sets off her glance; that blinded me through the tissue of her skin!*

*And then there is another blood line . . . Antonia's; the blood of the unfortunate Antonia, your blessed mother. This blood is like baptismal water. It is the blood of redemption. Only your mother's blood, Joaquína, can save your children, our grandchildren. It is this spotless blood which can redeem us.*

*Antonia must never see this journal; she must not see it. Let her leave this world, if she outlives me, without having more than guessed at our mystery—and our corruptibility.*

The betrothed quickly grew to understand and appreciate each other and to feel genuine affection. They came to realize that each was a victim of his own home, and of their individual ambients, both unfortunate: the one home frivolous and unfeeling, the other impassioned and stifling. They both sought support in Antonia. They felt a profound impulse to establish a home, a center of serene and self-sufficient love, of love which would be all-encompassing and would not romantically fix its gaze elsewhere or moon after other loves; their need was for a castle of solitude, where love could unite the two unfortunate families. They would make Abel, the painter, come to realize that the intimate life of the home is an imperishable reality of which art is but a bright reflection, when it is not a shadow. They would show Helena that perpetual youth is the property of the spirit able to submerge itself in the vital current of the family and its inheritance. Joaquín would be made to realize that although name and identity are lost with the loss of one's blood they are lost only to be joined in the new name and the new blood.

Antonia did not need to be shown anything, for she was a woman who had been born to live in the sweetness of custom.

Joaquín did in fact undergo a rebirth. He spoke of his old friend Abel with emotion and affection, and even confessed that it had been a stroke of good fortune to have lost Helena once and for all through Abel's intervention.

One time when he and his daughter were alone, he told her: "Now that everything seems to be taking a different and better turn, I can speak quite frankly. I did, at one time, love Helena. Or, at least I thought I did, and I courted her, to no avail. And the truth is she never gave me the slightest reason to hope for anything. Then I introduced her to Abel, who will now be your father-in-law, your second father, and the two of them were immediately drawn together. I took the entire episode as an affront, a mortal insult. . . . But what right did I have to her?"

"That's true. But men are like that in their demands."

"You're right, Daughter. I have acted like a madman, brooding upon a fancied insult, an imagined betrayal. . . ."

"Is that all, Father?"

"How do you mean, is that all?"

"Is that all there was to it, nothing more?"

"To my knowledge . . . no!" But as he said this, he closed his eyes and was unable to control the beating of his heart.

"Now you will be married," he went on, "and you will live with me. Yes, you will live with me, and I will make your husband—my new son—a great doctor, an artist in medicine, a complete artist, who at the very least will equal his father's fame."

"And he will record your work as he has told me."

"Yes, he will write what I have not been able to. . . ."

"He has told me that your career has demonstrated genius and that you have developed practices and made discoveries. . . ."

"Adulation on his part. . . ."

"He has told me privately. You are not known, not esteemed at your true worth, and he wants to write this account so that your work will become known."

"High time, at that. . . ."

"If fortune is good, it's never too late."

"Ah, Daughter, if instead of burying myself in patients, in this cursed practice which doesn't allow time to breathe or learn, if instead I had devoted myself to pure science, to research, the discovery for which Dr. Alvarez y García is so much lauded would have been my work, for I was on the verge of developing it. But this business of working for a living. . . ."

"We weren't in straits, you didn't have to do it."

"Yes, but . . . I don't know. Anyway, it's all past now and a new life begins. Now I shall give up my practice."

"Really and truly?"

"Yes, I shall give it over to your future husband, and simply keep an eye on how it goes. I shall lend him a guiding hand, and I will devote myself to my own work. We will all live together, and make another life. I can begin to live again, and I will be another man, another person. . . ."

"What a pleasure it is to hear you talk this way, Father. At last!"

"Does it please you to hear that I shall be another person?"

Joaquín's daughter looked at him closely as she sensed the undertones implicit in the question.

"Does it make you happy to hear that I shall be someone else?" the father asked the girl again.

"Yes, Father, it makes me happy!"

"In other words, the actual person, the person that I really am, strikes you as unfortunate?"

"And how does it strike you, Father?" the girl asked him resolutely, in her turn.

"Oh, don't let me say any more," he cried out.

And his daughter stopped his mouth with a kiss.

## CHAPTER XXX

"You already know why I've come," Abel said to Joaquín as soon as they were alone in the latter's office.

"Yes, I know. Your son has announced your visit."

"My son and soon yours. You don't know how happy it makes me. This is the way our friendship should culminate. My son is now nearly yours too. He already loves you as he would a father, and not just as a teacher. I'm ready to assert that he loves you more than he does me. . . ."

"No, no, not that. Don't say that."

"And what of it? Do you think I am jealous? I am incapable of jealousy. And listen, Joaquín, if there has been something standing between us before . . ."

"Please, Abel, don't say any more about. . . ."

"I must. Now that our two blood lines will be united, now that my son is to become yours, and your daughter is to become mine, we must settle that old score. We must be absolutely frank."

"No, no, nothing of the kind. And if you talk of it I'll leave."

"All right, then. But in any case I shall not forget what you said about my work the night of the supper."

"I wish you wouldn't talk about that either."

"About what shall I talk then?"

"Nothing of the past; nothing. Let's talk only about the future. . . ."

"Well, if you and I, at our age, are not to talk of the past, what are we to talk of? Why, we haven't anything left but the past."

"Don't say that," Joaquín almost cried out.

"We can't live now except from memories."

"Abel, please be quiet."

"And if the truth were known, it's better to live from memories than from hopes. The former have some basis in fact, but the latter . . . one cannot even know whether they'll ever be."

"But let's not go over our past," Joaquín insisted.

"We can talk of our children, then; in short, of our hopes."

"That's it. Let's talk of them, rather than of ourselves. . . ."

"In you my boy will have a teacher and a father. . . ."

"In any case, I hope to leave him my practice, give him at least those patients who are willing to make the change and whom I have already prepared for it. In acute cases I will be there to assist."

"Wonderful. Thank you, thank you."

"Then I will also give Joaquina a dowry. But they will live with me."

"My son has already told me. Still, I think it would be better if they had their own home: there is no house big enough for two families."

"No, I cannot be apart from my daughter."

"But you think we can live apart from our son, is that it?"

"You already live apart from him. . . . A man scarcely lives at home, a woman scarcely lives outside it. And I need my daughter."

"All right then . . . You see how amenable I am."

"This house will be yours, and Helena's. . . ."

"I appreciate your hospitality. It's something understood between us."

There followed a long discussion in which they arranged everything which concerned their two children's establishment as a family. When it came time to separate, Abel offered Joaquín his hand in a gesture of complete sincerity; he looked at his friend's eyes, and from the depths of his heart cried "Joaquín!" Tears came to the eyes of the doctor as he took the proffered hand.

At the end of a long moment Abel said: "I haven't seen you cry since we were boys, Joaquín."

"We won't see ourselves in that condition again, Abel."

"And that's the worst of it."

And they took leave of each other.

## CHAPTER XXXI

The sun, albeit an autumn sun, seemed to warm Joaquín's cold house following the marriage of his daughter. Joaquín himself seemed to quicken and come alive. He began to transfer his patients to the care of his son-in-law; serious cases he kept under advisement himself, and he let it be known that he acted in a consultative capacity in all matters.

The young Abel, Abelin, using the notes he had gotten from his father-in-law (whom he now called Father, addressing him with the intimate pronoun) and availing himself of the oral help of the doctor, had launched on the compilation of the volume which set forth the medical work of Joaquín Monegro. The youth had approached his subject with a veneration which would not have been possible on the part of the doctor himself. "It is better this way," Joaquín thought, "to have someone else write this account, as Plato did for Socrates." He himself could not, in good conscience and without seeming presumptuous and avid for the unattainable applause of posterity, detail his knowledge and skill. He would reserve his literary energies for other endeavors.

And it was at this point that he began the serious composition of his *Confession*, the intimate account of his struggle with the passion which consumed his life, the struggle against the demon which had possessed him from the first stirrings of conscience to the present moment. He wrote the account so that after his death his daughter might know of his effort. He addressed the narrative to his daughter; but he was so permeated with the profound tragedy of his life of passion, so self-centered in the story of it, that he entertained the hope that his daughter, or his grandchildren, would one day make the narrative known to the world, to a world which would be seized with both wonder and horror at this darkly afflicted hero who had lived and died in its midst without revealing the depths of his suffer‧ ing to those around him. For the truth was that Joaquín thought of himself as an exceptional spirit and, as such, more tormented and prone to pain than anyone else, a spirit marked by God with the sign of those predestined to greatness.

*My life, dear daughter, has been one long passion,* he wrote in the *Confession, and yet I would not have exchanged it for another. I have hated as no one else ever has, for I have felt more than anyone the supreme injustices of the world's favors. The way the parents of your husband acted towards me was neither human nor noble; what they did was infamous; but even worse, much worse, were the acts of every human being upon whom I have relied for love and support since the days of my childhood when I trusted everyone. Why have they rejected me? Why do they prefer the light-headed, the fickle, the egotists? My life has been made bitter by these people. And I have realized that the world is naturally unjust, and that I have not been born among my own. That was my chief misfortune, not to have been born among my own. The vulgarity, the common baseness of those surrounding me, led me to my downfall.*

At the same time that he put together his *Confession,* he was preparing, in case the first effort did not come to fruition, another literary endeavor which would make him eligible to the pantheon of immortals of his people and caste. The second work would be titled *Memoirs of a Doctor,* would be the harvest of a knowledge of the world, of passions, of life, joy and sadness, even of secret crimes, in short, the harvest he had gathered in his years of medical practice. It would be a mirror to life, but revealing the very entrails, the darkest corners of it; a descent into the abysses of human vileness. Into the book he would pour his soul, without speaking of himself; in it, by way of denuding the souls of others, he would denude his own; in it he would take vengeance on the vile world in which he had been forced to exist. When people saw themselves thus exposed and naked they would at first be astounded, but in the end they would admire and respect the author of the exposure; and in it, in this book, he would paint the definitive portraits—their names slightly altered in fictional guise—of Abel and Helena, and these portraits would be the ones to stand for all time. His portrait of that pair would be worth all the portraits Abel would ever paint. And

Joaquín savored the satisfaction of knowing that if he were successful in creating this literary portrayal of Abel Sanchez he would immortalize his subject more surely than all Abel's own painting would do, so that critics and commentators in a remote time would discover the actual person of the painter only when they penetrated the thin veil of fiction.

"Yes, Abel," Joaquín told himself, "your best opportunity of attaining what you have so long struggled for, the only thing for which you have striven, the only thing which interests you, for which you denigrated me, and even worse, ignored me, the best chance you have to perpetuate your memory does not lie with your paintings but rather with me, with whether or not I succeed in painting you just as you are, with my pen. And I will succeed, because I know you, because I have withstood you, because you have pressed upon me all my life. I shall unmask you for all time, and you will no longer be Abel Sanchez, but whatever name I give you. And when you are spoken of as the painter of your paintings, people will say rather: 'Ah, yes, that character of Joaquín Monegro's.' For in that sense you will be my creation, and you will live only as my work lives, and your name will follow along the ground behind me, dragged along in the mud at my heels, as the names of those put in the Inferno were dragged along by Dante. And you will be the perfect symbol of the invidious man."

Of the invidious man! For Joaquín persisted in believing that whatever passion animated Abel beneath his apparently impassive exterior of egotist, whatever feeling moved him was based on envy, his particular type of envy, and that from envy he had usurped, even as a child, the affection of playmates from Joaquín, and from envy had taken Helena from him later. And yet, why then had Abel allowed his own son to be taken away from him? "Ah," Joaquín told himself, "he simply is less concerned with the boy than with the renown of his own name. He doesn't believe in living on in his blood descendants, but only in those who admire his paintings, and he abandons his son to me so he may enjoy fame without competition from someone else with his name. But I shall unmask him."

He was disquieted by his age as he took up the writing of these *Memoirs*, for he had already reached his fifty-fifth year. Still, had not Cervantes begun his *Quixote* in his fifty-seventh year? And he bethought himself of all the other authors who had written their masterpieces after having passed his present age. Moreover, he felt strong, complete master of his mind and will, rich in experience, mature in judgment, his deep feelings and passion—which had been aroused for so many years—subdued and yet ebullient.

Now, in order to complete the work, he would hold himself steadily in check. Poor Abel, what a fate awaited him! He began to feel scorn and compassion for the painter. He looked upon him as a model and as a victim; he studied and observed him carefully, though the opportunity to do so was not very great, for Abel came very seldom to visit his son in his new home.

"Your father must be very busy," Joaquín would say to his son-in-law; "he scarcely appears here. Does he have some complaint against us, I wonder? Have we offended him, Antonia, or my daughter, or I, in some way? I would regret if . . ."

"No, no, Father" (for Abelín now addressed his father-in-law in this manner), "it is nothing of that sort. He doesn't stay at home either. Haven't I told you that he is not interested in anything but his own affairs, and these affairs center around his paintings and whatever. . . ."

"No, Son, don't exaggerate, there must be something else."

"No, that's all there is to it."

And, in order to hear the same explanation again, Joaquín would ask the same question again.

"How does it happen," he would ask Helena, "how does it happen Abel doesn't come here?"

"Oh, he is the same about going any place!" she would reply. For Helena, on the other hand, did visit her daughter-in-law at her home.

## CHAPTER XXXII

"But tell me," Joaquín said to his son-in-law one day, "why did it never occur to your father to train you in painting, to stir your interest in that direction?"

"I've never cared for it."

"That's beside the point. It would seem natural for him to have wanted to initiate you in his art. . . ."

"On the contrary, he was annoyed whenever I showed any interest in it. He never urged me or encouraged me to do even what other children do as a matter of course, to make drawings and figures."

"That's strange, very strange. And yet. . . ."

The young Abel was disturbed by the expression on his father-in-

law's face, by the unnatural glare in his eyes. He felt that something
writhed within him, something painful which he wished to be rid
of, some poisonous secretion. And Joaquín's words were followed by
a silence charged with bitterness, a silence which Joaquín broke by
saying:

"I simply do not understand why he did not wish to make you
into a painter. . . ."

"No, he simply did not want me to be what he was. . . ."

Another silence followed, which Joaquín again suddenly broke, as
if with heavy regret and with the air of a man who has decided to
make a clean breast of things:

"By heaven, I do understand it!"

Young Abel was shaken, without knowing well why, by the tone
with which his father-in-law uttered these words. "Why then . . . ?"
he asked.

"No, nothing." Joaquín appeared to have recovered and withdrawn
into himself.

"But you must tell me," the youth exclaimed, using the familiar
pronoun again, as if addressing a friend—a friend or an accomplice.
He was fearful, nevertheless, of hearing what he asked to hear.

"No, no, I don't want you to say later. . . ."

"This way it's worse, Father, than telling me directly, whatever it
is. Besides, I think I already know. . . ."

"What . . . ?" Joaquín asked, directing a piercing glance at his
son-in-law.

"That he perhaps feared I would some day eclipse him, his own
name. . . ."

"Yes," said Joaquín in a wrathful voice, "that's it exactly. Abel
Sanchez the son, or Abel Sanchez the Younger—that he could not
stand. And that later he should be remembered as your father
rather than you remembered as his son. This is a tragedy which has
happened more than once within a family. . . . For a son to out-
shine his father. . . ."

"But that is simply. . ." Abel broke off.

"That is simply envy, Son, envy pure and simple."

"Envy of a son! . . . On the part of a father?"

"Yes, and that is the most natural kind. Envy cannot exist between
two persons who scarcely know each other. A man from another
country or another time is not envied. The outsider, the foreigner is
not envied, only the man from the same town; not the man of an
older generation, but the contemporary, the comrade. And the

greatest envy is between brothers. Witness the legend of Cain and Abel. . . . Certainly the most terrible jealousy is that of a man who thinks his brother desires his wife, the sister-in-law. . . . And then there is the jealousy between fathers and sons. . . ."

"But what of the difference in age in this case?"

"It makes no difference. The fact that a being whom we created should come to obscure our own existence proves too much."

"And between master and disciple, then . . . ?"

Joaquín remained silent. For a moment he fixed his gaze on the floor; then he spoke, as if to the earth beneath his feet:

"Decidedly, envy is a form of family relation." And he added: "But let us talk of something else; and forget all this as if it had never been spoken. Do you hear?"

"No!"

"How do you mean, no?"

"I mean I did not hear what you said before."

"I wish neither of us might have heard it."

## CHAPTER XXXIII

Helena was in the habit of going to the home of her daughter-in-law with the purpose of introducing there, into this bourgeois home lacking distinction, a more refined tastefulness, a touch of greater elegance, or so she thought. She took it upon herself to correct, according to her lights, the deficiencies in the education of poor Joaquina, who had been brought up by a father filled with an unreasoning arrogance and an unfortunate mother who had to bear with a man rejected by another woman. And every day she expounded some lesson in manners and smart taste.

"All right, just as you wish," Antonia was always agreeable enough.

Joaquina's reaction was different: though she burned inwardly, she resigned herself; nevertheless, she felt that some day she would rebel; if she restrained herself, it was because of her husband's entreaties.

"It will be as *you* wish, madame," she said once, emphasizing the formal pronoun which they had never ceased to use between them; "I don't understand these matters, nor do they concern me. In all of this, it will be as you please. . . ."

"But it is not as I please, Daughter, but simply a matter of. . . ."

"It's all the same! I have been brought up in this house, a doctor's house, and when it's a question of hygiene, of health, or when later the child comes, and it's a question of raising it, I know what must be done; but now, in these niceties which you call matters of taste and refinement I must submit to one who has been formed in the house of an artist."

"But you mustn't get yourself into this state. . . ."

"Not at all, it's not that I get into a state. It's simply that you are always throwing it in our faces that what we do should not be done our way but some other way. After all, though, we are not arranging evening parties or tea-dances."

"I don't know where you have picked up this pretended scorn. . . . Yes, pretended, I say it's pretended. . . ."

"I have not said anything to indicate, madame, . . ."

"This pretended, this feigned scorn of all good form, of all social convention. A fine fix we would be in without them! . . . It would be utterly impossible to live!"

\*　　\*　　\*

Joaquina had been advised by both her father and her husband to take long walks, to expose to the sun and air the flesh and blood which was forming the flesh and blood of the coming child. Since the two men could not always accompany her and Antonia did not like to leave the house, Helena was usually the one to go with her. The mother-in-law was pleased to take these walks, to have Joaquina at her side like a younger sister (which was what people who did not know them took her to be), to overshadow her with the splendid beauty which the years had left intact. Beside her, the daughter-in-law was effaced, and Helena remained the object of the precipitous stares of the passers-by. Joaquina's attraction was of a completely different sort: it was a charm to be relished slowly by the eyes. Helena, on the other hand, dressed herself to dazzle the gaze of anyone who might be distracted. "I'll take the mother!" a passing young gallant provocatively murmured one day at Helena's side as he heard her call Joaquina "Daughter"; the older woman breathed heavier, moistening her lips with the end of her tongue.

"Listen, Daughter," she would tell Joaquina, "you must do your best to hide your condition. It is very unbecoming for a girl to let it be seen that she is pregnant. It looks brazen and ill-humored."

"I'm simply trying to stay as easy and comfortable as possible, and not pay any attention to what people think or don't think. . . . Even though I am in 'an interesting condition,' as affected people and wolves say, I don't pretend I am interesting or interested, in their sense, no matter what other women may have done while in this condition. I am not concerned. . . ."

"Well, you have to be concerned. You live in the world."

"And what difference does it make if people *do* know? . . . Or don't you want them to know, Mother, that you are on your way to becoming a grandmother?"

Helena was piqued both by the insinuation and the thought; but she controlled herself. "Well, listen, as far as age is concerned. . . ."

"Yes, as far as age is concerned, you could be a mother all over again," said Joaquina, wounding the other woman to the quick.

"Yes, of course," said Helena, choked and surprised, disarmed by the sharp attack on her. "But the idea that they should see you. . . ."

"No, you can rest easy on that score, because it's you they look at rather than at me. People remember that wonderful portrait of you, that work of art. . . ."

"Well, if I were in your place. . . ." began the mother-in-law.

"You in my place, Mother? And supposing you could join me in this same condition, would you?"

"Look, girl, if you go on in this vein, we will return to the house at once, and I shall never go out with you again, nor set foot in your house, in your father's house, that is. . . ."

"My house, madame, mine, and my husband's . . . and yours, too!"

"Where in heaven's name have you gotten this temper of yours?"

"Temper, is it? Ah, of course, temperament belongs only to artists."

"Oho, listen to our harmless little mouse, the one who was going to become a nun before her father hooked my son for her. . . ."

"I have already asked you, madame, not to repeat this lie. I know well enough what I did."

"And my son does too."

"Yes, he too knows what he has done. And let's not talk of it again."

## CHAPTER XXXIV

And the son of young Abel and Joaquina, in whom was mingled the blood of Abel Sanchez and Joaquín Monegro, was born into the world.

The first battle occurred over the name which should be given the child. The mother wanted the boy to be called Joaquín; Helena wanted his name to be Abel. The decision was left to Joaquín by Abel, by his son Abelin, and by Antonia. A veritable struggle took place thereupon in the soul of Monegro; the simple task of naming a new human being took on for him the character of a fateful augury, a magical determination; it was as if the future of the new spirit were being decided.

"His name should be Joaquín, the same as mine; after a while it would be written Joaquín S. Monegro, and eventually the S. would be left out, the S. which was the only remnant of the Sanchez, and *his* name, his son's name and his entire line would be absorbed into mine. . . . And yet, wouldn't it be better if his name were Abel Monegro, Abel S. Monegro, so that the Abel might be thus redeemed? Abel is his grandfather, but an Abel is also his father, my son-in-law, who now has become the same as a real son to me, my own Abel whom I have created. And what difference does it make if the new child is called Abel, if his other grandfather will not be remembered as Abel but as whatever I call him in my fictional memoirs, by whatever name I brand on his forehead? . . . But then again, . . ."

And while he thus wavered, it was Abel Sanchez the painter who finally decided the issue:

"Let him be called Joaquín. Abel the grandfather, Abel the father, Abel the son, three Abels. . . . It's too many. Besides, I don't like the name; it's the name of a victim. . . ."

"You were glad to give the name to your own son," Helena objected.

"It was your idea, and rather than make any objection. . . . But imagine what would have happened if instead of taking up medicine he had become a painter. . . . Abel Sanchez the Elder and Abel Sanchez the Younger. . . ."

"And there can not be more than one Abel Sanchez," interposed Joaquín, amused to have been proven so completely right in his conjecture.

"As far as I am concerned there could be a hundred of them," replied Abel. "I would always be myself."

"Who could doubt it?" asked his friend.

"An end to it, let him be called Joaquín. It's decided!"

"And let him not take up painting, eh?"

"Nor medicine either," Abel concluded, pretending to follow along with the pretended jest.

And the child was called Joaquín.

## CHAPTER XXXV

The newborn child's grandmother Antonia, who was the one to take care of it, would hug the infant to her breast as if to protect it from some imagined danger and whisper: "Sleep, my child, sleep, for the more you sleep the better, especially in this house, where it is better to be asleep than awake, and you will grow strong and healthy, and let us pray God that the two warring bloods do not quarrel in you; for otherwise what will become of you?"

And the child grew; he grew along with the written pages of the *Confession* and the *Memoirs* of his maternal grandfather, and with the artistic fame of his paternal grandfather. Abel's reputation as a painter was never greater than it now became; and he, for his part, seemed to occupy himself very little with whatever did not deal with this fame.

One morning, when he saw his grandchild sleeping in its cradle, he fixed his gaze on the infant with more than usual intensity and exclaimed: "What a beautiful study this would make!" And taking out a notebook he set about making a pencil sketch of the sleeping child.

"What would you call a finished drawing of such a subject?" Joaquín asked him. "A study of innocence?"

"The habit of giving titles to paintings is peculiar to the literati; something like the doctors' habit of giving names to diseases they can't cure."

"And whoever told you that the real purpose of medicine was to cure illnesses?"

"What is it then?"

"Knowledge; a knowledge of disease. The end of all science is knowledge."

"I had thought it was knowledge in order to cure. What use otherwise our having tasted the fruit of the knowledge of good and evil, if not to free ourselves of the evil?"

"And the end of art, what is it? What is the end purpose of this sketch you have just made of our grandchild?"

"That is its own end; it contains its purpose. It is an object of beauty and that's enough."

"What is the beautiful object, your sketch or our grandchild?"

"Both of them!"

"Do you perhaps think that your drawing is more beautiful than the little Joaquín?"

"Oh, now you're off on your mania! Joaquín, Joaquín!"

Antonia the grandmother came and took the child from its cradle and carried it off, as if to defend it from each of the grandfathers. Meanwhile she whispered to him: "Ah, my little one, my little one, little lamb of God, sun of this house, and angel without blemish, let them leave you alone, neither to draw you or treat you! Don't you be a model for any painter, or a patient for any doctor. . . . Let them have their art and their science, and you come with your grandmother, my little life, my tiny life. You are my life, our life, the sunshine warming this house. I will show you how to pray for your two grandfathers, and God will hear you. Come with me, my little life, lambkin without stain, little lamb of God." And Antonia would not stop to look at, nor did she care to see, Abel's sketch of the child.


## CHAPTER XXXVI

Joaquín anxiously followed, with his sickly anxiety, the growth in body and spirit of his grandson Joaquinito. Whom did he take after? Whom did he resemble? Which family was uppermost in him? He watched him all the more anxiously once he began to talk.

Joaquín was disturbed that the other grandfather, Abel, spent more and more time in his house, his son's house, now that the grandchild had been born, and he was amazed that the painter also saw to it that the child was frequently brought to his own home. Abel, that great and grandiose egotist—for such did his own son and his fellow parent-in-law consider him—seemed to have become intensely human, even somewhat like a child himself, in the presence of the newborn. He soon began to make drawings especially for the child, and gradually these began to delight the young Joaquín. "Little grandfather, Abelito, make saints!" And Abel never tired of drawing dogs, cats, horses, bulls, human figures. The child would ask for a horseman one time, two boys boxing another time, a boy running from a dog which ran after, or a repetition of all the previous scenes.

"Never in my life have I been happier to do something," Abel said. "This is pure pleasure; the rest is nonsense."

"You can put together an album of drawings for the children," Joaquín added.

"No, there would be no charm in that, not for the children. . . . That wouldn't be art, but rather. . . ."

"Pedagogy," interposed Joaquín.

"It would be that, whatever else it might be, but certainly not art. This is most like art, these drawings which our grandchild will tear up within half an hour."

"And if I were to save them?"

"Save them? What for?"

"I've heard of a book recently published containing drawings of this type which added greatly to the artist's reputation."

"I'm not making these drawings for publication, do you understand? And as regards reputation, which is one of your great preoccupations, you might as well know that I don't give a fig for it."

"Hypocrite! Why, it's the only thing that really does concern you. . . ."

"The only thing? It doesn't seem possible that you should accuse me of that. What concerns me now is this child; and that he may become a great artist."

"That he may inherit your genius, you mean?"

"And yours too."

The child watched the duel between the two grandfathers without comprehending, although he could guess at something amiss from their attitudes.

"What can be happening to my father," Abel's son asked Joaquín, "that he has become so crazy about his grandson? He never paid me the slightest attention. I don't recall, either, that he ever made me such drawings when I was a child."

"It's simply that we are becoming old," Joaquín answered, "and age teaches one a great deal."

"The other day, when the child asked him some question or other, I even saw him conceal some tears. The first tears I've ever seen from him."

"Oh, that's merely a cardiac reaction."

"How?"

"The truth is that your father is worn by the years and by work, by the effort of artistic endeavor and by his emotions. In short, he has a very weak heart, and any day. . . ."

"Any day what?"

"He will give you, that is to say us, a great shock. . . . I am actually glad that the occasion to tell you this has arrived. You might as well prepare your mother too."

"It's true he does complain of fatigue, of dyspnea. . . . Can it be . . . ?"

"Exactly. He has had me examine him without your knowledge, and I have done so. He needs attention."

And thus as soon as the weather began to get raw Abel stayed home and had the grandchild brought to him, a circumstance which embittered the other grandfather's entire day. "He is spoiling the child," Joaquín complained; "and he's trying to steal all his love; he wants to be first in his affection, and make up for his son's affection for me. He is doing it for revenge, yes, for vengeance. He wants to take away this last consolation from me. It's always he, the same one who took away my friend when we were children."

Meanwhile, Abel was instructing the child to love his other grandfather.

"I love you more," the child said to him one time.

"No, no. You mustn't love me more. You must love all of us the same. First, mother and father, and then the grandfathers, and each one the same. Your grandfather Joaquín is a very good man, he loves you very much, he buys you toys. . . ."

"You buy me toys too. . . ."

"He tells you stories. . . ."

"I like your drawings better. Will you make me a bull now, and a picador on horseback?"


## CHAPTER XXXVII

One day Joaquín came to see Abel. "Look, Abel," Joaquín said grimly as soon as they were alone, "I've come to talk to you about a serious matter, very serious, a matter of life and death."

"My illness?"

"No. But, if you will, of mine."

"Of yours?"

"Yes, mine. I've come to talk to you about our grandchild. Rather than beat around the bush, let me say that I think you should go away, far enough so that we don't see each other. I pray you, I beg you to do this. . . ."

"I, go away? Are you mad? Why should I go?"

"The child loves you and not me. That's clear. I don't know what you do to him . . . I don't want to know. . . ."

"I bewitch him, no doubt, or give him a potion. . . ."

"I don't know. Some perverse hold. . . . Your drawings are symptomatic. . . ."

"The drawings are evil too, then? You're not well, Joaquín."

"It may be that I am not well, but that no longer matters. I am not at an age to be cured. And if I am unwell, you should make allowances, show me some consideration. . . . Listen, Abel, you made my youth miserable, you have hounded me all my life long. . . ."

"I have?"

"Yes, you, you."

"I never knew it, then."

"Don't pretend. You have always despised and denigrated me."

"Look, if you continue in this way, I am leaving the room, because you will make me really ill. You know well enough that I am not in condition to listen to madness of this sort. Go away yourself, go to an institution where they can treat you or take care of you, and leave us alone."

"Abel, for the sole purpose of humiliating me, for the sole purpose of debasing me, you deprived me of Helena, you took her away from me. . . ."

"And haven't you had Antonia?"

"No, it was not for her sake you did it. It was an affront on your part, scorn, mockery. . . ."

"You're not well, Joaquín. I repeat, you are not well."

"You are worse off."

"As regards my body, that's true. I know I have not long to live. . . ."

"Too long."

"Ah, you want my death then?"

Joaquín's manner changed quickly. "No, Abel, no, I didn't say that." And then, with a plaintive note in his voice he added: "But please do go away from here. You can live somewhere else. Leave me the child . . . don't take him away from me . . . for the little time you have left. . . ."

"For the little time I have left then, let him stay with me."

"No, you pervert him with your tricks, you lure him away from me, you alienate him, you teach him to despise me. . . ."

"That's a lie! He has never heard from me, nor ever will, anything disparaging about you."

"It's sufficient that you sway him in some way, that you beguile him."

"And do you think that if I went away, that if I were to step out, he would therefore love you? Even if one wants to, Joaquín, it's impossible with you, it's impossible to love you. . . . You repel everyone, you reject them. . . ."

"You see, you see . . ."

"And if the boy does not love you as you want to be loved, to the exclusion of everyone else or more than anyone else is loved, it's because he senses the danger, because he fears. . . ."

"What does he fear? . . ." hissed Joaquín, turning pale.

"The contagion of your bad blood."

It was then that Joaquín rose, livid with anger. He came at Abel, and his hands went out like two claws for the sick man's throat.

"You thief!" he shrieked.

He had scarce laid hands on the victim before he drew back in horror. Abel gave a cry, clapped his hands to his chest, and murmured, "I'm dying!"

"An angina attack," thought Joaquín, "there's nothing to be done. It's the end!"

At that moment he heard the voice of the grandson calling, "Grandfather, grandfather." Joaquín turned around.

He heard his own voice: "Who are you calling? Which grandfather do you want? . . . Is it me you want?" The child was before him now, but was stricken dumb by the mystery lying there before him. "Come, tell me. Which grandfather were you calling? Was it me?"

The boy at length replied: "No. I was calling grandfather Abel."

"Abel was it? Well there you have him . . . dead. Do you know what that means, dead?"

Almost mechanically Joaquín raised the dead man's head and arranged his body in the armchair in which he had died. Then he turned to his grandson once more; he spoke in an unearthly voice:

"Yes, he's dead. And I killed him. Abel has been killed again by Cain, by your grandfather who is Cain. And now you have the power to kill me if you want. For he wanted to steal you away from me. He wanted to take away all your affections. And he has succeeded. . . . The fault was his." He was weeping now. "He wanted to rob me of you, who were the only consolation left for the poor Cain. Won't they leave Cain anything? Come to me now, and put your arms around me."

The child fled uncomprehending. He fled as if from a madman. And as he fled he called his grandmother Helena.

Alone, Joaquín continued to speak: "I killed him, but he was killing me. For over forty years he has been killing me. He poisoned all the walks of my life with his lording it over me, his triumphs and his celebration. He wanted to steal the child from me. . . ."

On hearing hurried footsteps Joaquín took hold of himself and turned. It was Helena who entered.

"What has happened. . . . What does the child mean? . . ."

"Your husband's sickness has come to a fatal end," said Joaquín coldly.

"You!"

"I was not able to do anything. One is always late in this type of case."

Helena fixed him with steady eyes: "You . . . It was you!"

Then, shaken and white, but maintaining her composure, she went to her dead husband's side.

## CHAPTER XXXVIII

A year passed during which Joaquín fell into a profound melancholy. He abandoned his *Memoirs*, and avoided seeing anyone, including his children. The death of Abel would have seemed a natural end to his gnawing disease, but a kind of blight had settled upon the house. For her part, Helena found that mourning and black suited her; she set about selling the remaining paintings left by her husband; she also seemed to have developed a certain aversion towards her small grandson. Meanwhile, another child had been born, so that there was now a granddaughter as well.

Joaquín himself was finally brought to bed by the onslaught of some obscure complaint. He felt himself slipping, at the boundary of death, and one day he summoned his family, his son-in-law's, his wife, and Helena.

"The child told you the truth," he blurted out at once, "it was I who killed Abel."

"Don't say such things, Father," his son-in-law pleaded.

"There's no time for either interruption or falsehoods. I killed him. Or just as well as killed him, for he died in my hands. . . ."

"That's another matter."

"He died when I seized him by the throat. It was all like a dream. My entire life has been a dream. But this was like a nightmare which happens just at the moment of waking, at dawn, between sleep and consciousness. I have not really lived nor slept . . . not even when awake. I no longer remember my parents; I don't want to remember them, and I trust that now that they are long dead, they have forgotten me. . . . And God, too, perhaps will forget me . . . in eternal forgetfulness perhaps there is peace. And you, too, my children, must forget me."

"That is not possible," exclaimed his son-in-law, and he took the doctor's hand and kissed it.

"Don't touch me! These are the hands which were at your father's neck when he died. Don't touch them. . . . But don't leave me yet. . . . Pray for me."

"Father, Father," cried his daughter, unable to say more.

"Why have I been so envious, so bad? What did I do to become that way? What mother's milk did I suck? Was there a philter, a potion of hate mixed with it? A potion in the blood? Why must I have been born into a country of hatreds? Into a land where the precept seem to be: 'Hate thy neighbor as thyself.' For I have lived hating myself; and here we all live hating ourselves. Still . . . bring the child."

"Father!"

"Bring the child!"

When the child was brought, he had him come near: "Do you forgive me?" he asked.

"There is no reason whatever to do so," interrupted Abel.

"Tell him you do," said the child's mother. "Go to your grandfather and tell him you do."

"Yes. . . ." whispered the boy.

"Tell me clearly, my child, tell me you forgive me."

"Yes, I do," said the child ingenuously.

"That's it. It's only from you I need forgiveness, from you who have not yet reached the age of reason, who are still innocent. . . . And don't forget your grandfather Abel, who made you drawings. Will you forget him?"

"No!"

"No, don't forget him, my child, don't forget him. . . . And you, Helena. . . ." Her gaze fixed before her, Helena was silent.

"And you, Helena. . . ." the dying man repeated.

"I, Joaquín, have forgiven you a long time ago."

"I didn't mean to ask you that. I only wanted to see you next to Antonia. Antonia. . . ."

That poor woman, her eyes swollen with tears, threw herself down on the bed by her husband, as if seeking to protect him.

"It is you, Antonia, who have been the real victim. You could not cure me, you could not make me good. . . ."

"But you have been, Joaquín. . . . You have suffered so much!"

"Yes, from a phthisis, a tuberculosis of the soul. But you could not make me good because I have not loved you."

"Don't say that!"

"I do say it, I must say it, I say it here before everyone. I have not loved you. If I had loved you I would have been saved. I have not loved you, and now it pains me that this was so. If we could begin all over again. . . ."

"Joaquín, Joaquín!" cried the poor woman from the depths of her broken heart. "Don't say such things. Have pity on me, have pity on your children, on the grandson who is listening to you even though he doesn't seem to understand, . . . perhaps tomorrow. . . ."

"That's why I've said it, out of pity. No, I have not loved you. I haven't wanted to love you. . . . If we were to start all over again! . . . Now, for it's now that. . . ."

His wife did not let him finish. She covered his dying mouth with her own, as if she wished to recover his last breath.

"I will save you, this will save you, Joaquín."

"Save me? What do you call salvation?"

"You can still live a few more years, if you want to. . . ."

"What for? So as finally to grow old, really old? No, old age isn't worth it, egotistic old age is no more than a state of infancy with a consciousness of death. An old man is a child who knows he will die. No, no, I don't want to become an old man. I would fight with my grandchildren from pure jealousy, I would grow to hate them. . . . No, no . . . enough of hatred! I could have loved you, I should have loved you, it would have been my salvation, but I did not."

He fell silent. He could not, or did not want to continue. He kissed the members of his family. A few hours later he gave his last weary breath.

[Translated by Anthony Kerrigan]

# NOW THAT YOU'VE READ UNAMUNO'S ABEL SANCHEZ:

In a conundrum characteristic of his thought, Miguel de Unamuno once wrote, "Some day we shall all die, even the dead." Yet, a sequent which would have delighted his taste for paradox, he himself looms larger in death than he did in life. His major efforts of the imagination, now that they are readily available in popular printings, are seen to have a universal dimension, despite their intensely Spanish spirit. *Abel Sanchez*, in particular, has perhaps a greater relevance today—considering the modern temper of alienation, conflict, and self-searching—than at any other time since its publication in 1917. By a growing number of readers, Unamuno is considered to be one of the significant spokesmen of our age. But spokesman he has become in spite of himself, for he made his name synonymous with dissent while he lived to pour out his passionate convictions in essays, criticism, philosophy, novels, and even in public meetings.

He was born in 1864 in the Basque seaport of Bilbao, and on both sides his people were Basques (his wedge-form face, with the craggy brows and the great breadth at the temples, is supposedly typical of this puzzling ethnic group). While yet an adolescent, Unamuno developed a deep interest in rationalistic philosophy, and almost defiantly forsook the faith of his family and his nation. In 1880, he entered the University of Madrid, and earned a doctorate with a dissertation on the Basque language, though he himself always wrote in pure Castilian. His uneventful life as a student gave no hint of his turbulent future, nor did the next seven years, during which he gave private lessons for a living, read enormously in all fields, and tried to obtain a teaching post.

At the age of twenty-seven, he received a chair in Greek at the University of Salamanca, and also married his Guernican sweetheart. During the decade of the nineties, Unamuno found life in Salamanca congenial; after his lectures, he would walk or read, and in the evenings enjoy the pleasures of family life (in 1897, the first of his ten children was born), or he would visit the Casino to debate the issues of the day. Good talk bubbled up readily and richly in his presence, and his friends remembered him primarily as a conversationalist during this period. When he did begin to write, he recorded spoken words—his conversations with himself and with others. It was agony for him to write, but he felt that only the written word could preserve his ideas. He translated Marxist books, tilted at the windmills of Spanish society, and fashioned a novel out of his youthful experiences during the Carlist wars.

On his reputation as a teacher, writer, and scholar, he was appointed rector of the University in 1901. In the following years, he added to that reputation a fame which spread through the Hispanic world on the wings of two books, *The Life of Don Quixote* (1905) and *The Tragic Sense of Life* (1912). Both express Unamuno's vigorous originality and his opposition to the dominant trends in European thought. In *Don Quixote*, he calls upon the knight-errant of La Mancha, the symbol of the heroic spirit, to return and to rescue the European soul from the chains of rationalism and materialism. *The Tragic Sense* shows Unamuno an existentialist, long before that mode of thought gained its wide currency. Here he states his fundamental belief that for the "man of flesh and blood," a man who for him was the real man and not an abstraction like "the common man" or "the economic man," neither blind faith (religion) nor sceptical rationalism (science) can furnish an adequate basis for existence. In Jose Mora's words, "The man of flesh and blood is not a person who turns from unreason and the dream world to embrace the implacable yet comforting light of reason, nor the person who escapes the rational universe to hide in the warm, trembling cosmos of faith, but one who vacillates incessantly between one and the other; a person who is, in fact, *composed of these two elements*." Thus, the man of flesh and blood lives at war with himself and never relinquishes his desire for peace; apparently split, he appears astride them both, sinking out of sight between them only to rise uncertainly again. Though he assailed rationalists before it was common to do so, he also saw that "the demands of reason are fully as imperious as those of life. The most potent urge of life, he says, is not only to continue living, but to transcend the mortality of the flesh. This urge is the origin of religion and the spur of all individual endeavor. The artist (such as Abel Sanchez, for example) creates out of his anxiety to perpetuate his name and fame, "to grasp at least at the shadow of immortality." This urge is also the source of all sin:

> From it springs envy, the cause, according to the biblical narrative, of the crime with which human history opened: the murder of Abel by his brother Cain. It was not a struggle for bread—it was a struggle to survive in God, in the divine memory. Envy is a thousand times more terrible than hunger, for it is spiritual hunger.

Hence, the only really burning problem for man is death and the possibility of life after death. The will to live, vital and affirmative, hungers after such immortality, but reason, unable to rise higher than scepticism, discounts it. Whether he knows it or not, man must live in the agony of this conflict. This agony is a necessary condition of existence. Yet it is out of this transcendental pessimism that Unamuno creates "a temporal and terrestrial optimism." In his will to live, which survives the onslaught of reason, he finds the basis of belief—or rather of the effort to believe, which he regards as the same thing.

Once man senses that he may return to nothingness despite his urge to live, he feels pity for himself. Self-pity leads to self-love ("to pity is to love"), and this self-love, founded as it is on a universal conflict, expands into a love of all that lives and therefore wants to survive. Hence, by an act of love springing from the selfish urge for immortality, we personalize everything and discover that "the Universe is also a Person possessing a Consciousness ("participated knowledge" or "co-feeling"), which in its turn suffers, pities, and loves. . . . And this Consciousness of the Universe, which love, personalizing all that it loves, discovers, is what we call God." In brief, Unamuno contends that man must suffer; suffering is the road to co-feeling and only through co-feeling can man exist vitally and act passionately, even though his existence and action may be ultimately meaningless.

In delineating this belief, which conditions nearly all of his work, including *Abel Sanchez*, Unamuno stirred the suspicions of heresy-hunters and political conservatives in powerful quarters. When he attacked the monarchy of Alfonso XIII for dictatorial tendencies, he was, in 1914, relieved of his rectorship by a government even less tolerant of political deviation than of possible heresy.

During the war which broke out in the same year, Unamuno espoused the Allied cause, and, in 1917, he visited the Italian front. Saddened by the sight of man's Cain complex unleashed on a vast scale, he wrote *Abel Sanchez*. After the war, he worked for the Republicans against the monarchy and resumed his attacks despite pointed warnings. In 1920, he was removed altogether from his university connections and given a suspended sentence for "lèse majesté." Uncowed, he took up service as the Republican deputy to the Cortes, the national legislative body, and when General Primo de Rivera's militarists assumed power, Unamuno vehemently denounced their rule.

For defying the dictatorship, he was exiled to a bleak Canary Island in 1924. The story of that island exile is told in the little volume of poems which was written at a later date, *De Fuertaventura A Paris*. It expresses the loneliness he felt as he walked the shore in the darkness, the bitterness that possessed him because he "who devoted his lifetime to working for the welfare of his beloved Spain was now in exile from that Spain." A Paris newspaper arranged for his escape by boat, and a few months later, the militarists lifted the unpopular sentence. But Unamuno refused to live in a Spain dominated by a dictator; instead, he chose voluntary exile in France. In the border town of Hendaye, he contributed many rousing articles to an anti-government publication, edited by exiled writers and smuggled into Spain. The further fruit of his six years' exile were two volumes of lyric poetry and a sequel to his *The Tragic Sense* called *The Agony of Christianity*. His presence and his writing in France must have contributed to the undercurrent of exististential thought beginning to develop in Europe under the influence of Heidegger and later Sartre.

With the monarchy tottering under the weight of grave social and political problems, the great objector, whose objections had not always been welcomed, returned from exile. He had caught the conscience of many a fellow Spaniard, if not his king, and was greeted with a hero's acclaim. He was soon restored to his professorship, and in 1931, following the establishment of the Second Republic, he was re-elected rector of Salamanca. At first, he supported the liberal government, but before long, almost as though possessed by the anti-spirit of his antagonist in *Abel Sanchez*, he voiced harsh criticism of the regime which he had helped into power, accusing it of radicalism in social matters and dogmatism in religious matters.

When the army, under Franco, rebelled against the badly-prepared attempt at democracy, Unamuno at the outset declared himself in favor of the rebels, not because he shared their fascist ideas, but because he hoped that the movement would save Spain from mass rule (which he feared was leading to materialism) and revive the "living tradition" of Quixote. But once he realized that the Fascists had nothing to do with the aspirations of his own spirit, he protested angrily. At the opening of the academic year at Salamanca (Franco's headquarters), on October 12, 1936, the old rector rose to speak out against the cult of violence personified in General Millan Astray, the man who invented the battle cry, "Long live Death!" Unamuno declared that there were patriots and anti-patriots in both camps, and that a divided Spain was a negative creation. He was shouted down by cries of "Death to the Intelligentsia!" but not before he had thundered, "You will conquer, but not convince."

Unamuno was relieved of his post again, and thereafter people avoided him, afraid even to greet him in the streets. He stayed in his home, as though under arrest, guarded by police, believing that the Nationalists were "the enemies of all that stands for the spirit in this world." Little is known about his last days, and the accounts we do have often conflict. According to his friend the Spanish scholar Ernest daCal, a group of young rebel officers went to pay him their respects. When the ailing old man saw them enter the room, he arose from his bed, and shook his clenched fist at them in a gesture of furious defiance. Then he collapsed across a chair with a cerebral hemorrhage. He died on the last day of 1936, a man of letters who in his own words "was no mere man of letters, but also a man."

Seventeen years after his death, at Salamanca's 700th anniversary celebration, the man and the man of letters received his due. Visitors from the world's leading universities lined up to visit his house and braved the rain to place wreaths on his tomb. Finally, they gathered in the Ceremonial Hall, and the name of the man once forbidden to these grounds echoed throughout the building as each visitor arose to congratulate the university. The rector of the University of Madrid delivered an eloquent eulogy to "one of the Spanish masters who will live forever" and cheers and applause filled the hall for long moments in tribute to his fame and memory.

Though his memory has endured through his philosophy, his popularity is spreading through his novels, only now gaining recognition outside the Hispanic world. In deference to the critics, he consented to call these works "nivola." Removed from contemporary literary techniques and fashions, they appear as simple interplays of personalities, without specific setting in time or place or scenery, and without psychological description (all of his work, Unamuno contended, is in novel form; that is, it depends for its structure upon what he termed "agonic" dialogue). Through this kind of interplay, he sought to probe the elemental forces that constitute human personality.

*Abel Sanchez* (this title is misleading, for the real hero is Joaquín Monegro) illustrates Unamuno's theory of the novel. The personality Unamuno explores is his own, and the interplay is between the components of his own make-up (though the prototype may have been Don Agustin del Canizo, an inseparable friend of Unamuno's who occupied the chair of pathology on the medical faculty at Salamanca). Hence, the novel becomes a play of his own passions, his own contradictions and conflicts, embodied in the two main characters. Though they co-exist, they can be distinguished easily, and their co-existence creates none of the awkwardness evident in Dostoyevsky's *The Double*. Abel is congenial, calm, reconciled, and reconciling. Joaquín (Jo-Cain) is antipathetic, restless, opposed and opposing. Abel is the yea-sayer, Joaquín the nay-sayer. One the artist and the other the inquirer, together they represent the fundamental qualities of their creator's spirit.

While distinct from one another, both characters are preoccupied by the same central preoccupation as was Unamuno. Each represents the one passion which obsessed the author, the lust for life, here and after. Abel, through his art, seeks to survive the nothingness that yawns before all flesh. Joaquín also desires immortality; but in his soul, waiting to possess and corrupt his passion for immortality, is the impulse of envy. Joaquín envies Abel his easy fame, the possible immortality inherent in his painting, and hates him with a passion derived from his own desire to live on forever. In the grip of this destructive passion, he re-enacts the crime of the Biblical Cain.

Yet it is Joaquín, not Abel, who has heroic proportions. Abel does not have Joaquín's passionate, desperate need for assurance that he is immortal. He can hardly be a tragic or tremendous figure, because he is not driven by a distorted impulse to his own destruction. Joaquín, on the other hand, grasps after immortality, hungers to perpetuate himself, and is vibrantly alive in his passionate obsession. By a subtle stroke, Unamuno suggests that Abel, bountifully blessed by God and the world's gifts, is responsible for Cain's envy and his own death. In the preface to the second edition of the book, Unamuno wrote, "In re-reading my *Abel Sanchez*, I have felt the greatness of my Joaquín's passion, and his moral superiority to all the Abels. The evil is not in Cain; it is in all the petty little Cains, and in all the petty little Abels." In the end, Unamuno could not pass pronouncement against his Cain.

By wrestling with the conflicts of the individual, Unamuno came to wrestle with conflicts of a broader scale. His quixotic and complex mind may have perceived in his own struggles of the soul a parable of all mankind. *Abel Sanchez* was written in 1917, the year he visited the Italian front during the first great war. His profound observations, reaching beyond the book's stormy surface, invite reflection upon a strife that was sundering almost the entire world. And Joaquín's last words may today be considered as containing an element of the prophetic: "No, no . . . enough of hatred! I could have loved you, I should have loved you, it would have been my salvation, but I did not." To a world threatened by total destruction, these words may well sound like the tolling of a warning bell.

## FOR FURTHER INFORMATION:

Arturo Barea. *Unamuno*. Yale University Press: New Haven, 1952.

Aubrey F. G. Bell. *Contemporary Spanish Literature*. Alfred Knopf: New York, 1933.

Anthony Kerrigan. "Introduction," *Abel Sanchez and Other Stories*. Henry Regnery Co.: Chicago, 1956.

Allen Lacy. *Miguel de Unamuno: The Rhetoric of Existence*. Mouton and Co.: The Hague, 1967.

Salvador de Madariaga. *The Genius of Spain and Other Essays*. Clarendon Press: Oxford, 1923.

Jose Ferrater Mora. *Unamuno: A Philosophy of Tragedy*. University of California Press: Berkeley and Los Angeles, 1962.

J. Lopez-Morillas. "Unamuno and Pascal: Notes on the Concept of Agony." *Publications of the Modern Language Association*, XLV (1950), 998-1010.

Margaret Rudd. *The Lonely Heretic*. University of Texas Press: Austin, 1963.

# THE PASTORAL SYMPHONY

## BY ANDRÉ GIDE

First published, 1919

# THE PASTORAL SYMPHONY

## First Note Book

10th February 189—

THE SNOW has been falling continuously for the last three days and all the roads are blocked. It has been impossible for me to go to R . . . , where I have been in the habit of holding a service twice a month for the last fifteen years. This morning not more than thirty of my flock were gathered together in La Brévine chapel.

I will take advantage of the leisure this enforced confinement affords me to think over the past and to set down how I came to take charge of Gertrude.

I propose to write here the whole history of her formation and development, for I seem to have called up out of the night her sweet and pious soul for no other end but adoration and love. Blessed be the Lord for having entrusted me with this task!

Two years and six months ago, I had just driven back one afternoon from La-Chaux-de-Founds, when a little girl, who was a stranger to me, came up in a great hurry to fetch me to a place about five miles off, where she said an old woman lay dying. My horse was still in the shafts, so I made the child get into the carriage, and set off at once, after having first provided myself with a lantern, as I thought it very likely I should not be able to get back before dark.

I had supposed myself to be perfectly acquainted with the whole country-side in the neighbourhood of my parish; but when we had passed La Saudraie farm, the child made me take a road which I had never ventured down before. About two miles further on, however, I recognized on the left hand side a mysterious little lake, where I had sometimes been to skate as a young man. I had not seen it for fifteen years, for none of my pastoral duties take me that way; I could not have said where it lay and it had so entirely dropped out of my mind that when I suddenly recognized it in the golden enchantment of the rose-flecked evening sky, I felt as though I had only seen it before in a dream.

The road ran alongside the stream that falls out of the lake, cut across the extreme end of the forest and then skirted a peat-moss. I had certainly never been there before.

The sun was setting and for a long time we had been driving in silence, when my young guide pointed out a cottage on the hill-side, which would have seemed uninhabited, but for a tiny thread of smoke that rose from the chimney, looking blue in the shade and brightening as it reached the gold of the sky. I tied the horse up to an apple-tree close by and then followed the child into the dark room where the old woman had just died.

The gravity of the landscape, the silence and solemnity of the hour had struck me to the heart. A woman, apparently still in her youth, was kneeling beside the bed. The child, whom I had taken to be the deceased woman's granddaughter, but who was only her servant, lighted a smoky tallow dip and then stood motionless at the foot of the bed. During our long drive I had tried to get her to talk, but had not succeeded in extracting two words from her.

The kneeling woman rose. She was not a relation, as I had at first supposed, but only a neighbour, a friend, whom the servant girl had fetched when she saw her mistress's strength failing, and who now offered to watch by the dead body. The old woman, she said, had passed away painlessly. We agreed together on the arrangements for the burial and the funeral service. As often before in this out of the world country, it fell to me to settle everything. I was a little uneasy, I admit, at leaving the house, in spite of the poverty of its appearance, in the sole charge of this neighbour and of the little servant girl. But it seemed very unlikely that there was any treasure hidden away in a corner of this wretched dwelling . . . and what else could I do? I inquired nevertheless whether the old woman had left any heirs.

Upon this, the woman took the tallow dip and held it up so as to light the corner of the hearth, and I could make out crouching in the fireplace, and apparently asleep, a nondescript looking creature, whose face was entirely hidden by a thick mass of hair.

"The blind girl there. She's a niece, the servant says. That's all that's left of the family, it seems. She must be sent to the workhouse; I don't see what else can be done with her."

I was shocked to hear the poor thing's future disposed of in this way in her presence and afraid such rough words might give her pain.

"Don't wake her up," I said softly, as a hint to the woman that she should at any rate lower her voice.

"Oh, I don't think she's asleep. But she's an idiot. She can't speak or understand anything, I'm told. I have been in the room since the morning and she has hardly so much as stirred. I thought at first she was deaf; the servant thinks not, but that the old woman was deaf herself and never uttered a word to her, nor to anyone else; she hadn't opened her mouth for a long time past except to eat and drink."

"How old is she?"

"About fifteen, I suppose. But as to that, I know no more about it than you do . . ."

It did not immediately occur to me to take charge of the poor, forlorn creature myself; but after I had prayed—or to be more accurate, while I was still praying on my knees between the woman and the little servant girl, who were both kneeling too—it suddenly came upon me that God had set a kind of obligation in my path, and that I could not shirk it without cowardice. When I rose, I had decided to take the girl away that very evening, though I had not actually asked myself what I should do with her afterwards, nor into whose charge I should put her. I stayed a few moments longer gazing at the old woman's sleeping face, with its puckered mouth, looking like a miser's purse with strings tightly drawn so as to let nothing escape. Then, turning towards the blind girl, I told the neighbour of my intention.

"Yes, it is better she should not be there tomorrow when they come to take the body away," said she. And that was all.

Many things would be easily accomplished but for the imaginary objections men sometimes take a pleasure in inventing. From our childhood upwards, how often have we been prevented from doing one thing or another we should have liked to do, simply by hearing people about us repeat: "He won't be able to! . . ."

The blind girl allowed herself to be taken away like a lifeless block.

The features of her face were regular, rather fine, but utterly expressionless. I took a blanket off the mattress where she must have usually slept, in a corner under a staircase that led from the room to the loft.

The neighbour was obliging and helped me to wrap her up carefully, for the night was very clear and chilly; after having lighted the carriage lamp, I started home, taking the girl with me. She sat huddled up against me—a soulless lump of flesh, with no sign of life beyond the communication of an obscure warmth. The whole way home I was thinking, "Is she asleep? And what can this black sheep be like? . . . And in what way do her waking hours differ from her sleeping? But this darkened body is surely tenanted; an immured soul is waiting there for a ray of Thy grace, O Lord, to touch it. Wilt Thou perhaps allow my love to dispel this dreadful darkness? . . ."

I have too much regard for the truth to pass over in silence the unpleasant welcome I had to encounter on my return home. My wife is a garden of all the virtues; and in the times of trouble we have sometimes gone through I have never for an instant had cause to doubt the stuff of which her heart is made; but it does not do to take her natural charity by surprise. She is an orderly person, careful neither to go beyond nor to fall short of her duty. Even her charity is measured, as though love were not an inexhaustible treasure. This is the only point on which we differ . . .

Her first thoughts, when she saw me bring home the poor girl that evening, broke from her in the following exclamation:

"What kind of job have you saddled yourself with now?"

As always happens when we have to come to an understanding, I began by telling the children—who were standing round, open-mouthed and full of curiosity and surprise—to leave the room. Ah! how different this welcome was from what I could have wished! Only my dear little Charlotte began to dance and clap her hands when she understood that something new, something alive was coming out of the carriage. But the others, who have been well trained by their mother, very soon damped the child's pleasure and made her fall into step.

There was a moment of great confusion. And as neither my wife nor the children yet knew that they had to do with a blind person, they could not understand the extreme care with which I guided her footsteps. I myself was disconcerted by the odd moans the poor afflicted creature began to utter as soon as I let go her hand, which I had held in mine during the whole drive. There was nothing human in the sounds she made; they were more like the plaintive whines of a puppy. Torn away for the first time as she had been from the narrow round of customary sensations that had formed her universe, her knees now failed her; but when I pushed forward a chair, she sank on to the floor in a heap, as if she were incapable of sitting down; I now led her up to the fireplace and she regained her calm a little as soon as she was able to crouch down in the same position in which I had first seen her beside the old woman's fire, leaning against the chimney-piece. In the carriage too, she had slipped off the seat and spent the whole drive huddled up at my feet. My wife, however, whose instinctive impulses are always the best, came to my help; it is her reflection which is constantly at odds with her heart and very often gets the better of it.

"What do you mean to do with *that?*" she asked when the girl had settled down.

I shivered in my soul at this use of the word "that," and had some difficulty in restraining a movement of indignation. As however, I was still under the spell of my long and peaceful meditation, I controlled myself. Turning towards the whole party, who were standing round in a circle, I placed my hand on the blind girl's head and said as solemnly as I could:

"I have brought back the lost sheep."

But Amélie will not admit that there can be anything unreasonable or super-reasonable in the teaching of the Gospel. I saw she was going to object, and it was then I made a sign to Jacques and Sarah who, as they are accustomed to our little conjugal differences and have not much natural curiosity (not enough, I often think) led the two younger children out of the room. Then, as my wife still remained silent and a little irritated, I thought, by the intruder's presence:

"You needn't mind speaking before her," I said. "The poor child doesn't understand."

Upon this Amélie began to protest that she had absolutely nothing to say—which is her usual prelude to the lengthiest explanations —and there was nothing for her to do but to submit, as usual, to all my most unpractical vagaries, however contrary to custom and good sense they might be. I have already said that I had not in the least made up my mind what I was going to do with the child. It had not occurred to me, or only in the vaguest way, that there was any possibility of taking her into our house permanently, and I may almost say it was Amélie herself who first suggested it to me, by asking whether I didn't think "there were enough of us in the house already?" Then she declared that I always hurried on ahead without taking any thought for those who could not keep up with me, that for her part she considered five children quite enough and that since the birth of Claude (who at that very moment set up a howl from his cradle, as if he had heard his name), she had as much as she could put up with and that she couldn't stand any more.

At the beginning of her outburst, some of Christ's words rose from my heart to my lips; I kept them back, however, for I never think it becoming to allege the authority of the Holy Book as an excuse for my conduct. But when she spoke of her fatigue, I was struck with confusion, for I must admit it has more than once happened to me to let my wife suffer from the consequences of my impulsive and inconsiderate zeal. In the mean time, however, her recriminations had enlightened me as to my duty; I begged Amélie therefore, as mildly as possible, to consider whether she would not have done the same in my place and whether she could have possibly abandoned a creature who had been so obviously left without anyone to help her; I added that I was under no illusion as to the extra fatigue the charge of this new inmate would add to the cares of the household, and that I regretted I was not more often able to help her with them. In this way I pacified her as best I could, begging her at the same time not to visit her anger on the innocent girl, who had done nothing to deserve it. Then I pointed out that Sarah was now old enough to be more of a help to her and that Jacques was no longer in need of her care. In short God put into my mouth the right words to help her to accept what I am sure she would have undertaken of her own accord, if the circumstances had given her time to reflect and if I had not forestalled her decision without consulting her.

I thought the cause was almost gained, and my dear Amélie was already approaching Gertrude with the kindest intentions; but her irritation suddenly blazed up again higher than ever when, on taking up the lamp to look at the child more closely, she discovered her to be in a state of unspeakable dirt.

"Why, she's filthy!" she cried. "Go and brush yourself quickly. No, not here. Go and shake your clothes outside. Oh dear! Oh dear! The children will be covered with them. There's nothing in the world I hate so much as vermin."

It cannot be denied that the poor child was crawling with them; and I could not prevent a feeling of disgust as I thought how close I had kept her to me during our long drive.

When I came back a few minutes later, having cleaned myself as best I could, I found my wife had sunk into an arm-chair and with her head in her hands was giving way to a fit of sobbing.

"I did not mean to put your fortitude to such a test," I said tenderly. "In any case it is late tonight and too dark to do anything. I will sit up and keep the fire in and the child can sleep beside it. Tomorrow we will cut her hair and clean her properly. You need not attend to her until you have got over your repugnance." And I begged her not to say anything to the children.

It was supper time. My protégée, at whom our old Rosalie cast many a scowling glance as she waited on us, greedily devoured the plateful of soup I handed her. The meal was a silent one. I should have liked to talk to the children and touch their hearts by making them understand and feel the strangeness of such a condition of total deprivation. I should have liked to rouse their pity, their sympathy for the guest God had sent us; but I was afraid of reviving Amélie's irritation. It seemed as though the word had been passed to take no notice of what had happened and to forget all about it, though certainly not one of us can have been thinking of anything else.

I was extremely touched when, more than an hour after everyone had gone to bed and Amélie had left me, I saw my little Charlotte steal gently through the half-open door in her nightdress and bare feet; she flung her arms round my neck and hugged me fiercely.

"I didn't say good-night to you properly," she murmured.

Then, pointing with her little forefinger to the blind girl, who was now peacefully slumbering and whom she had been curious to see again before going to sleep:

"Why didn't I kiss her too?" she whispered.

"You shall kiss her tomorrow. We must let her be now. She is asleep," I said, as I went with her to the door.

Then I sat down again and worked till morning, reading or preparing my next sermon.

"Certainly," I remember thinking to myself, "Charlotte seems much more affectionate than the elder children, but when they were her age, I believe they all got round me too. My big boy Jacques, nowadays so distant and reserved . . . One thinks them tender-hearted, when really they are only coaxing and wheedling one."

*February 27th*

The snow fell heavily again last night. The children are delighted because they say we shall soon be obliged to go out by the windows. It is a fact that this morning the front door is blocked and the only way out is by the wash-house. Yesterday I made sure the village was sufficiently provisioned, for we shall doubtless remain cut off from the rest of the world for some time to come. This is not the first winter we have been snowbound, but I cannot remember ever having seen so thick a fall. I take advantage of it to go on with the tale I began yesterday.

I have said that when I first brought home this afflicted child I had not clearly thought out what place she would take in our household. I knew the limits of my wife's powers of endurance; I knew the size of our house and the smallness of our income. I had acted, as usual, in the way that was natural to me, quite as much as on principle, and without for a moment calculating the expense into which my impulse might land me—a proceeding I have always thought contrary to the Gospels' teaching. But it is one thing to trust one's cares to God and quite another to shift them on to other people. I soon saw I had laid a heavy burden on Amélie's shoulders —so heavy that at first I felt struck with shame.

I helped her as best I could to cut the little girl's hair, and I saw that she did even that with disgust. But when it came to washing and cleaning her, I was obliged to leave it to my wife; and I realized that I perforce escaped the heaviest and most disagreeable tasks.

For the rest, Amélie ceased to make the slightest objection. She seemed to have thought things over during the night and resigned herself to her new duties; she even seemed to take some pleasure in them and I saw her smile when she had finished washing and dressing Gertrude. After her head had been shaved and I had rubbed it with ointment, a white cap was put on her; some of Sarah's old clothes and some clean linen took the place of the wretched rags Amélie threw into the fire. The name of Gertrude was chosen by Charlotte and immediately adopted by us all, in our ignorance of her real name, which the orphan girl herself was unaware of, and which I did not know how to find out. She must have been a little younger than Sarah, whose last year's clothes fitted her.

I must here confess the profound and overwhelming disappointment I felt during the first days. I had certainly built up a whole romance for myself on the subject of Gertrude's education, and the reality was a cruel disillusion. The indifference, the apathy of her countenance, or rather its total lack of expression froze my good intentions at their very source. She sat all day long by the fireside, seemingly on the defensive, and as soon as she heard our voices, still more when we came near her, her features appeared to harden; from being expressionless they became hostile; if anyone tried to attract her attention, she began to groan and grunt like an animal. This sulkiness only left her at meal times. I helped her myself and she flung herself on her food with a kind of bestial avidity which was most distressing to witness. And as love responds to love, so a feeling of aversion crept over me at this obstinate withholding of her soul. Yes truly, I confess that at the end of the first ten days I had begun to despair, and my interest in her was even so far diminished that I almost regretted my first impulse and wished I had never brought her home with me. And the absurd thing was that Amélie, being not unnaturally a little triumphant over feelings I was really unable to hide from her, seemed all the more lavish of care and kindness now that she saw Gertrude was becoming a burden to me, and that I felt her presence among us as a mortification.

This was how matters stood when I received a visit from my friend, Dr. Martins of Val Travers, in the course of one of his rounds. He was very much interested by what I told him of Gertrude's condition and was at first greatly astonished she should be so backward, considering her only infirmity was blindness; but I explained that in addition to this she had had to suffer from the deafness of the old woman who was her sole guardian and who never spoke to her, so that the poor child had been utterly neglected. He persuaded me that in that case I was wrong to despair, but that I was not employing the proper method.

"You are trying to build," he said, "before making sure of your foundations. You must reflect that her whole mind is in a state of chaos and that even its first lineaments are as yet unformed. The first thing to be done is to make her connect together one or two sensations of touch and taste and attach a sound to them—a word—to serve as a kind of label. This you must repeat over and over again indefatigably and then try and get her to say it after you.

"Above all, don't go too quickly; take her at regular hours and never for very long at a time. . . ."

"For the rest, this method," he added, after having described it to me minutely, "has nothing particularly magic about it. I did not invent it and other people have applied it. Don't you remember in the philosophy class at school, our professors told us of an analogous case à propos of Condillac and his animated statue . . . unless," he corrected himself, "I read it later in a psychological review . . . never mind; I was much struck by it and I even remember the name of the poor girl, who was still more afflicted than Gertrude, for she was a deaf-mute as well as blind. She was discovered somewhere in England towards the middle of last century by a doctor who devoted himself to educating her. Her name was Laura Bridgeman. The doctor kept a journal, as you ought to do, of the child's progress— or rather, in the first place, of his efforts to instruct her. For days and weeks he went on, first making her feel alternately two little objects, a pin and a pen, and then putting her fingers on the two words 'pin' and 'pen' written in a Braille book for the blind. For weeks and weeks there was no result. Her body seemed quite vacant. He did not lose courage, however. 'I felt like a person,' says he, 'leaning over the edge of a deep dark well and desperately dangling a rope in the hopes a hand would catch hold of it.' For he did not one moment doubt that someone was there at the bottom of the well and that in the end the rope would be caught hold of. And one day, at last, he saw Laura's impassive face light up with a kind of smile. I can well believe that tears of love and gratitude sprang to his eyes and that he straightway fell on his knees and gave thanks to God. Laura had understood at last what it was the doctor wanted. She was saved! From that day forward she was all attention; her progress was rapid; she was soon able to learn by herself and eventually became the head of an institution for the blind—unless that was some other person—for there have been other cases recently which the reviews and newspapers have been full of; they were all astonished —rather foolishly, in my opinion—that such creatures should be happy. For it is a fact that all these walled-up prisoners were happy, and as soon as they were able to express anything, it was their *happiness* they spoke of. The journalists of course went into ecstasies and pointed the 'moral' for people who 'enjoy' all their five senses and yet have the audacity to complain . . ."

Here an argument arose between Martins and me, for I objected to his pessimism and could not allow what he seemed to infer—that our senses serve in the long run only to make us miserable.

"That's not what I meant," he protested; "I merely wanted to say—first, that man's spirit imagines beauty, comfort and harmony more easily and gladly than it can the disorder and sin which everywhere tarnish, stain, degrade and mar this world—and further, that this state of things is revealed to us by our senses, which also help us to contribute to it. So that I feel inclined to put the words *'si sua mala nescient'* after Virgil's *'Fortunatos nimium,'* instead of *'si sua bona norint'* as we are taught. How happy men would be if they knew nothing of evil!"

Then he told me of one of Dickens's stories—which he thinks was directly inspired by Laura Bridgeman's case; he promised to send it to me, and four days later I received *The Cricket on the Hearth* which I read with the greatest pleasure. It is a rather lengthy but at times very touching tale of a little blind girl, maintained by her father, a poor toy-maker, in an illusory world of comfort, wealth and happiness. Dickens exerts all his art in representing this deception as an act of piety, but, thank Heaven, I shall not have to make use of any such falsehood with Gertrude.

The day after Martins' visit, I began to put his method into practice with all the application I was capable of. I am sorry now I did not take notes, as he advised, of Gertrude's first steps along the twilit path where I myself at first was but a groping guide. During the first weeks more patience was needed than can well be believed, not only because of the amount of time an education of this kind requires, but also because of the reproaches it brought me. It is painful for me to have to say that these reproaches came from Amélie; but for that matter, if I mention this here, it is because it has not left in me the slightest trace of animosity or bitterness—I declare this most solemnly, in case these lines should come to her eyes later on. (Does not Christ's teaching of the forgiveness of injuries follow immediately after the parable of the lost sheep?) More than that—at the very moment when I most suffered from her reproaches, I could not feel angry with her for disapproving the length of time I devoted to Gertrude. What I chiefly deplored was that she failed to believe that my efforts would be at all successful. Yes, it was her want of faith that grieved me—without, however, discouraging me. How often I heard her repeat: "If only any good were to come of it all! . . ." And she remained stubbornly convinced that my work was labour lost; so that naturally she thought it wrong of me to devote the time to Gertrude's education which she always declared would have been better employed otherwise.

And whenever I was occupied with Gertrude, she managed to make out that I was wanted at that moment for someone or something else, and that I was giving her time that ought to have been given to others. In fact, I think she felt a kind of maternal jealousy, for she more than once said to me: "You never took so much pains with any of your own children,"—which was true; for though I am very fond of my children, I have never thought it my business to take much pains with them.

It has often been my experience that the parable of the lost sheep is one of the most difficult of acceptance for certain people, who yet believe themselves to be profoundly Christian at heart. That each single sheep of the flock should be in turn more precious in the eyes of the shepherd than the rest of the flock as a whole, is beyond and above their power of conception. And the words, "If a man have a hundred sheep and one of them be gone astray, doth he not leave the ninety and nine and goeth into the mountains and seeketh that which is gone astray"—words all aglow with charity, such persons would, if they dared speak frankly, declare to be abominably unjust.

Gertrude's first smiles consoled me for everything and repaid me for my pains a hundredfold. For "and if so be that he find it, verily I say unto you, he rejoiceth more of that sheep, than of the ninety and nine which went not astray." Yes verily, the smile that dawned for me one morning on that marble face of hers, when she seemed suddenly touched to understanding and interest by what I had been trying for so many days to teach her, flooded my heart with a more seraphic joy than was ever given me by any child of my own.

*March 5th*

I noted this date as if it had been a birthday. It was not so much a smile as a transfiguration. Her features flashed into life—a sudden illumination, like the crimson glow that precedes dawn in the high Alps, thrilling the snowy peak on which it lights and calling it up out of darkness—such a flood, it seemed, of mystic colour; and I thought too of the pool of Bethesda at the moment the angel descends to stir the slumbering water. A kind of ecstasy rapt me at sight of the angelic expression that came over Gertrude's face so suddenly, for it was clear to me that this heavenly visitor was not so much intelligence as love. And in a very transport of gratitude I kissed her forehead and felt that I was offering thanks to God.

The progress she made after this was as rapid as the first steps had been slow. It is only with an effort that I can now recall our manner of proceeding; it seemed to me sometimes that Gertrude advanced by leaps and bounds, as though in defiance of all method. I can remember that at first I dwelt more on the qualities of objects than on their variety—hot, cold, sweet, bitter, rough, soft, light; and then on actions—to pick up, to put down, to remove, to approach, to tie, to cross, to assemble, to disperse, etc. . . . And very soon I abandoned all attempt at method and began to talk to her without troubling much as to whether her mind was always able to follow me; but I went slowly, inviting and provoking her questions as she seemed inclined. Certainly her mind was at work during the hours I left her to herself; for every time I came back to her after an absence, it was to find with fresh surprise that the wall of darkness that separated us had grown less thick. After all, I said to myself, it is so that the warmth of the air and the insistence of spring gradually triumph over winter. How often have I wondered at the melting of the snow; its white cloak seems to wear thin from underneath, while to all appearance it remains unchanged. Every winter Amélie falls into the trap: "The snow is as thick as ever," she declares. And indeed it still seems so, when all at once there comes a break and suddenly, in patches here and there, life once more shows through.

Fearing that Gertrude might become peaky if she continued to sit beside the fire like an old woman, I had begun to make her go out. But she refused to do this unless she held my arm. I realized from her surprise and fear when she first left the house, and before she was able to tell me so in words, that she had never as yet ventured out of doors. In the cottage where I had found her no one had cared for her further than to give her food and prevent her from dying—for I cannot say that anyone helped her to live. Her little universe of darkness was bounded by the walls of the single room she never left; she scarcely ventured on summer days as far as the threshold, when the door stood open to the great universe of light. She told me later that when she heard the birds' song she used to suppose it was simply the effect of light, like the gentle warmth which she felt on her cheeks and hands, and that, without precisely thinking about it, it seemed to her quite natural that the warm air should begin to sing, just as the water begins to boil on the fire. The truth is she did not trouble to think; she took no interest in anything and lived in a state of frozen numbness till the day I took charge of her. I remember her inexhaustible delight when I told her that the little voices came from living creatures, whose sole function apparently, was to express the joy that lies broadcast throughout all nature. (It was from that day that she began to say, "I am as joyful as a bird." And yet the idea that these songs proclaim the splendours of a spectacle she could not behold had begun by making her melancholy.

"Is the world really as beautiful as the birds say?" she would ask. "Why do people not tell us so oftener? Why do *you* never tell me so? Is it for fear of grieving me because I cannot see it? That would be wrong. I listen so attentively to the birds; I think I understand everything they say."

"People who can see do not hear them as well as you do, my Gertrude," I said, hoping to comfort her.

"Why don't other animals sing?" she went on. Sometimes her questions surprised me and left me perplexed for a moment, for she forced me to reflect on things I had hitherto taken for granted. It was thus it occurred to me for the first time that the closer an animal lives to the ground and the heavier its weight, the duller it is. I tried to make her understand this; and I told her of the squirrel and its gambols.

She asked me if the birds were the only animals that flew.

"There are butterflies too."

"And do they sing?"

"They have another way of telling their joy. It is painted on their wings . . ."

And I described the rainbow colours of the butterfly.

*February 28th*

Now let me turn back a little, for yesterday I allowed myself to be carried away.

In order to teach Gertrude, I had had to learn the Braille alphabet myself; but she was soon able to read much quicker than I could; I had some difficulty in deciphering the writing, and besides found it easier to follow with my eyes than with my fingers. For that matter, I was not the only one to give her lessons. And at first I was glad to be helped in this respect, for I have a great deal to do in the parish, the houses being so widely scattered that my visits to the poor and the sick sometimes oblige me to go far afield. Jacques had managed to break his arm while skating during the Christmas holidays, which he was spending with us; for during term time he goes to Lausanne, where he received his early education, and where he is studying at the Faculty of Theology. The fracture was not serious and Martins, whom I at once sent for, was easily able to set it without the help of a surgeon; but it was considered advisable for Jacques to keep indoors for some time. He now suddenly began to take an interest in Gertrude, to whom he had hitherto paid no attention, and occupied himself with helping me to teach her to read. His assistance only lasted the time of his convalescence—about three weeks—but during those weeks Gertrude's progress was very marked. She was now fired with extraordinary zeal. Her young intelligence, but yesterday so benumbed and torpid, its first steps hardly taken, and scarcely able to walk, seemed now already preparing to run. I wondered at the ease with which she succeeded in formulating her thoughts and at the rapidity with which she learnt to express herself—not childishly, but at once correctly, conveying her ideas by the help of images, taken in the most delightful and unexpected way from the objects we had just taught her to recognize, or from others we described to her, when we could not actually put them within her grasp; for she always used things she could touch or feel in order to explain what was beyond her reach, after the method of land-surveyors measuring distances.

But I think it is unnecessary to note here all the first steps of her education, doubtless the same in the early education of all blind people. I suppose too that in each case the teacher must have been plunged into a similar perplexity by the question of colours. (And this subject led me to the reflexion that there is nowhere any mention of colours in the Gospels.) I do not know how other people set about it; for my part, I began by naming the colours of the prism to her in the order in which they occur in the rainbow; but then a confusion was immediately set up in her mind between colour and brightness; and I realized that her imagination was unable to draw any distinction between the *quality* of the shade and what painters, I believe, call its *"value!"* She had the greatest difficulty in understanding that every colour in its turn might be more or less dark and that they might be mixed one with the other to an unlimited extent. It puzzled her exceedingly, and she came back to the subject again and again.

About this time the opportunity was given me of taking her to a concert at Neuchâtel. The part played by each instrument in the symphony suggested to me the idea of recurring to this question of colours. I bade Gertrude observe the different resonances of the brasses, the strings and the wood instruments, and that each of them was able in its own way to produce the whole series of sounds, from the lowest to the highest, with varying intensity. I asked her to imagine the colours of nature in the same way—the reds and oranges analogous to the sounds of the horns and trombones; the yellows and greens like those of the violins, cellos and double basses; the violets and blues suggested by the clarinets and oboes. A sort of inner rapture now took the place of all her doubts and uncertainties.

"How beautiful it must be!" she kept on repeating.

Then suddenly she added, "But the white? I can't understand now what the white can be like."

And I at once saw how insecure my comparison was.

"White," I tried however to explain, "is the extreme treble limit where all the tones are blended into one, just as black is the bass or dark limit."

But this did not satisfy me any more than it did her; and she pointed out at once that the wood instruments, the brasses and the violins remain distinct in the bass as well as in the treble parts. How often I have been obliged to remain puzzled and silent, as I did then, searching about for some comparison I might appeal to.

"Well," said I at last, "imagine white as something absolutely pure, something in which colour no longer exists, but only light; and black, on the contrary, something so full of colour that it has become dark . . ."

I recall this fragment of dialogue merely as an example of the difficulties which I encountered only too often. Gertrude had this good point, that she never pretended to understand, as so many people do, thus filling their minds with inaccurate or false statements, which in the end vitiate all their reasoning. So long as she could not form a clear idea of any notion, it remained a cause of anxiety and discomfort to her.

As regards what I have just related, the difficulty was increased by the fact that the notion of light and that of heat began by being closely associated with each other in her mind, and I had the greatest trouble afterwards in disconnecting them.

Thus, through these experiments with her, it was constantly brought home to me how greatly the visual world differs from the world of sound, and that any comparison between the two must necessarily be a lame one.

*February 29th*

I have been so full of my comparisons that I have not yet said what immense pleasure the Neuchâtel concert gave Gertrude. It was actually the *Pastoral Symphony* that was being played! I say *actually* because, as will be easily understood, there is no work I could have more wished her to hear. For a long time after we had left the concert-room, Gertrude remained silent, as though lost in ecstasy.

"Is what you see really as beautiful as that?" she asked at last.

"As beautiful as what, dear child?"

"As that 'scene on the bank of a stream?'"

I did not answer at once, for I was reflecting that those ineffable harmonies painted the world as it might have been, as it would be without evil and without sin, rather than the world as it really was. And I had never yet ventured to speak to Gertrude of evil and sin and death.

"Those who have eyes," I said at last, "do not know their happiness."

"But I who have not," she cried, "I know the happiness of hearing."

She pressed up against me as she walked and hung on to my arm in the way small children do.

"Pastor, do you feel how happy I am? No, no, I don't say so to please you. Look at me. Can't you see on people's faces whether they are speaking the truth? I always know by their voices. Do you remember the day you answered me that you weren't crying, when my aunt" (that is what she called my wife) "had reproached you with being no help to her? And I cried out, 'Pastor, that's not true!' Oh, I felt at once from your voice that you weren't telling me the truth; there was no need for me to feel your cheeks to know that you had been crying." And she repeated very loud: "No, there was no need for me to feel your cheeks"—which made me turn red, for we were still in the town and the passers-by turned round to look at us. She went on, however:

"You mustn't try to deceive me, you know. First of all because it would be very mean to try to deceive a blind person . . . and then, because you wouldn't succeed," she added laughing. "Tell me, pastor, you aren't unhappy, are you?"

I put her hand to my lips, as though to make her feel, without having to confess it, that part of my happiness came from her, and answered as I did so.

"No, Gertrude, I am not unhappy. How should I be unhappy?"

"And yet you cry sometimes?"

"I have cried sometimes."

"Not since that time?"

"No, I have not cried again since that time."

"And you have not felt inclined to cry?"

"No, Gertrude."

"And . . . tell me, have you felt inclined since then not to speak the truth?"

"No, dear child."

"Can you promise never to try to deceive me?"

"I promise."

"Well, tell me quickly then—am I pretty?"

This sudden question dumbfounded me . . . all the more because I had studiously avoided up till then taking any notice of Gertrude's undeniable beauty; and moreover I considered it perfectly unnecessary that she should be informed of it herself.

"What can it matter to you?" I said.

"I am anxious . . ." she went on, "I am anxious to know whether I do not . . . how shall I put it? . . . make too much of a discord in the symphony. Whom else should I ask, pastor?"

"It is not a pastor's business to concern himself with the beauty of people's faces," said I, defending myself as best I could.

"Why not?"

"Because the beauty of their souls suffices him."

"You had rather I thought myself ugly," was her reply with a charming pout; so that, giving up the struggle, I exclaimed:

"Gertrude, you know quite well you are pretty."

She was silent and her face took on an expression of great gravity which did not leave her until we got home.

On our return Amélie at once managed to make me feel she disapproved of the way I had been spending my day. She might have told me so before; but she had let Gertrude and me start without a word, according to her habit of letting people do things and of reserving to herself the right to blame them afterwards. For that matter, she did not actually reproach me; but her very silence was accusing; for surely it would have been natural to have inquired what we had heard, since she knew I was taking Gertrude to the concert. Would not the child's pleasure have been increased if she had felt the smallest interest had been taken in it? But Amélie did not remain entirely silent—she merely seemed to put a sort of affectation into avoiding any but the most indifferent topics; and it was not till evening, when the little ones had gone to bed, and after I had asked her in private and with some severity if she was vexed with me for taking Gertrude to the concert, that I got the following answer:

"You do things for her you would never have done for any of your own children."

So it was always the same grievance, and the same refusal to understand that the feast is prepared for the child who returns to us—not for those who have stayed at home . . . as we read in the parable. It grieved me too to see that she took no account of Gertrude's infirmity—poor Gertrude, who could hope for no other kind of pleasure. And if I providentially happened to be free that afternoon—I, who am as a rule so much in request—Amélie's reproach was all the more unfair, because she knew perfectly well that the other children were busy or occupied in one way or other, and that she herself did not care for music, so that even if she had all the time in the world, it would never enter her head to go to a concert, not even if it were given at our very door.

What distressed me still more was that Amélie had actually said this in front of Gertrude; for though I had taken my wife on one side, she had raised her voice so much that Gertrude heard her. I felt not so much sad as indignant, and a few moments later, when Amélie had left us, I went up to Gertrude and taking her frail little hand in mine, I lifted it to my face, "You see," I said, "this time I am not crying."

"No," answered she, trying to smile, "this time it is my turn." And as she looked up at me, I suddenly saw her face was flooded with tears.

*March 8th*

The only pleasure I can give Amélie is to refrain from doing the things she dislikes. These very negative signs of love are the only ones she allows me. The degree to which she has already narrowed my life is a thing she cannot realize. Oh, would to Heaven she would demand something difficult of me! How gladly I would undertake a rash—a dangerous task for her! But she seems to have a repugnance for everything that is not usual; so that for her, progress in life consists merely in adding like days to like days. She does not desire—she will not even accept—any new virtue, nor even an increase of the old ones. When it is not with disapproval, it is with mistrust that she views every effort of the soul to find in Christianity something other than the domestication of our instincts.

I must confess that I entirely forgot that afternoon at Neuchâtel, to go and pay our haberdasher's bill and to bring her back some reels of cotton she wanted. But I was more vexed with myself for this than she could have been; especially as I had been quite determined not to forget her commissions, being very well aware that "he that is faithful in that which is least is faithful also in much," and being afraid too of the conclusions she might draw from my forgetfulness. I should even have been glad if she had reproached me with it, for I certainly deserved reproaches. But, as often happens, the imaginary grievance outweighed the definite charge. Ah! how beautiful life would be and how bearable our wretchedness if we were content with real evils, without opening the doors to the phantoms and monsters of our imagination . . . But I am straying here into observations that would do better as the subject of a sermon— (Luke XII, 49. "Neither be ye of doubtful mind.") It is the history of Gertrude's intellectual and moral development that I purposed tracing here and I must now return to it.

I had hoped to follow its course step by step in this book and had begun to tell the story in detail. Not only however, do I lack time to note all its phases with minuteness, but I find it extremely difficult at the present moment to remember their exact sequence. Carried away by my tale, I began by setting down remarks of Gertrude's and conversations with her that are far more recent; a person reading these pages would no doubt be astonished at hearing her express herself so justly and reason so judiciously in such a little while. The fact is her progress was amazingly rapid; I often wondered at the promptness with which her mind fastened on the intellectual food I offered it, and indeed on everything it could catch hold of, absorbing it all by a constant process of assimilation and maturation. The way in which she forestalled my thoughts and outstripped them was a continual surprise to me, and often from one lesson to another, I ceased to recognize my pupil.

At the end of a very few months there was no appearance of her intelligence having lain dormant for so long. Even at this early stage she showed more sense and judgment than the generality of young girls, distracted as they are by the outside world and prevented from giving their best attention by a multitude of futile preoccupations. She was moreover a good deal older, I think, than we had at first supposed. Indeed it seemed as though she were determined to profit by her blindness, so that I actually wondered whether this infirmity was not in many ways an advantage. In spite of myself I compared her to Charlotte, so easily distracted by the veriest trifles, so that many a time while hearing the child say over her lessons, as I sometimes did, I found myself thinking, "Dear me! How much better she would listen, if only she could not see!"

Needless to say, Gertrude was a very eager reader, but as I wished as far as possible to keep in touch with the development of her mind, I preferred her not to read too much—or at any rate not much without me—and especially not the Bible—which may seem very strange for a Protestant. I will explain myself; but before touching on a question so important, I wish to relate a small circumstance which is connected with music and which should be placed, as far as I can remember, shortly after the concert at Neuchâtel.

Yes, the concert, I think, took place three weeks before the summer holidays which brought Jacques home. In the mean time I had often sat with Gertrude at the little harmonium of our chapel which is usually played by Mlle de la M . . . , with whom Gertrude is at present staying. Louise de la M . . . had not yet begun to give Gertrude music lessons. Notwithstanding my love for music, I do not know much about it, and I felt very little able to teach her anything when I sat beside her at the keyboard.

"No," she had said after the first gropings, "you had better leave me. I had rather try by myself."

And I left her all the more willingly that the chapel did not seem to me a proper place in which to be shut up alone with her, as much out of respect for the sanctity of the place as for fear of gossip—though as a rule I endeavour to disregard it; in this case, however, it is a matter that concerns not only me but her. So when a round of visits called me in that direction, I would take her to the church and leave her there, often for long hours together, and then would fetch her away on my return. In this way she spent her time patiently hunting out harmonies and I would find her again towards evening, pondering over some concord of sounds which had plunged her into a long ecstasy.

On one of the first days of August, barely more than six months ago, it so happened that I had gone to visit a poor widow in need of consolation, and had not found her in. I therefore returned at once to fetch Gertrude from the church where I had left her; she was not expecting me back so soon, and I was extremely surprised to find Jacques with her. Neither of them heard me come in, for the little noise I made was covered by the sound of the organ. It is not in my nature to play the spy, but everything that touches Gertrude touches me; so stepping as softly as I could, I stole up the few steps that lead to the gallery—an excellent post of observation. I must say that during the whole time I was there I did not hear a word from either of them that they might not have said before me. But he sat very close to her, and several times I saw him take her hand in order to guide her fingers over the keys. Was it not in itself strange that she should accept instructions and guidance from him, when she had previously refused them from me, preferring, she said, to prac- tice by herself? I was more astonished, more pained than I liked to own, and was just on the point of intervening, when I saw Jacques suddenly take out his watch.

"I must leave you now," he said, "my father will be coming back in a moment."

I saw him lift her unresisting hand to his lips; then he left. A few moments later I went noiselessly down the stairs and opened the church door so that she might hear me and think I had only just arrived.

"Well, Gertrude! Are you ready to come home? How is the organ getting on?"

"Very well," she answered in the most natural tone; "I have really made some progress today."

A great sadness filled my heart, but we neither of us made any allusion to the episode I have just described.

I was impatient to find myself alone with Jacques. My wife, Gertrude, and the children used as a rule to go to bed early after supper, while we two sat on late over our studies. I was waiting for this moment. But before speaking to him, I felt my heart bursting with such a mixture of feelings that I could not—or dared not— begin on the subject that was tormenting me. And it was he who abruptly broke the silence by announcing his intention of spending the rest of the holidays with us. Now a few days earlier he had spoken to us about a tour he wanted to make in the high Alps— a plan my wife and I heartily approved of; I knew his friend T . . . , who was to be his travelling companion, was counting on him; it was therefore quite obvious to me that this sudden change of plan was not unconnected with the scene I had just witnessed. I was at first stirred by violent indignation, but was afraid to give way to it lest it should put an end to my son's confidence altogether; I was afraid too of pronouncing words I should afterwards regret; so making a great effort over myself, I said as naturally as I could:

"I thought T . . . was counting on you."

"Oh," he answered, "not absolutely, and besides he will have no difficulty in finding someone else to go with him. I can rest here quite as well as in the Oberland, and I really think I can spend my time better than mountaineering."

"In fact," I said, "you have found something to occupy you at home."

He noticed some irony in the tone of my voice and looked at me, but being unable as yet to guess the motive of it, went on unconcernedly:

"You know I have always liked reading better than climbing."

"Yes, my dear boy," said I, returning his glance with one as searching; "but are not lessons in harmonium playing even more attractive than reading?"

No doubt he felt himself blush, for he put his hand to his forehead, as though to shade his eyes from the lamplight, but he recovered himself almost immediately, and went on in a voice I could have wished less steady:

"Do not blame me too much, Father. I did not mean to hide anything from you and you have only forestalled by a very little the confession I was preparing to make you."

He spoke deliberately, as if he were reading the words out of a book, finishing his sentences with as much calm as if it were a matter in which he had no concern. The extraordinary self-possession he showed brought my exasperation to a climax. Feeling that I was about to interrupt him, he raised his hand, as much as to say, "No, you can speak afterwards; let me finish first." But I seized his arm and shook it:

"Oh," I exclaimed impetuously, "I would rather never see you again than have you trouble the purity of Gertrude's soul. I don't want your confessions! To abuse infirmity, innocence, candour! What abominable cowardice! I should never have thought you capable of it. And to speak of it with such coldblooded concern! . . . Understand me; it is I who have charge of Gertrude and

I will not suffer you to speak to her, to touch her, to see her for one single day more."

"But, Father," he went on as calmly as ever, driving me almost beside myself, "you may be sure that I respect Gertrude as much as you do. You are making a strange mistake if you think there is anything reprehensible—I don't say in my conduct—but in my intentions and in my secret heart. I love Gertrude and respect her, I tell you, as much as I love her. The idea of troubling her, of abusing her innocence is as abominable to me as to you."

Then he protested that what he wanted was to be her help, her friend, her husband; that he had thought he ought not to speak to me about it until he had made up his mind to marry her; that Gertrude herself did not know of his intention and that he had wanted to speak to me about it first.

"This is the confession I had to make to you," he wound up; "and I have nothing else to confess, believe me."

These words filled me with stupour. As I listened, I felt my temples throbbing. I had been prepared with nothing but reproaches, and the fewer grounds he gave me for indignation the more at a loss I felt, so that at the end of his speech, I had nothing left to say.

"Let us go to bed," I said at last, after some moments of silence. "Tomorrow I will tell you what I think about it all."

"Tell me at any rate that you aren't still angry with me."

"I must have the night to think it over."


When I saw Jacques again the next morning, I seemed to be looking at him for the first time. I suddenly realized that my son was no longer a child but a young man: so long as I thought of him as a child, the love which I had accidentally discovered might appear monstrous. I had passed the whole night persuading myself that on the contrary it was perfectly natural and normal. Why was it that my dissatisfaction only became keener still? It was not till later that this became clear to me. In the mean time I had to speak to Jacques and tell him my decision. Now an instinct as sure as the voice of conscience warned me that this marriage must be prevented at all costs.

I took Jacques down to the bottom of the garden.

"Have you said anything to Gertrude?" I began by asking him.

"No," he answered; "perhaps she feels I love her, but I have not yet told her so."

"Then you must promise me not to speak of it yet awhile."

"I am determined to obey you, Father; but mayn't I know your reasons?"

I hesitated to give them, feeling doubtful whether those that first came into my mind were the wisest to put forward. To tell the truth, conscience rather than reason dictated my conduct.

"Gertrude is too young," I said at last. "You must reflect that she has not yet been confirmed. You know she was unhappily not like other children and did not begin to develop till very late. She is so trustful that she would no doubt be only too easily touched by the first words of love she heard. And that is why it is of importance not to say them. Your feelings, you say, are in no way reprehensible; I say they are wrong because they are premature. It is our duty to be prudent for Gertrude till she is able to be prudent for herself. It is a matter of conscience."

Jacques has one excellent point—that the simple words I often used to him as a child: "I appeal to your conscience" have always been sufficient to check him. Meanwhile, as I looked at him, I thought that if Gertrude were able to see, she could not fail to admire the tall slender figure, so straight and yet so lissom, the smooth forehead, the open look, the face, so childlike still, though now, as it were, overshadowed by a sudden gravity. He was bare-headed, and his fair hair, which was rather long at that time, curled a little at the temples and half hid his ears.

"There is another thing I want to ask you," I went on, rising from the bench where we had been sitting. "You had intended, you said, to go away the day after tomorrow; I beg you not to put off your journey. You were to remain away a whole month at least; I beg you not to shorten your absence by a single day. Is that agreed?"

"Very well, Father, I will obey."

I thought he turned extremely pale—so pale that the colour left even his lips. But I persuaded myself that such prompt submission argued no very great love, and I felt inexpressibly relieved. I was touched besides by his obedience.

"That's the child I love," I said gently. And drawing him to me, I put my lips to his forehead. There was a slight recoil on his part, but I refused to feel hurt by it.

*March 10th*

Our house is so small that we are obliged to live more or less on top of one another, which is sometimes very inconvenient for my work, although I keep a little room for myself upstairs where I can receive my visitors in private—and especially inconvenient when I want to speak to one of the family in private, without such an air of solemnity as would be the case if the interview took place in this little parlour of mine, which the children call my "sanctum" and into which they are forbidden to enter. On that particular morning, however, Jacques had gone to Neuchâtel to buy a pair of boots for his mountaineering, and as it was very fine, the children had gone out after lunch with Gertrude, whom they take charge of, while she at the same time takes charge of them. (It is a pleasure for me to note that Charlotte is particularly attentive to her.) At tea then, a meal we always take in the common sitting-room, I was quite naturally left alone with Amélie. This was just what I wanted, for I was longing to speak to her. It happens to me so rarely to have a tête-à-tête with her, that I felt almost shy, and the importance of what I had to say agitated me as much as if it had been a question not of Jacques' affairs but of my own. I felt too before I began to speak how two people who love one another and live practically the same life, can yet remain (or become) as much of an enigma to each other as if they lived behind stone walls. Words in this case—those spoken or those heard—have the pathetic sound of vain knocking against the resistance of that dividing barrier, which, unless watch be kept, will grow more and more impenetrable . . .

"Jacques was speaking to me last night and again this morning," I began, as she poured out the tea; and my voice was as faltering as Jacques' had been steady the day before. "He told me he loved Gertrude."

"It was quite right of him to tell you," said she, without looking at me and continuing her housewifely task, as if I had said the most natural thing in the world—or rather as if I had said nothing she did not already know.

"He told me he wanted to marry her; he is resolved to . . ."

"It was only to be expected," she murmured with a slight shrug of her shoulders.

"Then you suspected it?" I asked in some vexation.

"I've seen it coming on for a long while. But that's the kind of thing men never notice."

It would have been no use to protest, and besides there was perhaps some truth in her rejoinder, so, "In that case," I simply objected, "you might have warned me."

She gave me the little crooked smile with which she sometimes accompanies and screens her reticences, and then, with a sideways nod of her head,

"If I had to warn you," she said, "of everything you can't see for yourself, I should have my work cut out for me!"

What did she mean by this insinuation? I did not know or care to know, and went on, without attending to it.

"Well, but I want to hear what you think about it."

She sighed. Then, "You know, my dear, that I never approved of that child's staying with us."

I found it difficult not to be irritated by her harking back in this way to the past.

"Her staying with us is not what we are discussing," I said, but Amélie went on:

"I have always thought it would lead to no good."

With a strong desire to be conciliatory, I caught at her phrase:

"Then you think it would be no good if it led to such a marriage? That's just what I wanted to hear you say. I am glad we are of the same opinion." Then I added that Jacques had submitted quietly to the reasons I had given him, so that there was no need for her to be anxious; that it had been agreed he was to leave the next day for his trip and stay away a whole month.

"As I have no more wish than you that he should find Gertrude here when he comes back," I wound up, "I think the best thing would be to hand her over to the care of Mlle de la M . . . and I could continue to see her there. For there's no denying that I have very serious obligations to her. I have just been to sound our friend and she is quite ready to oblige us. In this way you will be rid of a presence that is painful to you. Louise de la M . . . will look after Gertrude; she seemed delighted with the arrangement; she is looking forward already to giving her harmony lessons."

Amélie seemed determined to remain silent, so that I went on:

"As we shall not want Jacques to see Gertrude there, I think it would be a good thing to warn Mlle de la M . . . of the state of affairs, don't you?"

I hoped by putting this question to get something out of her; but she kept her lips tightly shut, as if she had sworn not to speak. And I went on—not that I had anything more to add, but because I could not endure her silence:

"For that matter, perhaps Jacques will have got over his love by the time he gets back. At his age one hardly knows what one wants."

"And even later one doesn't always know," said she at last, rather oddly.

Her enigmatical and slightly oracular way of speaking irritated me, for I am too frank by nature to put up easily with mystery-making. Turning towards her, I begged her to explain what she meant to imply by that.

"Nothing, my dear," she answered sadly. "I was only thinking that a moment ago you were wishing to be warned of the things you didn't notice yourself."

"Well?"

"Well, I was thinking that it's not always easy to warn people."

I have said that I hate mysteries and I object on principle to hints and double meanings.

"When you want me to understand you, perhaps you will explain yourself more clearly," I replied, rather brutally, perhaps, and I was sorry as soon as I had said it; for I saw her lips tremble a moment. She turned her head aside, then got up and took a few hesitating —almost tottering steps about the room.

"But Amélie," I cried, "why do you go on being unhappy now that everything is all right again?"

I felt that my eyes embarrassed her, and it was with my back turned and my elbows on the table, resting my head in my hands, that I went on to say:

"I spoke to you unkindly just now. Forgive me."

At that I heard her come up behind me; then I felt her lay her fingers gently on my head, as she said tenderly and in a voice trembling with tears:

"My poor dear!"

Then she left the room quickly.

Amélie's words, which I then thought so mysterious, became clear to me soon after this; I have written them down as they struck me at the moment; and that day I only understood that it was time Gertrude should leave.

*March* 12*th*

I had imposed on myself the duty of devoting a little time daily
to Gertrude—a few hours or a few minutes, according to the occupations in hand. The day after this conversation with Amélie, I
had some free time, and as the weather was inviting, I took Gertrude
with me through the forest to that fold in the Jura where in the
clear weather one can see, through a curtain of branches and across
an immense stretch of land at one's feet, the wonder of the snowy
Alps emerging from a thin veil of mist. The sun was already declining
on the left when we reached our customary seat. A meadow of
thick, closely cropped grass sloped downwards at our feet; further
off, a few cows were grazing; each of them among these mountain
herds wears a bell at its neck.

"They outline the landscape," said Gertrude, as she listened to
their tinkling.

She asked me, as she does every time we go for a walk, to describe
the place where we had stopped.

"But you know it already," I said; "on the fringe of the forest,
where one can see the Alps."

"Can one see them clearly today?"

"Yes, in all their splendour."

"You told me they were a little different every day."

"What shall I compare them to this afternoon? To a thirsty mid-
summer's day. Before evening they will have melted into the air."

"I should like you to tell me if there are any lilies in the big
meadows before us?"

"No, Gertrude, lilies do not grow on these heights, or only a few
rare species."

"Not even the lilies called the lilies of the field?"

"There are no lilies in the fields."

"Not even in the fields round about Neuchâtel?"

"There are no lilies of the field."

"Then why did our Lord say 'Look at the lilies of the field'?"

"There were some in his day, no doubt, for him to say so; but they
have disappeared before men and their ploughs."

"I remember you have often told me that what this world most
needs is confidence and love. Don't you think that with a little more

confidence men would see them again? When I listen to His word, I assure you I see them. I will describe them to you, shall I? They are like bells of flame—great bells of azure, filled with the perfume of love and swinging in the evening breeze. Why do you say there are none there before us? I feel them. I see the meadow filled with them."

"They are not more beautiful than you see them, my Gertrude."

"Say they are not less beautiful."

"They are as beautiful as you see them."

"And yet I say unto you that even Solomon in all his glory was not arrayed like one of these," said she, quoting Christ's words; and when I heard her melodious voice, I felt I was listening to them for the first time. "In all his glory," she repeated thoughtfully, and was silent for a time. I went on:

"I have told you, Gertrude, that it is those who have eyes who cannot see." And a prayer rose from the bottom of my heart: "I thank thee O Lord, that thou revealest to the humble what thou hidest from the wise."

"If you knew," she exclaimed in a rapture of delight, "if you knew how easily I imagine it all! Would you like me to describe the landscape to you? . . . Behind us, above us, and around us are the great fir-trees, with their scent of resin and ruddy trunks, stretching out their long dark horizontal branches and groaning as the wind tries to bend them. At our feet, like an open book on the sloping desk of the mountain, lies the broad green meadow, shot with shifting colours—blue in the shade, golden in the sun, and speaking in clear words of flowers—gentians, pulsatillas, ranunculus and Solomon's beautiful lilies; the cows come and spell them out with their bells; and the angels come and read them—for you say that the eyes of men are closed. Below the book, I see a great smoky, misty river of milk, hiding abysses of mystery—an immense river, whose only shore is the beautiful, dazzling Alps far, far away in the distance . . . That's where Jacques is going. Tell me, is he really starting tomorrow?"

"He is to start tomorrow. Did he tell you so?"

"He didn't tell me so, but I guessed it. Will he be long away?"

"A month . . . Gertrude, I want to ask you something. Why didn't you tell me that he used to meet you in the church?"

"He came twice. Oh, I don't want to hide anything from you; but I was afraid of making you unhappy."

"It would make me unhappy if you didn't tell me."

Her hand sought mine.

"He was sad at leaving."

"Tell me, Gertrude . . . did he say he loved you?"

"He didn't say so, but I can feel it without being told. He doesn't love me as much as you do."

"And you, Gertrude, does it make you unhappy that he should go away?"

"I think it is better he should go. I couldn't respond."

"But tell me, does it make you unhappy that he should go?"

"You know, pastor, that it's you I love . . . Oh, why do you take your hand away? I shouldn't speak so, if you weren't married. But no one marries a blind girl. Then why shouldn't we love one another? Tell me, pastor, do you think there's anything wrong in it?"

"It's never in love that the wrong lies."

"I feel there is nothing but good in my heart. I don't want to make Jacques suffer. I don't want to make anyone suffer . . . . I only want to give happiness."

"Jacques was thinking of asking you to marry him."

"Will you let me speak to him before he goes? I should like to make him understand that he must give up loving me. Pastor, you understand, don't you, that I can't marry anyone? You'll let me speak to him, won't you?"

"This evening."

"No, tomorrow. Just before he leaves . . ."

The sun was setting in majestic splendour. The evening air was warm. We had risen and, talking as we went, we turned back along the somber homeward path.

## Second Note Book

*April 25th*

I have been obliged to put this book aside for some time. The snow melted at last and as soon as the roads were passable, there were a great many things to be done which I had been obliged to put off all the long while our village was isolated from the outer world. It was only yesterday I was able for the first time to find a few moments' leisure again.

Last night I read over everything I have written . . .

Now that I dare call by its name the feeling that so long lay unacknowledged in my heart, it seems almost incomprehensible that I should have mistaken it until this very day—incomprehensible that those words of Amélie's that I recorded here should have appeared mysterious—that even after Gertrude's naïve declarations, I should still have doubted that I loved her. The fact is that I would not then allow any love outside marriage could be permissible, nor at the same time would I allow that there could be anything whatever forbidden in the feeling that drew me so passionately to Gertrude.

The innocence of her avowals, their very frankness re-assured me. I told myself she was only a child. Real love would not go without confusion and blushes. As far as I was concerned, I persuaded myself I loved her as one loves an afflicted child. I tended her as one tends a sick person—and so I made a moral obligation, a duty of what was really a passionate inclination. Yes, truly, on the very evening she spoke to me in the way I have described, so happy was I, so light of heart that I misunderstood my real feelings and even as I transcribed our talk, I misunderstood them still. For I should have considered love reprehensible, and my conviction was that everything reprehensible must lie heavy on the soul; therefore, as I felt no weight on my soul, I had no thought of love.

These conversations were set down not only just as they occurred, but were also written while I was in the same frame of mind as when they took place; to tell the truth, it was only when I re-read them last night that I understood. . . . .

As soon as Jacques had gone (I had allowed Gertrude to speak to him before he left, and when he returned for the last few days of the holidays, he affected either to avoid her altogether or to speak to her only in my presence) our life slipped back into its usual peaceful course. Gertrude, as had been arranged, went to stay at Mlle Louise's, where I visited her every day. But, again in my fear of love, I made a point of not talking to her of anything likely to agitate us. I spoke to her only as a pastor and for the most part in Louise's presence, occupying myself chiefly with her religious instruction and with preparing her for Holy Communion, which she has just partaken of this Easter.

I too communicated on Easter day.

This was a fortnight ago. To my surprise Jacques, who was spending a week's holiday with us, did not accompany us to the Lord's

Table. And I greatly regret having to say that Amélie also abstained —for the first time since our marriage. It seemed as though the two of them had come to an understanding and resolved by their abstention from this solemn celebration to throw a shadow over my joy. Here again I congratulated myself that Gertrude could not see and that I was left to bear the weight of this shadow alone. I know Amélie too well not to be aware of all the blame she wished indirectly to convey by her conduct. She never openly disapproves of me, but she makes a point of showing her displeasure by leaving me in a sort of isolation.

I was profoundly distressed that a grievance of this kind—such a one, I mean, as I shrink from contemplating—should have so affected Amélie's soul as to turn her aside from her higher interests. And when I came home I prayed for her in all sincerity of heart.

As for Jacques' abstention, it was due to quite another motive, as I learnt from a conversation I had with him a little later on.

*May 3rd*

Gertrude's religious instruction has led me to re-read the Gospels with a fresh eye. It seems to me more and more that many of the notions that constitute our Christian faith originate not from Christ's own words but from St. Paul's commentaries.

This was, in fact, the subject of the discussion I have just had with Jacques. By disposition he is somewhat hard and rigid, and his mind is not sufficiently nourished by his heart; he is becoming traditionalist and dogmatic. He reproaches me with choosing out of the Christian doctrine "what pleases me." But I do not pick and choose among Christ's words. I simply, between Christ and St. Paul, choose Christ. He, on the contrary, for fear of finding them in opposition, refuses to dissociate them, refuses to feel any difference of inspiration between them, and makes objections when I say that in one case it is a man I hear, while in the other it is God. The more he argues, the more persuaded I am he does not feel that Christ's slightest word has a divine accent that is unique.

I search the Gospels, I search in vain for commands, threats, prohibitions . . . All of these come from St. Paul. And it is precisely because they are not to be found in the words of Christ that Jacques is disturbed. Souls like his think themselves lost as soon as they are deprived of their props, their hand-rails, their fences. And besides, they cannot endure others to enjoy a liberty they have resigned, and want to obtain by compulsion what would readily be granted by love.

"But, Father," he said, "I too desire the soul's happiness."

"No, my friend, you desire its submission."

I leave him the last word because I dislike arguing; but I know that happiness is endangered when one seeks to obtain it by what should on the contrary be the effect of happiness—and if it is true that the loving soul rejoices in a willing submission, nothing is further from happiness than submission without love.

For the rest Jacques reasons well, and if I were not distressed at seeing so much doctrinal harshness in so young a mind, I should no doubt admire the quality of his arguments and his unbending logic. It often seems to me that I am younger than he is—younger today than I was yesterday—and I repeat to myself the words:

"Except ye become as little children, ye shall not enter into the kingdom of Heaven."

Do I betray Christ, do I slight, do I profane the Gospels when I see in them above all a *method for attaining the life of blessedness?* The state of joy, which doubt and the hardness of our hearts alone prevent, is an obligation laid upon every Christian. Every living creature is more or less capable of joy. Every living creature ought to tend to joy. Gertrude's smile alone teaches me more in this respect than all my lessons teach her.

And these words of Christ's stood out before my eyes in letters of light: "If ye were blind ye should have no sin." Sin is that which darkens the soul—which prevents its joy. Gertrude's perfect happiness, which shines forth from her whole being, comes from the fact that she does not know sin. There is nothing in her but light and love.

I have put into her vigilant hands the four Gospels, the psalms, the Apocalypse, and the three Epistles of St. John, so that she may read, "God is light and in him is no darkness at all," as in the Gospel she has already heard the Saviour say, "I am the light of the world," I will not give her the Epistles of St. Paul, for if, being blind she knows not sin, what is the use of troubling her by letting her read, "sin by the commandment might become exceeding sinful" (Romans VII, 13) and the whole of the dialectic that follows, admirable as it may be.

*May 8th*

Dr. Martins came over yesterday from Chaux-de-Fond. He examined Gertrude's eyes for a long time with the ophthalmoscope. He told me he had spoken to Dr. Roux, the Lausanne specialist, about her and is to report his observations to him. They both have an idea that Gertrude might be operated on with success. But we have agreed to say nothing about it to her as long as things are not more certain. Martins is to come and let me know what they think after they have consulted. What would be the good of raising Gertrude's hopes if there is any risk of their being immediately extinguished? And besides is she not happy as she is? . . .

*May 10th*

At Easter Jacques and Gertrude saw each other again in my presence—at least, Jacques had a visit from Gertrude and spoke to her, only about trifles, however. He seemed less agitated than I feared; and I persuade myself afresh that if his love had really been very ardent, he would not have got over it so easily, even though Gertrude had told him last year before he went away that it was hopeless.

I notice that he no longer says "thou" to Gertrude but calls her "you," which is certainly preferable; however I had not asked him to do so and I am glad it was his own idea. There is undoubtedly a great deal of good in him.

I suspect, however, that this submission of Jacques' was not arrived at without a struggle. The unfortunate thing is that the constraint he has been obliged to impose on his feelings now seems to him good in itself; he would like to see it imposed on everyone; I felt this in the discussion I had with him which I have recorded further back. Is it not La Rochefoucauld who says that the mind is often the dupe of the heart? I need not say that, knowing Jacques as I do, I did not venture to point this out to him there and then, for I take him to be one of those people who are only made more obstinate by argument; but the very same evening I looked up what furnished me with a reply—and from St. Paul himself (I could only beat him with his own weapons), and left a little note in his room, in which I wrote out the text, "Let not him which eateth not judge him that eateth: for God has received him." (Romans XIV, 3.)

I might as well have copied out what follows: "I know and am persuaded by the Lord Jesus that there is nothing unclean of itself: but to him that esteemeth any thing to be unclean, to him it is unclean."—But I did not dare to, for I was afraid that Jacques might proceed to suspect me of some wrongful interpretation with regard to Gertrude—a suspicion which must not so much as cross his imagination for a second. Evidently it is here a question of food; but in how many passages of the Scriptures are we not called on to give the words a double and triple meaning? ("If thine eye" . . . the multiplication of the loaves; the miracle of Cana, etc. . . .) This is not a matter of logic-chopping; the meaning of this text is wide and deep: the restriction must not be dictated by the law but by love, and St. Paul exclaims immediately afterwards: "But if thy brother be grieved with thy meat, now walkest thou not charitably." It is where love fails that the chink in our armour lies. That is where the Evil One attacks us. Lord, remove from my heart all that does not belong to love . . . For I was wrong to provoke Jacques: the next morning I found on my table the same note on which I had written out the text; Jacques had simply written on the back of it another text from the same chapter: "Destroy not him with thy meat for whom Christ died." (Romans XIV, 15.)

I have re-read the whole chapter. It is the starting point for endless discussion. And is Gertrude to be tormented with these perplexities? Is the brightness of her sky to be darkened with these clouds? Am I not nearer Christ, do I not keep her nearer to Him, when I teach her, when I let her believe that the only sin is that which hurts the happiness of others or endangers our own?

Alas! There are some souls to whom happiness is uncongenial; they cannot, they do not know how to avail themselves of it . . . I am thinking of my poor Amélie. I never cease imploring her, urging her—I wish I could force her to be happy. Yes, I wish I could lift everyone among us up to God. But she will none of it; she curls up like certain flowers which never open to the sun. Everything she sees causes her uneasiness and distress.

"What's the good, my dear," she answered me the other day, "we can't all be blind."

Ah, how her irony grieves me! And what courage I need not to be disturbed by it! And yet it seems to me she ought to understand that this allusion to Gertrude's infirmity is particularly painful to me. She makes me feel indeed, that what I admire above all in Gertrude is her infinite mildness; I have never heard her express the slightest resentment against anyone. It is true I do not allow her to hear anything that might hurt her.

And as the soul that is happy diffuses happiness around it by the radiation of love, so everything in Amélie's neighbourhood becomes gloomy and morose. Amiel would say that her soul gives out black rays. When, after a harassing day of toil—visits to the sick, the poor, the afflicted—I come in at nightfall, tired out and with a heart longing for rest, affection, warmth, it is to find, more often than not, worries, recriminations and quarrels, which I dread a thousand times more than the cold, the wind and the rain out of doors. I know well enough that our old Rosalie invariably wants her own way, but she is not always in the wrong, nor Amélie always in the right when she tries to make her give in. I know that Gaspard and Charlotte are horribly unruly; but would not Amélie get better results if she scolded them less loudly and less constantly? So much nagging, so many reprimands and expostulations lose their edge like pebbles on the seashore; they are far less disturbing to the children than to me. I know that Claude is teething (at least that is what his mother declares every time he sets up a howl) but does it not encourage him to howl, for her or Sarah to run and pick him up and be for ever petting him? I am convinced he would not howl so often if he was left to howl once or twice to his heart's content when I am not there. But I know that is the very time they spoil him most.

Sarah is like her mother, and for that reason I should have wished to send her to school. She is not, alas, what her mother was at her age when we were first engaged, but what the material cares of life have made her—I was going to say the *cultivation* of the cares of life, for Amélie certainly does cultivate them. I find it indeed very difficult to recognize in her today the angel of those early times, who smiled encouragement on every high-minded impulse of my heart, who I dreamt would be the sharer of my every hope and fear, and whom I looked on as my guide and leader along the path to Heaven—or did love blind me in those days? . . . I cannot see that Sarah has any interests that are not vulgar; like her mother, she allows herself to be entirely taken up with paltry household matters; the very features of her face, unilluminated as they are by any inward flame, look dull and almost hard. She has no taste for poetry or for reading in general; I never overhear any conversation between her and her mother in which I have any inclination to take part, and I feel my isolation even more painfully when I am with them than when I retire to my study, as it is becoming my custom to do more and more often.

And I have also fallen into the habit this autumn—encouraged by the shortness of the days—of taking tea at Mlle de la M . . .'s whenever my rounds permit it, that is whenever I can get back early enough. I have not yet mentioned that since last November Mlle de la M . . . has extended her hospitality to three little blind girls, entrusted to her care by Martins. Gertrude is teaching them to read and to work at sundry little tasks over which they have already begun to be quite clever.

How restful, how comforting I find its warm friendly atmosphere every time I re-enter the Grange, and how much I miss it if I am obliged to let two or three days pass without going there. Mlle de la M . . . , it is hardly necessary to say, has sufficient means to take in and provide for Gertrude and the three little boarders without putting herself out in any way; three maid-servants help her with the greatest devotion and save her all fatigue. Can one imagine fortune and leisure better bestowed? Louise da la M . . . has always interested herself in the poor; she is a profoundly religious woman and seems hardly to belong to this earth or to live for anything but love; though her hair is already silvery under its lace cap, nothing can be more childlike than her laugh, nothing more harmonious than her movements, nothing more musical than her voice. Gertrude has caught her manners, her way of speaking, almost the intonation, not only of her voice, but of her mind, of her whole being—a likeness upon which I tease them both, but which neither of them will admit. How sweet it is, when I can find the time, to linger in their company, to see them sitting beside each other, Gertrude either leaning her head on her friend's shoulder, or clasping one of her hands in hers, while I read them some lines out of Lamartine or Hugo; how sweet to behold the beauties of such poetry reflected in the mirror of their limpid souls! Even the little pupils are touched by it. These children, in this atmosphere of peace and love develop astonishingly and their progress is wonderful. I smiled at first when Mlle Louise spoke of teaching them to dance—for their health's sake as much as for their amusement; but now I admire the rhythmic grace to which they have attained, though they themselves, alas, are unable to appreciate it. And yet Louise de la M . . . has persuaded me that though they cannot see, they do physically perceive the harmony of their movements. Gertrude takes part in their dances with the most charming grace and sweetness, and moreover seems to take the keenest pleasure in them. Or sometimes it is Louise de la M . . . who directs the little girls' movements and then Gertrude seats herself at the piano. Her progress in music is astonishing; she plays the organ in chapel now every Sunday. Every Sunday she comes to lunch with us; my children are delighted to see her, notwithstanding that their tastes are growing more and more divergent. Amélie is not too irritable and we get through the meal without a hitch. After lunch, the whole family goes back with Gertrude to the Grange and has tea there. It is a treat for my children and Louise enjoys spoiling them and loading them with cakes and sweetmeats. Amélie, who is far from being insensible to attentions of this kind, unbends at last and looks ten years younger. I think she would find it difficult now to do without this halt in the wearisome round of her daily life.

*May 18th*

Now that the fine weather has returned, I have been able to go out again with Gertrude—a thing I had not done for a long time (for there have been fresh falls of snow quite recently and the roads have been in a terrible state until only a few days ago) and it is a long time too since I have found myself alone with her.

We walked quickly; the sharp air coloured her cheeks and kept blowing her fair hair over her face. As we passed alongside a peatmoss, I picked one or two rushes that were in flower and slipped their stalks under her béret; then I twined them into her hair so as to keep them in place.

We had scarcely spoken to each other as yet in the astonishment of finding ourselves alone together, when Gertrude turned her sightless face towards me and asked abruptly:

"Do you think Jacques still loves me?"

"He has made up his mind to give you up," I replied at once.

"But do you think he knows you love me?" she went on.

Since the conversation which I have related above, more than six months had gone by without (strange to say) the slightest word of love having passed between us. We were never alone, as I have said, and it was better so . . . Gertrude's question made my heart beat so fast that I was obliged to slacken our pace a little.

"My dear Gertrude, everyone knows I love you," I cried. But she was not to be put off.

"No, no; you have not answered my question."

And after a moment's silence, she went on with lowered head:

"Aunt Amélie knows it; and I know it makes her sad."

"She would be sad any way," I protested with an unsteady voice; "it is her nature to be sad."

"Oh, you always try to reassure me," she answered with some impatience. "But I don't want to be reassured. There are a great many things, I feel sure, you don't tell me about for fear of troubling or grieving me; a great many things I don't know, so that sometimes . . ."

Her voice dropped lower and lower; she stopped as if for want of breath. And when, taking up her last words, I asked:

"So that sometimes? . . ."

"So that sometimes," she continued sadly, "I think all the happiness I owe you is founded upon ignorance."

"But Gertrude . . ."

"No, let me say this—I don't want a happiness of that kind. You must understand that I don't . . . I don't care about being happy. I would rather know. There are a great many things—sad things assured—that I can't see, but you have no right to keep them from me. I have reflected a great deal during these last winter months; I am afraid, you know, that the whole world is not as beautiful as you have made out, pastor—and in fact, that it is very far from it."

"It is true that man has often defaced it," I argued timidly, for the rush of her thoughts frightened me and I tried to turn it aside, though without daring to hope I should succeed. She seemed to be waiting for these words, for she seized on them at once as though they were the missing link in the chain:

"Exactly!" she cried; "I want to be sure of not adding to the evil."

For a long time we walked on very quickly and in silence. Everything I might have said was checked beforehand by what I felt she was thinking; I dreaded to provoke some sentence which might set both our fates trembling in the balance. And as I thought of what Martins had said as to the possibility of her regaining her sight, a dreadful anxiety gripped me.

"I wanted to ask you," she went on at last—"but I don't know how to say it. . . ."

Certainly she needed all her courage to speak, just as I needed all mine to listen. But how could I have foreseen the question that was tormenting her?

"Are the children of a blind woman always born blind?"

"No, Gertrude," I said, "except in very special cases. There is in fact no reason why they should be."

She seemed extremely reassured. I should have liked in my turn to ask her why she wanted to know this; I had not the courage and went on clumsily:

"But Gertrude, to have children, one must be married."

"Don't tell me that pastor, I know it's not true."

"I have told you what it was proper for me to tell you," I protested. "But it is true, the laws of nature do allow what is forbidden by the laws of man and God."

"You have often told me the laws of God were the laws of love."

"But such love as that is not the same that also goes by the name of Charity."

"Is it out of Charity you love me?"

"No, my Gertrude, you know it is not."

"Then you admit our love is outside the laws of God?"

"What do you mean?"

"Oh, you know well enough, and I ought not to be the one to say so."

I sought in vain for some way of evasion; the beating of my heart set all my arguments flying in confusion.

"Gertrude," I exclaimed wildly, ". . . you think your love wrong?" She corrected me;

"*Our* love . . . I say to myself I ought to think so."

"And then? . . ."

I heard what sounded like a note of supplication in my voice, while without waiting to take breath, she went on:

"But that I cannot stop loving you."

All this happened yesterday. I hesitated at first to write it down . . . I have no idea how our walk came to an end. We hurried along as if we were being pursued, while I held her arm tightly pressed against me. My soul was so absent from my body that I felt as if the smallest pebble in the path might send us both rolling to the ground.

*May 19th*
Martins came back this morning. Gertrude's is a case for operation. Roux is certain of it and wishes to have her under his care for
a time. I cannot refuse and yet, such is my cowardice, that I asked
to be allowed to reflect. I asked to have time to prepare her
gently . . . My heart should leap for joy, but it feels inexpressibly
heavy, weighed down by a sick misgiving. At the thought of having
to tell Gertrude her sight may be restored to her my heart fails me
altogether.

*May 19th Night*
I have seen Gertrude and I have not told her. At the Grange this
evening, there was no one in the drawing-room; I went upstairs to
her room. We were alone.
I held her long in my arms pressed to my heart. She made no
attempt to resist and as she raised her face to mine our lips met . . .

*May 21st*
O Lord, is it for us Thou hast clothed the night with such depth
and beauty? Is it for me? The air is warm and the moon shines in
at my open window as I sit listening to the vast silence of the skies.
Oh, from all creation rises a blended adoration which bears my
heart along, lost in an ecstasy that knows no words. I cannot—I
cannot pray with calm. If there is any limitation to love, it is set by
man and not by Thee, my God. However guilty my love may
appear in the eyes of men, oh tell me that in Thine it is sacred.
I try to rise above the idea of sin; but sin seems to me intolerable,
and I will not give up Christ. No, I will not admit that I sin in
loving Gertrude. I could only succeed in tearing this love from my
heart if I tore my heart out with it, and for what? If I did not
already love her, it would be my duty to love her for pity's sake; to

cease to love her would be to betray her; she needs my love . . .

Lord, I know not . . . I know nothing now but Thee. Be Thou my guide. Sometimes I feel that darkness is closing round me and that it is I who have been deprived of the sight that is to be restored to her.

Gertrude went into the Lausanne nursing-home yesterday and is not to come out for three weeks. I am expecting her return with extreme apprehension. Martins is to bring her back. She has made me promise not to try to see her before then.

*May 22nd*

A letter from Martins: the operation has been successful. God be thanked!

*May 24th*

The idea that she who loved me without seeing me must now see me causes me intolerable discomfort. Will she know me? For the first time in my life I consult the mirror. If I feel her eyes are less indulgent than her heart and less loving, what will become of me? O Lord, I sometimes think I have need of her love in order to love Thee!

*June 8th*

An unusual amount of work has enabled me to get through these last days with tolerable patience. Every occupation that takes me out of myself is a merciful one; but all day long and through all that happens her image is with me.

She is coming back tomorrow. Amélie, who during these last weeks has shown only the best side of herself and seems endeavouring to distract my thoughts, is preparing a little festivity with the children to welcome her return.

*June 9th*

Gaspard and Charlotte have picked what flowers they could find in the woods and fields. Old Rosalie has manufactured a monumental cake which Sarah is decorating with gold paper ornaments. We are expecting her this morning for lunch. I am writing to fill in the time of waiting. It is eleven o'clock. Every moment I raise my head and look out at the road along which Martins' carriage will come. I resist the temptation to go and meet them; it is better—especially for Amélie's sake—that I should not welcome her apart from the others. My heart leaps . . . Ah! Here they are!

*June 9th Evening*

Oh, in what abominable darkness I am plunged.

Pity, Lord, pity! I renounce loving her, but do Thou not let her die.

How right my fears were! What has she done? What did she want to do? Amélie and Sarah tell me they went with her as far as the door of the Grange, where Mlle de la M . . . was expecting her. So she must have gone out again . . . What happened?

I try to put my thoughts into some sort of order. The accounts they give are incomprehensible or contradictory. My mind is utterly confused . . . Mlle de la M . . .'s gardener has just brought her back to the Grange unconscious; he says he saw her walking by the river, then she crossed the garden bridge, then stooped and disappeared; but as he did not at first realize that she had fallen, he did not run to her help as he should have done; he found her at the little sluice, where she had been carried by the stream. When I saw her soon afterwards, she had not recovered consciousness; or at least had lost it again, for she came to for a moment, thanks to the prompt measures that were taken. Martins, who, thank Heaven, has not yet left, cannot understand the kind of stupor and lassitude in which she is now sunk. He has questioned her in vain; she seems either not to hear or else to be determined not to speak. Her breathing is very laboured and Martins is afraid of pneumonia; he has ordered sinapisms and cupping and has promised to come again tomorrow. The mistake was leaving her too long in her wet clothes while they were trying to bring her round; the water of the river is icy. Mlle de la M . . . , who is the only person who has succeeded in getting a few words from her, declares she wanted to pick some of the forget-me-nots that grow in abundance on this side of the river, and that, being still unaccustomed to measure distances, or else mistaking the floating carpet of flowers for solid ground, she suddenly lost her footing . . . If I could only believe it! If I could only persuade myself it was nothing but an accident, what a dreadful load would be lifted from my heart! During the whole meal, though it was so gay, the strange smile that never left her face made me uneasy; a forced smile, which I had never seen her wear before, but which I tried my utmost to believe was the smile of her newly-born sight; a smile which seemed to stream from her eyes on to her face like tears, and beside which, the vulgar mirth of the others seemed offensive. She did not join in the mirth; I felt as if she had discovered a secret she would surely have confided to me if we had been alone. She hardly spoke; but no one was surprised at that, because she is often silent when she is with others and all the more so when their merriment grows noisy.

Lord, I beseech Thee, let me speak to her. I must know or how can I continue to live? . . . And yet if she really wished to end her life, is it just because she *knew?* Knew what? Dear, what horrible thing can you have learnt? What did I hide from you that was so deadly? What can you so suddenly have seen?

I have been spending two hours at her bedside, my eyes never leaving her forehead, her pale cheeks, her delicate eyelids, shut down over some unspeakable sorrow, her hair still wet and like seaweed as it lies spread round about her on the pillow—listening to her difficult, irregular breathing.

*June 10th*

Mlle Louise sent for me this morning just as I was starting to go to the Grange. After a fairly quiet night, Gertrude has at last emerged from her torpor. She smiled when I went into the room and signed to me to come and sit by her bedside. I did not dare question her, and no doubt she was dreading my questions, for she said immediately, as though to forestall anything emotional:

"What do you call those little blue flowers that I wanted to pick by the river? Flowers the colour of the sky? Will you be cleverer than I and pick me a bunch of them? I should like to have them here beside my bed . . ."

The false cheerfulness of her voice was dreadful to me; and no doubt she was aware of it, for she added more gravely:

"I can't speak to you this morning; I am too tired. Go and pick those flowers for me, will you? You can come back again later."

And when an hour later, I brought her the bunch of forget-me-nots, Mlle Louise told me that Gertrude was resting and could not see me before evening.

I saw her again this evening. She was lying—almost sitting up in bed—propped against a pile of pillows. Her hair was now fastened up, with the forget-me-nots I had brought her twisted into the plaits above her forehead.

She was obviously very feverish and drew her breath with great difficulty. She kept the hand I put out to her in her burning hand; I remained standing beside her:

"I must confess something to you, pastor; because this evening I am afraid of dying," she said. "What I told you this morning was a lie. It was not to pick flowers . . . Will you forgive me if I say I wanted to kill myself?"

I fell on my knees beside the bed, still keeping her frail hand in mine; but she disengaged it and began to stroke my head, while I buried my face in the sheets so as to hide my tears and stifle my sobs.

"Do you think it was very wrong?" she went on tenderly; then, as I answered nothing:

"My friend, my friend," she said, "you must see that I take up too much room in your heart and in your life. When I came back to you, that was what struck me at once—or at any rate, that the place I took belonged to another and that it made her unhappy. My crime is that I did not feel it sooner; or rather—for indeed I knew it all along—that I allowed you to love me in spite of it. But when her face suddenly appeared to me—when I saw such unhappiness on her poor face, I could not bear the idea that that unhappiness was my work. . . . No, no, don't blame yourself for anything; but let me go, and give her back her joy."

The hand ceased stroking my head; I seized it and covered it with kisses and tears. But she drew it away impatiently and began to toss in the throes of some fresh emotion.

"That is not what I wanted to say to you; no, it's not that I wanted to say," she kept repeating, and I saw the sweat on her damp forehead. Then she closed her eyes and kept them shut for a time, as though to concentrate her thoughts or to recover her former state of blindness; and in a voice which at first was trailing and mournful, but which soon, as she reopened her eyes, grew louder, grew at last animated even to vehemence:

"When you gave me back my sight," she began, "my eyes opened on a world more beautiful than I had ever dreamt it could be; yes, truly, I had never imagined the daylight so bright, the air so brilliant, the sky so vast. But I had never imagined men's faces so full of care either; and when I went into your house, do you know what it was that struck me first? . . . Oh, it can't be helped, I must tell you: what I saw first of all was our fault, our sin. No, don't protest. You remember Christ's words, "If ye were blind ye should have no sin." But now I see . . . Get up, pastor. Sit there, beside me. Listen to me without interrupting. During the time I spent in the nursing-home, I read—or rather I had read to me some verses of the Bible I did not know—some you had never read me. I remember a text of St. Paul's which I repeated to myself all one day. 'For I was alive without the law once; but when the commandment came, sin revived and I died.' "

She spoke in a state of extreme excitement and in a very loud voice, almost shouting the last words, so that I was made uncomfortable by the idea that they might be heard outside the room; then she shut her eyes and repeated in a whisper as though for herself alone:

"Sin revived—and I died."

I shivered and my heart froze in a kind of terror. I tried to turn aside her thoughts:

"Who read you those texts?" I asked.

"Jacques," she said, opening her eyes and looking at me fixedly. "Did you know he was converted?"

It was more than I could bear; I was going to implore her to stop, but she had already gone on:

"My friend, I am going to grieve you very much; but there must be no falsehood between us now. When I saw Jacques, I suddenly realized it was not you I loved—but him. He had your face—I mean the face I imagined you had . . . Ah! why did you make me refuse him? I might have married him . . ."

"But Gertrude, you still can," I cried with despair in my heart.

"He is entering the priesthood," she said impetuously. Then, shaken by sobs, "Oh, I want to confess to him," she moaned in a kind of ecstasy. . . . "You see for yourself, there's nothing left me but to die. I am thirsty. Please call someone. I can't breathe. Leave me. I want to be alone. Ah! I had hoped that speaking to you would have brought me more relief. You must say good-bye. We must say good-bye. I cannot bear to be with you any more."

I left her. I called Mlle de la M . . . to take my place beside her; her extreme agitation made me fear the worst, but I could not help seeing that my presence did her harm. I begged that I might be sent for if there was a change for the worse.

*June 11th*

Alas! I was never to see her again alive. She died this morning after a night of delirium and exhaustion. Jacques, who at Gertrude's dying request was telegraphed for by Mlle de la M . . . , arrived a few hours after the end. He reproached me cruelly for not having called in a priest while there was yet time. But how could I have done so, when I was still unaware that during her stay at Lausanne, and evidently urged by him, Gertrude had abjured the Protestant faith? He told me in the same breath of his own conversion and Gertrude's. And so they both left me at the same time; it seemed as if, separated by me during their lifetime, they had planned to escape me here and be united to each other in God. But I tell myself that Jacques' conversion is more a matter of the head than the heart.

"Father," he said, "it is not fitting for me to make accusations against you; but it was the example of your error that guided me."

After Jacques had left again, I knelt down beside Amélie and asked her to pray for me, as I was in need of help. She simply repeated "Our Father . . ." but between each sentence she left long pauses which we filled with our supplication.

I would have wept, but I felt my heart more arid than the desert.

# NOW THAT YOU'VE READ GIDE'S
# THE PASTORAL SYMPHONY:

*The Pastoral Symphony* is a tender story of love, but its surface serenity masks calamitous tensions. It is with the revelation of these tensions, their forces and thrusts rather than the emotional avalanche they precipitate, that André Gide is concerned. The tensions in this short novel are not those of the ordinary love tale; they are spiritual and religious, reflecting the struggle which had waged for many years in the soul of the writer.

In 1916, two years before beginning *The Symphony*, Gide experienced a spiritual crisis. In two earlier novels he had revealed the two struggling, irreconcilable forces within him he now had, somehow, to reconcile: the hero of *The Immoralist* (1902) suddenly recognizes that the sexual desire he had so long repressed because of his moral training is a natural desire. A sense of freedom and serenity accompany this recognition, and the immoralist, for a time, joyfully ignores the moral and spiritual inclinations of his personality. Alissa, the heroine of the second novel, *Strait Is the Gate* (1909), aspires to a saintly life. She accedes to her spiritual longings, suppresses her desire for marriage, and lives a virtuous life of restraint and sacrifice which Gide describes with moving sincerity. Before she dies, however, Alissa suffers from the realization that she has sacrificed too much by suppressing her love. These companion novels dramatize the irreconcilable polarities (for the early Gide) of his nature—the carnal and the spiritual.

The struggle that reached its crisis in 1916 can be seen developing in Gide's early life. He was born in 1869 to strict Protestant parents. Gide's father, a law professor at the University of Paris, died when the writer was eleven years old, and his mother, a member of a wealthy Norman family, devoted her life to her only child. Juliette Gide, surrounded by Catholics even in her own family, was a staunch Protestant and always acted in accord with inflexible French Protestant principles. With the aid of her companion and childhood friend, Anna Shackleton, she occupied herself with the moral and intellectual training of her son.

As a young man Gide always carried in his pocket a small Bible. In his autobiography, *If It Die . . .* (1920), he describes the severe regimen he imposed upon himself in his effort to achieve sanctity by mortification of the flesh: he denied himself pleasures of the senses, slept on a board, plunged into a cold bath early in the morning. He knew the joy of spiritual and religious exaltation, and shortly after the death of his mother he married his cousin Madeleine, a woman of the same puritanical mold as the two women who had dominated his youth.

In his autobiography Gide also recalls his difficulties at school, his development of a nervous ailment to escape returning to classes after an illness, his early passion for entomology, the annual Spring visit to grandmother Gide's home in the South of France, and the frequent sojourns at La Roque in Normandy, the home of his maternal grandmother. He remembers his father reading Homer and Molière to him and the day his mother finally permitted him to read anything he wanted. One incident dominates these early recollections—the moment his love for Madeleine awakened. He had found his young cousin crying bitterly shortly after she had discovered that her mother was an adulteress. The boy was overwhelmed by a feeling of tenderness, and from that moment Madeleine embodied for Gide all his spiritual aspirations.

During his early years, music and the piano absorbed much of Gide's interest and time. He displayed, in fact, so fine a talent for the piano that one of his teachers wanted him to devote all his efforts to music. Madame Gide, however, insisted that her son continue his general studies. The writer's early interest in music never slackened. He wrote a book on Chopin, and derived much pleasure from Beethoven (composer of The Pastoral Symphony); he spent many hours at the piano, and, a born teacher, like the pastor of *The Symphony*, he enjoyed instructing a musically talented niece.

In his late teens Gide discovered the Greek poets and responded enthusiastically to their glorification of physical beauty. Though he became aware of physical desire at this time, the ardor of his religious beliefs and spiritual aspirations did not diminish. In this state he wrote his first book, *The Notebooks of André Walter* (1891), the journal of a young, poetic youth who passionately seeks complete spiritual union with Emmanuèle (a fictional creation based upon the character of Madeleine). Gide had only a small edition printed, and he sent a copy to Madeleine, hoping it would persuade her to marry him. She continued to resist his proposal, however, for several more years.

The young writer began to frequent the literary salons of Paris and, under the influence of the Symbolist poets he met, published a volume of poems. Then in 1893 he set off for a trip to North Africa. For the first time he traveled without his Bible. At the start of his journey he became seriously ill, and as he recovered he became more acutely conscious of his physical being. In the hot, sensuous climate of Africa he discovered in himself a compulsion for unconventional sexual behavior and experienced the pleasure and sense of release that acceding to the demands of the flesh provided. He came to the conclusion that life was good, that man should welcome experience, relish the joy it offered. The pagan in Gide, the lover of physical beauty and of sensual pleasure, was born and quickly matured under the hot African sun. Two mighty forces, the Pagan and the Christian, the carnal and the spiritual, were squared off in the arena of his soul. The struggle that was to produce some of the frankest writing of contemporary literature was almost ready to begin.

Until his mother died, in 1895, Gide devoted himself to sensuality; but immediately after her death, reaction set in; he renounced the life he had been living and turned to the person who was to him the incarnation of his spiritual longings. Once more he asked Madeleine Rondeaux to marry him, and this time she accepted. The marriage, in October, 1895, for Gide was an act of faith, prompted by the puritanical and spiritual forces in his personality. His love for Madeleine was the antithesis of the passion he had discovered in Africa. If he had hoped, however, that his union with Madeleine would eclipse the demon in him, on his wedding trip he realized that his demon was as powerful as his angel.

The terrible struggle began. The two extremes of his personality fought for dominance. Neither would be subdued, and Gide, with his keen analytical mind, watched and recorded in his Journals and his books the war raging so painfully in his soul. In these works Gide set forth his doctrine of sincerity, of knowing one's self completely, and living fully according to one's nature. Believing as he did, he could suppress neither of the extremes in his character; but, at the same time, the constant tugging in opposite directions was wearing him down physically and spiritually. Several of his Catholic friends recognized Gide's religious inclinations and hoped to bring about his conversion. He was unable, however, to find solace in the Church. Slowly, painfully, he began, in 1916, as Tolstoi had begun many years before, a study of the New Testament. In a notebook which he later published under the title *Numquid et tu . . . ?* he pondered the words of Christ and St. Paul. Finally his meditation and study brought him the peace he sought.

"It is never of Christ but of St. Paul that I run afoul—and it is in him, never in the Gospels, that I find again everything that had driven me away." There is no "prescription nor command" to be found, Gide declares, in the words of Christ. He quotes a passage from the "Epistle to the Romans": *I know and am persuaded by the Lord Jesus, that there is nothing unclean of itself: but to him that esteemeth any thing to be unclean, to him it is unclean.* The rules set down by men can destroy the state of innocence, the natural harmony of the human soul. The words of St. Paul take on new significance: *For I was alive without the law once: but when the commandment came, sin revived, and I died.* St. Paul is reborn into a state of grace when the commandment came; but,

Gide argues, "if one grants that the law precedes grace, cannot one admit a state of innocence preceding the law?" It is "that state of second innocence, that pure and laughing rapture," which man will achieve if he follow the admonition: *Except a man be born again*. The "secret of the higher felicity that Christ . . . reveals to us" is peace, happiness, now, in this life. "Joy. Joy. . . . I know that the secret of your gospel, Lord, lies altogether in this divine word: Joy. And is not that just what makes your word triumphant over all human teaching?—that it permits as much joy as the strength of each heart proposes." No true religion, Gide concluded, would insist that antagonism between the flesh and the spirit exists. Man could love life and God at the same time. Thus Gide reconciled his demon and his angel.

In *Numquid et tu . . . ?* Gide wrote: "The Christian artist is not he who paints saints and angels, any more than edifying subjects; but rather he who puts into practice the words of Christ—and I am amazed that no one has ever sought to bring out the *aesthetic* truth of the Gospels." When in 1918, he began to write the story of the blind girl, a story that had been germinating in his imagination for about twenty-five years, he utilized his own recent spiritual experiences. The arguments of the pastor in *The Symphony* are Gide's own arguments, some taken directly from *Numquid et tu . . . ?*

But the pastor is not Gide. With remarkable objectivity and clarity of thought, the writer recognized the inherent dangers of his interpretation of the Bible for a weak man to whom sincerity and knowledge of self are not cardinal principles. He portrays in the pastor a man who deludes himself into justifying his passion for Gertrude, the blind girl. (Originally, Gide titled his story *L'Aveugle*. The gender of the noun, meaning a blind person, is indefinite, and the title could apply to the physical blindness of Gertrude or the spiritual blindness of the pastor.) Gertrude is in that state of innocence preceding the law; in her love there is no evil; her desire for the pastor is natural and beautiful. It is in harmony with the world of beauty she imagines when she hears Beethoven's symphony. But the pastor can see the pain etched on his wife's face; his passion is not untainted like that of the blind girl for whom evil does not exist. In the Second Notebook he is dishonest with himself; he does not seek a way of life in Christ but merely an excuse for his desire.

Fifty years old when he published *The Symphony*, Gide felt that he was at last ready to write his fictional masterpiece, and a few years later he published *The Counterfeiters* (c.1925). All the qualities he had displayed in his previous works—the sense of humor and irony in *Lafacadio's Adventures* (1914), the frankness and audaciousness of *Corydon* (1924), the hatred of self-deception of *The Symphony*, and the beautiful style of all his writing were incorporated in this great novel. By 1924, Gide had become a respected literary figure, but his frank confessions and his plea to the young to live honestly, in freedom, according to their nature had made his a controversial name.

He increased the number of his enemies by becoming an advocate of Communism in the 1930's. Too individualistic to submit himself to party discipline, Gide, independently, supported the cause until he returned from a trip through the Soviet Union. What he saw there convinced him that Communism was not the panacea he had imagined, and he wrote two books presenting the reasons for his disillusionment. During World War II the writer was too old to join in active resistance, but he made his position clear, and in 1942 he went to Tunis and established a successor to the *Nouvelle Revue Française* (the important literary journal he had helped to found in 1908), then edited by a collaborator who was later executed for treason. The following year he wrote his final work of fiction, a short novel, *Theseus*, and after the war, in 1947, he received the Nobel prize for literature. On February 19, 1951 André Gide died, leaving behind him one of the frankest, most moving records of a human soul in the history of literature.

And André Gide's was a complex soul: he was able to submit to no philosophy; throughout his long career he sought and embraced many extremes in human thought and experience and then withdrew from them. Like Unamuno's, his writings abound in antithetical views asserted with equal force. Gide had no scruples about inconsistency and contradictions. His guiding principle was sincerity, knowledge of self, and then action, despite the consequences, upon that knowledge. He hated, above all, self-deception. Only by knowing himself completely and then making himself available to all experience, Gide believed, can man be free to live a full rich life. But knowing one's self is no easy task: it means accepting the multiple contradictions of the human personality. It demands unremitting sincerity and total honesty. It is a continuing process but a rewarding one because it guarantees against failure to take advantage of life's experiences, failure to realize in full the potential of one's personality.

## FOR FURTHER INFORMATION:

Germaine Brée. *Gide*. Rutgers University Press: New Brunswick, 1963.

Wallace Fowlie. *André Gide: His Life and Art*. Macmillan & Co.: New York, 1965.

André Gide. *If It Die . . .* (tr. Dorothy Bussy). Secker & Warburg: London, 1955.

André Gide. *Journals of André Gide*, Vol. II (tr. Justin O'Brien). Alfred Knopf: New York, 1948.

Albert Guerard. *André Gide*. Harvard University Press: Cambridge, 1951.

Justin O'Brien. *Portrait of André Gide*. Alfred Knopf: New York, 1953.

George Painter. *André Gide: A Critical Biography*. Atheneum Press: New York, 1968.

# MARIO AND THE MAGICIAN

## BY THOMAS MANN

First published, 1929

# MARIO AND THE MAGICIAN

THE ATMOSPHERE of Torre di Venere remains
unpleasant in the memory. From the first moment the air of the place
made us uneasy, we felt irritable, on edge; then at the end came the
shocking business of Cipolla, that dreadful being who seemed to in-
corporate, in so fateful and so humanly impressive a way, all the
peculiar evilness of the situation as a whole. Looking back, we had
the feeling that the horrible end of the affair had been preordained
and lay in the nature of things; that the children had to be present
at it was an added impropriety, due to the false colours in which
the weird creature presented himself. Luckily for them, they did
not know where the comedy left off and the tragedy began; and we
let them remain in their happy belief that the whole thing had been
a play up till the end.

Torre di Venere lies some fifteen kilometres from Portoclemente,
one of the most popular summer resorts on the Tyrrhenian Sea.
Portoclemente is urban and elegant and full to overflowing for months
on end. Its gay and busy main street of shops and hotels runs down
to a wide sandy beach covered with tents and pennanted sand-castles
and sunburnt humanity, where at all times a lively social bustle
reigns, and much noise. But this same spacious and inviting fine-
sanded beach, this same border of pine grove and near, presiding
mountains, continues all the way along the coast. No wonder then
that some competition of a quiet kind should have sprung up further
on. Torre di Venere—the tower that gave the town its name is
gone long since, one looks for it in vain—is an offshoot of the larger

resort, and for some years remained an idyll for the few, a refuge for more unworldly spirits. But the usual history of such places repeated itself: peace has had to retire further along the coast, to Marina Petriera and dear knows where else. We all know how the world at once seeks peace and puts her to flight—rushing upon her in the fond idea that they two will wed, and where she is, there it can be at home. It will even set up its Vanity Fair in a spot and be capable of thinking that peace is still by its side. Thus Torre—though its atmosphere so far is more modest and contemplative than that of Portoclemente—has been quite taken up, by both Italians and foreigners. It is no longer the thing to go to Portoclemente—though still so much the thing that it is as noisy and crowded as ever. One goes next door, so to speak: to Torre. So much more refined, even, and cheaper to boot. And the attractiveness of these qualities persists, though the qualities themselves long ago ceased to be evident. Torre has got a Grand Hotel. Numerous pensions have sprung up, some modest, some pretentious. The people who own or rent the villas and pinetas overlooking the sea no longer have it all their own way on the beach. In July and August it looks just like the beach at Portoclemente: it swarms with a screaming, squabbling, merrymaking crowd, and the sun, blazing down like mad, peels the skin off their necks. Garish little flat-bottomed boats rock on the glittering blue, manned by children, whose mothers hover afar and fill the air with anxious cries of Nino! and Sandro! and Bice! and Maria! Pedlars step across the legs of recumbent sun-bathers, selling flowers and corals, oysters, lemonade, and *cornetti al burro*, and crying their wares in the breathy, full-throated southern voice.

Such was the scene that greeted our arrival in Torre: pleasant enough, but after all, we thought, we had come too soon. It was the middle of August, the Italian season was still at its height, scarcely the moment for strangers to learn to love the special charms of the place. What an afternoon crowd in the cafés on the front! For instance, in the Esquisito, where we sometimes sat and were served by Mario, that very Mario of whom I shall have presently to tell. It is wellnigh impossible to find a table; and the various orchestras contend together in the midst of one's conversation with bewildering effect. Of course, it is in the afternoon that people come over from Portoclemente. The excursion is a favourite one for the restless denizens of that pleasure resort, and a Fiat motor-bus plies to and fro, coating inch-thick with dust the oleander and laurel hedges along the highroad—a notable if repulsive sight.

Yes, decidedly one should go to Torre in September, when the great public has left. Or else in May, before the water is warm enough to tempt the Southerner to bathe. Even in the before and after seasons Torre is not empty, but life is less national and more subdued. English, French, and German prevail under the tent-awnings and in the pension dining-rooms; whereas in August—in the Grand Hotel, at least, where, in default of private addresses, we had engaged rooms—the stranger finds the field so occupied by Florentine and Roman society that he feels quite isolated and even temporarily *déclassé.*

We had, rather to our annoyance, this experience on the evening we arrived, when we went in to dinner and were shown to our table by the waiter in charge. As a table, it had nothing against it, save that we had already fixed our eyes upon those on the veranda beyond, built out over the water, where little red-shaded lamps glowed—and there were still some tables empty, though it was as full as the dining-room within. The children went into raptures at the festive sight, and without more ado we announced our intention to take our meals by preference in the veranda. Our words, it appeared, were prompted by ignorance; for we were informed, with somewhat embarrassed politeness, that the cosy nook outside was reserved for the clients of the hotel: *ai nostri clienti.* Their clients? But we were their clients. We were not tourists or trippers, but boarders for a stay of some three or four weeks. However, we forbore to press for an explanation of the difference between the likes of us and that clientèle to whom it was vouchsafed to eat out there in the glow of the red lamps, and took our dinner by the prosaic common light of the dining-room chandelier—a thoroughly ordinary and monotonous hotel bill of fare, be it said. In Pensione Eleonora, a few steps landward, the table, as we were to discover, was much better.

And thither it was that we moved, three or four days later, before we had had time to settle in properly at the Grand Hotel. Not on account of the veranda and the lamps. The children, straightway on the best of terms with waiters and pages, absorbed in the joys of life on the beach, promptly forgot those colourful seductions. But now there arose, between ourselves and the veranda clientèle—or perhaps more correctly with the compliant management—one of those little unpleasantnesses which can quite spoil the pleasure of a holiday. Among the guests were some high Roman aristocracy, a Principe X and his family. These grand folk occupied rooms close to our own, and the Principessa, a great and a passionately maternal lady, was thrown into a panic by the vestiges of a whooping-cough which our little ones had lately got over, but which now and then still faintly troubled the unshatterable slumbers of our youngest-born. The nature of this illness is not clear, leaving some play for the imagination. So we took no offence at our elegant neighbour for clinging to the widely held view that whooping-cough is acoustically contagious and quite simply fearing lest her children yield to the bad example set by ours. In the fullness of her feminine self-confidence she protested to the management, which then, in the person of the proverbial frock-coated manager, hastened to represent to us, with many expressions of regret, that under the circumstances they were obliged to transfer us to the annex. We did our best to assure him that the disease was in its very last stages, that it was actually over, and presented no danger of infection to anybody. All that we gained was permission to bring the case before the hotel physician—not one chosen by us—by whose verdict we must then abide. We agreed, convinced that thus we should at once pacify the Princess and escape the trouble of moving. The doctor appeared, and behaved like a faithful and honest servant of science. He examined the child and gave his opinion: the disease was quite over, no danger of contagion was present. We drew a long breath and considered the incident closed—until the manager announced that despite the doctor's verdict it would still be necessary for us to give up our rooms and retire to the *dépendance*. Byzantinism like this outraged us. It is not likely that the Principessa was responsible for the wilful breach of faith. Very likely the fawning management had not even dared to tell her what the physician said. Anyhow, we made it clear to his understanding that we preferred to leave the hotel altogether and at once— and packed our trunks. We could do so with a light heart, having already set up casual friendly relations with Casa Eleonora. We had noticed its pleasant exterior and formed the acquaintance of its proprietor, Signora Angiolieri, and her husband: she slender and black-haired, Tuscan in type, probably at the beginning of the thirties, with the dead ivory complexion of the southern woman, he quiet and bald and carefully dressed. They owned a larger establishment in Florence and presided only in summer and early autumn over the branch in Torre di Venere. But earlier, before her marriage, our new landlady had been companion, fellow-traveller, wardrobe mistress, yes, friend, of Eleonora Duse and manifestly regarded that period as the crown of her career. Even at our first visit she spoke of it with animation. Numerous photographs of the great actress, with affectionate inscriptions, were displayed about the drawing-room, and other souvenirs of their life together adorned the little tables and étagères. This cult of a so interesting past was calculated, of course, to heighten the advantages of the signora's present business. Nevertheless our pleasure and interest were quite genuine as we were conducted through the house by its owner and listened to her sonorous and staccato Tuscan voice relating anecdotes of that immortal mistress, depicting her suffering saintliness, her genius, her profound delicacy of feeling.

Thither, then, we moved our effects, to the dismay of the staff of the Grand Hotel, who, like all Italians, were very good to children. Our new quarters were retired and pleasant, we were within easy reach of the sea through the avenue of young plane trees that ran down to the esplanade. In the clean, cool dining-room Signora Angiolieri daily served the soup with her own hands, the service was attentive and good, the table capital. We even discovered some Viennese acquaintances, and enjoyed chatting with them after luncheon, in front of the house. They, in their turn, were the means of our finding others—in short, all seemed for the best, and we were heartily glad of the change we had made. Nothing was now wanting to a holiday of the most gratifying kind.

And yet no proper gratification ensued. Perhaps the stupid occasion of our change of quarters pursued us to the new ones we had found. Personally, I admit that I do not easily forget these collisions with ordinary humanity, the naïve misuse of power, the injustice, the sycophantic corruption. I dwelt upon the incident too much, it irritated me in retrospect—quite futilely, of course, since such phenomena are only all too natural and all too much the rule. And we had not broken off relations with the Grand Hotel. The children were as friendly as ever there, the porter mended their toys, and we sometimes took tea in the garden. We even saw the Principessa. She would come out, with her firm and delicate tread, her lips emphatically corallined, to look after her children, playing under the supervision of their English governess. She did not dream that we were anywhere near, for so soon as she appeared in the offing we sternly forbade our little one even to clear his throat.

The heat—if I may bring it in evidence—was extreme. It was African. The power of the sun, directly one left the border of the indigo-blue wave, was so frightful, so relentless, that the mere thought of the few steps between the beach and luncheon was a burden, clad though one might be only in pyjamas. Do you care for that sort of thing? Weeks on end? Yes, of course, it is proper to the south, it is classic weather, the sun of Homer, the climate wherein human culture came to flower—and all the rest of it. But after a while it is too much for me, I reach a point where I begin to find it dull. The burning void of the sky, day after day, weighs one down; the high coloration, the enormous naïveté of the unrefracted light—they do, I dare say, induce light-heartedness, a carefree mood born of immunity from downpours and other meteorological caprices. But slowly, slowly, there makes itself felt a lack: the deeper, more complex needs of the northern soul remain unsatisfied. You are left barren—even, it may be, in time, a little contemptuous. True, without that stupid business of the whooping-cough I might not have been feeling these things. I was annoyed, very likely I wanted to feel them and so half-unconsciously seized upon an idea lying ready to hand to induce, or if not to induce, at least to justify and strengthen, my attitude. Up to this point, then, if you like, let us grant some ill will on our part. But the sea; and the mornings spent extended upon the fine sand in face of its eternal splendours—no, the sea could not conceivably induce such feelings. Yet it was none the less true that, despite all previous experience, we were not at home on the beach, we were not happy.

It was too soon, too soon. The beach, as I have said, was still in the hands of the middle-class native. It is a pleasing breed to look at, and among the young we saw much shapeliness and charm. Still, we were necessarily surrounded by a great deal of very average humanity—a middle-class mob, which, you will admit, is not more charming under this sun than under one's own native sky. The voices these women have! It was sometimes hard to believe that we were in the land which is the western cradle of the art of song. "*Fuggièro!*" I can still hear that cry, as for twenty mornings long I heard it close behind me, breathy, full-throated, hideously stressed, with a harsh open *e*, uttered in accents of mechanical despair. "*Fuggièro! Rispondi almeno!*" Answer when I call you! The *sp* in *rispondi* was pronounced like *shp*, as Germans pronounce it; and this, on top of what I felt already, vexed my sensitive soul. The cry was addressed to a repulsive youngster whose sunburn had made disgusting raw sores on his shoulders. He outdid anything I have ever seen for ill-breeding, refractoriness, and temper and was a great coward to boot, putting the whole beach in an uproar, one day, because of his outrageous sensitiveness to the slightest pain. A sand-crab had pinched his toe in the water, and the minute injury made him set up a cry of heroic proportions—the shout of an antique hero in his agony—that pierced one to the marrow and called up visions of some frightful tragedy. Evidently he considered himself not only wounded, but poisoned as well; he crawled out on the sand and lay in apparently intolerable anguish, groaning *"Ohi!"* and *"Ohimè!"* and threshing about with arms and legs to ward off his mother's tragic appeals and the questions of the bystanders. An audience gathered round. A doctor was fetched—the same who had pronounced objective judgment on our whooping-cough—and here again acquitted himself like a man of science. Good-naturedly he reassured the boy, telling him that he was not hurt at all, he should simply go into the water again to relieve the smart. Instead of which, Fuggièro was borne off the beach, followed by a concourse of people. But he did not fail to appear next morning, nor did he leave off spoiling our children's sand-castles. Of course, always by accident. In short, a perfect terror.

And this twelve-year-old lad was prominent among the influences that, imperceptibly at first, combined to spoil our holiday and render it unwholesome. Somehow or other, there was a stiffness, a lack of innocent enjoyment. These people stood on their dignity—just why, and in what spirit, it was not easy at first to tell. They displayed much self-respectingness; towards each other and towards the foreigner their bearing was that of a person newly conscious of a sense of honour. And wherefore? Gradually we realized the political implications and understood that we were in the presence of a national ideal. The beach, in fact, was alive with patriotic children—a phenomenon as unnatural as it was depressing. Children are a human species and a society apart, a nation of their own, so to speak. On the basis of their common form of life, they find each other out with the greatest ease, no matter how different their small vocabularies. Ours soon played with natives and foreigners alike. Yet they were plainly both puzzled and disappointed at times. There were wounded sensibilities, displays of assertiveness—or rather hardly assertiveness, for it was too self-conscious and too didactic to deserve the name. There were quarrels over flags, disputes about authority and precedence. Grown-ups joined in, not so much to pacify as to render judgment and enunciate principles. Phrases were dropped about the greatness and dignity of Italy, solemn phrases that spoilt the fun. We saw our two little ones retreat, puzzled and hurt, and were put to it to explain the situation. These people, we told them, were just passing through a certain stage, something rather like an illness, perhaps; not very pleasant, but probably unavoidable.

We had only our own carelessness to thank that we came to blows in the end with this "stage"—which, after all, we had seen and sized up long before now. Yes, it came to another "cross-purposes," so evidently the earlier ones had not been sheer accident. In a word, we became an offence to the public morals. Our small daughter—eight years old, but in physical development a good year younger and thin as a chicken—had had a good long bathe and gone playing in the warm sun in her wet costume. We told her that she might take off her bathing-suit, which was stiff with sand, rinse it in the sea, and put it on again, after which she must take care to keep it cleaner. Off goes the costume and she runs down naked to the sea, rinses her little jersey, and comes back. Ought we to have foreseen the outburst of anger and resentment which her conduct, and thus our conduct, called forth? Without delivering a homily on the subject, I may say that in the last decade our attitude towards the nude body and our feelings regarding it have undergone, all over the world, a fundamental change. There are things we "never think about" any more, and among them is the freedom we had permitted to this by no means provocative little childish body. But in these parts it was taken as a challenge. The patriotic children hooted. Fuggièro whistled on his fingers. The sudden buzz of conversation among the grown people in our neighbourhood boded no good. A gentleman in city togs, with a not very apropos bowler hat on the back of his head, was assuring his outraged womenfolk that he proposed to take punitive measures; he stepped up to us, and a philippic descended on our unworthy heads, in which all the emotionalism of the sense-loving south spoke in the service of morality and discipline. The offence against decency of which we had been guilty was, he said, the more to be condemned because it was also a gross ingratitude and an insulting breach of his country's hospitality. We had criminally injured not only the letter and spirit of the public bathing regulations, but also the honour of Italy; he, the gentleman in the city togs, knew how to defend that honour and proposed to see to it that our offence against the national dignity should not go unpunished.

We did our best, bowing respectfully, to give ear to this eloquence. To contradict the man, overheated as he was, would probably be to fall from one error into another. On the tips of our tongues we had various answers: as, that the word "hospitality," in its strictest sense, was not quite the right one, taking all the circumstances into consideration. We were not literally the guests of Italy, but of Signora Angiolieri, who had assumed the rôle of dispenser of hospitality some years ago on laying down that of familiar friend to Eleonora Duse. We longed to say that surely this beautiful country had not sunk so low as to be reduced to a state of hypersensitive prudishness. But we confined ourselves to assuring the gentleman that any lack of respect, any provocation on our parts, had been the furthest from our thoughts. And as a mitigating circumstance we pointed out the tender age and physical slightness of the little culprit. In vain. Our protests were waved away, he did not believe in them; our defence would not hold water. We must be made an example of. The authorities were notified, by telephone, I believe, and their representative appeared on the beach. He said the case was "*molto grave.*" We had to go with him to the Municipio up in the Piazza, where a higher official confirmed the previous verdict of "*molto grave,*" launched into a stream of the usual didactic phrases—the selfsame tune and words as the man in the bowler hat—and levied a fine and ransom of fifty lire. We felt that the adventure must willy-nilly be worth to us this much of a contribution to the economy of the Italian government; paid, and left. Ought we not at this point to have left Torre as well?

If we only had! We should thus have escaped that fatal Cipolla. But circumstances combined to prevent us from making up our minds to a change. A certain poet says that it is indolence that makes us endure uncomfortable situations. The *aperçu* may serve as an explanation for our inaction. Anyhow, one dislikes voiding the field immediately upon such an event. Especially if sympathy from other quarters encourages one to defy it. And in the Villa Eleonora they pronounced as with one voice upon the injustice of our punishment. Some Italian after-dinner acquaintances found that the episode put their country in a very bad light, and proposed taking the man in the bowler hat to task, as one fellow-citizen to another. But the next day he and his party had vanished from the beach. Not on our account, of course. Though it might be that the consciousness of his impending departure had added energy to his rebuke; in any case his going was a relief. And, furthermore, we stayed because our stay had by now become remarkable in our own eyes, which is worth something in itself, quite apart from the comfort or discomfort involved. Shall we strike sail, avoid a certain experience so soon as it seems not expressly calculated to increase our enjoyment or our self-esteem?

Shall we go away whenever life looks like turning in the slightest uncanny, or not quite normal, or even rather painful and mortifying? No, surely not. Rather stay and look matters in the face, brave them out; perhaps precisely in so doing lies a lesson for us to learn. We stayed on and reaped as the awful reward of our constancy the unholy and staggering experience with Cipolla.

I have not mentioned that the after season had begun, almost on the very day we were disciplined by the city authorities. The worshipful gentleman in the bowler hat, our denouncer, was not the only person to leave the resort. There was a regular exodus, on every hand you saw luggage-carts on their way to the station. The beach denationalized itself. Life in Torre, in the cafés and the pinetas, became more homelike and more European. Very likely we might even have eaten at a table in the glass veranda, but we refrained, being content at Signora Angiolieri's—as content, that is, as our evil star would let us be. But at the same time with this turn for the better came a change in the weather: almost to an hour it showed itself in harmony with the holiday calendar of the general public. The sky was overcast; not that it grew any cooler, but the unclouded heat of the entire eighteen days since our arrival, and probably long before that, gave place to a stifling sirocco air, while from time to time a little ineffectual rain sprinkled the velvety surface of the beach. Add to which, that two-thirds of our intended stay at Torre had passed. The colourless, lazy sea, with sluggish jellyfish floating in its shallows, was at least a change. And it would have been silly to feel retrospective longings after a sun that had caused us so many sighs when it burned down in all its arrogant power.

At this juncture, then, it was that Cipolla announced himself. Cavaliere Cipolla he was called on the posters that appeared one day stuck up everywhere, even in the dining-room of Pensione Eleonora. A travelling virtuoso, an entertainer, "*forzatore, illusionista, prestidigatore,*" as he called himself, who proposed to wait upon the highly respectable population of Torre di Venere with a display of extraordinary phenomena of a mysterious and staggering kind. A conjuror! The bare announcement was enough to turn our children's heads. They had never seen anything of the sort, and now our present holiday was to afford them this new excitement. From that moment on they besieged us with prayers to take tickets for the performance. We had doubts, from the first, on the score of the lateness of the hour, nine o'clock; but gave way, in the idea that we might see a little of what Cipolla had to offer, probably no great matter, and then go home. Besides, of course, the children could sleep late next day. We bought four tickets of Signora Angiolieri herself, she having taken a number of the stalls on commission to sell them to her guests. She could not vouch for the man's performance, and we had no great expectations. But we were conscious of a need for diversion, and the children's violent curiosity proved catching.

The Cavaliere's performance was to take place in a hall where during the season there had been a cinema with a weekly programme. We had never been there. You reached it by following the main street under the wall of the "*palazzo*," a ruin with a "For sale" sign, that suggested a castle and had obviously been built in lordlier days. In the same street were the chemist, the hairdresser, and all the better shops; it led, so to speak, from the feudal past the bourgeois into the proletarian, for it ended off between two rows of poor fishing-huts, where old women sat mending nets before the doors. And here, among the proletariat, was the hall, not much more, actually, than a wooden shed, though a large one, with a turreted entrance, plastered on either side with layers of gay placards. Some while after dinner, then, on the appointed evening, we wended our way thither in the dark, the children dressed in their best and blissful with the sense of so much irregularity. It was sultry, as it had been for days; there was heat lightning now and then, and a little rain; we proceeded under umbrellas. It took us a quarter of an hour.

Our tickets were collected at the entrance, our places we had to find ourselves. They were in the third row left, and as we sat down we saw that, late though the hour was for the performance, it was to be interpreted with even more laxity. Only very slowly did an audience—who seemed to be relied upon to come late—begin to fill the stalls. These comprised the whole auditorium; there were no boxes. This tardiness gave us some concern. The children's cheeks were already flushed as much with fatigue as with excitement. But even when we entered, the standing-room at the back and in the side aisles was already well occupied. There stood the manhood of Torre di Venere, all and sundry, fisherfolk, rough-and-ready youths with bare forearms crossed over their striped jerseys. We were well pleased with the presence of this native assemblage, which always adds colour and animation to occasions like the present; and the children were frankly delighted. For they had friends among these people—acquaintances picked up on afternoon strolls to the further ends of the beach. We would be turning homeward, at the hour when the sun dropped into the sea, spent with the huge effort it had made and gilding with reddish gold the oncoming surf; and we would come upon bare-legged fisherfolk standing in rows, bracing and hauling with long-drawn cries as they drew in the nets and harvested in dripping baskets their catch, often so scanty, of *frutta di mare*. The children looked on, helped to pull, brought out their little stock of Italian words, made friends. So now they exchanged nods with the "standing-room" clientèle; there was Guiscardo, there Antonio, they knew them by name and waved and called across in half-whispers, getting answering nods and smiles that displayed rows of healthy white teeth. Look, there is even Mario, Mario from the Esquisito, who brings us the chocolate. He wants to see the conjuror, too, and he must have come early, for he is almost in front; but he does not see us, he is not paying attention; that is a way he has, even though he is a waiter. So we wave instead to the man who lets out the little boats on the beach; he is there too, standing at the back.

It had got to a quarter past nine, it got to almost half past. It was natural that we should be nervous. When would the children get to bed? It had been a mistake to bring them, for now it would be very hard to suggest breaking off their enjoyment before it had got well under way. The stalls had filled in time; all Torre, apparently, was there: the guests of the Grand Hotel, the guests of Villa Eleonora, familiar faces from the beach. We heard English and German and the sort of French that Rumanians speak with Italians. Madame Angiolieri herself sat two rows behind us, with her quiet, bald-headed spouse, who kept stroking his moustache with the two middle fingers of his right hand. Everybody had come late, but nobody too late. Cipolla made us wait for him.

He made us wait. That is probably the way to put it. He heightened the suspense by his delay in appearing. And we could see the point of this, too—only not when it was carried to extremes. Towards half past nine the audience began to clap—an amiable way of expressing justifiable impatience, evincing as it does an eagerness to applaud. For the little ones, this was a joy in itself—all children love to clap. From the popular sphere came loud cries of *"Pronti!"* *"Cominciamo!"* And lo, it seemed now as easy to begin as before it had been hard. A gong sounded, greeted by the standing rows with a many-voiced "Ah-h!" and the curtains parted. They revealed a platform furnished more like a schoolroom than like the theatre of a conjuring performance—largely because of the blackboard in the left foreground. There was a common yellow hat-stand, a few ordinary straw-bottomed chairs, and further back a little round table holding a water carafe and glass, also a tray with a liqueur glass and a flask of pale yellow liquid. We had still a few seconds of time to let these things sink in. Then, with no darkening of the house, Cavaliere Cipolla made his entry.

He came forward with a rapid step that expressed his eagerness to appear before his public and gave rise to the illusion that he had already come a long way to put himself at their service—whereas, of course, he had only been standing in the wings. His costume supported the fiction. A man of an age hard to determine, but by no means young; with a sharp, ravaged face, piercing eyes, compressed lips, small black waxed moustache, and a so-called imperial in the curve between mouth and chin. He was dressed for the street with a sort of complicated evening elegance, in a wide black pelerine with velvet collar and satin lining; which, in the hampered state of his arms, he held together in front with his white-gloved hands. He had a white scarf round his neck; a top hat with a curving brim sat far back on his head. Perhaps more than anywhere else the eighteenth century is still alive in Italy, and with it the charlatan and mountebank type so characteristic of the period. Only there, at any rate, does one still encounter really well-preserved specimens. Cipolla had in his whole appearance much of the historic type; his very clothes helped to conjure up the traditional figure with its blatantly, fantastically foppish air. His pretentious costume sat upon him, or rather hung upon him, most curiously, being in one place drawn too tight, in another a mass of awkward folds. There was something not quite in order about his figure, both front and back—that was plain later on. But I must emphasize the fact that there was not a trace of personal jocularity or clownishness in his pose, manner, or behavior. On the contrary, there was complete seriousness, an absence of any humorous appeal; occasionally even a cross-grained pride, along with that curious, self-satisfied air so characteristic of the deformed. None of all this, however, prevented his appearance from being greeted with laughter from more than one quarter of the hall.

All the eagerness had left his manner. The swift entry had been merely an expression of energy, not of zeal. Standing at the footlights he negligently drew off his gloves, to display long yellow hands, one of them adorned with a seal ring with a lapis-lazuli in a high setting. As he stood there, his small hard eyes, with flabby pouches beneath them, roved appraisingly about the hall, not quickly, rather in a considered examination, pausing here and there upon a face with his lips clipped together, not speaking a word. Then with a display of skill as surprising as it was casual, he rolled his gloves into a ball and tossed them across a considerable distance into the glass on the table. Next from an inner pocket he drew forth a packet of cigarettes; you could see by the wrapper that they were the cheapest sort the government sells. With his fingertips he pulled out a cigarette and lighted it, without looking, from a quick-firing benzine lighter. He drew the smoke deep into his lungs and let it out again, tapping his foot, with both lips drawn in an arrogant grimace and the grey smoke streaming out between broken and saw-edged teeth.

With a keenness equal to his own his audience eyed him. The youths at the rear scowled as they peered at this cocksure creature to search out his secret weaknesses. He betrayed none. In fetching out and putting back the cigarettes his clothes got in his way. He had to turn back his pelerine, and in so doing revealed a riding-whip with a silver claw-handle that hung by a leather thong from his left forearm and looked decidedly out of place. You could see that he had on not evening clothes but a frock-coat, and under this, as he lifted it to get at his pocket, could be seen a striped sash worn about the body. Somebody behind me whispered that this sash went with his title of Cavaliere. I give the information for what it may be worth —personally, I never heard that the title carried such insignia with it. Perhaps the sash was sheer pose, like the way he stood there, without a word, casually and arrogantly puffing smoke into his audience's face.

People laughed, as I said. The merriment had become almost general when somebody in the "standing seats," in a loud, dry voice, remarked: "*Buona sera.*"

Cipolla cocked his head. "Who was that?" asked he, as though he had been dared. "Who was that just spoke? Well? First so bold and now so modest? *Paura*, eh?" He spoke with a rather high, asthmatic voice, which yet had a metallic quality. He waited.

"That was me," a youth at the rear broke into the stillness, seeing himself thus challenged. He was not far from us, a handsome fellow in a woollen shirt, with his coat hanging over one shoulder. He wore his curly, wiry hair in a high, dishevelled mop, the style affected by the youth of the awakened Fatherland; it gave him an African appearance that rather spoiled his looks. "*Bè!* That was me. It was your business to say it first, but I was trying to be friendly."

More laughter. The chap had a tongue in his head. "*Ha sciolto la scilinguágnolo,*" I heard near me. After all, the retort was deserved.

"Ah, bravo!" answered Cipolla. "I like you, *giovanotto.* Trust me,

I've had my eye on you for some time. People like you are just in my line. I can use them. And you are the pick of the lot, that's plain to see. You do what you like. Or is it possible you have ever not done what you liked—or even, maybe, what you didn't like? What somebody else liked, in short? Hark ye, my friend, that might be a pleasant change for you, to divide up the willing and the doing and stop tackling both jobs at once. Division of labour, *sistema americano, sa'!* For instance, suppose you were to show your tongue to this select and honourable audience here—your whole tongue, right down to the roots?"

"No, I won't," said the youth, hostilely. "Sticking out your tongue shows a bad bringing-up."

"Nothing of the sort," retorted Cipolla. "You would only be *doing* it. With all due respect to your bringing-up, I suggest that before I count ten, you will perform a right turn and stick out your tongue at the company here further than you knew yourself that you could stick it out."

He gazed at the youth, and his piercing eyes seemed to sink deeper into their sockets. "*Uno!*" said he. He had let his riding-whip slide down his arm and made it whistle once through the air. The boy faced about and put out his tongue, so long, so extendedly, that you could see it was the very uttermost in tongue which he had to offer. Then he turned back, stony-faced, to his former position.

"That was me," mocked Cipolla, with a jerk of his head towards the youth. "*Bè!* That was me." Leaving the audience to enjoy its sensations, he turned towards the little round table, lifted the bottle, poured out a small glass of what was obviously cognac, and tipped it up with a practised hand.

The children laughed with all their hearts. They had understood practically nothing of what had been said, but it pleased them hugely that something so funny should happen, straightaway, between that queer man up there and somebody out of the audience. They had no preconception of what an "evening" would be like and were quite ready to find this a priceless beginning. As for us, we exchanged a glance and I remember that involuntarily I made with my lips the sound that Cipolla's whip had made when it cut the air. For the rest, it was plain that people did not know what to make of a preposterous beginning like this to a sleight-of-hand performance. They could not see why the *giovanotto*, who after all in a way had been their spokesman, should suddenly have turned on them to vent his incivility. They felt that he had behaved like a silly ass and withdrew their countenances from him in favour of the artist, who now came back from his refreshment table and addressed them as follows:

"Ladies and gentlemen," said he, in his wheezing, metallic voice, "you saw just now that I was rather sensitive on the score of the rebuke this hopeful young linguist saw fit to give me"—"*questo linguista di belle speranze*" was what he said, and we all laughed at the pun. "I am a man who sets some store by himself, you may take it from me. And I see no point in being wished a good-evening unless it is done courteously and in all seriousness. For anything else there is no occasion. When a man wishes me a good-evening and he wishes himself one, for the audience will have one only if I do. So this lady-killer of Torre di Venere" (another thrust) "did well to testify that I have one tonight and that I can dispense with any wishes of his in the matter. I can boast of having good evenings almost without exception. One not so good does come my way now and again, but very seldom. My calling is hard and my health not of the best. I have a little physical defect which prevented me from doing my bit in the war for the greater glory of the Fatherland. It is perforce with my mental and spiritual parts that I conquer life—which after all only means conquering oneself. And I flatter myself that my achievements have aroused interest and respect among the educated public. The leading newspapers have lauded me, the *Corriere della Sera* did me the courtesy of calling me a phenomenon, and in Rome the brother of the *Duce* honoured me by his presence at one of my evenings. I should not have thought that in a relatively less important place" (laughter here, at the expense of poor little Torre) "I should have to give up the small personal habits which brilliant and elevated audiences had been ready to overlook. Nor did I think I had to stand being heckled by a person who seems to have been rather spoilt by the favours of the fair sex." All this of course at the expense of the youth whom Cipolla never tired of presenting in the guise of *donnaiuolo* and rustic Don Juan. His persistent thin-skinnedness and animosity were in striking contrast to the self-confidence and the worldly success he boasted of. One might have assumed that the *giovanotto* was merely the chosen butt of Cipolla's customary professional sallies, had not the very pointed witticisms betrayed a genuine antagonism. No one looking at the physical parts of the two men need have been at a loss for the explanation, even if the deformed man had not constantly played on the other's supposed success with the fair sex. "Well," Cipolla went on, "before beginning our entertainment this evening, perhaps you will permit me to make myself comfortable."

And he went towards the hat-stand to take off his things.

"*Parla benissimo*," asserted somebody in our neighbourhood. So far, the man had done nothing; but what he had said was accepted as an achievement, by means of that he had made an impression. Among southern peoples speech is a constituent part of the pleasure of living, it enjoys far livelier social esteem than in the north. That national cement, the mother tongue, is paid symbolic honours down here, and there is something blithely symbolical in the pleasure people take in their respect for its forms and phonetics. They enjoy speaking, they enjoy listening; and they listen with discrimination. For the way a man speaks serves as a measure of his personal rank; carelessness and clumsiness are greeted with scorn, elegance and mastery are rewarded with social éclat. Wherefore the small man too, where it is a question of getting his effect, chooses his phrase nicely and turns it with care. On this count, then, at least, Cipolla had won his audience; though he by no means belonged to the class of men which the Italian, in a singular mixture of moral and æsthetic judgments, labels "*simpatico*."

After removing his hat, scarf, and mantle he came to the front of the stage, settling his coat, pulling down his cuffs with their large cuff-buttons, adjusting his absurd sash. He had very ugly hair; the top of his head, that is, was almost bald, while a narrow, black-varnished frizz of curls ran from front to back as though stuck on; the side hair, likewise blackened, was brushed forward to the corners of the eyes—it was, in short, the hairdressing of an old-fashioned circus-director, fantastic, but entirely suited to his outmoded personal type and worn with so much assurance as to take the edge off the public's sense of humour. The little physical defect of which he had warned us was now all too visible, though the nature of it was even now not very clear: the chest was too high, as is usual in such cases; but the corresponding malformation of the back did not sit between the shoulders, it took the form of a sort of hips or buttocks hump, which did not indeed hinder his movements but gave him a grotesque and dipping stride at every step he took. However, by mentioning his deformity beforehand he had broken the shock of it, and a delicate propriety of feeling appeared to reign throughout the hall.

"At your service," said Cipolla. "With your kind permission, we will begin the evening with some arithmetical tests."

Arithmetic? That did not sound much like sleight-of-hand. We began to have our suspicions that the man was sailing under a false flag, only we did not yet know which was the right one. I felt sorry on the children's account; but for the moment they were content simply to be there.

The numerical test which Cipolla now introduced was as simple as it was baffling. He began by fastening a piece of paper to the upper right-hand corner of the blackboard; then lifting it up, he wrote something underneath. He talked all the while, relieving the dryness of his offering by a constant flow of words, and showed himself a practised speaker, never at a loss for conversational turns of phrase. It was in keeping with the nature of his performance, and at the same time vastly entertained the children, that he went on to eliminate the gap between stage and audience, which had already been bridged over by the curious skirmish with the fisher lad: he had representatives from the audience mount the stage, and himself descended the wooden steps to seek personal contact with his public. And again, with individuals, he fell into his former taunting tone. I do not know how far that was a deliberate feature of his system; he preserved a serious, even a peevish air, but his audience, at least the more popular section, seemed convinced that that was all part of the game. So then, after he had written something and covered the writing by the paper, he desired that two persons should come up on the platform and help to perform the calculations. They would not be difficult, even for people not clever at figures. As usual, nobody volunteered, and Cipolla took care not to molest the more select portion of his audience. He kept to the populace. Turning to two sturdy young louts standing behind us, he beckoned them to the front, encouraging and scolding by turns. They should not stand there gaping, he said, unwilling to oblige the company. Actually, he got them in motion; with clumsy tread they came down the middle aisle, climbed the steps, and stood in front of the blackboard, grinning sheepishly at their comrades' shouts and applause. Cipolla joked with them for a few minutes, praised their heroic firmness of limb and the size of their hands, so well calculated to do this service for the public. Then he handed one of them the chalk and told him to write down the numbers as they were called out. But now the creature declared that he could not write! *"Non so scrivere,"* said he in his gruff voice, and his companion added that neither did he.

God knows whether they told the truth or whether they wanted to make game of Cipolla. Anyhow, the latter was far from sharing the general merriment which their confession aroused. He was insulted and disgusted. He sat there on a straw-bottomed chair in the centre of the stage with his legs crossed, smoking a fresh cigarette out of his cheap packet; obviously it tasted the better for the cognac he had indulged in while the yokels were stumping up the steps. Again he inhaled the smoke and let it stream out between curling lips. Swinging his leg, with his gaze sternly averted from the two shamelessly chuckling creatures and from the audience as well, he stared into space as one who withdraws himself and his dignity from the contemplation of an utterly despicable phenomenon.

"Scandalous," said he, in a sort of icy snarl. "Go back to your places! In Italy everybody can write—in all her greatness there is no room for ignorance and unenlightenment. To accuse her of them, in the hearing of this international company, is a cheap joke, in which you yourselves cut a very poor figure and humiliate the government and the whole country as well. If it is true that Torre di Venere is indeed the last refuge of such ignorance, then I must blush to have visited the place—being, as I already was, aware of its inferiority to Rome in more than one respect—"

Here Cipolla was interrupted by the youth with the Nubian coiffure and his jacket across his shoulder. His fighting spirit, as we now saw, had only abdicated temporarily, and he now flung himself into the breach in defence of his native heath. "That will do," said he loudly. "That's enough jokes about Torre. We all come from the place and we won't stand strangers making fun of it. These two chaps are our friends. Maybe they are no scholars, but even so they may be straighter than some folks in the room who are so free with their boasts about Rome, though they did not build it either."

That was capital. The young man had certainly cut his eye-teeth. And this sort of spectacle was good fun, even though it still further delayed the regular performance. It is always fascinating to listen to an altercation. Some people it simply amuses, they take a sort of killjoy pleasure in not being principals. Others feel upset and uneasy, and my sympathies are with these latter, although on the present occasion I was under the impression that all this was part of the show—the analphabetic yokels no less than the *giovanotto* with the jacket. The children listened well pleased. They understood not at all, but the sound of the voices made them hold their breath. So this was a "magic evening"—at least it was the kind they have in Italy. They expressly found it "lovely."

Cipolla had stood up and with two of his scooping strides was at the footlights.

"Well, well, see who's here!" said he with grim cordiality. "An old acquaintance! A young man with his heart at the end of his tongue" (he used the word *linguaccia,* which means a coated tongue, and gave rise to much hilarity). "That will do, my friends," he turned to the yokels. "I do not need you now, I have business with this deserving young man here, *con questo torregiano di Venere,* this tower of Venus, who no doubt expects the gratitude of the fair as a reward for his prowess—"

"*Ah, non scherziamo!* We're talking earnest," cried out the youth. His eyes flashed, and he actually made as though to pull off his jacket and proceed to direct methods of settlement.

Cipolla did not take him too seriously. We had exchanged apprehensive glances; but he was dealing with a fellow-countryman and had his native soil beneath his feet. He kept quite cool and showed complete mastery of the situation. He looked at his audience, smiled, and made a sideways motion of the head towards the young cockerel as though calling the public to witness how the man's bumptiousness only served to betray the simplicity of his mind. And then, for the second time, something strange happened, which set Cipolla's calm superiority in an uncanny light, and in some mysterious and irritating way turned all the explosiveness latent in the air into matter for laughter.

Cipolla drew still nearer to the fellow, looking him in the eye with a peculiar gaze. He even came half-way down the steps that led into the auditorium on our left, so that he stood directly in front of the trouble-maker, on slightly higher ground. The riding-whip hung from his arm.

"My son, you do not feel much like joking," he said. "It is only too natural, for anyone can see that you are not feeling too well. Even your tongue, which leaves something to be desired on the score of cleanliness, indicates acute disorder of the gastric system. An evening entertainment is no place for people in your state; you yourself, I can tell, were of several minds whether you would not do better to put on a flannel bandage and go to bed. It was not good judgment to drink so much of that very sour white wine this afternoon. Now you have such a colic you would like to double up with the pain. Go ahead, don't be embarrassed. There is a distinct relief that comes from bending over, in cases of intestinal cramp."

He spoke thus, word for word, with quiet impressiveness and a kind of stern sympathy, and his eyes, plunged the while deep in the young man's, seemed to grow very tired and at the same time burning above their enlarged tear-ducts—they were the strangest eyes, you could tell that not manly pride alone was preventing the young adversary from withdrawing his gaze. And presently, indeed, all trace of its former arrogance was gone from the bronzed young face. He looked open-mouthed at the Cavaliere and the open mouth was drawn in a rueful smile.

"Double over," repeated Cipolla. "What else can you do? With a colic like that you *must* bend. Surely you will not struggle against the performance of a perfectly natural action just because somebody suggests it to you?"

Slowly the youth lifted his forearms, folded and squeezed them across his body; it turned a little sideways, then bent, lower and lower, the feet shifted, the knees turned inward, until he had become a picture of writhing pain, until he all but grovelled upon the ground. Cipolla let him stand for some seconds thus, then made a short cut through the air with his whip and went with his scooping stride back to the little table, where he poured himself out a cognac.

"*Il boit beaucoup,*" asserted a lady behind us. Was that the only thing that struck her? We could not tell how far the audience grasped the situation. The fellow was standing upright again, with a sheepish grin—he looked as though he scarcely knew how it had all happened. The scene had been followed with tense interest and applauded at the end; there were shouts of "*Bravo, Cipolla!*" and "*Bravo, giovanotto!*" Apparently the issue of the duel was not looked upon as a personal defeat for the young man. Rather the audience encouraged him as one does an actor who succeeds in an unsympathetic rôle. Certainly his way of screwing himself up with cramp had been highly picturesque, its appeal was directly calculated to impress the gallery—in short, a fine dramatic performance. But I am not sure how far the audience were moved by that natural tactfulness in which the south excels, or how far it penetrated into the nature of what was going on.

The Cavaliere, refreshed, had lighted another cigarette. The numerical tests might now proceed. A young man was easily found in the back row who was willing to write down on the blackboard the numbers as they were dictated to him. Him too we knew; the whole entertainment had taken on an intimate character through our acquaintance with so many of the actors. This was the man who worked at the greengrocer's in the main street; he had served us several times, with neatness and dispatch. He wielded the chalk with clerkly confidence, while Cipolla descended to our level and walked with his deformed gait through the audience, collecting numbers as they were given, in two, three, and four places, and calling them out to the grocer's assistant, who wrote them down in a column. In all this, everything on both sides was calculated to amuse, with its jokes and its oratorical asides. The artist could not fail to hit on foreigners, who were not ready with their figures, and with them he was elaborately patient and chivalrous, to the great amusement of the natives, whom he reduced to confusion in their turn, by making them translate numbers that were given in English or French. Some people gave dates concerned with great events in Italian history. Cipolla took them up at once and made patriotic comments. Somebody shouted "Number one!" The Cavaliere, incensed at this as at every attempt to make game of him, retorted over his shoulder that he could not take less than two-place figures. Whereupon another joker cried out "Number two!" and was greeted with the applause and laughter which every reference to natural functions is sure to win among southerners.

When fifteen numbers stood in a long straggling row on the board, Cipolla called for a general adding-match. Ready reckoners might add in their heads, but pencil and paper were not forbidden. Cipolla, while the work went on, sat on his chair near the blackboard, smoked and grimaced, with the complacent, pompous air cripples so often have. The five-place addition was soon done. Somebody announced the answer, somebody else confirmed it, a third had arrived at a slightly different result, but the fourth agreed with the first and second. Cipolla got up, tapped some ash from his coat, and lifted the paper at the upper right-hand corner of the board to display the writing. The correct answer, a sum close on a million, stood there; he had written it down beforehand.

Astonishment, and loud applause. The children were overwhelmed. How had he done that, they wanted to know. We told them it was a trick, not easily explainable offhand. In short, the man was a conjuror. This was what a sleight-of-hand evening was like, so now they knew. First the fisherman had cramp, and then the right answer was written down beforehand—it was all simply glorious, and we saw with dismay that despite the hot eyes and the hand of the clock at almost half past ten, it would be very hard to get them away. There would be tears. And yet it was plain that this magician did not "magick"—at least not in the accepted sense, of manual dexterity—

and that the entertainment was not at all suitable for children. Again, I do not know, either, what the audience really thought. Obviously there was grave doubt whether its answers had been given of "free choice"; here and there an individual might have answered of his own motion, but on the whole Cipolla certainly selected his people and thus kept the whole procedure in his own hands and directed it towards the given result. Even so, one had to admire the quickness of his calculations, however much one felt disinclined to admire anything else about the performance. Then his patriotism, his irritable sense of dignity—the Cavaliere's own countrymen might feel in their element with all that and continue in a laughing mood; but the combination certainly gave us outsiders food for thought.

Cipolla himself saw to it—though without giving them a name— that the nature of his powers should be clear beyond a doubt to even the least-instructed person. He alluded to them, of course, in his talk—and he talked without stopping—but only in vague, boastful, self-advertising phrases. He went on awhile with experiments on the same lines as the first, merely making them more complicated by introducing operations in multiplying, subtracting, and dividing; then he simplified them to the last degree in order to bring out the method. He simply had numbers "guessed" which were previously written under the paper; and the guess was nearly always right. One guesser admitted that he had had in mind to give a certain number, when Cipolla's whip went whistling through the air, and a quite different one slipped out, which proved to be the "right" one. Cipolla's shoulders shook. He pretended admiration for the powers of the people he questioned. But in all his compliments there was something sneering and derogatory; the victims could scarcely have relished them much, although they smiled, and although they might easily have set down some part of the applause to their own credit. Moreover, I had not the impression that the artist was popular with his public. A certain ill will and reluctance were in the air, but courtesy kept such feelings in check, as did Cipolla's competency and his stern self-confidence. Even the riding-whip, I think, did much to keep rebellion from becoming overt.

From tricks with numbers he passed to tricks with cards. There were two packs, which he drew out of his pockets, and so much I still remember, that the basis of the tricks he played with them was as follows: from the first pack he drew three cards and thrust them without looking at them inside his coat. Another person then drew three out of the second pack, and these turned out to be the same as the first three—not invariably all the three, for it did happen that only two were the same. But in the majority of cases Cipolla triumphed, showing his three cards with a little bow in acknowledgment of the applause with which his audience conceded his possession of strange powers—strange whether for good or evil. A young man in the front row, to our right, an Italian, with proud, finely chiselled features, rose up and said that he intended to assert his own will in his choice and consciously to resist any influence, of whatever sort. Under these circumstances, what did Cipolla think would be the result? "You will," answered the Cavaliere, "make my task somewhat more difficult thereby. As for the result, your resistance will not alter it in the least. Freedom exists, and also the will exists; but freedom of the will does not exist, for a will that aims at its own freedom aims at the unknown. You are free to draw or not to draw. But if you draw, you will draw the right cards—the more certainly, the more wilfully obstinate your behaviour."

One must admit that he could not have chosen his words better, to trouble the waters and confuse the mind. The refractory youth hesitated before drawing. Then he pulled out a card and at once demanded to see if it was among the chosen three. "But why?" queried Cipolla. "Why do things by halves?" Then, as the other defiantly insisted, "E servito," said the juggler, with a gesture of exaggerated servility; and held out the three cards fanwise, without looking at them himself. The left-hand card was the one drawn.

Amid general applause, the apostle of freedom sat down. How far Cipolla employed small tricks and manual dexterity to help out his natural talents, the deuce only knew. But even without them the result would have been the same: the curiosity of the entire audience was unbounded and universal, everybody both enjoyed the amazing character of the entertainment and unanimously conceded the professional skill of the performer. "Lavora bene," we heard, here and there in our neighbourhood; it signified the triumph of objective judgment over antipathy and repressed resentment.

After his last, incomplete, yet so much the more telling success, Cipolla had at once fortified himself with another cognac. Truly he did "drink a lot," and the fact made a bad impression. But obviously he needed the liquor and the cigarettes for the replenishment of his energy, upon which, as he himself said, heavy demands were made in all directions. Certainly in the intervals he looked very ill, exhausted and hollow-eyed. Then the little glassful would redress the

balance, and the flow of lively, self-confident chatter run on, while
the smoke he inhaled gushed out grey from his lungs. I clearly recall
that he passed from the card-tricks to parlour games—the kind based
on certain powers which in human nature are higher or else lower
than human reason: on intuition and "magnetic" transmission; in
short, upon a low type of manifestation. What I do not remember
is the precise order things came in. And I will not bore you with
a description of these experiments; everybody knows them, everybody has at one time or another taken part in this finding of hidden
articles, this blind carrying out of a series of acts, directed by a force
that proceeds from organism to organism by unexplored paths.
Everybody has had his little glimpse into the equivocal, impure,
inexplicable nature of the occult, has been conscious of both curiosity
and contempt, has shaken his head over the human tendency of those
who deal in it to help themselves out with humbuggery, though, after
all, the humbuggery is no disproof whatever of the genuineness of
the other elements in the dubious amalgam. I can only say here
that each single circumstance gains in weight and the whole greatly
in impressiveness when it is a man like Cipolla who is the chief
actor and guiding spirit in the sinister business. He sat smoking at
the rear of the stage, his back to the audience while they conferred.
The object passed from hand to hand which it was his task to find,
with which he was to perform some action agreed upon beforehand.
Then he would start to move zigzag through the hall, with his head
thrown back and one hand outstretched, the other clasped in that
of a guide who was in the secret but enjoined to keep himself
perfectly passive, with his thoughts directed upon the agreed goal.
Cipolla moved with the bearing typical in these experiments: now
groping upon a false start, now with a quick forward thrust, now
pausing as though to listen and by sudden inspiration correcting his
course. The rôles seemed reversed, the stream of influence was moving
in the contrary direction, as the artist himself pointed out, in his
ceaseless flow of discourse. The suffering, receptive, performing part
was now his, the will he had before imposed on others was shut out,
he acted in obedience to a voiceless common will which was in the
air. But he made it perfectly clear that it all came to the same thing.
The capacity for self-surrender, he said, for becoming a tool, for
the most unconditional and utter self-abnegation, was but the reverse
side of that other power to will and to command. Commanding and
obeying formed together one single principle, one indissoluble unity;
he who knew how to obey knew also how to command, and con-

versely; the one idea was comprehended in the other, as people and leader were comprehended in one another. But that which was *done*, the highly exacting and exhausting performance, was in every case his, the leader's and mover's, in whom the will became obedience, the obedience will, whose person was the cradle and womb of both, and who thus suffered enormous hardship. Repeatedly he emphasized the fact that his lot was a hard one—presumably to account for his need of stimulant and his frequent recourse to the little glass.

Thus he groped his way forward, like a blind seer, led and sustained by the mysterious common will. He drew a pin set with a stone out of its hiding-place in an Englishwoman's shoe, carried it, halting and pressing on by turns, to another lady—Signora Angiolieri —and handed it to her on bended knee, with the words it had been agreed he was to utter. "I present you with this in token of my respect," was the sentence. Their sense was obvious, but the words themselves not easy to hit upon, for the reason that they had been agreed on in French; the language complication seemed to us a little malicious, implying as it did a conflict between the audience's natural interest in the success of the miracle, and their desire to witness the humiliation of this presumptuous man. It was a strange sight: Cipolla on his knees before the signora, wrestling, amid efforts at speech, after knowledge of the preordained words. "I must say something," he said, "and I feel clearly what it is I must say. But I also feel that if it passed my lips it would be wrong. Be careful not to help me unintentionally!" he cried out, though very likely that was precisely what he was hoping for. "*Pensez très fort*," he cried all at once, in bad French, and then burst out with the required words—in Italian, indeed, but with the final substantive pronounced in the sister tongue, in which he was probably far from fluent: he said *vénération* instead of *venerazione*, with an impossible nasal. And this partial success, after the complete success before it, the finding of the pin, the presentation of it on his kness to the right person—was almost more impressive than if he had got the sentence exactly right, and evoked bursts of admiring applause.

Cipolla got up from his knees and wiped the perspiration from his brow. You understand that this experiment with the pin was a single case, which I describe because it sticks in my memory. But he changed his method several times and improvised a number of variations suggested by his contact with his audience; a good deal of time thus went by. He seemed to get particular inspiration from the person of our landlady; she drew him on to the most extraordinary displays of clairvoyance. "It does not escape me, madame," he said to her, "that there is something unusual about you, some special and honourable distinction. He who has eyes to see decries about your lovely brow an aureola—if I mistake not, it once was stronger than now—a slowly paling radiance . . . hush, not a word! Don't help me. Beside you sits your husband—yes?" He turned towards the silent Signor Angiolieri. "You are the husband of this lady, and your happiness is complete. But in the midst of this happiness memories rise . . . the past, signora, so it seems to me, plays an important part in your present. You knew a king . . . has not a king crossed your path in bygone days?"

"No," breathed the dispenser of our midday soup, her golden-brown eyes gleaming in the noble pallor of her face.

"No? No, not a king; I meant that generally, I did not mean literally a king. Not a king, not a prince, and a prince after all, a king of a loftier realm; it was a great artist, at whose side you once—you would contradict me, and yet I am not wholly wrong. Well, then! It was a woman, a great, a world-renowned woman artist, whose friendship you enjoyed in your tender years, whose sacred memory overshadows and transfigures your whole existence. Her name? Need I utter it, whose fame has long been bound up with the Fatherland's immortal as its own? Eleonora Duse," he finished, softly and with much solemnity.

The little woman bowed her head, overcome. The applause was like a patriotic demonstration. Nearly everyone there knew about Signora Angiolieri's wonderful past; they were all able to confirm the Cavaliere's intuition—not least the present guests of Casa Eleonora. But we wondered how much of the truth he had learned as the result of professional inquiries made on his arrival. Yet I see no reason at all to cast doubt, on rational grounds, upon powers which, before our very eyes, became fatal to their possessor.

At this point there was an intermission. Our lord and master withdrew. Now I confess that almost ever since the beginning of my tale I have looked forward with dread to this moment in it. The thoughts of men are mostly not hard to read; in this case they are very easy. You are sure to ask why we did not choose this moment to go away—and I must continue to owe you an answer. I do not know why. I cannot defend myself. By this time it was certainly eleven, probably later. The children were asleep. The last series of tests had been too long, nature had had her way. They were sleeping in our laps, the little one on mine, the boy on his mother's. That was, in a way, a consolation; but at the same time it was also ground for compassion and a clear leading to take them home to bed. And I give you my word that we wanted to obey this touching admonition, we seriously wanted to. We roused the poor things and told them it was now high time to go. But they were no sooner conscious than they began to resist and implore—you know how horrified children are at the thought of leaving before the end of a thing. No cajoling has any effect, you have to use force. It was so lovely, they wailed. How did we know what was coming next? Surely we could not leave until after the intermission; they liked a little nap now and again—only not go home, only not go to bed, while the beautiful evening was still going on!

We yielded, but only for the moment, of course—so far as we knew—only for a little while, just a few minutes longer. I cannot excuse our staying, scarcely can I even understand it. Did we think, having once said A, we had to say B—having once brought the children hither we had to let them stay? No, it is not good enough. Were we ourselves so highly entertained? Yes, and no. Our feelings for Cavaliere Cipolla were of a very mixed kind, but so were the feelings of the whole audience, if I mistake not, and nobody left. Were we under the sway of a fascination which emanated from this man who took so strange a way to earn his bread; a fascination which he gave out independently of the programme and even between the tricks and which paralysed our resolve? Again, sheer curiosity may account for something. One was curious to know how such an evening turned out; Cipolla in his remarks having all along hinted that he had tricks in his bag stranger than any he had yet produced.

But all that is not it—or at least it is not all of it. More correct it would be to answer the first question with another. Why had we not left Torre di Venere itself before now? To me the two questions are one and the same, and in order to get out of the impasse I might simply say that I had answered it already. For, as things had been in Torre in general: queer, uncomfortable, troublesome, tense, oppressive, so precisely they were here in this hall tonight. Yes, more than precisely. For it seemed to be the fountainhead of all the uncanniness and all the strained feelings which had oppressed the atmosphere of our holiday. This man whose return to the stage we were awaiting was the personification of all that; and, as we had not gone away in general, so to speak, it would have been inconsistent to do it in the particular case. You may call this an explanation, you may call it inertia, as you see fit. Any argument more to the purpose I simply do not know how to adduce.

Well, there was an interval of ten minutes, which grew into nearly twenty. The children remained awake. They were enchanted by our compliance, and filled the break to their own satisfaction by renewing relations with the popular sphere, with Antonio, Guiscardo, and the canoe man. They put their hands to their mouths and called messages across, appealing to us for the Italian words. "Hope you have a good catch tomorrow, a whole netful!" They called to Mario, Esquisito Mario: "*Mario, una cioccolata e biscotti!*" And this time he heeded and answered with a smile: "*Subito, signorini!*" Later we had reason to recall this kindly, if rather absent and pensive smile.

Thus the interval passed, the gong sounded. The audience, which had scattered in conversation, took their places again, the children sat up straight in their chairs with their hands in their laps. The curtain had not been dropped. Cipolla came forward again, with his dipping stride, and began to introduce the second half of the programme with a lecture.

Let me state once for all that this self-confident cripple was the most powerful hypnotist I have ever seen in my life. It was pretty plain now that he threw dust in the public eye and advertised himself as a prestidigitator on account of police regulations which would have prevented him from making his living by the exercise of his powers. Perhaps this eye-wash is the usual thing in Italy; it may be permitted or even connived at by the authorities. Certainly the man had from the beginning made little concealment of the actual nature of his operations; and this second half of the programme was quite frankly and exclusively devoted to one sort of experiment. While he still practised some rhetorical circumlocutions, the tests themselves were one long series of attacks upon the will-power, the loss or compulsion of volition. Comic, exciting, amazing by turns, by midnight they were still in full swing; we ran the gamut of all the phenomena this natural-unnatural field has to show, from the unimpressive at one end of the scale to the monstrous at the other. The audience laughed and applauded as they followed the grotesque details; shook their heads, clapped their knees, fell very frankly under the spell of this stern, self-assured personality. At the same time I saw signs that they were not quite complacent, not quite unconscious of the peculiar ignominy which lay, for the individual and for the general, in Cipolla's triumphs.

Two main features were constant in all the experiments: the liquor glass and the claw-handled riding-whip. The first was always invoked to add fuel to his demoniac fires; without it, apparently, they might have burned out. On this score we might even have felt pity for the man; but the whistle of his scourge, the insulting symbol of his domination, before which we all cowered, drowned out every sensation save a dazed and outbraved submission to his power. Did he then lay claim to our sympathy to boot? I was struck by a remark he made—it suggested no less. At the climax of his experiments, by stroking and breathing upon a certain young man who had offered himself as a subject and already proved himself a particularly susceptible one, he had not only put him into the condition known as deep trance and extended his insensible body by neck and feet across the backs of two chairs, but had actually sat down on the rigid form as on a bench, without making it yield. The sight of this unholy figure in a frock-coat squatted on the stiff body was horrible and incredible; the audience, convinced that the victim of this scientific diversion must be suffering, expressed its sympathy: "*Ah, poveretto!*" Poor soul, poor soul! "*Poor soul!*" Cipolla mocked them, with some bitterness. "Ladies and gentlemen, you are barking up the wrong tree. *Sono io il poveretto*. I am the person who is suffering. I am the one to be pitied." We pocketed the information. Very good. Maybe the experiment was at his expense, maybe it was he who had suffered the cramp when the *giovanotto* over there had made the faces. But appearances were all against it; and one does not feel like saying *poveretto* to a man who is suffering to bring about the humiliation of others.

I have got ahead of my story and lost sight of the sequence of events. To this day my mind is full of the Cavaliere's feats of endurance; only I do not recall them in their order—which does not matter. So much I do know that the longer and more circumstantial tests, which got the most applause, impressed me less than some of the small ones which passed quickly over. I remember the young man whose body Cipolla converted into a board, only because of the accompanying remarks which I have quoted. An elderly lady in a cane-seated chair was lulled by Cipolla in the delusion that she was on a voyage to India and gave a voluble account of her adventures by land and sea. But I found this phenomenon less impressive than one which followed immediately after the intermission. A tall, well-built, soldierly man was unable to lift his arm, after the hunchback had told him that he could not and given a cut through the air with his whip. I can still see the face of that stately, mustachioed colonel smiling and clenching his teeth as he struggled to regain his lost freedom of action. A staggering performance! He seemed to be exerting his will, and in vain; the trouble, however, was probably simply that he could not will. There was involved here that recoil of the will upon itself which paralyses choice—as our tyrant had previously explained to the Roman gentleman.

Still less can I forget the touching scene, at once comic and horrible, with Signora Angiolieri. The Cavaliere, probably in his first bold survey of the room, had spied out her ethereal lack of resistance to his power. For actually he bewitched her, literally drew her out of her seat, out of her row, and away with him whither he willed. And in order to enhance his effect, he bade Signor Angiolieri call upon his wife by her name, to throw, as it were, all the weight of his existence and his rights in her into the scale, to rouse by the voice of her husband everything in his spouse's soul which could shield her virtue against the evil assaults of magic. And how vain it all was! Cipolla was standing at some distance from the couple, when he made a single cut with his whip through the air. It caused our landlady to shudder violently and turn her face towards him. "Sofronia!" cried Signor Angiolieri—we had not known that Signora Angiolieri's name was Sofronia. And he did well to call, everybody saw that there was no time to lose. His wife kept her face turned in the direction of the diabolical Cavaliere, who with his ten long yellow fingers was making passes at his victim, moving backwards as he did so, step by step. Then Signora Angiolieri, her pale face gleaming, rose up from her seat, turned right round, and began to glide after him. Fatal and forbidding sight! Her face as though moon-struck, stiff-armed, her lovely hands lifted a little at the wrists, the feet as it were together, she seemed to float slowly out of her row and after the tempter. "Call her, sir, keep on calling," prompted the redoubtable man. And Signor Angiolieri, in a weak voice, called: "Sofronia!" Ah, again and again he called; as his wife went further off he even curved one hand round his lips and beckoned with the other as he called. But the poor voice of love and duty echoed unheard, in vain, behind the lost one's back; the signora swayed along, moon-struck, deaf, enslaved; she glided into the middle aisle and down it towards the fingering hunchback, towards the door. We were convinced, we were driven to the conviction, that she would have followed her master, had he so willed it, to the ends of the earth.

"*Accidente!*" cried out Signor Angiolieri, in genuine affright, springing up as the exit was reached. But at the same moment the

Cavaliere put aside, as it were, the triumphal crown and broke off. "Enough, signora, I thank you," he said, and offered his arm to lead her back to her husband. "Signor," he greeted the latter, "here is your wife. Unharmed, with my compliments, I give her into your hands. Cherish with all the strength of your manhood a treasure which is so wholly yours, and let your zeal be quickened by knowing that there are powers stronger than reason or virtue, and not always so magnanimously ready to relinquish their prey!"

Poor Signor Angiolieri, so quiet, so bald! He did not look as though he would know how to defend his happiness, even against powers much less demoniac than these which were now adding mockery to frightfulness. Solemnly and pompously the Cavaliere retired to the stage, amid applause to which his eloquence gave double strength. It was this particular episode, I feel sure, that set the seal upon his ascendancy. For now he made them dance, yes, literally; and the dancing lent a dissolute, abandoned, topsy-turvy air to the scene, a drunken abdication of the critical spirit which had so long resisted the spell of this man. Yes, he had had to fight to get the upper hand —for instance against the animosity of the young Roman gentleman, whose rebellious spirit threatened to serve others as a rallying-point. But it was precisely upon the importance of example that the Cavaliere was so strong. He had the wit to make his attack at the weakest point and to choose as his first victim that feeble, ecstatic youth whom he had previously made into a board. The master had but to look at him, when this young man would fling himself back as though struck by lightning, place his hands rigidly at his sides, and fall into a state of military somnambulism, in which it was plain to any eye that he was open to the most absurd suggestion that might be made to him. He seemed quite content in his abject state, quite pleased to be relieved of the burden of voluntary choice. Again and again he offered himself as a subject and gloried in the model facility he had in losing consciousness. So now he mounted the platform, and a single cut of the whip was enough to make him dance to the Cavaliere's orders, in a kind of complacent ecstasy, eyes closed, head nodding, lank limbs flying in all directions.

It looked unmistakably like enjoyment, and other recruits were not long in coming forward: two other young men, one humbly and one well dressed, were soon jigging alongside the first. But now the gentleman from Rome bobbed up again, asking defiantly if the Cavaliere would engage to make him dance too, even against his will.

"Even against your will," answered Cipolla, in unforgettable accents. That frightful *"anche se non vuole"* still rings in my ears. The struggle began. After Cipolla had taken another little glass and lighted a fresh cigarette he stationed the Roman at a point in the middle aisle and himself took up a position some distance behind him, making his whip whistle through the air as he gave the order: *"Balla!"* His opponent did not stir. *"Balla!"* repeated the Cavaliere incisively, and snapped his whip. You saw the young man move his neck round in his collar; at the same time one hand lifted slightly at the wrist, one ankle turned outward. But that was all, for the time at least; merely a tendency to twitch, now sternly repressed, now seeming about to get the upper hand. It escaped nobody that here a heroic obstinacy, a fixed resolve to resist, must needs be conquered; we were beholding a gallant effort to strike out and save the honour of the human race. He twitched but danced not; and the struggle was so prolonged that the Cavaliere had to divide his attention between it and the stage, turning now and then to make his riding-whip whistle in the direction of the dancers, as it were to keep them in leash. At the same time he advised the audience that no fatigue was involved in such activities, however long they went on, since it was not the automatons up there who danced, but himself. Then once more his eye would bore itself into the back of the Roman's neck and lay siege to the strength of purpose which defied him.

One saw it waver, that strength of purpose, beneath the repeated summons and whip-crackings. Saw with an objective interest which yet was not quite free from traces of sympathetic emotion—from pity, even from a cruel kind of pleasure. If I understand what was going on, it was the negative character of the young man's fighting position which was his undoing. It is likely that *not* willing is not a practicable state of mind; *not* to want to do something may be in the long run a mental content impossible to subsist on. Between not willing a certain thing and not willing at all—in other words, yielding to another person's will—there may lie too small a space for the idea of freedom to squeeze into. Again, there were the Cavaliere's persuasive words, woven in among the whip-crackings and commands, as he mingled effects that were his own secret with others of a bewilderingly psychological kind. *"Balla!"* said he. "Who wants to torture himself like that? Is forcing yourself your idea of freedom? *Una ballatina!* Why, your arms and legs are aching for it. What a relief to give way to them—there, you are dancing already! That is no struggle any more, it is a pleasure!" And so it was. The jerking and twitching of the refractory youth's limbs had at last got the upper hand; he lifted his arms, then his knees, his joints quite suddenly relaxed, he flung his legs and danced, and amid bursts of applause the Cavaliere led him to join the row of puppets on the stage. Up there we could see his face as he "enjoyed" himself; it was clothed in a broad grin and the eyes were half-shut. In a way, it was consoling to see that he was having a better time than he had had in the hour of his pride.

His "fall" was, I may say, an epoch. The ice was completely broken, Cipolla's triumph had reached its height. The Circe's wand, that whistling leather whip with the claw handle, held absolute sway. At one time—it must have been well after midnight—not only were there eight or ten persons dancing on the little stage, but in the hall below a varied animation reigned, and a long-toothed Anglo-Saxoness in a pince-nez left her seat of her own motion to perform a tarantella in the centre aisle. Cipolla was lounging in a cane-seated chair at the left of the stage, gulping down the smoke of a cigarette and breathing it impudently out through his bad teeth. He tapped his foot and shrugged his shoulders, looking down upon the abandoned scene in the hall; now and then he snapped his whip backwards at a laggard up on the stage. The children were awake at the moment. With shame I speak of them. For it was not good to be here, least of all for them; that we had not taken them away can only be explained by saying that we had caught the general devil-may-careness of the hour. By that time it was all one. Anyhow, thank goodness, they lacked understanding for the disreputable side of the entertainment, and in their innocence were perpetually charmed by the unheard-of indulgence which permitted them to be present at such a thing as a magician's "evening." Whole quarter-hours at a time they drowsed on our laps, waking refreshed and rosy-cheeked, with sleep-drunk eyes, to laugh to bursting at the leaps and jumps the magician made those people up there make. They had not thought it would be so jolly; they joined with their clumsy little hands in every round of applause. And jumped for joy upon their chairs, as was their wont, when Cipolla beckoned to their friend Mario from the Esquisito, beckoned to him just like a picture in a book, holding his hand in front of his nose and bending and straightening the forefinger by turns.

Mario obeyed. I can see him now going up the stairs to Cipolla, who continued to beckon him, in that droll, picture-book sort of way. He hesitated for a moment at first; that, too, I recall quite clearly. During the whole evening he had lounged against a wooden pillar at the side entrance, with his arms folded, or else with his hands thrust into his jacket pockets. He was on our left, near the youth with the militant hair, and had followed the performance attentively, so far as we had seen, if with no particular animation and God knows how much comprehension. He could not much relish being summoned thus, at the end of the evening. But it was only too easy to see why he obeyed. After all, obedience was his calling in life; and then, how should a simple lad like him find it within his human capacity to refuse compliance to a man so throned and crowned as Cipolla at that hour? Willy-nilly he left his column and with a word of thanks to those making way for him he mounted the steps with a doubtful smile on his full lips.

Picture a thickset youth of twenty years, with clipt hair, a low forehead, and heavy-lidded eyes of an indefinite grey, shot with green and yellow. These things I knew from having spoken with him, as we often had. There was a saddle of freckles on the flat nose, the whole upper half of the face retreated behind the lower, and that again was dominated by thick lips that parted to show the salivated teeth. These thick lips and the veiled look of the eyes lent the whole face a primitive melancholy—it was that which had drawn us to him from the first. In it was not the faintest trace of brutality—indeed, his hands would have given the lie to such an idea, being unusually slender and delicate even for a southerner. They were hands by which one liked being served.

We knew him humanly without knowing him personally, if I may make that distinction. We saw him nearly every day, and felt a certain kindness for his dreamy ways, which might at times be actual inattentiveness, suddenly transformed into a redeeming zeal to serve. His mien was serious, only the children could bring a smile to his face. It was not sulky, but uningratiating, without intentional effort to please—or, rather, it seemed to give up being pleasant in the conviction that it could not succeed. We should have remembered Mario in any case, as one of those homely recollections of travel which often stick in the mind better than more important ones. But of his circumstances we knew no more than that his father was a petty clerk in the Municipio and his mother took in washing.

His white waiter's coat became him better than the faded striped suit he wore, with a gay coloured scarf instead of a collar, the ends tucked into his jacket. He neared Cipolla, who however did not leave off that motion of his finger before his nose, so that Mario had to come still closer, right up to the chair-seat and the master's legs. Whereupon the latter spread out his elbows and seized the lad, turning him so that we had a view of his face. Then gazed him briskly up and down, with a careless, commanding eye.

"Well, *ragazzo mio*, how comes it we make acquaintance so late in the day? But believe me, I made yours long ago. Yes, yes, I've had you in my eye this long while and known what good stuff you were made of. How could I go and forget you again? Well, I've had a good deal to think about. . . . Now tell me, what is your name? The first name, that's all I want."

"My name is Mario," the young man answered, in a low voice.

"Ah, Mario. Very good. Yes, yes, there is such a name, quite a common name, a classic name too, one of those which preserve the heroic traditions of the Fatherland. *Bravo! Salve!*" And he flung up his arm slantingly above his crooked shoulder, palm outward, in the Roman salute. He may have been slightly tipsy by now, and no wonder; but he spoke as before, clearly, fluently, and with emphasis. Though about this time there had crept into his voice a gross, autocratic note, and a kind of arrogance was in his sprawl.

"Well, now, Mario *mio*," he went on, "it's a good thing you came this evening, and that's a pretty scarf you've got on; it is becoming to your style of beauty. It must stand you in good stead with the girls, the pretty pretty girls of Torre—"

From the row of youths, close by the place where Mario had been standing, sounded a laugh. It came from the youth with the militant hair. He stood there, his jacket over his shoulder, and laughed outright, rudely and scornfully.

Mario gave a start. I think it was a shrug, but he may have started and then hastened to cover the movement by shrugging his shoulders, as much as to say that the neckerchief and the fair sex were matters of equal indifference to him.

The Cavaliere gave a downward glance.

"We needn't trouble about him," he said. "He is jealous, because your scarf is so popular with the girls, maybe partly because you and I are so friendly up here. Perhaps he'd like me to put him in mind of his colic—I could do it free of charge. Tell me, Mario. You've come here this evening for a bit of fun—and in the daytime you work in an ironmonger's shop?"

"In a café," corrected the youth.

"Oh, in a café. That's where Cipolla nearly came a cropper! What you are is a cup-bearer, a Ganymede—I like that, it is another classical allusion—*Salvietta!*" Again the Cavaliere saluted, to the huge gratification of his audience.

Mario smiled too. "But before that," he interpolated, in the interest of accuracy, "I worked for a while in a shop in Portoclemente." He seemed visited by a natural desire to assist the prophecy by dredging out its essential features.

"There, didn't I say so? in an ironmonger's shop?"

"They kept combs and brushes," Mario got round it.

"Didn't I say that you were not always a Ganymede? Not always at the sign of the serviette? Even when Cipolla makes a mistake, it is a kind that makes you believe in him. Now tell me: Do you believe in me?"

An indefinite gesture.

"A half-way answer," commented the Cavaliere. "Probably it is not easy to win your confidence. Even for me, I can see, it is not so easy. I see in your features a reserve, a sadness, *un tratto di malinconia* . . . tell me" (he seized Mario's hand persuasively) "have you troubles?"

"*Nossignore,*" answered Mario, promptly and decidedly.

"You *have* troubles," insisted the Cavaliere, bearing down the denial by the weight of his authority. "Can't I see? Trying to pull the wool over Cipolla's eyes, are you? Of course, about the girls—it is a girl, isn't it? You have love troubles?"

Mario gave a vigorous head-shake. And again the *giovanotto's* brutal laugh rang out. The Cavaliere gave heed. His eyes were roving about somewhere in the air; but he cocked an ear to the sound, then swung his whip backwards, as he had once or twice before in his conversation with Mario, that none of his puppets might flag in their zeal. The gesture had nearly cost him his new prey: Mario gave a sudden start in the direction of the steps. But Cipolla had him in his clutch.

"Not so fast," said he. "That would be fine, wouldn't it? So you want to skip, do you, Ganymede, right in the middle of the fun, or, rather, when it is just beginning? Stay with me, I'll show you something nice, I'll convince you. You have no reason to worry, I promise you. This girl—you know her and others know her too—what's her name? Wait! I read the name in your eyes, it is on the tip of my tongue and yours too—"

"Silvestra!" shouted the *giovanotto* from below.

The Cavaliere's face did not change.

"Aren't there the forward people?" he asked, not looking down, more as in undisturbed converse with Mario. "Aren't there the young fighting-cocks that crow in season and out? Takes the word out of your mouth, the conceited fool, and seems to think he has some special right to it. Let him be. But Silvestra, your Silvestra—ah, what a girl that is! What a prize! Brings your heart into your mouth to see her walk or laugh or breathe, she is so lovely. And her round arms when she washes, and tosses her head back to get the hair out of her eyes! An angel from paradise!"

Mario stared at him, his head thrust forward. He seemed to have forgotten the audience, forgotten where he was. The red rings round his eyes had got larger, they looked as though they were painted on. His thick lips parted.

"And she makes you suffer, this angel," went on Cipolla, "or, rather, you make yourself suffer for her—there is a difference, my lad, a most important difference, let me tell you. There are misunderstandings in love, maybe nowhere else in the world are there so many. I know what you are thinking: what does this Cipolla, with his little physical defect, know about love? Wrong, all wrong, he knows a lot. He has a wide and powerful understanding of its workings, and it pays to listen to his advice. But let's leave Cipolla out, cut him out altogether and think only of Silvestra, your peerless Silvestra! What! Is she to give any young gamecock the preference, so that he can laugh while you cry? To prefer him to a chap like you, so full of feeling and so sympathetic? Not very likely, is it? It is impossible—we know better, Cipolla and she. If I were to put myself in her place and choose between the two of you, a tarry lout like that —a codfish, a sea-urchin—and a Mario, a knight of the serviette, who moves among gentlefolk and hands round refreshments with an air—my word, but my heart would speak in no uncertain tones—it knows to whom I gave it long ago. It is time that he should see and understand, my chosen one! It is time that you see me and recognize me, Mario, my beloved! Tell me, who am I?"

It was grisly, the way the betrayer made himself irresistible, wreathed and coquetted with his crooked shoulder, languished with the puffy eyes, and showed his splintered teeth in a sickly smile. And alas, at his beguiling words, what was come of our Mario? It is hard for me to tell, hard as it was for me to see; for here was nothing less than an utter abandonment of the inmost soul, a public exposure of timid and deluded passion and rapture. He put his hands across his mouth, his shoulders rose and fell with his pantings. He could not, it was plain, trust his eyes and ears for joy, and the one thing he forgot was precisely that he could not trust them. "Silvestra!" he breathed, from the very depths of his vanquished heart.

"Kiss me!" said the hunchback. "Trust me, I love thee. Kiss me here." And with the tip of his index finger, hand, arm, and little finger outspread, he pointed to his cheek, near the mouth. And Mario bent and kissed him.

It had grown very still in the room. That was a monstrous moment, grotesque and thrilling, the moment of Mario's bliss. In that evil span of time, crowded with a sense of the illusiveness of all joy, one sound became audible, and that not quite at once, but on the instant of the melancholy and ribald meeting between Mario's lips and the repulsive flesh which thrust itself forward for his caress. It was the sound of a laugh, from the *giovanotto* on our left. It broke into the dramatic suspense of the moment, coarse, mocking, and yet—or I must have been grossly mistaken—with an undertone of compassion for the poor bewildered, victimized creature. It had a faint ring of that *"Poveretto"* which Cipolla had declared was wasted on the wrong person, when he claimed the pity for his own.

The laugh still rang in the air when the recipient of the caress gave his whip a little swish, low down, close to his chair-leg, and Mario started up and flung himself back. He stood in that posture staring, his hands one over the other on those desecrated lips. Then he beat his temples with his clenched fists, over and over; turned and staggered down the steps, while the audience applauded, and Cipolla sat there with his hands in his lap, his shoulders shaking. Once below, and even while in full retreat, Mario hurled himself round with legs flung wide apart; one arm flew up, and two flat shattering detonations crashed through applause and laughter.

There was instant silence. Even the dancers came to a full stop and stared about, struck dumb. Cipolla bounded from his seat. He stood with his arms spread out, slanting as though to ward everybody off, as though next moment he would cry out: "Stop! Keep back! Silence! What was that?" Then, in that instant, he sank back in his seat, his head rolling on his chest; in the next he had fallen sideways to the floor, where he lay motionless, a huddled heap of clothing, with limbs awry.

The commotion was indescribable. Ladies hid their faces, shuddering, on the breasts of their escorts. There were shouts for a doctor, for the police. People flung themselves on Mario in a mob, to disarm him, to take away the weapon that hung from his fingers—that small, dull-metal, scarcely pistol-shaped tool with hardly any barrel—in how strange and unexpected a direction had fate levelled it!

And now—now finally, at last—we took the children and led them towards the exit, past the pair of *carabinieri* just entering. Was that the end, they wanted to know, that they might go in peace? Yes, we assured them, that was the end. An end of horror, a fatal end. And yet a liberation—for I could not, and I cannot, but find it so!

[Translated by H. T. Lowe-Porter]

# NOW THAT YOU'VE READ MANN'S
# MARIO AND THE MAGICIAN:

For some years before his death, Thomas Mann had been not only Germany's most distinguished novelist since Goethe, but also perhaps the world's most eminent man of letters (an eminence that only a few men, of the stature of André Gide, George Bernard Shaw, William Faulkner, or T. S. Eliot, might safely have challenged). His position rests most solidly on three works: *Buddenbrooks, The Magic Mountain,* and *Joseph and His Brethren.* In size, scope, and significance, these literary leviathans swamp most competition out of sight.

Master of the major opus, Mann was no less the master of the minor medium. Among his outstanding pieces of shorter fiction are *Death in Venice* and *Mario and the Magician,* the best of his several tales with Italian settings. Both are high aesthetic achievements, and both fascinate us by the illuminating insights they throw upon the mysterious and irrational human urges that destroy self-discipline and dignity. But while *Death in Venice* emphasizes the moral implications of these underground forces, *Mario and the Magician* examines their political implications—or to be more precise, the imperative interaction between the two. That this political allegory, as memorable and timely now as when it was written in 1929, should have come from a man who called himself "non-political" will seem inevitable enough to those familiar with the milieu in which Mann moved and matured as an artist.

He was born in Lubeck, the second of five children, amid surroundings which combined middle-class prosperity with the provincial aspects of an ancient port. His father was an important grain merchant and a senator of the city, his mother a lady of mixed German and Portuguese Creole stock. His parents gave him a happy childhood and a rich family life, but his school days were less joyful. Planning to take him into the family business, the father sent young Mann to the *Realgymnasium* (secondary school); the Prussian spirit of the institution, the appalling manners of the masters who regarded him as an oddity because he wrote verses, left Mann with a permanent hatred of the German education system, on which he later took handsome literary revenge in both *Buddenbrooks* and *Tonio Kroger*.

The first crisis in his life at Lubeck was the unexpected death of his father, when Mann was fifteen. The business, unsteady for some years, had to be liquidated, and the family moved to Munich, leaving Mann in Lubeck to finish his schooling. After graduation, he followed his family and soon found a position in a Munich fire-insurance office. While working there, he wrote his first published story, *Gefallen*, a little work about a "fallen" woman. It was clear that Mann's ambitions did not run in the direction of business, and after a year, he left the office to become an auditor at the University of Munich, there participating fully in its cultural life.

Meanwhile, his elder brother, Heinrich, the novelist, was living in Rome. On his urging, Mann came to Italy, and together the brothers spent a summer in the Sabine Hills (where *Buddenbrooks* was begun) and the winter in Rome. However, like Tonio Kroger, Mann was not fond of Italians then, and soon returned to his mother's home in Munich.

There he joined the editorial staff of the journal *Simplicissimus*, and continued working on *Buddenbrooks* until its completion in 1900. The book was not really successful until a five-mark edition appeared the following year, and then the twenty-six-year-old author became famous for this panorama of the decline and fall of a bourgeois family through four generations. (With twenty printings in the first American edition alone, it remains today his most popular book.) Three years afterwards, the *Tonio Kroger* volume of stories was published to critical accolades, and after these successes, Mann's social horizon began to expand. He fell in love with Katja Pringsheim, the daughter of a Munich professor, and, in 1905, married her. Within four years, the couple were parents of a girl and boy: Erika, later an actress, authoress, and wife of the poet W. H. Auden, and Klaus, the writer and authority on André Gide. Four other children subsequently completed the family.

Between the years 1904-1911, Mann published several minor pieces. Among the most interesting was the fragmentary *The Confessions of the Swindler Felix Krull*, containing a cynical portrait of a mesmerizing stage artist which Mann may have developed into Cipolla in *Mario*. In 1912, Katja Mann was found to be suffering from a lung condition and had to spend a period in a Swiss sanatorium. The previous spring, Mann had spent a short vacation with Katja and the children on the Lido at Venice, and during and after her convalescence he wove his impressions of that city into his study of a gifted but death-possessed artist, *Death in Venice*. When it appeared immediately before World War I, it had a profound impact upon the German and French public, for Mann seemed to be articulating current half-felt fears for the future of Western European civilization.

As a rather short "humorous pendant" to the "triumph of drunken disorder over the forces of a life consecrated to rule and discipline," Mann began to sketch out *The Magic Mountain*. But in 1914 the world tottered, and he found himself unable to work on the novel. Before this time, preoccupied with his own highly personal problem of the artist's nature and his relation to society, Mann had not felt the need to take an attitude toward European politics; but now he could not resume his creative activities until he had clarified his ideas about the war, and above all, about his relationship to the rapidly-advancing tide of democracy.

Out of these concerns came *The Reflections of a Non-Political Man* (1917), a book unimportant as art but important to the understanding of Mann's thought. In it, Mann emphasizes his conviction that politics is foreign to his own and the German nature; only more repugnant to him are liberal democracy and universal suffrage. He attacks England, France, and especially Italy ("Diese Romanen haben kein Gewissen in dem Augen"), and upholds Germany as the land of protest against the domination of Europe by the Franco-Anglo-Roman tradition. Though the book does contain flashes of the detached and humane man of letters, it is nationalistic and narrow in its attitudes.

With this tract out of his system, he returned to *The Magic Mountain* and completed it in 1924. The seed of a comic novel had grown into a tremendous structure built upon his experiences as a visitor to the sanatorium where his wife had stayed. If *Death in Venice* is about the decay of a man, and *Buddenbrooks* about the decay of a family, *The Magic Mountain* is about the decay of a whole society. It marks a significant turning point in Mann's intellectual development. The young officer who represents that national pride which was so much a part of the author's make-up is permitted to die half-way through the book, while the engineer, influenced by a liberal-minded old Italian, becomes the symbol of the young German republic seeking new directions. Though not yet an open advocate of democracy, Mann was becoming increasingly democratic in his views. His comment about one of the novel's characters is self-revealing: "One must have knowledge of sin in order to find redemption."

After the war, Mann's services as a writer and lecturer were in great demand. In the middle twenties, he visited the countries of western Europe, addressing large crowds everywhere, and his journeys to Italy and the Middle East provided him with the material for *Mario* and for his Joseph tetralogy. Between 1924-1929, Mann moved farther and farther away from the arch-conservatism he had once advocated. For example, in a notable Munich speech, he appealed to his audience to resist the harmful spirit of anti-semitism and hysterical nationalism which already were making themselves felt in Germany. Even before Hitler came to power, the "non-political" man of 1917 was pointing out the dangerous trends at home. In 1929, Mann became an international hero: he won the Nobel Prize for Literature and made his first decisive literary protest against Fascism, in *Mario and the Magician*.

*Mario* is, on the surface, a simple account of an incident which occurs during a vacation the narrator spends with his family at a Tyrrhenian resort, but beneath this surface the careful reader discovers important depths. The natives, who represent all levels of Italian society, from the illiterate peasants to the sophisticated patricians, have submitted to the spirit of nationalism. They are, the narrator observes early, "a society passing through a certain stage, something like an illness"; they are ready prey for predatory power. Casually at first but then with swiftly-mounting clarity, Mann sifts the situation which makes Cipolla's mesmerism possible. We see a people who are about to be tricked, deluded, and coerced, but who are at least partially responsible for their own degradation because of their spiritual and moral poverty, because without their consent the action could not be willed. Ironically and significantly, it is the adults, not the innocent children, who are corrupted by the evil influence.

As the action develops, the focus shifts subtly from the audience to the stage artist who bends the audience to his will. Cipolla (this Italian word for "onion" carries a sly reference to Mussolini's bald pate) and his magic reveal the tactics of fascism. Slowly and carefully, Cipolla makes the crowd forget the meaning of his cruel, claw-handled whip, makes them entirely oblivious to the aura of aberration and decay which he emits. He begins this feat with the simple folk, the gullible populace, and passes up through the "more select portion of his audience." His performance advances from the comic and harmless through the grotesque and to the horrible. The jigging gentleman of Rome at the climax of the political parallels symbolizes with terrifying emotional force "the drunken abdication of the critical spirit which had so long resisted" the spell of the magician (one is reminded of the kind of image which brings Orwell's *1984* to its conclusion).

Opposed to the symbols of death and debility is Mario, the symbol of life and resistance. At first, he seems the least likely to break the grip of Cipolla, but when pushed to the critical point, he draws upon inner reserves of decency and dignity, and at the ominous crack of the whip, shatters the evil spell. As a liberating force against tyranny, human dignity is seen to be stronger than either free will or consciousness. Mario emerges as the essential human being, disappointed by misfortune yet unbowed by it, whom Mann later urged to resist the irrational forces seeking control of his people.

Interwoven with this political and moral motif is a variation on a Mann theme: the artist (in this case, an *artiste*) as a daemonic, despicable, special case who carries within him a potentiality for great evil. Though repulsive in every respect, he wields strange power over people. That this power also leads to his own disaster is further proof of the dangers inherent in possessing such special gifts.

With firmness and courage, Mann continued to oppose the antidemocratic forces engulfing much of Europe. In the early thirties, he condemned Nazism, then making rapid headway in Germany, and also those intellectuals who were creating an atmosphere in which it could thrive. If the Nazis came to power, he said, they would turn the German people into a race of primitive, blue-eyed, heel-clicking robots. However, it was his 1933 lecture critical of Wagner, their idol, that finally angered the Nazis. While he was lecturing in Switzerland, his children telephoned that "the weather was unpleasant at home." Thomas Mann had begun his exile.

In 1936, he was deprived of his citizenship and, soon afterwards, of the honorary doctorate (restored after the war) previously conferred by the University of Bonn. Now he saw clearly that the Nazis meant barbarism at home and war abroad, and he predicted their ultimate defeat. The Nazis retaliated by burning his books, but Mann continued to direct against the Hitler regime his outspoken articles, speeches, and broadcasts, later collected under the titles of *Achtung, Europa!* and *Listen, Germany.* This era marks Mann's declaration of independence from the theories which had once led him to think an artist could be a complete human being without worrying about politics.

After making some visits to the United States, Mann settled in Princeton, lecturing at the University, and in 1941, moved to Southern California, joining a colony of German exiles including Bruno Walter, Arnold Schönberg, and Franz Werfel. Under the "Egyptian sky of California," he concluded his great Joseph tetralogy, and during the war, wrote the masterpiece of his twilight years, *Doctor Faustus.* Though its protagonist is a great musician, the book is not primarily about music. The protagonist stands for Germany itself; he is the genius who has abandoned moral considerations in his struggle for knowledge and power. His surrender to the devil is plainly a symbolic act.

But Mann never ceased to love the land that had denied him, and in 1949, he visited Germany for the first time in sixteen years. He received tumultuous ovations in both the Western and Eastern sectors from a people hungry for a symbol of German humanitarianism. In 1952, he returned to Europe once more, this time to take up permanent residence in Zurich, where he developed *The Confessions of the Swindler Felix Krull* into a full-length novel of the same title. This was his last testament. On August 12, 1955, "a shocked and respectful world received the news of his decease."

## FOR FURTHER INFORMATION:

Joseph Gerard Brennan. *Thomas Mann's World.* Columbia University Press: New York, 1942.

Henry Hatfield. *Thomas Mann.* New Directions: Norfolk, 1951.

J. M. Lindsay. *Thomas Mann.* Basil Blackwell: Oxford, 1954.

*Thomas Mann: A Collection of Critical Essays.* Edited by Henry C. Hatfield. Prentice-Hall: Englewood Cliffs, N.J., 1964.

*The Stature of Thomas Mann: A Critical Anthology by Many Hands.* Edited by Charles Neider. New Directions: Norfolk, 1947.

*Germanic Review.* December 1950, XXV (a Thomas Mann issue).

Joseph P. Stern. *Thomas Mann.* Columbia University Press: New York, 1967.

Andrew White. *Thomas Mann.* Grove Press: New York, 1967.

# OLD MAN

## BY WILLIAM FAULKNER

First published, 1939

# OLD MAN

## CHAPTER I

**O**NCE (it was in Mississippi, in May, in the flood year 1927) there were two convicts. One of them was about twenty-five, tall, lean, flat-stomached, with a sunburned face and Indian-black hair and pale, china-colored outraged eyes—an outrage directed not at the men who had foiled his crime, not even at the lawyers and judges who had sent him here, but at the writers, the uncorporeal names attached to the stories, the paper novels—the Diamond Dicks and Jesse James and such—whom he believed had led him into his present predicament through their own ignorance and gullibility regarding the medium in which they dealt and took money for, in accepting information on which they placed the stamp of verisimilitude and authenticity (this so much the more criminal since there was no sworn notarised statement attached and hence so much the quicker would the information be accepted by one who expected the same unspoken good faith, demanding, asking, expecting no certification, which he extended along with the dime or fifteen cents to pay for it) and retailed for money and which on actual application proved to be impractical and (to the convict) criminally false; there would be times when he would halt his mule and plow in mid-furrow (there is no walled penitentiary in Mississippi; it is a cotton plantation which the convicts work under the rifles and shotguns of guards and trusties) and muse with a kind of enraged impotence, fumbling among the rubbish left him by his one and only experience with courts and law, fumbling until the meaningless and verbose shibboleth took form at last (himself seeking justice at the same blind fount where he had met justice and been hurled back and down): Using the mails to defraud: who felt that he had been defrauded by the third-class mail system not of crass and stupid money which he did not particularly want anyway, but of liberty and honor and pride.

He was in for fifteen years (he had arrived shortly after his nineteenth birthday) for attempted train robbery. He had laid his plans in advance, he had followed his printed (and false) authority to the letter; he had saved the paperbacks for two years, reading and re-reading them, memorising them, comparing and weighing story and method against story and method, taking the good from each and discarding the dross as his workable plan emerged, keeping his mind open to make the subtle last-minute changes, without haste and without impatience, as the newer pamphlets appeared on their appointed days as a conscientious dressmaker makes the subtle alterations in a court presentation costume as the newer bulletins appear. And then when the day came, he did not even have a chance to go through the coaches and collect the watches and the rings, the brooches and the hidden money-belts, because he had been captured as soon as he entered the express car where the safe and the gold would be. He had shot no one because the pistol which they took away from him was not that kind of a pistol although it was loaded; later he admitted to the District Attorney that he had got it, as well as the dark lantern in which a candle burned and the black handkerchief to wear over the face, by peddling among his pinehill neighbors subscriptions to the *Detectives' Gazette*. So now from time to time (he had ample leisure for it) he mused with that raging impotence, because there was something else he could not tell them at the trial, did not know how to tell them. It was not the money he had wanted. It was not riches, not the crass loot; that would have been merely a bangle to wear upon the breast of his pride like the Olympic runner's amateur medal—a symbol, a badge to show that he too was the best at his chosen gambit in the living and fluid world of his time. So that at times as he trod the richly shearing black earth behind his plow or with a hoe thinned the sprouting cotton and corn or lay on his sullen back in his bunk after supper, he cursed in a harsh steady unrepetitive stream, not at the living men who had put him where he was but at what he did not even know were pennames, did not even know were not actual men but merely the designations of shades who had written about shades.

The second convict was short and plump. Almost hairless, he was quite white. He looked like something exposed to light by turning over rotting logs or planks and he too carried (though not in his eyes like the first convict) a sense of burning and impotent outrage. So it did not show on him and hence none knew it was there. But then nobody knew very much about him, including the people who had sent him here. His outrage was directed at no printed word but at the paradoxical fact that he had been forced to come here of his own free choice and will. He had been forced to choose between the Mississippi State penal farm and the Federal Penitentiary at Atlanta, and the fact that he, who resembled a hairless and pallid slug, had chosen the out-of-doors and the sunlight was merely another manifestation of the close-guarded and solitary enigma of his character, as something recognizable roils momentarily into view from beneath stagnant and opaque water, then sinks again. None of his fellow prisoners knew what his crime had been, save that he was in for a hundred and ninety-nine years—this incredible and impossible period of punishment or restraint itself carrying a vicious and fabulous quality which indicated that his reason for being here was such that the very men, the paladins and pillars of justice and equity who had sent him here had during that moment become blind apostles not of mere justice but of all human decency, blind instruments not of equity but of all human outrage and vengeance, acting in a savage personal concert, judge, lawyer and jury, which certainly abrogated justice and possibly even law. Possibly only the Federal and State's Attorneys knew what the crime actually was. There had been a woman in it and a stolen automobile transported across a State line, a filling station robbed and the attendant shot to death. There had been a second man in the car at the time and anyone could have looked once at the convict (as the two attorneys did) and known he would not even have had the synthetic courage of alcohol to pull trigger on anyone. But he and the woman and the stolen car had been captured while the second man, doubtless the actual murderer, had escaped, so that, brought to bay at last in the State's Attorney's office, harried, dishevelled and snarling, the two grimly implacable and viciously gleeful attorneys in his front and the now raging woman held by two policemen in the anteroom in his rear, he was given his choice. He could be tried in Federal Court under the Mann Act and for the automobile, that is, by electing to pass through the anteroom where the woman raged he could take his chances on the lesser crime in Federal Court, or by accepting a sentence for manslaughter in the State Court he would be permitted to quit the room by a back entrance, without having to pass the woman. He had chosen; he stood at the bar and heard a judge, (who looked down at him as if the District Attorney actually had turned over a rotten plank with his toe and exposed him) sentence him to a hundred and ninety-nine years at the State Farm. Thus (he had ample leisure too; they had tried to teach him to plow and had failed, they had put him in the blacksmith shop and the foreman trusty himself had asked to have him removed: so that now, in a long apron like a woman, he cooked and swept and dusted in the deputy wardens' barracks) he too mused at times with that sense of impotence and outrage though it did not show on him as on the first convict since he leaned on no halted broom to do it and so none knew it was there.

It was this second convict who, toward the end of April, began to read aloud to the others from the daily newspapers when, chained ankle to ankle and herded by armed guards, they had come up from the fields and had eaten supper and were gathered in the bunkhouse. It was the Memphis newspaper which the deputy wardens had read at breakfast; the convict read aloud from it to his companions who could have had but little active interest in the outside world, some of whom could not have read it for themselves at all and did not even know where the Ohio and Missouri river basins were, some of whom had never seen the Mississippi River although for past periods ranging from a few days to ten and twenty and thirty years (and for future periods ranging from a few months to life) they had plowed and planted and eaten and slept beneath the shadow of the levee itself, knowing only that there was water beyond it from hearsay and because now and then they heard the whistles of steamboats from beyond it and, during the last week or so had seen the stacks and pilot houses moving along the sky sixty feet above their heads.

But they listened, and soon even those who like the taller convict had probably never before seen more water than a horse pond would hold knew what thirty feet on a river gauge at Cairo or Memphis meant and could (and did) talk glibly of sandboils. Perhaps what actually moved them were the accounts of the conscripted levee gangs, mixed blacks and whites working in double shifts against the steadily rising water; stories of men, even though they were Negroes, being forced like themselves to do work for which they received no other pay than coarse food and a place in a mudfloored tent to sleep on—stories, pictures, which emerged from the shorter convict's reading voice; the mudsplashed white men with the inevitable shotguns, the antlike lines of Negroes carrying sandbags, slipping and crawling up the steep face of the revetment to hurl their futile ammunition into the face of a flood and return for more. Or perhaps it was more than this. Perhaps they watched the approach of the disaster with that same amazed and incredulous hope of the slaves—the lions and bears and elephants, the grooms and bathmen and pastrycooks—who watched the mounting flames of Rome from Ahenobarbus' gardens. But listen they did and presently it was May and the wardens' newspaper began to talk in headlines two inches tall—those black staccato slashes of ink which, it would almost seem, even the illiterate should be able to read: *Crest Passes Memphis at Midnight 4000 Homeless in White River Basin Governor Calls out National Guard Martial Law Declared in Following Counties Red Cross Train with President Hoover Leaves Washington Tonight;* then, three evenings later (It had been raining all day—not the vivid brief thunderous downpours of April and May, but the slow steady gray rain of November and December before a cold north wind. The men had not gone to the fields at all during the day, and the very second-hand optimism of the almost twenty-four-hour-old news seemed to contain its own refutation.): *Crest Now Below Memphis 22,000 Refugees Safe at Vicksburg Army Engineers Say Levees Will Hold.*

"I reckon that means it will bust tonight," one convict said.

"Well, maybe this rain will hold on until the water gets here," a second said. They all agreed to this because what they meant, the living unspoken thought among them, was that if the weather cleared, even though the levees broke and the flood moved in upon the Farm itself, they would have to return to the fields and work, which they would have had to do. There was nothing paradoxical in this, although they could not have expressed the reason for it which they instinctively perceived: that the land they farmed and the substance they produced from it belonged neither to them who worked it nor to those who forced them at guns' point to do so, that as far as either—convicts or guards—were concerned, it could have been pebbles they put into the ground and papier-mâché cotton- and corn-sprouts which they thinned. So it was that, what between the sudden wild hoping and the idle day and the evening's headlines, they were sleeping restlessly beneath the sound of the rain on the tin roof when at midnight the sudden glare of the electric bulbs and the guards' voices waked them and they heard the throbbing of the waiting trucks.

"Turn out of there!" the deputy shouted. He was fully dressed—rubber boots, slicker and shotgun. "The levee went out at Mound's Landing an hour ago. Get up out of it!"

## CHAPTER II

When the belated and streaming dawn broke the two convicts, along with twenty others, were in a truck. A trusty drove, two armed guards sat in the cab with him. Inside the high, stall-like topless body the convicts stood, packed like matches in an upright box or like the pencil-shaped ranks of cordite in a shell, shackled by the ankles to a single chain which wove among the motionless feet and swaying legs and a clutter of picks and shovels among which they stood, and was riveted by both ends to the steel body of the truck.

Then and without warning they saw the flood about which the plump convict had been reading for two weeks or more. The road ran south. It was built on a raised levee, known locally as a dump, about eight feet above the flat surrounding land, bordered on both sides by the barrow pits from which the earth of the levee had been excavated. These barrow pits had held water all winter from the fall rains, not to speak of the rain of yesterday, but now they saw that the pit on either side of the road had vanished and instead there lay a flat still sheet of brown water which extended into the fields beyond the pits, ravelled out into long motionless shreds in the bottom of the plow furrows and gleaming faintly in the gray light like the bars of a prone and enormous grating. And then (the truck was moving at good speed) as they watched quietly (they had not been talking much anyway but now they were all silent and quite grave, shifting and craning as one to look soberly off to the west side of the road) the crests of the furrows vanished too and they now looked at a single perfectly flat and motionless steel-colored sheet in which the telephone poles and the straight hedgerows which marked section lines seemed to be fixed and rigid as though set in concrete.

It was perfectly motionless, perfectly flat. It looked, not innocent, but bland. It looked almost demure. It looked as if you could walk on it. It looked so still that they did not realize it possessed motion until they came to the first bridge. There was a ditch under the bridge, a small stream, but ditch and stream were both invisible now, indicated only by the rows of cypress and bramble which marked its course. Here they both saw and heard movement—the slow profound eastward and upstream ("It's running backward," one convict said quietly.) set of the still rigid surface, from beneath which came a deep faint subaquean rumble which (though none in the truck could have made the comparison) sounded like a subway train passing far beneath the street and which inferred a terrific and secret speed. It was as if the water itself were in three strata, separate and distinct, the bland and unhurried surface bearing a frothy scum and a miniature flotsam of twigs and screening as though by vicious calculation the rush and fury of the flood itself, and beneath this in turn the original stream, trickle, murmuring along in the opposite direction, following undisturbed and unaware its appointed course and serving its Lilliputian end, like a thread of ants between the rails on which an express train passes, they (the ants) as unaware of the power and fury as if it were a cyclone crossing Saturn.

Now there was water on both sides of the road and now, as if once they had become aware of movement in the water the water seemed to have given over deception and concealment, they seemed to be able to watch it rising up the flanks of the dump; trees which a few miles back had stood on tall trunks above the water now seemed to burst from the surface at the level of the lower branches like decorative shrubs on barbered lawns. The truck passed a Negro cabin. The water was up to the window ledges. A woman clutching two children squatted on the ridgepole, a man and a halfgrown youth, standing waist-deep, were hoisting a squealing pig onto the slanting roof of a barn, on the ridgepole of which sat a row of chickens and a turkey. Near the barn was a haystack on which a cow stood tied by a rope to the center pole and bawling steadily; a yelling Negro boy on a saddleless mule which he flogged steadily, his legs clutching the mule's barrel and his body leaned to the drag of a rope attached to a second mule, approached the haystack, splashing and floundering. The woman on the housetop began to shriek at the passing truck, her voice carrying faint and melodious across the brown water, becoming fainter and fainter as the truck passed and went on, ceasing at last, whether because of distance or because she had stopped screaming those in the truck did not know.

Then the road vanished. There was no perceptible slant to it yet it had slipped abruptly beneath the brown surface with no ripple, no ridgy demarcation, like a flat thin blade slipped obliquely into flesh by a delicate hand, annealed into the water without disturbance, as if it had existed so for years, had been built that way. The truck stopped. The trusty descended from the cab and came back and dragged two shovels from among their feet, the blades clashing again the serpentining of the chain about their ankles. "What is it?" one said. "What are you fixing to do?" The trusty didn't answer. He returned to the cab, from which one of the guards had descended, without his shotgun. He and the trusty, both in hip boots and each carrying a shovel, advanced into the water, gingerly, probing and feeling ahead with the shovel handles. The same convict spoke again. He was a middle-aged man with a wild thatch of iron-gray hair and a slightly mad face. "What the hell are they doing?" he said. Again nobody answered him. The truck moved, on into the water, behind the guard and the trusty, beginning to push ahead of itself a thick slow viscid ridge of chocolate water. Then the gray-haired convict began to scream. "God damn it, unlock the chain!" He began to struggle, thrashing violently about him, striking at the men nearest him until he reached the cab, the roof of which he now hammered on with his fists, screaming. "God damn it, unlock us! Unlock us! Son of a bitch!" he screamed, addressing no one. "They're going to drown us! Unlock the chain!" But for all the answer he got the men within radius of his voice might have been dead. The truck crawled on, the guard and the trusty feeling out the road ahead with the reversed shovels, the second guard at the wheel, the twenty-two convicts packed like sardines into the truck itself. They crossed another bridge—two delicate and paradoxical iron railings slanting out of the water, travelling parallel to it for a distance, then slanting down into it again with an outrageous quality almost significant yet apparently meaningless like something in a dream not quite nightmare. The truck crawled on.

Along toward noon they came to a town, their destination. The streets were paved; now the wheels of the truck made a sound like tearing silk. Moving faster now, the guard and the trusty in the cab again, the truck even had a slight bone in its teeth, its bow-wave spreading beyond the submerged sidewalks and across the adjacent lawns, lapping against the stoops and porches of houses where people stood among piles of furniture. They passed through the business district; a man in hip boots, emerged knee-deep in water from a store, dragging a flat-bottomed skiff containing a steel safe.

At last they reached the railroad. It crossed the street at right angles, cutting the town in two. It was on a dump, a levee, also, eight or ten feet above the town itself; the street ran blankly into it and turned at right angles beside a cotton compress and a loading platform on stilts at the level of a freight car door. On this platform was a khaki army tent and a uniformed National Guard sentry with a rifle and bandolier.

The truck turned and crawled out of the water and up the ramp which cotton wagons used and where trucks and private cars filled with household goods came and unloaded onto the platform. They were unlocked from the chain in the truck and shackled ankle to ankle in pairs they mounted the platform and into an apparently inextricable jumble of beds and trunks, gas and electric stoves, radios and tables and chairs and framed pictures which a chain of Negroes under the eye of an unshaven white man in muddy corduroy and hip boots carried piece by piece into the compress, at the door of which another guardsman stood with his rifle, they (the convicts) not stopping here but herded on by the two guards with their shot-guns, into the dim and cavernous building where among the piled heterogeneous furniture the ends of cotton bales and the mirrors on dressers and sideboards gleamed with an identical mute and un-reflecting concentration of pallid light.

They passed on through, onto the loading platform where the army tent and the first sentry were. They waited here. Nobody told them for what nor why. While the two guards talked with the sentry before the tent the convicts sat in a line along the edge of the platform like buzzards on a fence, their shackled feet dangling above the brown motionless flood out of which the railroad embank-ment rose, pristine and intact, in a kind of paradoxical denial and repudiation of change and portent, not talking, just looking quietly across the track to where the other half of the amputated town seemed to float, house shrub and tree, ordered and pageant-like and without motion, upon the limitless liquid plain beneath the thick gray sky.

After a while the other four trucks from the Farm arrived. They came up, bunched closely, radiator to tail light, with their four separate sounds of tearing silk and vanished beyond the compress. Presently the ones on the platform heard the feet, the mute clashing of the shackles, the first truckload emerged from the compress, the second, the third; there were more than a hundred of them now in their bed-ticking overalls and jumpers and fifteen or twenty guards with rifles and shotguns. The first lot rose and they mingled, paired, twinned by their clanking and clashing umbilicals; then it began to rain, a slow steady drizzle like November instead of May. Yet not one of them made any move toward the open door of the compress.

They did not even look toward it, with longing or hope or without it. If they thought at all, they doubtless knew that the available space in it would be needed for furniture, even if it were not already filled. Or perhaps they knew that, even if there were room in it, it would not be for them, not that the guards would wish them to get wet but that the guards would not think about getting them out of the rain. So they just stopped talking and with their jumper collars turned up and shackled in braces like dogs at a field trial they stood, immobile, patient, almost ruminant, their backs turned to the rain as sheep and cattle do.

After another while they became aware that the number of soldiers had increased to a dozen or more, warm and dry beneath rubberised ponchos, there was an officer with a pistol at his belt, then and without making any move toward it, they began to smell food and, turning to look, saw an army field kitchen set up just inside the compress door. But they made no move, they waited until they were herded into line, they inched forward, their heads lowered and patient in the rain, and received each a bowl of stew, a mug of coffee, two slices of bread. They ate this in the rain. They did not sit down because the platform was wet, they squatted on their heels as country men do, hunching forward, trying to shield the bowls and mugs into which nevertheless the rain splashed steadily as into miniature ponds and soaked, invisible and soundless, into the bread.

After they had stood on the platform for three hours, a train came for them. Those nearest the edge saw it, watched it—a passenger coach apparently running under its own power and trailing a cloud of smoke from no visible stack, a cloud which did not rise but instead shifted slowly and heavily aside and lay upon the surface of the aqueous earth with a quality at once weightless and completely spent. It came up and stopped, a single old fashioned open-ended wooden car coupled to the nose of a pushing switch engine considerably smaller. They were herded into it, crowding forward to the other end where there was a small cast iron stove. There was no fire in it, nevertheless they crowded about it—the cold and voiceless lump of iron stained with fading tobacco and hovered about by the ghosts of a thousand Sunday excursions to Memphis or Moorhead and return— the peanuts, the bananas, the soiled garments of infants—huddling, shoving for places near it. "Come on, come on," one of the guards shouted. "Sit down, now." At last three of the guards, laying aside their guns, came among them and broke up the huddle, driving them back into seats.

There were not enough seats for all. The others stood in the aisle, they stood braced, they heard the air hiss out of the released brakes, the engine whistled four blasts, the car came into motion with a snapping jerk; the platform, the compress fled violently as the train seemed to transpose from immobility to full speed with that same quality of unreality with which it had appeared, running backward now though with the engine in front where before it had moved forward but with the engine behind.

When the railroad in its turn ran beneath the surface of the water, the convicts did not even know it. They felt the train stop, they heard the engine blow a long blast which wailed away unechoed across the waste, wild and forlorn, and they were not even curious; they sat or stood behind the rain-streaming windows as the train crawled on again, feeling its way as the truck had while the brown water swirled between the trucks and among the spokes of the driving wheels and lapped in cloudy steam against the dragging fire-filled belly of the engine; again it blew four short harsh blasts filled with the wild triumph and defiance yet also with repudiation and even farewell, as if the articulated steel itself knew it did not dare stop and would not be able to return. Two hours later in the twilight they saw through the streaming windows a burning plantation house. Juxtaposed to nowhere and neighbored by nothing it stood, a clear steady pyrelike flame rigidly fleeing its own reflection, burning in the dusk above the watery desolation with a quality paradoxical, outrageous and bizarre.

Sometime after dark the train stopped. The convicts did not know where they were. They did not ask. They would no more have thought of asking where they were than they would have asked why and what for. They couldn't even see, since the car was unlighted and the windows fogged on the outside by rain and on the inside by the engendered heat of the packed bodies. All they could see was a milky and sourceless flick and glare of flashlights. They could hear shouts and commands, then the guards inside the car began to shout; they were herded to their feet and toward the exit, the ankle chains clashing and clanking. They descended into a fierce hissing of steam, through ragged wisps of it blowing past the car. Laid-to alongside the train and resembling a train itself was a thick blunt motor launch to which was attached a string of skiffs and flat boats. There were more soldiers; the flashlights played on the rifle barrels and bandolier buckles and flicked and glinted on the ankle chains of the convicts as they stepped gingerly down into knee-deep water and entered the boats; now car and engine both vanished completely in steam as the crew began dumping the fire from the firebox.

After another hour they began to see lights ahead—a faint wavering row of red pin-pricks extending along the horizon and apparently hanging low in the sky. But it took almost another hour to reach them while the convicts squatted in the skiffs, huddled into the soaked garments (they no longer felt the rain any more at all as separate drops) and watched the lights draw nearer and nearer until at last the crest of the levee defined itself; now they could discern a row of army tents stretching along it and people squatting about the fires, the wavering reflections from which, stretching across the water, revealed an involved mass of other skiffs tied against the flank of the levee which now stood high and dark overhead. Flashlights glared and winked along the base, among the tethered skiffs; the launch, silent now, drifted in.

When they reached the top of the levee they could see the long line of khaki tents, interspersed with fires about which people—men, women and children, Negro and white—crouched or stood among shapeless bales of clothing, their heads turning, their eyeballs glinting in the firelight as they looked quietly at the striped garments and the chains; further down the levee, huddled together too though untethered, was a drove of mules and two or three cows. Then the taller convict became conscious of another sound. He did not begin to hear it all at once, he suddenly became aware that he had been hearing it all the time, a sound so much beyond all his experience and his powers of assimilation that up to this point he had been as oblivious of it as an ant or a flea might be of the sound of the avalanche on which it rides, he had been travelling upon water since early afternoon and for seven years now he had run his plow and harrow and planter within the very shadow of the levee on which he now stood, but this profound deep whisper which came from the further side of it he did not at once recognise. He stopped. The line of convicts behind jolted into him like a line of freight cars stopping, with an iron clashing like cars. "Get on!" a guard shouted.

"What's that?" the convict said. A Negro man squatting before the nearest fire answered him:

"Dat's him. Dat's de Ole Man."

"The old man?" the convict said.

"Get on! Get on up there!" the guard shouted. They went on; they passed another huddle of mules, the eyeballs rolling too, the long morose faces turning into and out of the firelight; they passed them and reached a section of empty tents, the light pup tents of a military campaign, made to hold two men. The guards herded the convicts into them, three brace of shackled men to each tent.

They crawled in on all fours, like dogs into cramped kennels, and settled down. Presently the tent became warm from their bodies. Then they became quiet and then all of them could hear it, they lay listening to the bass whisper deep, strong and powerful. "The old man?" the train-robber convict said.

"Yah," another said. "He don't have to brag."

At dawn the guards waked them by kicking the soles of the projecting feet. Opposite the muddy landing and the huddle of skiffs an army field kitchen was set up, already they could smell the coffee. But the taller convict at least, even though he had had but one meal yesterday and that at noon in the rain, did not move at once toward the food. Instead and for the first time he looked at the River within whose shadow he had spent the last seven years of his life but had never seen before; he stood in quiet and amazed surmise and looked at the rigid steel-colored surface not broken into waves but merely slightly undulant. It stretched from the levee on which he stood, further than he could see—a slowly and heavily roiling chocolate-frothy expanse broken only by a thin line a mile away as fragile in appearance as a single hair, which after a moment he recognised. *It's another levee,* he thought quietly. *That's what we look like from there. That's what I am standing on looks like from there.* He was prodded from the rear; a guard's voice carried forward: "Go on! Go on! You'll have plenty of time to look at that!"

They received the same stew and coffee and bread as the day before; they squatted again with their bowls and mugs as yesterday, though it was not raining yet. During the night an intact wooden barn had floated up. It now lay jammed by the current against the levee while a crowd of Negroes swarmed over it, ripping off the shingles and planks and carrying them up the bank; eating steadily and without haste, the taller convict watched the barn dissolve rapidly down to the very water-line exactly as a dead fly vanished beneath the moiling industry of a swarm of ants.

They finished eating. Then it began to rain again, as upon a signal, while they stood or squatted in their harsh garments which had not dried out during the night but had merely become slightly warmer than the air. Presently they were haled to their feet and told off into two groups, one of which was armed from a stack of mud-clogged picks and shovels nearby, and marched away up the levee. A little later the motor launch with its train of skiffs came up across what was, fifteen feet beneath its keel, probably a cotton field, the skiffs loaded to the gunwales with Negroes and a scattering of white people nursing bundles on their laps. When the engine shut off the faint plinking of a guitar came across the water. The skiffs warped in and unloaded; the convicts watched the men and women and children struggle up the muddy slope, carrying heavy towsacks and bundles wrapped in quilts. The sound of the guitar had not ceased and now the convicts saw him—a young, black, lean-hipped man, the guitar slung by a piece of cotton plow line about his neck. He mounted the levee, still picking it. He carried nothing else, no food, no change of clothes, not even a coat.

The taller convict was so busy watching this that he did not hear the guard until the guard stood directly beside him shouting his name. "Wake up!" the guard shouted. "Can you fellows paddle a boat?"

"Paddle a boat where?" the taller convict said.

"In the water," the guard said. "Where in hell do you think?"

"I ain't going to paddle no boat nowhere out yonder," the tall convict said, jerking his head toward the invisible river beyond the levee behind him.

"No, it's on this side," the guard said. He stooped swiftly and unlocked the chain which joined the tall convict and the plump hairless one. "It's just down the road a piece." He rose. The two convicts followed him down to the boats. "Follow them telephone poles until you come to a filling station. You can tell it, the roof is still above water. It's on a bayou and you can tell the bayou because the tops of the trees are sticking up. Follow the bayou until you come to a cypress snag with a woman in it. Pick her up and then cut straight back west until you come to a cotton house with a fellow sitting on the ridgepole—" He turned, looking at the two convicts, who stood perfectly still, looking first at the skiff and then at the water with intense sobriety. "Well? What are you waiting for?"

"I can't row a boat," the plump convict said.

"Then it's high time you learned," the guard said. "Get in."

The tall convict shoved the other forward. "Get in," he said. "That water aint going to hurt you. Aint nobody going to make you take a bath."

As, the plump one in the bow and the other in the stern, they shoved away from the levee, they saw other pairs being unshackled and manning the other skiffs. "I wonder how many more of them fellows are seeing this much water for the first time in their lives too," the tall convict said. The other did not answer. He knelt in the bottom of the skiff, pecking gingerly at the water now and then with his paddle. The very shape of his thick soft back seemed to wear that expression of wary and tense concern.

Some time after midnight a rescue boat filled to the guard rail with homeless men and women and children docked at Vicksburg. It was a steamer, shallow of draft; all day long it had poked up and down cypress- and gum-choked bayous and across cotton fields (where at times instead of swimming it waded) gathering its sorry cargo from the tops of houses and barns and even out of trees, and now it warped into that mushroom city of the forlorn and despairing where kerosene flares smoked in the drizzle and hurriedly strung electrics glared upon the bayonets of martial policemen and the red cross brassards and doctors and nurses and canteen-workers. The bluff overhead was almost solid with tents, yet still there were more people than shelter for them; they sat or lay, single and by the whole families, under what shelter they could find or sometimes under the rain itself, in the little death of profound exhaustion while the doctors and the nurses and the soldiers stepped over and around and among them.

Among the first to disembark was one of the penitentiary deputy wardens, followed closely by the plump convict and another white man—a small man with a gaunt unshaven wan face still wearing an expression of incredulous outrage. The deputy warden seemed to know exactly where he wished to go. Followed closely by his two companions he threaded his way swiftly among the piled furniture and the sleeping bodies and stood presently in a fiercely lighted and hastily established temporary office, almost a military post of command in fact, where the Warden of the Penitentiary sat with two army officers wearing majors' leaves. The deputy warden spoke without preamble. "We lost a man," he said. He called the tall convict's name.

"Lost him?" the Warden said.

"Yah. Drowned." Without turning his head he spoke to the plump convict. "Tell him," he said.

"He was the one that said he could row a boat," the plump convict said. "I never. I told him myself—" he indicated the deputy warden with a jerk of his head "—I couldn't. So when we got to the bayou—"

"What's this?" the Warden said.

"The launch brought word in," the deputy warden said. "Woman in a cypress snag on the bayou, then this fellow—" he indicated the third man; the Warden and the two officers looked at the third man "—on a cotton house. Never had room in the launch to pick them up. Go on."

"So we come to where the bayou was," the plump convict continued in a voice perfectly flat, without any inflection whatever. "Then the boat got away from him. I dont know what happened. I was just sitting there because he was so positive he could row a boat. I never saw any current. Just all of a sudden the boat whirled clean around and began to run fast backward like it was hitched to a train and it whirled around again and I happened to look up and there was a limb right over my head and I grabbed it just in time and that boat was snatched out from under me like you'd snatch off a sock and I saw it one time more upside down and that fellow that said he knew all about rowing holding to it with one hand and still holding the paddle in the other—" He ceased. There was no dying fall to his voice, it just ceased and the convict stood looking quietly at a half-full quart of whiskey sitting on the table.

"How do you know he's drowned?" the Warden said to the deputy. "How do you know he didn't just see his chance to escape, and took it?"

"Escape where?" the other said. "The whole Delta's flooded. There's fifteen foot of water for fifty miles, clean back to the hills. And that boat was upside down."

"That fellow's drowned," the plump convict said. "You dont need to worry about him. He's got his pardon; it wont cramp nobody's hand signing it, neither."

"And nobody else saw him?" the Warden said. "What about the woman in the tree?"

"I dont know," the deputy said. "I aint found her yet. I reckon some other boat picked her up. But this is the fellow on the cotton house."

Again the Warden and the two officers looked at the third man, at the gaunt, unshaven wild face in which an old terror, an old blending of fear and impotence and rage still lingered. "He never came for you?" the Warden said. "You never saw him?"

"Never nobody came for me," the refugee said. He began to tremble though at first he spoke quietly enough. "I set there on that sonabitching cotton house, expecting hit to go any minute. I saw that launch and them boats come up and they never had no room for me. Full of bastard niggers and one of them setting there playing a guitar but there wasn't no room for me. A guitar!" he cried; now he began to scream, trembling, slavering, his face twitching and jerking. "Room for a bastard nigger guitar but not for me—"

"Steady now," the Warden said. "Steady now."

"Give him a drink," one of the officers said. The Warden poured the drink. The deputy handed it to the refugee, who took the glass in both jerking hands and tried to raise it to his mouth. They watched him for perhaps twenty seconds, then the deputy took the glass from him and held it to his lips while he gulped, though even then a thin trickle ran from each corner of his mouth, into the stubble on his chin.

"So we picked him and—" the deputy called the plump convict's name now "—both up just before dark and come on in. But that other fellow is gone."

"Yes," the Warden said. "Well. Here I haven't lost a prisoner in ten years, and now, like this—I'm sending you back to the Farm tomorrow. Have his family notified, and his discharge papers filled out at once."

"All right," the deputy said. "And listen, chief. He wasn't a bad fellow and maybe he never had no business in that boat. Only he did say he could paddle one. Listen. Suppose I write on his discharge, Drowned while trying to save lives in the great flood of nineteen twenty-seven, and send it down for the Governor to sign it. It will be something nice for his folks to have, to hang on the wall when neighbors come in or something. Maybe they will even give his folks a cash bonus because after all they sent him to the Farm to raise cotton, not to fool around in a boat in a flood."

"All right," the Warden said. "I'll see about it. The main thing is to get his name off the books as dead before some politician tries to collect his food allowance."

"All right," the deputy said. He turned and herded his companions out. In the drizzling darkness again he said to the plump convict: "Well, your partner beat you. He's free. He's done served his time out but you've got a right far piece to go yet."

"Yah," the plump convict said. "Free. He can have it."

## CHAPTER III

As the short convict had testified, the tall one, when he returned to the surface, still retained what the short one called the paddle. He clung to it, not instinctively against the time when he would be back inside the boat and would need it, because for a time he did not believe he would ever regain the skiff or anything else that would support him, but because he did not have time to think about turning it loose. Things had moved too fast for him. He had not been warned, he had felt the first snatching tug of the current, he had seen the skiff begin to spin and his companion vanish violently upward like in a translation out of Isaiah, then he himself was in the water, struggling against the drag of the paddle which he did not know he still held each time he fought back to the surface and grasped at the spinning skiff which at one instant was ten feet away and the next poised above his head as though about to brain him, until at last he grasped the stern, the drag of his body becoming a rudder to the skiff, the two of them, man and boat and with the paddle perpendicular above them like a jackstaff, vanishing from the view of the short convict (who had vanished from that of the tall one with the same celerity though in a vertical direction) like a tableau snatched offstage intact with violent and incredible speed.

He was now in the channel of a slough, a bayou, in which until today no current had run probably since the old subterranean outrage which had created the country. There was plenty of current in it now though; from his trough behind the stern he seemed to see the trees and sky rushing past with vertiginous speed, looking down at him between the gouts of cold yellow in lugubrious and mournful amazement. But they were fixed and secure in something; he thought of that, he remembered in an instant of despairing rage the firm earth fixed and founded strong and cemented fast and stable forever by the generations of laborious sweat, somewhere beneath him, beyond the reach of his feet, when, and again without warning, the stern of the skiff struck him a stunning blow across the bridge of his nose. The instinct which had caused him to cling to it now caused him to fling the paddle into the boat in order to grasp the gunwale with both hands just as the skiff pivoted and spun away again. With both hands free he now dragged himself over the stern and lay prone on his face, streaming with blood and water and panting, not with exhaustion but with that furious rage which is terror's aftermath.

But he had to get up at once because he believed he had come much faster (and so farther) than he had. So he rose, out of the watery scarlet puddle in which he had lain, streaming, the soaked denim heavy as iron on his limbs, the black hair plastered to his skull, the blood-infused water streaking his jumper, and dragged his forearm gingerly and hurriedly across his lower face and glanced at it then grasped the paddle and began to try to swing the skiff back upstream. It did not even occur to him that he did not know where his companion was, in which tree among all which he had passed or might pass. He did not even speculate on that for the reason that he knew so incontestably that the other was upstream from him, and after his recent experience the mere connotation of the term upstream carried a sense of such violence and force and speed that the conception of it as other than a straight line was something which the intelligence, reason, simply refused to harbor, like the notion of a rifle bullet the width of a cotton field.

The bow began to swing back upstream. It turned readily, it outpaced the aghast and outraged instant in which he realised it was swinging far too easily, it had swung on over the arc and lay broadside to the current and began again that vicious spinning while he sat, his teeth bared in his bloody streaming face while his spent arms flailed the impotent paddle at the water, that innocent-appearing medium which at one time had held him in iron-like and shifting convolutions like an anaconda yet which now seemed to offer no more resistance to the thrust of his urge and need than so much air, like air; the boat which had threatened him and at last actually struck him in the face with the shocking violence of a mule's hoof now seemed to poise weightless upon it like a thistle bloom, spinning like a wind vane while he flailed at the water and thought of, envisioned, his companion safe, inactive and at ease in the tree with nothing to do but wait, musing with impotent and terrified fury upon that arbitrariness of human affairs which had abrogated to the one the secure tree and to the other the hysterical and unmanageable boat for the very reason that it knew that he alone of the two of them would make any attempt to return and rescue his companion.

The skiff had paid off and now ran with the current again. It seemed again to spring from immobility into incredible speed, and he thought he must already be miles away from where his companion had quitted him, though actually he had merely described a big circle since getting back into the skiff, and the object (a clump of cypress trees choked by floating logs and debris) which the skiff was now about to strike was the same one it had careened into before when the stern had struck him. He didn't know this because he had not yet ever looked higher than the bow of the boat. He didn't look higher now, he just saw that he was going to strike; he seemed to feel run through the very insentient fabric of the skiff a current of eager gleeful vicious incorrigible wilfulness; and he who had never ceased to flail at the bland treacherous water with what he had believed to be the limit of his strength now from somewhere, some ultimate absolute reserve, produced a final measure of endurance, will to endure which adumbrated mere muscle and nerves, continuing to flail the paddle right up to the instant of striking, completing one last reach thrust and recover out of pure desperate reflex, as a man slipping on ice reaches for his hat and money-pocket, as the skiff struck and hurled him once more flat on his face in the bottom of it.

This time he did not get up at once. He lay flat on his face, slightly spread-eagled and in an attitude almost peaceful, a kind of abject meditation. He would have to get up sometime, he knew that, just as all life consists of having to get up sooner or later and then having to lie down again sooner or later after a while. And he was not exactly exhausted and he was not particularly without hope and he did not especially dread getting up. It merely seemed to him that he had accidentally been caught in a situation in which time and environment, not himself, was mesmerised; he was being toyed with by a current of water going nowhere, beneath a day which would wane toward no evening; when it was done with him it would spew him back into the comparatively safe world he had been snatched violently out of and in the meantime it did not much matter just what he did or did not do. So he lay on his face, now not only feeling but hearing the strong quiet rustling of the current on the underside of the planks, for a while longer. Then he raised his head and this time touched his palm gingerly to his face and looked at the blood again, then he sat up onto his heels and leaning over the gunwale he pinched his nostrils between thumb and finger and expelled a gout of blood and was in the act of wiping his fingers on his thigh when a voice slightly above his line of sight said quietly, "It's taken you a while," and he who up to this moment had had neither reason nor time to raise his eyes higher than the bows looked up and saw, sitting in a tree and looking at him, a woman. She was not ten feet away. She sat on the lowest limb of one of the trees holding the jam he had grounded on, in a calico wrapper and an army private's tunic and a sunbonnet, a woman whom he did not even bother to examine since that first startled glance had been ample to reveal to him all the generations of her life and background, who could have been his sister if he had a sister, his wife if he had not entered the penitentiary at an age scarcely out of adolescence and some years younger than that at which even his prolific and monogamous kind married—a woman who sat clutching the trunk of the tree, her stockingless feet in a pair of man's unlaced brogans less than a yard from the water, who was very probably somebody's sister and quite certainly (or certainly should have been) somebody's wife, though this too he had entered the penitentiary too young to have had more than mere theoretical female experience to discover yet. "I thought for a minute you wasn't aiming to come back."

"Come back?"

"After the first time. After you run into this brush pile the first time and got into the boat and went on." He looked about, touching his face tenderly again; it could very well be the same place where the boat had hit him in the face.

"Yah," he said. "I'm here now though."

"Could you maybe get the boat a little closer? I taken a right sharp strain getting up here; maybe I better . . ." He was not listening; he had just discovered that the paddle was gone; this time when the skiff hurled him forward he had flung the paddle not into it but beyond it. "It's right there in them brush tops," the woman said. "You can get it. Here. Catch a holt of this." It was a grapevine. It had grown up into the tree and the flood had torn the roots loose. She had taken a turn with it about her upper body; she now loosed it and swung it out until he could grasp it. Holding to the end of the vine he warped the skiff around the end of the jam, picking up the paddle, and warped the skiff on beneath the limb and held it and now he watched her move, gather herself heavily and carefully to descend—that heaviness which was not painful but just excruciatingly careful, that profound and almost lethargic awkwardness which added nothing to the sum of that first aghast amazement which had served already for the catafalque of invincible dream since even in durance he had continued (and even with the old avidity, even though they had caused his downfall) to consume the impossible pulp-printed fables carefully censored and as carefully smuggled into the penitentiary; and who to say what Helen, what living Garbo, he had not dreamed of rescuing from what craggy pinnacle or dragoned keep when he and his companion embarked in the skiff. He watched her, he made no further effort to help her beyond holding the skiff savagely steady while she lowered herself from the limb—the entire body, the deformed swell of belly bulging the calico, suspended by its arms, thinking, *And this is what I get. This, out of all the female meat that walks, is what I have to be caught in a runaway boat with.*

"Where's that cottonhouse?" he said.

"Cottonhouse?"

"With that fellow on it. The other one."

"I don't know. It's a right smart of cottonhouses down here. With folks on them too, I reckon." She was examining him. "You're bloody as a hog," she said. "You look like a convict."

"Yah," he snarled. "I feel like I done already been hung. Well, I got to pick up my pardner and then find that cottonhouse." He cast off. That is, he released his hold on the vine. That was all he had to do, for even while the bow of the skiff hung high on the log jam and even while he held it by the vine in the comparatively dead water behind the jam, he felt steadily and constantly the whisper, the strong purring power of the water just one inch beyond the frail planks on which he squatted and which, as soon as he released the vine, took charge of the skiff not with one powerful clutch but in a series of touches light, tentative, and catlike; he realised now that he had entertained a sort of foundationless hope that the added weight might make the skiff more controllable. During the first moment or two he had a wild (and still foundationless) belief that it had; he had got the head upstream and managed to hold it so by terrific exertion continued even after he discovered that they were travelling straight enough but stern-first and continued somehow even after the bow began to wear away and swing: the old irresistible movement which he knew well by now, too well to fight against it, so that he let the bow swing on downstream with the hope of utilising the skiff's own momentum to bring it through the full circle and so upstream again, the skiff travelling broadside then bow-first then broadside again, diagonally across the channel, toward the other wall of submerged trees; it began to flee beneath him with terrific speed, they were in an eddy but did not know it; he had no time to draw conclusions or even wonder; he crouched, his teeth bared in his blood-caked and swollen face, his lungs bursting, flailing at the water while the trees stooped hugely down at him. The skiff struck, spun, struck again; the woman half lay in the bow, clutching the gunwales, as if she were trying to crouch behind her own pregnancy; he banged now not at the water but at living sapblooded wood with the paddle, his desire now not to go anywhere, reach any destination, but just to keep the skiff from beating itself to fragments against the tree trunks. Then something exploded, this time against the back of his head, and stooping trees and dizzy water, the woman's face and all, fled together and vanished in bright soundless flash and glare.

An hour later the skiff came slowly up an old logging road and so out of the bottom, the forest, and into (or onto) a cottonfield— a gray and limitless desolation now free of turmoil, broken only by a thin line of telephone poles like a wading millipede. The woman was now paddling, steadily and deliberately, with that curious lethargic care, while the convict squatted, his head between his knees, trying to stanch the fresh and apparently inexhaustible flow of blood from his nose with handfuls of water. The woman ceased paddling, the skiff drifted on, slowly, while she looked about. "We're done out," she said.

The convict raised his head and also looked about. "Out where?"

"I thought maybe you might know."

"I dont even know where I used to be. Even if I knowed which way was north, I wouldn't know if that was where I wanted to go." He cupped another handful of water to his face and lowered his hand and regarded the resulting crimson marbling on his palm, not with dejection, not with concern, but with a kind of sardonic and vicious bemusement. The woman watched the back of his head.

"We got to get somewhere."

"Dont I know it? A fellow on a cottonhouse. Another in a tree. And now that thing in your lap."

"It wasn't due yet. Maybe it was having to climb that tree quick yesterday, and having to set in it all night. I'm doing the best I can. But we better get somewhere soon."

"Yah," the convict said. "I thought I wanted to get somewhere too and I aint had no luck at it. You pick out a place to get to now and we'll try yours. Gimme that oar." The woman passed him the paddle. The boat was a double-ender; he had only to turn around.

"Which way you fixing to go?" the woman said.

"Never mind that. You just keep on holding on." He began to paddle, on across the cottonfield. It began to rain again, though not hard at first. "Yah," he said. "Ask the boat. I been in it since breakfast and I aint never knowed, where I aimed to go or where I was going either."

That was about one oclock. Toward the end of the afternoon the skiff (they were in a channel of some sort again, they had been in it for some time; they had got into it before they knew it and too late to get out again, granted there had been any reason to get out, as, to the convict anyway, there was certainly none and the fact that their speed had increased again was reason enough to stay in it) shot out upon a broad expanse of debris-filled water which the convict recognised as a river and, from its size, the Yazoo River though it was little enough he had seen of this country which he had not quitted for so much as one single day in the last seven years of his life. What he did not know was that it was now running backward. So as soon as the drift of the skiff indicated the set of the current, he began to paddle in that direction which he believed to be downstream, where he knew there were towns—Yazoo City, and as a last resort, Vicksburg, if his luck was that bad, if not smaller towns whose names he did not know but where there would be people, houses, something, anything he might reach and surrender his charge to and turn his back on her forever, on all pregnant and female life forever and return to that monastic existence of shotguns and shackles where he would be secure from it. Now, with the imminence of habitations, release from her, he did not even hate her. When he looked upon the swelling and unmanageable body before him it seemed to him that it was not the woman at all but rather a separate demanding threatening inert yet living mass of which both he and she were equally victims; thinking, as he had been for the last three or four hours, of that minute's—nay, second's—aberration of eye or hand which would suffice to precipitate her into the water to be dragged down to death by that senseless millstone which in its turn would not even have to feel agony, he no longer felt any glow of revenge toward her as its custodian, he felt sorry for her as he would for the living timber in a barn which had to be burned to rid itself of vermin.

He paddled on, helping the current, steadily and strongly, with a calculated husbandry of effort, toward what he believed was downstream, towns, people, something to stand upon, while from time to time the woman raised herself to bail the accumulated rain from the skiff. It was raining steadily now though still not hard, still without passion, the sky, the day itself dissolving without grief; the skiff moved in a nimbus, an aura of gray gauze which merged almost without demarcation with the roiling spittle-frothed debris-choked water. Now the day, the light, definitely began to end and the convict permitted himself an extra notch or two of effort because it suddenly seemed to him that the speed of the skiff had lessened. This was actually the case though the convict did not know it. He merely took it as a phenomenon of the increasing obfuscation, or at most as a result of the long day's continuous effort with no food, complicated by the ebbing and fluxing phases of anxiety and impotent rage at his absolutely gratuitous predicament. So he stepped up his stroke a beat or so, not from alarm but on the contrary, since he too had received that lift from the mere presence of a known stream, a river known by its ineradicable name to generations of men who had been drawn to live beside it as man always has been drawn to dwell beside water, even before he had a name for water and fire, drawn to the living water, the course of his destiny and his actual physical appearance rigidly coerced and postulated by it. So he was not alarmed. He paddled on, upstream without knowing it, unaware that all the water which for forty hours now had been pouring through the levee break to the north was somewhere ahead of him, on its way back to the River.

It was full dark now. That is, night had completely come, the gray dissolving sky had vanished, yet as though in perverse ratio surface visibility had sharpened, as though the light which the rain of the afternoon had washed out of the air had gathered upon the water as the rain itself had done, so that the yellow flood spread on before him now with a quality almost phosphorescent, right up to the instant where vision ceased. The darkness in fact had its advantages; he could now stop seeing the rain. He and his garments had been wet for more than twenty-four hours now so he had long since stopped feeling it, and now that he could no longer see it either it had in a certain sense ceased for him. Also, he now had to make no effort even not to see the swell of his passenger's belly. So he was paddling on, strongly and steadily, not alarmed and not concerned but just exasperated because he had not yet begun to see any reflection on the clouds which would indicate the city or cities which he believed he was approaching but which were actually now miles behind him, when he heard a sound. He did not know what it was because he had never heard it before and he would never be expected to hear such again since it is not given to every man to hear such at all and to none to hear it more than once in his life. And he was not alarmed now either because there was not time, for although the visibility ahead, for all its clarity, did not extend very far, yet in the next instant to the hearing he was also seeing something such as he had never seen before. This was that the sharp line where the phosphorescent water met the darkness was now about ten feet higher than it had been an instant before and that it was curled forward upon itself like a sheet of dough being rolled out for a pudding. It reared, stooping; the crest of it swirled like the mane of a galloping horse and, phosphorescent too, fretted and flickered like fire. And while the woman huddled in the bows, aware or not aware the convict did not know which, he (the convict), his swollen and blood-streaked face gaped in an expression of aghast and incredulous amazement, continued to paddle directly into it. Again he simply had not had time to order his rhythm-hypnotised muscles to cease. He continued to paddle though the skiff had ceased to move forward at all but seemed to be hanging in space while the paddle still reached thrust recovered and reached again; now instead of space the skiff became abruptly surrounded by a welter of fleeing debris—planks, small buildings, the bodies of drowned yet antic animals, entire trees leaping and diving like porpoises above which the skiff seemed to hover in weightless and airy indecision like a bird above a fleeing countryside, undecided where to light or whether to light at all, while the convict squatted in it still going through the motions of paddling, waiting for an opportunity to scream. He never found it. For an instant the skiff seemed to stand erect on its stern and then shoot scrabbling and scrambling up the curling wall of water like a cat, and soared on above the licking crest itself and hung cradled into the high actual air in the limbs of a tree, from which bower of new-leafed boughs and branches the convict, like a bird in its nest and still waiting his chance to scream and still going through the motions of paddling though he no longer even had the paddle now, looked down upon a world turned to furious motion and in incredible retrograde.

Some time about midnight, accompanied by a rolling cannonade of thunder and lightning like a battery going into action, as though some forty hours' constipation of the elements, the firmament itself, were discharging in clapping and glaring salute to the ultimate acquiescence to desperate and furious motion, and still leading its charging welter of dead cows and mules and outhouses and cabins and hencoops, the skiff passed Vicksburg. The convict didn't know it. He wasn't looking high enough above the water; he still squatted, clutching the gunwales and glaring at the yellow turmoil about him out of which entire trees, the sharp gables of houses, the long mournful heads of mules which he fended off with a splintered length of plank snatched from he knew not where in passing (and which seemed to glare reproachfully back at him with sightless eyes, in limber-lipped and incredulous amazement) rolled up and then down again, the skiff now travelling forward now sideways now sternward, sometimes in the water, sometimes riding for yards upon the roofs of houses and trees and even upon the backs of the mules as though even in death they were not to escape that burden-bearing doom with which their eunuch race was cursed. But he didn't see Vicksburg; the skiff, travelling at express speed, was in a seething gut between soaring and dizzy banks with a glare of light above them but he did not see it; he saw the flotsam ahead of him divide violently and begin to climb upon itself, mounting, and he was sucked through the resulting gap too fast to recognise it as the trestling of a railroad bridge; for a horrible moment the skiff seemed to hang in static indecision before the looming flank of a steamboat as though undecided whether to climb over it or dive under it, then a hard icy wind filled with the smell and taste and sense of wet and boundless desolation blew upon him; the skiff made one long bounding lunge as the convict's native state, in a final paroxysm, regurgitated him onto the wild bosom of the Father of Waters.

This is how he told about it seven weeks later, sitting in new bedticking garments, shaved and with his hair cut again, on his bunk in the barracks:

During the next three or four hours after the thunder and lightning had spent itself the skiff ran in pitch streaming darkness upon a roiling expanse which, even if he could have seen, apparently had no boundaries. Wild and invisible, it tossed and heaved about and beneath the boat, ridged with dirty phosphorescent foam and filled with a debris of destruction—objects nameless and enormous and invisible which struck and slashed at the skiff and whirled on. He did not know he was now upon the River. At that time he would have refused to believe it, even if he had known. Yesterday he had known he was in a channel by the regularity of the spacing between the bordering trees. Now, since even by daylight he could have seen no boundaries, the last place under the sun (or the streaming sky rather) he would have suspected himself to be would have been a river; if he had pondered at all about his present whereabouts, about the geography beneath him, he would merely have taken himself to be travelling at dizzy and inexplicable speed above the largest cotton-field in the world; if he who yesterday had known he was in a river, had accepted that fact in good faith and earnest, then had seen that river turn without warning and rush back upon him with furious and deadly intent like a frenzied stallion in a lane—if he had suspected for one second that the wild and limitless expanse on which he now found himself was a river, consciousness would simply have refused; he would have fainted.

When daylight—a gray and ragged dawn filled with driving scud between icy rain-squalls—came and he could see again, he knew he was in no cottonfield. He knew that the wild water on which the skiff tossed and fled flowed above no soil tamely trod by man, behind the straining and surging buttocks of a mule. That was when it occurred to him that its present condition was no phenomenon of a decade, but that the intervening years during which it consented to bear upon its placid and sleepy bosom the frail mechanicals of man's clumsy contriving was the phenomenon and this the norm and the river was now doing what it liked to do, had waited patiently the ten years in order to do, as a mule will work for you ten years for the privilege of kicking you once. And he also learned something else about fear too, something he had even failed to discover on that other occasion when he was really afraid—that three or four seconds of that night in his youth while he looked down the twice-flashing pistol barrel of the terrified mail clerk before the clerk could be persuaded that his (the convict's) pistol would not shoot: that if you just held on long enough a time would come in fear after which it would no longer be agony at all but merely a kind of horrible outrageous itching, as after you have been burned bad.

He did not have to paddle now, he just steered (who had been without food for twenty-four hours now and without any sleep to speak of for fifty) while the skiff sped on across that boiling desolation where he had long since begun to not dare believe he could possibly be where he could not doubt he was, trying with his fragment of splintered plank merely to keep the skiff intact and afloat among the houses and trees and dead animals (the entire towns, stores, residences, parks and farmyards, which leaped and played about him like fish), not trying to reach any destination, just trying to keep the skiff afloat until he did. He wanted so little. He wanted nothing for himself. He just wanted to get rid of the woman, the belly, and he was trying to do that in the right way, not for himself, but for her. He could have put her back into another tree at any time—

"Or you could have jumped out of the boat and let her and it drown," the plump convict said. "Then they could have given you the ten years for escaping and then hung you for the murder and charged the boat to your folks."

"Yah," the tall convict said.—But he had not done that. He wanted to do it the right way, find somebody, anybody he could surrender her to, something solid he could set her down on and then jump back into the river, if that would please anyone. That was all he wanted—just to come to something, anything. That didn't seem like a great deal to ask. And he couldn't do it. He told how the skiff fled on—

"Didn't you pass nobody?" the plump convict said. "No steamboat, nothing?"

"I dont know," the tall one said.—while he tried merely to keep it afloat, until the darkness thinned and lifted and revealed—

"Darkness?" the plump convict said. "I thought you said it was already daylight."

"Yah," the tall one said. He was rolling a cigarette, pouring the tobacco carefully from a new sack, into the creased paper. "This was another one. They had several while I was gone."—the skiff to be moving still rapidly up a winding corridor bordered by drowned trees which the convict recognised again to be a river running again in the direction that, until two days ago, had been upstream. He was not exactly warned through instinct that this one, like that of two days ago, was in reverse. He would not say that he now believed himself to be in the same river, though he would not have been surprised to find that he did believe this, existing now, as he did and had and apparently was to continue for an unnamed period, in a state in which he was toy and pawn on a vicious and inflammable geography. He merely realised that he was in a river again, with all the subsequent inferences of a comprehensible, even if not familiar, portion of the earth's surface. Now he believed that all he had to do would be to paddle far enough and he would come to something horizontal and above water even if not dry and perhaps even populated; and, if fast enough, in time, and that his only other crying urgency was to refrain from looking at the woman who, as vision, the incontrovertible and apparently inescapable presence of his passenger, returned with dawn, had ceased to be a human being and (you could add twenty-four more hours to the first twenty-four and the first fifty now, even counting the hen. It was dead, drowned, caught by one wing under a shingle on a roof which had rolled momentarily up beside the skiff yesterday and he had eaten some of it raw though the woman would not) had become instead one single inert monstrous sentient womb from which, he now believed, if he would only turn his gaze away and keep it away, would disappear, and if he could only keep his gaze from pausing again at the spot it occupied, would not return. That's what he was doing this time when he discovered the wave was coming.

He didn't know how he discovered it was coming back. He heard no sound, it was nothing felt nor seen. He did not even believe that finding the skiff to be now in slack water—that is, that the motion of the current which, whether right or wrong, had at least been horizontal, had now stopped that and assumed a vertical direction—was sufficient to warn him. Perhaps it was just an invincible and almost fanatic faith in the inventiveness and innate viciousness of that medium on which his destiny was now cast, apparently forever; a sudden conviction far beyond either horror or surprise that now was none too soon for it to prepare to do whatever it was it intended doing. So he whirled the skiff, spun it on its heel like a running horse, whereupon, reversed, he could not even distinguish the very channel he had come up. He did not know whether he simply could not see it or if it had vanished some time ago and he not aware at the time; whether the river had become lost in a drowned world or if the world had become drowned in one limitless river. So now he could not tell if he were running directly before the wave or quartering across its line of charge; all he could do was keep that sense of swiftly accumulating ferocity behind him and paddle as fast as his spent and now numb muscles could be driven, and try not to look at the woman, to wrench his gaze from her and keep it away until he reached something flat and above water. So, gaunt, hollow-eyed, striving and wrenching almost physically at his eyes as if they were two of those suction-tipped rubber arrows shot from the toy gun of a child, his spent muscles obeying not will now but that attenuation beyond mere exhaustion which, mesmeric, can continue easier than cease, he once more drove the skiff full tilt into something it could not pass and, once more hurled violently forward onto his hands and knees, crouching, he glared with his wild swollen face up at the man with the shotgun and said in a harsh, croaking voice: "Vicksburg? Where's Vicksburg?"

Even when he tried to tell it, even after the seven weeks and he safe, secure, riveted warranted and doubly guaranteed by the ten years they had added to his sentence for attempted escape, something of the old hysteric incredulous outrage came back into his face, his voice, his speech. He never did even get on the other boat.

He told how he clung to a strake (it was a dirty unpainted shanty boat with a drunken rake of tin stove pipe, it had been moving when he struck it and apparently it had not even changed course even though the three people on it must have been watching him all the while—a second man, barefoot and with matted hair and beard also at the steering sweep, and then—he did not know how long—a woman leaning in the door, in a filthy assortment of men's garments, watching him too with the same cold speculation) being dragged violently along, trying to state and explain his simple (and to him at least) reasonable desire and need; telling it, trying to tell it, he could feel again the old unforgettable affronting like an ague fit as he watched the abortive tobacco rain steadily and faintly from between his shaking hands and then the paper itself part with a thin dry snapping report:

"Burn my clothes?" the convict cried. "Burn them?"

"How in hell do you expect to escape in them billboards?" the man with the shotgun said. He (the convict) tried to tell it, tried to explain as he had tried to explain not to the three people on the boat alone but to the entire circumambience—desolate water and forlorn trees and sky—not for justification because he needed none and knew that his hearers, the other convicts, required none from him, but rather as, on the point of exhaustion, he might have picked dreamily and incredulously at a suffocation. He told the man with the gun how he and his partner had been given the boat and told to pick up a man and a woman, how he had lost his partner and failed to find the man, and now all in the world he wanted was something flat to leave the woman on until he could find an officer, a sheriff. He thought of home, the place where he had lived almost since childhood, his friends of years whose ways he knew and who knew his ways, the familiar fields where he did work he had learned to do well and to like, the mules with characters he knew and respected as he knew and respected the characters of certain men; he thought of the barracks at night, with screens against the bugs in summer and good stoves in winter and someone to supply the fuel and the food too; the Sunday ball games and the picture shows—things which, with the exception of the ball games, he had never known before. But most of all, his own character (Two years ago they had offered to make a trusty of him. He would not longer need to plow or feed stock, he would only follow those who did with a loaded gun, but he declined. "I reckon I'll stick to plowing," he said, absolutely without humor. "I done already tried to use a gun one time too many.") his good name, his responsibility not only toward those who were responsible toward him but to himself, his own honor in the doing of what was asked of him, his pride in being able to do it, no matter what it was. He thought of this and listened to the man with the gun talking about escape and it seemed to him that, hanging there, being dragged violently along (it was here he said that he first noticed the goats' beards of moss in the trees, though it could have been there for several days so far as he knew. It just happened that he first noticed it here.) that he would simply burst.

"Cant you get it into your head that the last thing I want to do is run away?" he cried. "You can set there with that gun and watch me; I give you fair lief. All I want is to put this woman—"

"And I told you she could come aboard," the man with the gun said in his level voice. "But there aint no room on no boat of mine for nobody hunting a sheriff in no kind of clothes, let alone a penitentiary suit."

"When he steps aboard, knock him in the head with the gun barrel," the man at the sweep said. "He's drunk."

"He aint coming aboard," the man with the gun said. "He's crazy."

Then the woman spoke. She didn't move, leaning in the door, in a pair of faded and patched and filthy overalls like the two men: "Give them some grub and tell them to get out of here." She moved, she crossed the deck and looked down at the convict's companion with her cold sullen face. "How much more time have you got?"

"It wasn't due till next month," the woman in the boat said. "But I—" The woman in overalls turned to the man with the gun.

"Give them some grub," she said. But the man with the gun was still looking down at the woman in the boat.

"Come on," he said to the convict. "Put her aboard, and beat it."

"And what'll happen to you," the woman in overalls said, "when you try to turn her over to an officer. When you lay alongside a sheriff and the sheriff asks you who you are?" Still the man with the gun didn't even look at her. He hardly even shifted the gun across his arm as he struck the woman across the face with the back of his other hand, hard. "You son of a bitch," she said. Still the man with the gun did not even look at her.

"Well?" he said to the convict.

"Dont you see I cant?" the convict cried. "Cant you see that?"

Now, he said, he gave up. He was doomed. That is, he knew now that he had been doomed from the very start never to get rid of her, just as the ones who sent him out with the skiff knew that he never would actually give up; when he recognised one of the objects which the woman in overalls was hurling into the skiff to be a can of condensed milk, he believed it to be a presage, gratuitous and irrevocable as a death-notice over the telegraph, that he was not even to find a flat stationary surface in time for the child to be born on it. So he told how he held the skiff alongside the shanty-boat while the first tentative toying of the second wave made up beneath him, while the woman in overalls passed back and forth between house and rail, flinging the food—the hunk of salt meat, the ragged and filthy quilt, the scorched lumps of cold bread which she poured into the skiff from a heaped dishpan like so much garbage—while he clung to the strake against the mounting pull of the current, the new wave which for the moment he had forgotten because he was still trying to state the incredible simplicity of his desire and need until the man with the gun (the only one of the three who wore shoes) began to stamp at his hands, he snatching his hands away one at a time to avoid the heavy shoes, then grasping the rail again until the man with the gun kicked at his face, he flinging himself sideways to avoid the shoe and so breaking his hold on the rail, his weight canting the skiff off at a tangent on the increasing current so that it began to leave the shanty boat behind and he paddling again now, violently, as a man hurries toward the precipice for which he knows at last he is doomed, looking back at the other boat, the three faces sullen derisive and grim and rapidly diminishing across the widening water and at last, apoplectic, suffocating with the intolerable fact not that he had been refused but that he had been refused so little, had wanted so little, asked for so little, yet there had been demanded of him in return the one price out of all breath which (they must have known) if he could have paid it, he would not have been where he was, asking what he asked, raising the paddle and shaking it and screaming curses back at them even after the shotgun flashed and the charge went scuttering past along the water to one side.

So he hung there, he said, shaking the paddle and howling, when suddenly he remembered that other wave, the second wall of water full of houses and dead mules building up behind him back in the swamp. So he quit yelling then and went back to paddling. He was not trying to outrun it. He just knew from experience that when it overtook him, he would have to travel in the same direction it was moving in anyway, whether he wanted to or not, and when it did overtake him, he would begin to move too fast to stop, no matter what places he might come to where he could leave the woman, land her in time. Time: that was his itch now, so his only chance was to stay ahead of it as long as he could and hope to reach something before it struck. So he went on, driving the skiff with muscles which had been too tired so long they had quit feeling it, as when a man has had bad luck for so long that he ceases to believe it is even bad, let alone luck. Even when he ate—the scorched lumps the size of baseballs and the weight and durability of cannel coal even after having lain in the skiff's bilge where the shanty boat woman had thrown them—the iron-like lead-heavy objects which no man would have called bread outside of the crusted and scorched pan in which they had cooked—it was with one hand, begrudging even that from the paddle.

He tried to tell that too—that day while the skiff fled on among the bearded trees while every now and then small quiet tentative exploratory feelers would come up from the wave behind and toy for a moment at the skiff, light and curious, then go on with a faint hissing sighing, almost a chuckling, sound, the skiff going on, driving on with nothing to see but trees and water and solitude: until after a while it no longer seemed to him that he was trying to put space and distance behind him or shorten space and distance ahead but that both he and the wave were now hanging suspended simultaneous and unprogressing in pure time, upon a dreamy desolation in which he paddled on not from any hope even to reach anything at all but merely to keep intact what little of distance the length of the skiff provided between himself and the inert and inescapable mass of female meat before him; then night and the skiff rushing on, fast since any speed over anything unknown and invisible is too fast, with nothing before him and behind him the outrageous idea of a volume of moving water toppling forward, its crest frothed and shredded like fangs, and then dawn again (another of those dreamlike alterations day to dark then back to day again with that quality truncated, anachronic and unreal as the waxing and waning of lights in a theatre scene) and the skiff emerging now with the woman no longer supine beneath the shrunken soaked private's coat but sitting bolt upright, gripping the gunwales with both hands, her eyes closed and her lower lip caught between her teeth and he driving the splintered board furiously now, glaring at her out of his wild swollen sleepless face and crying, croaking, "Hold on! For God's sake hold on!"

"I'm trying to," she said. "But hurry! Hurry!" He told it, the unbelievable: hurry, hasten: the man falling from a cliff being told to catch onto something and save himself; the very telling of it emerging shadowy and burlesque, ludicrous, comic and mad, from the ague of unbearable forgetting with a quality more dreamily furious than any fable behind proscenium lights:

He was in a basin now—"A basin?" the plump convict said. "That's what you wash in."

"All right," the tall one said harshly, above his hands. "I did." With a supreme effort he stilled them long enough to release the two bits of cigarette paper and watched them waft in light fluttering indecision to the floor between his feet, holding his hands motionless even for a moment longer—a basin, a broad peaceful yellow sea which had an abruptly and curiously ordered air, giving him, even at that moment, the impression that it was accustomed to water even if not total submersion; he even remembered the name of it, told to him two or three weeks later by someone: Atchafalaya—

"Louisiana?" the plump convict said. "You mean you were clean out of Mississippi? Hell fire." He stared at the tall one. "Shucks," he said. "That aint but just across from Vicksburg."

"They never named any Vicksburg across from where I was," the tall one said. "It was Baton Rouge they named." And now he began to talk about a town, a little neat white portrait town nestling among enormous very green trees, appearing suddenly in the telling as it probably appeared in actuality, abrupt and airy and mirage-like and incredibly serene before him behind a scattering of boats moored to a line of freight cars standing flush to the doors in water. And now he tried to tell that too: how he stood waist-deep in water for a moment looking back and down at the skiff in which the woman half lay, her eyes still closed, her knuckles white on the gunwales and a tiny thread of blood creeping down her chin from her chewed lip, and he looking down at her in a kind of furious desperation.

"How far will I have to walk?" she said.

"I dont know, I tell you!" he cried. "But it's land somewhere yonder! It's land, houses."

"If I try to move, it wont even be born inside a boat," she said. "You'll have to get closer."

"Yes," he cried, wild, desperate, incredulous. "Wait. I'll go surrender, then they will have—" He didn't finish, wait to finish; he told that too: himself splashing, stumbling, trying to run, sobbing and grasping; now he saw it—another loading platform standing above the yellow flood, the khaki figures on it as before, identical, the same; he said how the intervening days since that first innocent morning telescoped, vanished as if they had never been, the two contiguous succeeding instants (succeeding? simultaneous) and he transported across no intervening space but merely turned in his own footsteps, plunging, splashing, his arms raised, croaking harshly. He heard the startled shout, "There's one of them!", the command, the clash of equipment, the alarmed cry: "There he goes! There he goes!"

"Yes!" he cried, running, plunging, "here I am! Here! Here!" running on, into the first scattered volley, stopping among the bullets, waving his arms, shrieking, "I want to surrender! I want to surrender!" watching not in terror but in amazed and absolutely unbearable outrage as a squatting clump of the khaki figures parted and he saw the machine gun, the blunt thick muzzle slant and drop and probe toward him and he still screaming in his hoarse crow's voice, "I want to surrender! Cant you hear me?" continuing to scream even as he whirled and plunged splashing, ducking, went completely under and heard the bullets going thuck-thuck-thuck on the water above him and he scrabbling still on the bottom, still trying to scream even before he regained his feet and still all submerged save his plunging unmistakable buttocks, the outraged screaming bubbling from his mouth and about his face since he merely wanted to surrender. Then he was comparatively screened, out of range, though not for long. That is (he didn't tell how nor where) there was a moment in which he paused, breathed for a second before running again, the course back to the skiff open for the time being though he could still hear the shouts behind him and now and then a shot, and he panting, sobbing, a long savage tear in the flesh of one hand, got when and how he did not know, and he wasting precious breath, speaking to no one now any more than the scream of the dying rabbit is addressed to any mortal ear but rather an indictment of all breath and its folly and suffering, its infinite capacity for folly and pain, which seems to be its only immortality: "All in the world I want is just to surrender."

He returned to the skiff and got in and took up his splintered plank. And now when he told this, despite the fury of element which climaxed it, it (the telling) became quite simple; he now even creased another cigarette paper between fingers which did not tremble at all and filled the paper from the tobacco sack without spilling a flake, as though he had passed from the machine-gun's barrage into a bourne beyond any more amazement: so that the subsequent part of his narrative seemed to reach his listeners as though from beyond a sheet of slightly milky though still transparent glass, as something not heard but seen—a series of shadows, edgeless yet distinct, and smoothly flowing, logical and unfrantic and making no sound: They were in the skiff, in the center of the broad placid trough which had no boundaries and down which the tiny forlorn skiff flew to the irresistible coercion of a current going once more he knew not where, the neat small liveoak-bowered towns unattainable and miragelike and apparently attached to nothing upon the airy and unchanging horizon. He did not believe them, they did not matter, he was doomed; they were less than the figments of smoke or of delirium, and he driving his unceasing paddle without destination or even hope now, looking now and then at the woman sitting with her knees drawn up and locked and her entire body one terrific clench while the threads of bloody saliva crept from her teeth-clenched lower lip. He was going nowhere and fleeing from nothing, he merely continued to paddle because he had paddled so long now that he believed if he stopped his muscles would scream in agony. So when it happened he was not surprised. He heard the sound which he knew well (he had heard it but once before, true enough, but no man needed hear it but once) and he had been expecting it; he looked back, still driving the paddle, and saw it, curled, crested with its strawlike flotsam of trees and debris and dead beasts and he glared over his shoulder at it for a full minute out of that attenuation far beyond the point of outragement where even suffering, the capability of being further affronted, had ceased, from which he now contemplated with savage and invulnerable curiosity the further extent to which his now anesthetised nerves could bear, what next could be invented for them to bear, until the wave actually began to rear above his head into its thunderous climax. Then only did he turn his head. His stroke did not falter, it neither slowed nor increased; still paddling with that spent hypnotic steadiness, he saw the swimming deer. He did not know what it was nor that he had altered the skiff's course to follow it, he just watched the swimming head before him as the wave boiled down and the skiff rose bodily in the old familiar fashion on a welter of tossing trees and houses and bridges and fences, he still paddling even while the paddle found no purchase save air and still paddled even as he and the deer shot forward side by side at arm's length, he watching the deer now, watching the deer begin to rise out of the water bodily until it was actually running along upon the surface, rising still, soaring clear of the water altogether, vanishing upward in a dying crescendo of splashings and snapping branches, its damp scut flashing upward, the entire animal vanishing upward as smoke vanishes. And now the skiff struck and canted and he was out of it too, standing knee-deep, springing out and falling to his knees, scrambling up, glaring after the vanished deer. "Land!" he croaked. "Land! Hold on! Just hold on!" He caught the woman beneath the arms, dragging her out of the boat, plunging and panting after the vanished deer. Now earth actually appeared—an acclivity smooth and swift and steep, bizarre, solid and unbelievable; an Indian mound, and he plunging at the muddy slope, slipping back, the woman struggling in his muddy hands.

"Let me down!" she cried. "Let me down!" But he held her, panting, sobbing, and rushed again at the muddy slope; he had almost reached the flat crest with his now violently unmanageable burden when a stick under his foot gathered itself with thick convulsive speed. *It was a snake,* he thought as his feet fled beneath him and with the indubitable last of his strength he half pushed and half flung the woman up the bank as he shot feet first and face down back into that medium upon which he had lived for more days and nights than he could remember and from which he himself had never completely emerged, as if his own failed and spent flesh were attempting to carry out his furious unflagging will for severance at any price, even that of drowning, from the burden with which, unwitting and without choice, he had been doomed. Later it seemed to him that he had carried back beneath the surface with him the sound of the infant's first mewling cry.

## CHAPTER IV

When the woman asked him if he had a knife, standing there in the streaming bed-ticking garments which had got him shot at, the second time by a machine gun, on the two occasions when he had seen any human life after leaving the levee four days ago, the convict felt exactly as he had in the fleeing skiff when the woman suggested that they had better hurry. He felt the same outrageous affronting of a condition purely moral, the same raging impotence to find any answer to it; so that, standing above her, spent suffocating and inarticulate, it was a full minute before he comprehended that she was now crying, "The can! The can in the boat!" He did not anticipate what she could want with it; he did not even wonder nor stop to ask. He turned running; this time he thought, *It's another moccasin* as the thick body truncated in that awkward reflex which had nothing of alarm in it but only alertness, he not even shifting his stride though he knew his running foot would fall within a yard of the flat head. The bow of the skiff was well up the slope now where the wave had set it and there was another snake just crawling over the stern into it and as he stooped for the bailing can he saw something else swimming toward the mound, he didn't know what —a head, a face at the apex of a vee of ripples. He snatched up the can; by pure juxtaposition of it and water he scooped it full, already turning. He saw the deer again, or another one. That is, he saw a deer—a side glance, the light smoke-colored phantom in a cypress vista then gone, vanished, he not pausing to look after it, galloping back to the woman and kneeling with the can to her lips until she told him better.

It had contained a pint of beans or tomatoes, something, hermetically sealed and opened by four blows of an axe heel, the metal flap turned back, the jagged edges razor-sharp. She told him how, and he used this in lieu of a knife, he removed one of his shoelaces and cut it in two with the sharp tin. Then she wanted warm water— "If I just had a little hot water," she said in a weak serene voice without particular hope; only when he thought of matches it was again a good deal like when she had asked him if he had a knife, until she fumbled in the pocket of the shrunken tunic (it had a darker double vee on one cuff and a darker blotch on the shoulder where service stripes and a divisional emblem had been ripped off but this meant nothing to him) and produced a match-box contrived by telescoping two shotgun shells. So he drew her back a little from the water and went to hunt wood dry enough to burn, thinking this time, *It's just another snake*, only, he said, he should have thought *ten thousand other snakes*: and now he knew it was not the same deer because he saw three at one time, does or bucks he did not know which since they were all antlerless in May and besides he had never seen one of any kind anywhere before except on a Christmas card; and then the rabbit, drowned, dead anyway, already torn open, the bird, the hawk, standing upon it—the erected crest, the hard, vicious, patrician nose, the intolerant omnivorous yellow eye—and he kicking at it, kicking it lurching and broad-winged into the actual air.

When he returned with the wood and the dead rabbit, the baby, wrapped in the tunic, lay wedged between two cypress-knees and the woman was not in sight, though while the convict knelt in the mud, blowing and nursing his meagre flame, she came slowly and weakly from the direction of the water. Then, the water heated at last and there produced from some where he was never to know, she herself perhaps never to know until the need comes, no woman perhaps ever to know, only no woman will even wonder, that square of something somewhere between sackcloth and silk—squatting, his own wet garments steaming in the fire's heat, he watched her bathe the child with a savage curiosity and interest that became amazed unbelief, so that at last he stood above them both, looking down at the tiny terra-cotta colored creature resembling nothing, and thought, *And this is all. This is what severed me violently from all I ever knew and did not wish to leave and cast me upon a medium I was born to fear, to fetch up at last in a place I never saw before and where I do not even know where I am.*

Then he returned to the water and refilled the bailing can. It was drawing toward sunset now (or what would have been sunset save for the high prevailing overcast) of this day whose beginning he could not even remember; when he returned to where the fire burned in the interlaced gloom of the cypresses, even after this short absence, evening had definitely come, as though darkness too had taken refuge upon that quarter-acre mound, that earthen Ark out of Genesis, that dim wet cypress-choked life-teeming constricted desolation in what direction and how far from what and where he had no more idea than of the day of the month, and had now with the setting of the sun crept forth again to spread upon the waters. He stewed the rabbit in sections while the fire burned redder and redder in the darkness where the shy wild eyes of small animals—once the tall mild almost plate-sized stare of one of the deer—glowed and vanished and glowed again, the broth hot and rank after the four days; he seemed to hear the roar of his own saliva as he watched the woman sip the first canful. Then he drank too; they ate the other fragments which had been charring and scorching on willow twigs; it was full night now. "You and him better sleep in the boat," the convict said. "We want to get an early start tomorrow." He shoved the bow of the skiff off the land so it would lie level, he lengthened the painter with a piece of grapevine and returned to the fire and tied the grapevine about his wrist and lay down. It was mud he lay upon, but it was solid underneath, it was earth, it did not move; if you fell upon it you broke your bones against its incontrovertible passivity sometimes but it did not accept you substanceless and enveloping and suffocating, down and down and down; it was hard at times to drive a plow through, it sent you spent, weary, and cursing its light-long insatiable demands back to your bunk at sunset at times but it did not snatch you violently out of all familiar knowing and sweep you thrall and impotent for days against any returning. *I dont know where I am and I dont reckon I know the way back to where I want to go,* he thought. *But at least the boat has stopped long enough to give me a chance to turn it around.*

He waked at dawn, the light faint, the sky jonquil-colored; the day would be fine. The fire had burned out; on the opposite side of the cold ashes lay three snakes motionless and parallel as underscoring, and in the swiftly making light others seemed to materialize: earth which an instant before had been mere earth broke up into motionless coils and loops, branches which a moment before had been mere branches now become immobile ophidian festoons even as the convict stood thinking about food, about something hot before they started. But he decided against this, against wasting this much time, since there still remained in the skiff quite a few of the rocklike objects which the shanty woman had flung into it, besides (thinking this) no matter how fast nor successfully he hunted, he would never be able to lay up enough food to get them back to where they wanted to go. So he returned to the skiff, paying himself back to it by his vine-spliced painter, back to the water on which a low mist thick as cotton batting (though apparently not very tall, deep), lay, into which the stern of the skiff was already beginning to disappear although it lay with its prow almost touching the mound. The woman waked, stirred. "We fixing to start now?" she said.

"Yah," the convict said. "You aint aiming to have another one this morning, are you?" He got in and shoved the skiff clear of the land, which immediately began to dissolve into the mist. "Hand me the oar," he said over his shoulder, not turning yet.

"The oar?"

He turned his head. "The oar. You're laying on it." But she was not, and for an instant during which the mound, the island continued to fade slowly into the mist which seemed to enclose the skiff in weightless and impalpable wool like a precious or fragile bauble or jewel, the convict squatted not in dismay but in that frantic and astonished outrage of a man who, having just escaped a falling safe, is struck by the following two-ounce paper weight which was sitting on it: this the more unbearable because he knew that never in his life had he less time to give way to it. He did not hesitate. Grasping the grapevine end he sprang into the water, vanishing in the violent action of climbing and reappeared still climbing and (who had never learned to swim) plunged and threshed on toward the almost-vanished mound, moving through the water then upon it as the deer had done yesterday and scrabbled up the muddy slope and lay gasping and panting, still clutching the grapevine end.

Now the first thing he did was to choose what he believed to be the most suitable tree (for an instant in which he knew he was insane he thought of trying to saw it down with the flange of the bailing can) and build a fire against the butt of it. Then he went to seek food. He spent the next six days seeking it while the tree burned through and fell and burned through again at the proper length and he nursing little constant cunning flames along the flanks of the log to make it paddle-shaped, nursing them at night too while the woman and the baby (it was eating, nursing now, he turning his back or even returning into the woods each time she prepared to open the faded tunic) slept in the skiff. He learned to watch for stooping hawks and so found more rabbits and twice possums; they ate some drowned fish which gave them both a rash and then a violent flux and one snake which the woman thought was turtle and which did them no harm, and one night it rained and he got up and dragged brush, shaking the snakes (he no longer thought, *It aint nothing but another moccasin*, he just stepped aside for them as they, when there was time, telescoped sullenly aside for him) out of it with the older former feeling of personal invulnerability and built a shelter and the rain stopped at once and did not recommence and the woman went back to the skiff.

Then one night—the slow tedious charring log was almost a paddle now—one night and he was in bed, in his bed in the bunkhouse and it was cold, he was trying to pull the covers up only his mule wouldn't let him, prodding and bumping heavily at him, trying to get into the narrow bed with him and now the bed was cold too and wet and he was trying to get out of it only the mule would not let him, holding him by his belt in its teeth, jerking and bumping him back into the cold wet bed and, leaning, gave him a long swipe across the face with its cold limber musculated tongue and he walked to no fire, no coal even beneath where the almost-finished paddle had been charring and something else prolonged and coldly limber passed swiftly across his body where he lay in four inches of water while the nose of the skiff alternately tugged at the grapevine tied about his waist and bumped and shoved him back into the water again. Then something else came up and began to nudge at his ankle (the log, the oar, it was) even as he groped frantically for the skiff, hearing the swift rustling going to and fro inside the hull as the woman began to thrash about and scream. "Rats!" she cried. "It's full of rats!"

"Lay still!" he cried. "It's just snakes. Cant you hold still long enough for me to find the boat?" Then he found it, he got into it with the unfinished paddle; again the thick muscular body convulsed under his foot; it did not strike; he would not have cared, glaring astern where he could see a little—the faint outer luminosity of the open water. He poled toward it, thrusting aside the snake-looped branches, the bottom of the skiff resounding faintly to thick solid plops, the woman shrieking steadily. Then the skiff was clear of the trees, the mound, and now he could feel the bodies whipping about his ankles and hear the rasp of them as they went over the gunwale. He drew the log in and scooped it forward along the bottom of the boat and up and out; against the pallid water he could see three more of them in lashing convolutions before they vanished. "Shut up!" he cried. "Hush! I wish I was a snake so I could get out too!"

When once more the pale and heatless wafer disc of the early sun stared down at the skiff (whether they were moving or not the convict did not know) in its nimbus of fine cotton batting, the convict was hearing again that sound which he had heard twice before and would never forget—that sound of deliberate and irresistible and monstrously disturbed water. But this time he could not tell from what direction it came. It seemed to be everywhere, waxing and fading; it was like a phantom behind the mist, at one instant miles away, the next on the point of overwhelming the skiff within the next second; suddenly, in the instant he would believe (his whole weary body would spring and scream) that he was about to drive the skiff point-blank into it and with the unfinished paddle of the color and texture of sooty bricks, like something gnawed out of an old chimney by beavers and weighing twenty-five pounds, he would whirl the skiff frantically and find the sound dead ahead of him again. Then something bellowed tremendously above his head, he heard human voices, a bell jangled and the sound ceased and the mist vanished as when you draw your hand across a frosted pane, and the skiff now lay upon a sunny glitter of brown water flank to flank with, and about thirty yards away from, a steamboat. The decks were crowded and packed with men and women and children sitting or standing beside and among a homely conglomeration of hurried furniture, who looked mournfully and silently down into the skiff while the convict and the man with a megaphone in the pilot house talked to each other in alternate puny shouts and roars above the chuffing of the reversed engines:

"What in hell are you trying to do? Commit suicide?"

"Which is the way to Vicksburg?"

"Vicksburg? Vicksburg? Lay alongside and come aboard."

"Will you take the boat too?"

"Boat? Boat?" Now the megaphone cursed, the roaring waves of blasphemy and biological supposition empty cavernous and bodiless in turn, as if the water, the air, the mist had spoken it, roaring the words then taking them back to itself and no harm done, no scar, no insult left anywhere. "If I took aboard every floating sardine can you sonabitchin mushrats want me to I wouldn't even have room forrard for a leadsman. Come aboard! Do you expect me to hang here on stern engines till hell freezes?"

"I aint coming without the boat," the convict said. Now another voice spoke, so calm and mild and sensible that for a moment it sounded more foreign and out of place than even the megaphone's bellowing and bodiless profanity:

"Where is it you are trying to go?"

"I aint trying," the convict said. "I'm going. Parchman." The man who had spoken last turned and appeared to converse with a third man in the pilot house. Then he looked down at the skiff again.

"Carnarvon?"

"What?" the convict said. "Parchman?"

"All right. We're going that way. We'll put you off where you can get home. Come aboard."

"The boat too?"

"Yes, yes. Come along. We're burning coal just to talk to you." So the convict came alongside then and watched them help the woman and baby over the rail and he came aboard himself, though he still held to the end of the vine-spliced painter until the skiff was hoisted onto the boiler deck. "My God," the man, the gentle one, said, "is that what you have been using for a paddle?"

"Yah," the convict said. "I lost the plank."

"The plank," the mild man (the convict told how he seemed to whisper it), "the plank. Well. Come along and get something to eat. Your boat is all right now."

"I reckon I'll wait here," the convict said. Because now, he told them, he began to notice for the first time that the other people, the other refugees who crowded the deck, who had gathered in a quiet circle about the upturned skiff on which he and the woman sat, the grapevine painter wrapped several times about his wrist and clutched in his hand, staring at him and the woman with queer hot mournful intensity, were not white people—

"You mean niggers?" the plump convict said.

"No. Not Americans."

"Not Americans? You was clean out of *America* even?"

"I dont know," the tall one said. "They called it Atchafalaya."—Because after a while he said, "What?" to the man and the man did it again, gobble-gobble—

"Gobble-gobble?" the plump convict said.

"That's the way they talked," the tall one said. "Gobble-gobble, whang, caw-caw-to-to."—And he sat there and watched them gobbling at one another and then looking at him again, then they fell back and the mild man (he wore a Red Cross brassard) entered, followed by a waiter with a tray of food. The mild man carried two glasses of whiskey.

"Drink this," the mild man said. "This will warm you." The woman took hers and drank it but the convict told how he looked at his and thought, *I aint tasted whiskey in seven years.* He had not tasted it but once before that; it was at the still itself back in a pine hollow; he was seventeen, he had gone there with four companions, two of whom were grown men, one of twenty-two or -three, the other about forty; he remembered it. That is, he remembered perhaps a third of that evening—a fierce turmoil in the hell-colored firelight, the shock of blows about his head (and likewise of his own fists on other hard bone), then the waking to a splitting and blinding sun in a place, a cowshed, he had never seen before and which later turned out to be twenty miles from his home. He said he thought of this and he looked about at the faces watching him and he said,

"I reckon not."

"Come, come," the mild man said. "Drink it."

"I dont want it."

"Nonsense," the mild man said. "I'm a doctor. Here. Then you can eat." So he took the glass and even then he hesitated but again the mild man said, "Come along, down with it; you're still holding us up," in that voice still calm and sensible but a little sharp too—the voice of a man who could keep calm and affable because he wasn't used to being crossed—and he drank the whiskey and even in the second between the sweet full fire in his belly and when it began to happen he was trying to say, "I tried to tell you! I tried to!" But it was too late now in the pallid sunglare of the tenth day of terror and hopelessness and despair and impotence and rage and outrage and it was himself and the mule, his mule (they had let him name it—John Henry) which no man save he had plowed for five years now and whose ways and habits he knew and respected and who knew his ways and habits so well that each of them could anticipate the other's very movements and intentions; it was himself and the mule, the little gobbling faces flying before them, the familiar hard skull-bones shocking against his fists, his voice shouting, "Come on, John Henry! Plow them down! Gobble them down, boy!" even as the bright hot red wave turned back, meeting it joyously, happily, lifted, poised, then hurling through space, triumphant and yelling, then again the old shocking blow at the back of his head: he lay on the deck, flat on his back and pinned arm and leg and cold sober again, his nostrils gushing again, the mild man stooping over him with behind the thin rimless glasses the coldest eyes the convict had ever seen—eyes which the convict said were not looking at him but at the gushing blood with nothing in the world in them but complete impersonal interest.

"Good man," the mild man said. "Plenty of life in the old carcass yet, eh? Plenty of good red blood too. Anyone ever suggest to you that you were hemophilic?" ("What?" the plump convict said. "Hemophilic? You know what that means?" The tall convict had his cigarette going now, his body jackknifed backward into the coffinlike space between the upper and lower bunks, lean, clean, motionless, the blue smoke wreathing across his lean dark aquiline shaven face. "That's a calf that's a bull and a cow at the same time."

"No, it aint," a third convict said. "It's a calf or a colt that aint neither one."

"Hell fire," the plump one said. "He's got to be one or the other to keep from drounding." He had never ceased to look at the tall one in the bunk; now he spoke to him again: "You let him call you that?") The tall one had done so. He did not answer the doctor (this was where he stopped thinking of him as the mild man) at all. He could not move either, though he felt fine, he felt better than he had in ten days. So they helped him to his feet and steadied him over and lowered him onto the upturned skiff beside the woman, where he sat bent forward, elbows on knees in the immemorial attitude, watching his own bright crimson staining the mud-trodden deck, until the doctor's clean clipped hand appeared under his nose with a phial.

"Smell," the doctor said. "Deep." The convict inhaled, the sharp ammoniac sensation burned up his nostrils and into his throat. "Again," the doctor said. The convict inhaled obediently. This time he choked and spat a gout of blood, his nose now had no more feeling than a toenail, other than it felt about the size of a ten-inch shovel, and as cold.

"I ask you to excuse me," he said. "I never meant—"

"Why?" the doctor said. "You put up as pretty a scrap against forty or fifty men as I ever saw. You lasted a good two seconds. Now you can eat something. Or do you think that will send you haywire again?"

They both ate, sitting on the skiff, the gobbling faces no longer watching them now, the convict gnawing slowly and painfully at the thick sandwich, hunched, his face laid sideways to the food and parallel to the earth as a dog chews; the steamboat went on. At noon there were bowls of hot soup and bread and more coffee; they ate this, too, sitting side by side on the skiff, the grapevine still wrapped about the convict's wrist. The baby waked and nursed and slept again and they talked quietly:

"Was it Parchman he said he was going to take us?"

"That's where I told him I wanted to go."

"It never sounded exactly like Parchman to me. It sounded like he said something else." The convict had thought that too. He had been thinking about that fairly soberly ever since they boarded the steamboat and soberly indeed ever since he had remarked the nature of the other passengers, those men and women definitely a little shorter than he and with skin a little different in pigmentation from any sunburn, even though the eyes were sometimes blue or gray, who talked to one another in a tongue he had never heard before and who apparently did not understand his own, people the like of whom he had never seen about Parchman nor anywhere else and whom he did not believe were going there or beyond there either. But after his hill-billy country fashion and kind he would not ask, because to his raising asking information was asking a favor and you did not ask favors of strangers; if they offered them perhaps you accepted and you expressed gratitude almost tediously recapitulant, but you did not ask. So he would watch and wait, as he had done before, and do or try to do to the best of his ability what the best of his judgment dictated.

So he waited, and in midafternoon the steamboat chuffed and thrust through a willow-choked gorge and emerged from it, and now the convict knew it was the River. He could believe it now—the tremendous reach, yellow and sleepy in the afternoon—("Because it's too big," he told them soberly. "Aint no flood in the world big enough to make it do more than stand a little higher so it can look back and see just where the flea is, just exactly where to scratch. It's the little ones, the little piddling creeks that run backward one day and forward the next and come busting down on a man full of dead mules and hen houses.")—and the steamboat moving up this now (*like a ant crossing a plate,* the convict thought, sitting beside the woman on the upturned skiff, the baby nursing again, apparently looking too out across the water where, a mile away on either hand, the twin lines of levee resembled parallel unbroken floating thread) and then it was nearing sunset and he began to hear, to notice, the voices of the doctor and of the man who had first bawled at him through the megaphone now bawling again from the pilot house overhead:

"Stop? Stop? Am I running a street car?"

"Stop for the novelty then," the doctor's pleasant voice said. "I dont know how many trips back and forth you have made in yonder nor how many of what you call mushrats you have fetched out. But this is the first time you ever had two people—no, three—who not only knew the name of some place they wished to go to but were actually trying to get there." So the convict waited while the sun slanted more and more and the steamboat-ant crawled steadily on across its vacant and gigantic plate turning more and more to copper. But he did not ask, he just waited. *Maybe it was Carrollton he said,* he thought. *It begun with a* C. But he did not believe that either. He did not know where he was, but he did not know that this was not anywhere near the Carrollton he remembered from that day seven years ago when, shackled wrist to wrist with the deputy sheriff, he had passed through it on the train—the slow spaced repeated shattering banging of trucks where two railroads crossed, a random scattering of white houses tranquil among trees on green hills lush with summer, a pointing spire, the finger of the hand of God. But there was no river there. *And you aint never close to this river without knowing it*, he thought. *I dont care who you are nor where you have been all your life.* Then the head of the steamboat began to swing across the stream, its shadow swinging too, travelling long before it across the water, toward the vacant ridge of willow-massed earth empty of all life. There was nothing there at all, the convict could not even see either earth or water beyond it; it was as though the steamboat were about to crash slowly through the thin low frail willow barrier and embark into space, or lacking this, slow and back and fill and disembark him into space, granted it was about to disembark him, granted this was that place which was not near Parchman and was not Carrollton either, even though it did begin with c. Then he turned his head and saw the doctor stooping over the woman, pushing the baby's eyelid up with his forefinger, peering at it.

"Who else was there when he came?" the doctor said.

"Nobody," the convict said.

"Did it all yourselves, eh?"

"Yes," the convict said. Now the doctor stood up and looked at the convict.

"This is Carnarvon," he said.

"Carnarvon?" the convict said. "That aint—" Then he stopped, ceased. And now he told about that—the intent eyes as dispassionate as ice behind the rimless glasses, the clipped quick-tempered face that was not accustomed to being crossed or lied to either. ("Yes," the plump convict said. "That's what I was aiming to ask. Them clothes. Anybody would know them. How if this doctor was as smart as you claim he was—"

"I had slept in them for ten nights, mostly in the mud," the tall one said. "I had been rowing since midnight with that sapling oar I had tried to burn out that I never had time to scrape the soot off. But it's being scared and worried and then scared and then worried again in clothes for days and days and days that changes the way they look. I dont mean just your pants." He did not laugh. "Your face too. That doctor knowed."

"All right," the plump one said. "Go on.")

"I know it," the doctor said. "I discovered that while you were lying on the deck yonder sobering up again. Now dont lie to me. I dont like lying. This boat is going to New Orleans."

"No," the convict said immediately, quietly, with absolute finality. He could hear them again—the thuck-thuck-thuck on the water where an instant before he had been. But he was not thinking of the bullets. He had forgotten them, forgiven them. He was thinking of himself crouching, sobbing, panting before running again—the voice, the indictment, the cry of final and irrevocable repudiation of the old primal faithless Manipulator of all the lust and folly and injustice: *All in the world I wanted was just to* *surrender;* thinking of it, remembering it but without heat now, without passion now and briefer than an epitaph: No. *I tried that once. They shot at me.*

"So you dont want to go to New Orleans. And you didn't exactly plan to go to Carnarvon. But you will take Carnarvon in preference to New Orleans." The convict said nothing. The doctor looked at him, the magnified pupils like the heads of two bridge nails. "What were you in for? Hit him harder than you thought, eh?"

"No. I tried to rob a train."

"Say that again." The convict said it again. "Well? Go on. You dont say that in the year 1927 and just stop, man." So the convict told it, dispassionately too—about the magazines, the pistol which would not shoot, the mask and the dark lantern in which no draft had been arranged to keep the candle burning so that it died almost with the match but even then left the metal too hot to carry, won with subscriptions. *Only it aint my eyes or my mouth either he's* *watching,* he thought. *It's like he is watching the way my hair grows* *on my head.* "I see," the doctor said. "But something went wrong. But you've had plenty of time to think about it since. To decide what was wrong, what you failed to do."

"Yes," the convict said. "I've thought about it a right smart since."

"So next time you are not going to make that mistake."

"I dont know," the convict said. "There aint going to be a next time."

"Why? If you know what you did wrong, they wont catch you next time."

The convict looked at the doctor steadily. They looked at each other steadily; the two sets of eyes were not so different after all. "I reckon I see what you mean," the convict said presently. "I was eighteen then. I'm twenty-five now."

"Oh," the doctor said. Now (the convict tried to tell it) the doctor did not move, he just simply quit looking at the convict. He produced a pack of cheap cigarettes from his coat. "Smoke?" he said.

"I wouldn't care for none," the convict said.

"Quite," the doctor said in that affable clipped voice. He put the cigarettes away. "There has been conferred upon my race (the

Medical race) also the power to bind and to loose, if not by Jehovah perhaps, certainly by the American Medical Association—on which incidentally, in this day of Our Lord, I would put my money, at any odds, at any amount, at any time. I dont know just how far out of bounds I am on this specific occasion but I think we'll put it to the touch." He cupped his hands to his mouth, toward the pilot house overhead. "Captain!" he shouted. "We'll put these three passengers ashore here." He turned to the convict again. "Yes," he said, "I think I shall let your native State lick its own vomit. Here." Again his hand emerged from his pocket, this time with a bill in it.

"No," the convict said.

"Come, come; I dont like to be disputed either."

"No," the convict said. "I aint got any way to pay it back."

"Did I ask you to pay it back?"

"No," the convict said. "I never asked to borrow it either."

So once more he stood on dry land, who had already been toyed with twice by that risible and concentrated power of water, once more than should have fallen to the lot of any one man, any one lifetime, yet for whom there was reserved still another unbelievable recapitulation, he and the woman standing on the empty levee, the sleeping child wrapped in the faded tunic and the grapevine painter still wrapped about the convict's wrist, watching the steamboat back away and turn and once more crawl onward up the platter-like reach of vacant water burnished more and more to copper, its trailing smoke roiling in slow copper-edged gouts, thinning out along the water, fading, stinking away across the vast serene desolation, the boat growing smaller and smaller until it did not seem to crawl at all but to hang stationary in the airy substanceless sunset, dissolving into nothing like a pellet of floating mud.

Then he turned and for the first time looked about him, behind him, recoiling, not through fear but through pure reflex and not physically but the soul, the spirit, that profound sober alert attentiveness of the hillman who will not ask anything of strangers, not even information, thinking quietly, No. This aint Carrollton neither. Because he now looked down the almost perpendicular landward slope of the levee through sixty feet of absolute space, upon a surface, a terrain flat as a waffle and of the color of a waffle or perhaps of the summer coat of a claybank horse and possessing that same piled density of a rug or peltry, spreading away without undulation yet with that curious appearance of imponderable solidity like fluid, broken here and there by thick humps of arsenical green which nevertheless still seemed to possess no height and by writhen veins of the color of ink which he began to suspect to be actual water but with judgment reserved, with judgment still reserved even when presently he was walking in it. That's what he said, told: So they went on. He didn't tell how he got the skiff single-handed up the revetment and across the crown and down the opposite sixty foot drop, he just said he went on, in a swirling cloud of mosquitoes like hot cinders, thrusting and plunging through the saw-edged grass which grew taller than his head and which whipped back at his arms and face like limber knives, dragging by the vine-spliced painter the skiff in which the woman sat, slogging and stumbling knee-deep in something less of earth than water, along one of those black winding channels less of water than earth: and then (he was in the skiff too now, paddling with the charred log, what footing there had been having given away beneath him without warning thirty minutes ago, leaving only the air-filled bubble of his jumperback ballooning lightly on the twilit water until he rose to the surface and scrambled into the skiff) the house, the cabin a little larger than a horse-box, of cypress boards and an iron roof, rising on ten-foot stilts slender as spiders' legs, like a shabby and death-stricken (and probably poisonous) wading creature which had got that far into that flat waste and died with nothing nowhere in reach or sight to lie down upon, a pirogue tied to the foot of a crude ladder, a man standing in the open door holding a lantern (it was that dark now) above his head, gobbling down at them.

He told it—of the next eight or nine or ten days, he did not remember which, while the four of them—himself and the woman and baby and the little wiry man with rotting teeth and soft wild bright eyes like a rat or a chipmunk, whose language neither of them could understand—lived in the room and a half. He did not tell it that way, just as he apparently did not consider it worth the breath to tell how he had got the hundred-and-sixty-pound skiff singlehanded up and across and down the sixty-foot levee. He just said, "After a while we come to a house and we stayed there eight or nine days then they blew up the levee with dynamite so we had to leave." That was all. But he remembered it, but quietly now, with the cigar now, the good one the Warden had given him (though not lighted yet) in his peaceful and steadfast hand, remembering that first morning when he waked on the thin pallet beside his host (the woman and baby had the one bed) with the fierce sun already latticed through the warped rough planking of the wall, and stood on the rickety porch looking out upon that flat fecund waste neither earth nor water, where even the senses doubted which was which, which rich and massy air and which mazy and impalpable vegetation, and thought quietly. *He must do something here to eat and live. But I dont know what. And until I can go on again, until I can find where I am and how to pass that town without them seeing me I will have to help him do it so we can eat and live too, and I dont know what.* And he had a change of clothing too, almost at once on that first morning, not telling any more than he had about the skiff and the levee how he had begged borrowed or bought from the man whom he had not laid eyes on twelve hours ago and with whom on the day he saw him for the last time he still could exchange no word, the pair of dungaree pants which even the Cajan had discarded as no longer wearable, filthy, buttonless, the legs slashed and frayed into fringe like that on an 1890 hammock, in which he stood naked from the waist up and holding out to her the mud-caked and soot-stained jumper and overall when the woman waked on that first morning in the crude bunk nailed into one corner and filled with dried grass, saying, "Wash them. Good. I want all them stains out. All of them."

"But the jumper," she said. "Aint he got ere old shirt too? That sun and them mosquitoes—" But he did not even answer, and she said no more either, though when he and the Cajan returned at dark the garments were clean, stained a little still with the old mud and soot, but clean, resembling again what they were supposed to resemble as (his arms and back already a fiery red which would be blisters by tomorrow) he spread the garments out and examined them and then rolled them up carefully in a six-months-old New Orleans paper and thrust the bundle behind a rafter, where it remained while day followed day and the blisters on his back broke and suppurated and he would sit with his face expressionless as a wooden mask beneath the sweat while the Cajan doped his back with something on a filthy rag from a filthy saucer, she still saying nothing since she too doubtless knew what his reason was, not from that rapport of the wedded conferred upon her by the two weeks during which they had jointly suffered all the crises emotional social economic and even moral which do not always occur even in the ordinary fifty married years (the old married: you have seen them, the electroplate reproductions, the thousand identical coupled faces with only a collarless stud or a fichu out of Louisa Alcott to denote the sex, looking in pairs like the winning braces of dogs after a field trial, out from among the packed columns of disaster and alarm and baseless assurance and hope and incredible insensitivity and insulation from tomorrow propped by a thousand morning sugar bowls or coffee urns; or singly, rocking on porches or sitting in the sun beneath the tobacco-stained porticoes of a thousand county courthouses, as though with the death of the other having inherited a sort of rejuvenescence, immortality; relict, they take a new lease on breath and seem to live forever, as though that flesh which the old ceremony or ritual had morally purified and made legally one had actually become so with long tedious habit and he or she who entered the ground first took all of it with him or her, leaving only the old permanent enduring bone, free and trammeless)—not because of this but because she too had stemmed at some point from the same dim hillbred Abraham.

So the bundle remained behind the rafter and day followed day while he and his partner (he was in partnership now with his host, hunting alligators on shares, on the halvers he called it—"Halvers?" the plump convict said. "How could you make a business agreement with a man you claim you couldn't even talk to?"

"I never had to talk to him," the tall one said. "Money aint got but one language.") departed at dawn each day, at first together in the pirogue but later singly, the one in the pirogue and the other in the skiff, the one with the battered and pitted rifle, the other with the knife and a piece of knotted rope and a lightwood club the size and weight and shape of a Thuringian mace, stalking their pleistocene nightmares up and down the secret inky channels which writhed the flat brass-colored land. He remembered that too: that first morning when turning in the sunrise from the rickety platform he saw the hide nailed drying to the wall and stopped dead, looking at it quietly, thinking quietly and soberly, *So that's it. That's what he does in order to eat and live,* knowing it was a hide, a skin, but from what animal, by association, ratiocination or even memory of any picture out of his dead youth, he did not know but knowing that it was the reason, the explanation, for the little lost spider-legged house (which had already begun to die, to rot from the legs upward almost before the roof was nailed on) set in that teeming and myriad desolation, enclosed and lost within the furious embrace of flowing mare earth and stallion sun, divining through pure rapport of kind for kind, hill-billy and bayou-rat the two one and identical because of the same grudged dispensation and niggard fate of hard and unceasing travail not to gain future security, a balance in the bank or even in a buried soda can for slothful and easy old age, but just permission to endure and endure to buy air to feel and sun to drink for each's little while, thinking (the convict), *Well, anyway I am going to find out what it is sooner than I expected to,* and did so, re-entered the house where the woman was just waking in the one sorry built-in straw-filled bunk which the Cajan had surrendered to her, and ate the breakfast (the rice, a semi-liquid mess violent with pepper and mostly fish considerably high, the chicory-thickened coffee) and, shirtless, followed the little scuttling bobbing bright-eyed rotten-toothed man down the crude ladder and into the pirogue. He had never seen a pirogue either and he believed that it would not remain upright—not that it was light and precariously balanced with its open side upward but that there was inherent in the wood, the very log, some dynamic and unsleeping natural law, almost will, which its present position outraged and violated—yet accepting this too as he had the fact that that hide had belonged to something larger than any calf or hog and that anything which looked like that on the outside would be more than likely to have teeth and claws too, accepting this, squatting in the pirogue, clutching both gunwales, rigidly immobile as though he had an egg filled with nitroglycerin in his mouth and scarcely breathing, thinking, *If that's it, then I can do it too and even if he cant tell me how I reckon I can watch him and find out.* And he did this too, he remembered it, quietly even yet, thinking, *I thought that was how to do it and I reckon I would still think that even if I had it to do again now for the first time*—the brazen day already fierce upon his naked back, the crooked channel like a voluted thread of ink, the pirogue moving steadily to the paddle which both entered and left the water without a sound; then the sudden cessation of the paddle behind him and the fierce hissing gobble of the Cajan at his back and he squatting bate-breathed and with that intense immobility of complete sobriety of a blind man listening while the frail wooden shell stole on at the dying apex of its own parted water. Afterward he remembered the rifle too—the rust-pitted single-shot weapon with a clumsily wired stock and a muzzle you could have driven a whiskey cork into, which the Cajan had brought into the boat—but not now; now he just squatted, crouched, immobile, breathing with infinitesimal care, his sober unceasing gaze going here and there constantly as he thought, *What? What? I not only dont know what I am looking for, I dont even know where to look for it.* Then he felt the motion of the pirogue as the Cajan moved and then the tense gobbling hissing actually, hot rapid and repressed, against his neck and ear, and glancing downward saw projecting between his own arm and body from behind the Cajan's hand holding the knife, and glaring again saw the flat thick spit of mud which as he looked at it divided and became a thick mud-colored log which in turn seemed, still immobile, to leap suddenly against his retinae in three—no, four—dimensions: volume, solidity, shape, and another: not fear but pure and intense speculation and he looking at the scaled motionless shape, thinking not, *It looks dangerous* but *It looks big*, thinking, *Well, maybe a mule standing in a lot looks big to a man that never walked up to one with a halter before*, thinking, *Only if he could just tell me what to do it would save time*, the pirogue drawing nearer now, creeping now, with no ripple now even and it seemed to him that he could even hear his companion's held breath and he taking the knife from the other's hand now and not even thinking this since it was too fast, a flash; it was not a surrender, not a resignation, it was too calm, it was a part of him, he had drunk it with his mother's milk and lived with it all his life: *After all a man cant only do what he has to do, with what he has to do it with, with what he has learned, to the best of his judgment. And I reckon a hog is still a hog, no matter what it looks like. So here goes*, sitting still for an instant longer until the bow of the pirogue grounded lighter than the falling of a leaf and stepped out of it and paused just for one instant while the words *It does look big* stood for just a second, unemphatic and trivial, somewhere where some fragment of his attention could see them and vanished, and stooped straddling, the knife driving even as he grasped the near foreleg, this all in the same instant when the lashing tail struck him a terrific blow upon the back. But the knife was home, he knew that even on his back in the mud, the weight of the thrashing beast longwise upon him, its ridged back clutched to his stomach, his arm about its throat, the hissing head clamped against his jaw, the furious tail lashing and flailing, the knife in his other hand probing for the life and finding it, the hot fierce gush: and now sitting beside the profound upbellied carcass, his head again between his knees in the old attitude while his own blood freshened the other which drenched him, thinking, *It's my durn nose again.*

So he sat there, his head, his streaming face, bowed between his knees in an attitude not of dejection but profoundly bemused, contemplative, while the shrill voice of the Cajan seemed to buzz at him from an enormous distance; after a time he even looked up at the antic wiry figure bouncing hysterically about him, the face wild and grimacing, the voice gobbling and high; while the convict, holding his face carefully slanted so the blood would run free looked at him with the cold intentness of a curator or custodian paused before one of his own glass cases, the Cajan threw up the rifle, cried "Boom-boom-boom!" flung it down and in pantomime re-enacted the recent scene then whirled his hands again, crying "Magnifique! Magnifique! Cent d'argent! mille d'argent! Tout l'argent sous le ciel de Dieu!" But the convict was already looking down again, cupping the coffee-colored water to his face, watching the constant bright carmine marble it, thinking, *It's a little late to be telling me that now*, and not even thinking this long because presently they were in the pirogue again, the convict squatting again with that unbreathing rigidity as though he were trying by holding his breath to decrease his very weight, the bloody skin in the bows before him and he looking at it, thinking. *And I cant even ask him how much my half will be.*

But this not for long either, because as he was to tell the plump convict later, money has but one language. He remembered that too (they were at home now, the skin spread on the platform, where for the woman's benefit now the Cajan once more went through the pantomine—the gun which was not used, the hand-to-hand battle; for the second time the invisible alligator was slain and amid cries, the victor rose and found this time that not even the woman was watching him. She was looking at the once more swollen and inflamed face of the convict. "You mean it kicked you right in the face?" she said.

"Nah," the convict said harshly, savagely. "It never had to. I done seem to got to where if that boy was to shoot me in the tail with a bean blower my nose would bleed.")—remembered that too but he did not try to tell it. Perhaps he could not have—how two people who could not even talk to one another made an agreement which both not only understood but which each knew the other would hold true and protect (perhaps for this reason) better than any written and witnessed contract. They even discussed and agreed somehow that they should hunt separately, each in his own vessel, to double the chances of finding prey. But this was easy: the convict could almost understand the words in which the Cajan said, "You do not need me and the rifle; we will only hinder you, be in your way." And more than this, they even agreed about the second time the invisible alligator was slain amid who—friend, neighbor, perhaps one in business in that line—from whom they could rent a second rifle; in their two patois, the one bastard English, the other bastard French—the one volatile, with his wild bright eyes and his voluble mouth full of stumps of teeth, the other sober, almost grim, swollen-faced and with his naked back blistered and scoriated like so much beef—they discussed this, squatting on either side of the pegged-out hide like two members of a corporation facing each other across a mahogany board table, and decided against it, the convict deciding: "I reckon not," he said. "I reckon if I had knowed enough to wait to start out with a gun, I still would. But since I done already started out without one, I dont reckon I'll change." Because it was a question of the money in terms of time, days. (Strange to say, that was the one thing which the Cajan could not tell him: how much the half would be. But the convict knew it was half.) He had so little of them. He would have to move on soon, thinking (the convict), *All this durn foolishness will stop soon and I can get on back*, and then suddenly he found he was thinking, *Will have to get on back*, and he became quite still and looked about at the rich strange desert which surrounded him, in which he was temporarily lost in peace and hope and into which the last seven years had sunk like so many trivial pebbles into a pool, leaving no ripple, and he thought quietly, with a kind of bemused amazement, *Yes. I reckon I had done forgot how good making money was. Being let to make it.*

So he used no gun, his the knotted rope and the Thuringian mace, and each morning he and the Cajan took their separate ways in the two boats to comb and creep the secret channels about the lost land from (or out of) which now and then still other pint-sized dark men appeared gobbling, abruptly and as though by magic from nowhere, in other hollowed logs, to follow quietly and watched him at his single combats—men named Tine and Toto and Theule, who were not much larger than and looked a good deal like the muskrats which the Cajan (the host did this too, supplied the kitchen too, he expressed this too like the rifle business, in his own tongue, the convict comprehending this too as though it had been English. Do not concern yourself about food, O Hercules. Catch alligators; I will supply the pot.") took now and then from traps as you take a shoat pig at need from a pen, and varied the eternal rice and fish (the convict did tell this: how at night, in the cabin, the door and one sashless window battened against mosquitoes—a form, a ritual, as empty as crossing the finger or knocking on wood—sitting beside the bug-swirled lantern on the plank table in a temperature close to blood heat he would look down at the swimming segment of meat on his sweating plate and think, *It must be Theule. He was the fat one.*)—day following day, unemphatic and identical, each like the one before and the one which would follow while his theoretical half of a sum to be reckoned in pennies, dollars, or tens of dollars he did not know, mounted—the mornings when he set forth to find waiting for him like the *matador* his *aficionados* the small clump of constant and deferential pirogues, the hard noons when ringed half about by little motionless shells he fought his solitary combats, the evenings, the return, the pirogues departing one by one into inlets and passages which during the first few days he could not even distinguish, then the platform in the twilight where before the static woman and the usually nursing infant and the one or two bloody hides of the day's take the Cajan would perform his ritualistic victorious pantomime before the two growing rows of knifemarks in one of the boards of the wall; then the nights when, the woman and child in the single bunk and the Cajan already snoring on the pallet and the reeking lantern set close, he (the convict) would sit on his naked heels, sweating steadily, his face worn and calm, immersed and indomitable, his bowed back raw and savage as beef beneath the suppurant old blisters and the fierce welts of tails, and scrape and chip at the charred sapling which was almost a paddle now, pausing now and then to raise his head while the cloud of mosquitoes about it whined and whirled, to stare at the wall before him until after a while the crude boards themselves must have dissolved away and let his blank unseeing gaze go on and on unhampered, through the rich oblivious darkness, beyond it even perhaps, even perhaps beyond the seven wasted years during which, so he had just realised, he had been permitted to toil but not to work. Then he would retire himself, he would take a last look at the rolled bundle behind the rafter and blow out the lantern and lie down as he was beside his snoring partner, to lie sweating (on his stomach, he could not bear the touch of anything to his back) in the whining ovenlike darkness filled with the forlorn bellowing of alligators, thinking not, *They never gave me time to learn* but *I had forgot how good it is to work.*

Then on the tenth day it happened. It happened for the third time. At first he refused to believe it, not that he felt that now he had served out and discharged his apprenticeship to mischance, had with the birth of the child reached and crossed the crest of his Golgotha and would now be, possibly not permitted so much as ignored, to descend the opposite slope free-wheeling. That was not his feeling at all. What he declined to accept was the fact that a power, a force such as that which had been consistent enough to concentrate upon him with deadly undeviation for weeks, should with all the wealth of cosmic violence and disaster to draw from, have been so barren of invention and imagination, so lacking in pride of artistry and

craftsmanship, as to repeat itself twice. Once he had accepted, twice
he even forgave, but three times he simply declined to believe, particularly when he was at last persuaded to realise that this third time
was to be instigated not by the blind potency of volume and motion
but by human direction and hands: that now the cosmic joker, foiled
twice, had stooped in its vindictive concentration to the employing
of dynamite.

He did not tell that. Doubtless he did not know himself how it
happened, what was happening. But he doubtless remembered it (but
quietly above the thick rich-colored pristine cigar in his clean steady
hand), what he knew, divined of it. It would be evening, the ninth
evening, he and the woman on either side of their host's empty place
at the evening meal, he hearing the voices from without but not
ceasing to eat, still chewing steadily, because it would be the same
as though he was seeing them anyway—the two or three or four pirogues floating on the dark water beneath the platform on which the
host stood, the voices gobbling and jabbering, incomprehensible and
filled not with alarm and not exactly with rage or ever perhaps absolute surprise but rather just cacophony like those of disturbed marsh
fowl, he (the convict) not ceasing to chew but just looking up quietly
and maybe without a great deal of interrogation or surprise too as the
Cajan burst in and stood before them, wild-faced, glaring, his blackened teeth gaped against the inky orifice of his distended mouth,
watching (the convict) while the Cajan went through his violent
pantomime of violent evacuation, ejection, scooping something invisible into his arms and hurling it out and downward and in the
instant of completing the gesture changing from instigator to victim of that which he had sent into pantomimic motion, clasping
his head and, bowed over and not otherwise moving, seeming to be
swept on and away before it, crying "Boom! Boom! Boom!", the convict watching him, his jaw not chewing now, for just that moment,
thinking, *What? What is it he is trying to tell me?* thinking (this is
a flash too, since he could not have expressed this, and hence did not
even know that he had ever thought it) that though his life had been
cast here, circumscribed by this environment, accepted by this environment and accepting it in turn (and he had done well here—
this quietly, soberly indeed, if he had been able to phrase it, thinking
it instead of merely knowing it—better than he had ever done, who
had not even known until now how good work, making money, could
be) yet it was not his life, he still and would ever be no more than
the water bug upon the surface of the pond, the plumbless and lurk-

ing depths of which he would never know, his only actual contact with it being the instants when on lonely and glaring mudspits under the pitiless sun and amphitheatred by his motionless and riveted semicircle of watching pirogues, he accepted the gambit which he had not elected, entered the lashing radius of the armed tail and beat at the thrashing and hissing head with his lightwood club, or this failing, embraced without hesitation the armored body itself with the frail web of flesh and bone in which he walked and lived and sought the raging life with an eight-inch knife-blade.

So he and the woman merely watched the Cajan as he acted out the whole charade of eviction—the little wiry man gesticulant and wild, his hysterical shadow leaping and falling upon the rough wall as he went through the pantomime of abandoning the cabin, gathering in pantomime his meagre belongings from the walls and corners—objects which no other man would want and only some power or force like blind water or earthquake or fire would ever dispossess him of, the woman watching too, her mouth slightly open upon a mass of chewed food, on her face an expression of placid astonishment, saying, "What? What's he saying?"

"I don't know," the convict said. "But I reckon if it's something we ought to know we will find it out when it's ready for us to." Because he was not alarmed, though by now he had read the other's meaning plainly enough. *He's fixing to leave*, he thought. *He's telling me to leave too*—this later, after they had quitted the table and the Cajan and the woman had gone to bed and the Cajan had risen from the pallet and approached the convict and once more went through the pantomime of abandoning the cabin, this time as one repeats a speech which may have been misunderstood, tediously, carefully repetitional as to a child, seeming to hold the convict with one hand while he gestured, talked, with the other, gesturing as though in single syllables, the convict (squatting, the knife open and the almost-finished paddle across his lap) watching, nodding his head, even speaking in English: "Yah; sure. You bet. I got you."—trimming again at the paddle but no faster, with no more haste than on any other night, serene in his belief that when the time came for him to know whatever it was, that would take care of itself, having already and without even knowing it, even before the possibility, the question, ever arose, declined, refused to accept even the thought of moving also, thinking about the hides, thinking, *If there was just some way he could tell me where to carry my share to get the money* but thinking this only for an instant between two delicate strokes of the blade because almost at once he thought, *I reckon as long as I can catch them I wont have no big trouble finding whoever it is that will buy them.*

So the next morning he helped the Cajan load his few belongings—the pitted rifle, a small bundle of clothing (again they traded, who could not even converse with one another, this time the few cooking vessels, a few rusty traps by definite allocation, and something embracing and abstractional which included the stove, the crude bunk, the house or its occupancy—something—in exchange for one alligator hide)—into the pirogue, then, squatting and as two children divide sticks they divided the hides, separating them into two piles, one-for-me-and-one-for-you, two-for-me-and-two-for-you, and the Cajan loaded his share and shoved away from the platform and paused again, though this time he only put the paddle down, gathered something invisibly into his two hands and flung it violently upward, crying "Boom? Boom?" on a rising inflection, nodding violently to the half-naked and savagely scoriated man on the platform who stared with a sort of grim equability back at him and said, "Sure. Boom. Boom." Then the Cajan went on. He did not look back. They watched him, already paddling rapidly, or the woman did; the convict had already turned.

"Maybe he was trying to tell us to leave too," she said.

"Yah," the convict said. "I thought of that last night. Hand me the paddle." She fetched it to him—the sapling, the one he had been trimming at nightly, not quite finished yet though one more evening would do it (he had been using a spare one of the Cajan's. The other had offered to let him keep it, to include it perhaps with the stove and the bunk and the cabin's freehold, but the convict had declined. Perhaps he had computed it by volume against so much alligator hide, this weighed against one more evening with the tedious and careful blade.) and he departed too with his knotted rope and mace, in the opposite direction, as though not only not content with refusing to quit the place he had been warned against, he must establish and affirm the irrevocable finality of his refusal by penetrating even further and deeper into it. And then and without warning the high fierce drowsing of his solitude gathered itself and struck at him.

He could not have told this if he had tried—this not yet mid-morning and he going on, alone for the first time, no pirogue emerging anywhere to fall in behind him, but he had not expected this anyway, he knew that the others would have departed too; it was not this, it was his very solitude, his desolation which was now his alone and in full since he had elected to remain; the sudden cessation of the paddle, the skiff shooting on for a moment yet while he thought, *What? What?* Then, *No. No. No*, as the silence and solitude and emptiness roared down upon him in a jeering bellow: and now reversed, the skiff spun violently on its heel, he the betrayed driving furiously back toward the platform where he knew it was already too late, that citadel where the very crux and dear breath of his life—the being allowed to work and earn money, that right and privilege which he believed he had earned to himself unaided, asking no favor of anyone or anything save the right to be let alone to pit his will and strength against the sauric protagonist of a land, a region, which he had not asked to be projected into—was being threatened, driving the home-made paddle in grim fury, coming in sight of the platform at last and seeing the motor launch lying alongside it with no surprise at all but actually with a kind of pleasure as though at a visible justification of his outrage and fear, the privilege of saying I *told you so* to his own affronting, driving on toward it in a dream-like state in which there seemed to be no progress at all, in which, unimpeded and suffocating, he strove dreamily with a weightless oar, with muscles without strength or resiliency, at a medium without resistance, seeming to watch the skiff creep infinitesimally across the sunny water and up to the platform while a man in the launch (there were five of them in all) gobbled at him in that same tongue he had been hearing constantly now for ten days and still knew no word of, just as a second man, followed by the woman carrying the baby and dressed again for departure in the faded tunic and the sunbonnet, emerged from the house, carrying (the man carried several other things but the convict saw nothing else) the paper-wrapped bundle which the convict had put behind the rafter ten days ago and no other hand had touched since, he (the convict) on the platform too now, holding the skiff's painter in one hand and the bludgeon-like paddle in the other, contriving to speak to the woman at last in a voice dreamy and suffocating and incredibly calm: "Take it away from him and carry it back into the house."

"So you can talk English, can you?" the man in the launch said. "Why didn't you come out like they told you to last night?"

"Out?" the convict said. Again he even looked, glared, at the man in the launch, contriving even again to control his voice: "I aint got time to take trips. I'm busy," already turning to the woman again, his mouth already open to repeat as the dreamy buzzing voice of the man came to him and he turning once more, in a terrific and absolutely unbearable exasperation, crying, "Flood? What flood? Hell a mile, it's done passed me twice months ago! It's gone! What flood? and then (he did not think this in actual words either but he knew it, suffered that flashing insight into his own character or destiny: how there was a peculiar quality of repetitiveness about his present fate, how not only the almost seminal crises recurred with a certain monotony, but the very physical circumstances followed a stupidly unimaginative pattern) the man in the launch said, "Take him" and he was on his feet for a few minutes, yet, lashing and striking in panting fury, then once more on his back on hard unyielding planks while the four men swarmed over him in a fierce wave of hard bones and panting curses and at last the thin dry vicious snapping of handcuffs.

"Damn it, are you mad?" the man in the launch said. "Cant you understand they are going to dynamite that levee at noon today— Come on," he said to the others. "Get him aboard. Let's get out of here."

"I want my hides and boat," the convict said.

"Damn your hides," the man in the launch said. "If they dont get that levee blowed pretty soon you can hunt plenty more of them on the capitol steps at Baton Rouge. And this is all the boat you will need and you can say your prayers about it."

"I aint going without my boat," the convict said. He said it calmly and with complete finality, so calm, so final that for almost a minute nobody answered him, they just stood looking quietly down at him as he lay, half-naked, blistered and scarred, helpless and manacled hand and foot, on his back, delivering his ultimatum in a voice peaceful and quiet as that in which you talk to your bedfellow before going to sleep. Then the man in the launch moved; he spat quietly over the side and said in a voice as calm and quiet as the convict's:

"All right. Bring his boat." They helped the woman, carrying the baby and the paper-wrapped parcel, into the launch. Then they helped the convict to his feet and into the launch too, the shackles on his wrists and ankles clashing. "I'd unlock you if you'd promise to behave yourself," the man said. The convict did not answer this at all.

"I want to hold the rope," he said.

"The rope?"

"Yes," the convict said. "The rope." So they lowered him into the stern and gave him the end of the painter after it had passed the towing cleat, and they went on. The convict did not look back. But then, he did not look forward either, he lay half sprawled, his shackled legs before him, the end of the skiff's painter in one shackled hand. The launch made two other stops; when the hazy wafer of the intolerable sun began to stand once more directly overhead there were fifteen people in the launch; and then the convict, sprawled and motionless, saw the flat brazen land begin to rise and become a greenish-black mass of swamp, bearded and convoluted, this in turn stopping short off and there spread before him an expanse of water embraced by a blue dissolution of shore line and glittering thinly under the noon, larger than he had ever seen before, the sound of the launch's engine ceasing, the hull sliding on behind its fading bow-wave. "What are you doing?" the leader said.

"It's noon," the helmsman said. "I thought we might hear the dynamite." So they all listened, the launch lost of all forward motion, rocking slightly, the glitter-broken small waves slapping and whispering at the hull, but no sound, no tremble even, came anywhere under the fierce hazy sky; the long moment gathered itself and turned on and noon was past. "All right," the leader said. "Let's go." The engine started again, the hull began to gather speed. The leader came aft and stooped over the convict, key in hand. "I guess you'll have to behave now, whether you want to or not," he said, unlocking the manacles. "Wont you?"

"Yes," the convict said. They went on; after a time the shore vanished completely and a little sea got up. The convict was free now but he lay as before, the end of the skiff's painter in his hand, bent now with three or four turns about his wrist; he turned his head now and then to look back at the towing skiff as it slewed and bounced in the launch's wake; now and then he even looked out over the lake, the eyes alone moving, the face grave and expressionless, thinking, *This is a greater immensity of water, of waste and desolation, than I have ever seen before*; perhaps not; thinking three or four hours later, the shoreline raised again and broken into a clutter of sailing sloops and power cruisers, *These are more boats than I believed existed, a maritime race of which I also had no cognizance* or perhaps not thinking it but just watching as the launch opened the shored gut of the ship canal, the low smoke of the city beyond it, then a wharf, the launch slowing in; a quiet crowd of people watching with that same forlorn passivity he had seen before and whose race he did recognise even though he had not seen Vicksburg when he passed it—the brand, the unmistakable hallmark of the violently homeless, he more so than any, who would have permitted no man to call him one of them.

"All right," the leader said to him. "Here you are."

"The boat," the convict said.

"You've got it. What do you want me to do—give you a receipt for it?"

"No," the convict said. "I just want the boat."

"Take it. Only you ought to have a bookstrap or something to carry it in." ("Carry it in?" the plump convict said. "Carry it where? Where would you have to carry it?")

He (the tall one) told that: how he and the woman disembarked and how one of the men helped him haul the skiff up out of the water and how he stood there with the end of the painter wrapped around his wrist and the man bustled up, saying, "All right. Next load! Next load!" and how he told this man too about the boat and the man cried, "Boat? Boat?" and how he (the convict) went with them when they carried the skiff over and racked, berthed, it with the others and how he lined himself up by a coca-cola sign and the arch of a draw bridge so he could find the skiff again quick when he returned, and how he and the woman (he carrying the paper-wrapped parcel) were herded into a truck and after a while the truck began to run in traffic, between close houses, then there was a big building, an armory—

"Armory?" the plump one said. "You mean a jail."

"No. It was a kind of warehouse, with people with bundles laying on the floor." And how he thought maybe his partner might be there and how he even looked about for the Cajan while waiting for a chance to get back to the door again, where the soldier was and how he got back to the door at last, the woman behind him and his chest actually against the dropped rifle.

"Gwan, gwan," the soldier said. "Get back. They'll give you some clothes in a minute. You cant walk around the streets that way. And something to eat too. Maybe your kinfolks will come for you by that time." And he told that too: how the woman said,

"Maybe if you told him you had some kinfolks here he would let us out." And how he did not; he could not have expressed this either, it was too deep, too ingrained; he had never yet had to think it into words through all the long generations of himself—his hill-man's sober and jealous respect not for truth but for the power, the strength, of lying—not to be niggard with lying but rather to use it with respect and even care, delicate quick and strong, like a fine and fatal blade. And how they fetched him clothes—a blue jumper and overalls, and then food too (a brisk starched young woman saying, "But the baby must be bathed, cleaned. It will die if you dont" and the woman saying, "Yessum. He might holler some, he aint never been bathed before. But he's a good baby.") and now it was night, the unshaded bulbs harsh and savage and forlorn above the snorers and he rising, gripping the woman awake, and then the window. He told that: how there were doors in plenty, leading he did not know where, but he had a hard time finding a window they could use but he found one at last, he carrying the parcel and the baby too while he climbed through first—"You ought to tore up a sheet and slid down it," the plump convict said. But he needed no sheet, there were cobbles under his feet now, in the rich darkness. The city was there too but he had not seen it yet and would not— the low constant glare; Bienville had stood there too, it had been the figment of an emasculate also calling himself Napoleon but no more, Andrew Jackson had found it one step from Pennsylvania Avenue. But the convict found it considerably further than one step back to the ship canal and the skiff, the coca-cola sign dim now, the draw bridge arching spidery against the jonquil sky at dawn: nor did he tell, any more than about the sixty-foot levee, how he got the skiff back into the water. The lake was behind him now; there was but one direction he could go. When he saw the River again he knew it at once. He should have; it was now ineradicably a part of his past, his life; it would be a part of what he would bequeath, if that were in store for him. But four weeks later it would look different from what it did now, and did: he (the old man) had recovered from his debauch, back in banks again, the Old Man, rippling placidly toward the sea, brown and rich as chocolate be- tween levees whose inner faces were wrinkled as though in a frozen and aghast amazement, crowned with the rich green of summer in the willows; beyond them, sixty feet below, slick mules squatted against the broad pull of middle-busters in the richened soil which would not need to be planted, which would need only to be shown a cotton seed to sprout and make, there would be the symmetric miles of strong stalks by July, purple bloom in August, in September the black fields snowed over, spilled, the middles dragged smooth by the long sacks, the long black limber hands plucking, the hot air filled with the whine of gins, the September air then but now June air heavy with locust and (the towns) the smell of new paint and the sour smell of the paste which holds wall paper—the towns, the villages, the little lost wood landings on stilts on the inner face of the levee, the lower storeys bright and rank under the new paint and paper and even the marks on spile and post and tree of May's raging water-height fading beneath each bright silver gust of summer's loud and inconstant rain; there was a store at the levee's lip, a few saddled and rope-bridled mules in the sleepy dust, a few dogs, a handful of Negroes sitting on the steps beneath the chewing tobacco and malaria medicine signs, and three white men, one of them a deputy sheriff canvassing for votes to beat his superior (who had given him his job) in the August primary, all pausing to watch the skiff emerge from the glitter-glare of the afternoon water and approach and land, a woman carrying a child stepping out, then a man, a tall man who, approaching, proved to be dressed in a faded but recently washed and quite clean suit of penitentiary clothing, stopping in the dust where the mules dozed and watching with pale cold humorless eyes while the deputy sheriff was still making toward his armpit that gesture which everyone present realised was to have produced a pistol in one flashing motion for a considerable time while still nothing came of it. It was apparently enough for the newcomer, however.

"You a officer?" he said.

"You damn right I am," the deputy said. "Just let me get this damn gun—"

"All right," the other said. "Yonder's your boat, and here's the woman. But I never did find that bastard on the cottonhouse."

## CHAPTER V

One of the Governor's young men arrived at the Penitentiary the next morning. That is, he was fairly young (he would not see thirty again though without doubt he did not want to, there being that about him which indicated a character which never had and never would want anything it did not, or was not about to, possess), a Phi Beta Kappa out of an Eastern university, a colonel on the Governor's staff who did not buy it with a campaign contribution, who had stood in his negligent Eastern-cut clothes and his arched nose and lazy contemptuous eyes on the galleries of any number of little lost backwoods stores and told his stories and received the guffaws of his overalled and spitting hearers and with the same look in his eyes fondled infants named in memory of the last administration and in honor (or hope) of the next and (it was said of him and doubtless not true) by lazy accident the behinds of some who were not infants any longer though still not old enough to vote. He was in the Warden's office with a briefcase, and presently the deputy warden of the levee was there too. He would have been sent for presently though not yet, but he came anyhow, without knocking, with his hat on, calling the Governor's young man loudly by a nickname and striking him with a flat hand on the back and lifted one thigh to the Warden's desk, almost between the Warden and the caller, the emissary. Or the vizier with the command, the knotted cord, as began to appear immediately.

"Well," the Governor's young man said, "you've played the devil, haven't you?" The Warden had a cigar. He had offered the caller one. It had been refused, though presently, while the Warden looked at the back of his neck with hard immobility even a little grim, the deputy leaned and reached back and opened the desk drawer and took one.

"Seems straight enough to me," the Warden said. "He got swept away against his will. He came back as soon as he could and surrendered."

"He even brought that damn boat back," the deputy said. "If he'd a throwed the boat away he could a walked back in three days. But no sir. He's got to bring the boat back. 'Here's your boat and here's the woman but I never found no bastard on no cottonhouse.'" He slapped his knee, guffawing. "Them convicts. A mule's got twice as much sense."

"A mule's got twice as much sense as anything except a rat," the emissary said in his pleasant voice. "But that's not the trouble."

"What is the trouble?" the Warden said.

"This man is dead."

"Hell fire, he aint dead," the deputy said. "He's up yonder in that bunkhouse right now, lying his head off probly. I'll take you up there and you can see him." The Warden was looking at the deputy.

"Look," he said. "Bledsoe was trying to tell me something about that Kate mule's leg. You better go up to the stable and—"

"I done tended to it," the deputy said. He didn't even look at the Warden. He was watching, talking to, the emissary. "No sir. He aint—"

"But he has received an official discharge as being dead. Not a pardon nor a parole either: a discharge. He's either dead, or free.

In either case he doesn't belong here." Now both the Warden and the deputy looked at the emissary, the deputy's mouth open a little, the cigar poised in his hand to have its tip bitten off. The emissary spoke pleasantly, extremely distinctly: "On a report of death forwarded to the Governor by the Warden of the Penitentiary." The deputy closed his mouth, though otherwise he didn't move. "On the official evidence of the officer delegated at the time to the charge and returning of the body of the prisoner to the Penitentiary." Now the deputy put the cigar into his mouth and got slowly off the desk, the cigar rolling across his lip as he spoke:

"So that's it. I'm to be it, am I?" He laughed shortly, a stage laugh, two notes. "When I done been right three times running through three separate administrations? That's on a book somewhere too. Somebody in Jackson can find that too. And if they cant, I can show—"

"Three administrations?" the emissary said. "Well, well. That's pretty good."

"You damn right it's good," the deputy said. "The woods are full of folks that didn't." The Warden was again watching the back of the deputy's neck.

"Look," he said. "Why dont you step up to my house and get that bottle of whiskey out of the sideboard and bring it down here?"

"All right," the deputy said. "But I think we better settle this first. I'll tell you what we'll do—"

"We can settle it quicker with a drink or two," the Warden said. "You better step on up to your place and get a coat so the bottle—"

"That'll take too long," the deputy said. "I wont need no coat." He moved to the door, where he stopped and turned. "I'll tell you what to do. Just call twelve men in here and tell him it's a jury—he never seen but one before and he wont know no better—and try him over for robbing that train. Hamp can be the judge."

"You cant try a man twice for the same crime," the emissary said. "He might know that even if he doesn't know a jury when he sees one."

"Look," the Warden said.

"All right. Just call it a new train robbery. Tell him it happened yesterday, tell him he robbed another train while he was gone and just forgot it. He couldn't help himself. Besides, he wont care. He'd just as lief be here as out. He wouldn't have nowhere to go if he was out. None of them do. Turn one loose and be damned if he aint right back here by Christmas like it was a reunion or something, for doing the very same thing they caught him at before." He guffawed again. "Them convicts."

"Look," the Warden said. "While you're there, why dont you open the bottle and see if the liquor's any good. Take a drink or two. Give yourself time to feel it. If it's not good, no use in bringing it."

"O. K.," the deputy said. He went out this time.

"Couldn't you lock the door?" the emissary said. The Warden squirmed faintly. That is, he shifted his position in his chair.

"After all, he's right," he said. "He's guessed right three times now. And he's kin to all the folks in Pittman County except the niggers."

"Maybe we can work fast then." The emissary opened the brief-case and took out a sheaf of papers. "So there you are," he said.

"There what are?"

"He escaped."

"But he came back voluntarily and surrendered."

"But he escaped."

"All right," the Warden said. "He escaped. Then what?" Now the emissary said look. That is, he said,

"Listen. I'm on per diem. That's tax-payers, votes. And if there's any possible chance for it to occur to anyone to hold an investigation about this, there'll be ten senators and twenty-five representatives here on a special train maybe. On per diem. And it will be mighty hard to keep some of them from going back to Jackson by way of Memphis or New Orleans—on per diem."

"All right," the Warden said. "What does he say to do?"

"This. That man left here in charge of one specific officer. But he was delivered back here by a different one."

"But he surren—" This time the Warden stopped of his own accord. He looked, stared almost, at the emissary. "All right. Go on."

"In specific charge of an appointed and delegated officer, who returned here and reported that the body of the prisoner was no longer in his possession; that, in fact, he did not know where the prisoner was. That's correct, isn't it?" The Warden said nothing. "Isn't that correct?" the emissary said, pleasantly, insistently.

"But you cant do that to him. I tell you he's kin to half the—"

"That's taken care of. The Chief has made a place for him on the highway patrol."

"Hell," the Warden said. "He cant ride a motorcycle. I dont even let him try to drive a truck."

"He wont have to. Surely an amazed and grateful State can supply the man who guessed right three times in succession in Mississippi general elections with a car to ride in and somebody to run it if necessary. He wont even have to stay in it all the time. Just so he's near enough so when an inspector sees the car and stops and blows the horn of it he can hear it and come out."

"I still dont like it," the Warden said.

"Neither do I. Your man could have saved all of this if he had just gone on and drowned himself, as he seems to have led everybody to believe he had. But he didn't. And the Chief says do. Can you think of anything better?" The Warden sighed.

"No," he said.

"All right." The emissary opened the papers and uncapped a pen and began to write. "Attempted escape from the Penitentiary, ten years' additional sentence," he said. "Deputy Warden Buckworth transferred to Highway Patrol. Call it for meritorious service even if you want to. It wont matter now. Done?"

"Done," the Warden said.

"Then suppose you send for him. Get it over with." So the Warden sent for the tall convict and he arrived presently, saturnine and grave, in his new bed-ticking, his jowls blue and close under the sunburn, his hair recently cut and neatly parted and smelling faintly of the prison barber's (the barber was in for life, for murdering his wife, still a barber) pomade. The Warden called him by name.

"You had bad luck, didn't you?" The convict said nothing. "They are going to have to add ten years to your time."

"All right," the convict said.

"It's hard luck. I'm sorry."

"All right," the convict said. "If that's the rule." So they gave him the ten years more and the Warden gave him the cigar and now he sat, jackknifed backward into the space between the upper and lower bunks, the unlighted cigar in his hand while the plump convict and four others listened to him. Or questioned him, that is, since it was all done, finished, now and he was safe again, so maybe it wasn't even worth talking about any more.

"All right," the plump one said. "So you come back into the River. Then what?"

"Nothing. I rowed."

"Wasn't it pretty hard rowing coming back?"

"The water was still high. It was running pretty hard still. I never made much speed for the first week or two. After that it got better." Then, suddenly and quietly, something—the inarticulateness, the innate and inherited reluctance for speech, dissolved and he found himself listening to himself, telling it quietly, the words coming not fast but easily to the tongue as he required them: How he paddled on (he found out by trying it that he could make better speed, if you could call it speed, next the bank—this after he had been carried suddenly and violently out to midstream before he could prevent it and found himself, the skiff, travelling back toward the region from which he had just escaped and he spent the better part of the morning getting back inshore and up to the canal again from which he had emerged at dawn) until night came and they tied up to the bank and ate some of the food he had secreted in his jumper before leaving the armory in New Orleans and the woman and the infant slept in the boat as usual and when daylight came they went on and tied up again that night too and the next day the food gave out and he came to a landing, a town, he didn't notice the name of it, and he got a job. It was a cane farm—

"Cane?" one of the other convicts said. "What does anybody want to raise cane for? You cut cane. You have to fight it where I come from. You burn it just to get shut of it."

"It was sorghum," the tall convict said.

"Sorghum?" another said. "A whole farm just raising sorghum? *Sorghum?* What did they do with it?" The tall one didn't know. He didn't ask, he just came up the levee and there was a truck waiting full of niggers and a white man said, "You there. Can you run a shovel plow?" and the convict said, "Yes," and the man said, "Jump in then," and the convict said, "Only I've got a—"

"Yes," the plump one said. "That's what I been aiming to ask. What did—" The tall convict's face was grave, his voice was calm, just a little short:

"They had tents for the folks to live in. They were behind." The plump one blinked at him.

"Did they think she was your wife?"

"I dont know. I reckon so." The plump one blinked at him.

"Wasn't she your wife? Just from time to time kind of, you might say?" The tall one didn't answer this at all. After a moment he raised the cigar and appeared to examine a loosening of the wrapper because after another moment he licked the cigar carefully near the end. "All right," the plump one said. "Then what?" So he worked there four days. He didn't like it. Maybe that was why: that he too could not quite put credence in that much of what he believed to be sorghum. So when they told him it was Saturday and paid him and the white man told him about somebody who was going to Baton Rouge the next day in a motor boat, he went to see the man and took the six dollars he had earned and bought food with it and tied the skiff behind the motor boat and went to Baton Rouge. It didn't take long and even after they left the motor boat at Baton Rouge and he was paddling again it seemed to the convict that the River was lower and the current not so fast, so hard, so they made fair speed, tying up to the bank at night among the willows, the woman and baby sleeping in the skiff as of old. Then the food gave out again. This time it was a wood landing, the wood stacked and waiting, a wagon and team being unladen of another load. The men with the wagon told him about the sawmill and helped him drag the skiff up the levee; they wanted to leave it there but he would not so they loaded it onto the wagon too and he and the woman got on the wagon too and they went to the sawmill. They gave them one room in a house to live in here. They paid two dollars a day and furnish. The work was hard. He liked it. He stayed there eight days.

"If you liked it so well, why did you quit?" the plump one said. The tall convict examined the cigar again, holding it up where the light fell upon the rich chocolate-colored flank.

"I got in trouble," he said.

"What trouble?"

"Woman. It was a fellow's wife."

"You mean you had been toting one piece up and down the country day and night for over a month, and now the first time you have a chance to stop and catch your breath almost you got to get in trouble over another one?" The tall convict had thought of that. He remembered it: how there were times, seconds, at first when if it had not been for the baby he might have, might have tried. But they were just seconds because in the next instant his whole being would seem to flee the very idea in a kind of savage and horrified revulsion; he would find himself looking from a distance at this millstone which the force and power of blind and risible Motion had fastened upon him, thinking, saying aloud actually, with harsh and savage outrage even though it had been two years since he had had a woman and that a nameless and not young Negress, a casual, a straggler whom he had caught more or less by chance on one of the fifth-Sunday visiting days, the man—husband or sweetheart— whom she had come to see having been shot by a trusty a week or so previous and she had not heard about it: "She aint even no good to me for that."

"But you got this one, didn't you?" the plump convict said.

"Yah," the tall one said. The plump one blinked at him.

"Was it good?"

"It's all good," one of the others said. "Well? Go on. How many more did you have on the way back? Sometimes when a fellow starts getting it it looks like he just cant miss even if—" That was all, the convict told them. They left the sawmill fast, he had no time to buy food until they reached the next landing. There he spent the whole sixteen dollars he had earned and they went on. The River was lower now, there was no doubt of it, and sixteen dollars' worth looked like a lot of food and he thought maybe it would do, would be enough. But maybe there was more current in the River still than it looked like. But this time it was Mississippi, it was cotton; the plow handles felt right to his palms again, the strain and squat of the slick buttocks against the middle buster's blade was what he knew, even though they paid but a dollar a day here. But that did it. He told it: they told him it was Saturday again and paid him and he told about it— night, a smoked lantern and a disc of worn and barren earth as smooth as silver, a circle of crouching figures, the importunate murmurs and ejaculations, the meagre piles of worn bills beneath the crouching knees, the dotted cubes clicking and scuttering in the dust; that did it. "How much did you win?" the second convict said.

"Enough," the tall one said.

"But how much?"

"Enough," the tall one said. It was enough exactly; he gave it all to the man who owned the second motor boat (he would not need food now), he and the woman in the launch now and the skiff towing behind, the woman with the baby and the paper-wrapped parcel beneath his peaceful hand, on his lap; almost at once he recognised, not Vicksburg because he had never seen Vicksburg, but the trestle beneath which on his roaring wave of trees and houses and dead animals he had shot, accompanied by thunder and lightning, a month and three weeks ago; he looked at it once without heat, even without interest as the launch went on. But now he began to watch the bank, the levee. He didn't know how he would know but he knew he would, and then it was early afternoon and sure enough the moment came and he said to the launch owner: "I reckon this will do."

"Here?" the launch owner said. "This dont look like anywhere to me."

"I reckon this is it," the convict said. So the launch put inshore, the engine ceased, it drifted up and lay against the levee and the owner cast the skiff loose.

"You better let me take you on until we come to something," he said. "That was what I promised."

"I reckon this will do," the convict said. So they got out and he stood with the grapevine painter in his hand while the launch purred again and drew away, already curving; he did not watch it. He laid the bundle down and made the painter fast to a willow root and picked up the bundle and turned. He said no word, he mounted the levee, passing the mark, the tide-line of the old raging, dry now and lined, traversed by shallow and empty cracks like foolish and deprecatory senile grins, and entered a willow clump and removed the overalls and shirt they had given him in New Orleans and dropped them without even looking to see where they fell and opened the parcel and took out the other, the known, the desired, faded a little, stained and worn, but clean, recognisable, and put them on and returned to the skiff and took up the paddle. The woman was already in it.

The plump convict stood blinking at him. "So you come back," he said. "Well well." Now they all watched the tall convict as he bit the end from the cigar neatly and with complete deliberation and spat it out and licked the bite smooth and damp and took a match from his pocket and examined the match for a moment as though to be sure it was a good one, worthy of the cigar perhaps, and raked it up his thigh with the same deliberation—a motion almost too slow to set fire to it, it would seem—and held it until the flame burned clear and free of sulphur, then put it to the cigar. The plump one watched him, blinking rapidly and steadily. "And they give you ten years more for running. That's bad. A fellow can get used to what they give him at first, to start off with, I dont care how much it is, even a hundred and ninety-nine years. But ten more years. Ten years more, on top of that. When you never expect it. Ten more years to have to do without no society, no female companionship—" He blinked steadily at the tall convict. But he (the tall convict) had thought of that too. He had had a sweetheart. That is, he had gone to church singings and picnics with her—a girl a year or so younger than he, short-legged, with ripe breasts and a heavy mouth and dull eyes like ripe muscadines, who owned a baking-powder can almost full of ear-rings and brooches and rings bought (or presented at suggestion) from ten-cent stores. Presently he had divulged his plan to her, and there were times later when, musing, the thought occurred to him that possibly if it had not been for her he would not actually have attempted it—this a mere feeling, unworded, since he could not have phrased this either: that who to know what Capone's uncandled bridehood she might not have dreamed to be her destiny and fate, what fast car filled with authentic colored glass and machine guns, running traffic lights. But that was all past and done when the notion first occurred to him, and in the third month of his incarceration she came to see him. She wore ear-rings and a bracelet or so which he had never seen before and it never became quite clear how she had got that far from home, and she cried violently for the first three minutes though presently (and without his ever knowing either exactly how they had got separated or how she had made the acquaintance) he saw her in animated conversation with one of the guards. But she kissed him before she left that evening and said she would return the first chance she got, clinging to him, sweating a little, smelling of scent and soft young female flesh, slightly pneumatic. But she didn't come back though he continued to write to her, and seven months later he got an answer. It was a postcard, a colored lithograph of a Birmingham hotel, a childish X inked heavily across one window, the heavy writing on the reverse slanted and primer-like too: *This is where were honnymonning at. Your friend (Mrs) Vernon Waldrip*

The plump convict stood blinking at the tall one, rapidly and steadily. "Yes, sir," he said. "It's them ten more years that hurt. Ten more years to do without a woman, no woman a tall a fellow wants—" He blinked steadily and rapidly, watching the tall one. The other did not move, jackknifed backward between the two bunks, grave and clean, the cigar burning smoothly and richly in his clean steady hand, the smoke wreathing upward across his face saturnine, humorless, and calm. "Ten more years—"

"Women—!" the tall convict said.

# NOW THAT YOU'VE READ FAULKNER'S
# THE OLD MAN:

On December 10, 1950, William Faulkner of Oxford, Mississippi, self-styled "farmer"—and formerly at one time or another, a postmaster, bookstore clerk, and boiler-room tender—received the Nobel Prize for literature. In his acceptance speech Faulkner deplored the despairing attitude of modern writers. He declared that the human spirit would prevail and urged young writers to write about man's soul, his spirit, his capacity for sacrifice and endurance. A writer, he said, should help man to endure by reminding him of his courage and honor, his compassion, hope, and pride.

To some readers of Faulkner's *The Sound and the Fury, As I Lay Dying, Sanctuary, Light in August, Absalom, Absalom!,* these statements came as a surprise. The major themes in these novels had, to them seemed to be despair, human degradation, man's inability to cope with a mechanized, commercialized society. But such readers had ignored or failed to mark the note of hope in each novel. There is, as Faulkner has said, "always some one person who survives, who triumphs over his fate." Usually, this one person is in the background, overshadowed by involuted, incestuous Southerners living in the past and incapable of coping with the modern commercial world. *Light in August,* for instance, opens and closes with the story of the simple Lena Grove, who plays only a minor role in the rest of the novel. In *Old Man* (1939), however, Faulkner devotes the entire novel to one of those who survive. That the hero of this short novel embodies the virtues which will enable man to endure is clear to any reader, but the reason Faulkner chose a social outcast, a convict, simple and unintelligent, to dramatize his belief that the human spirit will prevail is not clear until *Old Man* is seen in the perspective of Faulkner's background and of his other works.

William Faulkner is a Southerner. According to family legend, his great-grandfather arrived in Ripley, Mississippi, sometime around 1839. He quickly established himself in the community and a short while later became involved in a feud, as a consequence of which he killed two men in self-defense. At the outbreak of the Civil War he raised a volunteer regiment and led it into battle. After the war, Colonel Falkner (the *u* is a recent addition) built a small railroad and wrote *The White Rose of Memphis*, a best selling novel. He died in 1889, eight years before the birth (1897) of his great-grandson and namesake, cut down by the bullet of a former partner. He remains alive, however, as Colonel Sartoris in Faulkner's stories (for example, *The Unvanquished*, 1938) and in his novels, a symbol of the strong men who pioneered the South and of the fine qualities of pre-war plantation society.

Colonel Falkner's son and grandson lived and died in Oxford County, and there his great-grandson still lives in a colonial mansion just outside the town of Oxford. The Southern society into which William Faulkner was born just before the turn of the century was a sick society. A new aggressive commercial group was undermining the social and economic power of the older families, still staggering from the disaster of the Civil War. The moral and social values of the pre-bellum South were struggling with those of the newly entrenched business group, but there was no clear-cut battle and no clear-cut decision. The values of the new society were opportunistic and selfish, but the Old South, for all its admirable code of chivalry, courage, honesty, pride, had allowed a people to be enslaved. The Civil War not only devastated the plantations and the manor houses; it also forced the Southern conscience to admit to itself, even if it could not do so openly, the terrible guilt attendant upon this enslavement—a guilt which chivalric virtues had hitherto helped to keep quiescent.

Faulkner grew up among people who had known and loved the Old South and who, in their hearts and in their stories, kept the past alive. Their children were born into two worlds, the harsh reality of the present and the grand romance of the past. Faulkner listened to the stories and remembered them. "I always write," he has said, "out of my personal experience, out of events I've been present at, out of stories I've heard from people." At an early age he began to entertain his companions with his own stories, but his first literary ambition was to be a poet. ("I think that every novelist is a failed poet.") Though he did not finish high school, he read extensively under the guidance of an educated friend. In 1918, he enlisted in the Canadian Air Force (he was too short for the American), and retained his interest in flying (*Pylon*, 1935) until a brother was killed in a plane the writer owned. After the war, Faulkner returned to Oxford and became something of a town character. The monocle he at that time sported increased the town's astonishment at the young man who preferred doing odd jobs to settling down in a steady position. But Faulkner was determined to become a writer and spent his time reading, and working on his poems. Not until he was in New Orleans, where he had gone to work on a newspaper, did he decide to try writing a novel, *Soldier's Pay* (1926).

In his third novel, *Sartoris* (1929), the story of the son and great-grandson of Colonel Sartoris, Faulkner began to use his own heritage and write about the Southern world which he knew so intimately, understood, loved and hated. Almost all Faulkner's characters are Southerners and almost all his fiction is set in a specific section of the South, Yoknapatawpha, a mythical county approximating Lafayette County, Mississippi. If Faulkner's vision were superficial he would be no more than a first rate regional writer, but his vision is profound: it penetrates beyond the specific and the local. As "the stereopticon condenses into one instantaneous field the myriad minutiae of its scope," Faulkner's novels condense modern society into Yoknapatawpha County. His characters, though Southerners, are images of modern man. Their violence, incest, fear, retreat from life, alcoholism, suicide are symbols of the tragic confusion—produced by conflicting moral values—that Faulkner sees in his contemporaries.

In *The Sound and the Fury* (1929), published immediately after *Sartoris*, he portrays two generations of the Compson family in varying stages of moral degeneration. From the reality of the present, Mr. Compson takes refuge in cynicism and alcohol, Mrs. Compson in a world of fantasy. One of their four children, Benjy, is an idiot; their only daughter, Caddy, is sexually promiscuous; Jason is selfish, corrupt, vicious, having disassociated himself from the past and become a part of the new commercialized society; and Quentin commits suicide.

Quentin idealizes the old traditions of chivalry, honor, and pride, and learns that he cannot apply these values to the present, which is reflected in his sister's immorality. His father's cynical reaction to Caddy's loss of chastity taunts him. Quentin will not believe, with his father, that time levels everything, that his anguish is meaningless and only momentary. Though his suicide is a desperate act, it is also a vain attempt to defy the instability of man's values. But Quentin is no innocent victim. He is tortured by incestuous desires for his sister.

*The Sound and the Fury* was an immediate critical success but not until he published *Sanctuary* (1931) did Faulkner know popular acclaim. In that novel, Temple Drake, the daughter of an old Southern family, is unnaturally violated by the emasculated Popeye, that horrible symbol of a mechanized society. But Temple, like Quentin and like the modern South, is not simply a victim. She has that within her which makes her contribute to her further degradation. Rather than face her own guilt she hands the innocent Goodwin over to the mob to be burned alive.

In *Absalom, Absalom!* (1936), set chronologically earlier than *The Sound and the Fury*, Quentin Compson tries to explain to his Canadian roommate what the South means to him. He tells the story of Thomas Sutpen, a strong, ambitious, courageous man who came to Mississippi with the grand design of forming a dynasty, but who brought tragedy upon his children by his refusal to acknowledge as his son the child of a former wife who had Negro blood. Quentin's combined feeling of love for the kind of people he tells about and hate for what they have done to their descendants is poignantly expressed at the end of the novel when his friend asks him why he hates the South and he answers, "*I don't hate it! I don't hate it! I don't hate it!*"

The violence, which Faulkner uses to symbolize the moral confusion of the modern world, in these novels and in his other fiction, is often misinterpreted. Many readers see only the violence and not its significance and condemn the novels as exaggerated and false pictures of the South and of society at large. Faulkner's work, for obvious reasons, was unpopular for a long time with many people in Oxford, but though the famous novelist could easily have settled in any large city and enjoyed the life of a literary celebrity, he seldom, until recently, left his home town. Even when he worked for Hollywood studios he did most of his script-writing at home.

There is much to keep Faulkner in Oxford. For one thing he is close to the woods where he hunted as a boy and where he discovered the antidote to the moral confusion which was his heritage. That discovery he described explicitly in a short novel, *The Bear* (1940). Ike McCaslin, under the tutelage of Sam Fathers, learns to be a hunter, a man "with the will and hardihood to endure and the humility and skill to survive." Sam Fathers, part Negro, part Chickasaw, is not tainted by the sin of slavery. He is "taintless and incorruptible" and he lives in harmony with Nature, by the simple primitive code of the forest. Ike McCaslin learns the code, gives up his land, the symbol of his moral heritage, and becomes a carpenter. There is no possibility of freeing one's self from inherited guilt, Faulkner seems to be saying, except by cutting through the complexity and confusion of modern life and accepting the codes and the values not of "the wise of the earth because . . . maybe the wise no longer have any heart, but . . . the doomed and lowly of the earth who have nothing else . . . but heart."

The code of the "lowly," Ike McCaslin describes as " 'Courage and honor and pride, and pity and love of justice and of liberty. They all touch the heart, and what the heart holds to becomes truth, as far as we know truth." These values Faulkner further dramatizes in the character of Dilsey, the Negro of *The Sound and the Fury*, who "will endure" because she is brave, honest, and generous, has pity, forbearance and fidelity; in the simple Lena Grove of *Light in August*; and in the protagonist of *Old Man*.

The tall unnamed convict of *Old Man*, who loses his freedom because of his romantic imagination, discovers in prison not only the joy of his muscles as he strains behind the plow, but also a womb-like safety from the confusion of modern society. As he battles the river to complete his mission he becomes a symbol of pristine man, struggling instinctively for survival, motivated by a primitive, natural code of courage, self-respect, and decency.

*Old Man* was published originally with another short novel, *The Wild Palms*. Faulkner alternated sections of the two stories though they had no apparent relation. The book was an experiment in literary counterpoint: the hopeful, positive theme of *Old Man* set against the tragic, negative theme of its companion story. The juxtaposition of the two themes in this book is, actually, no more than an elaboration of the technique Faulkner consistently uses in his novels to interweave his thread of hope into the fabric of despair.

Faulkner's is a complicated, penetrating vision of life and the human personality, and to communicate it he uses a style that captures the uninhibited flow of human thought as it merges past and present, and that also captures the despair, the confusion of modern man. The involuted, often tortuous sentences, the spastic unravelling of the story drag the reader inexorably into Faulkner's world. In *Old Man*, the style carries us as the river carries the tall convict to a world and life beyond the confines of the intellect; it creates the feeling of the river's power, of the tortured physical struggles of the convict, of his inarticulateness.

*Old Man* is not only an excellent example of Faulkner's power as a story-teller, it also reflects his compassion for the human being and his belief in basic moral values. The convict has none of the qualities that make a person socially appealing—wit, charm, grace; all he possesses are the moral virtues of the natural, the "taintless and incorruptible" man—dignity, courage, honor, will—the virtues that allow man to endure.


## FOR FURTHER INFORMATION:

Cleanth Brooks. *William Faulkner: The Yoknapatawpha Country*. Yale University Press: New Haven, 1963.

Hoffman & Vickery (eds.). *William Faulkner: Three Decades of Criticism*. Michigan State University Press: East Lansing, 1960.

Michael Millgate. *The Achievement of William Faulkner*. Random House: New York, 1966.

Olga Vickery. *The Novels of William Faulkner: A Critical Interpretation*. Louisiana State University Press: Baton Rouge, 1959.

Edmond L. Volpe. *A Reader's Guide to William Faulkner*. Farrar, Straus: New York, 1964.

Hyatt Waggoner. *William Faulkner: From Jefferson to the World*. University of Kentucky Press: Lexington, 1959.

# THE STRANGER

## BY ALBERT CAMUS

First published, 1942

# THE STRANGER

## Part One

### CHAPTER I

MOTHER died today. Or, maybe, yesterday; I can't
be sure. The telegram from the Home says: YOUR MOTHER PASSED
AWAY. FUNERAL TOMORROW. DEEP SYMPATHY. Which leaves the matter
doubtful; it could have been yesterday.

The Home for Aged Persons is at Marengo, some fifty miles from
Algiers. With the two-o'clock bus I should get there well before nightfall. Then I can spend the night there, keeping the usual vigil beside
the body, and be back here by tomorrow evening. I have fixed up
with my employer for two days' leave; obviously, under the circumstances, he couldn't refuse. Still, I had an idea he looked annoyed,
and I said, without thinking: "Sorry, sir, but it's not my fault, you
know."

Afterwards it struck me I needn't have said that. I had no reason
to excuse myself; it was up to him to express his sympathy and so
forth. Probably he will do so the day after tomorrow, when he sees
me in black. For the present, it's almost as if Mother weren't really
dead. The funeral will bring it home to me, put an official seal on it,
so to speak. . . .

I took the two-o'clock bus. It was a blazing hot afternoon. I'd
lunched, as usual, at Céleste's restaurant. Everyone was most kind,
and Céleste said to me, "There's no one like a mother." When I left
they came with me to the door. It was something of a rush, getting
away, as at the last moment I had to call in at Emmanuel's place
to borrow his black tie and mourning band. He lost his uncle a few
months ago.

I had to run to catch the bus. I suppose it was my hurrying like that, what with the glare off the road and from the sky, the reek of gasoline, and the jolts, that made me feel so drowsy. Anyhow, I slept most of the way. When I woke I was leaning against a soldier; he grinned and asked me if I'd come from a long way off, and I just nodded, to cut things short. I wasn't in a mood for talking.

The Home is a little over a mile from the village. I went there on foot. I asked to be allowed to see Mother at once, but the door-keeper told me I must see the warden first. He wasn't free, and I had to wait a bit. The doorkeeper chatted with me while I waited; then he led me to the office. The warden was a very small man, with gray hair, and a Legion of Honor rosette in his buttonhole. He gave me a long look with his watery blue eyes. Then we shook hands, and he held mine so long that I began to feel embarrassed. After that he consulted a register on his table, and said:

"Madame Meursault entered the Home three years ago. She had no private means and depended entirely on you."

I had a feeling he was blaming me for something, and started to explain. But he cut me short.

"There's no need to excuse yourself, my boy. I've looked up the record and obviously you weren't in a position to see that she was properly cared for. She needed someone to be with her all the time, and young men in jobs like yours don't get too much pay. In any case, she was much happier in the Home."

I said, "Yes, sir; I'm sure of that."

Then he added: "She had good friends here, you know, old folks like herself, and one gets on better with people of one's own generation. You're much too young; you couldn't have been much of a companion to her."

That was so. When we lived together, Mother was always watching me, but we hardly ever talked. During her first few weeks at the Home she used to cry a good deal. But that was only because she hadn't settled down. After a month or two she'd have cried if she'd been told to leave the Home. Because this, too, would have been a wrench. That was why, during the last year, I seldom went to see her. Also, it would have meant losing my Sunday—not to mention the trouble of going to the bus, getting my ticket, and spending two hours on the journey each way.

The warden went on talking, but I didn't pay much attention. Finally he said:

"Now, I suppose you'd like to see your mother?"

I rose without replying, and he led the way to the door. As we were going down the stairs he explained:

"I've had the body moved to our little mortuary—so as not to upset the other old people, you understand. Every time there's a death here, they're in a nervous state for two or three days. Which means, of course, extra work and worry for our staff."

We crossed a courtyard where there were a number of old men, talking amongst themselves in little groups. They fell silent as we came up with them. Then, behind our backs, the chattering began again. Their voices reminded me of parakeets in a cage, only the sound wasn't quite so shrill. The warden stopped outside the entrance of a small, low building.

"So here I leave you, Monsieur Meursault. If you want me for anything, you'll find me in my office. We propose to have the funeral tomorrow morning. That will enable you to spend the night beside your mother's coffin, as no doubt you would wish to do. Just one more thing; I gathered from your mother's friends that she wished to be buried with the rites of the Church. I've made arrangements for this; but I thought I should let you know."

I thanked him. So far as I knew, my mother, though not a professed atheist, had never given a thought to religion in her life.

I entered the mortuary. It was a bright, spotlessly clean room, with whitewashed walls and a big sky-light. The furniture consisted of some chairs and trestles. Two of the latter stood open in the center of the room and the coffin rested on them. The lid was in place, but the screws had been given only a few turns and their nickeled heads stuck out above the wood, which was stained dark walnut. An Arab woman—a nurse, I supposed—was sitting beside the bier; she was wearing a blue smock and had a rather gaudy scarf wound round her hair.

Just then the keeper came up behind me. He'd evidently been running, as he was a little out of breath.

"We put the lid on, but I was told to unscrew it when you came, so that you could see her."

While he was going up to the coffin I told him not to trouble.

"Eh? What's that?" he exclaimed. "You don't want me to . . . ?"

"No," I said.

He put back the screwdriver in his pocket and stared at me. I realized then that I shouldn't have said, "No," and it made me rather embarrassed. After eying me for some moments he asked:

"Why not?" But he didn't sound reproachful; he simply wanted to know.

"Well, really I couldn't say," I answered.

He began twiddling his white mustache; then, without looking at me, said gently:

"I understand."

He was a pleasant-looking man, with blue eyes and ruddy cheeks. He drew up a chair for me near the coffin, and seated himself just behind. The nurse got up and moved toward the door. As she was going by, the keeper whispered in my ear:

"It's a tumor she has, poor thing."

I looked at her more carefully and I noticed that she had a bandage round her head, just below her eyes. It lay quite flat across the bridge of her nose, and one saw hardly anything of her face except that strip of whiteness.

As soon as she had gone, the keeper rose.

"Now I'll leave you to yourself."

I don't know whether I made some gesture, but instead of going he halted behind my chair. The sensation of someone posted at my back made me uncomfortable. The sun was getting low and the whole room was flooded with a pleasant, mellow light. Two hornets were buzzing overhead, against the skylight. I was so sleepy I could hardly keep my eyes open. Without looking round, I asked the keeper how long he'd been at the Home. "Five years." The answer came so pat that one could have thought he'd been expecting my question.

That started him off, and he became quite chatty. If anyone had told him ten years ago that he'd end his days as doorkeeper at a home at Marengo, he'd never have believed it. He was sixty-four, he said, and hailed from Paris.

When he said that, I broke in. "Ah, you don't come from here?"

I remembered then that, before taking me to the warden, he'd told me something about Mother. He had said she'd have to be buried mighty quickly because of the heat in these parts, especially down in the plain. "At Paris they keep the body for three days, sometimes four." After that he had mentioned that he'd spent the best part of his life in Paris, and could never manage to forget it. "Here," he had said, "things have to go with a rush, like. You've hardly time to get used to the idea that someone's dead, before you're hauled off to the funeral." "That's enough," his wife put in. "You didn't ought to say such things to the poor young gentleman." The old fellow had blushed and begun to apologize. I had told him it was quite all right. As a matter of fact, I found it rather interesting, what he'd been telling me; I hadn't thought of that before.

Now he went on to say that he'd entered the Home as an ordinary inmate. But he was still quite hale and hearty, and when the keeper's job fell vacant, he offered to take it on.

I pointed out that, even so, he was really an inmate like the others, but he wouldn't hear of it. He was "an official, like." I'd been struck before by his habit of saying "they" or, less often, "them old folks," when referring to inmates no older than himself. Still, I could see his point of view. As doorkeeper he had a certain standing, and some authority over the rest of them.

Just then the nurse returned. Night had fallen very quickly; all of a sudden, it seemed, the sky went black above the skylight. The keeper switched on the lamps, and I was almost blinded by the blaze of light.

He suggested I should go to the refectory for dinner, but I wasn't hungry. Then he proposed bringing me a mug of *café au lait*. As I am very partial to *café au lait* I said, "Thanks," and a few minutes later he came back with a tray. I drank the coffee, and then I wanted a cigarette. But I wasn't sure if I should smoke, under the circumstances—in Mother's presence. I thought it over; really it didn't seem to matter, so I offered the keeper a cigarette, and we both smoked.

After a while he started talking again.

"You know, your mother's friends will be coming soon, to keep vigil with you beside the body. We always have a 'vigil' here, when anyone dies. I'd better go and get some chairs and a pot of black coffee."

The glare off the white walls was making my eyes smart, and I asked him if he couldn't turn off one of the lamps. "Nothing doing," he said. They'd arranged the lights like that; either one had them all on or none at all. After that I didn't pay much more attention to him. He went out, brought some chairs, and set them out round the coffin. On one he placed a coffeepot and ten or a dozen cups. Then he sat down facing me, on the far side of Mother. The nurse was at the other end of the room, with her back to me. I couldn't see what she was doing, but by the way her arms moved I guessed that she was knitting. I was feeling very comfortable; the coffee had warmed me up, and through the open door came scents of flowers and breaths of cool night air. I think I dozed off for a while.

I was wakened by an odd rustling in my ears. After having had my eyes closed, I had a feeling that the light had grown even stronger than before. There wasn't a trace of shadow anywhere, and every object, each curve or angle, seemed to score its outline on one's eyes. The old people, Mother's friends, were coming in. I counted ten in all, gliding almost soundlessly through the bleak white glare. None of the chairs creaked when they sat down. Never in my life had I seen anyone so clearly as I saw these people; not a detail of their clothes or features escaped me. And yet I couldn't hear them, and it was hard to believe they really existed.

Nearly all the women wore aprons, and the strings drawn tight round their waists made their big stomachs bulge still more. I'd never yet noticed what big paunches old women usually have. Most of the men, however, were as thin as rakes, and they all carried sticks. What struck me most about their faces was that one couldn't see their eyes, only a dull glow in a sort of nest of wrinkles.

On sitting down, they looked at me, and wagged their heads awkwardly, their lips sucked in between their toothless gums. I couldn't decide if they were greeting me and trying to say something, or if it was due to some infirmity of age. I inclined to think that they were greeting me, after their fashion, but it had a queer effect, seeing all those old fellows grouped round the keeper, solemnly eying me and dandling their heads from side to side. For a moment I had an absurd impression that they had come to sit in judgment on me.

A few minutes later one of the women started weeping. She was in the second row and I couldn't see her face because of another woman in front. At regular intervals she emitted a little choking sob; one had a feeling she would never stop. The others didn't seem to notice. They sat in silence, slumped in their chairs, staring at the coffin or at their walking sticks or any object just in front of them, and never took their eyes off it. And still the woman sobbed. I was rather surprised, as I didn't know who she was. I wanted her to stop crying, but dared not speak to her. After a while the keeper bent toward her and whispered in her ear; but she merely shook her head, mumbled something I couldn't catch, and went on sobbing as steadily as before.

The keeper got up and moved his chair beside mine. At first he kept silent; then, without looking at me, he explained.

"She was devoted to your mother. She says your mother was her only friend in the world, and now she's all alone."

I had nothing to say, and the silence lasted quite a while. Presently the woman's sighs and sobs became less frequent, and, after blowing her nose and snuffling for some minutes, she, too, fell silent.

I'd ceased feeling sleepy, but I was very tired and my legs were aching badly. And now I realized that the silence of these people was telling on my nerves. The only sound was a rather queer one; it came only now and then, and at first I was puzzled by it. However, after listening attentively, I guessed what it was; the old men were sucking at the insides of their cheeks, and this caused the odd, wheezing noises that had mystified me. They were so much absorbed in their thoughts that they didn't know what they were up to. I even had an impression that the dead body in their midst meant nothing at all to them. But now I suspect that I was mistaken about this.

We all drank the coffee, which the keeper handed round. After that, I can't remember much; somehow the night went by. I can recall only one moment; I had opened my eyes and I saw the old men sleeping hunched up on their chairs, with one exception. Resting his chin on his hands clasped round his stick, he was staring hard at me, as if he had been waiting for me to wake. Then I fell asleep again. I woke up after a bit, because the ache in my legs had developed into a sort of cramp.

There was a glimmer of dawn above the skylight. A minute or two later one of the old men woke up and coughed repeatedly. He spat into a big check handkerchief, and each time he spat it sounded as if he were retching. This woke the others, and the keeper told them it was time to make a move. They all got up at once. Their faces were ashen gray after the long, uneasy vigil. To my surprise each of them shook hands with me, as though this night together, in which we hadn't exchanged a word, had created a kind of intimacy between us.

I was quite done in. The keeper took me to his room, and I tidied myself up a bit. He gave me some more "white" coffee, and it seemed to do me good. When I went out, the sun was up and the sky mottled red above the hills between Marengo and the sea. A morning breeze was blowing and it had a pleasant salty tang. There was the promise of a very fine day. I hadn't been in the country for ages, and I caught myself thinking what an agreeable walk I could have had, if it hadn't been for Mother.

As it was, I waited in the courtyard, under a plane tree. I sniffed the smells of the cool earth and found I wasn't sleepy any more.

Then I thought of the other fellows in the office. At this hour they'd be getting up, preparing to go to work; for me this was always the worst hour of the day. I went on thinking, like this, for ten minutes or so; then the sound of a bell inside the building attracted my attention. I could see movements behind the windows; then all was calm again. The sun had risen a little higher and was beginning to warm my feet. The keeper came across the yard and said the warden wished to see me. I went to his office and he got me to sign some document. I noticed that he was in black, with pin-stripe trousers. He picked up the telephone receiver and looked at me.

"The undertaker's men arrived some moments ago, and they will be going to the mortuary to screw down the coffin. Shall I tell them to wait, for you to have a last glimpse of your mother?"

"No," I said.

He spoke into the receiver, lowering his voice.

"That's all right, Figeac. Tell the men to go there now."

He then informed me that he was going to attend the funeral, and I thanked him. Sitting down behind his desk, he crossed his short legs and leaned back. Besides the nurse on duty, he told me, he and I would be the only mourners at the funeral. It was a rule of the Home that inmates shouldn't attend funerals, though there was no objection to letting some of them sit up beside the coffin, the night before.

"It's for their own sakes," he explained, "to spare their feelings. But in this particular instance I've given permission to an old friend of your mother to come with us. His name is Thomas Pérez." The warden smiled. "It's a rather touching little story in its way. He and your mother had become almost inseparable. The other old people used to tease Pérez about having a fiancée. 'When are you going to marry her?' they'd ask. He'd turn it with a laugh. It was a standing joke, in fact. So, as you can guess, he feels very badly about your mother's death. I thought I couldn't decently refuse him permission to attend the funeral. But, on our medical officer's advice, I forbade him to sit up beside the body last night."

For some time we sat there without speaking. Then the warden got up and went to the window. Presently he said:

"Ah, there's the padre from Marengo. He's a bit ahead of time."

He warned me that it would take us a good three quarters of an hour, walking to the church, which was in the village. Then we went downstairs.

The priest was waiting just outside the mortuary door. With him were two acolytes, one of whom had a censer. The priest was stooping over him, adjusting the length of the silver chain on which it hung. When he saw us he straightened up and said a few words to me, addressing me as, "My son." Then he led the way into the mortuary.

I noticed at once that four men in black were standing behind the coffin and the screws in the lid had now been driven home. At the same moment I heard the warden remark that the hearse had arrived, and the priest starting his prayers. Then everybody made a move. Holding a strip of black cloth, the four men approached the coffin, while the priest, the boys, and myself filed out. A lady I hadn't seen before was standing by the door. "This is Monsieur Meursault," the warden said to her. I didn't catch her name, but I gathered she was a nursing sister attached to the Home. When I was introduced, she bowed, without the trace of a smile on her long, gaunt face. We stood aside from the doorway to let the coffin by; then, following the bearers down a corridor, we came to the front entrance, where a hearse was waiting. Oblong, glossy, varnished black all over, it vaguely reminded me of the pen trays in the office.

Beside the hearse stood a quaintly dressed little man, whose duty it was, I understood, to supervise the funeral, as a sort of master of ceremonies. Near him, looking constrained, almost bashful, was old M. Pérez, my mother's special friend. He wore a soft felt hat with a pudding-basin crown and a very wide brim—he whisked it off the moment the coffin emerged from the doorway—trousers that concertina'd on his shoes, a black tie much too small for his high white double collar. Under a bulbous, pimply nose, his lips were trembling. But what caught my attention most was his ears; pendulous, scarlet ears that showed up like blobs of sealing wax on the pallor of his cheeks and were framed in wisps of silky white hair.

The undertaker's factotum shepherded us to our places, with the priest in front of the hearse, and the four men in black on each side of it. The warden and myself came next, and, bringing up the rear, old Pérez and the nurse.

The sky was already a blaze of light, and the air stoking up rapidly. I felt the first waves of heat lapping my back, and my dark suit made things worse. I couldn't imagine why we waited so long for getting under way. Old Pérez, who had put on his hat, took it off again. I had turned slightly in his direction and was looking at him when the warden started telling me more about him. I remember his saying that old Pérez and my mother used often to have a longish stroll together in the cool of the evening; sometimes they went as far as the village, accompanied by a nurse, of course.

I looked at the countryside, at the long lines of cypresses sloping up toward the skyline and the hills, the hot red soil dappled with vivid green, and here and there a lonely house sharply outlined against the light—and I could understand Mother's feelings. Evenings in these parts must be a sort of mournful solace. Now, in the full glare of the morning sun, with everything shimmering in the heat haze, there was something inhuman, discouraging, about this landscape.

At last we made a move. Only then I noticed that Pérez had a slight limp. The old chap steadily lost ground as the hearse gained speed. One of the men beside it, too, fell back and drew level with me. I was surprised to see how quickly the sun was climbing up the sky, and just then it struck me that for quite a while the air had been throbbing with the hum of insects and the rustle of grass warming up. Sweat was running down my face. As I had no hat I tried to fan myself with my handkerchief.

The undertaker's man turned to me and said something that I didn't catch. At the same time he wiped the crown of his head with a handkerchief that he held in his left hand, while with his right he tilted up his hat. I asked him what he'd said. He pointed upward.

"Sun's pretty bad today, ain't it?"

"Yes," I said.

After a while he asked: "Is it your mother we're burying?"

"Yes," I said again.

"What was her age?"

"Well, she was getting on." As a matter of fact, I didn't know exactly how old she was.

After that he kept silent. Looking back, I saw Pérez limping along some fifty yards behind. He was swinging his big felt hat at arm's length, trying to make the pace. I also had a look at the warden. He was walking with carefully measured steps, economizing every gesture. Beads of perspiration glistened on his forehead, but he didn't wipe them off.

I had an impression that our little procession was moving slightly faster. Wherever I looked I saw the same sun-drenched countryside, and the sky was so dazzling that I dared not raise my eyes. Presently we struck a patch of freshly tarred road. A shimmer of heat played over it and one's feet squelched at each step, leaving bright black gashes. In front, the coachman's glossy black hat looked like a lump of the same sticky substance, poised above the hearse. It gave one a queer, dreamlike impression, that blue-white glare overhead and all this blackness round one: the sleek black of the hearse, the dull black of the men's clothes, and the silvery-black gashes in the road. And then there were the smells, smells of hot leather and horse dung from the hearse, veined with whiffs of incense smoke. What with these and the hangover from a poor night's sleep, I found my eyes and thoughts growing blurred.

I looked back again. Pérez seemed very far away now, almost hidden by the heat haze; then, abruptly, he disappeared altogether. After puzzling over it for a bit, I guessed that he had turned off the road into the fields. Then I noticed that there was a bend of the road a little way ahead. Obviously Pérez, who knew the district well, had taken a short cut, so as to catch up with us. He rejoined us soon after we were round the bend; then began to lose ground again. He took another short cut and met us again farther on; in fact, this happened several times during the next half-hour. But soon I lost interest in his movements; my temples were throbbing and I could hardly drag myself along.

After that everything went with a rush; and also with such precision and matter-of-factness that I remember hardly any details. Except that when we were on the outskirts of the village the nurse said something to me. Her voice took me by surprise; it didn't match her face at all; it was musical and slightly tremulous. What she said was: "If you go too slowly there's the risk of a heatstroke. But, if you go too fast, you perspire, and the cold air in the church gives you a chill." I saw her point; either way one was in for it.

Some other memories of the funeral have stuck in my mind. The old boy's face, for instance, when he caught up with us for the last time, just outside the village. His eyes were streaming with tears, of exhaustion or distress, or both together. But because of the wrinkles they couldn't flow down. They spread out, crisscrossed, and formed a smooth gloss on the old, worn face.

And I can remember the look of the church, the villagers in the street, the red geraniums on the graves, Pérez's fainting fit—he crumpled up like a rag doll—the tawny-red earth pattering on Mother's coffin, the bits of white roots mixed up with it; then more people, voices, the wait outside a café for the bus, the rumble of the engine, and my little thrill of pleasure when we entered the first brightly lit streets of Algiers, and I pictured myself going straight to bed and sleeping twelve hours at a stretch.

## CHAPTER II

On waking I understood why my employer had looked rather cross when I asked for my two days off; it's a Saturday today. I hadn't thought of this at the time; it only struck me when I was getting out of bed. Obviously he had seen that it would mean my getting four days' holiday straight off, and one couldn't expect him to like that. Still, for one thing, it wasn't my fault if Mother was buried yesterday and not today; and then, again, I'd have had my Saturday and Sunday off in any case. But naturally this didn't prevent me from seeing my employer's point.

Getting up was an effort, as I'd been really exhausted by the previous day's experiences. While shaving, I wondered how to spend the morning, and decided that a swim would do me good. So I caught the streetcar that goes down to the harbor.

It was quite like old times; a lot of young people were in the swimming pool, amongst them Marie Cardona, who used to be a typist at the office. I was rather keen on her in those days, and I fancy she liked me, too. But she was with us so short a time that nothing came of it.

While I was helping her to climb on to a raft, I let my hand stray over her breasts. Then she lay flat on the raft, while I trod water. After a moment she turned and looked at me. Her hair was over her eyes and she was laughing. I clambered up on to the raft, beside her. The air was pleasantly warm, and, half jokingly, I let my head sink back upon her lap. She didn't seem to mind, so I let it stay there. I had the sky full in my eyes, all blue and gold, and I could feel Marie's stomach rising and falling gently under my head. We must have stayed a good half-hour on the raft, both of us half asleep. When the sun got too hot she dived off and I followed. I caught up with her, put my arm round her waist, and we swam side by side. She was still laughing.

While we were drying ourselves on the edge of the swimming pool she said: "I'm browner than you." I asked her if she'd come to the movies with me that evening. She laughed again and said, "Yes," if I'd take her to the comedy everybody was talking about, the one with Fernandel in it.

When we had dressed, she stared at my black tie and asked if I was in mourning. I explained that my mother had died. "When?" she asked, and I said, "Yesterday." She made no remark, though I thought she shrank away a little. I was just going to explain to her that it wasn't my fault, but I checked myself, as I remembered having said the same thing to my employer, and realizing then it sounded rather foolish. Still, foolish or not, somehow one can't help feeling a bit guilty, I suppose.

Anyhow, by evening Marie had forgotten all about it. The film was funny in parts, but some of it was downright stupid. She pressed her leg against mine while we were in the picture house, and I was fondling her breast. Toward the end of the show I kissed her, but rather clumsily. Afterward she came back with me to my place.

When I woke up, Marie had gone. She'd told me her aunt expected her first thing in the morning. I remembered it was a Sunday, and that put me off; I've never cared for Sundays. So I turned my head and lazily sniffed the smell of brine that Marie's head had left on the pillow. I slept until ten. After that I stayed in bed until noon, smoking cigarettes. I decided not to lunch at Céleste's restaurant as I usually did; they'd be sure to pester me with questions, and I dislike being questioned. So I fried some eggs and ate them off the pan. I did without bread as there wasn't any left, and I couldn't be bothered going down to buy it.

After lunch I felt at loose ends and roamed about the little flat. It suited us well enough when Mother was with me, but now that I was by myself it was too large and I'd moved the dining table into my bedroom. That was now the only room I used; it had all the furniture I needed: a brass bedstead, a dressing table, some cane chairs whose seats had more or less caved in, a wardrobe with a tarnished mirror. The rest of the flat was never used, so I didn't trouble to look after it.

A bit later, for want of anything better to do, I picked up an old newspaper that was lying on the floor and read it. There was an advertisement of Kruschen Salts and I cut it out and pasted it into an album where I keep things that amuse me in the papers. Then I washed my hands and, as a last resource, went out on to the balcony.

My bedroom overlooks the main street of our district. Though it was a fine afternoon, the paving blocks were black and glistening.

What few people were about seemed in an absurd hurry. First of all there came a family going for their Sunday-afternoon walk; two small boys in sailor suits, with short trousers hardly down to their knees, and looking rather uneasy in their Sunday best; then a little girl with a big pink bow and black patent-leather shoes. Behind them was their mother, an enormously fat woman in a brown silk dress, and their father, a dapper little man, whom I knew by sight. He had a straw hat, a walking stick, and a butterfly tie. Seeing him beside his wife, I understood why people said he came of a good family and had married beneath him.

Next came a group of young fellows, the local "bloods," with sleek oiled hair, red ties, coats cut very tight at the waist, braided pockets, and square-toed shoes. I guessed they were going to one of the big theaters in the center of the town. That was why they had started out so early and were hurrying to the streetcar stop, laughing and talking at the top of their voices.

After they had passed, the street gradually emptied. By this time all the matinees must have begun. Only a few shopkeepers and cats remained about. Above the sycamores bordering the road the sky was cloudless, but the light was soft. The tobacconist on the other side of the street brought a chair out on to the pavement in front of his door and sat astride it, resting his arms on the back. The streetcars which a few minutes before had been crowded were now almost empty. In the little café, Chez Pierrot, beside the tobacconist's, the waiter was sweeping up the sawdust in the empty restaurant. A typical Sunday afternoon. . . .

I turned my chair round and seated myself like the tobacconist, as it was more comfortable that way. After smoking a couple of cigarettes I went back to the room, got a tablet of chocolate, and returned to the window to eat it. Soon after, the sky clouded over, and I thought a summer storm was coming. However, the clouds gradually lifted. All the same, they had left in the street a sort of threat of rain, which made it darker. I stayed watching the sky for quite a while.

At five there was a loud clanging of streetcars. They were coming from the stadium in our suburb where there had been a football match. Even the back platforms were crowded and people were standing on the steps. Then another streetcar brought back the teams. I knew they were the players by the little suitcase each man carried. They were bawling out their team song, "Keep the ball rolling, boys." One of them looked up at me and shouted, "We licked them!" I waved my hand and called back, "Good work!" From now on there was a steady stream of private cars.

The sky had changed again; a reddish glow was spreading up beyond the housetops. As dusk set in, the street grew more crowded. People were returning from their walks, and I noticed the dapper little man with the fat wife among the passers-by. Children were whimpering and trailing wearily after their parents. After some minutes the local picture houses disgorged their audiences. I noticed that the young fellows coming from them were taking longer strides and gesturing more vigorously than at ordinary times; doubtless the picture they'd been seeing was of the wild-West variety. Those who had been to the picture houses in the middle of the town came a little later, and looked more sedate, though a few were still laughing. On the whole, however, they seemed languid and exhausted. Some of them remained loitering in the street under my window. A group of girls came by, walking arm in arm. The young men under my window swerved so as to brush against them, and shouted humorous remarks, which made the girls turn their heads and giggle. I recognized them as girls from my part of the town, and two or three of them, whom I knew, looked up and waved to me.

Just then the street lamps came on, all together, and they made the stars that were beginning to glimmer in the night sky paler still. I felt my eyes getting tired, what with the lights and all the movement I'd been watching in the street. There were little pools of brightness under the lamps, and now and then a streetcar passed, lighting up a girl's hair, or a smile, or a silver bangle.

Soon after this, as the streetcars became fewer and the sky showed velvety black above the trees and lamps, the street grew emptier, almost imperceptibly, until a time came when there was nobody to be seen and a cat, the first of the evening, crossed, unhurrying, the deserted street.

It struck me that I'd better see about some dinner. I had been leaning so long on the back of my chair, looking down, that my neck hurt when I straightened myself up. I went down, bought some bread and spaghetti, did my cooking, and ate my meal standing. I'd intended to smoke another cigarette at my window, but the night had turned rather chilly and I decided against it. As I was coming back, after shutting the window, I glanced at the mirror and saw reflected in it a corner of my table with my spirit lamp and some bits of bread beside it. It occurred to me that somehow I'd got through another Sunday, that Mother now was buried, and tomorrow I'd be going back to work as usual. Really, nothing in my life had changed.

## CHAPTER III

I had a busy morning in the office. My employer was in a good humor. He even inquired if I wasn't too tired, and followed it up by asking what Mother's age was. I thought a bit, then answered, "Round about sixty," as I didn't want to make a blunder. At which he looked relieved—why, I can't imagine—and seemed to think that closed the matter.

There was a pile of bills of lading waiting on my desk, and I had to go through them all. Before leaving for lunch I washed my hands. I always enjoyed doing this at midday. In the evening it was less pleasant, as the roller towel, after being used by so many people, was sopping wet. I once brought this to my employer's notice. It was regrettable, he agreed—but, to his mind, a mere detail. I left the office building a little later than usual, at half-past twelve, with Emmanuel, who works in the Forwarding Department. Our building overlooks the sea, and we paused for a moment on the steps to look at the shipping in the harbor. The sun was scorching hot. Just then a big truck came up, with a din of chains and backfires from the engine, and Emmanuel suggested we should try to jump it. I started to run. The truck was well away, and we had to chase it for quite a distance. What with the heat and the noise from the engine, I felt half dazed. All I was conscious of was our mad rush along the water front, among cranes and winches, with dark hulls of ships alongside and masts swaying in the offing. I was the first to catch up with the truck. I took a flying jump, landed safely, and helped Emmanuel to scramble in beside me. We were both of us out of breath, and the bumps of the truck on the roughly laid cobbles made things worse. Emmanuel chuckled, and panted in my ear, "We've made it!"

By the time we reached Céleste's restaurant we were dripping with sweat. Céleste was at his usual place beside the entrance, with his apron bulging on his paunch, his white mustache well to the fore. When he saw me he was sympathetic and "hoped I wasn't feeling too badly." I said, "No," but I was extremely hungry. I ate very quickly and had some coffee to finish up. Then I went to my place and took a short nap, as I'd drunk a glass of wine too many.

When I woke I smoked a cigarette before getting off my bed. I was a bit late and had to run for the streetcar. The office was stifling, and I was kept hard at it all the afternoon. So it came as a relief when we closed down and I was strolling slowly along the wharves in the coolness. The sky was green, and it was pleasant to be out-of-doors after the stuffy office. However, I went straight home, as I had to put some potatoes on to boil.

The hall was dark and, when I was starting up the stairs, I almost bumped into old Salamano, who lived on the same floor as I. As usual, he had his dog with him. For eight years the two had been inseparable. Salamano's spaniel is an ugly brute, afflicted with some skin disease—mange, I suspect; anyhow, it has lost all its hair and its body is covered with brown scabs. Perhaps through living in one small room, cooped up with his dog, Salamano has come to resemble it. His towy hair has gone very thin, and he has reddish blotches on his face. And the dog has developed something of its master's queer hunched-up gait; it always has its muzzle stretched far forward and its nose to the ground. But, oddly enough, though so much alike, they detest each other.

Twice a day, at eleven and six, the old fellow takes his dog for a walk, and for eight years that walk has never varied. You can see them in the rue de Lyon, the dog pulling his master along as hard as he can, till finally the old chap misses a step and nearly falls. Then he beats his dog and calls it names. The dog cowers and lags behind, and it's his master's turn to drag him along. Presently the dog forgets, starts tugging at the leash again, gets another hiding and more abuse. Then they halt on the pavement, the pair of them, and glare at each other; the dog with terror and the man with hatred in his eyes. Every time they're out, this happens. When the dog wants to stop at a lamppost, the old boy won't let him, and drags him on, and the wretched spaniel leaves behind him a trail of little drops. But, if he does it in the room, it means another hiding.

It's been going on like this for eight years, and Céleste always says it's a "crying shame," and something should be done about it; but really one can't be sure. When I met him in the hall, Salamano was bawling at his dog, calling him a bastard, a lousy mongrel, and so forth, and the dog was whining. I said, "Good evening," but the old fellow took no notice and went on cursing. So I thought I'd ask him what the dog had done. Again he didn't answer, but went on shouting, "You bloody cur!" and the rest of it. I couldn't see very clearly, but he seemed to be fixing something on the dog's collar. I raised my voice a little. Without looking round, he mumbled in a sort of suppressed fury: "He's always in the way, blast him!" Then he started up the stairs, but the dog tried to resist and flattened itself out on the floor, so he had to haul it up on the leash, step by step.

Just then another man who lives on my floor came in from the street. The general idea hereabouts is that he's a pimp. But if you ask him what his job is, he says he's a warehouseman. One thing's sure: he isn't popular in our street. Still, he often has a word for me, and drops in sometimes for a short talk in my room, because I listen to him. As a matter of fact, I find what he says quite interesting. So, really I've no reason for freezing him off. His name is Sintès; Raymond Sintès. He's short and thick-set, has a nose like a boxer's, and always dresses very sprucely. He, too, once said to me, referring to Salamano, that it was "a damned shame" and asked me if I wasn't disgusted by the way the old man served his dog. I answered: "No."

We went up the stairs together, Sintès and I, and when I was turning in at my door, he said:

"Look here! How about having some grub with me? I've a black pudding and some wine."

It struck me that this would save my having to cook my dinner, so I said, "Thanks very much."

He, too, has only one room, and a little kitchen without a window. I saw a pink-and-white plaster angel above his bed, and some photos of sporting champions and naked girls pinned to the opposite wall. The bed hadn't been made and the room was dirty. He began by lighting a paraffin lamp; then fumbled in his pocket and produced a rather grimy bandage, which he wrapped round his right hand. I asked him what the trouble was. He told me he'd been having a roughhouse with a fellow who'd annoyed him.

"I'm not one who looks for trouble," he explained, "only I'm a bit short-tempered. That fellow said to me, challenging-like, 'Come down off that streetcar, if you're a man.' I says, 'You keep quiet, I ain't done nothing to you.' Then he said I hadn't any guts. Well, that settled it. I got down off the streetcar and I said to him, 'You better keep your mouth shut, or I'll shut it for you.' 'I'd like to see you try!' says he. Then I gave him one across the face, and laid him out good and proper. After a bit I started to help him get up, but all he did was to kick at me from where he lay. So I gave him one with my knee and a couple more swipes. He was bleeding like a pig when I'd done with him. I asked him if he'd had enough, and he said, 'Yes.'"

Sintès was busy fixing his bandage while he talked, and I was sitting on the bed.

"So you see," he said, "it wasn't my fault; he was asking for it, wasn't he?"

I nodded, and he added:

"As a matter of fact, I rather want to ask your advice about something; it's connected with this business. You've knocked about the world a bit, and I daresay you can help me. And then I'll be your pal for life; I never forget anyone who does me a good turn."

When I made no comment, he asked me if I'd like us to be pals. I replied that I had no objection, and that appeared to satisfy him. He got out the black pudding, cooked it in a frying pan, then laid the table, putting out two bottles of wine. While he was doing this he didn't speak.

We started dinner, and then he began telling me the whole story, hesitating a bit at first.

"There's a girl behind it—as usual. We slept together pretty regular. I was keeping her, as a matter of fact, and she cost me a tidy sum. That fellow I knocked down is her brother."

Noticing that I said nothing, he added that he knew what the neighbors said about him, but it was a filthy lie. He had his principles like everybody else, and a job in a warehouse.

"Well," he said, "to go on with my story . . . I found out one day that she was letting me down." He gave her enough money to keep her going, without extravagance, though; he paid the rent of her room and twenty francs a day for food. "Three hundred francs for rent, and six hundred for her grub, with a little present thrown in now and then, a pair of stockings or whatnot. Say, a thousand francs a month. But that wasn't enough for my fine lady; she was always grumbling that she couldn't make both ends meet with what I gave her. So one day I says to her, 'Look here, why not get a job for a few hours a day? That'd make things easier for me, too. I bought you a new dress this month, I pay your rent and give you twenty francs a day. But you go and waste your money at the café with a pack of girls. You give them coffee and sugar. And, of course, the money comes out of my pocket. I treat you on the square, and that's how you pay me back.' But she wouldn't hear of working, though she kept on saying she couldn't make do with what I gave her. And then one day I found out she was doing me dirt."

He went on to explain that he'd found a lottery ticket in her bag, and, when he asked where the money'd come from to buy it, she wouldn't tell him. Then, another time, he'd found a pawn ticket for two bracelets that he'd never set eyes on.

"So I knew there was dirty work going on, and I told her I'd have nothing more to do with her. But, first, I gave her a good hiding, and I told her some home truths. I said that there was only one thing interested her and that was getting into bed with men whenever she'd the chance. And I warned her straight, 'You'll be sorry one day, my girl, and wish you'd got me back. All the girls in the street, they're jealous of your luck in having me to keep you.'"

He'd beaten her till the blood came. Before that he'd never beaten her. "Well, not hard, anyhow; only affectionately-like. She'd howl a bit, and I had to shut the window. Then, of course, it ended as per usual. But this time I'm done with her. Only, to my mind, I ain't punished her enough. See what I mean?"

He explained that it was about this he wanted my advice. The lamp was smoking, and he stopped pacing up and down the room, to lower the wick. I just listened, without speaking. I'd had a whole bottle of wine to myself and my head was buzzing. As I'd used up my cigarettes I was smoking Raymond's. Some late streetcars passed, and the last noises of the street died off with them. Raymond went on talking. What bored him was that he had "a sort of lech on her" as he called it. But he was quite determined to teach her a lesson.

His first idea, he said, had been to take her to a hotel, and then call in the special police. He'd persuade them to put her on the register as a "common prostitute," and that would make her wild. Then he'd looked up some friends of his in the underworld, fellows who kept tarts for what they could make out of them, but they had practically nothing to suggest. Still, as he pointed out, that sort of thing should have been right up their street; what's the good of being in that line if you don't know how to treat a girl who's let you down? When he told them that, they suggested he should "brand" her. But that wasn't what he wanted, either. It would need a lot of thinking out. . . . But, first, he'd like to ask me something. Before he asked it, though, he'd like to have my opinion of the story he'd been telling, in a general way.

I said I hadn't any, but I'd found it interesting.

Did I think she really had done him dirt?

I had to admit it looked like that. Then he asked me if I didn't think she should be punished and what I'd do if I were in his shoes.

I told him one could never be quite sure how to act in such cases, but I quite understood his wanting her to suffer for it.

I drank some more wine, while Raymond lit another cigarette and began explaining what he proposed to do. He wanted to write her a letter, "a real stinker, that'll get her on the raw," and at the same time make her repent of what she'd done. Then, when she came back, he'd go to bed with her and, just when she was "properly primed up," he'd spit in her face and throw her out of the room. I agreed it wasn't a bad plan; it would punish her, all right.

But, Raymond told me, he didn't feel up to writing the kind of letter that was needed, and that was where I could help. When I didn't say anything, he asked me if I'd mind doing it right away, and I said, "No," I'd have a shot at it.

He drank off a glass of wine and stood up. Then he pushed aside the plates and the bit of cold pudding that was left, to make room on the table. After carefully wiping the oilcloth, he got a sheet of squared paper from the drawer of his bedside table; after that, an envelope, a small red wooden penholder, and a square inkpot with purple ink in it. The moment he mentioned the girl's name I knew she was a Moor.

I wrote the letter. I didn't take much trouble over it, but I wanted to satisfy Raymond, as I'd no reason not to satisfy him. Then I read out what I'd written. Puffing at his cigarette, he listened, nodding now and then. "Read it again, please," he said. He seemed delighted. "That's the stuff," he chuckled. "I could tell you was a brainy sort, old boy, and you know what's what."

At first I hardly noticed that "old boy." It came back to me when he slapped me on the shoulder and said, "So now we're pals, ain't we?" I kept silent and he said it again. I didn't care one way or the other, but as he seemed so set on it, I nodded and said, "Yes."

He put the letter into the envelope and we finished off the wine. Then both of us smoked for some minutes, without speaking. The street was quite quiet, except when now and again a car passed. Finally, I remarked that it was getting late, and Raymond agreed. "Time's gone mighty fast this evening," he added, and in a way that was true. I wanted to be in bed, only it was such an effort making a move. I must have looked tired, for Raymond said to me, "You mustn't let things get you down." At first I didn't catch his meaning. Then he explained that he had heard of my mother's death; anyhow, he said, that was something bound to happen one day or another. I appreciated that, and told him so.

When I rose, Raymond shook hands very warmly, remarking that men always understood each other. After closing the door behind me I lingered for some moments on the landing. The whole building was as quiet as the grave, a dank, dark smell rising from the well hole of the stairs. I could hear nothing but the blood throbbing in my ears, and for a while I stood still, listening to it. Then the dog began to moan in old Salamano's room, and through the sleep-bound house the little plaintive sound rose slowly, like a flower growing out of the silence and the darkness.

## CHAPTER IV

I had a busy time in the office throughout the week. Raymond dropped in once to tell me he'd sent off the letter. I went to the pictures twice with Emmanuel, who doesn't always understand what's happening on the screen and asks me to explain it. Yesterday was Saturday, and Marie came as we'd arranged. She had a very pretty dress, with red and white stripes, and leather sandals, and I couldn't take my eyes off her. One could see the outline of her firm little breasts, and her sun-tanned face was like a velvety brown flower. We took the bus and went to a beach I know, some miles out of Algiers. It's just a strip of sand between two rocky spurs, with a line of rushes at the back, along the tide line. At four o'clock the sun wasn't too hot, but the water was pleasantly tepid, and small, languid ripples were creeping up the sand.

Marie taught me a new game. The idea was, while one swam, to suck in the spray off the waves and, when one's mouth was full of foam, to lie on one's back and spout it out against the sky. It made a sort of frothy haze that melted into the air or fell back in a warm shower on one's cheeks. But very soon my mouth was smarting with all the salt I'd drawn in; then Marie came up and hugged me in the water, and pressed her mouth to mine. Her tongue cooled my lips, and we let the waves roll us about for a minute or two before swimming back to the beach.

When we had finished dressing, Marie looked hard at me. Her eyes were sparkling. I kissed her; after that neither of us spoke for quite a while. I pressed her to my side as we scrambled up the foreshore. Both of us were in a hurry to catch the bus, get back to my place, and tumble on to the bed. I'd left my window open, and it was pleasant to feel the cool night air flowing over our sunburned bodies.

Marie said she was free next morning, so I proposed she should have luncheon with me. She agreed, and I went down to buy some meat. On my way back I heard a woman's voice in Raymond's room. A little later old Salamano started grumbling at his dog and presently there was a sound of boots and paws on the wooden stairs; then, 'Filthy brute! Get on, you cur!" and the two of them went out into the street. I told Marie about the old man's habits, and it made her laugh. She was wearing one of my pajama suits, and had the sleeves rolled up. When she laughed I wanted her again. A moment later she asked me if I loved her. I said that sort of question had no meaning, really; but I supposed I didn't. She looked sad for a bit, but when we were getting our lunch ready she brightened up and started laughing, and when she laughs I always want to kiss her. It was just then that the row started in Raymond's room.

First we heard a woman saying something in a high-pitched voice; then Raymond bawling at her, "You let me down, you bitch! I'll learn you to let me down!" There came some thuds, then a piercing scream—it made one's blood run cold—and in a moment there was a crowd of people on the landing. Marie and I went out to see. The woman was still screaming and Raymond still knocking her about. Marie said, wasn't it horrible! I didn't answer anything. Then she asked me to go and fetch a policeman, but I told her I didn't like policemen. However, one turned up presently; the lodger on the second floor, a plumber, came up with him. When he banged on the door the noise stopped inside the room. He knocked again, and, after a moment the woman started crying, and Raymond opened the door. He had a cigarette dangling from his underlip and a rather sickly smile.

"Your name?" Raymond gave his name. "Take that cigarette out of your mouth when you're talking to me," the policeman said gruffly. Raymond hesitated, glanced at me, and kept the cigarette in his mouth. The policeman promptly swung his arm and gave him a good hard smack on the left cheek. The cigarette shot from his lips and dropped a yard away. Raymond made a wry face, but said nothing for a moment. Then in a humble tone he asked if he mightn't pick up his cigarette.

The officer said, "Yes," and added: "But don't you forget next time that we don't stand for any nonsense, not from guys like you."

Meanwhile the girl went on sobbing and repeating: "He hit me, the coward. He's a pimp."

"Excuse me, officer," Raymond put in, "but is that in order, calling a man a pimp in the presence of witnesses?"

The policeman told him to shut his trap.

Raymond then turned to the girl. "Don't you worry, my pet. We'll meet again."

"That's enough," the policeman said, and told the girl to go away. Raymond was to stay in his room till summoned to the police station. "You ought to be ashamed of yourself," the policeman added, "getting so tight you can't stand steady. Why, you're shaking all over!"

"I'm not tight," Raymond explained. "Only when I see you standing there and looking at me, I can't help trembling. That's only natural."

Then he closed his door, and we all went away. Marie and I finished getting our lunch ready. But she hadn't any appetite, and I ate nearly all. She left at one, and then I had a nap.

Toward three there was a knock at my door and Raymond came in. He sat down on the edge of my bed and for a minute or two said nothing. I asked him how it had gone off. He said it had all gone quite smoothly at first, as per program, only then she'd slapped his face and he'd seen red, and started thrashing her. As for what happened after that, he needn't tell me, as I was there.

"Well," I said, "you taught her a lesson, all right, and that's what you wanted, isn't it?"

He agreed, and pointed out that whatever the police did, that wouldn't change the fact she'd had her punishment. As for the police, he knew exactly how to handle them. But he'd like to know if I'd expected him to return the blow when the policeman hit him.

I told him I hadn't expected anything whatsoever and, anyhow, I had no use for the police. Raymond seemed pleased and asked if I'd like to come out for a stroll with him. I got up from the bed and started brushing my hair. Then Raymond said that what he really wanted was for me to act as his witness. I told him I had no objection; only I didn't know what he expected me to say.

"It's quite simple," he replied. "You've only got to tell them that the girl had let me down."

So I agreed to be his witness.

We went out together, and Raymond stood me a brandy in a café. Then we had a game of billiards; it was a close game and I lost by only a few points. After that he proposed going to a brothel, but I refused; I didn't feel like it. As we were walking slowly back he told me how pleased he was at having paid out his mistress so satisfactorily. He made himself extremely amiable to me, and I quite enjoyed our walk.

When we were nearly home I saw old Salamano on the doorstep; he seemed very excited. I noticed that his dog wasn't with him. He was turning like a teetotum, looking in all directions, and sometimes peering into the darkness of the hall with his little bloodshot eyes. Then he'd mutter something to himself and start gazing up and down the street again.

Raymond asked him what was wrong, but he didn't answer at once. Then I heard him grunt, "The bastard! The filthy cur!" When I asked him where his dog was, he scowled at me and snapped out, "Gone!" A moment later, all of a sudden, he launched out into it.

"I'd taken him to the Parade Ground as usual. There was a fair on, and you could hardly move for the crowd. I stopped at one of the booths to look at the Handcuff King. When I turned to go, the dog was gone. I'd been meaning to get a smaller collar, but I never thought the brute could slip it and get away like that."

Raymond assured him the dog would find its way home, and told him stories of dogs that had traveled miles and miles to get back to their masters. But this seemed to make the old fellow even more worried than before.

"Don't you understand, they'll do away with him; the police, I mean. It's not likely anyone will take him in and look after him; with all those scabs he puts everybody off."

I told him that there was a pound at the police station, where stray dogs are taken. His dog was certain to be there and he could get it back on payment of a small charge. He asked me how much the charge was, but there I couldn't help him. Then he flew into a rage again.

"Is it likely I'd give money for a mutt like that? No damned fear! They can kill him, for all I care." And he went on calling his dog the usual names.

Raymond gave a laugh and turned into the hall. I followed him upstairs, and we parted on the landing. A minute or two later I heard Salamano's footsteps and a knock on my door.

When I opened it, he halted for a moment in the doorway. "Excuse me . . . I hope I'm not disturbing you."

I asked him in, but he shook his head. He was staring at his toe caps, and the gnarled old hands were trembling. Without meeting my eyes, he started talking.

"They won't really take him from me, will they, Monsieur Meursault? Surely they wouldn't do a thing like that. If they do—I don't know what will become of me."

I told him that, so far as I knew, they kept stray dogs in the pound for three days, waiting for their owners to call for them. After that they disposed of the dogs as they thought fit.

He stared at me in silence for a moment, then said, "Good evening." After that I heard him pacing up and down his room for quite a while. Then his bed creaked. Through the wall there came to me a little wheezing sound, and I guessed that he was weeping. For some reason, I don't know what, I began thinking of Mother. But I had to get up early next day; so, as I wasn't feeling hungry, I did without supper, and went straight to bed.

## CHAPTER V

Raymond rang me up at the office. He said that a friend of his—to whom he'd spoken about me—invited me to spend next Sunday at his little seaside bungalow just outside Algiers. I told him I'd have been delighted; only I had promised to spend Sunday with a girl. Raymond promptly replied that she could come, too. In fact, his friend's wife would be very pleased not to be the only woman in a party of men.

I'd have liked to hang up at once, as my employer doesn't approve of my using the office phone for private calls. But Raymond asked me to hold on; he had something else to tell me, and that was why he'd rung me up, though he could have waited till the evening to pass on the invitation.

"It's like this," he said. "I've been shadowed all the morning by some Arabs. One of them's the brother of that girl I had the row with. If you see him hanging round the house when you come back, pass me the word."

I promised to do so.

Just then my employer sent for me. For a moment I felt uneasy, as I expected he was going to tell me to stick to my work and not waste time chattering with friends over the phone. However, it was nothing of the kind. He wanted to discuss a project he had in view, though so far he'd come to no decision. It was to open a branch at Paris, so as to be able to deal with the big companies on the spot, without postal delays, and he wanted to know if I'd like a post there.

"You're a young man," he said, "and I'm pretty sure you'd enjoy living in Paris. And, of course, you could travel about France for some months in the year."

I told him I was quite prepared to go; but really I didn't care much one way or the other.

He then asked if a "change of life," as he called it, didn't appeal to me, and I answered that one never changed his way of life; one life was as good as another, and my present one suited me quite well.

At this he looked rather hurt, and told me that I always shilly-shallied, and that I lacked ambition—a grave defect, to his mind, when one was in business.

I returned to my work. I'd have preferred not to vex him, but I saw no reason for "changing my life." By and large it wasn't an unpleasant one. As a student I'd had plenty of ambition of the kind he meant. But, when I had to drop my studies, I very soon realized all that was pretty futile.

Marie came that evening and asked me if I'd marry her. I said I didn't mind; if she was keen on it, we'd get married.

Then she asked me again if I loved her. I replied, much as before, that her question meant nothing or next to nothing—but I supposed I didn't.

"If that's how you feel," she said, "why marry me?"

I explained that it had no importance really, but, if it would give her pleasure, we could get married right away. I pointed out that, anyhow, the suggestion came from her; as for me, I'd merely said, "Yes."

Then she remarked that marriage was a serious matter.

To which I answered: "No."

She kept silent after that, staring at me in a curious way. Then she asked:

"Suppose another girl had asked you to marry her—I mean, a girl you liked in the same way as you like me—would you have said 'Yes' to her, too?"

"Naturally."

Then she said she wondered if she really loved me or not. I, of course, couldn't enlighten her as to that. And, after another silence, she murmured something about my being "a queer fellow." "And

I daresay that's why I love you," she added. "But maybe that's why one day I'll come to hate you."

To which I had nothing to say, so I said nothing.

She thought for a bit, then started smiling and, taking my arm, repeated that she was in earnest; she really wanted to marry me.

"All right," I answered. "We'll get married whenever you like." I then mentioned the proposal made by my employer, and Marie said she'd love to go to Paris.

When I told her I'd lived in Paris for a while, she asked me what it was like.

"A dingy sort of town, to my mind. Masses of pigeons and dark courtyards. And the people have washed-out, white faces."

Then we went for a walk all the way across the town by the main streets. The women were good-lookers, and I asked Marie if she, too, noticed this. She said, "Yes," and that she saw what I meant. After that we said nothing for some minutes. However, as I didn't want her to leave me, I suggested we should dine together at Céleste's. She'd have loved to dine with me, she said, only she was booked up for the evening. We were near my place, and I said, "Au revoir, then."

She looked me in the eyes.

"Don't you want to know what I'm doing this evening?"

I did want to know, but I hadn't thought of asking her, and I guessed she was making a grievance of it. I must have looked embarrassed, for suddenly she started laughing and bent toward me, pouting her lips for a kiss.

I went by myself to Céleste's. When I had just started my dinner an odd-looking little woman came in and asked if she might sit at my table. Of course she might. She had a chubby face like a ripe apple, bright eyes, and moved in a curiously jerky way, as if she were on wires. After taking off her close-fitting jacket she sat down and started studying the bill of fare with a sort of rapt attention. Then she called Céleste and gave her order, very fast but quite distinctly; one didn't lose a word. While waiting for the hors d'oeuvre she opened her bag, took out a slip of paper and a pencil, and added up the bill in advance. Diving into her bag again, she produced a purse and took from it the exact sum, plus a small tip, and placed it on the cloth in front of her.

Just then the waiter brought the hors d'oeuvre, which she proceeded to wolf down voraciously. While waiting for the next course, she produced another pencil, this time a blue one, from her bag, and the radio magazine for the coming week, and started making ticks against almost all the items of the daily programs. There were a dozen pages in the magazine, and she continued studying them closely throughout the meal. When I'd finished mine she was still ticking off items with the same meticulous attention. Then she rose, put on her jacket again with the same abrupt, robotlike gestures, and walked briskly out of the restaurant.

Having nothing better to do, I followed her for a short distance. Keeping on the curb of the pavement, she walked straight ahead, never swerving or looking back, and it was extraordinary how fast she covered the ground, considering her smallness. In fact, the pace was too much for me, and I soon lost sight of her and turned back homeward. For a moment the "little robot" (as I thought of her) had much impressed me, but I soon forgot about her.

As I was turning in at my door I ran into old Salamano. I asked him into my room, and he informed me that his dog was definitely lost. He'd been to the pound to inquire, but it wasn't there, and the staff told him it had probably been run over. When he asked them whether it was any use inquiring about it at the police station, they said the police had more important things to attend to than keeping records of stray dogs run over in the streets. I suggested he should get another dog, but, reasonably enough, he pointed out that he'd become used to this one, and it wouldn't be the same thing.

I was seated on my bed, with my legs up, and Salamano on a chair beside the table, facing me, his hands spread on his knees. He had kept on his battered felt hat and was mumbling away behind his draggled yellowish mustache. I found him rather boring, but I had nothing to do and didn't feel sleepy. So, to keep the conversation going, I asked some questions about his dog—how long he had had it and so forth. He told me he had got it soon after his wife's death. He'd married rather late in life. When a young man, he wanted to go on the stage; during his military service he'd often played in the regimental theatricals and acted rather well, so everybody said. However, finally, he had taken a job in the railway, and he didn't regret it, as now he had a small pension. He and his wife had never hit it off very well, but they'd got used to each other, and when she died he felt lonely. One of his mates on the railway whose bitch had just had pups had offered him one, and he had taken it, as a companion. He'd had to feed it from the bottle at first. But, as a dog's life is shorter than a man's, they'd grown old together, so to speak.

"He was a cantankerous brute," Salamano said. "Now and then we had some proper set-tos, he and I. But he was a good mutt all the same."

I said he looked well bred, and that evidently pleased the old man.

"Ah, but you should have seen him before his illness!" he said. "He had a wonderful coat; in fact, that was his best point, really. I tried hard to cure him; every mortal night after he got that skin disease I rubbed an ointment in. But his real trouble was old age, and there's no curing that."

Just then I yawned, and the old man said he'd better make a move. I told him he could stay, and that I was sorry about what had happened to his dog. He thanked me, and mentioned that my mother had been very fond of his dog. He referred to her as "your poor mother," and was afraid I must be feeling her death terribly. When I said nothing he added hastily and with a rather embarrassed air that some of the people in the street said nasty things about me because I'd sent my mother to the Home. But he, of course, knew better; he knew how devoted to my mother I had always been.

I answered—why, I still don't know—that it surprised me to learn I'd produced such a bad impression. As I couldn't afford to keep her here, it seemed the obvious thing to do, to send her to a home. "In any case," I added, "for years she'd never had a word to say to me, and I could see she was moping, with no one to talk to."

"Yes," he said, "and at a home one makes friends, anyhow."

He got up, saying it was high time for him to be in bed, and added that life was going to be a bit of a problem for him, under the new conditions. For the first time since I'd known him he held out his hand to me—rather shyly, I thought—and I could feel the scales on his skin. Just as he was going out of the door, he turned and, smiling a little, said:

"Let's hope the dogs won't bark again tonight. I always think it's mine I hear. . . ."

## CHAPTER VI

It was an effort waking up that Sunday morning; Marie had to jog my shoulders and shout my name. As we wanted to get into the water early, we didn't trouble about breakfast. My head was aching slightly and my first cigarette had a bitter taste. Marie told me I looked like a mourner at a funeral, and I certainly did feel very limp. She was wearing a white dress and had her hair loose. I told her she looked quite ravishing like that, and she laughed happily.

On our way out we banged on Raymond's door, and he shouted that he'd be with us in a jiffy. We went down to the street and, because of my being rather under the weather and our having kept the blind down in my room, the glare of the morning sun hit me in the eyes like a clenched fist.

Marie, however, was almost dancing with delight, and kept repeating, "What a heavenly day!" After a few minutes I was feeling better, and noticed that I was hungry. I mentioned this to Marie, but she paid no attention. She was carrying an oilcloth bag in which she had stowed our bathing kit and a towel. Presently we heard Raymond shutting his door. He was wearing blue trousers, a short-sleeved white shirt, and a straw hat. I noticed that his forearms were rather hairy, but the skin was very white beneath. The straw hat made Marie giggle. Personally, I was rather put off by his getup. He seemed in high spirits and was whistling as he came down the stairs. He greeted me with, "Hello, old boy!" and addressed Marie as "Mademoiselle."

On the previous evening we had visited the police station, where I gave evidence for Raymond—about the girl's having been false to him. So they let him off with a warning. They didn't check my statement.

After some talk on the doorstep we decided to take the bus. The beach was within easy walking distance, but the sooner we got there the better. Just as we were starting for the bus stop, Raymond plucked my sleeve and told me to look across the street. I saw some Arabs lounging against the tobacconist's window. They were staring at us silently, in the special way these people have—as if we were blocks of stone or dead trees. Raymond whispered that the second Arab from the left was "his man," and I thought he looked rather worried. However, he assured me that all that was ancient history. Marie, who hadn't followed his remarks, asked, "What is it?"

I explained that those Arabs across the way had a grudge against Raymond. She insisted on our going at once. Then Raymond laughed, and squared his shoulders. The young lady was quite right, he said. There was no point in hanging about here. Halfway to the bus stop he glanced back over his shoulder and said the Arabs weren't following. I, too, looked back. They were exactly as before, gazing in the same vague way at the spot where we had been.

When we were in the bus, Raymond, who now seemed quite at ease, kept making jokes to amuse Marie. I could see he was attracted by her, but she had hardly a word for him. Now and again she would catch my eye and smile.

We alighted just outside Algiers. The beach is not far from the bus stop; one has only to cross a patch of highland, a sort of plateau, which overlooks the sea and shelves down steeply to the sands. The ground here was covered with yellowish pebbles and wild lilies that showed snow-white against the blue of the sky, which had already the hard, metallic glint it gets on very hot days. Marie amused herself swishing her bag against the flowers and sending the petals showering in all directions. Then we walked between two rows of little houses with wooden balconies and green or white palings. Some of them were half hidden in clumps of tamarisks; others rose naked from the stony plateau. Before we came to the end of it, the sea was in full view; it lay smooth as a mirror, and in the distance a big headland jutted out over its black reflection. Through the still air came the faint buzz of a motor engine and we saw a fishing boat very far out, gliding almost imperceptibly across the dazzling smoothness.

Marie picked some rock irises. Going down the steep path leading to the sea, we saw some bathers already on the sands.

Raymond's friend owned a small wooden bungalow at the near end of the beach. Its back rested against the cliffside, while the front stood on piles, which the water was already lapping. Raymond introduced us to his friend, whose name was Masson. He was tall, broad-shouldered, and thick-set; his wife was a plump, cheerful little woman who spoke with a Paris accent.

Masson promptly told us to make ourselves at home. He had gone out fishing, he said, first thing in the morning, and there would be fried fish for lunch. I congratulated him on his little bungalow, and he said he always spent his week ends and holidays here. "With the missus, needless to say," he added. I glanced at her, and noticed that she and Marie seemed to be getting on well together; laughing and chattering away. For the first time, perhaps, I seriously considered the possibility of my marrying her.

Masson wanted to have a swim at once, but his wife and Raymond were disinclined to move. So only the three of us, Marie, Masson, and myself, went down to the beach. Marie promptly plunged in, but Masson and I waited for a bit. He was rather slow of speech and had, I noticed, a habit of saying "and what's more" between his phrases—even when the second added nothing really to the first. Talking of Marie, he said: "She's an awfully pretty girl, and what's more, charming."

But I soon ceased paying attention to this trick of his; I was basking in the sunlight, which, I noticed, was making me feel much better. The sand was beginning to stoke up underfoot and, though I was eager for a dip, I postponed it for a minute or two more. At last I said to Masson: "Shall we go in now?" and plunged. Masson walked in gingerly and only began to swim when he was out of his depth. He swam hand over hand and made slow headway, so I left him behind and caught up with Marie. The water was cold and I felt all the better for it. We swam a long way out, Marie and I, side by side, and it was pleasant feeling how our movements matched, hers and mine, and how we were both in the same mood, enjoying every moment.

Once we were out in the open, we lay on our backs and, as I gazed up at the sky, I could feel the sun drawing up the film of salt water on my lips and cheeks. We saw Masson swim back to the beach and slump down on the sand under the sun. In the distance he looked enormous, like a stranded whale. Then Marie proposed that we should swim tandem. She went ahead and I put my arms round her waist from behind and while she drew me forward with her arm strokes, I kicked out behind to help us on.

That sound of little splashes had been in my ears for so long that I began to feel I'd had enough of it. So I let go of Marie and swam back at an easy pace, taking long, deep breaths. When I made the beach I stretched myself belly downward beside Masson, resting my face on the sand. I told him "it was fine" here, and he agreed. Presently Marie came back. I raised my head to watch her approach. She was glistening with brine and holding her hair back. Then she lay down beside me, and what with the combined warmth of our bodies and the sun, I felt myself dropping off to sleep.

After a while Marie tugged my arm and said Masson had gone to his place; it must be nearly lunchtime. I rose at once, as I was feeling hungry, but Marie told me I hadn't kissed her once since the early morning. That was so—though I'd wanted to, several times. "Let's go into the water again," she said, and we ran into the sea and lay flat amongst the ripples for a moment. Then we swam a few strokes, and when we were almost out of our depth she flung her arms round me and hugged me. I felt her legs twining round mine, and my senses tingled.

When we got back, Masson was on the steps of his bungalow, shouting to us to come. I told him I was ravenously hungry, and he promptly turned to his wife and said he'd taken quite a fancy to me. The bread was excellent, and I had my full share of the fish. Then came some steak and potato chips. None of us spoke while eating. Masson drank a lot of wine and kept refilling my glass the moment it was empty. By the time coffee was handed round I was feeling slightly muzzy, and I started smoking one cigarette after another. Masson, Raymond, and I discussed a plan of spending the whole of August on the beach together, sharing expenses.

Suddenly Marie exclaimed: "I say! Do you know the time? It's only half-past eleven!"

We were all surprised at that, and Masson remarked that we'd had a very early lunch, but really lunch was a movable feast, you had it when you felt like it.

This set Marie laughing, I don't know why. I suspect she'd drunk a bit too much.

Then Masson asked if I'd like to come with him for a stroll on the beach.

"My wife always has a nap after lunch," he said. "Personally I find it doesn't agree with me; what I need is a short walk. I'm always telling her it's much better for the health. But, of course, she's entitled to her own opinion."

Marie proposed to stay and help with the washing up. Mme Masson smiled and said that, in that case, the first thing was to get the men out of the way. So we went out together, the three of us.

The light was almost vertical and the glare from the water seared one's eyes. The beach was quite deserted now. One could hear a faint tinkle of knives and forks and crockery in the shacks and bungalows lining the foreshore. Heat was welling up from the rocks, and one could hardly breathe.

At first Raymond and Masson talked of things and people I didn't know. I gathered that they'd been acquainted for some time and had even lived together for a while. We went down to the water's edge and walked along it; now and then a longer wave wet our canvas shoes. I wasn't thinking of anything, as all that sunlight beating down on my bare head made me feel half asleep.

Just then Raymond said something to Masson that I didn't quite catch. But at the same moment I noticed two Arabs in blue dungarees a long way down the beach, coming in our direction. I gave Raymond a look and he nodded, saying, "That's him." We walked steadily on. Masson wondered how they'd managed to track us here. My impression was that they had seen us taking the bus and noticed Marie's oilcloth bathing bag; but I didn't say anything.

Though the Arabs walked quite slowly, they were much nearer already. We didn't change our pace, but Raymond said:

"Listen! If there's a roughhouse, you, Masson, take on the second one. I'll tackle the fellow who's after me. And you, Meursault, stand by to help if another one comes up, and lay him out."

I said, "Right," and Masson put his hands in his pockets.

The sand was as hot as fire, and I could have sworn it was glowing red. The distance between us and the Arabs was steadily decreasing. When we were only a few steps away the Arabs halted. Masson and I slowed down, while Raymond went straight up to his man. I couldn't hear what he said, but I saw the native lowering his head, as if to butt him in the chest. Raymond lashed out promptly and shouted to Masson to come. Masson went up to the man he had been marking and struck him twice with all his might. The fellow fell flat into the water and stayed there some seconds with bubbles coming up to the surface round his head. Meanwhile Raymond had been slogging the other man, whose face was streaming with blood. He glanced at me over his shoulder and shouted:

"Just you watch! I ain't finished with him yet!"

"Look out!" I cried. "He's got a knife."

I spoke too late. The man had gashed Raymond's arm and his mouth as well.

Masson sprang forward. The other Arab got up from the water and placed himself behind the fellow with the knife. We didn't dare to move. The two natives backed away slowly, keeping us at bay with the knife and never taking their eyes off us. When they were at a safe distance they swung round and took to their heels. We stood stock-still, with the sunlight beating down on us. Blood was dripping from Raymond's wounded arm, which he was squeezing hard above the elbow.

Masson remarked that there was a doctor who always spent his Sundays here, and Raymond said: "Good. Let's go to him at once." He could hardly get the words out, as the blood from his other wound made bubbles in his mouth.

We each gave him an arm and helped him back to the bungalow. Once we were there he told us the wounds weren't so very deep and he could walk to where the doctor was. Marie had gone quite pale, and Mme Masson was in tears.

Masson and Raymond went off to the doctor's while I was left behind at the bungalow to explain matters to the women. I didn't much relish the task and soon dried up and started smoking, staring at the sea.

Raymond came back at about half-past one, accompanied by Masson. He had his arm bandaged and a strip of sticking plaster on the corner of his mouth. The doctor had assured him it was nothing serious, but he was looking very glum. Masson tried to make him laugh, but without success.

Presently Raymond said he was going for a stroll on the beach. I asked him where he proposed to go, and he mumbled something about "wanting to take the air." We—Masson and I—then said we'd go with him, but he flew into a rage and told us to mind our own business. Masson said we mustn't insist, seeing the state he was in. However, when he went out, I followed him.

It was like a furnace outside, with the sunlight splintering into flakes of fire on the sand and sea. We walked for quite a while, and I had an idea that Raymond had a definite idea where he was going; but probably I was mistaken about this.

At the end of the beach we came to a small stream that had cut a channel in the sand, after coming out from behind a biggish rock. There we found our two Arabs again, lying on the sand in their blue dungarees. They looked harmless enough, as if they didn't bear any malice, and neither made any move when we approached. The man who had slashed Raymond stared at him without speaking. The other man was blowing down a little reed and extracting from it three notes of the scale, which he played over and over again, while he watched us from the corner of an eye.

For a while nobody moved; it was all sunlight and silence except for the tinkle of the stream and those three little lonely sounds. Then Raymond put his hand to his revolver pocket, but the Arabs still didn't move. I noticed the man playing on the reed had his big toes splayed out almost at right angles to his feet.

Still keeping his eyes on his man, Raymond said to me: "Shall I plug him one?"

I thought quickly. If I told him not to, considering the mood he was in, he might very well fly into a temper and use his gun. So I said the first thing that came into my head.

"He hasn't spoken to you yet. It would be a lowdown trick to shoot him like that, in cold blood."

Again, for some moments one heard nothing but the tinkle of the stream and the flute notes weaving through the hot, still air.

"Well," Raymond said at last, "if that's how you feel, I'd better say something insulting, and if he answers back I'll loose off."

"Right," I said. "Only, if he doesn't get out his knife you've no business to fire."

Raymond was beginning to fidget. The Arab with the reed went on playing, and both of them watched all our movements.

"Listen," I said to Raymond. "You take on the fellow on the right, and give me your revolver. If the other one starts making trouble or gets out his knife, I'll shoot."

The sun glinted on Raymond's revolver as he handed it to me. But nobody made a move yet; it was just as if everything had closed in on us so that we couldn't stir. We could only watch each other, never lowering our eyes; the whole world seemed to have come to a standstill on this little strip of sand between the sunlight and the sea, the twofold silence of the reed and stream. And just then it crossed my mind that one might fire, or not fire—and it would come to absolutely the same thing.

Then, all of a sudden, the Arabs vanished; they'd slipped like lizards under cover of the rock. So Raymond and I turned and walked back. He seemed happier, and began talking about the bus to catch for our return.

When we reached the bungalow Raymond promptly went up the wooden steps, but I halted on the bottom one. The light seemed thudding in my head and I couldn't face the effort needed to go up the steps and make myself amiable to the women. But the heat was so great that it was just as bad staying where I was, under that flood of blinding light falling from the sky. To stay, or to make a move—it came to much the same. After a moment I returned to the beach, and started walking.

There was the same red glare as far as eye could reach, and small waves were lapping the hot sand in little, flurried gasps. As I slowly walked toward the boulders at the end of the beach I could feel my temples swelling under the impact of the light. It pressed itself on me, trying to check my progress. And each time I felt a hot blast strike my forehead, I gritted my teeth, I clenched my fists in my trouser pockets and keyed up every nerve to fend off the sun and the dark befuddlement it was pouring into me. Whenever a blade of vivid light shot upward from a bit of shell or broken glass lying on the sand, my jaws set hard. I wasn't going to be beaten, and I walked steadily on.

The small black hump of rock came into view far down the beach. It was rimmed by a dazzling sheen of light and feathery spray, but I was thinking of the cold, clear stream behind it, and longing to hear again the tinkle of running water. Anything to be rid of the glare, the sight of women in tears, the strain and effort—and to retrieve the pool of shadow by the rock and its cool silence!

But when I came nearer I saw that Raymond's Arab had returned. He was by himself this time, lying on his back, his hands behind his head, his face shaded by the rock while the sun beat on the rest of his body. One could see his dungarees steaming in the heat. I was rather taken aback; my impression had been that the incident was closed, and I hadn't given a thought to it on my way here.

On seeing me, the Arab raised himself a little, and his hand went to his pocket. Naturally, I gripped Raymond's revolver in the pocket of my coat. Then the Arab let himself sink back again, but without taking his hand from his pocket. I was some distance off, at least ten yards, and most of the time I saw him as a blurred dark form wobbling in the heat haze. Sometimes, however, I had glimpses of his eyes glowing between the half-closed lids. The sound of the waves was even lazier, feebler, than at noon. But the light hadn't changed; it was pounding as fiercely as ever on the long stretch of sand that ended at the rock. For two hours the sun seemed to have made no progress; becalmed in a sea of molten steel. Far out on the horizon a steamer was passing; I could just make out from the corner of an eye the small black moving patch, while I kept my gaze fixed on the Arab.

It struck me that all I had to do was to turn, walk away, and think no more about it. But the whole beach, pulsing with heat, was pressing on my back. I took some steps toward the stream. The Arab didn't move. After all, there was still some distance between us. Perhaps because of the shadow on his face, he seemed to be grinning at me.

I waited. The heat was beginning to scorch my cheeks; beads of sweat were gathering in my eyebrows. It was just the same sort of heat as at my mother's funeral, and I had the same disagreeable sensations—especially in my forehead, where all the veins seemed to be bursting through the skin. I couldn't stand it any longer, and took another step forward. I knew it was a fool thing to do; I wouldn't get out of the sun by moving on a yard or so. But I took that step, just one step, forward. And then the Arab drew his knife and held it up toward me, athwart the sunlight.

A shaft of light shot upward from the steel, and I felt as if a long, thin blade transfixed my forehead. At the same moment all the sweat that had accumulated in my eyebrows splashed down on my eyelids, covering them with a warm film of moisture. Beneath a veil of brine and tears my eyes were blinded; I was conscious only of the cymbals of the sun clashing on my skull, and, less distinctly, of the keen blade of light flashing up from the knife, scarring my eyelashes, and gouging into my eyeballs.

Then everything began to reel before my eyes, a fiery gust came from the sea, while the sky cracked in two, from end to end, and a great sheet of flame poured down through the rift. Every nerve in my body was a steel spring, and my grip closed on the revolver. The trigger gave, and the smooth underbelly of the butt jogged my palm. And so, with that crisp, whipcrack sound, it all began. I shook off my sweat and the clinging veil of light. I knew I'd shattered the balance of the day, the spacious calm of this beach on which I had been happy. But I fired four shots more into the inert body, on which they left no visible trace. And each successive shot was another loud, fateful rap on the door of my undoing.

# Part Two

## CHAPTER I

I was questioned several times immediately after my arrest. But they were all formal examinations, as to my identity and so forth. At the first of these, which took place at the police station, nobody seemed to have much interest in the case. However, when I was brought before the examining magistrate a week later, I noticed that he eyed me with distinct curiosity. Like the others, he began by asking my name, address, and occupation, the date and place of my birth. Then he inquired if I had chosen a lawyer to defend me. I answered, "No," I hadn't thought about it, and asked him if it was really necessary for me to have one.

"Why do you ask that?" he said. I replied that I regarded my case as very simple. He smiled. "Well, it may seem so to you. But we've got to abide by the law, and, if you don't engage a lawyer, the court will have to appoint one for you."

It struck me as an excellent arrangement that the authorities should see to details of this kind, and I told him so. He nodded, and agreed that the Code was all that could be desired.

At first I didn't take him quite seriously. The room in which he interviewed me was much like an ordinary sitting room, with curtained windows, and a single lamp standing on the desk. Its light fell on the armchair in which he'd had me sit, while his own face stayed in shadow.

I had read descriptions of such scenes in books, and at first it all seemed like a game. After our conversation, however, I had a good look at him. He was a tall man with clean-cut features, deep-set blue eyes, a big gray mustache, and abundant, almost snow-white hair, and he gave me the impression of being highly intelligent and, on the whole, likable enough. There was only one thing that put one off: his mouth had now and then a rather ugly twist; but it seemed to be only a sort of nervous tic. When leaving, I very nearly held out my hand and said, "Good-by"; just in time I remembered that I'd killed a man.

Next day a lawyer came to my cell; a small, plump, youngish man with sleek black hair. In spite of the heat—I was in my shirt sleeves— he was wearing a dark suit, stiff collar, and a rather showy tie, with broad black and white stripes. After depositing his brief case on my bed, he introduced himself, and added that he'd perused the record of my case with the utmost care. His opinion was that it would need cautious handling, but there was every prospect of my getting off, provided I followed his advice. I thanked him, and he said: "Good. Now let's get down to it."

Sitting on the bed, he said that they'd been making investigations into my private life. They had learned that my mother died recently in a home. Inquiries had been conducted at Marengo and the police informed that I'd shown "great callousness" at my mother's funeral.

"You must understand," the lawyer said, "that I don't relish having to question you about such a matter. But it has much importance, and, unless I find some way of answering the charge of 'callousness,' I shall be handicapped in conducting your defense. And that is where you, and only you, can help me."

He went on to ask if I had felt grief on that "sad occasion." The question struck me as an odd one; I'd have been much embarrassed if I'd had to ask anyone a thing like that.

I answered that, of recent years, I'd rather lost the habit of noting my feelings, and hardly knew what to answer. I could truthfully say I'd been quite fond of Mother—but really that didn't mean much. All normal people, I added as an afterthought, had more or less desired the death of those they loved, at some time or another.

Here the lawyer interrupted me, looking greatly perturbed.

"You must promise me not to say anything of that sort at the trial, or to the examining magistrate."

I promised, to satisfy him, but I expalined that my physical condition at any given moment often influenced my feelings. For instance, on the day I attended Mother's funeral, I was fagged out and only half awake. So, really, I hardly took stock of what was happening. Anyhow, I could assure him of one thing: that I'd rather Mother hadn't died.

The lawyer, however, looked displeased. "That's not enough," he said curtly.

After considering for a bit he asked me if he could say that on that day I had kept my feelings under control.

"No," I said. "That wouldn't be true."

He gave me a queer look, as if I slightly revolted him; then informed me, in an almost hostile tone, that in any case the head of the Home and some of the staff would be cited as witnesses.

"And that might do you a very nasty turn," he concluded.

When I suggested that Mother's death had no connection with the charge against me, he merely replied that this remark showed I'd never had any dealings with the law.

Soon after this he left, looking quite vexed. I wished he had stayed longer and I could have explained that I desired his sympathy, not for him to make a better job of my defense, but, if I might put it so, spontaneously. I could see that I got on his nerves; he couldn't make me out, and, naturally enough, this irritated him. Once or twice I had a mind to assure him that I was just like everybody else; quite an ordinary person. But really that would have served no great purpose, and I let it go—out of laziness as much as anything else.

Later in the day I was taken again to the examining magistrate's office. It was two in the afternoon and, this time, the room was flooded with light—there was only a thin curtain on the window—and extremely hot.

After inviting me to sit down, the magistrate informed me in a very polite tone that, "owing to unforeseen circumstances," my lawyer was unable to be present. I should be quite entitled, he added, to reserve my answers to his questions until my lawyer could attend.

To this I replied that I could answer for myself. He pressed a bell push on his desk and a young clerk came in and seated himself just behind me. Then we—I and the magistrate—settled back in our chairs and the examination began. He led off by remarking that I had the reputation of being a taciturn, rather self-centered person, and he'd like to know what I had to say to that. I answered:

"Well, I rarely have anything much to say. So, naturally I keep my mouth shut."

He smiled as on the previous occasion, and agreed that that was the best of reasons. "In any case," he added, "it has little or no importance."

After a short silence he suddenly leaned forward, looked me in the eyes, and said, raising his voice a little:

"What really interests me is—you!"

I didn't know what he meant, so I made no comment.

"There are several things," he continued, "that puzzle me about your crime. I feel sure that you will help me to understand them."

When I replied that really it was quite simple, he asked me to give him an account of what I'd done that day. As a matter of fact, I had already told him at our first interview—in a summary sort of way, of course—about Raymond, the beach, our swim, the fight, then the beach again, and the five shots I'd fired. But I went over it all again, and after each phrase he nodded. "Quite so, quite so." When I described the body lying on the sand, he nodded more emphatically, and said, "Good!" I was tired of repeating the same story; I felt as if I'd never talked so much in all my life before.

After another silence he stood up and said he'd like to help me; I interested him, and, with God's help, he would do something for me in my trouble. But, first, he must put a few more questions.

He began by asking bluntly if I'd loved my mother.

"Yes," I replied, "like everybody else." The clerk behind me, who had been typing away at a steady pace, must just then have hit the wrong keys, as I heard him pushing the carrier back and crossing something out.

Next, without any apparent logical connection, the magistrate sprang another question.

"Why did you fire five consecutive shots?"

I thought for a bit; then explained that they weren't quite consecutive. I fired one at first, and the other four after a short interval.

"Why did you pause between the first and second shot?"

I seemed to see it hovering again before my eyes, the red glow of the beach, and to feel that fiery breath on my cheeks—and, this time, I made no answer.

During the silence that followed, the magistrate kept fidgeting, running his fingers through his hair, half rising, then sitting down again. Finally, planting his elbows on the desk, he bent toward me with a queer expression.

"But why, *why* did you go on firing at a prostrate man?"

Again I found nothing to reply.

The magistrate drew his hand across his forehead and repeated in a slightly different tone:

"I ask you 'Why?' I insist on your telling me."

I still kept silent.

Suddenly he rose, walked to a file cabinet standing against the opposite wall, pulled a drawer open, and took from it a silver crucifix, which he was waving as he came back to the desk.

"Do you know who this is?" His voice had changed completely; it was vibrant with emotion.

"Of course I do," I answered.

That seemed to start him off; he began speaking at a great pace. He told me he believed in God, and that even the worst of sinners could obtain forgiveness of Him. But first he must repent, and become like a little child, with a simple, trustful heart, open to conviction. He was leaning right across the table, brandishing his crucifix before my eyes.

As a matter of fact, I had great difficulty in following his remarks, as, for one thing, the office was so stifling hot and big flies were buzzing round and settling on my cheeks; also because he rather alarmed me. Of course, I realized it was absurd to feel like this, considering that, after all, it was I who was the criminal. However, as he continued talking, I did my best to understand, and I gathered that there was only one point in my confession that badly needed clearing up—the fact that I'd waited before firing a second time. All the rest was, so to speak, quite in order; but that completely baffled him.

I started to tell him that he was wrong in insisting on this; the point was of quite minor importance. But, before I could get the words out, he had drawn himself up to his full height and was asking me very earnestly if I believed in God. When I said, "No," he plumped down into his chair indignantly.

That was unthinkable, he said; all men believe in God, even those who reject Him. Of this he was absolutely sure; if ever he came to doubt it, his life would lose all meaning. "Do you wish," he asked indignantly, "my life to have no meaning?" Really I couldn't see how my wishes came into it, and I told him as much.

While I was talking, he thrust the crucifix again just under my nose and shouted: "I, anyhow, am a Christian. And I pray Him to forgive you for your sins. My poor young man, how can you not believe that He suffered for your sake?"

I noticed that his manner seemed genuinely solicitous when he said, "My poor young man"—but I was beginning to have enough of it. The room was growing steadily hotter.

As I usually do when I want to get rid of someone whose conversation bores me, I pretended to agree. At which, rather to my surprise, his face lit up.

"You see! You see! Now won't you own that you believe and put your trust in Him?"

I must have shaken my head again, for he sank back in his chair, looking limp and dejected.

For some moments there was a silence during which the typewriter, which had been clicking away all the time we talked, caught up with the last remark. Then he looked at me intently and rather sadly.

"Never in all my experience have I known a soul so case-hardened as yours," he said in a low tone. "All the criminals who have come before me until now wept when they saw this symbol of our Lord's sufferings."

I was on the point of replying that was precisely because they *were* criminals. But then I realized that I, too, came under that description. Somehow it was an idea to which I never could get reconciled.

To indicate, presumably, that the interview was over, the magistrate stood up. In the same weary tone he asked me a last question: Did I regret what I had done?

After thinking a bit, I said that what I felt was less regret than a kind of vexation—I couldn't find a better word for it. But he didn't seem to understand. . . . This was as far as things went at that day's interview.

I came before the magistrate many times more, but on these occasions my lawyer always accompanied me. The examinations were confined to asking me to amplify my previous statements. Or else the magistrate and my lawyer discussed technicalities. At such times they

took very little notice of me, and, in any case, the tone of the examinations changed as time went on. The magistrate seemed to have
lost interest in me, and to have come to some sort of decision about
my case. He never mentioned God again or displayed any of the
religious fervor I had found so embarrassing at our first interview.
The result was that our relations became more cordial. After a few
questions, followed by an exchange of remarks with the lawyer, the
magistrate closed the interview. My case was "taking its course," as
he put it. Sometimes, too, the conversation was of a general order,
and the magistrate and lawyer encouraged me to join in it. I began
to breathe more freely. Neither of the two men, at these times,
showed the least hostility toward me, and everything went so smoothly,
so amiably, that I had an absurd impression of being "one of the
family." I can honestly say that during the eleven months these
examinations lasted I got so used to them that I was almost surprised
at having ever enjoyed anything better than those rare moments when
the magistrate, after escorting me to the door of the office, would
pat my shoulder and say in a friendly tone: "Well, Mr. Antichrist,
that's all for the present!" After which I was made over to my jailers.

## CHAPTER II

There are some things of which I've never cared to talk.
And, a few days after I'd been sent to prison, I decided that this phase
of my life was one of them. However, as time went by, I came to
feel that this aversion had no real substance. In point of fact, during
those early days, I was hardly conscious of being in prison; I had
always a vague hope that something would turn up, some agreeable
surprise.

The change came soon after Marie's first and only visit. From the
day when I got her letter telling me they wouldn't let her come to
see me any more, because she wasn't my wife—it was from that day
that I realized that this cell was my last home, a dead end, so to
speak.

On the day of my arrest they put me in a biggish room with several
other prisoners, mostly Arabs. They grinned when they saw me enter,
and asked me what I'd done. I told them I'd killed an Arab, and
they kept mum for a while. But presently night began to fall, and
one of them explained to me how to lay out my sleeping mat. By

rolling up one end one makes a sort of bolster. All night I felt bugs crawling over my face.

Some days later I was put by myself in a cell, where I slept on a plank bed hinged to the wall. The only other furniture was a latrine bucket and a tin basin. The prison stands on rising ground, and through my little window I had glimpses of the sea. One day when I was hanging on the bars, straining my eyes toward the sunlight playing on the waves, a jailer entered and said I had a visitor. I thought it must be Marie, and so it was.

To go to the Visitors' Room, I was taken along a corridor, then up a flight of steps, then along another corridor. It was a very large room, lit by a big bow window, and divided into three compartments by high iron grilles running transversally. Between the two grilles there was a gap of some thirty feet, a sort of no man's land between the prisoners and their friends. I was led to a point exactly opposite Marie, who was wearing her striped dress. On my side of the rails were about a dozen other prisoners, Arabs for the most part. On Marie's side were mostly Moorish women. She was wedged between a small old woman with tight-set lips and a fat matron, without a hat, who was talking shrilly and gesticulated all the time. Because of the distance between the visitors and prisoners I found I, too, had to raise my voice.

When I came into the room the babel of voices echoing on the bare walls, and the sunlight streaming in, flooding everything in a harsh white glare, made me feel quite dizzy. After the relative darkness and the silence of my cell it took me some moments to get used to these conditions. After a bit, however, I came to see each face quite clearly, lit up as if a spotlight played on it.

I noticed a prison official seated at each end of the no man's land between the grilles. The native prisoners and their relations on the other side were squatting opposite each other. They didn't raise their voices and, in spite of the din, managed to converse almost in whispers. This murmur of voices coming from below made a sort of accompaniment to the conversations going on above their heads. I took stock of all this very quickly and moved a step forward toward Marie. She was pressing her brown, sun-tanned face to the bars and smiling as hard as she could. I thought she was looking very pretty, but somehow couldn't bring myself to tell her so.

"Well?" she asked, pitching her voice very high. "What about it? Are you all right, have you everything you want?"

"Oh, yes. I've everything I want."

We were silent for some moments; Marie went on smiling. The fat woman was bawling at the prisoner beside me, her husband presumably, a tall, fair, pleasant-looking man.

"Jeanne refused to have him," she yelled.

"That's just too bad," the man replied.

"Yes, and I told her you'd take him back the moment you got out; but she wouldn't hear of it."

Marie shouted across the gap that Raymond sent me his best wishes, and I said, "Thanks." But my voice was drowned by my neighbor's, asking "if he was quite fit."

The fat woman gave a laugh. "Fit? I should say he is! The picture of health."

Meanwhile the prisoner on my left, a youngster with thin, girlish hands, never said a word. His eyes, I noticed, were fixed on the little old woman opposite him, and she returned his gaze with a sort of hungry passion. But I had to stop looking at them as Marie was shouting to me that we mustn't lose hope.

"Certainly not," I answered. My gaze fell on her shoulders, and I had a sudden longing to squeeze them, through the thin dress. Its silky texture fascinated me, and I had a feeling that the hope she spoke of centered on it, somehow. I imagine something of the same sort was in Marie's mind, for she went on smiling, looking straight at me.

"It'll all come right, you'll see, and then we shall get married."

All I could see of her now was the white flash of her teeth, and the little puckers round her eyes. I answered: "Do you really think so?" but chiefly because I felt it up to me to answer something.

She started talking very fast in the same high-pitched voice.

"Yes, you'll be acquitted, and we'll go bathing again, Sundays."

The woman beside me was still yelling away, telling her husband that she'd left a basket for him in the prison office. She gave a list of the things she'd brought and told him to mind and check them carefully, as some had cost quite a lot. The youngster on my other side and his mother were still gazing mournfully at each other, and the murmur of the Arabs droned on below us. The light outside seemed to be surging up against the window, seeping through, and smearing the faces of the people facing it with a coat of yellow oil.

I began to feel slightly squeamish, and wished I could leave. The strident voice beside me was jarring on my ears. But, on the other hand, I wanted to have the most I could of Marie's company. I've no idea how much time passed. I remember Marie's describing to me her work, with that set smile always on her face. There wasn't a moment's letup in the noise—shouts, conversations, and always that muttering undertone. The only oasis of silence was made by the young fellow and the old woman gazing into each other's eyes.

Then, one by one, the Arabs were led away; almost everyone fell silent when the first one left. The little old woman pressed herself against the bars and at the same moment a jailer tapped her son's shoulder. He called, "Au revoir, Mother," and, slipping her hand between the bars, she gave him a small, slow wave with it.

No sooner was she gone than a man, hat in hand, took her place. A prisoner was led up to the empty place beside me, and the two started a brisk exchange of remarks—not loud, however, as the room had become relatively quiet. Someone came and called away the man on my right, and his wife shouted at him—she didn't seem to realize it was no longer necessary to shout—"Now, mind you look after yourself, dear, and don't do anything rash!"

My turn came next. Marie threw me a kiss. I looked back as I walked away. She hadn't moved; her face was still pressed to the rails, her lips still parted in that tense, twisted smile.

Soon after this I had a letter from her. And it was then that the things I've never liked to talk about began. Not that they were particularly terrible; I've no wish to exaggerate and I suffered less than others. Still, there was one thing in those early days that was really irksome: my habit of thinking like a free man. For instance, I would suddenly be seized with a desire to go down to the beach for a swim. And merely to have imagined the sound of ripples at my feet, the smooth feel of the water on my body as I struck out, and the wonderful sensation of relief it gave brought home still more cruelly the narrowness of my cell.

Still, that phase lasted a few months only. Afterward, I had prisoner's thoughts. I waited for the daily walk in the courtyard or a visit from my lawyer. As for the rest of the time, I managed quite well, really. I've often thought that had I been compelled to live in the trunk of a dead tree, with nothing to do but gaze up at the patch of sky just overhead, I'd have got used to it by degrees. I'd have learned to watch for the passing of birds or drifting clouds, as I had come to watch for my lawyer's odd neckties, or, in another world, to wait patiently till Sunday for a spell of love-making with Marie. Well, here, anyhow, I wasn't penned in a hollow tree trunk. There were others in the world worse off than I. I remembered it had been one of Mother's pet ideas—she was always voicing it—that in the long run one gets used to anything.

Usually, however, I didn't think things out so far. Those first months were trying, of course; but the very effort I had to make helped me through them. For instance, I was plagued by the desire for a woman—which was natural enough, considering my age. I never thought of Marie especially. I was obsessed by thoughts of this woman or that, of all the ones I'd had, all the circumstances under which I'd loved them; so much so that the cell grew crowded with their faces, ghosts of my old passions. That unsettled me, no doubt; but, at least, it served to kill time.

I gradually became quite friendly with the chief jailer, who went the rounds with the kitchen hands at mealtimes. It was he who brought up the subject of women. "That's what the men here grumble about most," he told me.

I said I felt like that myself. "There's something unfair about it," I added, "like hitting a man when he's down."

"But that's the whole point of it," he said; "that's why you fellows are kept in prison."

"I don't follow."

"Liberty," he said, "means that. You're being deprived of your liberty."

It had never before struck me in that light, but I saw his point. "That's true," I said. "Otherwise it wouldn't be a punishment."

The jailer nodded. "Yes, you're different, you can use your brains. The others can't. Still, those fellows find a way out; they do it by themselves." With which remark the jailer left my cell. Next day I did like the others.

The lack of cigarettes, too, was a trial. When I was brought to the prison, they took away my belt, my shoelaces, and the contents of my pockets, including my cigarettes. Once I had been given a cell to myself I asked to be given back, anyhow, the cigarettes. Smoking was forbidden, they informed me. That, perhaps, was what got me down the most; in fact, I suffered really badly during the first few days. I even tore off splinters from my plank bed and sucked them. All day long I felt faint and bilious. It passed my understanding why I shouldn't be allowed even to smoke; it could have done no one any harm. Later on, I understood the idea behind it; this privation, too, was part of my punishment. But, by the time I understood, I'd lost the craving, so it had ceased to be a punishment.

Except for these privations I wasn't too unhappy. Yet again, the whole problem was: how to kill time. After a while, however, once I'd learned the trick of remembering things, I never had a moment's boredom. Sometimes I would exercise my memory on my bedroom and, starting from a corner, make the round, noting every object I saw on the way. At first it was over in a minute or two. But each time I repeated the experience, it took a little longer. I made a point of visualizing every piece of furniture, and each article upon or in it, and then every detail of each article, and finally the details of the details, so to speak: a tiny dent or incrustation, or a chipped edge, and the exact grain and color of the woodwork. At the same time I forced myself to keep my inventory in mind from start to finish, in the right order and omitting no item. With the result that, after a few weeks, I could spend hours merely in listing the objects in my bedroom. I found that the more I thought, the more details, half-forgotten or malobserved, floated up from my memory. There seemed no end to them.

So I learned that even after a single day's experience of the outside world a man could easily live a hundred years in prison. He'd have laid up enough memories never to be bored. Obviously, in one way, this was a compensation.

Then there was sleep. To begin with, I slept badly at night and never in the day. But gradually my nights became better, and I managed to doze off in the daytime as well. In fact, during the last months, I must have slept sixteen or eighteen hours out of the twenty-four. So there remained only six hours to fill—with meals, relieving nature, my memories . . . and the story of the Czech.

One day, when inspecting my straw mattress, I found a bit of newspaper stuck to its underside. The paper was yellow with age, almost transparent, but I could still make out the letter print. It was the story of a crime. The first part was missing, but I gathered that its scene was some village in Czechoslovakia. One of the villagers had left his home to try his luck abroad. After twenty-five years, having made a fortune, he returned to his country with his wife and child. Meanwhile his mother and sister had been running a small hotel in the village where he was born. He decided to give them a surprise and, leaving his wife and child in another inn, he went to stay at his mother's place, booking a room under an assumed name. His mother and sister completely failed to recognize him. At dinner that evening he showed them a large sum of money he had on him, and in the course of the night they slaughtered him with a hammer.

After taking the money they flung the body into the river. Next morning his wife came and, without thinking, betrayed the guest's identity. His mother hanged herself. His sister threw herself into a well. I must have read that story thousands of times. In one way it sounded most unlikely; in another, it was plausible enough. Anyhow, to my mind, the man was asking for trouble; one shouldn't play fool tricks of that sort.

So, what with long bouts of sleep, my memories, readings of that scrap of newspaper, the tides of light and darkness, the days slipped by. I'd read, of course, that in jail one ends up by losing track of time. But this had never meant anything definite to me. I hadn't grasped how days could be at once long and short. Long, no doubt, as periods to live through, but so distended that they ended up by overlapping on each other. In fact, I never thought of days as such; only the words "yesterday" and "tomorrow" still kept some meaning.

When, one morning, the jailer informed me I'd now been six months in jail, I believed him—but the words conveyed nothing to my mind. To me it seemed like one and the same day that had been going on since I'd been in my cell, and that I'd been doing the same thing all the time.

After the jailer left me I shined up my tin pannikin and studied my face in it. My expression was terribly serious, I thought, even when I tried to smile. I held the pannikin at different angles, but always my face had the same mournful, tense expression.

The sun was setting and it was the hour of which I'd rather not speak—"the nameless hour," I called it—when evening sounds were creeping up from all the floors of the prison in a sort of stealthy procession. I went to the barred window and in the last rays looked once again at my reflected face. It was as serious as before; and that wasn't surprising, as just then I was feeling serious. But, at the same time, I heard something that I hadn't heard for months. It was the sound of a voice; my own voice, there was no mistaking it. And I recognized it as the voice that for many a day of late had been sounding in my ears. So I knew that all this time I'd been talking to myself.

And something I'd been told came back; a remark made by the nurse at Mother's funeral. No, there was no way out, and no one can imagine what the evenings are like in prison.

## CHAPTER III

On the whole I can't say that those months passed slowly; another summer was on its way almost before I realized the first was over. And I knew that with the first really hot days something new was in store for me. My case was down for the last sessions of the Assize Court, and those sessions were due to end some time in June.

The day on which my trial started was one of brilliant sunshine. My lawyer assured me the case would take only two or three days. "From what I hear," he added, "the court will dispatch your case as quickly as possible, as it isn't the most important one on the Cause List. There's a case of parricide immediately after, which will take them some time."

They came for me at half-past seven in the morning and I was conveyed to the law courts in a prison van. Two policemen led me into a small room that smelled of darkness. We sat near a door through which came sounds of voices, shouts, chairs scraping on the floor; a vague hubbub which reminded me of one of those small-town "socials" when, after the concert's over, the hall is cleared for dancing.

One of my policemen told me the judges hadn't arrived yet, and offered me a cigarette, which I declined. After a bit he asked me if I was feeling nervous. I said, "No," and that the prospect of witnessing a trial rather interested me; I'd never had occasion to attend one before.

"Maybe," the other policeman said. "But after an hour or two one's had enough of it."

After a while a small electric bell purred in the room. They unfastened my handcuffs, opened the door, and led me to the prisoner's dock.

There was a great crowd in the courtroom. Though the Venetian blinds were down, light was filtering through the chinks, and the air stiflingly hot already. The windows had been kept shut. I sat down, and the police officers took their stand on each side of my chair.

It was then that I noticed a row of faces opposite me. These people were staring hard at me, and I guessed they were the jury. But somehow I didn't see them as individuals. I felt as you do just after boarding a streetcar and you're conscious of all the people on the opposite seat staring at you in the hope of finding something in your appearance to amuse them. Of course, I knew this was an absurd comparison; what these people were looking for in me wasn't anything to laugh at, but signs of criminality. Still, the difference wasn't so very great, and, anyhow, that's the idea I got.

What with the crowd and the stuffiness of the air I was feeling a bit dizzy. I ran my eyes round the courtroom but couldn't recognize any of the faces. At first I could hardly believe that all these people had come on my account. It was such a new experience, being a focus of interest; in the ordinary way no one ever paid much attention to me.

"What a crush!" I remarked to the policeman on my left, and he explained that the newspapers were responsible for it.

He pointed to a group of men at a table just below the jury box. "There they are!"

"Who?" I asked, and he replied, "The press." One of them, he added, was an old friend of his.

A moment later the man he'd mentioned looked our way and, coming to the dock, shook hands warmly with the policeman. The journalist was an elderly man with a rather grim expression, but his manner was quite pleasant. Just then I noticed that almost all the people in the courtroom were greeting each other, exchanging remarks and forming groups—behaving, in fact, as in a club where the company of others of one's own tastes and standing makes one feel at ease. That, no doubt, explained the odd impression I had of being *de trop* here, a sort of gate-crasher.

However, the journalist addressed me quite amiably, and said he hoped all would go well for me. I thanked him, and he added with a smile:

"You know, we've been featuring you a bit. We're always rather short of copy in the summer, and there's been precious little to write about except your case and the one that's coming on after it. I expect you've heard about it; it's a case of parricide."

He drew my attention to one of the group at the press table, a plump, small man with huge black-rimmed glasses, who made me think of an overfed weasel.

"That fellow's the special correspondent of one of the Paris dailies. As a matter of fact, he didn't come on your account. He was sent for the parricide case, but they've asked him to cover yours as well."

It was on the tip of my tongue to say, "That was very kind of them," but then I thought it would sound silly. With a friendly wave of his hand he left us, and for some minutes nothing happened.

Then, accompanied by some colleagues, my lawyer bustled in, in his gown. He went up to the press table and shook hands with the journalists. They remained laughing and chatting together, all seemingly very much at home here, until a bell rang shrilly and everyone went to his place. My lawyer came up to me, shook hands, and advised me to answer all the questions as briefly as possible, not to volunteer information, and to rely on him to see me through.

I heard a chair scrape on my left, and a tall, thin man wearing pince-nez settled the folds of his red gown as he took his seat. The Public Prosecutor, I gathered. A clerk of the court announced that Their Honors were entering, and at the same moment two big electric fans started buzzing overhead. Three judges, two in black and the third in scarlet, with brief cases under their arms, entered and walked briskly to the bench, which was several feet above the level of the courtroom floor. The man in scarlet took the central, high-backed chair, placed his cap of office on the table, ran a handkerchief over his small bald crown, and announced that the hearing would now begin.

The journalists had their fountain pens ready; they all wore the same expression of slightly ironical indifference, with the exception of one, a much younger man than his colleagues, in gray flannels with a blue tie, who, leaving his pen on the table, was gazing hard at me. He had a plain, rather chunky face; what held my attention were his eyes, very pale, clear eyes, riveted on me, though not betraying any definite emotion. For a moment I had an odd impression, as if I were being scrutinized by myself. That—and the fact that I was unfamiliar with court procedure—may explain why I didn't follow very well the opening phases: the drawing of lots for the jury, the various questions put by the presiding judge to the Prosecutor, the foreman of the jury, and my counsel (each time he spoke all the jurymen's heads swung round together toward the bench), the hurried reading of the charge sheet, in the course of which I recognized some familiar names of people and places; then some supplementary questions put to my lawyer.

Next, the Judge announced that the court would call over the witness list. Some of the names read out by the clerk rather surprised me. From among the crowd, which until now I had seen as a mere blur of faces, rose, one after the other, Raymond, Masson, Salamano, the doorkeeper from the Home, old Pérez, and Marie, who gave me a little nervous wave of her hand before following the others out by a side door. I was thinking how strange it was I hadn't noticed any of them before when I heard the last name called, that of Céleste. As he rose, I noticed beside him the quaint little woman with a mannish coat and brisk, decided air, who had shared my table at the restaurant. She had her eyes fixed on me, I noticed. But I hadn't time to wonder about her; the Judge had started speaking again.

He said that the trial proper was about to begin, and he need hardly say that he expected the public to refrain from any demonstration whatsoever. He explained that he was there to supervise the proceedings, as a sort of umpire, and he would take a scrupulously impartial view of the case. The verdict of the jury would be interpreted by him in a spirit of justice. Finally, at the least sign of a disturbance he would have the court cleared.

The day was stoking up. Some of the public were fanning themselves with newspapers, and there was a constant rustle of crumpled paper. On a sign from the presiding judge the clerk of the court brought three fans of plaited straw, which the three judges promptly put in action.

My examination began at once. The Judge questioned me quite calmly and even, I thought, with a hint of cordiality. For the nth time I was asked to give particulars of my identity and, though heartily sick of this formality, I realized that it was natural enough; after all, it would be a shocking thing for the court to be trying the wrong man.

The Judge then launched into an account of what I'd done, stopping after every two or three sentences to ask me, "Is that correct?" To which I always replied, "Yes, sir," as my lawyer had advised me. It was a long business, as the Judge lingered on each detail. Meanwhile the journalists scribbled busily away. But I was sometimes conscious of the eyes of the youngest fixed on me; also those of the queer little robot woman. The jurymen, however, were all gazing at the red-robed judge, and I was again reminded of the row of passengers on one side of a tram. Presently he gave a slight cough, turned some pages of his file, and, still fanning his face, addressed me gravely.

He now proposed, he said, to trench on certain matters which, on a superficial view, might seem foreign to the case, but actually were highly relevant. I guessed that he was going to talk about Mother, and at the same moment realized how odious I would find this. His first question was: Why had I sent my mother to an institution? I replied that the reason was simple; I hadn't enough money to see that she was properly looked after at home. Then he asked if the parting hadn't caused me distress. I explained that neither Mother nor I expected much of one another—or, for that matter, of anybody else; so both of us had got used to the new conditions easily enough. The Judge then said that he had no wish to press the point, and asked the Prosecutor if he could think of any more questions that should be put to me at this stage.

The Prosecutor, who had his back half turned to me, said, without looking in my direction, that, subject to His Honor's approval, he would like to know if I'd gone back to the stream with the intention of killing the Arab. I said, "No." In that case, why had I taken a revolver with me, and why go back precisely to that spot? I said it was a matter of pure chance. The Prosecutor then observed in a nasty tone: "Very good. That will be all for the present."

I couldn't quite follow what came next. Anyhow, after some palavering among the bench, the Prosecutor, and my counsel, the presiding judge announced that the court would now rise; there was an adjournment till the afternoon, when evidence would be taken.

Almost before I knew what was happening I was rushed out to the prison van, which drove me back, and I was given my midday meal. After a short time, just enough for me to realize how tired I was feeling, they came for me. I was back in the same room, confronting the same faces, and the whole thing started again. But the heat had meanwhile much increased, and by some miracle fans had been procured for everyone: the jury, my lawyer, the Prosecutor, and some of the journalists, too. The young man and the robot woman were still at their places. But they were not fanning themselves and, as before, they never took their eyes off me.

I wiped the sweat from my face, but I was barely conscious of where or who I was until I heard the warden of the Home called to the witness box. When asked if my mother had complained about my conduct, he said, "Yes," but that didn't mean much; almost all the inmates of the Home had grievances against their relatives. The Judge asked him to be more explicit; did she reproach me with having sent her to the Home, and he said, "Yes," again. But this time he didn't qualify his answer.

To another question he replied that on the day of the funeral he was somewhat surprised by my calmness. Asked to explain what he meant by "my calmness," the warden lowered his eyes and stared at his shoes for a moment. Then he explained that I hadn't wanted to see Mother's body, or shed a single tear, and that I'd left immediately the funeral ended, without lingering at her grave. Another thing had surprised him. One of the undertaker's men told him that I didn't know my mother's age. There was a short silence; then the Judge asked him if he might take it that he was referring to the prisoner in the dock. The warden seemed puzzled by this, and the Judge explained: "It's a formal question. I am bound to put it."

The Prosecutor was then asked if he had any questions to put, and he answered loudly: "Certainly not! I have all I want." His tone and the look of triumph on his face, as he glanced at me, were so marked that I felt as I hadn't felt for ages. I had a foolish desire to burst into tears. For the first time I'd realized how all these people loathed me.

After asking the jury and my lawyer if they had any questions, the Judge heard the doorkeeper's evidence. On stepping into the box the man threw a glance at me, then looked away. Replying to questions, he said that I'd declined to see Mother's body, I'd smoked cigarettes and slept, and drunk *café au lait*. It was then I felt a sort of wave of indignation spreading through the courtroom, and for the first time I understood that I was guilty. They got the doorkeeper to repeat what he had said about the coffee and my smoking.

The Prosecutor turned to me again, with a gloating look in his eyes. My counsel asked the doorkeeper if he, too, hadn't smoked. But the Prosecutor took strong exception to this. "I'd like to know," he cried indignantly, "who is on trial in this court. Or does my friend think that by aspersing a witness for the prosecution he will shake the evidence, the abundant and cogent evidence, against his client?" None the less, the Judge told the doorkeeper to answer the question.

The old fellow fidgeted a bit. Then, "Well, I know I didn't ought to have done it," he mumbled, "but I did take a cigarette from the young gentleman when he offered it—just out of politeness."

The Judge asked me if I had any comment to make. "None," I said, "except that the witness is quite right. It's true I offered him a cigarette."

The doorkeeper looked at me with surprise and a sort of gratitude. Then, after hemming and hawing for a bit, he volunteered the statement that it was he who'd suggested I should have some coffee.

My lawyer was exultant. "The jury will appreciate," he said, "the importance of this admission."

The Prosecutor, however, was promptly on his feet again. "Quite so," he boomed above our heads. "The jury will appreciate it. And they will draw the conclusion that, though a third party might inadvertently offer him a cup of coffee, the prisoner, in common decency, should have refused it, if only out of respect for the dead body of the poor woman who had brought him into the world."

After which the doorkeeper went back to his seat.

When Thomas Pérez was called, a court officer had to help him to the box. Pérez stated that, though he had been a great friend of my mother, he had met me once only, on the day of the funeral. Asked how I had behaved that day, he said:

"Well, I was most upset, you know. Far too much upset to notice things. My grief sort of blinded me, I think. It had been a great shock, my dear friend's death; in fact, I fainted during the funeral. So I didn't hardly notice the young gentleman at all."

The Prosecutor asked him to tell the court if he'd seen me weep. And when Pérez answered, "No," added emphatically: "I trust the jury will take note of this reply."

My lawyer rose at once, and asked Pérez in a tone that seemed to me needlessly aggressive:

"Now, think well, my man! Can you swear you saw he didn't shed a tear?"

Pérez answered, "No."

At this some people tittered, and my lawyer, pushing back one sleeve of his gown, said sternly:

"That is typical of the way this case is being conducted. No attempt is being made to elicit the true facts."

The Prosecutor ignored this remark; he was making dabs with his pencil on the cover of his brief, seemingly quite indifferent.

There was a break of five minutes, during which my lawyer told me the case was going very well indeed. Then Céleste was called. He was announced as a witness for the defense. The defense meant me.

Now and again Céleste threw me a glance; he kept squeezing his Panama hat between his hands as he gave evidence. He was in his best suit, the one he wore when sometimes of a Sunday he went with me to the races. But evidently he hadn't been able to get his collar on; the top of his shirt, I noticed, was secured only by a brass stud. Asked if I was one of his customers, he said, "Yes, and a friend as well." Asked to state his opinion of me, he said that I was "all right" and, when told to explain what he meant by that, he replied that everyone knew what that meant. "Was I a secretive sort of man?" "No," he answered, "I shouldn't call him that. But he isn't one to waste his breath, like a lot of folks."

The Prosecutor asked him if I always settled my monthly bill at his restaurant when he presented it. Céleste laughed. "Oh, he paid on the nail, all right. But the bills were just details-like, between him and me." Then he was asked to say what he thought about the crime. He placed his hands on the rail of the box and one could see he had a speech all ready.

"To my mind it was just an accident, or a stroke of bad luck, if you prefer. And a thing like that takes you off your guard."

He wanted to continue, but the Judge cut him short. "Quite so. That's all, thank you."

For a bit Céleste seemed flabbergasted; then he explained that he hadn't finished what he wanted to say. They told him to continue, but to make it brief.

He only repeated that it was "just an accident."

"That's as it may be," the Judge observed. "But what we are here for is to try such accidents, according to law. You can stand down."

Céleste turned and gazed at me. His eyes were moist and his lips trembling. It was exactly as if he'd said: "Well, I've done my best for you, old man. I'm afraid it hasn't helped much. I'm sorry."

I didn't say anything, or make any movement, but for the first time in my life I wanted to kiss a man.

The Judge repeated his order to stand down, and Céleste returned to his place among the crowd. During the rest of the hearing he remained there, leaning forward, elbows on knees and his Panama between his hands, not missing a word of the proceedings.

It was Marie's turn next. She had a hat on and still looked quite pretty, though I much preferred her with her hair free. From where I was I had glimpses of the soft curve of her breasts, and her underlip had the little pout that always fascinated me. She appeared very nervous.

The first question was: How long had she known me? Since the time when she was in our office, she replied. Then the Judge asked her what were the relations between us, and she said she was my girl friend. Answering another question, she admitted promising to marry me. The Prosecutor, who had been studying a document in front of him, asked her rather sharply when our "liaison" had begun. She gave the date. He then observed with a would-be casual air that apparently she meant the day following my mother's funeral. After letting this sink in he remarked in a slightly ironic tone that obviously this was a "delicate topic" and he could enter into the young lady's feelings, but—and here his voice grew sterner—his duty obliged him to waive considerations of delicacy.

After making this announcement he asked Marie to give a full account of our doings on the day when I had "intercourse" with her for the first time. Marie wouldn't answer at first, but the Prosecutor insisted, and then she told him that we had met at the baths, gone together to the pictures, and then to my place. He then informed the court that, as a result of certain statements made by Marie at the proceedings before the magistrate, he had studied the movie programs of that date, and turning to Marie asked her to name the film that we had gone to see. In a very low voice she said it was a picture with Fernandel in it. By the time she had finished, the courtroom was so still you could have heard a pin drop.

Looking very grave, the Prosecutor drew himself up to his full height and, pointing at me, said in such a tone that I could have sworn he was genuinely moved:

"Gentlemen of the jury, I would have you note that on the next day after his mother's funeral that man was visiting the swimming pool, starting a liaison with a girl, and going to see a comic film. That is all I wish to say."

When he sat down there was the same dead silence. Then all of a sudden Marie burst into tears. He'd got it all wrong, she said; it wasn't a bit like that really, he'd bullied her into saying the opposite of what she meant. She knew me very well, and she was sure I hadn't done anything really wrong—and so on. At a sign from the presiding judge, one of the court officers led her away, and the hearing continued.

Hardly anyone seemed to listen to Masson, the next witness. He stated that I was a respectable young fellow; "and, what's more, a very decent chap." Nor did they pay any more attention to Salamano, when he told them how kind I'd always been to his dog, or when, in answer to a question about my mother and myself, he said that Mother and I had very little in common and that explained why I'd fixed up for her to enter the Home. "You've got to understand," he added. "You've got to understand." But no one seemed to understand. He was told to stand down.

Raymond was the next, and last, witness. He gave me a little wave of his hand and led off by saying I was innocent. The Judge rebuked him.

"You are here to give evidence, not your views on the case, and you must confine yourself to answering the questions put you."

He was then asked to make clear his relations with the deceased, and Raymond took this opportunity of explaining that it was he, not I, against whom the dead man had a grudge, because he, Raymond, had beaten up his sister. The Judge asked him if the deceased had no reason to dislike me, too. Raymond told him that my presence on the beach that morning was a pure coincidence.

"How comes it then," the Prosecutor inquired, "that the letter which led up to this tragedy was the prisoner's work?"

Raymond replied that this, too, was due to mere chance.

To which the Prosecutor retorted that in this case "chance" or "mere coincidence" seemed to play a remarkably large part. Was it by chance that I hadn't intervened when Raymond assaulted his mistress? Did this convenient term "chance" account for my having vouched for Raymond at the police station and having made, on that occasion, statements extravagantly favorable to him? In conclusion he asked Raymond to state what were his means of livelihood.

On his describing himself as a warehouseman, the Prosecutor informed the jury it was common knowledge that the witness lived on the immoral earnings of women. I, he said, was this man's intimate friend and associate; in fact, the whole background of the crime was of the most squalid description. And what made it even more odious was the personality of the prisoner, an inhuman monster wholly without a moral sense.

Raymond began to expostulate, and my lawyer, too, protested. They were told that the Prosecutor must be allowed to finish his remarks.

"I have nearly done," he said; then turned to Raymond. "Was the prisoner your friend?"

"Certainly. We were the best of pals, as they say."

The Prosecutor then put me the same question. I looked hard at Raymond, and he did not turn away.

Then, "Yes," I answered.

The Prosecutor turned toward the jury.

"Not only did the man before you in the dock indulge in the most shameful orgies on the day following his mother's death. He killed a man cold-bloodedly, in pursuance of some sordid vendetta in the underworld of prostitutes and pimps. That, gentlemen of the jury, is the type of man the prisoner is."

No sooner had he sat down than my lawyer, out of all patience, raised his arms so high that his sleeves fell back, showing the full length of his starched shirt cuffs.

"Is my client on trial for having buried his mother, or for killing a man?" he asked.

There were some titters in court. But then the Prosecutor sprang to his feet and, draping his gown round him, said he was amazed at his friend's ingenuousness in failing to see that between these two elements of the case there was a vital link. They hung together psychologically, if he might put it so. "In short," he concluded, speaking with great vehemence, "I accuse the prisoner of behaving at his mother's funeral in a way that showed he was already a criminal at heart."

These words seemed to take much effect on the jury and public. My lawyer merely shrugged his shoulders and wiped the sweat from his forehead. But obviously he was rattled, and I had a feeling things weren't going well for me.

Soon after this incident the court rose. As I was being taken from the courthouse to the prison van, I was conscious for a few brief moments of the once familiar feel of a summer evening out-of-doors. And, sitting in the darkness of my moving cell, I recognized, echoing in my tired brain, all the characteristic sounds of a town I'd loved, and of a certain hour of the day which I had always particularly enjoyed. The shouts of newspaper boys in the already languid air, the last calls of birds in the public garden, the cries of sandwich vendors, the screech of streetcars at the steep corners of the upper town, and that faint rustling overhead as darkness sifted down upon the harbor—all these sounds made my return to prison like a blind man's journey along a route whose every inch he knows by heart.

Yes, this was the evening hour when—how long ago it seemed!—I always felt so well content with life. Then, what awaited me was a night of easy, dreamless sleep. This was the same hour, but with a difference; I was returning to a cell, and what awaited me was a night haunted by forebodings of the coming day. And so I learned that familiar paths traced in the dusk of summer evenings may lead as well to prisons as to innocent, untroubled sleep.

## CHAPTER IV

It is always interesting, even in the prisoner's dock, to hear oneself being talked about. And certainly in the speeches of my lawyer and the prosecuting counsel a great deal was said about me; more, in fact, about me personally than about my crime.

Really there wasn't any very great difference between the two speeches. Counsel for the defense raised his arms to heaven and pleaded guilty, but with extenuating circumstances. The Prosecutor made similar gestures; he agreed that I was guilty, but denied extenuating circumstances.

One thing about this phase of the trial was rather irksome. Quite often, interested as I was in what they had to say, I was tempted to put in a word, myself. But my lawyer had advised me not to. "You won't do your case any good by talking," he had warned me. In fact, there seemed to be a conspiracy to exclude me from the proceedings; I wasn't to have any say and my fate was to be decided out of hand.

It was quite an effort at times for me to refrain from cutting them all short, and saying: "But, damn it all, who's on trial in this court, I'd like to know? It's a serious matter for a man, being accused of murder. And I've something really important to tell you."

However, on second thoughts, I found I had nothing to say. In any case, I must admit that hearing oneself talked about loses its interest very soon. The Prosecutor's speech, especially, began to bore me before he was halfway through it. The only things that really caught my attention were occasional phrases, his gestures, and some elaborate tirades—but these were isolated patches.

What he was aiming at, I gathered, was to show that my crime was premeditated. I remember his saying at one moment, "I can prove this, gentlemen of the jury, to the hilt. First, you have the facts of the crime; which are as clear as daylight. And then you have what I may call the night side of this case, the dark workings of a criminal mentality."

He began by summing up the facts, from my mother's death onward. He stressed my heartlessness, my inability to state Mother's age, my visit to the swimming pool where I met Marie, our matinee at the pictures where a Fernandel film was showing, and finally my return with Marie to my rooms. I didn't quite follow his remarks at first, as he kept on mentioning "the prisoner's mistress," whereas for me she was just "Marie." Then he came to the subject of Raymond. It seemed to me that his way of treating the facts showed a certain shrewdness. All he said sounded quite plausible. I'd written the letter in collusion with Raymond so as to entice his mistress to his room and subject her to ill-treatment by a man "of more than dubious reputation." Then, on the beach, I'd provoked a brawl with Raymond's enemies, in the course of which Raymond was wounded. I'd asked him for his revolver and gone back by myself with the intention of using it. Then I'd shot the Arab. After the first shot I waited. Then, "to be certain of making a good job of it," I fired four more shots deliberately, point-blank, and in cold blood, at my victim.

"That is my case," he said. "I have described to you the series of events which led this man to kill the deceased, fully aware of what he was doing. I emphasize this point. We are not concerned with an act of homicide committed on a sudden impulse which might serve as extenuation. I ask you to note, gentlemen of the jury, that the prisoner is an educated man. You will have observed the way in which he answered my questions; he is intelligent and he knows the value of words. And I repeat that it is quite impossible to assume that, when he committed the crime, he was unaware what he was doing."

I noticed that he laid stress on my "intelligence." It puzzled me rather why what would count as a good point in an ordinary person should be used against an accused man as an overwhelming proof of his guilt. While thinking this over, I missed what he said next, until I heard him exclaim indignantly: "And has he uttered a word of regret for his most odious crime? Not one word, gentlemen. Not once in the course of these proceedings did this man show the least contrition."

Turning toward the dock, he pointed a finger at me, and went on in the same strain. I really couldn't understand why he harped on this point so much. Of course, I had to own that he was right; I didn't feel much regret for what I'd done. Still, to my mind he overdid it, and I'd have liked to have a chance of explaining to him, in a quite friendly, almost affectionate way, that I have never been able to regret anything in all my life. I've always been far too much absorbed in the present moment, or the immediate future, to think back. Of course, in the position into which I had been forced, there was no question of my speaking to anyone in that tone. I hadn't the right to show any friendly feeling or possess good intentions. And I tried to follow what came next, as the Prosecutor was now considering what he called my "soul."

He said he'd studied it closely—and had found a blank, "literally nothing, gentlemen of the jury." Really, he said, I had no soul, there was nothing human about me, not one of those moral qualities which normal men possess had any place in my mentality. "No doubt," he added, "we should not reproach him with this. We cannot blame a man for lacking what it was never in his power to acquire. But in a criminal court the wholly passive ideal of tolerance must give place to a sterner, loftier ideal, that of justice. Especially when this lack of every decent instinct is such as that of the man before you, a menace to society." He proceeded to discuss my conduct toward my mother, repeating what he had said in the course of the hearing. But he spoke at much greater length of my crime—at such length, indeed, that I lost the thread and was conscious only of the steadily increasing heat.

A moment came when the Prosecutor paused and, after a short silence, said in a low, vibrant voice: "This same court, gentlemen, will be called on to try tomorrow that most odious of crimes, the murder of a father by his son." To his mind, such a crime was almost unimaginable. But, he ventured to hope, justice would be meted out without paltering. And yet, he made bold to say, the horror that even the crime of parricide inspired in him paled beside the loathing inspired by my callousness.

"This man, who is morally guilty of his mother's death, is no less unfit to have a place in the community than that other man who did to death the father that begat him. And, indeed, the one crime led on to the other; the first of these two criminals, the man in the dock, set a precedent, if I may put it so, and authorized the second crime. Yes, gentlemen, I am convinced"—here he raised his voice a tone—"that you will not find I am exaggerating the case against the prisoner when I say that he is also guilty of the murder to be tried tomorrow in this court. And I look to you for a verdict accordingly."

The Prosecutor paused again, to wipe the sweat off his face. He then explained that his duty was a painful one, but he would do it without flinching. "This man has, I repeat, no place in a community whose basic principles he flouts without compunction. Nor, heartless as he is, has he any claim to mercy. I ask you to impose the extreme penalty of the law; and I ask it without a qualm. In the course of a long career, in which it has often been my duty to ask for a capital sentence, never have I felt that painful duty weigh so little on my mind as in the present case. In demanding a verdict of murder without extenuating circumstances, I am following not only the dictates of my conscience and a sacred obligation, but also those of the natural and righteous indignation I feel at the sight of a criminal devoid of the least spark of human feeling."

When the Prosecutor sat down there was a longish silence. Personally I was quite overcome by the heat and my amazement at what I had been hearing. The presiding judge gave a short cough, and asked me in a very low tone if I had anything to say. I rose, and as I felt in the mood to speak, I said the first thing that crossed my mind: that I'd had no intention of killing the Arab. The Judge replied that this statement would be taken into consideration by the court. Meanwhile he would be glad to hear, before my counsel addressed the court, what were the motives of my crime. So far, he must admit, he hadn't fully understood the grounds of my defense.

I tried to explain that it was because of the sun, but I spoke too quickly and ran my words into each other. I was only too conscious that it sounded nonsensical, and, in fact, I heard people tittering.

My lawyer shrugged his shoulders. Then he was directed to address the court, in his turn. But all he did was to point out the lateness of the hour and to ask for adjournment till the following afternoon. To this the judge agreed.

When I was brought back next day, the electric fans were still churning up the heavy air and the jurymen plying their gaudy little fans in a sort of steady rhythm. The speech for the defense seemed to me interminable. At one moment, however, I pricked up my ears; it was when I heard him saying: "It is true I killed a man." He went on in the same strain, saying "I" when he referred to me. It seemed so queer that I bent toward the policeman on my right and asked him to explain. He told me to shut up; then, after a moment, whispered: "They all do that." It seemed to me that the idea behind it was still further to exclude me from the case, to put me off the map, so to speak, by substituting the lawyer for myself. Anyway, it hardly mattered; I already felt worlds away from this courtroom and its tedious "proceedings."

My lawyer, in any case, struck me as feeble to the point of being ridiculous. He hurried through his plea of provocation, and then he, too, started in about my soul. But I had an impression that he had much less talent than the Prosecutor.

"I, too," he said, "have closely studied this man's soul; but, unlike my learned friend for the prosecution, I have found something there. Indeed, I may say that I have read the prisoner's mind like an open book." What he had read there was that I was an excellent young fellow, a steady, conscientious worker who did his best by his employer; that I was popular with everyone and sympathetic in others' troubles. According to him I was a dutiful son, who had supported his mother as long as he was able. After anxious consideration I had reached the conclusion that, by entering a home, the old lady would have comforts that my means didn't permit me to provide for her. "I am astounded, gentlemen," he added, "by the attitude taken up by my learned friend in referring to this Home. Surely if proof be needed of the excellence of such institutions, we need only remember that they are promoted and financed by a government department." I noticed that he made no reference to the funeral, and this seemed to me a serious omission. But, what with his long-windedness, the endless days and hours they had been discussing my "soul," and the rest of it, I found that my mind had gone blurred; everything was dissolving into a grayish, watery haze.

Only one incident stands out; toward the end, while my counsel rambled on, I heard the tin trumpet of an ice-cream vendor in the street, a small, shrill sound cutting across the flow of words. And then a rush of memories went through my mind—memories of a life which was mine no longer and had once provided me with the surest, humblest pleasures: warm smells of summer, my favorite streets, the sky at evening, Marie's dresses and her laugh. The futility of what was happening here seemed to take me by the throat, I felt like vomiting, and I had only one idea: to get it over, to go back to my cell, and sleep . . . and sleep.

Dimly I heard my counsel making his last appeal.

"Gentlemen of the jury, surely you will not send to his death a decent, hard-working young man, because for one tragic moment he lost his self-control? Is he not sufficiently punished by the lifelong remorse that is to be his lot? I confidently await your verdict, the only verdict possible—that of homicide with extenuating circumstances."

The court rose, and the lawyer sat down, looking thoroughly exhausted. Some of his colleagues came to him and shook his hand. "You put up a magnificent show, old man," I heard one of them say. Another lawyer even called me to witness: "Fine, wasn't it?" I agreed, but insincerely; I was far too tired to judge if it had been "fine" or otherwise.

Meanwhile the day was ending and the heat becoming less intense.

By some vague sounds that reached me from the street I knew that the cool of the evening had set in. We all sat on, waiting. And what we all were waiting for really concerned nobody but me. I looked round the courtroom. It was exactly as it had been on the first day. I met the eyes of the journalist in gray and the robot woman. This reminded me that not once during the whole hearing had I tried to catch Marie's eye. It wasn't that I'd forgotten her; only I was too preoccupied. I saw her now, seated between Céleste and Raymond. She gave me a little wave of her hand, as if to say, "At last!" She was smiling, but I could tell that she was rather anxious. But my heart seemed turned to stone, and I couldn't even return her smile.

The judges came back to their seats. Someone read out to the jury, very rapidly, a string of questions. I caught a word here and there. "Murder of malice aforethought . . . Provocation . . . Extenuating circumstances." The jury went out, and I was taken to the little room where I had already waited. My lawyer came to see me; he was very talkative and showed more cordiality and confidence than ever before. He assured me that all would go well and I'd get off with a few years' imprisonment or transportation. I asked him what were the chances of getting the sentence quashed. He said there was no chance of that. He had not raised any point of law, as this was apt to prejudice the jury. And it was difficult to get a judgment quashed except on technical grounds. I saw his point, and agreed. Looking at the matter dispassionately, I shared his view. Otherwise there would be no end to litigation. "In any case," the lawyer said, "you can appeal in the ordinary way. But I'm convinced the verdict will be favorable."

We waited for quite a while, a good three quarters of an hour, I should say. Then a bell rang. My lawyer left me, saying:

"The foreman of the jury will read out the answers. You will be called on after that to hear the judgment."

Some doors banged. I heard people hurrying down flights of steps, but couldn't tell whether they were near by or distant. Then I heard a voice droning away in the courtroom.

When the bell rang again and I stepped back into the dock, the silence of the courtroom closed in round me, and with the silence came a queer sensation when I noticed that, for the first time, the young journalist kept his eyes averted. I didn't look in Marie's direction. In fact, I had no time to look, as the presiding judge had already started pronouncing a rigmarole to the effect that "in the name of the French people" I was to be decapitated in some public place.

It seemed to me then that I could interpret the look on the faces of those present; it was one of almost respectful sympathy. The policemen, too, handled me very gently. The lawyer placed his hand on my wrist. I had stopped thinking altogether. I heard the Judge's voice asking if I had anything more to say. After thinking for a moment, I answered, "No." Then the policemen led me out.

## CHAPTER V

I have just refused, for the third time, to see the prison chaplain. I have nothing to say to him, don't feel like talking—and shall be seeing him quite soon enough, anyway. The only thing that interests me now is the problem of circumventing the machine, learning if the inevitable admits a loophole.

They have moved me to another cell. In this one, lying on my back, I can see the sky, and there is nothing else to see. All my time is spent in watching the slowly changing colors of the sky, as day moves on to night. I put my hands behind my head, gaze up, and wait.

This problem of a loophole obsesses me; I am always wondering if there have been cases of condemned prisoners' escaping from the implacable machinery of justice at the last moment, breaking through the police cordon, vanishing in the nick of time before the guillotine falls. Often and often I blame myself for not having given more attention to accounts of public executions. One should always take an interest in such matters. There's never any knowing what one may come to. Like everyone else I'd read descriptions of executions in the papers. But technical books dealing with this subject must certainly exist; only I'd never felt sufficiently interested to look them up. And in these books I might have found escape stories. Surely they'd have told me that in one case, anyhow, the wheels had stopped; that once, if only once, in that inexorable march of events, chance or luck had played a happy part. Just once! In a way I think that single instance would have satisfied me. My emotion would have done the rest. The papers often talk of "a debt owed to society"—a debt which, according to them, must be paid by the offender. But talk of that sort doesn't touch the imagination. No, the one thing that counted for me was the possibility of making a dash for it and defeating their bloodthirsty rite; of a mad stampede to freedom that would anyhow give me a moment's hope, the gambler's last throw. Naturally, all that "hope" could come to was to be knocked down at the corner of a street or picked off by a bullet in my back. But, all things considered, even this luxury was forbidden me; I was caught in the rattrap irrevocably.

Try as I might, I couldn't stomach this brutal certitude. For really, when one came to think of it, there was a disproportion between the judgment on which it was based and the unalterable sequence of events starting from the moment when that judgment was delivered. The fact that the verdict was read out at eight P.M. rather than at five, the fact that it might have been quite different, that it was given by men who change their underclothes, and was credited to so vague an entity as the "French people"—for that matter, why not to the Chinese or the German people?—all these facts seemed to deprive the court's decision of much of its gravity. Yet I could but recognize that, from the moment the verdict was given, its effects became as cogent, as tangible, as, for example, this wall against which I was lying pressing my back to it.

When such thoughts crossed my mind, I remembered a story Mother used to tell me about my father. I never set eyes on him. Perhaps the only things I really knew about him were what Mother had told me. One of these was that he'd gone to see a murderer executed. The mere thought of it turned his stomach. But he'd seen it through and, on coming home, was violently sick. At the time, I found my father's conduct rather disgusting. But now I understood; it was so natural. How had I failed to recognize that nothing was more important than an execution; that, viewed from one angle, it's the only thing that can genuinely interest a man? And I decided that, if ever I got out of jail, I'd attend every execution that took place. I was unwise, no doubt, even to consider this possibility. For, the moment I'd pictured myself in freedom, standing behind a double rank of policemen—on the right side of the line, so to speak —the mere thought of being an onlooker who comes to see the show, and can go home and vomit afterward, flooded my mind with a wild, absurd exultation. It was a stupid thing to let my imagination run away with me like that; a moment later I had a shivering fit and had to wrap myself closely in my blanket. But my teeth went on chattering; nothing would stop them.

Still, obviously, one can't be sensible all the time. Another equally ridiculous fancy of mine was to frame new laws, altering the penalties. What was wanted, to my mind, was to give the criminal a chance, if only a dog's chance; say, one chance in a thousand. There might be some drug, or combination of drugs, which would kill the patient (I thought of him as "the patient") nine hundred and ninety times in a thousand. That he should know this was, of course, essential. For after taking much thought, calmly, I came to the conclusion that what was wrong about the guillotine was that the condemned man had no chance at all, absolutely none. In fact, the patient's death had been ordained irrevocably. It was a foregone conclusion. If by some fluke the knife didn't do its job, they started again. So it came to this, that—against the grain, no doubt—the condemned man had to hope the apparatus was in good working order! This, I thought, was a flaw in the system; and, on the face of it, my view was sound enough. On the other hand, I had to admit it proved the efficiency of the system. It came to this; the man under sentence was obliged to collaborate mentally, it was in his interest that all should go off without a hitch.

Another thing I had to recognize was that, until now, I'd had wrong ideas on the subject. For some reason I'd always supposed that one had to go up steps and climb on to a scaffold, to be guillotined. Probably that was because of the 1789 Revolution; I mean, what I'd learned about it at school, and the pictures I had seen. Then one morning I remembered a photograph the newspapers had featured on the occasion of the execution of a famous criminal. Actually the apparatus stood on the ground; there was nothing very impressing about it, and it was much narrower than I'd imagined. It struck me as rather odd that picture had escaped my memory until now. What had struck me at the time was the neat appearance of the guillotine; its shining surfaces and finish reminded me of some laboratory instrument. One always has exaggerated ideas about what one doesn't know. Now I had to admit it seemed a very simple process, getting guillotined; the machine is on the same level as the man, and he walks toward it as he steps forward to meet somebody he knows. In a sense, that, too, was disappointing. The business of climbing a scaffold, leaving the world below, so to speak, gave something for a man's imagination to get hold of. But, as it was, the machine dominated everything; they killed you discreetly, with a hint of shame and much efficiency.

There were two other things about which I was always thinking:

the dawn and my appeal. However, I did my best to keep my mind off these thoughts. I lay down, looked up at the sky, and forced myself to study it. When the light began to turn green I knew that night was coming. Another thing I did to deflect the course of my thoughts was to listen to my heart. I couldn't imagine that this faint throbbing which had been with me for so long would ever cease. Imagination has never been one of my strong points. Still, I tried to picture a moment when the beating of my heart no longer echoed in my head. But, in vain. The dawn and my appeal were still there. And I ended by believing it was a silly thing to try to force one's thoughts out of their natural groove.

They always came for one at dawn; that much I knew. So, really, all my nights were spent in waiting for that dawn. I have never liked being taken by surprise. When something happens to me I want to be ready for it. That's why I got into the habit of sleeping off and and on in the daytime and watching through the night for the first hint of daybreak in the dark dome above. The worst period of the night was that vague hour when, I knew, they usually come; once it was after midnight I waited, listening intently. Never before had my ears perceived so many noises, such tiny sounds. Still, I must say I was lucky in one respect; never during any of those periods did I hear footsteps. Mother used to say that however miserable one is, there's always something to be thankful for. And each morning, when the sky brightened and light began to flood my cell, I agreed with her. Because I might just as well have heard footsteps, and felt my heart shattered into bits. Even though the faintest rustle sent me hurrying to the door and, pressing an ear to the rough, cold wood, I listened so intently that I could hear my breathing, quick and hoarse like a dog's panting—even so there was an end; my heart hadn't split, and I knew I had another twenty-four hours' respite.

Then all day there was my appeal to think about. I made the most of this idea, studying my effects so as to squeeze out the maximum of consolation. Thus, I always began by assuming the worst; my appeal was dismissed. That meant, of course, I was to die. Sooner than others, obviously. "But," I reminded myself, "it's common knowledge that life isn't worth living, anyhow." And, on a wide view, I could see that it makes little difference whether one dies at the age of thirty or threescore and ten—since, in either case, other men and women will continue living, the world will go on as before. Also, whether I died now or forty years hence, this business of dying had to be got through, inevitably. Still, somehow this line of thought wasn't as consoling as it should have been; the idea of all those years of life in hand was a galling reminder! However, I could argue myself out of it, by picturing what would have been my feelings when my term was up, and death had cornered me. Once you're up against it, the precise manner of your death has obviously small importance. Therefore—but it was hard not to lose the thread of the argument leading up to that "therefore"—I should be prepared to face the dismissal of my appeal.

At this stage, but only at this stage, I had, so to speak, the *right*, and accordingly I gave myself leave, to consider the other alternative; that my appeal was successful. And then the trouble was to calm down that sudden rush of joy rushing through my body and even bringing tears to my eyes. But it was up to me to bring my nerves to heel and steady my mind; for even in considering this possibility, I had to keep some order in my thoughts, so as to make my consolations, as regards the first alternative, more plausible. When I'd succeeded, I had earned a good hour's peace of mind; and that, anyhow, was something.

It was at one of these moments that I refused once again to see the chaplain. I was lying down and could mark the summer evening coming on by a soft golden glow spreading across the sky. I had just turned down my appeal, and felt my blood circulating with slow, steady throbs. No, I didn't want to see the chaplain. . . . Then I did something I hadn't done for quite a while; I fell to thinking about Marie. She hadn't written for ages; probably, I surmised, she had grown tired of being the mistress of a man sentenced to death. Or she might be ill, or dead. After all, such things happen. How could I have known about it, since, apart from our two bodies, separated now, there was no link between us, nothing to remind us of each other? Supposing she were dead, her memory would mean nothing; I couldn't feel an interest in a dead girl. This seemed to me quite normal; just as I realized people would soon forget me once I was dead. I couldn't even say that this was hard to stomach; really, there's no idea to which one doesn't get acclimatized in time.

My thoughts had reached this point when the chaplain walked in, unannounced. I couldn't help giving a start on seeing him. He noticed this evidently, as he promptly told me not to be alarmed. I reminded him that usually his visits were at another hour, and for a pretty grim occasion. This, he replied, was just a friendly visit; it had no concern with my appeal, about which he knew nothing. Then he sat down on my bed, asking me to sit beside him. I refused—

not because I had anything against him; he seemed a mild, amiable man.

He remained quite still at first, his arms resting on his knees, his eyes fixed on his hands. They were slender but sinewy hands, which made me think of two nimble little animals. Then he gently rubbed them together. He stayed so long in the same position that for a while I almost forgot he was there.

All of a sudden he jerked his head up and looked me in the eyes. "Why," he asked, "don't you let me come to see you?"

I explained that I didn't believe in God.

"Are you really so sure of that?"

I said I saw no point in troubling my head about the matter; whether I believed or didn't was, to my mind, a question of so little importance.

He then leaned back against the wall, laying his hands flat on his thighs. Almost without seeming to address me, he remarked that he'd often noticed one fancies one is quite sure about something, when in point of fact one isn't. When I said nothing, he looked at me again, and asked:

"Don't you agree?"

I said that seemed quite possible. But, though I mightn't be so sure about what interested me, I was absolutely sure about what didn't interest me. And the question he had raised didn't interest me at all.

He looked away and, without altering his posture, asked if it was because I felt utterly desperate that I spoke like this. I explained that it wasn't despair I felt, but fear—which was natural enough.

"In that case," he said firmly, "God can help you. All the men I've seen in your position turned to Him in their time of trouble."

Obviously, I replied, they were at liberty to do so, if they felt like it. I, however, didn't want to be helped, and I hadn't time to work up interest for something that didn't interest me.

He fluttered his hands fretfully; then, sitting up, smoothed out his cassock. When this was done he began talking again, addressing me as "my friend." It wasn't because I'd been condemned to death, he said, that he spoke to me in this way. In his opinion every man on the earth was under sentence of death.

There, I interrupted him; that wasn't the same thing, I pointed out, and, what's more, could be no consolation.

He nodded. "Maybe. Still, if you don't die soon, you'll die one day. And then the same question will arise. How will you face that terrible, final hour?"

I replied that I'd face it exactly as I was facing it now.

Thereat he stood up, and looked me straight in the eyes. It was a trick I knew well. I used to amuse myself trying it on Emmanuel and Céleste, and nine times out of ten they'd look away uncomfortably. I could see the chaplain was an old hand at it, as his gaze never faltered. And his voice was quite steady when he said: "Have you no hope at all? Do you really think that when you die you die outright, and nothing remains?"

I said: "Yes."

He dropped his eyes and sat down again. He was truly sorry for me, he said. It must make life unbearable for a man, to think as I did.

The priest was beginning to bore me, and, resting a shoulder on the wall, just beneath the little skylight, I looked away. Though I didn't trouble much to follow what he said, I gathered he was questioning me again. Presently his tone became agitated, urgent, and, as I realized that he was genuinely distressed, I began to pay more attention.

He said he felt convinced my appeal would succeed, but I was saddled with a load of guilt, of which I must get rid. In his view man's justice was a vain thing; only God's justice mattered. I pointed out that the former had condemned me. Yes, he agreed, but it hadn't absolved me from my sin. I told him that I wasn't conscious of any "sin"; all I knew was that I'd been guilty of a criminal offense. Well, I was paying the penalty of that offense, and no one had the right to expect anything more of me.

Just then he got up again, and it struck me that if he wanted to move in this tiny cell, almost the only choice lay between standing up and sitting down. I was staring at the floor. He took a single step toward me, and halted, as if he didn't dare to come nearer. Then he looked up through the bars at the sky.

"You're mistaken, my son," he said gravely. "There's more that might be required of you. And perhaps it *will* be required of you."

"What do you mean?"

"You might be asked to see . . ."

"To see what?"

Slowly the priest gazed round my cell, and I was struck by the sadness of his voice when he replied:

"These stone walls, I know it only too well, are steeped in human suffering. I've never been able to look at them without a shudder. And yet—believe me, I am speaking from the depths of my heart —I *know* that even the wretchedest among you have sometimes seen, taking form against that grayness, a divine face. It's that face you are asked to see."

This roused me a little. I informed him that I'd been staring at those walls for months; there was nobody, nothing in the world, I knew better than I knew them. And once upon a time, perhaps, I used to try to see a face. But it was a sun-gold face, lit up with desire—Marie's face. I had no luck; I'd never seen it, and now I'd given up trying. Indeed, I'd never seen anything "taking form," as he called it, against those gray walls.

The chaplain gazed at me with a sort of sadness. I now had my back to the wall and light was flowing over my forehead. He muttered some words I didn't catch; then abruptly asked if he might kiss me. I said, "No." Then he turned, came up to the wall, and slowly drew his hand along it.

"Do you really love these earthly things so very much?" he asked in a low voice.

I made no reply.

For quite a while he kept his eyes averted. His presence was getting more and more irksome, and I was on the point of telling him to go, and leave me in peace, when all of a sudden he swung round on me, and burst out passionately:

"No! No! I refuse to believe it. I'm sure you've often wished there was an afterlife."

Of course I had, I told him. Everybody has that wish at times. But that had no more importance than wishing to be rich, or to swim very fast, or to have a better-shaped mouth. It was in the same order of things. I was going on in the same vein, when he cut in with a question. How did I picture the life after the grave?

I fairly bawled out at him: "A life in which I can remember this life on earth. That's all I want of it." And in the same breath I told him I'd had enough of his company.

But, apparently, he had more to say on the subject of God. I went close up to him and made a last attempt to explain that I'd very little time left, and I wasn't going to waste it on God.

Then he tried to change the subject by asking me why I hadn't once addressed him as "Father," seeing that he was a priest. That irritated me still more, and I told him he wasn't my father; quite the contrary, he was on the others' side.

"No, no, my son," he said, laying his hand on my shoulder. "I'm on *your* side, though you don't realize it—because your heart is hardened. But I shall pray for you."

Then, I don't know how it was, but something seemed to break inside me, and I started yelling at the top of my voice. I hurled insults at him, I told him not to waste his rotten prayers on me; it was better to burn than to disappear. I'd taken him by the neckband of his cassock, and, in a sort of ecstasy of joy and rage, I poured out on him all the thoughts that had been simmering in my brain. He seemed so cocksure, you see. And yet none of his certainties was worth one strand of a woman's hair. Living as he did, like a corpse, he couldn't even be sure of being alive. It might look as if my hands were empty. Actually, I was sure of myself, sure about everything, far surer than he; sure of my present life and of the death that was coming. That, no doubt, was all I had; but at least that certainty was something I could get my teeth into—just as it had got its teeth into me. I'd been right, I was still right, I was always right. I'd passed my life in a certain way, and I might have passed it in a different way, if I'd felt like it. I'd acted thus, and I hadn't acted otherwise; I hadn't done x, whereas I had done y or z. And what did that mean? That, all the time, I'd been waiting for this present moment, for that dawn, tomorrow's or another day's, which was to justify me. Nothing, nothing had the least importance, and I knew quite well why. He, too, knew why. From the dark horizon of my future a sort of slow, persistent breeze had been blowing toward me, all my life long, from the years that were to come. And on its way that breeze had leveled out all the ideas that people tried to foist on me in the equally unreal years I then was living through. What difference could they make to me, the deaths of others, or a mother's love, or his God; or the way a man decides to live, the fate he thinks he chooses, since one and the same fate was bound to "choose" not only me but thousands of millions of privileged people who, like him, called themselves my brothers. Surely, surely he must see that? Every man alive was privileged; there was only one class of men, the privileged class. All alike would be condemned to die one day; his turn, too, would come like the others'. And what difference could it make if, after being charged with murder, he were executed because he didn't weep at his mother's funeral, since it all came to the same thing in the end? The same thing for Salamano's wife and for Salamano's dog. That little robot woman was as "guilty" as the girl from Paris who had married Masson, or as Marie, who wanted me to marry her. What did it matter if Raymond was as much my pal as Céleste, who was a far worthier man? What did it matter if at this very moment Marie was kissing a new boy friend? As a condemned man himself, couldn't he grasp what I meant by that dark wind blowing from my future? . . .

I had been shouting so much that I'd lost my breath, and just then the jailers rushed in and started trying to release the chaplain from my grip. One of them made as if to strike me. The chaplain quietened them down, then gazed at me for a moment without speaking. I could see tears in his eyes. Then he turned and left the cell.

Once he'd gone, I felt calm again. But all this excitement had exhausted me and I dropped heavily on to my sleeping plank. I must have had a longish sleep, for, when I woke, the stars were shining down on my face. Sounds of the countryside came faintly in, and the cool night air, veined with smells of earth and salt, fanned my cheeks. The marvelous peace of the sleepbound summer night flooded through me like a tide. Then, just on the edge of daybreak, I heard a steamer's siren. People were starting on a voyage to a world which had ceased to concern me forever. Almost for the first time in many months I thought of my mother. And now, it seemed to me, I understood why at her life's end she had taken on a "fiancé"; why she'd played at making a fresh start. There, too, in that Home where lives were flickering out, the dusk came as a mournful solace. With death so near, Mother must have felt like someone on the brink of freedom, ready to start life all over again. No one, no one in the world had any right to weep for her. And I, too, felt ready to start life all over again. It was as if that great rush of anger had washed me clean, emptied me of hope, and, gazing up at the dark sky spangled with its signs and stars, for the first time, the first, I laid my heart open to the benign indifference of the universe. To feel it so like myself, indeed, so brotherly, made me realize that I'd been happy, and that I was happy still. For all to be accomplished, for me to feel less lonely, all that remained to hope was that on the day of my execution there should be a huge crowd of spectators and that they should greet me with howls of execration.

[Translated by Stuart Gilbert]

# NOW THAT YOU'VE READ CAMUS'
# THE STRANGER:

*The Stranger* is a shocking story, with a central character who is indeed a stranger. Written in a precise, epigrammatic prose, the short novel combines dramatic action—a funeral, a love affair, a murder, a trial, a death cell scene—with social criticism and philosophy. Its author, Albert Camus, was, like Sartre, Malraux, and other of his French contemporaries, not only a fine creative writer but also a profound thinker and a man who took seriously his role as a social being. He traveled extensively, served as a delegate to UNESCO, asserted his views on many important national and international issues, and made a deep impression on modern thought in France and throughout the world.

Camus was born in Algeria, in 1913, less than a year before the outbreak of World War I. His father, an agricultural worker, was killed in the battle of the Marne. "I grew up," wrote Camus, "with all the men of my age, to the drums of the first World War, and our history since, has not ceased to be murder, injustice, or violence." His mother moved from the village of Mondovi to Algiers and worked hard at humble tasks to support her two sons. Camus spent his early years in a two-room apartment which he, his older brother, and his mother shared with a grandmother and a sick uncle.

At the local public school his ability attracted the attention of a teacher who tutored him and helped him win a scholarship to the *lycée*. When he had completed the course there, he enrolled in the University of Algiers, supporting himself with odd jobs. His major interest was philosophy and the Greek classics; and planning to become a teacher, he completed a *licence* (equivalent to the American Master's degree). In 1936 he presented a thesis on Plotinus and St. Augustine for the *diplome d'études superieures*. A handsome, tall, broad-shouldered, black-haired, robust young man, he relished a sense of well being and enjoyed athletic activities. He played football at the University and loved to swim in the Mediterranean and to lie in the hot Algerian sun. He responded wholeheartedly to life and all its experiences, and his student years were eventful: he began to write; he joined the Communist party but left it, disillusioned, a year later; he married and was divorced within a year; he worked as an actor with a touring theatrical group, and later established his own *avant garde* theater.

Then in 1937, at the age of twenty-four, Camus became critically ill with tuberculosis. The athletic, life-loving young man was forced into intimate companionship with death. He had to curtail his activities, but he refused to be dominated by the specter that shadowed him; in fact, he made death serve him. He formulated his philosophy as he slowly recovered, and during the next four years he began writing seriously. As soon as he could, he plunged again into an active life. At the start of World War II he tried, unsuccessfully, to enlist. He married a second time and became the father of two children. He went to Paris, and during the occupation participated actively in the French resistance movement by editing an underground paper, *Combat*. Before he left Algiers he had completed *The Stranger* (1942) and *The Myth of Sisyphus* (1943), a philosophical essay. During the war years, besides his journalistic activities, he wrote plays and worked on a long novel, *The Plague* (1947).

After the war he continued his many activities. He was connected with the publishing house of Gallimard, and continued to travel extensively. In 1945 he came to the United States for a three month visit and left with many pleasant memories of the country. His post-war plays *L'Etat de Seige* and *Les Justes* were successfully staged and he adapted for the French stage *Requiem for a Nun* by William Faulkner, whom he considered "*the* great American writer, the only one in the great tradition of the American nineteenth century—a creator of myths, a creator of a universe." In *The Rebel* (1951) Camus further developed his philosophy. His novel, *The Fall* (1956), deals with a Joseph Conrad theme: the brave man who suddenly turns coward. The hero of *The Fall*, Camus said in an interview, is "a less brilliant Lord Jim." In 1957, Camus was awarded the Nobel Prize for Literature.

Albert Camus' love of life and his intimate acquaintance with death as an individual and as a member of a war-scarred generation are reflected in *The Stranger*. The short novel embodies the ideas which he formulated and presented in his philosophical works. Camus' ideas, though individual, belong (as do Unamuno's) in the broad stream of contemporary thought called Existentialism. He rejects the traditional view that there is a divine purpose in the universe and in human life. Man, animals, plants live and die; there is no God and therefore no supernatural intelligence directs this process. Man is a part of the natural, purposeless world, chained to it by his mortality; but at the same time separated from it by his consciousness. Man is unique because he alone is conscious of his mortality. Consciousness, the ability to think, brings with it a desire, an instinctive need for understanding why evil, pain, and death are a part of life. The human being seeks explanations and creates them. But there is no explanation that is not created by man. The truth is that life is without purpose and without meaning. What Camus calls The Absurd is this peculiar situation in which man, like the animal, is a part of the world but is at the same time set apart from it by his ability to think and his knowledge that he must suffer and die.

Man can be blind to the absurdity of his condition. He can close his mind to the truth by living like an automaton, existing in a stifling routine. But then all of a sudden, a tragic accident, a horrible illness, and he must face, like Iván Ilých in Tolstoy's story, the inevitability of his extinction. As Camus describes it in *The Myth of Sisyphus*:

> The stage sets collapse. Rising, streetcar, four hours in the office or the factory, meal, streetcar, four hours of work, meal, sleep, and Monday Tuesday Wednesday Thursday Friday and Saturday according to the same rhythm—this path is easily followed most of the time. But one day the "why" arises and everything begins in the weariness tinged with amazement. "Begins"—this is important. Weariness comes at the end of the acts of a mechanical life, but at the same time it inaugurates the impulse of consciousness. It awakens consciousness and provokes what follows. What follows is the gradual return into the chain or it is the definitive awakening. At the end of the awakening comes, in time, the consequence: suicide or recovery.

To awaken to the absurdity of man's condition, to realize suddenly that life is meaningless, that the things he considers so important are really without value forces the human mind to ask: why continue to live? why not commit suicide?

Camus' answer to this question is courageous and resonant: man has within him the strength to accept the absurdity of his condition and live, even though he is aware that life is meaningless. Though without purpose or meaning, life is the only thing that man has, the only reality he can know, and once he recognizes this and strips away his illusions he discovers that there is much in life he can enjoy and relish. Someone reaching this stage of thought would not necessarily have to be a hedonist. By facing, honestly, his own mortality he can come to recognize that he shares the inevitability of death with all men, and with this recognition comes love and compassion. Upon this feeling of love for one's fellow men is erected a moral code.

Camus places the full and terrible burden of living and dying upon the human being; he extends no hope of divine aid, of immortality; he makes each man responsible only to himself and to his fellow man for his acts and for his life. It is a grim, almost overwhelming burden, but Camus believes man is capable of shouldering it.

Some of these ideas Camus dramatized in *The Stranger*. The central character Meursault, a breathing robot in the first part of the novel, commits a pointless murder. It is the chance occurrence that forces him to face his own mortality; his routine life collapses and he awakens. Meursault is condemned, for not accepting its illusions, by the society that fosters the automaton existence he exemplifies in the extreme. At the end of the story he shares with every man a condemnation to death and he realizes there is no escape. In his death cell he rejects the priest's belief in a divine purpose in the world and in man's existence. As soon as Meursault recognizes that death is a bond that ties him to his fellow man, he is no longer a stranger. He awaits his execution, convinced that though life is meaningless, it is worthwhile because there is nothing else.

In his protagonist's final attitude, Camus suggests to modern man a way of life, a suggestion he develops in *The Plague*. The routine of an entire city collapses as the plague sweeps through it. The death rate rises daily and the people are isolated from the rest of the world. Their usual concerns become insignificant and they must, like Meursault in *The Stranger*, face the reality of imminent death. Meursault's death-cell conclusions Camus expands and dramatizes in the person of Dr. Rieux, the narrator and protagonist of *The Plague*. The rejection of religion is symbolized by the death of a priest, and the awakening of love and compassion for one's fellows by Rieux's feeling of spiritual unity with a coworker. Unselfishly, heroically the representative group surrounding Rieux work harmoniously together to fight the plague. Their acceptance of imminent death does not make them selfish; it makes Christian morality meaningful to them.

Though these novels reflect Camus' ideas, they are by no means philosophical tracts. *The Stranger* and *The Plague* are fiction, working out in human terms, dramatically and symbolically, Camus' ideas about life and his fellow man.

## FOR FURTHER INFORMATION:

Germaine Brée. *Camus*. Rutgers University Press: New Brunswick, 1959.

John Cruickshank. *Albert Camus and the Literature of Revolt*. Oxford University Press: New York, 1963.

Thomas Hanna. *The Thought and Art of Albert Camus*. Regnery: Chicago, 1958.

Emmett Parker. *Albert Camus, the Artist in the Arena*. University of Wisconsin Press: Madison, 1965.

Philip Thody. *Albert Camus, 1933–1960*. Macmillan & Co.: New York, 1962.

Carl A. Viggiani. "Camus' L'Etranger," *Publications of the Modern Language Association,* LXXI (1956), 865–887.

# THE MAN WHO LIVED
# UNDERGROUND

## BY RICHARD WRIGHT

First published, 1944

# THE MAN WHO LIVED UNDERGROUND

**I**'VE got to hide, he told himself. His chest heaved as he waited, crouching in a dark corner of the vestibule. He was tired of running and dodging. Either he had to find a place to hide, or he had to surrender. A police car swished by through the rain, its siren rising sharply. They're looking for me all over . . . He crept to the door and squinted through the fogged plate glass. He stiffened as the siren rose and died in the distance. Yes, he had to hide, but where? He gritted his teeth. Then a sudden movement in the street caught his attention. A throng of tiny columns of water snaked into the air from the perforations of a manhole cover. The columns stopped abruptly, as though the perforations had become clogged; a gray spout of sewer water jutted up from underground and lifted the circular metal cover, juggled it for a moment, then let it fall with a clang.

He hatched a tentative plan: he would wait until the siren sounded far off, then he would go out. He smoked and waited, tense. At last the siren gave him his signal; it wailed, dying, going away from him. He stepped to the sidewalk, then paused and looked curiously at the open manhole, half expecting the cover to leap up again. He went to the center of the street and stooped and peered into the hole, but could see nothing. Water rustled in the black depths.

He started with terror; the siren sounded so near that he had the idea that he had been dreaming and had awakened to find the car upon him. He dropped instinctively to his knees and his hands grasped the rim of the manhole. The siren seemed to hoot directly above him and with a wild gasp of exertion he snatched the cover far enough off to admit his body. He swung his legs over the opening and lowered himself into watery darkness. He hung for an eternal moment to the rim by his finger tips, then he felt rough metal prongs and at once he knew that sewer workmen used these ridges to lower themselves into manholes. Fist over fist, he let his body sink until he could feel no more prongs. He swayed in dank space; the siren seemed to howl at the very rim of the manhole. He dropped and was washed violently into an ocean of warm, leaping water. His head was battered against a wall and he wondered if this were death. Frenziedly his fingers clawed and sank into a crevice. He steadied himself and measured the strength of the current with his own muscular tension. He stood slowly in water that dashed past his knees with fearful velocity.

He heard a prolonged scream of brakes and the siren broke off. Oh, God! They had found him! Looming above his head in the rain a white face hovered over the hole. "How did this damn thing get off?" he heard a policeman ask. He saw the steel cover move slowly until the hole looked like a quarter moon turned black. "Give me a hand here," someone called. The cover clanged into place, muffling the sights and sounds of the upper world. Knee-deep in the pulsing current, he breathed with aching chest, filling his lungs with the hot stench of yeasty rot.

From the perforations of the manhole cover, delicate lances of hazy violet sifted down and wove a mottled pattern upon the surface of the streaking current. His lips parted as a car swept past along the wet pavement overhead, its heavy rumble soon dying out, like the hum of a plane speeding through a dense cloud. He had never thought that cars could sound like that; everything seemed strange and unreal under here. He stood in darkness for a long time, knee-deep in rustling water, musing.

The odor of rot had become so general that he no longer smelled it. He got his cigarettes, but discovered that his matches were wet. He searched and found a dry folder in the pocket of his shirt and manged to strike one; it flared weirdly in the wet gloom, glowing greenishly, turning red, orange, then yellow. He lit a crumpled cigarette; then, by the flickering light of the match, he looked for support so that he would not have to keep his muscles flexed against the pouring water. His pupils narrowed and he saw to either side of him two steaming walls that rose and curved inward some six feet above his head to form a dripping, mouse-colored dome. The bottom of the sewer was a sloping V-trough. To the left, the sewer vanished in ashen fog. To the right was a steep down-curve into which water plunged.

He saw now that had he not regained his feet in time, he would have been swept to death, or had he entered any other manhole he would have probably drowned. Above the rush of the current he heard sharper juttings of water; tiny streams were spewing into the sewer from smaller conduits. The match died; he struck another and saw a mass of debris sweep past him and clog the throat of the down-curve. At once the water began rising rapidly. Could he climb out before he drowned? A long hiss sounded and the debris was sucked from sight; the current lowered. He understood now what had made the water toss the manhole cover; the down-curve had become temporarily obstructed and the perforations had become clogged.

He was in danger; he might slide into a down-curve; he might wander with a lighted match into a pocket of gas and blow himself up; or he might contract some horrible disease . . . Though he wanted to leave, an irrational impulse held him rooted. To the left, the convex ceiling swooped to a height of less than five feet. With cigarette slanting from pursed lips, he waded with taut muscles, his feet sloshing over the slimy bottom, his shoes sinking into spongy slop, the slate-colored water cracking in creamy foam against his knees. Pressing his flat left palm against the lowered ceiling, he struck another match and saw a metal pole nestling in a niche of the wall. Yes, some sewer workman had left it. He reached for it, then jerked his head away as a whisper of scurrying life whisked past and was still. He held the match close and saw a huge rat, wet with slime, blinking beady eyes and baring tiny fangs. The light blinded the rat and the frizzled head moved aimlessly. He grabbed the pole and let it fly against the rat's soft body; there was shrill piping and the grizzly body splashed into the dun-colored water and was snatched out of sight, spinning in the scuttling stream.

He swallowed and pushed on, following the curve of the misty cavern, sounding the water with the pole. By the faint light of another manhole cover he saw, amid loose wet brick, a hole with walls of damp earth leading into blackness. Gingerly he poked the pole into it; it was hollow and went beyond the length of the pole. He shoved the pole before him, hoisted himself upward, got to his hands and knees, and crawled. After a few yards he paused, struck to wonderment by the silence; it seemed that he had traveled a million miles away from the world. As he inched forward again he could sense the bottom of the dirt tunnel becoming dry and lowering slightly. Slowly he rose and to his astonishment he stood erect. He could not hear the rustling of the water now and he felt confoundingly alone, yet lured by the darkness and silence.

He crept a long way, then stopped, curious, afraid. He put his right foot forward and it dangled in space; he drew back in fear. He thrust the pole outward and it swung in emptiness. He trembled, imagining the earth crumbling and burying him alive. He scratched a match and saw that the dirt floor sheered away steeply and widened into a sort of cave some five feet below him. An old sewer, he muttered. He cocked his head, hearing a feathery cadence which he could not identify. The match ceased to burn.

Using the pole as a kind of ladder, he slid down and stood in darkness. The air was a little fresher and he could still hear vague noises. Where was he? He felt suddenly that someone was standing near him and he turned sharply, but there was only darkness. He poked cautiously and felt a brick wall; he followed it and the strange sounds grew louder. He ought to get out of here. This was crazy. He could not remain here for any length of time; there was no food and no place to sleep. But the faint sounds tantalized him; they were strange but familiar. Was it a motor? A baby crying? Music? A siren? He groped on, and the sounds came so clearly that he could feel the pitch and timbre of human voices. Yes, singing! That was it! He listened with open mouth. It was a church service. Enchanted, he groped toward the waves of melody.

> *Jesus, take me to your home above*
> *And fold me in the bosom of Thy love. . .*

The singing was on the other side of the brick wall. Excited, he wanted to watch the service without being seen. Whose church was it? He knew most of the churches in this area above ground, but the singing sounded too strange and detached for him to guess. He looked to the left, to the right, down to the black dirt, then upward and was startled to see a bright sliver of light slicing the darkness like the blade of a razor. He struck one of his two remaining matches and saw rusty pipes running along an old concrete ceiling. Photographically he located the exact position of the pipes in his mind. The match flame sank and he sprang upward; his hands clutched a pipe. He swung his legs and tossed his body onto the bed of pipes and they creaked, swaying up and down; he thought that the tier was about to crash, but nothing happened. He edged to the crevice and saw a segment of black men and women, dressed in white robes, singing, holding tattered songbooks in their black palms. His first impulse was to laugh, but he checked himself.

What was he doing? He was crushed with a sense of guilt. Would God strike him dead for that? The singing swept on and he shook his head, disagreeing in spite of himself. They oughtn't to do that, he thought. But he could think of no reason *why* they should not do it. Just singing with the air of the sewer blowing in on them . . . He felt that he was gazing upon something abysmally obscene, yet he could not bring himself to leave.

After a long time he grew numb and dropped to the dirt. Pain throbbed in his legs and a deeper pain, induced by the sight of those black people groveling and begging for something they could never get, churned in him. A vague conviction made him feel that those people should stand unrepentant and yield no quarter in singing and praying, yet *he* had run away from the police, had pleaded with them to believe in *his* innocence. He shook his head, bewildered.

How long had he been down here? He did not know. This was a new kind of living for him; the intensity of feelings he had experienced when looking at the church people sing made him certain that he had been down here a long time, but his mind told him that the time must have been short. In this darkness the only notion he had of time was when a match flared and measured time by its fleeting light. He groped back through the hole toward the sewer and the waves of song subsided and finally he could not hear them at all. He came to where the earth hole ended and he heard the noise of the current and time lived again for him, measuring the moments by the wash of the water.

The rain must have slackened, for the flow of water had lessened and came only to his ankles. Ought he to go up into the streets and take his chances on hiding somewhere else? But they would surely catch him. The mere thought of dodging and running again from the police made him tense. No, he would stay and plot how to elude them. But what could he do down here? He walked forward into the sewer and came to another manhole cover; he stood beneath it, debating. Fine pencils of gold spilled suddenly from the little circles in the manhole cover and trembled on the surface of the current. Yes, street lamps . . . It must be night . . .

He went forward for about a quarter of an hour, wading aimlessly, poking the pole carefully before him. Then he stopped, his eyes fixed and intent. What's that? A strangely familiar image attracted and repelled him. Lit by the yellow stems from another manhole cover was a tiny nude body of a baby snagged by debris and half-submerged in water. Thinking that the baby was alive, he moved impulsively to save it, but his roused feelings told him that it was dead, cold, nothing, the same nothingness he had felt while watching the men and women singing in the church. Water blossomed about the tiny legs, the tiny arms, the tiny head, and rushed onward. The eyes were closed, as though in sleep; the fists were clenched, as though in protest; and the mouth gaped black in a soundless cry.

He straightened and drew in his breath, feeling that he had been staring for all eternity at the ripples of veined water skimming impersonally over the shriveled limbs. He felt as condemned as when the policemen had accused him. Involuntarily he lifted his hand to brush the vision away, but his arm fell listlessly to his side. Then he acted; he closed his eyes and reached forward slowly with the soggy shoe of his right foot and shoved the dead baby from where it had been lodged. He kept his eyes closed, seeing the little body twisting in the current as it floated from sight. He opened his eyes, shivered, placed his knuckles in the sockets, hearing the water speed in the somber shadows.

He tramped on, sensing at times a sudden quickening in the current as he passed some conduit whose waters were swelling the stream that slid by his feet. A few minutes later he was standing under another manhole cover, listening to the faint rumble of noises above ground. Streetcars and trucks, he mused. He looked down and saw a stagnant pool of gray-green sludge; at intervals a balloon pocket rose from the scum, glistening a bluish-purple, and burst. Then another. He turned, shook his head, and tramped back to the dirt cave by the church, his lips quivering.

Back in the cave, he sat and leaned his back against a dirt wall. His body was trembling slightly. Finally his senses quieted and he slept. When he awakened he felt stiff and cold. He had to leave this foul place, but leaving meant facing those policemen who had wrongly accused him. No, he could not go back above-ground. He remembered the beating they had given him and how he had signed his name to a confession, a confession which he had not even read. He had been too tired when they had shouted at him, demanding that he sign his name; he had signed it to end his pain.

He stood and groped about in the darkness. The church singing had stopped. How long had he slept? He did not know. But he felt refreshed and hungry. He doubled his fist nervously, realizing that he could not make a decision. As he walked about he stumbled over an old rusty iron pipe. He picked it up and felt a jagged edge. Yes, there was a brick wall and he could dig into it. What would he find? Smiling, he groped to the brick wall, sat, and began digging idly into damp cement. I can't make any noise, he cautioned himself. As time passed he grew thirsty, but there was no water. He had to kill time or go aboveground. The cement came out of the wall easily; he extracted four bricks and felt a soft draft blowing into his face. He stopped, afraid. What was beyond? He waited a long time and nothing happened; then he began digging again, soundlessly, slowly; he enlarged the hole and crawled through into a dark room and collided with another wall. He felt his way to the right; the wall ended and his fingers toyed in space, like the antennae of an insect.

He fumbled on and his feet struck something hollow, like wood. What's this? He felt with his fingers. Steps . . . He stooped and pulled off his shoes and mounted the stairs and saw a yellow chink of light shining and heard a low voice speaking. He placed his eye to a keyhole and saw the nude waxen figure of a man stretched out upon a white table. The voice, low-pitched and vibrant, mumbled indistinguishable words, neither rising nor falling. He craned his neck and squinted to see the man who was talking, but he could not locate him. Above the naked figure was suspended a huge glass container filled with a blood-red liquid from which a white rubber tube dangled. He crouched closer to the door and saw the tip end of a black object lined with pink satin. A coffin, he breathed. This is an undertaker's establishment . . . A fine-spun lace of ice covered his body and he shuddered. A throaty chuckle sounded in the depths of the yellow room.

He turned to leave. Three steps down it occurred to him that a light switch should be nearby; he felt along the wall, found an electric button, pressed it, and a blinding glare smote his pupils so hard that he was sightless, defenseless. His pupils contracted and he wrinkled his nostrils at a peculiar odor. At once he knew that he had been dimly aware of this odor in the darkness, but the light had brought it sharply to his attention. Some kind of stuff they use to embalm, he thought. He went down the steps and saw piles of lumber, coffins, and a long workbench. In one corner was a tool chest. Yes, he could use tools, could tunnel through walls with them. He lifted the lid of the chest and saw nails, a hammer, a crowbar, a screwdriver, a light bulb, and a long length of electric wire. Good!

He would lug these back to his cave.

He was about to hoist the chest to his shoulders when he dis-covered a door behind the furnace. Where did it lead? He tried to open it and found it securely bolted. Using the crowbar so as to make no sound, he pried the door open; it swung on creaking hinges, outward. Fresh air came to his face and he caught the faint roar of faraway sound. Easy now, he told himself. He widened the door and a lump of coal rattled toward him. A coalbin . . . Evidently the door led into another basement. The roaring noise was louder now, but he could not identify it. Where was he? He groped slowly over the coal pile, then ranged in darkness over a gritty floor. The roaring noise seemed to come from above him, then below. His fingers followed a wall until he touched a wooden ridge. A door, he breathed.

The noise died to a low pitch; he felt his skin prickle. It seemed that he was playing a game with an unseen person whose intelligence outstripped his. He put his ear to the flat surface of the door. Yes, voices . . . Was this a prize fight stadium? The sound of the voices came near and sharp, but he could not tell if they were joyous or despairing. He twisted the knob until he heard a soft click and felt the springy weight of the door swinging toward him. He was afraid to open it, yet captured by curiosity and wonder. He jerked the door wide and saw on the far side of the basement a furnace glowing red. Ten feet away was still another door, half ajar. He crossed and peered through the door into an empty, high-ceilinged corridor that ter-minated in a dark complex of shadow. The belling voices rolled about him and his eagerness mounted. He stepped into the corridor and the voices swelled louder. He crept on and came to a narrow stairway leading circularly upward; there was no question but that he was going to ascend those stairs.

Mounting the spiraled staircase, he heard the voices roll in a steady wave, then leap to crescendo, only to die away, but always remaining audible. Ahead of him glowed red letters: E—X—I—T. At the top of the steps he paused in front of a black curtain that fluttered un-certainly. He parted the folds and looked into a convex depth that gleamed with clusters of shimmering lights. Sprawled below him was a stretch of human faces, tilted upward, chanting, whistling, screaming, laughing. Dangling before the faces, high upon a screen of silver, were jerking shadows. A movie, he said with slow laughter breaking from his lips.

He stood in a box in the reserved section of a movie house and the impulse he had had to tell the people in the church to stop their singing seized him. These people were laughing at their lives, he thought with amazement. They were shouting and yelling at the animated shadows of themselves. His compassion fired his imagination and he stepped out of the box, walked out upon thin air, walked on down to the audience; and, hovering in the air just above them, he stretched out his hand to touch them . . . His tension snapped and he found himself back in the box, looking down into the sea of faces. No; it could not be done; he could not awaken them. He sighed. Yes, these people were children, sleeping in their living, awake in their dying.

He turned away, parted the black curtain, and looked out. He saw no one. He started down the white stone steps and when he reached the bottom he saw a man in trim blue uniform coming toward him. So used had he become to being underground that he thought that he could walk past the man, as though he were a ghost. But the man stopped. And he stopped.

"Looking for the men's room, sir?" the man asked, and, without waiting for an answer, he turned and pointed. "This way, sir. The first door to your right."

He watched the man turn and walk up the steps and go out of sight. Then he laughed. What a funny fellow! He went back to the basement and stood in the red darkness, watching the glowing embers in the furnace. He went to the sink and turned the faucet and the water flowed in a smooth silent stream that looked like a spout of blood. He brushed the mad image from his mind and began to wash his hands leisurely, looking about for the usual bar of soap. He found one and rubbed it in his palms until a rich lather bloomed in his cupped fingers, like a scarlet sponge. He scrubbed and rinsed his hands meticulously, then hunted for a towel; there was none. He shut off the water, pulled off his shirt, dried his hands on it; when he put it on again he was grateful for the cool dampness that came to his skin.

Yes, he was thirsty; he turned on the faucet again, bowled his fingers and when the water bubbled over the brim of his cupped palms, he drank in long, slow swallows. His bladder grew tight; he shut off the water, faced the wall, bent his head, and watched a red stream strike the floor. His nostrils wrinkled against acrid wisps of vapor; though he had tramped in the waters of the sewer, he stepped back from the wall so that his shoes, wet with sewer slime, would not touch his urine.

He heard footsteps and crawled quickly into the coalbin. Lumps rattled noisily. The footsteps came into the basement and stopped.

Who was it? Had someone heard him and come down to investigate? He waited, crouching, sweating. For a long time there was silence, then he heard the clang of metal and a brighter glow lit the room. Somebody's tending the furnace, he thought. Footsteps came closer and he stiffened. Looming before him was a white face lined with coal dust, the face of an old man with watery blue eyes. Highlights spotted his gaunt cheekbones, and he held a huge shovel. There was a screechy scrape of metal against stone, and the old man lifted a shovelful of coal and went from sight.

The room dimmed momentarily, then a yellow glare came as coal flared at the furnace door. Six times the old man came to the bin and went to the furnace with shovels of coal, but not once did he lift his eyes. Finally he dropped the shovel, mopped his face with a dirty handkerchief, and sighed: "Wheeew!" He turned slowly and trudged out of the basement, his footsteps dying away.

He stood, and lumps of coal clattered down the pile. He stepped from the bin and was startled to see the shadowy outline of an electric bulb hanging above his head. Why had not the old man turned it on? Oh, yes . . . He understood. The old man had worked here for so long that he had no need for light; he had learned a way of seeing in his dark world, like those sightless worms that inch along underground by a sense of touch.

His eyes fell upon a lunch pail and he was afraid to hope that it was full. He picked it up; it was heavy. He opened it. *Sandwiches!* He looked guiltily around; he was alone. He searched farther and found a folder of matches and a half-empty tin of tobacco; he put them eagerly into his pocket and clicked off the light. With the lunch pail under his arm, he went through the door, groped over the pile of coal, and stood again in the lighted basement of the undertaking establishment. I've got to get those tools, he told himself. And turn off that light. He tiptoed back up the steps and switched off the light; the invisible voice still droned on behind the door. He crept down and, seeing with his fingers, opened the lunch pail and tore off a piece of paper bag and brought out the tin and spilled grains of tobacco into the makeshift concave. He rolled it and wet it with spittle, then inserted one end into his mouth and lit it: he sucked smoke that bit his lungs. The nicotine reached his brain, went out along his arms to his finger tips, down to his stomach, and over all the tired nerves of his body.

He carted the tools to the hole he had made in the wall. Would the noise of the falling chest betray him? But he would have to take a chance; he had to have those tools. He lifted the chest and shoved it; it hit the dirt on the other side of the wall with a loud clatter. He waited, listening; nothing happened. Head first, he slithered through and stood in the cave. He grinned, filled with a cunning idea. Yes, he would now go back into the basement of the undertaking establishment and crouch behind the coal pile and dig another hole. Sure! Fumbling, he opened the tool chest and extracted a crowbar, a screwdriver, and a hammer; he fastened them securely about his person.

With another lumpish cigarette in his flexed lips, he crawled back through the hole and over the coal pile and sat, facing the brick wall. He jabbed with the crowbar and the cement sheered away; quicker than he thought, a brick came loose. He worked an hour; the other bricks did not come easily. He sighed, weak from effort. I ought to rest a little, he thought. I'm hungry. He felt his way back to the cave and stumbled along the wall till he came to the tool chest. He sat upon it, opened the lunch pail, and took out two thick sandwiches. He smelled them. Pork chops . . . His mouth watered. He closed his eyes and devoured a sandwich, savoring the smooth rye bread and juicy meat. He ate rapidly, gulping down lumpy mouthfuls that made him long for water. He ate the other sandwich and found an apple and gobbled that up too, sucking the core till the last trace of flavor was drained from it. Then, like a dog, he ground the meat bones with his teeth, enjoying the salty, tangy marrow. He finished and stretched out full length on the ground and went to sleep. . . .

. . . His body was washed by cold water that gradually turned warm and he was buoyed upon a stream and swept out to sea where waves rolled gently and suddenly he found himself walking upon the water how strange and delightful to walk upon the water and he came upon a nude woman holding a nude baby in her arms and the woman was sinking into the water holding the baby above her head and screaming *help* and he ran over the water to the woman and he reached her just before she went down and he took the baby from her hands and stood watching the breaking bubbles where the woman sank and he called *lady* and still no answer yes dive down there and rescue that woman but he could not take this baby with him and he stooped and laid the baby tenderly upon the surface of the water expecting it to sink but it floated and he leaped into the water and held his breath and strained his eyes to see through the gloomy volume of water but there was no woman and he opened his mouth and called *lady* and the water bubbled and his chest ached and his arms were tired but he could not see the woman and he called again *lady lady* and his feet touched sand at the bottom of the sea and his chest felt as though it would burst and he bent his knees and propelled himself upward and water rushed past him and his head bobbed out and he breathed deeply and looked around where was the baby the baby was gone and he rushed over the water looking for the baby calling *where is it* and the empty sky and sea threw back his voice *where is it* and he began to doubt that he could stand upon the water and then he was sinking and as he struggled the water rushed him downward spinning dizzily and he opened his mouth to call for help and water surged into his lungs and he choked . . .

He groaned and leaped erect in the dark, his eyes wide. The images of terror that thronged his brain would not let him sleep. He rose, made sure that the tools were hitched to his belt, and groped his way to the coal pile and found the rectangular gap from which he had taken the bricks. He took out the crowbar and hacked. Then dread paralyzed him. How long had he slept? Was it day or night now? He had to be careful. Someone might hear him if it were day. He hewed softly for hours at the cement, working silently. Faintly quivering in the air above him was the dim sound of yelling voices. Crazy people, he muttered. They're still there in that movie . . .

Having rested, he found the digging much easier. He soon had a dozen bricks out. His spirits rose. He took out another brick and his fingers fluttered in space. Good! What lay ahead of him? Another basement? He made the hole larger, climbed through, walked over an uneven floor and felt a metal surface. He lighted a match and saw that he was standing behind a furnace in a basement; before him, on the far side of the room, was a door. He crossed and opened it; it was full of odds and ends. Daylight spilled from a window above his head.

Then he was aware of a soft, continuous tapping. What was it? A clock? No, it was louder than a clock and more irregular. He placed an old empty box beneath the window, stood upon it, and looked into an areaway. He eased the window up and crawled through; the sound of the tapping came clearly now. He glanced about; he was alone. Then he looked upward at a series of window ledges. The tapping identified itself. That's a typewriter, he said to himself. It seemed to be coming from just above. He grasped the ridges of a rain pipe and lifted himself upward; through a half-inch opening of window he saw a doorknob about three feet away. No, it was not a doorknob; it was a small circular disk made of stainless steel with many fine markings upon it. He held his breath; an eerie white hand, seemingly detached from its arm, touched the metal knob and whirled it, first to the left, then to the right. It's a safe! . . . Suddenly he could see the dial no more; a huge metal door swung slowly toward him and he was looking into a safe filled with green wads of paper money, rows of coins wrapped in brown paper, and glass jars and boxes of various sizes. His heart quickened. Good Lord! The white hand went in and out of the safe, taking wads of bills and cylinders of coins. The hand vanished and he heard the muffled click of the big door as it closed. Only the steel dial was visible now. The typewriter still tapped in his ears, but he could not see it. He blinked, wondering if what he had seen was real. There was more money in that safe than he had seen in all his life.

As he clung to the rain pipe, a daring idea came to him and he pulled the screwdriver from his belt. If the white hand twirled that dial again, he would be able to see how far to left and right it spun and he would have the combination! His blood tingled. I can scratch the numbers right here, he thought. Holding the pipe with one hand, he made the sharp edge of the screwdriver bite into the brick wall. Yes, he could do it. Now, he was set. Now, he had a reason for staying here in the underground. He waited for a long time, but the white hand did not return. Goddamn! Had he been more alert, he could have counted the twirls and he would have had the combination. He got down and stood in the areaway, sunk in reflection.

How could he get into that room? He climbed back into the basement and saw wooden steps leading upward. Was that the room where the safe stood? Fearing that the dial was now being twirled, he clambered through the window, hoisted himself up the rain pipe, and peered; he saw only the naked gleam of the steel dial. He got down and doubled his fists. Well, he would explore the basement. He returned to the basement room and mounted the steps to the door and squinted through the keyhole; all was dark, but the tapping was still somewhere near, still faint and directionless. He pushed the door in; along one wall of a room was a table piled with radios and electrical equipment. A radio shop, he muttered.

Well, he could rig up a radio in his cave. He found a sack, slid the radio into it, and slung it across his back. Closing the door, he went down the steps and stood again in the basement, disappointed. He had not solved the problem of the steel dial and he was irked. He set the radio on the floor and again hoisted himself through the window and up the rain pipe and squinted; the metal door was swinging shut. Goddamn! He's worked the combination again. If I had been patient, I'd have had it! How could he get into that room? He *had* to get into it. He could jimmy the window, but it would be much better if he could get in without any traces. To the right of him, he calculated, should be the basement of the building that held the safe; therefore, if he dug a hole right *here*, he ought to reach his goal.

He began a quiet scraping; it was hard work, for the bricks were not damp. He eventually got one out and lowered it softly to the floor. He had to be careful; perhaps people were beyond this wall. He extracted a second layer of brick and found still another. He gritted his teeth, ready to quit. I'll dig one more, he resolved. When the next brick came out he felt air blowing into his face. He waited to be challenged, but nothing happened.

He enlarged the hole and pulled himself through and stood in quiet darkness. He scratched a match to flame and saw steps; he mounted and peered through a keyhole: Darkness . . . He strained to hear the typewriter, but there was only silence. Maybe the office had closed? He twisted the knob and swung the door in; a frigid blast made him shiver. In the shadows before him were halves and quarters of hogs and lambs and steers hanging from metal hooks on the low ceiling, red meat encased in folds of cold white fat. Fronting him was frost-coated glass from behind which came indistinguishable sounds. The odor of fresh raw meat sickened him and he backed away. A meat market, he whispered.

He ducked his head, suddenly blinded by light. He narrowed his eyes; the red-white rows of meat were drenched in yellow glare. A man wearing a crimson spotted jacket came in and took down a bloody meat cleaver. He eased the door to, holding it ajar just enough to watch the man, hoping that the darkness in which he stood would keep him from being seen. The man took down a hunk of steer and placed it upon a bloody wooden block and bent forward and whacked with the cleaver. The man's face was hard, square, grim; a jet of mustache smudged his upper lip and a glistening cowlick of hair fell over his left eye. Each time he lifted the cleaver and brought it down upon the meat, he let out a short, deep-chested grunt. After he had cut the meat, he wiped blood off the wooden block with a sticky wad of gunny sack and hung the cleaver upon a hook. His face was proud as he placed the chunk of meat in the crook of his elbow and left.

The door slammed and the light went off; once more he stood in shadow. His tension ebbed. From behind the frosted glass he heard the man's voice: "Forty-eight cents a pound, ma'am." He shuddered, feeling that there was something he had to do. But what? He stared fixedly at the cleaver, then he sneezed and was terrified for fear that the man had heard him. But the door did not open. He took down the cleaver and examined the sharp edge smeared with cold blood. Behind the ice-coated glass a cash register rang with a vibrating, musical tinkle.

Absent-mindedly holding the meat cleaver, he rubbed the glass with his thumb and cleared a spot that enabled him to see into the front of the store. The shop was empty, save for the man who was now putting on his hat and coat. Beyond the front window a wan sun shone in the streets; people passed and now and then a fragment of laughter or the whir of a speeding auto came to him. He peered closer and saw on the right counter of the shop a mosquito netting covering pears, grapes, lemons, oranges, bananas, peaches, and plums. His stomach contracted.

The man clicked out the light and he gritted his teeth, muttering, Don't lock the icebox door . . . The man went through the door of the shop and locked it from the outside. Thank God! Now, he would eat some more! He waited, trembling. The sun died and its rays lingered on in the sky, turning the streets to dusk. He opened the door and stepped inside the shop. In reverse letters across the front window was: NICK'S FRUITS AND MEATS. He laughed, picked up a soft ripe yellow pear and bit into it; juice squirted; his mouth ached as his saliva glands reacted to the acid of the fruit. He ate three pears, gobbled six bananas, and made away with several oranges, taking a bite out of their tops and holding them to his lips and squeezing them as he hungrily sucked the juice.

He found a faucet, turned it on, laid the cleaver aside, pursed his lips under the stream until his stomach felt about to burst. He straightened and belched, feeling satisfied for the first time since he had been underground. He sat upon the floor, rolled and lit a cigarette, his bloodshot eyes squinting against the film of drifting smoke. He watched a patch of sky turn red, then purple; night fell and he lit another cigarette, brooding. Some part of him was trying to remember the world he had left, and another part of him did not want to remember it. Sprawling before him in his mind was his wife, Mrs. Wooten for whom he worked, the three policemen who had picked him up . . . He possessed them now more completely than he had ever possessed them when he had lived aboveground. How this had come about he could not say, but he had no desire to go back to them. He laughed, crushed the cigarette, and stood up.

He went to the front door and gazed out. Emotionally he hovered between the world aboveground and the world underground. He longed to go out, but sober judgment urged him to remain here. Then impulsively he pried the lock loose with one swift twist of the crowbar; the door swung outward. Through the twilight he saw a white man and a white woman coming toward him. He held himself tense, waiting for them to pass; but they came directly to the door and confronted him.

"I want to buy a pound of grapes," the woman said.

Terrified, he stepped back into the store. The white man stood to one side and the woman entered.

"Give me a pound of dark ones," the woman said.

The white man came slowly forward, blinking his eyes.

"Where's Nick?" the man asked.

"Were you just closing?" the woman asked.

"Yes, ma'am," he mumbled. For a second he did not breathe, then he mumbled again: "Yes, ma'am."

"I'm sorry," the woman said.

The street lamps came on, lighting the store somewhat. Ought he run? But that would raise an alarm. He moved slowly, dreamily, to a counter and lifted up a bunch of grapes and showed them to the woman.

"Fine," the woman said. "But isn't that more than a pound?"

He did not answer. The man was staring at him intently.

"Put them in a bag for me," the woman said, fumbling with her purse.

"Yes, ma'am."

He saw a pile of paper bags under a narrow ledge; he opened one and put the grapes in.

"Thanks," the woman said, taking the bag and placing a dime in his dark palm.

"Where's Nick?" the man asked again. "At supper?"

"Sir? Yes, sir," he breathed.

They left the store and he stood trembling in the doorway. When they were out of sight, he burst out laughing and crying. A trolley car rolled noisily past and he controlled himself quickly. He flung the dime to the pavement with a gesture of contempt and stepped into the warm night air. A few shy stars trembled above him. The look of things was beautiful, yet he felt a lurking threat. He went to an unattended newsstand and looked at a stack of papers. He saw a headline: HUNT NEGRO FOR MURDER.

He felt that someone had slipped up on him from behind and was stripping off his clothes; he looked about wildly, went quickly back into the store, picked up the meat cleaver where he had left it near the sink, then made his way through the icebox to the basement. He stood for a long time, breathing heavily. They know I didn't do anything, he muttered. But how could he prove it? He had signed a confession. Though innocent, he felt guilty, condemned. He struck a match and held it near the steel blade, fascinated and repelled by the dried blotches of blood. Then his fingers gripped the handle of the cleaver with all the strength of his body, he wanted to fling the cleaver from him, but he could not. The match flame wavered and fled; he struggled through the hole and put the cleaver in the sack with the radio. He was determined to keep it, for what purpose he did not know.

He was about to leave when he remembered the safe. Where was it? He wanted to give up, but felt that he ought to make one more try. Opposite the last hole he had dug, he tunneled again, plying the crowbar. Once he was so exhausted that he lay on the concrete floor and panted. Finally he made another hole. He wriggled through and his nostrils filled with the fresh smell of coal. He struck a match; yes, the usual steps led upward. He tiptoed to a door and eased it open. A fair-haired white girl stood in front of a steel cabinet, her blue eyes wide upon him. She turned chalky and gave a high-pitched scream. He bounded down the steps and raced to his hole and clambered through, replacing the bricks with nervous haste. He paused, hearing loud voices.

"What's the matter, Alice?"

"A man . . ."

"What man? Where?"

"A man was at that door . . ."

"Oh, nonsense!"

"He was looking at me through the door!"

"Aw, you're dreaming."

"I *did* see a man!"

The girl was crying now.

"There's nobody here."

Another man's voice sounded.

"What is it, Bob?"

"Alice says she saw a man in here, in that door!"

"Let's take a look."

He waited, poised for flight. Footsteps descended the stairs.

"There's nobody down here."

"The window's locked."

"And there's no door."

"You ought to fire that dame."

"Oh, I don't know. Women are that way."

"She's too hysterical."

The men laughed. Footsteps sounded again on the stairs. A door slammed. He sighed, relieved that he had escaped. But he had not done what he had set out to do; his glimpse of the room had been too brief to determine if the safe was there. He had to know. Boldly he groped through the hole once more; he reached the steps and pulled off his shoes and tip-toed up and peered through the keyhole. His head accidentally touched the door and it swung silently in a fraction of an inch; he saw the girl bent over the cabinet, her back to him. Beyond her was the safe. He crept back down the steps, thinking exultingly: I found it!

Now he had to get the combination. Even if the window in the areaway was locked and bolted, he could gain entrance when the office closed. He scoured through the holes he had dug and stood again in the basement where he had left the radio and the cleaver. Again he crawled out of the window and lifted himself up the rain pipe and peered. The steel dial showed lonely and bright, reflecting the yellow glow of an unseen light. Resigned to a long wait, he sat and leaned against the wall. From far off came the faint sounds of life aboveground; once he looked with a baffled expression at the dark sky. Frequently he rose and climbed the pipe to see the white hand spin the dial, but nothing happened. He bit his lip with impatience. It was not the money that was luring him, but the mere fact that he could get it with impunity. Was the hand now twirling the dial? He rose and looked, but the white hand was not in sight.

Perhaps it would be better to watch continuously? Yes; he clung to the pipe and watched the dial until his eyes thickened with tears. Exhausted, he stood again in the areaway. He heard a door being shut and he clawed up the pipe and looked. He jerked tense as a vague figure passed in front of him. He stared unblinkingly, hugging the pipe with one hand and holding the screw-

driver with the other, ready to etch the combination upon the wall.
His ears caught: *Dong . . . Dong . . . Dong . . . Dong . . . Dong
. . . Dong . . . Dong . . .* Seven o'clock, he whispered. Maybe they
were closing now? What kind of a store would be open as late as this?
he wondered. Did anyone live in the rear? Was there a night watchman? Perhaps the safe was *already* locked for the night! Goddamn!
While he had been eating in that shop, they had locked up everything . . . Then, just as he was about to give up, the white hand
touched the dial and turned it once to the right and stopped at six.
With quivering fingers, he etched 1—R—6 upon the brick wall with
the tip of the screwdriver. The hand twirled the dial twice to the
left and stopped at two, and he engraved 2—L—2 upon the wall.
The dial was spun four times to the right and stopped at six again;
he wrote 4—R—6. The dial rotated three times to the left and was
centered straight up and down; he wrote 3—L—o. The door swung
open and again he saw the piles of green money and the rows of
wrapped coins. I got it, he said grimly.

Then he was stone still, astonished. There were two hands now.
A right hand lifted a wad of green bills and deftly slipped it up the
sleeve of a left arm. The hands trembled; again the right hand
slipped a packet of bills up the left sleeve. He's stealing, he said to
himself. He grew indignant, as if the money belonged to him.
Though *he* had planned to steal the money, he despised and pitied
the man. He felt that his stealing the money and the man's stealing
were two entirely different things. He wanted to steal the money
merely for the sensation involved in getting it, and he had no intention whatever of spending a penny of it; but he knew that the
man who was now stealing it was going to spend it, perhaps for
pleasure. The huge steel door closed with a soft click.

Though angry, he was somewhat satisfied. The office would close
soon. I'll clean the place out, he mused. He imagined the entire
office staff cringing with fear; the police would question everyone
for a crime they had not committed, just as they had questioned
him. And they would have no idea of how the money had been
stolen until they discovered the holes he had tunneled in the walls
of the basements. He lowered himself and laughed mischievously,
with the abandoned glee of an adolescent.

He flattened himself against the wall as the window above him
closed with rasping sound. He looked; somebody was bolting the
window securely with a metal screen. That won't help you, he
snickered to himself. He clung to the rain pipe until the yellow

light in the office went out. He went back into the basement, picked up the sack containing the radio and cleaver, and crawled through the two holes he had dug and groped his way into the basement of the building that held the safe. He moved in slow motion, breathing softly. Be careful now, he told himself. There might be a night watchman . . . In his memory was the combination written in bold white characters as upon a blackboard. Eel-like he squeezed through the last hole and crept up the steps and put his hand on the knob and pushed the door in about three inches. Then his courage ebbed; his imagination wove dangers for him.

Perhaps the night watchman was waiting in there, ready to shoot. He dangled his cap on a forefinger and poked it past the jamb of the door. If anyone fired, they would hit his cap; but nothing happened. He widened the door, holding the crowbar high above his head, ready to beat off an assailant. He stood like that for five minutes; the rumble of a streetcar brought him to himself. He entered the room. Moonlight floated in from a side window. He confronted the safe, then checked himself. Better take a look around first . . . He stepped about and found a closed door. Was the night watchman in there? He opened it and saw a washbowl, a faucet, and a commode. To the left was still another door that opened into a huge dark room that seemed empty; on the far side of that room he made out the shadow of still another door. Nobody's here, he told himself.

He turned back to the safe and fingered the dial; it spun with ease. He laughed and twirled it just for fun. Get to work, he told himself. He turned the dial to the figures he saw on the blackboard of his memory; it was so easy that he felt that the safe had not been locked at all. The heavy door eased loose and he caught hold of the handle and pulled hard, but the door swung open with a slow momentum of its own. Breathless, he gaped at wads of green bills, rows of wrapped coins, curious glass jars full of white pellets, and many oblong green metal boxes. He glanced guiltily over his shoulder; it seemed impossible that someone should not call to him to stop.

They'll be surprised in the morning, he thought. He opened the top of the sack and lifted a wad of compactly tied bills; the money was crisp and new. He admired the smooth, cleancut edges. The fellows in Washington sure know how to make this stuff, he mused. He rubbed the money with his fingers, as though expecting it to reveal hidden qualities. He lifted the wad to his nose and smelled the fresh odor of ink. Just like any other paper, he mumbled. He dropped the wad into the sack and picked up another. Holding the bag, he thought and laughed.

There was in him no sense of possessiveness; he was intrigued with the form and color of the money, with the manifold reactions which he knew that men aboveground held toward it. The sack was one-third full when it occurred to him to examine the denominations of the bills; without realizing it, he had put many wads of one-dollar bills into the sack. Aw, nuts, he said in disgust. Take the big ones . . . He dumped the one-dollar bills onto the floor and swept all the hundred-dollar bills he could find into the sack, then he raked in rolls of coins with crooked fingers.

He walked to a desk upon which sat a typewriter, the same machine which the blond girl had used. He was fascinated by it; never in his life had he used one of them. It was a queer instrument of business, something beyond the rim of his life. Whenever he had been in an office where a girl was typing, he had almost always spoken in whispers. Remembering vaguely what he had seen others do, he inserted a sheet of paper into the machine; it went in lopsided and he did not know how to straighten it. Spelling in a soft diffident voice, he pecked out his name on the keys: *freddaniels*. He looked at it and laughed. He would learn to type correctly one of these days.

Yes, he would take the typewriter too. He lifted the machine and placed it atop the bulk of money in the sack. He did not feel that he was stealing, for the cleaver, the radio, the money, and the typewriter were all on the same level of value, all meant the same thing to him. They were the serious toys of the men who lived in the dead world of sunshine and rain he had left, the world that had condemned him, branded him guilty.

But what kind of a place is this? He wondered. What was in that dark room to his rear? He felt for his matches and found that he had only one left. He leaned the sack against the safe and groped forward into the room, encountering smooth, metallic objects that felt like machines. Baffled, he touched a wall and tried vainly to locate an electric switch. Well, he *had* to strike his last match. He knelt and struck it, cupping the flame near the floor with his palms. The place seemed to be a factory, with benches and tables. There were bulbs with green shades spaced about the tables; he turned on a light and twisted it low so that the glare was limited. He saw a half-filled packet of cigarettes and appropriated it. There were stools at the benches and he concluded that men worked here at some trade. He wandered and found a few half-used folders of matches. If only he could find more cigarettes! But there were none.

But what kind of a place was this? On a bench he saw a pad of paper captioned: PEER'S—MANUFACTURING JEWELERS. His lips formed an "O," then he snapped off the light and ran back to the safe and lifted one of the glass jars and stared at the tiny white pellets. Gingerly he picked up one and found that it was wrapped in tissue paper. He peeled the paper and saw a glittering stone that looked like glass, glinting white and blue sparks. Diamonds, he breathed.

Roughly he tore the paper from the pellets and soon his palm quivered with precious fire. Trembling, he took all four glass jars from the safe and put them into the sack. He grabbed one of the metal boxes, shook it, and heard a tinny rattle. He pried off the lid with the screwdriver. Rings! Hundreds of them . . . Were they worth anything? He scooped up a handful and jets of fire shot fitfully from the stones. These are diamonds too, he said. He pried open another box. Watches! A chorus of soft, metallic ticking filled his ears. For a moment he could not move, then he dumped all the boxes into the sack.

He shut the safe door, then stood looking around, anxious not to overlook anything. Oh! He had seen a door in the room where the machines were. What was in there? More valuables? He re-entered the room, crossed the floor, and stood undecided before the door. He finally caught hold of the knob and pushed the door in; the room beyond was dark. He advanced cautiously inside and ran his fingers along the wall for the usual switch, then he was stark still. *Something had moved in the room!* What was it? Ought he to creep out, taking the rings and diamonds and money? Why risk what he already had? He waited and the ensuing silence gave him confidence to explore further. Dare he strike a match? Would not a match flame make him a good target? He tensed again as he heard a faint sigh; he was now convinced that there was something alive near him, something that lived and breathed. On tiptoe he felt slowly along the wall, hoping that he would not collide with anything. Luck was with him; he found the light switch.

No; don't turn the light on . . . Then suddenly he realized that he did not know in what direction the door was. Goddamn! He had to turn the light on or strike a match. He fingered the switch for a long time, then thought of an idea. He knelt upon the floor, reached his arm up to the switch and flicked the button, hoping that if anyone shot, the bullet would go above his head. The moment the light came on he narrowed his eyes to see quickly. He sucked in his breath and his body gave a violent twitch and was still. In front of him, so close that it made him want to bound up and scream, was a human face.

He was afraid to move lest he touch the man. If the man had opened his eyes at that moment, there was no telling what he might have done. The man—long and rawboned—was stretched out on his back upon a little cot, sleeping in his clothes, his head cushioned by a dirty pillow; his face, clouded by a dark stubble of beard, looked straight up to the ceiling. The man sighed, and he grew tense to defend himself; the man mumbled and turned his face away from the light. I've got to turn off that light, he thought. Just as he was about to rise, he saw a gun and cartridge belt on the floor at the man's side. Yes, he would take the gun and cartridge belt, not to use them, but just to keep them, as one takes a memento from a country fair. He picked them up and was about to click off the light when his eyes fell upon a photograph perched upon a chair near the man's head; it was the picture of a woman, smiling, shown against a background of open fields; at the woman's side were two young children, a boy and a girl. He smiled indulgently; he could send a bullet into that man's brain and time would be over for him . . .

He clicked off the light and crept silently back into the room where the safe stood; he fastened the cartridge belt about him and adjusted the holster at his right hip. He strutted about the room on tiptoe, lolling his head nonchalantly, then paused, abruptly pulled the gun, and pointed it with grim face toward an imaginary foe. "Boom!" he whispered fiercely. Then he bent forward with silent laughter. That's just like they do it in the movies, he said.

He contemplated his loot for a long time, then got a towel from the washroom and tied the sack securely. When he looked up he was momentarily frightened by his shadow looming on the wall before him. He lifted the sack, dragged it down the basement steps, lugged it across the basement, gasping for breath. After he had struggled through the hole, he clumsily replaced the bricks, then tussled with the sack until he got it to the cave. He stood in the dark, wet with sweat, brooding about the diamonds, the rings, the watches, the money; he remembered the singing in the church, the people yelling in the movie, the dead baby, the nude man stretched out upon the white table . . . He saw these items hovering before his eyes and felt that some dim meaning linked them together, that some magical relationship made them kin. He stared with vacant eyes, convinced that all of these images, with their tongueless reality, were striving to tell him something . . .

Later, seeing with his fingers, he untied the sack and set each item neatly upon the dirt floor. Exploring, he took the bulb, the socket, and the wire out of the tool chest; he was elated to find a double socket at one end of the wire. He crammed the stuff into his pockets and hoisted himself upon the rusty pipes and squinted into the church; it was dim and empty. Somewhere in this wall were live electric wires; but where? He lowered himself, groped and tapped the wall with the butt of the screwdriver, listening vainly for hollow sounds. I'll just take a chance and dig, he said.

For an hour he tried to dislodge a brick, and when he struck a match, he found that he had dug a depth of only an inch! No use in digging here, he sighed. By the flickering light of a match, he looked upward, then lowered his eyes, only to glance up again, startled. Directly above his head, beyond the pipes, was a wealth of electric wiring. I'll be damned, he snickered.

He got an old dull knife from the chest and, seeing again with his fingers, separated the two strands of wire and cut away the insulation. Twice he received a slight shock. He scraped the wiring clean and managed to join the two twin ends, then screwed in the bulb. The sudden illumination blinded him and he shut his lids to kill the pain in his eyeballs. I've got that much done, he thought jubilantly.

He placed the bulb on the dirt floor and the light cast a blatant glare on the bleak clay walls. Next he plugged one end of the wire that dangled from the radio into the light socket and bent down and switched on the button; almost at once there was the harsh sound of static, but no words or music. Why won't it work? he wondered. Had he damaged the mechanism in any way? Maybe it needed grounding? Yes . . . He rummaged in the tool chest and found another length of wire, fastened it to the ground of the radio, and then tied the opposite end to a pipe. Rising and growing distinct, a slow strain of music entranced him with its measured sound. He sat upon the chest, deliriously happy.

Later he searched again in the chest and found a half-gallon can of glue; he opened it and smelled a sharp odor. Then he recalled that he had not even looked at the money. He took a wad of green bills and weighed it in his palm, then broke the seal and held one of the bills up to the light and studied it closely. *The United States of America will pay to the bearer on demand one hundred dollars*, he read in slow speech; then: *This note is legal tender for all debts, public and private*. . . . He broke into a musing laugh, feeling that he was reading of the doings of people who lived on some far-off planet. He turned the bill over and saw on the other side of it a delicately beautiful building gleaming with paint and set amidst green grass. He had no desire whatever to count the money; it was what it stood for—the various currents of life swirling aboveground —that captivated him. Next he opened the rolls of coins and let them slide from their paper wrappings to the ground; the bright, new gleaming pennies and nickles and dimes piled high at his feet, a glowing mound of shimmering copper and silver. He sifted them through his fingers, listening to their tinkle as they struck the conical heap.

Oh, yes! He had forgotten. He would now write his name on the typewriter. He inserted a piece of paper and poised his fingers to write. But what was his name? He stared, trying to remember. He stood and glared about the dirt cave, his name on the tip of his lips. But it would not come to him. Why was he here? Yes, he had been running away from the police. But why? His mind was blank. He bit his lips and sat again, feeling a vague terror. But why worry? He laughed, then pecked slowly: *itwasalonghotday*. He was deter- mined to type the sentence without making any mistakes. How did one make capital letters? He experimented and luckily discovered how to lock the machine for capital letters and then shift it back to lower case. Next he discovered how to make spaces, then he wrote neatly and correctly: *It was a long hot day*. Just why he selected that sentence he did not know; it was merely the ritual of per- forming the thing that appealed to him. He took the sheet out of the machine and looked around with stiff neck and hard eyes and spoke to an imaginary person:

"Yes, I'll have the contracts ready tomorrow."

He laughed. That's just the way they talk, he said. He grew weary of the game and pushed the machine aside. His eyes fell upon the can of glue, and a mischievous idea bloomed in him, filling him with nervous eagerness. He leaped up and opened the can of glue, then broke the seals on all the wads of money. I'm going to have some wallpaper, he said with a luxurious, physical laugh that made him bend at the knees. He took the towel with which he had tied the sack and balled it into a swab and dipped it into the can of glue and dabbed glue onto the wall; then he pasted one green bill by the side of another. He stepped back and cocked his head. Jesus! That's funny . . . He slapped his thighs and guffawed. He had triumphed over the world aboveground! He was free! If only people could see this! He wanted to run from this cave and yell his discovery to the world.

He swabbed all the dirt walls of the cave and pasted them with green bills; when he had finished the walls blazed with a yellow-green fire. Yes, this room would be his hide-out; between him and the world that had branded him guilty would stand this mocking symbol. He had not stolen the money; he had simply picked it up, just as a man would pick up firewood in a forest. And that was how the world aboveground now seemed to him, a wild forest filled with death.

The walls of money finally palled on him and he looked about for new interests to feed his emotions. The cleaver! He drove a nail into the wall and hung the bloody cleaver upon it. Still another idea welled up. He pried open the metal boxes and lined them side by side on the dirt floor. He grinned at the gold and fire. From one box he lifted up a fistful of ticking gold watches and dangled them by their gleaming chains. He stared with an idle smile, then began to wind them up; he did not attempt to set them at any given hour, for there was no time for him now. He took a fistful of nails and drove them into the papered walls and hung the watches upon them, letting them swing down by their glittering chains, trembling and ticking busily against the backdrop of green with the lemon sheen of the electric light shining upon the metal watch casings, converting the golden disks into blobs of liquid yellow. Hardly had he hung up the last watch than the idea extended itself; he took more nails from the chest and drove them into the green paper and took the boxes of rings and went from nail to nail and hung up the golden bands. The blue and white sparks from the stones filled the cave with brittle laughter, as though enjoying his hilarious secret. People certainly can do some funny things, he said to himself.

He sat upon the tool chest, alternately laughing and shaking his head soberly. Hours later he became conscious of the gun sagging at his hip and he pulled it from the holster. He had seen men fire guns in movies, but somehow his life had never led him into contact with firearms. A desire to feel the sensation others felt in firing came over him. But someone might hear . . . Well, what if they did? They would not know where the shot had come from. Not in their wildest notions would they think that it had come from under the streets! He tightened his fingers on the trigger; there was a deafening report and it seemed that the entire underground had caved in upon his eardrums; and in the same instant there flashed an orange-blue spurt of flame that died quickly but lingered on as a vivid after-image. He smelled the acrid stench of burnt powder filling his lungs and he dropped the gun abruptly.

The intensity of his feelings died and he hung the gun and cartridge belt upon the wall. Next he lifted the jars of diamonds and turned them bottom upward, dumping the white pellets upon the ground. One by one he picked them up and peeled the tissue paper from them and piled them in a neat heap. He wiped his sweaty hands on his trousers, lit a cigarette, and commenced playing another game. He imagined that he was a rich man who lived aboveground in the obscene sunshine and he was strolling through a park of a summer morning, smiling, nodding to his neighbors, sucking an after-breakfast cigar. Many times he crossed the floor of the cave, avoiding the diamonds with his feet, yet subtly gauging his footsteps so that his shoes, wet with sewer slime, would strike the diamonds at some undetermined moment. After twenty minutes of sauntering, his right foot smashed into the heap and diamonds lay scattered in all directions, glinting with a million tiny chuckles of icy laughter. Oh, shucks, he mumbled in mock regret, intrigued by the damage he had wrought. He continued walking, ignoring the brittle fire. He felt that he had a glorious victory locked in his heart.

He stooped and flung the diamonds more evenly over the floor and they showered rich sparks, collaborating with him. He went over the floor and trampled the stones just deeply enough for them to be faintly visible, as though they were set deliberately in the prongs of a thousand rings. A ghostly light bathed the cave. He sat on the chest and frowned. Maybe *any*thing's right, he mumbled. Yes, if the world as men had made it was right, then anything else was right, any act a man took to satisfy himself, murder, theft, torture.

He straightened with a start. What was happening to him? He was drawn to these crazy thoughts, yet they made him feel vaguely guilty. He would stretch out upon the ground, then get up; he would want to crawl again through the holes he had dug, but would restrain himself; he would think of going again up into the streets, but fear would hold him still. He stood in the middle of the cave, surrounded by green walls and a laughing floor, trembling. He was going to do something, but what? Yes, he was afraid of himself, afraid of doing some nameless thing.

To control himself, he turned on the radio. A melancholy piece of music rose. Brooding over the diamonds on the floor was like looking up into a sky full of restless stars; then the illusion turned into its opposite: he was high up in the air looking down at the twinkling lights of a sprawling city. The music ended and a man recited news events. In the same attitude in which he had contemplated the city, so now, as he heard the cultivated tone, he looked down upon land and sea as men fought, as cities were razed, as planes scattered death upon open towns, as long lines of trenches wavered and broke. He heard the names of generals and the names of mountains and the names of countries and the names and numbers of divisions that were in action on different battle fronts. He saw black smoke billowing from the stacks of warships as they neared each other over wastes of water and he heard their huge thunder as red-hot shells screamed across the surface of night seas. He saw hundreds of planes wheeling and droning in the sky and heard the clatter of machine guns as they fought each other and he saw planes falling in plumes of smoke and blaze of fire. He saw steel tanks rumbling across fields of ripe wheat to meet other tanks and there was a loud clang of steel as numberless tanks collided. He saw troops with fixed bayonets charging in waves against other troops who held fixed bayonets and men groaned as steel ripped into their bodies and they went down to die . . . The voice of the radio faded and he was staring at the diamonds on the floor at his feet.

He shut off the radio, fighting an irrational compulsion to act. He walked aimlessly about the cave, touching the walls with his finger tips. Suddenly he stood still. *What was the matter with him?* Yes, he knew . . . It was these walls; these crazy walls were filling him with a wild urge to climb out into the dark sunshine aboveground. Quickly he doused the light to banish the shouting walls, then sat again upon the tool chest. Yes, he was trapped. His muscles were flexed taut and sweat ran down his face. He knew now that he could not stay here and he could not go out. He lit a cigarette with shaking fingers; the match flame revealed the green-papered walls with militant distinctness; the purple on the gun barrel glinted like a threat; the meat cleaver brooded with its eloquent splotches of blood; the mound of silver and copper smoldered angrily; the diamonds winked at him from the floor; and the gold watches ticked and trembled, crowning time the king of consciousness, defining the limits of living . . . The match blaze died and he bolted from where he stood and collided brutally with the nails upon the walls. The spell was broken. He shuddered, feeling that, in spite of his fear, sooner or later he would go up into that dead sunshine and somehow say something to somebody about all this.

He sat again upon the tool chest. Fatigue weighed upon his forehead and eyes. Minutes passed and he relaxed. He dozed, but his imagination was alert. He saw himself rising, wading again in the sweeping water of the sewer; he came to a manhole and climbed out and was amazed to discover that he had hoisted himself into a room filled with armed policemen who were watching him intently. He jumped awake in the dark; he had not moved. He sighed, closed his eyes, and slept again; this time his imagination designed a scheme of protection for him. His dreaming made him feel that he was standing in a room watching over his own nude body lying stiff and cold upon a white table. At the far end of the room he saw a crowd of people huddled in a corner, afraid of his body. Though lying dead upon the table, he was standing in some mysterious way at his side, warding off the people, guarding his body, and laughing to himself as he observed the situation. They're scared of me, he thought.

He awakened with a start, leaped to his feet, and stood in the center of the black cave. It was a full minute before he moved again. He hovered between sleeping and waking, unprotected, a prey of wild fears. He could neither see nor hear. One part of him was asleep; his blood coursed slowly and his flesh was numb. On the other hand he was roused to a strange, high pitch of tension. He lifted his fingers to his face, as though about to weep. Gradually his hands lowered and he struck a match, looking about, expecting to see a door through which he could walk to safety; but there was no door, only the green walls and the moving floor. The match flame died and it was dark again.

Five minutes later he was still standing when the thought came to him that he had been asleep. Yes . . . But he was not yet fully awake; he was still queerly blind and deaf. How long had he slept? Where was he? Then suddenly he recalled the green-papered walls of the cave and in the same instant he heard loud singing coming from the church beyond the wall. Yes, they woke me up, he muttered. He hoisted himself and lay atop the bed of pipes and brought his face to the narrow slit. Men and women stood here and there between pews. A song ended and a young black girl tossed back her head and closed her eyes and broke plaintively into another hymn:

> *Glad, glad, glad, oh, so glad*
> *I got Jesus in my soul . . .*

Those few words were all she sang, but what her words did not say, her emotions said as she repeated the lines, varying the mood and tempo, making her tone express meanings which her conscious mind did not know. Another woman melted her voice with the girl's, and then an old man's voice merged with that of the two women. Soon the entire congregation was singing:

> *Glad, glad, glad, oh, so glad*
> *I got Jesus in my soul . . .*

They're wrong, he whispered in the lyric darkness. He felt that their search for a happiness they could never find made them feel that they had committed some dreadful offense which they could not remember or understand. He was now in possession of the feeling that had gripped him when he had first come into the underground. It came to him in a series of questions: Why was this sense of guilt so seemingly innate, so easy to come by, to think, to feel, so verily physical? It seemed that when one felt this guilt one was retracing in one's feelings a faint pattern designed long before; it seemed that one was always trying to remember a gigantic shock that had left a haunting impression upon one's body which one could not forget or shake off, but which had been forgotten by the conscious mind, creating in one's life a state of eternal anxiety.

He had to tear himself away from this; he got down from the pipes. His nerves were so taut that he seemed to feel his brain pushing through his skull. He felt that he had to do something, but he could not figure out what it was. Yet he knew that if he stood here until he made up his mind, he would never move. He crawled through the hole he had made in the brick wall and the exertion afforded him respite from tension. When he entered the basement of the radio store, he stopped in fear, hearing loud voices.

"Come on, boy! Tell us what you did with the radio!"

"Mister, I didn't steal the radio! I swear!"

He heard a dull thumping sound and he imagined a boy being struck violently.

"Please, mister!"

"Did you take it to a pawn shop?"

"No, sir! I didn't steal the radio! I got a radio at home," the boy's voice pleaded hysterically. "Go to my home and look!"

There came to his ears the sound of another blow. It was so funny that he had to clap his hand over his mouth to keep from laughing out loud. They're beating some poor boy, he whispered to himself, shaking his head. He felt a sort of distant pity for the boy and wondered if he ought to bring back the radio and leave it in the basement. No. Perhaps it was a good thing that they were beating the boy; perhaps the beating would bring to the boy's attention, for the first time in his life, the secret of his existence, the guilt that he could never get rid of.

Smiling, he scampered over a coal pile and stood again in the basement of the building where he had stolen the money and jewelry. He lifted himself into the areaway, climbed the rain pipe, and squinted through a two-inch opening of window. The guilty familiarity of what he saw made his muscles tighten. Framed before him in a bright tableau of daylight was the night watchman sitting upon the edge of a chair, stripped to the waist, his head sagging forward, his eyes red and puffy. The watchman's face and shoulders were stippled with red and black welts. Back of the watchman stood the safe, the steel door wide open showing the empty vault. Yes, they think he did it, he mused.

Footsteps sounded in the room and a man in a blue suit passed in front of him, then another, then still another. Policemen, he breathed. Yes, they were trying to make the watchman confess, just as they had once made him confess to a crime he had not done. He stared into the room, trying to recall something. Oh . . . Those were the same policemen who had beaten him, had made him sign that paper when he had been too tired and sick to care. Now, they were doing the same thing to the watchman. His heart pounded as he saw one of the policemen shake a finger into the watchman's face.

"Why don't you admit it's an inside job, Thompson?" the policeman said.

"I've told you all I know," the watchman mumbled through swollen lips.

"But nobody was here but you!" the policeman shouted.

"I was sleeping," the watchman said. "It was wrong, but I was sleeping all that night!"

"Stop telling us that lie!"

"It's the truth!"

"When did you get the combination?"

"I don't know how to open the safe," the watchman said.

He clung to the rain pipe, tense; he wanted to laugh, but he controlled himself. He felt a great sense of power; yes, he could go back to the cave, rip the money off the walls, pick up the diamonds and rings, and bring them here and write a note, telling them where to look for their foolish toys. No . . . What good would that do? It was not worth the effort. The watchman was guilty; although he was not guilty of the crime of which he had been accused, he was guilty, had always been guilty. The only thing that worried him was that the man who had been really stealing was not being accused. But he consoled himself: they'll catch him sometime during his life.

He saw one of the policemen slap the watchman across the mouth.

"Come clean, you bastard!"

"I've told you all I know," the watchman mumbled like a child.

One of the police went to the rear of the watchman's chair and jerked it from under him; the watchman pitched forward upon his face.

"Get up!" a policeman said.

Trembling, the watchman pulled himself up and sat limply again in the chair.

"Now, are you going to talk?"

"I've told you all I know," the watchman gasped.

"Where did you hide the stuff?"

"I didn't take it!"

"Thompson, your brains are in your feet," one of the policemen said. "We're going to string you up and get them back into your skull."

He watched the policemen clamp handcuffs on the watchman's wrists and ankles; then they lifted the watchman and swung him upside-down and hoisted his feet to the edge of a door. The watchman hung, head down, his eyes bulging. They're crazy, he whispered to himself as he clung to the ridges of the pipe.

"You going to talk?" a policeman shouted into the watchman's ear.

He heard the watchman groan.

"We'll let you hang there till you talk, see?"

He saw the watchman close his eyes.

"Let's take 'im down. He passed out," a policeman said.

He grinned as he watched them take the body down and dump it carelessly upon the floor. The policeman took off the handcuffs.

"Let 'im come to. Let's get a smoke," a policeman said.

The three policemen left the scope of his vision. A door slammed.

He had an impulse to yell to the watchman that he could escape through the hole in the basement and live with him in the cave. But he wouldn't understand, he told himself. After a moment he saw the watchman rise and stand, swaying from weakness. He stumbled across the room to a desk, opened a drawer, and took out a gun. He's going to kill himself, he thought, intent, eager, detached, yearning to see the end of the man's actions. As the watchman stared vaguely about he lifted the gun to his temple; he stood like that for some minutes, biting his lips until a line of blood etched its way down a corner of his chin. No, he oughtn't do that, he said to himself in a mood of pity.

"Don't!" he half whispered and half yelled.

The watchman looked wildly about; he had heard him. But it did not help; there was a loud report and the watchman's head jerked violently and he fell like a log and lay prone, the gun clattering over the floor.

The three policemen came running into the room with drawn guns. One of the policemen knelt and rolled the watchman's body over and stared at a ragged, scarlet hole in the temple.

"Our hunch was right," the kneeling policeman said. "He was guilty, all right."

"Well, this ends the case," another policeman said.

"He knew he was licked," the third one said with grim satisfaction.

He eased down the rain pipe, crawled back through the holes he had made, and went back into his cave. A fever burned in his bones. He had to act, yet he was afraid. His eyes stared in the darkness as though propped open by invisible hands, as though they had become lidless. His muscles were rigid and he stood for what seemed to him a thousand years.

When he moved again his actions were informed with precision, his muscular system reinforced from a reservoir of energy. He crawled through the hole of earth, dropped into the gray sewer current, and sloshed ahead. When his right foot went forward at a street inter-section, he fell backward and shot down into water. In a spasm of terror his right hand grabbed the concrete ledge of a down-curve and he felt the streaking water tugging violently at his body. The current reached his neck and for a moment he was still. He knew if he moved clumsily he would be sucked under. He held onto the ledge with both hands and slowly pulled himself up. He sighed, standing once more in the sweeping water, thankful that he had missed death.

He waded on through sludge, moving with care, until he came to a web of light sifting down from a manhole cover. He saw steel hooks running up the side of the sewer wall; he caught hold and lifted himself and put his shoulder to the cover and moved it an inch. A crash of sound came to him as he looked into a hot glare of sunshine through which blurred shapes moved. Fear scalded him and he dropped back into the pallid current and stood paralyzed in the shadows. A heavy car rumbled past overhead, jarring the pavement, warning him to stay in his world of dark light, knocking the cover back into place with an imperious clang.

He did not know how much fear he felt, for fear claimed him completely; yet it was not a fear of the police or of people, but a cold dread at the thought of the actions he knew he would perform if he went out into that cruel sunshine. His mind said no; his body said yes; and his mind could not understand his feelings. A low whine broke from him and he was in the act of uncoiling. He climbed upward and heard the faint honking of auto horns. Like a frantic cat clutching a rag, he clung to the steel prongs and heaved his shoulder against the cover and pushed it off halfway. For a split second his eyes were drowned in the terror of yellow light and he was in a deeper darkness than he had ever known in the underground.

Partly out of the hole, he blinked, regaining enough sight to make out meaningful forms. An odd thing was happening: No one was rushing forward to challenge him. He had imagined the moment of his emergence as a desperate tussle with men who wanted to cart him off to be killed; instead, life froze about him as the traffic stopped. He pushed the cover aside, stood, swaying in a world so fragile that he expected it to collapse and drop him into some deep void. But nobody seemed to pay him heed. The cars were now swerving to shun him and the gaping hole.

"Why in hell don't you put up a red light, dummy?" a raucous voice yelled.

He understood; they thought that he was a sewer workman. He walked toward the sidewalk, weaving unsteadily through the moving traffic.

"Look where you're going, nigger!"

"That's right! Stay there and get killed!"

"You blind, you bastard?"

"Go home and sleep your drunk off!"

A policeman stood at the curb, looking in the opposite direction.

When he passed the policeman, he feared that he would be grabbed, but nothing happened. Where was he? Was this real? He wanted to look about to get his bearings, but felt that something awful would happen to him if he did. He wandered into a spacious doorway of a store that sold men's clothing and saw his reflection in a long mirror: his cheekbones protruded from a hairy black face; his greasy cap was perched askew upon his head and his eyes were red and glassy. His shirt and trousers were caked with mud and hung loosely. His hands were gummed with a black stickiness. He threw back his head and laughed so loudly that passers-by stopped and stared.

He ambled on down the sidewalk, not having the merest notion of where he was going. Yet, sleeping within him, was the drive to go somewhere and say something to somebody. Half an hour later his ears caught the sound of spirited singing.

> The Lamb, the Lamb, the Lamb
> I hear thy voice a-calling
> The Lamb, the Lamb, the Lamb
> I feel thy grace a-falling

A church! He exclaimed. He broke into a run and came to brick steps leading downward to a subbasement. This is it! The church into which he had peered. Yes, he was going in and tell them. What? He did not know; but, once face to face with them, he would think of what to say. Must be Sunday, he mused. He ran down the steps and jerked the door open; the church was crowded and a deluge of song swept over him.

> The Lamb, the Lamb, the Lamb
> Tell me again your story
> The Lamb, the Lamb, the Lamb
> Flood my soul with your glory

He stared at the singing faces with a trembling smile.

"Say!" he shouted.

Many turned to look at him, but the song rolled on. His arm was jerked violently.

"I'm sorry, Brother, but you can't do that in here," a man said.

"But, mister!"

"You can't act rowdy in God's house," the man said.

"He's filthy," another man said.

"But I want to tell 'em," he said loudly.

"He stinks," someone muttered.

The song had stopped, but at once another one began.

> Oh, wondrous sight upon the cross
> > Vision sweet and divine
> Oh, wondrous sight upon the cross
> > Full of such love sublime

He attempted to twist away, but other hands grabbed him and rushed him into the doorway.

"Let me alone!" he screamed, struggling.

"Get out!"

"He's drunk," somebody said. "He ought to be ashamed!"

"He acts crazy!"

He felt that he was failing and he grew frantic.

"But, mister, let me tell—"

"Get away from this door, or I'll call the police!"

He stared, his trembling smile fading in a sense of wonderment.

"The police," he repeated vacantly.

"Now, get!"

He was pushed toward the brick steps and the door banged shut. The waves of song came.

> Oh, wondrous sight, wondrous sight
> > Lift my heavy heart above
> Oh, wondrous sight, wondrous sight
> > Fill my weary soul with love

He was smiling again now. Yes, the police . . . That was it! Why had he not thought of it before? The idea had been deep down in him, and only now did it assume supreme importance. He looked up and saw a street sign: COURT STREET—HARTSDALE AVENUE. He turned and walked northward, his mind filled with the image of the police station. Yes, that was where they had beaten him, accused him, and had made him sign a confession of his guilt. He would go there and clear up everything, make a statement. What statement? He did not know. He was the statement, and since it was all so clear to him, surely he would be able to make it clear to others.

He came to the corner of Hartsdale Avenue and turned westward. Yeah, there's the station . . . A policeman came down the steps and walked past him without a glance. He mounted the stone steps and went through the door, paused; he was in a hallway where several policemen were standing, talking, smoking. One turned to him.

"What do you want, boy?"

He looked at the policeman and laughed.

"What in hell are you laughing about?" the policeman asked.

He stopped laughing and stared. His whole being was full of what he wanted to say to them, but he could not say it.

"Are you looking for the Desk Sergeant?"

"Yes, sir," he said quickly; then: "Oh, no, sir."

"Well, make up your mind, now."

Four policemen grouped themselves around him.

"I'm looking for the men," he said.

"What men?"

Peculiarly, at that moment he could not remember the names of the policemen; he recalled their beating him, the confession he had signed, and how he had run away from them. He saw the cave next to the church, the money on the walls, the guns, the rings, the cleaver, the watches, and the diamonds on the floor.

"They brought me here," he began.

"When?"

His mind flew back over the blur of the time lived in the underground blackness. He had no idea of how much time had elapsed, but the intensity of what had happened to him told him that it could not have transpired in a short space of time, yet his mind told him that time must have been brief.

"It was a long time ago." He spoke like a child relating a dimly remembered dream. "It was a long time," he repeated, following the promptings of his emotions. "They beat me . . . I was scared . . . I ran away."

A policeman raised a finger to his temple and made a derisive circle.

"Nuts," the policeman said.

"Do you know what place this is, boy?"

"Yes, sir. The police station," he answered sturdily, almost proudly.

"Well, who do you want to see?"

"The men," he said again, feeling that surely they knew the men. "You know the men," he said in a hurt tone.

"What's your name?"

He opened his lips to answer and no words came. He had forgotten. But what did it matter if he had? It was not important.

"Where do you live?"

Where did he live? It had been so long ago since he had lived up here in this strange world that he felt it was foolish even to try to remember. Then for a moment the old mood that had dominated him in the underground surged back. He leaned forward and spoke eagerly.

"They said I killed the woman."

"What woman?" a policeman asked.

"And I signed a paper that said I was guilty," he went on, ignoring their questions. "Then I ran off . . ."

"Did you run off from an institution?"

"No, sir," he said, blinking and shaking his head. "I came from under the ground. I pushed off the manhole cover and climbed out . . ."

"All right, now," a policeman said, placing an arm about his shoulder. "We'll send you to the psycho and you'll be taken care of."

"Maybe he's a Fifth Columnist!" a policeman shouted.

There was laughter and, despite his anxiety, he joined in. But the laughter lasted so long that it irked him.

"I got to find those men," he protested mildly.

"Say, boy, what have you been drinking?"

"Water," he said. "I got some water in a basement."

"Were the men you ran away from dressed in white, boy?"

"No, sir," he said brightly. "They were men like you."

An elderly policeman caught hold of his arm.

"Try and think hard. Where did they pick you up?"

He knitted his brows in an effort to remember, but he was blank inside. The policeman stood before him demanding logical answers and he could no longer think with his mind; he thought with his feelings and no words came.

"I was guilty," he said. "Oh, no, sir. I wasn't then, I mean, mister!"

"Aw, talk sense. Now, where did they pick you up?"

He felt challenged and his mind began reconstructing events in reverse; his feelings ranged back over the long hours and he saw the cave, the sewer, the bloody room where it was said that a woman had been killed.

"Oh, yes, sir," he said, smiling. "I was coming from Mrs. Wooten's."

"Who is she?"

"I work for her."

"Where does she live?"

"Next door to Mrs. Peabody, the woman who was killed."

The policemen were very quiet now, looking at him intently.

"What do you know about Mrs. Peabody's death, boy?"

"Nothing, sir. But they said I killed her. But it doesn't make any difference. I'm guilty!"

"What are you talking about, boy?"

His smile faded and he was possessed with memories of the underground; he saw the cave next to the church and his lips moved to speak. But how could he say it? The distance between what he felt and what these men meant was vast. Something told him, as he stood there looking into their faces, that he would never be able to tell them, that they would never believe him even if he told them.

"All the people I saw was guilty," he began slowly.

"Aw, nuts," a policeman muttered.

"Say," another policeman said, "that Peabody woman was killed over on Winewood. That's Number Ten's beat."

"Where's Number Ten?" a policeman asked.

"Upstairs in the swing room," someone answered.

"Take this boy up, Sam," a policeman ordered.

"O.K. Come along, boy."

An elderly policeman caught hold of his arm and led him up a flight of wooden stairs, down a long hall, and to a door.

"Squad Ten!" the policeman called through the door.

"What?" a gruff voice answered.

"Someone to see you!"

"About what?"

The old policeman pushed the door in and then shoved him into the room.

He stared, his lips open, his heart barely beating. Before him were the three policemen who had picked him up and had beaten him to extract the confession. They were seated about a small table, playing cards. The air was blue with smoke and sunshine poured through a high window, lighting up fantastic smoke shapes. He saw one of the policemen look up; the policeman's face was tired and a cigarette dropped limply from one corner of his mouth and both of his fat, puffy eyes were squinting and his hands gripped his cards.

"Lawson!" the man exclaimed.

The moment the man's name sounded he remembered the names of all of them: Lawson, Murphy, and Johnson. How simple it was. He waited, smiling, wondering how they would react when they knew that he had come back.

"Looking for me?" the man who had been called Lawson mumbled, sorting his cards. "For what?"

So far only Murphy, the red-headed one, had recognized him.

"Don't you-all remember me?" he blurted, running to the table.

All three of the policemen were looking at him now. Lawson, who seemed the leader, jumped to his feet.

"Where in hell have you been?"

"Do you know 'im, Lawson?" the old policeman asked.

"Huh?" Lawson frowned. "Oh, yes. I'll handle 'im." The old policeman left the room and Lawson crossed to the door and turned the key in the lock. "Come here, boy," he ordered in a cold tone.

He did not move; he looked from face to face. Yes, he would tell them about his cave.

"He looks batty to me," Johnson said, the one who had not spoken before.

"Why in hell did you come back here?" Lawson said.

"I—I just didn't want to run away no more," he said. "I'm all right, now." He paused; the men's attitude puzzled him.

"You've been hiding, huh?" Lawson asked in a tone that denoted that he had not heard his previous words. "You told us you were sick, and when we left you in the room, you jumped out of the window and ran away."

Panic filled him. Yes, they were indifferent to what he would say! They were waiting for him to speak and they would laugh at him. He had to rescue himself from this bog; he had to force the reality of himself upon them.

"Mister, I took a sackful of money and pasted it on the walls . . ." he began.

"I'll be damned," Lawson said.

"Listen," said Murphy, "let me tell you something for your own good. We don't want you, see? You're free, free as air. Now go home and forget it. It was all a mistake. We caught the guy who did the Peabody job. He wasn't colored at all. He was an Eyetalian."

"Shut up!" Lawson yelled. "Have you no sense!"

"But I want to tell 'im," Murphy said.

"We can't let this crazy fool go," Lawson exploded. "He acts nuts, but this may be a stunt . . ."

"I was down in the basement," he began in a childlike tone, as though repeating a lesson learned by heart; "and I went into a movie . . ." His voice failed. He was getting ahead of his story. First, he ought to tell them about the singing in the church, but what words could he use? He looked at them appealingly. "I went into a shop and took a sackful of money and diamonds and watches and rings . . . I didn't steal 'em, I'll give 'em all back. I just took 'em to play with . . ." He paused, stunned by their disbelieving eyes.

Lawson lit a cigarette and looked at him coldly.

"What did you do with the money?" he asked in a quiet, waiting voice.

"I pasted the hundred-dollar bills on the walls."

"What walls?" Lawson asked.

"The walls of the dirt room," he said, smiling, "the room next to the church. I hung up the rings and the watches and I stamped the diamonds into the dirt . . ." He saw that they were not understanding what he was saying. He grew frantic to make them believe, his voice tumbled on eagerly. "I saw a dead baby and a dead man . . ."

"Aw, you're nuts," Lawson snarled, shoving him into a chair.

"But mister . . ."

"Johnson, where's the paper he signed?" Lawson asked.

"What paper?"

"The confession, fool!"

Johnson pulled out his billfold and extracted a crumpled piece of paper.

"Yes, sir, mister," he said, stretching forth his hand. "That's the paper I signed . . ."

Lawson slapped him and he would have toppled had his chair not struck a wall behind him. Lawson scratched a match and held the paper over the flame; the confession burned down to Lawson's fingertips.

He stared, thunderstruck; the sun of the underground was fleeting and the terrible darkness of the day stood before him. They did not believe him, but he *had* to make them believe him!

"But mister . . ."

"It's going to be all right, boy," Lawson said with a quiet, soothing laugh. "I've burned your confession, see? You didn't sign anything." Lawson came close to him with the black ashes cupped in his palm. "You don't remember a thing about this, do you?"

"Don't you-all be scared of me," he pleaded, sensing their uneasiness. "I'll sign another paper, if you want me to. I'll show you the cave."

"What's your game, boy?" Lawson asked suddenly.

"What are you trying to find out?" Johnson asked.

"Who sent you here?" Murphy demanded.

"Nobody sent me, mister," he said. "I just want to show you the room . . ."

"Aw, he's plumb bats," Murphy said. "Let's ship 'im to the psycho."

"No," Lawson said. "He's playing a game and I wish to God I knew what it was."

There flashed through his mind a definite way to make them believe him; he rose from the chair with nervous excitement.

"Mister, I saw the night watchman blow his brains out because you accused him of stealing," he told them. "But he didn't steal the money and diamonds. I took 'em."

Tigerishly Lawson grabbed his collar and lifted him bodily.

"*Who told you about that?*"

"Don't get excited, Lawson," Johnson said. "He read about it in the papers."

Lawson flung him away.

"He couldn't have," Lawson said, pulling papers from his pocket. "I haven't turned in the reports yet."

"Then how *did* he find out?" Murphy asked.

"Let's get out of here," Lawson said with quick resolution. "Listen, boy, we're going to take you to a nice, quiet place, see?"

"Yes, sir," he said. "And I'll show you the underground."

"Goddamn," Lawson muttered, fastening the gun at his hip. He narrowed his eyes at Johnson and Murphy. "Listen," he spoke just above a whisper, "say nothing about this, you hear?"

"O.K.," Johnson said.

"Sure," Murphy said.

Lawson unlocked the door and Johnson and Murphy led him down the stairs. The hallway was crowded with policemen.

"What have you got there, Lawson?"

"What did he do, Lawson?"

"He's psycho, ain't he, Lawson?"

Lawson did not answer; Johnson and Murphy led him to the car parked at the curb, pushed him into the back seat. Lawson got behind the steering wheel and the car rolled forward.

"What's up, Lawson?" Murphy asked.

"Listen," Lawson began slowly, "we tell the papers that he spilled about the Peabody job, then he escapes. The Wop is caught and we tell the papers that we steered them wrong to trap the real guy, see? Now this dope shows up and acts nuts. If we let him go, he'll squeal that we framed him, see?"

"I'm all right, mister," he said, feeling Murphy's and Johnson's arm locked rigidly into his. "I'm guilty . . . I'll show you everything in the underground. I laughed and laughed . . ."

"Shut that fool up!" Lawson ordered.

Johnson tapped him across the head with a blackjack and he fell back against the seat cushion, dazed.

"Yes, sir," he mumbled. "I'm all right."

The car sped along Hartsdale Avenue, then swung onto Pine Street and rolled to State Street, then turned south. It slowed to a stop, turned in the middle of a block, and headed north again.

"You're going around in circles, Lawson," Murphy said.

Lawson did not answer; he was hunched over the steering wheel. Finally he pulled the car to a stop at a curb.

"Say, boy, tell us the truth," Lawson asked quietly. "Where did you hide?"

"I didn't hide, mister."

The three policemen were staring at him now; he felt that for the first time they were willing to understand him.

"Then what happened?"

"Mister, when I looked through all of those holes and saw how people were living, I loved 'em . . ."

"Cut out that crazy talk!" Lawson snapped. "Who sent you back here?"

"Nobody, mister."

"Maybe he's talking straight," Johnson ventured.

"All right," Lawson said. "Nobody hid you. Now, tell us *where* you hid."

"I went underground . . ."

"What goddamn underground do you keep talking about?"

"I just went . . ." He paused and looked into the street, then pointed to a manhole cover. "I went down in there and stayed."

"In the *sewer?*"

"Yes, sir."

The policemen burst into a sudden laugh and ended quickly. Lawson swung the car around and drove to Woodside Avenue; he brought the car to a stop in front of a tall apartment building.

"What're we going to do, Lawson?" Murphy asked.

"I'm taking him up to my place," Lawson said. "We've got to wait until night. There's nothing we can do now."

They took him out of the car and led him into a vestibule.

"Take the steps," Lawson muttered.

They led him up four flights of stairs and into the living room of a small apartment. Johnson and Murphy let go of his arms and he stood uncertainly in the middle of the room.

"Now, listen, boy," Lawson began, "forget those wild lies you've been telling us. Where did you hide?"

"I just went underground, like I told you."

The room rocked with laughter. Lawson went to a cabinet and got a bottle of whisky; he placed glasses for Johnson and Murphy. The three of them drank.

He felt that he could not explain himself to them. He tried to muster all the sprawling images that floated in him; the images stood out sharply in his mind, but he could not make them have the meaning for others that they had for him. He felt so helpless that he began to cry.

"He's nuts, all right," Johnson said. "All nuts cry like that."

Murphy crossed the room and slapped him.

"Stop that raving!"

A sense of excitement flooded him; he ran to Murphy and grabbed his arm.

"Let me show you the cave," he said. "Come on, and you'll see!"

Before he knew it a sharp blow had clipped him on the chin; darkness covered his eyes. He dimly felt himself being lifted and laid out on the sofa. He heard low voices and struggled to rise, but hard hands held him down. His brain was clearing now. He pulled to a sitting posture and stared with glazed eyes. It had grown dark. How long had he been out?

"Say, boy," Lawson said soothingly, "will you show us the underground?"

His eyes shone and his heart swelled with gratitude. Lawson believed him! He rose, glad; he grabbed Lawson's arm, making the policeman spill whisky from the glass to his shirt.

"Take it easy, goddammit," Lawson said.

"Yes, sir."

"O.K. We'll take you down. But you'd better be telling us the truth, you hear?"

He clapped his hands in wild joy.

"I'll show you everything!"

He had triumphed at last! He would now do what he had felt was compelling him all along. At last he would be free of his burden.

"Take 'im down," Lawson ordered.

They led him down to the vestibule; when he reached the sidewalk he saw that it was night and a fine rain was falling.

"It's just like when I went down," he told them.

"What?" Lawson asked.

"The rain," he said, sweeping his arm in a wide arc. "It was raining when I went down. The rain made the water rise and lift the cover off."

"Cut it out," Lawson snapped.

They did not believe him now, but they would. A mood of high selflessness throbbed in him. He could barely contain his rising spirits. They would see what he had seen; they would feel what he had felt. He would lead them through all the holes he had dug and . . . He wanted to make a hymn, prance about in physical ecstasy, throw his arm about the policemen in fellowship.

"Get into the car," Lawson ordered.

He climbed in and Johnson and Murphy sat at either side of him; Lawson slid behind the steering wheel and started the motor.

"Now, tell us where to go," Lawson said.

"It's right around the corner from where the lady was killed," he said.

The car rolled slowly and he closed his eyes, remembering the song he had heard in the church, the song that had wrought him to such a high pitch of terror and pity. He sang softly, lolling his head:

> *Glad, glad, glad, oh, so glad*
> *I got Jesus in my soul . . .*

"Mister," he said, stopping his song, "you ought to see how funny the rings look on the wall." He giggled. "I fired a pistol, too. Just once, to see how it felt."

"What do you suppose he's suffering from?" Johnson asked.

"Delusions of grandeur, maybe," Murphy said.

"Maybe it's because he lives in a white man's world," Lawson said.

"Say, boy, what did you eat down there?" Murphy asked, prodding Johnson anticipatorily with his elbow.

"Pears, oranges, bananas, and pork chops," he said.

The car filled with laughter.

"You didn't eat any watermelon?" Lawson asked, smiling.

"No, sir," he answered calmly. "I didn't see any."

The three policemen roared harder and louder.

"Boy, you're sure some case," Murphy said, shaking his head in wonder.

The car pulled to a curb.

"All right, boy," Lawson said. "Tell us where to go."

He peered through the rain and saw where he had gone down. The streets, save for a few dim lamps glowing softly through the rain, were dark and empty.

"Right there, mister," he said, pointing.

"Come on; let's take a look," Lawson said.

"Well, suppose he did hide down there," Johnson said, "what is that supposed to prove?"

"I don't believe he hid down there," Murphy said.

"It won't hurt to look," Lawson said. "Leave things to me."

Lawson got out of the car and looked up and down the street.

He was eager to show them the cave now. If he could show them what he had seen, then they would feel what he had felt and they in turn would show it to others and those others would feel as they had felt, and soon everybody would be governed by the same impulse of pity.

"Take 'im out," Lawson ordered.

Johnson and Murphy opened the door and pushed him out; he stood trembling in the rain, smiling. Again Lawson looked up and down the street; no one was in sight. The rain came down hard, slanting like black wires across the wind-swept air.

"All right," Lawson said. "Show us."

He walked to the center of the street, stopped and inserted a finger in one of the tiny holes of the cover and tugged, but he was too weak to budge it.

"Did you really go down in there, boy?" Lawson asked; there was a doubt in his voice.

"Yes, sir. Just a minute. I'll show you."

"Help 'im get that damn thing off," Lawson said.

Johnson stepped forward and lifted the cover; it clanged against the wet pavement. The hole gaped round and black.

"I went down in there," he announced with pride.

Lawson gazed at him for a long time without speaking, then he reached his right hand to his holster and drew his gun.

"Mister, I got a gun just like that down there," he said, laughing and looking into Lawson's face. "I fired it once then hung it on the wall. I'll show you."

"Show us how you went down," Lawson said quietly.

"I'll go down first, mister, and then you-all can come after me, hear?" he spoke like a little boy playing a game.

"Sure, sure," Lawson said soothingly. "Go ahead. We'll come."

He looked brightly at the policemen; he was bursting with happiness. He bent down and placed his hands on the rim of the hole and sat on the edge, his feet dangling into watery darkness. He heard the familiar drone of the gray current. He lowered his body and hung for a moment by his fingers, then he went downward on the steel prongs, hand over hand, until he reached the last rung. He dropped and his feet hit the water and he felt the stiff current trying to suck him away. He balanced himself quickly and looked back upward at the policemen.

"Come on, you-all!" he yelled, casting his voice above the rustling at his feet.

The vague forms that towered above him in the rain did not move. He laughed, feeling that they doubted him. But, once they saw the things he had done, they would never doubt again.

"Come on! The cave isn't far!" he yelled. "But be careful when your feet hit the water, because the current's pretty rough down here!"

Lawson still held the gun. Murphy and Johnson looked at Lawson quizzically.

"What are we going to do, Lawson?" Murphy asked.

"We are not going to follow that crazy nigger down into that sewer, are we?" Johnson asked.

"Come on, you-all!" he begged in a shout.

He saw Lawson raise the gun and point it directly at him. Lawson's face twitched, as though he were hesitating.

Then there was a thunderous report and a streak of fire ripped through his chest. He was hurled into the water, flat on his back. He looked in amazement at the blurred white faces looming above him. They shot me, he said to himself. The water flowed past him, blossoming in foam about his arms, his legs, and his head. His jaw sagged and his mouth gaped soundless. A vast pain gripped his head and gradually squeezed out consciousness. As from a great distance he heard hollow voices.

"What did you shoot him for, Lawson?"

"I had to."

"Why?"

"You've got to shoot his kind. They'd wreck things."

As though in a deep dream, he heard a metallic clank; they had replaced the manhole cover, shutting out forever the sound of wind and rain. From overhead came the muffled roar of a powerful motor and the swish of a speeding car. He felt the strong tide pushing him slowly into the middle of the sewer, turning him about. For a split second there hovered before his eyes the glittering cave, the shouting walls, and the laughing floor . . . Then his mouth was full of thick, bitter water. The current spun him around. He sighed and closed his eyes, a whirling object rushing alone in the darkness, veering, tossing, lost in the heart of the earth.

# NOW THAT YOU'VE READ WRIGHT'S THE MAN WHO LIVED UNDERGROUND

Richard Wright has generally been thought of as a proletarian writer, but the existentialist short novel *The Man Who Lived Underground* is typical of Wright's exploration of the effects of social and metaphysical alienation. Its theme is one Wright grappled with throughout his career as a writer. Fred Daniels, the protagonist of *The Man Who Lived Underground*, is a ready target for the police because he is black, but in the dark loneliness of the underground world he experiences the fear and trembling, the terror and dread that is common to modern man. Alienated from God, twentieth-century man exists on a small, insignificant planet lost in the vast reaches of space. The product of a chance union of natural elements, he must discover in the natural world and in his own nature a meaning and purpose for his existence. Fred Daniels, who is suddenly cut off from the moral values and religious myths of society, confronts the terrifying reality of a man alone in the universe. His experience makes him aware that the values of society make man blind to the reality of his metaphysical condition and alienate him from his fellow man. Trembling with the excitement of discovery, Daniels emerges from the underground, certain that if he can communicate what he has learned, men will be united in peace and harmony.

Fred Daniel's desire to liberate his fellow man by exposing the terrible consequences of living by values that alienate man from man is not unlike the aspiration of Richard Wright. Early in life he rejected the idea of a moral, God-directed universe. The human condition is created by man and it is within man's power to improve that condition. Like most protest writers who emphasize the sordid aspects of human life and the brutality and irrationality of human conduct, Wright had faith in man's rationality. Progress toward a more humane society was possible if evil was exposed and if man could learn more about the laws that governed his personality, society, and history.

A product of the age of science, Wright was an agnostic in search of a God. He sought a unifying, all-embracing natural concept that would bring order out of chaos. In his search for understanding, he studied many of the major concepts of twentieth century thought—Marxism, Freudianism, existentialism. He once described fiction as the exploration of an idea, and to a great extent his novels and stories reflect his intellectual concerns. He began his career as a Marxian writer of naturalistic fiction, exposing the brutal effects of racism in America on both the victims and the oppressors. But early in the 1940's he began to question the Marxian ideology and its implementation by the Communist party. When the "god" of Marxism failed him, as had the God of traditional religion failed him in his youth, he embarked upon his own intellectual voyage to discover the secret of man's nature and the meaning of his existence. *The Man Who Lived Underground* marks the beginning of that search which continued until his death in 1960. It was written and published in the early 1940's and was eventually included in a collection of stories entitled *Eight Men* (1961).

Though Wright was very much involved with ideas, his narratives are structured upon violence, flight, and pursuit. The impelling force in all of his fiction is anger. The record he has provided of his early years in his autobiography *Black Boy* (1945) reveals that the anger to which he gave literary form had its origin in a personal struggle to maintain integrity and to achieve self-fulfillment in a society that alienated him because he was black. His rise from dire poverty in Natchez, Mississippi to international fame as a major author in American literature, admired and befriended by such literary luminaries as Gertrude Stein, André Gide and Albert Camus is an heroic demonstration of the power of will against almost overwhelming odds. After reading *Black Boy*, which is Wright's finest non-fiction book, William Faulkner wrote to him expressing his admiration and suggesting that, as an artist, his obligation was to translate his experiences into fiction. And that, in fact, is what Wright did in those stories and novels in which he so effectively depicted the frustration, alienation and smoldering anger of the American Negro.

Richard Wright was born in 1908. His father, a tenant farmer, deserted his wife and two young sons when Wright was about six. His mother, though trained as a grade school teacher, had to work as a domestic. Her desperate search for work led her from town to town in Tennessee and in neighboring states, and not until he was in the eighth grade did Wright complete a full year in one school. When she could find work, Mrs. Wright's earnings were meager, and her children often went hungry. While still young, she suffered a stroke that made her a semi-invalid for life, dependent upon her family for shelter and support. After an unhappy period in an orphanage, the two boys were taken in by relatives. Eventually, Wright was re-united with his mother in the home of his maternal grandmother, a rigid Seventh-Day Adventist.

In his autobiography, Wright dwells upon the determined efforts of this religious woman to make him a God-fearing Christian. Though the religious symbols and services appealed to his sensibilities, he almost instinctively resisted what he later described as the myth that, by promising peace after life made people accept passively unnecessary suffering. The "meaning of living," he wrote, "came only when one was struggling to wring a meaning out of meaningless suffering." The vigorous battles waged by the grandmother and an aunt to save the young boy's soul frequently verged on physical violence. Wright's feeling of alienation from his family increased and he dreamed of being free and independent. Reading became a refuge from the daily reality of poverty, the suffering of his mother, the oppressiveness of family and community. He dreamed of being a writer, and he avidly read whatever magazines and books he could find. Neither the black nor the white society in the South expected a young black to be interested in books, and when he completed the nine grades of formal schooling available to blacks and went to work in Memphis, Wright had to connive to use the public library. He finally was able to read a whole book by H. L. Mencken, whose attacks on American society in magazine essays had fascinated him, by making believe that he was an errand boy sent by a white man to get books. The indictments of society in the novels of Theodore Dreiser and Sinclair Lewis revealed to him the kind of fiction that he wanted to write. "My reading," he said in *Black Boy*, "had created a vast sense of distance between me and the world in which I lived and tried to make a living. . . . My days and nights were one long quiet, continuously contained dream of terror, tension, and anxiety."

Wright's struggle for intellectual freedom and growth was necessitated, to a great extent, by the humiliating position assigned the black in Southern society. He had little awareness of the white world until he began to work, but by the time he was in his early teens he "had already grown to feel that there existed men against whom I was powerless, who could violate my life at will." And soon, at the mere mention of whites, he wrote, tension "would set in . . . and a vast complex of emotions, involving the whole of my personality would be aroused. It was as though I was continuously reacting to the threat of some natural force whose hostile behavior could not be predicted." The squalid condition of the economically deprived Southern blacks was only one of the effects of the prejudice to which they were subjected. The whole pattern of Negro life, Wright saw as an adaptation to fear. To protect their lives and the lives of their children, they cultivated passivity, sought refuge in religion, adopted the values and aspirations of the white society. They put on masks in their relations with white people, acting as the white people expected them to act. Such a protective fragmentation of personality kept hidden the resentment and hatred that continual humiliation and fear inevitably produced. It became increasingly clear to Wright that he could preserve his integrity only by fleeing the South, and finally in 1927 he had saved enough to make his way to Chicago. But he could not leave behind his resentment and anger:

> The white South said that it knew "niggers," and I was what the white South called a "nigger." Well, the white South had never known me—never known what I thought, what I felt. . . . The pressures of southern living kept me from being the kind of person that I might have been. I had been what my surroundings had demanded, what my family—conforming to the dictates of the whites above them had exacted of me, and what the whites had said that I must be. Never being fully able to be myself, I had slowly learned that the South could recognize but a part of a man, could accept but a fragment of his personality, and all the rest—the best and deepest things of heart and mind—were tossed away in blind ignorance and hate.

In Chicago, Wright very soon discovered that he had not escaped poverty and racial prejudice. He had to work at menial jobs to keep alive, and he learned that life in the urban ghetto was, in many ways, more depressing than life in the rural South. The frustration and alienation of the urban black were intensified by a greater awareness of life's possibilities and the illusion of greater opportunity. Wright qualified for a position as a postal clerk in the Chicago post office, but he knew financial security for only a short time. In the 1930's the national economy collapsed and he worked intermittently. His determination to become a writer never flagged, and eager for association with people who had similar interests, he joined the local John Reed Club, a cultural organization of the Communist party. The writers and artists that he met readily accepted him and took seriously his literary aspirations. He read Marx and Lenin, and the oppression of the American black seemed to him directly related to the oppression of the working classes. He embraced the tenets of Communism and in 1934 he joined the Communist party.

His poems and essays began to appear in left-wing journals, and in 1937 he was sent to New York to write for the *Daily Worker*. During the period that he was most active as a member of the party, however, Wright was reading Dostoyevsky, Nietzsche, Freud, and the existentialist philosophers. He began to have doubts about the all-embracing Marxian view of man and human history, and he began to resent the restraints that the party imposed upon the artistic freedom of its writers. Some time before he officially resigned from the party in 1944, he had concluded that the liberation of the American Negro, which was his central concern, was only of peripheral interest to the Communist party leaders.

In 1938, Wright published his first book, a collection of stories entitled *Uncle Tom's Children*. Drawing upon his early experiences and impressions, he portrayed in these stories the fear that dominated the lives of Southern blacks, their dire poverty and their continual humiliation by warped, brutal whites. Several of the stories reveal Wright's hope for a united effort by blacks to resist oppression and an alliance with the Communists. In his first attempt at a novel, also written during the late 1930's, Wright shifted from the rural to the urban black, focusing his attention upon the psychological and social problems of the Negro who had left the rural South for the urban ghetto. *Lawd Today* was not published during Wright's lifetime, perhaps, as some critics have suggested, because the author knew that his realistic portrait of a black postal worker would not win the approval of the Communist party, which wanted its writers to depict the Negro as an exploited victim of a capitalist society. Though the novel has many artistic weaknesses, it is an important prelude to Wright's later fiction. The narrative centers upon one day—February 12—in the life of Jake Jackson, who awakens in the morning from a dream of running upstairs and never reaching the top, to his return home, drunk and angry, early the next morning. Wright's characterization of his protagonist is an attack upon the bourgeois aspirations of blacks who accept the tawdry values and dreams of a society that excludes them. Jake uses hair straightener each morning, takes much pride in the ten suits hanging in his closet and dreams of being part of the world portrayed in the American movie. He plays the daily numbers, eager for the luck that will free him from his mounting debts, from his boring work in the post office, from his sick wife. Wright's portrait of Jake Jackson, combining satire with understanding and sympathy is not unlike Sinclair Lewis's portraits of white middle class Americans. Jake Jackson's activities throughout the day expose the frustrations which eventually ferment into rage. In the final scene of the novel, Jackson returns home and beats his helpless wife.

In *Native Son* (1940), Wright once again explores the suppressed anger of the American black, whose aspirations are thwarted and whose ego is humiliated by white society. This is the novel that first brought him international prominence. The protagonist, Bigger Thomas, "knew that the moment he allowed what his life meant to enter fully into his consciousness, he would kill himself or someone else." Trapped in a situation in which his responses are controlled by his fear of white people, the young Bigger, unwittingly, kills a white girl. However, his subsequent actions—his scheme to get ransom, his flight from the police, and the murder of his girl friend—are deliberate and conscious acts, assertions of his individual will. Bigger had grown up in a world in which white people did not see Bigger Thomas; when they looked at him they saw a Negro. Only through murder is he freed from the degrading prison of that abstraction. Looking at the white girl's dead body, he thinks: "She was dead and he had killed her. He was a murderer, a Negro murderer, a black murderer." Bigger sees himself, subsequently, as the embodiment of the white man's fear of the Negro. And as such he makes the white world aware of Bigger Thomas as an entity. Wright's powerful narrative, presenting the murderer as a creation of a corrupt society, is masterful and convincing. The novel ends, as does Dreiser's *An American Tragedy*, with a trial that forcefully indicts American society. But if social determinism accounts for Bigger's alienation and his first murder, it does not fully explain Bigger's subsequent violence. Initially, fear and frustration make Bigger a murderer, but it is his newly discovered sense of identity as a criminal that governs his future actions.

This nascent image of existential man, which is buried under the naturalistic superstructure of *Native Son*, Wright developed in the short novel *The Man Who Lived Underground*, and in his next full novel, *The Outsider*. He began work on the short novel not long after the publication of *Native Son*. In the spring of 1942, he published two short portions from it in *Accent* with the subtitle "Two Excerpts from a Novel." The complete story was published in 1944 in *Cross-Section: A Collection of New American Writing*. In this initial study of the metaphysically alienated man, which shows the influence of Dostoyevsky's *Notes from Underground*, Wright uncovered humanistic impulses deep within the psyche of his protagonist. In *The Outsider* (1953), however, he explored the anti-humanistic, criminal impulses of Damon Cross, his protagonist. Apparently no longer satisfied with his earlier view of man as the creation of society, Wright sought, in this novel, to probe the nature of the human being for the clue to man's failure as a social being. He provides Damon Cross a maximum of freedom by liberating him from any allegiance to traditional moral codes and presents him as a Nietzschean man of instinct and will. Like Jake Jackson, Damon Cross is a black postal worker who feels oppressed by his job, his debts, and his family. Mistakenly identified as the dead victim of a subway accident, he decides to flee Chicago. While awaiting his opportunity to board a train for New York, he hides in a small hotel, where he is seen by a friend. To preserve his freedom, Cross kills the man. He feels neither guilt nor remorse. In New York, he assumes a new name and identity. The dominant drive in Cross's nature is the need for satisfying his ego by wielding power over others. In a world without a god, man's instinct is to seek the power of a god. Cross's acts of violence are passionless expressions of his freedom and his will. When he becomes involved with the Communist party, he quickly perceives that its leaders are mirrors of himself. They seek power and use Marxian ideology, as leaders before them had used other ideologies, to gain control over the minds of weaker people.

Wright, obviously, has rejected Marx's view of man and of human history. Man is governed by his need to assert his significance, make his existence meaningful by expressing his ego, and the violence that characterizes human history is the individual's search for power.

Whether Wright rejected this view of man or backed away, perhaps, from its pessimistic implications concerning man's power to change and improve his social condition is not clear from the fiction that follows. Psychological determinism is the theme that *Savage Holiday* (1954) explores. The puritanic, tautly disciplined life of the central character, a white man, as well as his murder of a woman to whom he has proposed are traced to an early traumatic relationship with his mother. The characters in this overformulistic Freudian novel never come to life, and *Savage Holiday* is Wright's weakest work of fiction. In his final novel *The Long Dream* (1958), Wright returns to the American South to analyze the many complex psychological and social forces that contribute to the development of his young hero's character and to his eventual decision to flee the South for Paris, a decision that Wright himself had made in 1946.

Through the efforts of Gertrude Stein, the French government invited Wright to visit Paris in 1945. He was impressed by the cordiality of his reception by French artists and by the indifference of the French to the color of his skin. He felt free, for the first time in his life, from the tensions that dominated the life of a black man in the United States, and the following year he brought his wife and daughter to France, where he lived until his death. His self-imposed exile did not alter his commitment to the struggle for the liberation of black people from oppression. In 1948, with other writers, including André Gide and Albert Camus, he helped to found *Présence Africaine*, a journal devoted to African culture, and he published three books all dealing with the plight of colored people struggling for independence. *Black Power* (1954) records a trip to the African Gold Coast and his hopes for the newly emerging nation. In 1955 he attended the conference of twenty-nine African and Asian nations at Bandung, and in *The Color Curtain* (1956) expressed his hope for a union of the colored nations as a third force in the world. *White Man, Listen* (1957) is a collection of essays, offered originally as lectures, urging the white nations to allow the emerging black nations to develop freely and determine their own destinies.

Despite the continuing influence of these essays and travel books and the impetus that Wright personally gave to the struggle of the American black for equality and dignity, his real contribution was as a man of letters, as an artist who gave literary form to the anger and violence that grew out of his experiences as a black. As Ralph Ellison has written, "Wright saw his destiny—that combination of forces before which man feels powerless—in terms of a quick and casual violence inflicted upon him by both family and community. His response was likewise violent, and it has been his need to give that violence significance which has shaped his writing."

The alienation of the American Negro became for Wright a symbol of the human condition in a meaningless universe, and within a compelling narrative structure of violence, flight, and pursuit, he dramatized not only the anguish of the American black but the anxiety and dread of modern man.

## FOR FURTHER INFORMATION:

James Baldwin. "Many Thousands Gone," *Notes of a Native Son*. Beacon Press: Boston, 1955, pp. 24-26; Bantam Books, Inc.: New York, 1964, pp. 18-36.

——. "Alas Poor Richard (i. Eight Men; ii. The Exile; Alas, Poor Richard)," *Nobody Knows My Name*. The Dial Press: New York, 1961, pp. 181-215.

Russell Carl Brignano. *Richard Wright: An Introduction to the Man and His Works*. University of Pittsburg Press: Pittsburgh, 1970.

Ralph Ellison. "Richard Wright's Blues," *Shadow and Act*. Random House: New York, 1964; Signet Edition, New American Library: New York, 1966, pp. 89-104.

Edward Margolies. *The Art of Richard Wright*. Southern Illinois University Press: Carbondale and Edwardsville, 1969.

Dan McCall. *The Example of Richard Wright*. Harcourt, Brace & World, Inc.: New York, 1969.

Constance Webb. *Richard Wright: A Biography*. G. P. Putnam's Sons: New York, 1968.

# *AGOSTINO*

## BY ALBERTO MORAVIA

First published, 1944

# AGOSTINO

**D**URING those days of early summer Agostino and his mother used to go out every morning on a bathing raft. The first few times his mother had taken a boatman, but Agostino so plainly showed his annoyance at the man's presence that from then on the oars were entrusted to him. It gave him intense pleasure to row on that calm, transparent, early morning sea; and his mother sat facing him, as gay and serene as the sea and sky, and talked to him in a soft voice, just as if he had been a man instead of a thirteen-year-old boy. Agostino's mother was a tall, beautiful woman, still in her prime, and Agostino felt a sense of pride each time he set out with her on one of those morning expeditions. It seemed to him that all the bathers on the beach were watching them, admiring his mother and envying him. In the conviction that all eyes were upon them his voice sounded to him stronger than usual, and he felt as if all his movements had something symbolic about them, as if they were part of a play; as if he and his mother, instead of being on the beach, were on a stage, under the eager eyes of hundreds of spectators. Sometimes his mother would appear in a new dress, and he could not resist remarking on it aloud, in the secret hope that others would hear. Now and again she would send him to fetch something or other from the beach cabin, while she stood waiting for him by the boat. He would obey with a secret joy, happy if he could prolong their departure even by a few minutes. At last they would get on the raft, and Agostino would take the oars and row out to sea. But for quite a long time he would remain under the disturbing influence of his filial vanity. When they were some way from the shore his mother would tell him to stop rowing, put on her rubber bathing cap, take off her sandals and slip into the water. Agostino would follow her. They swam round and round the empty raft with its floating oars, talking gaily together, their voices ringing clear in the silence of the calm, sunlit sea. Sometimes his mother would point to a piece of cork bobbing up and down a short distance from them, and challenge him to race her to it. She gave him a few yards start, and they would swim as hard as they could toward the cork. Or they would have diving competitions from the platform of the raft, splashing up the pale, smooth water as they plunged in. Agostino would watch his mother's body sink down deeper and deeper through a froth of green bubbles; then suddenly he would dive in after her, eager to follow wherever she might go, even to the bottom of the sea. As he flung himself into the furrow his mother had made it seemed to him that even that cold, dense water must keep some trace of the passage of her beloved body. When their swim was over they would climb back onto the raft, and gazing all round her on the calm, luminous sea his mother would say: "How beautiful it is, isn't it?" Agostino made no reply, because he felt that his own enjoyment of the beauty of sea and sky was really due above all to his deep sense of union with his mother. Were it not for this intimacy, it sometimes entered his head to wonder what would remain of all that beauty. They would stay out a long time, drying themselves in the sun, which toward midday got hotter and hotter; then his mother, stretched out at full length on the platform between the two floats, with her long hair trailing in the water and her eyes closed, would fall into a doze, while Agostino would keep watch from his seat on the bench, his eyes fixed on his mother, and hardly breathing for fear of disturbing her slumber. Suddenly she would open her eyes and say what a delightful novelty it was to lie on one's back with one's eyes shut and to feel the water rocking underneath; or she would ask Agostino to pass her her cigarette case or, better still, to light one for her himself and give it to her. All of which he would do with fervent and tremulous care. While his mother smoked, Agostino would lean forward with his back to her, but with his head on one side so that he could watch the clouds of blue smoke which indicated the spot where his mother's head was resting, with her hair spread out round her on the water. Then, as she never could have enough of the sun, she would ask Agostino to row on and not turn around, while she would take off her brassière and let down her bathing suit so as to expose her whole body to the sunlight. Agostino would go on rowing, proud of her injunction not to look as if he were being allowed to take part in a ritual. And not only did he never dream of looking around, but he felt that her body, lying so close behind him, naked in the sun, was surrounded by a halo of mystery to which he owed the greatest reverence.

One morning his mother was sitting as usual under the great beach umbrella, with Agostino beside her on the sand, waiting for the moment of their daily row. Suddenly a tall shadow fell between him and the sun. He looked up and saw a dark, sunburnt young man shaking hands with his mother. He did not pay much attention to him, thinking it was one of his mother's casual acquaintances; he only drew back a little, waiting for the conversation to be over. But the young man did not accept the invitation to sit down; pointing to the white raft in which he had come, he invited the mother to go for a row. Agostino was sure his mother would refuse this invitation as she had many previous ones; so that his surprise was great when he saw her accept at once, and immediately begin to put her things together—her sandals, bathing cap and purse, and then get up from her chair. His mother had accepted the young man's invitation with exactly the same spontaneity and simple friendliness which she would have shown toward her son; and with a like simplicity she now turned to Agostino, who sat waiting with his head down, letting the sand trickle through his fingers, and told him to have a sun bath, for she was going out for a short turn in the boat and would be back soon. The young man, meanwhile, as if quite sure of himself, had gone off in the direction of the raft, while the woman walked submissively behind him with her usual calm, majestic gait. Her son, watching them, could not help saying to himself that the young man must now be feeling the same pride and vanity and excitement which he himself always felt when he set out in a boat with his mother. He watched her get onto the float: the young man leaned backward and pushed with his feet against the sandy bottom; then, with a few vigorous strokes, lifted the raft out of the shallow water near the shore. The young man was rowing now, and his mother sat facing him, holding onto the seat with both hands and apparently chatting with him. Gradually the raft grew smaller and smaller, till it entered the region of dazzling light which the sun shed on the surface of the water, and slowly became absorbed into it.

Left alone, Agostino stretched himself out in his mother's deck chair and with one arm behind his head lay gazing up at the sky, seemingly lost in reflection and indifferent to his surroundings. He felt that all the people on the beach must have noticed him going off every day with his mother, and therefore it could not have escaped them that today his mother had left him behind and gone off with the young man of the bathing raft. So he was determined to give no sign at all of the disappointment and disillusion which filled him with such bitterness. But however much he tried to adopt an air of calm composure, he felt at the same time that everyone must be noticing how forced and artificial his attitude was. What hurt him still more was not so much that his mother had preferred the young man's company to his as the alacrity with which she had accepted the invitation—almost as if she had anticipated it. It was as if she had decided beforehand not to lose any opportunity, and when one offered itself to accept it without hesitation. Apparently she had been bored all those times she had been alone with him on the raft, and had only gone with him for lack of something better to do. A memory came back to his mind that increased his discomfiture. It had happened at a dance to which he had been taken by his mother. A girl cousin was with them who, in despair at not being asked by anyone else, had consented to dance once or twice with him, though he was only a boy in short trousers. She had danced reluctantly and looked very cross and out of temper, and Agostino, though preoccupied with his own steps, was aware of her contemptuous and unflattering sentiments toward himself. He had, however, asked her for a third dance, and had been quite surprised to see her suddenly smile and leap from her chair, shaking out the folds of her dress with both hands. But instead of rushing into his arms she had turned her back on him and joined a young man who had motioned to her over Agostino's shoulder. The whole scene lasted only five seconds, and no one noticed anything except Agostino himself. But he felt utterly humiliated and was sure everyone had seen how he had been snubbed.

And now, after his mother had gone off with the young man, he compared the two happenings and found them identical. Like his cousin, his mother had only waited for an opportunity to abandon him. Like his cousin, and with the same exaggerated readiness, she had accepted the first offer that presented itself. And in each case it had been his fate to come tumbling down from an illusory height and to lie bruised and wounded at the bottom.

That day his mother stayed out for about two hours. From under his big umbrella he saw her step on to the shore, shake hands with the young man and move slowly off toward the beach cabin, stooping a little under the heat of the midday sun. The beach was deserted by now, and this was a relief to Agostino, who was always convinced that all eyes were fixed on them. "What have you been doing?" his mother asked casually. "I have had great fun," began Agostino, and he made up a story of how *he* had been bathing too with the boys from the next beach cabin. But his mother was not listening; she had hurried off to dress. Agostino decided that as soon as he saw the raft appear the next day he would make some excuse to leave so as not to suffer the indignity of being left behind again. But when the next day came he had just started away when he heard his mother calling him back. "Come along," she said, as she got up and collected her belongings, "we're going out to swim." Agostino followed her, thinking that she meant to dismiss the young man and go out alone with him. The young man was standing on the raft waiting for her. She greeted him and said simply: "I'm bringing my son, too." So Agostino, much as he disliked it, found himself sitting beside his mother facing the young man, who was rowing.

Agostino had always seen his mother in a certain light—calm, dignified and reserved. During this outing he was shocked to see the change which had taken place, not only in her manner of talking but, as it seemed, even in herself. One could scarcely believe she was the same person. They had hardly put out to sea before she made some stinging personal remark, quite lost on Agostino, which started a curious, private conversation. As far as he could make out it concerned a lady friend of the young man who had rejected his advances in favor of a rival. But this only led up to the real matter of their conversation, which seemed to be alternately insinuating, exacting, contemptuous and teasing. His mother appeared to be the more aggressive and the more susceptible of the two, for the young man contented himself with replying in a calm, ironical tone, as if he were quite sure of himself. At times his mother seemed displeased, even positively angry with the young man, and then Agostino was glad. But immediately after she would disappoint him by some flattering phrase which destroyed the illusion. Or in an offended voice she would address to the young man a string of mysterious reproaches. But instead of being offended, Agostino would see his face light up with an expression of fatuous vanity, and concluded that those reproaches were only a cover for some affectionate meaning which he was unable to fathom. As for himself, both his mother and the young man seemed to be unaware of his existence; he might as well not have been there, and his mother carried this obliviousness so far as to remind the young man that if she had gone out alone with him the day before, this was a mistake on her part which she did not intend to repeat. In the future she would bring her son with her. Agostino felt this to be decidedly insulting, as if he was something with no will of its own, merely an object to be disposed of as her caprice or convenience might see fit.

Only once did his mother seem aware of his presence, and that was when the young man, letting go the oars for a moment, leaned forward with an intensely malicious expression on his face and murmured something in an undertone which Agostino could not understand. His mother started, pretending to be terribly shocked, and cried out, pointing to Agostino sitting by her, "Let us at least spare this innocent!" Agostino trembled with rage at hearing himself called innocent, as if a dirty rag had been thrown at him which he could not avoid.

When they were some way out from shore, the young man suggested a swim to his companion. Agostino, who had often admired the ease and simplicity with which his mother slipped into the water, was painfully struck by all the unfamiliar movements she now put into that familiar action. The young man had time to dive in and come up again to the surface, while she still stood hesitating and dipping one toe after another into the water, apparently pretending to be timid or shy. She made a great fuss about going in, laughing and protesting and holding on to the seat with both hands, till at last she dropped in an almost indecent attitude over the side and let herself fall clumsily into the arms of her companion. They dived together and came up together to the surface. Agostino, huddled on the seat, saw his mother's smiling face quite close to the young man's grave, brown one, and it seemed to him that their cheeks touched. He could see their two bodies disporting themselves in the limpid water, their hips and legs touching, and looking as if they longed to interlace with each other. Agostino looked first at them and then at the distant shore, with a shameful sense of being in the way. Catching sight of his frowning face, his mother, who was having her second dip, called up to him: "Why are you so serious? Don't you see how lovely it is in here? Goodness! what a serious son I've got"; a remark which filled Agostino with a sense of shame and humiliation. He made no reply, and contented himself with looking elsewhere. The swim was a long one. His mother and her companion disported themselves in the water like two dolphins, and seemed to have forgotten him entirely. At last they got back onto the raft. The young man sprang on at one bound, and then leaned over the edge to assist his companion, who was calling him to help her get out of the water. Agostino saw how in raising her the young man gripped her brown flesh with his fingers, just where the arm is softest and biggest, between the shoulder and the armpit. Then she sat down beside Agostino, panting and laughing, and with her pointed nails held her wet suit away from her, so that it should not cling to her breasts. Agostino remembered that when they were alone his mother was strong enough to climb into the boat without anyone's aid, and attributed her appeal for help and her bodily postures, which seemed to draw attention to her feminine disabilities, to the new spirit which had already produced such unpleasant changes in her. Indeed, he could not help thinking that his mother, who was naturally a tall, dignified woman, resented her size as a positive drawback from which she would have liked to rid herself; and her dignity as a tiresome habit which she was trying to replace by a sort of tomboy gaucherie.

When they were both back on the raft, the return journey began. This time the oars were entrusted to Agostino, while the other two sat down on the platform which joined the two floats. He rowed gently in the burning sun, wondering constantly about the meaning of the sounds and laughter and movements of which he was conscious behind his back. From time to time his mother, as if suddenly aware of his presence, would reach up with one arm and try to stroke the back of his neck, or she would tickle him under the arm and ask if he were tired. "No, I am not tired," he replied. He heard the young man say laughingly: "Rowing's good for him," which made him plunge in the oar savagely. His mother was sitting with her head resting against his seat and her long legs stretched out; that he knew, but it seemed to him that she did not stay in that position; once, for instance, a short skirmish seemed to be going on; his mother made a stifled sound as if she were being suffocated and the raft lurched to one side. For a moment Agostino's cheek came into contact with his mother's body, which seemed vast to him—like the sky—and pulsing with a life over which she had no control. She stood with her legs apart, holding on to her son's shoulders, and said: "I will only sit down again if you promise to be good." "I promise," rejoined the young man with mock solemnity. She let herself down again awkwardly on to the platform, and it was then her body brushed her son's cheek. The moisture of her body confined in its wet bathing suit remained on his skin, but its heat seemed to overpower its dampness and though he felt a tormenting sense of uneasiness, even of repugnance, he persisted in not drying away the traces.

As they approached the shore the young man sprang lightly to the rower's seat and seized the oars, pushing Agostino away and forcing him to take the place left empty beside his mother. She put her arm round his waist and asked how he felt, and if he was happy. She herself seemed in the highest spirits, and began singing, another most unusual thing with her. She had a sweet voice, and put in some pathetic trills which made Agostino shiver. While she sang she continued to hold him close to her, wetting him with the water from her damp bathing suit, which seemed to exude a violent animal heat. And so they came in to the shore, the young man rowing, the woman singing and caressing her son, who submitted with a feeling of utter boredom; making up a picture which Agostino felt to be false, and contrived for appearance sake.

Next day the young man appeared again. Agostino's mother insisted on her son coming and the scenes of the day before repeated themselves. Then after a few days' interval they went out again. And at last, with their apparently growing intimacy, he came to fetch her daily, and each time Agostino was obliged to go too, to listen to their conversation and to watch them bathing. He hated these expeditions, and invented a thousand reasons for not going. He would disappear and not show himself till his mother, having called him repeatedly and hunted for him everywhere, succeeded at last in unearthing him; but then he came less in response to her appeals than because her disappointment and vexation aroused his pity. He kept completely silent on the float, hoping they would understand and leave him alone, but in the end he proved weaker and more susceptible to pity than his mother or the young man. It was enough for them just to have him there; as for his feelings, he came to see that they counted for less than nothing. So, in spite of all his attempts to escape, the expeditions continued.

One day Agostino was sitting on the sand behind his mother's deck chair, waiting for the white raft to appear on the sea and for his mother to wave her hand in greeting and call to the young man by name. But the usual hour for his appearance passed, and his mother's disappointed and cross expression clearly showed that she had given up all hope of his coming. Agostino had often wondered what he should feel in such a case, and had supposed that his joy would have been at least as great as his mother's disappointment. But he was surprised to feel instead a vague disappointment, and he realized that the humiliations and resentments of those daily outings had become almost a necessity of life to him. Therefore, with a confused and unconscious desire to inflict pain on his mother, he asked her more than once if they were not going out for their usual row. She replied each time that she didn't know, but that probably they wouldn't be going today. She lay in the deck chair with a book open in her lap, but she wasn't reading and her eyes continually wandered out to sea, as if seeking some particular object among the many boats and bathers with which the water was already swarming. After sitting a long time behind his mother's chair, drawing patterns in the sand, Agostino came round to her and said in a tone of voice which he felt to be teasing and even mocking: "Mamma, do you mean to say that we're not going out on the raft today?" His mother may have felt the mockery in his voice and the desire to make her suffer, or his few rash words may have sufficed to release her long pent-up irritation. She raised her hand with an involuntary gesture and gave him a sharp slap on the cheek, which did not really hurt, probably because she regretted it almost before the blow fell. Agostino said nothing, but leaping up off the sand in one bound, he went away with his head hanging down, in the direction of the beach cabin. "Agostino! . . . Agostino! . . ." he heard his name called several times. Then the calling stopped, and looking back he fancied he saw among the throng of boats the young man's white raft. But he no longer worried about that, he was like someone who has found a treasure and hastens to hide it away so that he may examine it alone. For it was with just such a sense of discovery that he ran away to nurse his injury; something so novel to him as to seem almost incredible.

His cheek burned, his eyes were full of tears which he could not keep back; and fearing lest his sobs should break out before he got into shelter, he ran doubled up. The accumulated bitterness of all those days when he had been compelled to accompany the young man and his mother came surging back on him, and he felt that if only he could have a good cry it would release something in him and help him to understand the meaning of all these strange happenings. The simplest thing seemed to be to shut himself up in the beach cabin. His mother was probably already out in the boat and no one would disturb him. Agostino climbed the steps hurriedly, opened the door and, leaving it ajar, sat down on a stool in the corner.

He huddled up with his knees tucked into his chest and his head against the wall, and holding his face between his hands, started weeping conscientiously. The slap he had received kept rising up before him, and he wondered why, when it seemed so hard, his mother's hand had been so soft and irresolute. With the bitter sense of humiliation aroused in him by the blow were mixed a thousand other sensations, even more disagreeable, which had wounded his feelings during these last days. There was one above all which kept returning to his mind: the image of his mother's body in its damp tricot pressed against his cheek, quivering with a sort of imperious vitality. And just as great clouds of dust fly out from old clothes when they are beaten, so, as the result of that blow to his suffering and bewildered consciousness, there arose in him again the sensation of his mother's body pressed against his cheek. Indeed, that sensation seemed at times to take the place of the slap; at others, the two became so mixed that he felt both the throbbing of her body and the burning blow. But while it seemed to him natural that the slap on his cheek should keep flaring up like a fire which is gradually going out, he could not understand why the earlier sensation so persistently recurred. Why, among so many others, was it just that one which haunted him? He could not have explained it, but he thought that as long as he lived he would only have to carry his memory back to that moment in his life in order to have fresh against his cheek the pulse of her body and the rough texture of the damp tricot.

He went on crying softly to himself so as not to interrupt the painful workings of his memory, at the same time rubbing away from his wet skin with the tips of his fingers the tears which continued to fall slowly but uninterruptedly from his eyes. It was dark and stuffy in the cabin. Suddenly he had a feeling of someone opening the door, and he almost hoped that his mother, repenting of what she had done, would lay her hand affectionately on his shoulder and turn his face toward her. And his lips had already begun to shape the word "Mamma" when he heard a step in the cabin and the door pulled to, without any hand touching his shoulder or stroking his head.

He raised his head and looked up. Close to the half-open door he saw a boy of about his own age standing in an attitude of someone on the lookout. He had on a pair of short trousers rolled up at the bottom, and an open sailor blouse with a great hole in the back. A thin ray of sunshine falling through a gap in the roof of the cabin lit up the thick growth of auburn curls round his neck. His feet were bare; holding the door ajar with his hands, he was gazing intently at something on the beach and did not seem to be aware of Agostino's presence. Agostino dried his eyes with the back of his hand and said: "Hello, what do you want?" The boy turned around, making a sign not to speak. He had an ugly, freckled face, the most remarkable feature of which was the rapid movement of his hard blue eyes. Agostino thought he recognized him. Probably he was the son of a fisherman or beach attendant, and he had doubtless seen him pushing out the boats or doing something about the beach.

"We're playing cops and robbers," said the boy, after a moment, turning to Agostino. "They mustn't see me."

"Which are you?" asked Agostino, hastily drying his eyes.

"A robber, of course," replied the other without looking around.

Agostino went on watching the boy. He couldn't make up his mind whether he liked him, but his voice had a rough touch of dialect which piqued him and aroused his curiosity. Besides, he felt instinctively that this boy's hiding in the cabin just at that moment was an opportunity—he could not have explained of what sort—but certainly an opportunity he must not miss.

"Will you let me play too?" he asked. The boy turned round and stared at him rudely. "How do you get into it?" he said quickly. "We're all pals playing together."

"Well," said Agostino, with shameless persistence, "let me play too."

The boy shrugged his shoulders. "It's too late now. We've almost finished the game."

"Well, in the next game."

"There won't be any more," said the boy, looking him over doubtfully, but as if struck by his persistence. "Afterwards we're going to the pine woods."

"I'll go with you, if you'll let me."

The boy seemed amused and began to laugh rather contemptuously. "You're a fine one, you are. But we don't want you."

Agostino had never been in such a position before. But the same instinct which prompted him to ask the boy if he might join their game suggested to him now a means by which he might make himself acceptable.

"Look here," he said hesitatingly, "if you . . . if you'll let me join your gang, I . . . I'll give you something."

The other turned round at once with greedy eyes.

"What'll you give me?"

"Whatever you like."

Agostino pointed to a big model of a sailboat, with all its sails attached, which was lying on the floor of the cabin among a lot of other toys.

"I'll give you that."

"What use is that to me?" replied the boy, shrugging his shoulders.

"You could sell it," Agostino suggested.

"They'd never take it," said the boy, with the air of one who knows. "They'd say it was stolen goods."

Agostino looked all round him despairingly. His mother's clothes were hanging on pegs, her shoes were on the floor, on the table was a handkerchief and a scarf or two. There was absolutely nothing in the cabin which seemed a suitable offering.

"Say," said the boy, seeing his bewilderment, "got any cigarettes?"

Agostino remembered that that very morning his mother had put two boxes of a very good brand in the big bag which was hanging from a peg; and he hastened to reply, triumphantly, "Yes, I have. Would you like some?"

"I *don't* think!" said the other, with scornful irony. "Are you stupid! Give them here, quick."

Agostino took down the bag, felt about in it and pulled out the two boxes. He held them out to the boy, as if he were not quite sure how many he wanted.

"I'll take both," he said lightly, seizing the boxes. He looked at the label and clicked his tongue approvingly and said: "You must be rich, eh?"

Agostino didn't know what to answer. The boy went on: "I'm Berto. What's your name?"

Agostino told him. But the other had ceased to pay any attention. His impatient fingers had already torn open one of the boxes, breaking the seals on its paper wrapping. He took out a cigarette and put it between his lips. Then he took a match from his pocket and struck it against the wall of the cabin; and after inhaling a mouthful of smoke and puffing it out through his nose, he resumed his watching position at the crack of the door.

"Come on, let's go," he said, after a moment, making Agostino a sign to follow him. They left the cabin one behind the other. When they got to the beach Berto made straight for the road behind the row of beach cabins.

As they walked along the burning sand between the low bushes of broom and thistles, he said: "Now we're going to the Cave . . . they've gone on past . . . they're looking for me lower down."

"Where is the Cave?" asked Agostino.

"At the Vespucci Baths," replied the boy. He held his cigarette ostentatiously between two fingers, as if to display it, and voluptuously inhaled great mouthfuls of smoke. "Don't you smoke?" he said.

"I don't care about it," said Agostino, ashamed to confess that he had never even dreamed of smoking. But Berto laughed. "Why don't you say straight out that your mother won't let you? Speak the truth." His way of saying this was contemptuous rather than friendly. He offered Agostino a cigarette, saying: "Go ahead, you smoke too."

They had reached the sea-front and were walking barefoot on the sharp flints between dried-up flower beds. Agostino put the cigarette to his lips and took a few puffs, inhaling a little smoke which he at once let out again instead of swallowing it.

Berto laughed derisively.

"You call that smoking!" he exclaimed. "That's not the way to do it. Look." He took the cigarette and inhaled deeply, rolling his sulky eyes all the while; then he opened his mouth wide and put it quite close to Agostino's eyes. There was nothing to be seen in his mouth, except his tongue curled up at the back.

"Now watch," said Berto, shutting his mouth again. And he puffed a cloud of smoke straight into Agostino's face. Agostino coughed and laughed nervously at the same time. "It's your turn now," said Berto.

A trolley passed them, whistling, its window curtains flapping in the breeze. Agostino inhaled a fresh mouthful and with a great effort swallowed the smoke. But it went the wrong way and he had a dreadful fit of coughing. Berto took the cigarette and gave him a great slap on the back, saying: "Bravo! There's no doubt about your being a smoker."

After this experiment they walked on in silence past a whole series of bath establishments, with their rows of cabins painted in bright colors, great striped umbrellas slanting in all directions, and absurd triumphal arches. The beach between the cabins was packed with noisy holiday-makers and the sparkling sea swarmed with bathers.

"Where is Vespucci?" asked Agostino, who had to walk very fast to keep up with his new friend.

"It's the last one of all."

Agostino began to wonder whether he ought not to turn back. If his mother hadn't gone out on the raft after all, she would certainly be looking for him. But the memory of that slap put his scruples to rest. In going with Berto he almost felt as if he were pursuing a mysterious and justified vendetta.

Suddenly Berto stopped and said: "How about letting the smoke out through your nose? Can you do that?" Agostino shook his head, and his companion, holding the stump of his cigarette between his lips, inhaled the smoke and expelled it through his nostrils. "Now," he went on, "I'm going to let it out through my eyes. But you must put your hand on my chest and look me straight in the face." Agostino went up to him quite innocently and put his hand on Berto's chest and fixed his eyes on Berto's, expecting to see smoke come out of them.

But Berto treacherously pressed the lighted cigarette down hard on the back of his hand and threw the butt away, jumping for joy and shouting: "Oh! you silly idiot! You just don't know anything." Agostino was almost blind with pain, and his first impulse was to fling himself on Berto and strike him. But Berto, as if he saw what was coming, stood still and clenched his fists, and with two sharp blows in the stomach almost knocked the breath out of Agostino's body.

"I'm not one for words," he said savagely. "If you ask for it you'll get it." Agostino, infuriated, rushed at him again, but he felt terribly weak and certain of being defeated. This time Berto seized him by the head, and taking it under his arm almost strangled him. Agostino did not even attempt to resist, but in a stifled voice implored him to let go. Berto released him and sprang back, planting his feet firmly on the ground in a fighting stance. But Agostino had heard the vertebrae of his neck crack, and was stupefied by the boy's extraordinary brutality. It seemed incredible that he, Agostino, who had always been kind to everyone, should suddenly be treated with such savage and deliberate cruelty. His chief feeling was one of amazement at such barbarousness. It overwhelmed him, but at the same time fascinated him because of its very novelty and because it was so monstrous.

"I haven't done you any harm," he panted. "I gave you those cigarettes . . . and you . . ." He couldn't finish. His eyes filled with tears.

"Uh, you crybaby," retorted Berto. "Want your cigarettes back? I don't want them. Take them back to Mamma."

"It doesn't matter," said Agostino, shaking his head disconsolately. "I only just said it for something to say. Please keep them."

"Well, let's get on," said Berto. "We're almost there."

The burn on Agostino's hand was hurting him badly. Raising it to his lips he looked about him. On that part of the beach there were very few cabins, five or six in all, scattered about at some distance from each other. They were miserable huts of rough wood. The sand between them was deserted and the sea was equally empty. There were a few women in the shade of a boat pulled up out of reach of the tide, some standing, some lying stretched out on the sand, all dressed in antiquated bathing suits, with long drawers edged with white braid, all busy drying themselves and exposing their white limbs to the sun. A signboard painted blue bore the inscription: "Amerigo Vespucci Baths." A low green shack half-buried in the sand evidently belonged to the bath man. Beyond this the shore stretched away as far as the eye could see, without either cabins or houses, a solitude of windswept sand between the sparkling blue sea and the dusty green of the pine trees.

One entire side of the man's hut was hidden from the road by sand dunes, which were higher at this point. Then, when you had climbed to the top of the dunes, you saw a patched, faded awning of rusty red, which seemed to have been cut out of an old sail. This awning was attached at one end to two poles driven into the sand, and at the other to the hut.

"That's our cave," said Berto.

Under the awning a man seated at a rickety table was in the act of lighting a cigarette. Two or three boys were stretched on the sand around him. Berto took a flying leap and landed at the man's feet, crying: "Cave!" Agostino approached rather timidly. "This is Pisa," said Berto, pointing to him. He was surprised to hear himself called by this nickname so soon. It was only five minutes ago that he had told Berto he was born at Pisa. Agostino lay down on the ground beside the others. The sand was not so clean as it was on the beach; bits of coconut shell and wooden splinters, fragments of earthenware and all sorts of rubbish were mixed up in it. Here and there it was caked and hard from the pails of dirty water which had been thrown out of the hut. Agostino noticed that the boys, four in all, were poorly dressed. Like Berto they were evidently the sons of sailors or bath men. "He was at the Speranza," burst out Berto, without drawing breath. "He says he wants to play at cops and robbers too, but the game's over, isn't it? I told you the game would be over."

At that moment there was a cry of "It's not fair! It's not fair!" Agostino, looking up, saw another gang of boys running from the direction of the sea, probably the cops. First came a thickset, stumpy youth of about seventeen in a bathing costume; next, to his great surprise, a Negro; the third was fair, and by his carriage and physical beauty struck Agostino as being better bred than the others. But as he got nearer, his ragged bathing suit, full of holes, and a certain coarseness in his handsome face with beautiful blue eyes, showed that he too belonged to the people. After these three boys came four more, all about the same age, between thirteen and fourteen. The big, thickset boy was so much older than the others that at first it seemed odd that he should mix with such children. But his pasty face, the color of half-baked bread; the thick, expressionless features, and an almost brutish stupidity were sufficient explanation of the company he kept. He had hardly any neck, and his smooth, hairless torso was as wide at the waist and hips as at the shoulders. "You hid in a cabin," he shouted at Berto. "I dare you to deny it! Cabins are out of bounds by the rules of the game."

"It's a lie!" retorted Berto, with equal violence. "Isn't it, Pisa?" he added, suddenly turning to Agostino. "I didn't hide in a cabin, did I? We were both standing by the hut of the Speranza, and we saw you go by, didn't we, Pisa?"

"You did hide in my cabin, you know," said Agostino, who was incapable of telling a lie. "There, you see!" shouted the other, brandishing his fist under Berto's nose. "I'll bash your head in, you liar!"

"Spy!" yelled Berto in Agostino's face. "I told you to stay where you were. Go back to Mamma, that's the place for you." He was filled with uncontrollable rage, a bestial fury which amazed and mystified Agostino. But in springing to punish him one of the cigarette boxes tumbled out of his pocket. He stooped to pick it up, but the big boy was quicker still, and darting down he pounced on the box and waved it in the air, crying triumphantly: "Cigarettes! Cigarettes!"

"Give them back," shouted Berto, hurling himself upon the big boy. "They're mine. Pisa gave them to *me*. You just give them back."

The other took a step back and waited till Berto was within range. Then he held the box of cigarettes in his mouth and began to pummel Berto's stomach methodically with his two fists. Finally he kicked Berto's feet from under and brought him down with a crash. "Give me them back!" Berto went on shouting, while he rolled in the sand. But the big boy, with a stupid laugh, called out: "He's got some more . . . at him, boys." And with a unanimity which surprised Agostino all the boys flung themselves upon Berto. For a moment there was nothing to be seen but a writhing mass of bodies tangled together in a cloud of sand at the feet of the man, who went on smoking calmly at the table. At last, the fair boy, who seemed to be the most agile, disentangled himself from the heap and got up, triumphantly waving the second box of cigarettes. Then the others got up, one by one; and last of all Berto. His ugly, freckled little face was convulsed with fury. "Swine! Thieves!" he bellowed, shaking his fist and sobbing.

It was a strange and novel impression for Agostino to see his tormentor tormented in his turn, and treated as pitilessly as he himself had just been. "Swine! Swine!" Berto screamed again. The big boy went up to him and gave him a resounding box on the ear, which made his companions dance for joy. "Do you want any more?" Berto rushed like a mad one to the corner of the hut and, bending down, grabbed hold of a large rock with both hands and flung it at his enemy, who with a derisive whistle sprang aside to avoid it. "You swine!" yelled Berto again, still sobbing with rage, but withdrawing himself prudently behind a corner of the hut. His sobs were loud and furious, as if giving vent to some frightful bitterness, but his companions had ceased to take any interest in him. They were all stretched out again on the sand. The big boy opened one box of cigarettes, and the fair boy another. Suddenly the man, who had remained seated at the little table without moving during the fight, said: "Hand over those cigarettes."

Agostino looked at him. He was a tall, fat man of about fifty. He had a cold and deceptively good-natured face. He was bald, with a curious saddle-shaped forehead and twinkling eyes; a red, aquiline nose with wide nostrils full of little scarlet veins horrible to look at. He had a drooping mustache, which hid a rather crooked mouth, and a cigar between his lips. He was wearing a faded shirt and a pair of blue cotton trousers with one leg down to his ankle and the other rolled up below his knee. A black sash was wound round his stomach. One detail in particular added to Agostino's first feeling of revulsion, the fact that Saro—for this was his name—had six fingers instead of five on both hands. This made them look enormous, and his fingers like abbreviated tentacles. Agostino could not take his eyes off those hands; he could not make up his mind whether Saro had two first or two middle or two third fingers. They all seemed of equal length, except the little finger, which stuck out from his hand like a small branch at the base of a knotty tree trunk. Saro took the cigar out of his mouth and repeated simply: "What about those cigarettes?"

The fair boy got up and put his box on the table. "Good for you, Sandro," said Saro.

"And supposing I won't give you them?" shouted the elder boy defiantly.

"Give them up, Tortima; you'd better," called out several voices at once. Tortima looked all round and then at Saro, who with the six fingers of his right hand on the box of cigarettes, kept his half-closed little eyes fixed on him. Then, with the remark: "All right, but it isn't fair," he came over and put his box down on the table too.

"And now I'll divide them," said Saro, in a soft, affable voice. Without removing his cigar, he screwed up his eyes, opened one of the boxes, took out a cigarette with his stumpy, multiple fingers, which looked incapable of gripping it, and threw it to the Negro, with a "Catch, Homs!" Then he took another and threw it to one of the others; a third he threw into the joined palms of Sandro; a fourth straight at Tortima's stolid face—and so with all the rest. "Do you want one?" he asked Berto, who, swallowing back his sobs, had come silently back to join the others. He nodded sulkily, and was thrown one. When each of the boys had received his cigarette, Saro was about to shut the box, which was still half-full, when he stopped and said to Agostino: "What about you, Pisa?" Agostino would have liked to refuse, but Berto gave him a dig in the ribs and whispered: "Ask for one, idiot, we'll smoke it together afterward." So Agostino said he would like one, and he too had his cigarette. Then Saro shut the box.

"What about the rest? What about the rest?" shouted all the boys at once.

"You shall have the rest another day," replied Saro calmly. "Pisa, take these cigarettes and go put them in the hut." There was complete silence. Agostino nervously took both boxes, and, stepping over the boys' prostrate bodies, crossed to the shed. It appeared to consist of one room only, and he liked its smallness, which made it seem like a house in a fairy tale. It had a low ceiling with white-washed beams, and the walls were of unplaned planks. Two tiny windows, complete with window sill, little square panes of glass, latches, curtains, even a vase or two of flowers, diffused a mild light. One corner was occupied by the bed, neatly made up, with a clean pillowcase and red counterpane; in another stood a round table and three stools. On the marble top of a big chest stood two of those bottles which have sailboats or steamships imprisoned inside them. Sails were hung on hooks all round the walls, and there were pairs of oars and other sea tackle. Agostino thought how he should love to own a cottage as cosy and convenient as this. He went up to the table, on which lay a big, cracked china bowl full of half-smoked cigarettes, put down his two boxes and went out again into the sunlight.

All the boys were lying face downward on the sand around Saro, smoking with great demonstrations of enjoyment. And meanwhile they were discussing something about which they did not seem to agree. Sandro was just saying: "I tell you it *is* him."

"His mother's a real beauty," said an admiring voice. "She's the best looker on the beach. Homs and me got under the cabin one day to see her undress, but her chemise fell just above the crack we were looking through and we couldn't see anything at all. Her legs, gee, and her breasts. . . ."

"You never see the husband anywhere about," said a third voice.

"You needn't worry, she satisfies herself. . . . D'you know who with? That young guy from Villa Sorriso . . . the dark one. He takes her out every day on his raft."

"He's not the only one either. She'd take anyone on," said someone maliciously.

"But I know it's not him," insisted another.

"Say, Pisa," said Sandro suddenly. "Isn't that your mother, that lady at the Speranza? She's tall and dark, with long legs, and wears a striped two-piece bathing suit . . . and she's got a mole on the left side of her mouth."

"Yes, why?" asked Agostino, nervously.

"It *is* her, it *is* her," cried Berto triumphantly. And then, in a burst of jealous spite: "You're just their blind, aren't you? You all go out together, her and you, and her gigolo. You're their blind, aren't you?" At these words everyone roared with laughter. Even Saro smiled under his mustache. "I don't know what you mean," said Agostino, blushing and only half-understanding. He wanted to protest, but their coarse jokes aroused in him a curious and unexpected sense of sadistic satisfaction. As if by their words the boys had, all unawares, avenged the humiliations which his mother had inflicted on him all these days past. At the same time he was struck dumb with horror at their knowing so much about his private affairs.

"Innocent little lamb," said the same malicious voice. "I'd like to know what they're up to; they always go a long way out," said Tortima with mock gravity. "Come on, tell us what they do. He kisses her, eh?" He put the back of his hand to his lips and gave it a smacking kiss.

"It's quite true," said Agostino, flushing with shame; "we do go a long way out to swim."

"Oh yes, to swim!" came sarcastically from several voices at once.

"My mother does swim, and so does Renzo."

"Ah, yes, Renzo, that's his name," affirmed the boy, as if recovering a lost thread in his memory. "Renzo, that tall dark fellow."

"And what do Renzo and Mamma do together?" suddenly asked Berto, quite restored. "Is it this they do?" and he made an expressive gesture with his hand, "And you just look on, eh?"

"I?" questioned Agostino, turning around with a look of terror.

They all burst out laughing and smothered their merriment in the sand. But Saro continued to observe him attentively, without moving. Agostino looked around despairingly, as if to implore aid.

Saro seemed to be struck by his look. He took his cigar out of his mouth, and said: "Can't you see he knows absolutely nothing?"

The din was immediately silenced. "How do you mean, he doesn't know?" asked Tortima, who hadn't understood.

"He just doesn't know," repeated Saro, simply. And turning to Agostino, he said in a softer voice: "Speak up, Pisa. A man and woman, what is it they do together? Don't you know?"

They all listened breathlessly. Agostino stared at Saro, who continued to smoke and watch him through half-closed eyelids. He looked round at the boys, who were evidently bursting with stifled laughter, and repeated mechanically, through the cloud which seemed to cover his sight: "A man and a woman?"

"Yes, your mother and Renzo," explained Berto brutally.

Agostino wanted to say "Don't talk about my mother," but the question awoke in him a whole swarm of sensations and memories, and he was too upset to say anything at all. "He doesn't know," said Saro abruptly, shifting his cigar from one corner of his mouth to the other. "Which of you boys is going to tell him?" Agostino looked around bewildered. It was like being at school, but what a strange schoolmaster! What odd schoolfellows! "Me, me, me! . . ." all the boys shouted at once. Saro's glance rested dubiously on all those faces burning with eagerness to be the first to speak. Then he said: "You don't really know either, any of you. You've only got

it from hearsay. . . . Let someone tell him who really knows."
Agostino saw them all eyeing each other in silence. Then someone
said: "Tortima." An expression of vanity lit up the youth's face. He
was just going to get up when Berto said, with hatred in his voice:
"He made it all up, himself. . . . It's a pack of lies. . . ."

"What d'you mean, a pack of lies?" shouted Tortima, flinging
himself upon Berto. "It's you who tells lies, you bastard!" But this
time Berto was too quick for him, and from behind the corner of
the hut he began making faces and putting out his tongue at
Tortima, his red, freckled face distorted by hatred. Tortima contented himself with threatening him with his fist and shouting:
"You dare come back!" But somehow Berto's intervention had
wrecked his chances, and the boys with one accord voted for Sandro.
His arms crossed over his broad brown chest on which shone a few
golden hairs, Sandro, handsome and elegant, advanced into the
circle of boys stretched out on the sand. Agostino noticed that his
strong, bronzed legs looked as if they were dusted over with gold.
A few hairs also showed through the gaps in his bathing trunks.
"It's quite simple," he said in a strong, clear voice. And speaking
slowly with the aid of gestures which were significant without being
coarse, he explained to Agostino what he now felt he had always
known but had somehow forgotten, as in a deep sleep. Sandro's
explanation was followed by other less sober ones. Some of the boys
made vulgar gestures with their hands, others dinned into Agostino's
ears coarse words which he had never heard before; two of them said:
"We'll show him what they do," and gave a demonstration on the
hot sand, jerking and writhing in each other's arms. Sandro, satisfied
with his success, went off alone to finish his cigar. "Do you understand now?" asked Saro, as soon as the din had died down. Agostino
nodded. In reality he hadn't so much understood as absorbed the
notion, rather as one absorbs a medicine or poison, the effect of which
is not immediately felt but will be sure to manifest itself later on.
The idea was not in his empty, bewildered and anguished mind, but
in some other part of his being; in his embittered heart, or deep in
his breast, which received it with amazement. It was like some
bright, dazzling object, which one cannot look at for the radiance it
emits, so that one can only guess its real shape. He felt it was something he had always possessed but only now experienced in his blood.

"Renzo and Pisa's mother," he heard someone say close beside
him. "I'll be Renzo and you be Pisa's mother. Let's try." He turned
suddenly and saw Berto, who with an awkward, ceremonious gesture

was making a bow to another boy. "Madam, may I have the honor of your company on my raft? I'm going for a swim. Pisa will accompany us." Then suddenly blind rage took possession of him and flinging himself upon Berto he yelled: "I forbid you to talk about my mother." But before he knew what had happened he was lying on his back on the sand, with Berto's knee holding him down and Berto's fists raining blows on his face. He wanted to cry, but realizing that his tears would only be an opening for more jeers, he controlled them with great effort. Then, covering his face with his arm, he lay as still as death. Berto left him alone after a bit, and feeling very ill-treated he went and sat down at Saro's feet. The boys were already busy talking about something else. One of them suddenly asked Agostino: "Are you rich, you people?"

Agostino was so intimidated that he hardly knew what to say. But he replied: "I think so."

"How much? . . . A million? Two millions? . . . Three millions?"

"I don't know," said Agostino, feeling bothered.

"Got a big house?"

"Yes," said Agostino; and somewhat reassured by the more courteous turn of the conversation, pride of possession prompted him to add: "We have twenty rooms."

"Bum . . ." came incredulously from someone.

"We've got two reception rooms and then there's my father's study . . ."

"Aha!" said a scornful voice.

"Or it *used* to be my father's," Agostino hastened to add, half-hoping that this detail might make them feel a little more sympathetic towards him. "My father is dead."

There was a moment's silence. "So your mother's a widow?" said Tortima.

"Well, of course," came from several mocking voices. "That's not saying anything," protested Tortima. "She might have married again."

"No, she hasn't married again," said Agostino.

"And have you got a car?"

"Yes."

"And a chauffeur?"

"Yes."

"Tell your mother I'm ready to be her chauffeur," shouted someone.

"And what do you do in those reception rooms?" asked Tortima, on whom Agostino's account seemed to make more impression than on anyone else. "Do you give dances?"

"Yes, my mother has receptions," replied Agostino.

"Lots of pretty women, you bet," said Tortima, as if speaking to himself. "How many people come?"

"I don't really know."

"How many?"

"Twenty or thirty," said Agostino, who by now felt quite at his ease and was rather gratified by his success.

"Twenty or thirty . . . What do they do?"

"What do you expect them to do?" asked Berto ironically. "I suppose they dance and amuse themselves. They're rich . . . not like us. They make love, I suppose."

"No, they don't make love," said Agostino conscientiously, for the sake of showing that he knew perfectly well what they meant.

Tortima seemed to be struggling with an idea which he was unable to formulate. At last he said: "But supposing I was to appear at one of those receptions, and say: 'I've come too.' What would you do?" As he spoke he got up and marched forward impudently, with his hands on his hips and his chest stuck out. The boys burst out laughing. "I should ask you to go away," said Agostino simply, emboldened by the laughter of the boys.

"And supposing I refused to go away?"

"I should make our men turn you out."

"Have you got menservants?"

"No, but my mother hires waiters when she has a reception."

"Bah, just like your father." One of the boys was evidently the son of a waiter.

"And supposing I resisted, and broke that waiter's nose for him, and then marched into the middle of the room and shouted, 'You're a lot of rogues and bitches, the whole lot of you.' What would you say?" insisted Tortima, advancing threateningly upon Agostino, and turning his fist round and round, as if to let him smell it. But this time they all turned against Tortima, not so much from a wish to protect Agostino as from the desire to hear more details of his fabulous wealth.

"Leave him alone . . . they'd kick you out, and a good thing too," was heard on all sides. Berto said sneeringly: "What have you got to do with it? Your father's a boatman and you'll be a boatman too; and if you did turn up at Pisa's house you certainly wouldn't shout anything. I can see you," he added, getting up and mimicking Tortima's supposed humility in Agostino's house . . . " 'Excuse me, is Mr. Pisa at home? Excuse me . . . I just came . . . Oh, he can't? . . . Never mind, please excuse me . . . I'm so sorry . . . I'll come another time.' Oh, I can see you. Why, you'd bow down to the ground."

All the boys burst out laughing. Tortima, who was as stupid as he was brutal, didn't dare stand up to their taunts. But in order to get even he said to Agostino: "Can you make an iron arm?"

"An iron arm?" repeated Agostino.

"He don't know what an iron arm is," said several voices, derisively. Sandro came over and took hold of Agostino's arm and doubled it up, and told him to stay with his hand in the air and his elbow in the sand. Meanwhile Tortima lay face downward on the sand and placed his arm in a similar position. "You push from one side," said Sandro, "and Tortima will push from the other."

Agostino took Tortima's hand. The latter at one stroke brought down his arm and got up triumphantly.

"Let me try," said Berto. He brought down Agostino's arm just as easily and got up in his turn. "Me too, me too!" cried all the others. One after another they all beat Agostino. At last it was the Negro's turn, and someone said: "If you let Homs beat you, well, your arm must be made of putty." Agostino made up his mind not to let the Negro beat him.

The Negro's arms were thin, the color of roasted coffee. He thought his own looked stronger. "Come on, Pisa," said Homs, with sham bravado, as he lay down facing him. He had a weak voice, like a woman's, and when he brought his face to within an inch of Agostino's, he saw that his nose, instead of being flat, as you might have expected, was almost aquiline, and curved in on itself like a black, shiny curl of flesh, with a pale, almost yellow mole above one nostril. Nor were his lips broad and thick like a Negro's, but thin and violet-colored. He had round eyes with large whites, on which his protuberant forehead with its great mop of sooty wool seemed to press. "Come on, Pisa, I won't hurt you," he said, putting his delicate hand with its thin, rose-nailed fingers in Agostino's. Agostino saw that by raising himself slightly on his shoulder he could easily have brought his whole weight to bear on his hand, and this simple fact allowed him at first to keep Homs under his control. For quite a while they competed without either of them getting the upper hand, surrounded by a circle of admiring boys. Agostino's face wore a look of great concentration; he was putting his whole strength into the effort; whereas the Negro made fearful grimaces, grinding his white teeth and screwing up his eyes. Suddenly a surprised voice proclaimed: "Pisa's winning!" But at that very moment Agostino felt an excruciating pain running from his shoulder right down his arm; he could bear no more, and gave in, saying: "No, he's stronger than me." "You'll beat me next time," said the Negro, in an unpleasantly honeyed voice, as he rose from the ground. "Fancy Homs beating you too, you're good for nothing," sneered Tortima. But the other boys seemed tired of ragging Agostino. "How about a swim?" said someone. "Yes, yes, a swim!" they all cried, and they set off by leaps and bounds over the hot sand to the sea. Agostino, trailing behind, saw them turning somersaults like fish into the shallow water with shouts and screams of joy. As he reached the water's edge Tortima emerged, bottom first, like a huge sea-animal, and called out: "Dive in, Pisa. What are you doing?"

"But I'm dressed," said Agostino.

"Get undressed then," returned Tortima crossly. Agostino tried to escape, but it was too late. Tortima caught hold of him and dragged him along, struggling and pulling his tormentor over with him. He only let him go when he had almost suffocated him by holding his head under water. Then with a "Good-bye, Pisa," he swam off. Some way out Agostino could see Sandro standing in an elegant posture on a raft, in the middle of a swarm of boys, all trying to climb on to the floats. Wet and panting he returned to the beach and stood a few moments watching the raft going further and further out to sea, all alone under the blinding sunshine. Then hurrying along the burnished sand at the water's edge, he made his way back to the Speranza.


It was not so late as he feared. When he reached the bathing place he found that his mother had not yet returned. The beach was emptying; only a few isolated bathers still loitered in the dazzling water. The majority were trailing languidly off in single file under the midday sun up the tiled path which led from the beach. Agostino sat down under the big umbrella and waited. He thought his mother was staying out an unusually long time. He forgot that the young man had arrived much later than usual with his raft and that it was not his mother who had wanted to go out alone, but he who had disappeared; and said to himself that those two had certainly profited by his absence to do what Saro and the boys had suggested. He no longer felt any jealousy about this, but experienced a new and strange quiver of curiosity and secret approval, as if he were himself an accomplice. It was quite natural for his mother to behave like that with the young man, to go out with him every day on the float, and at a safe distance from prying eyes to fling herself into his arms. It was natural, and he was now perfectly well able to accept the fact. These thoughts passed through his mind as he sat scanning the sea for the return of the lovers. At length the raft appeared, a bright speck on the sea, and as it drew rapidly nearer he could see his mother sitting on the bench and the young man rowing. Every stroke of the oars as they rose and fell left a glittering track in the water. He got up and went down to the water's edge. He wanted to see his mother land, and to discover some traces of the intimacy at which he had assisted so long without understanding, and which, in the light of the revelations that Saro and the boys had made, must surely be brazenly advertised in their behavior. As the raft came near the shore his mother waved to him, then sprang gaily into the water and was soon at his side. "Are you hungry? We'll go and have something to eat at once. . . . Good-bye, good-bye till tomorrow. . . ." she added in a caressing voice, turning to wave to the young man. Agostino thought she seemed happier than usual, and as he followed her across the beach he could not help thinking there had been a note of joyous intoxication in her farewell to the young man; as if what her son's presence had hitherto prevented had actually taken place that day. But his observations and suspicions went no further than this; for apart from her naïve joy, which was something quite different from her customary dignity, he could not really picture what might have happened while they were out together, nor imagine what their relations actually were. Though he scrutinized her face, her neck, her hands, her body with a new and cruel awareness, they did not seem to bear any trace of the kisses and caresses they had received. The more Agostino watched his mother the more dissatisfied he felt. "You were alone today . . . without me . . ." he began, as they approached the cabin; almost hoping she would say: "Yes, and at last we were able to make love." But his mother only seemed to treat this remark as an allusion to the slap she had given him, and to his running away. "Don't let's say any more about that," she said, stopping and putting her arm around his shoulders, and looking at him with her laughing, excited eyes. "I know you love me; give me a kiss and we won't say any more about it, eh?" Agostino suddenly felt his lips against her neck—that neck whose chaste perfume and warmth had been so sweet to him. But now he fancied he felt beneath his lips, however faintly, a stirring of something new, as it were a sharp quiver of reaction to the young man's kisses. Then she ran up the steps to the cabin, and he lay down on the sand, his face burning with a shame he could not comprehend.

Later, as they were walking back together, he stirred up these new mysterious feelings in his troubled mind. Before, when he had been ignorant of good and evil, his mother's relations with the young man had seemed to him mysteriously tinged with guilt, but now that Saro and his disciples had opened his eyes, he was, strange to say, full of doubt and unsatisfied curiosity. It was indeed the frank jealousy of his childish love for his mother which had first aroused his sensibilities; whereas now, in the clear, cruel light of day, this love, though as great as ever, was replaced by a bitter, disillusioned curiosity compared with which those early, faint evidences seemed insipid and insufficient. Formerly, every word and gesture which he felt unbecoming had offended without enlightening him, and he wished he had not seen them. Now that he came to look back, those small, tasteless gestures which used to scandalize him seemed mere trifles, and he almost wished he could surprise his mother in some of the shameless attitudes into which Saro and the boys had so recently initiated him.

He would never have hit so soon on the idea of spying on his mother with the direct intention of destroying the halo of dignity and respect which had hitherto enveloped her, had he not that very day been driven by chance to take a step in that direction. When they reached home mother and son ate their luncheon in silence. His mother seemed distrait, and Agostino, full of new and, to him, incredible thoughts, was unusually silent. But after lunch he suddenly felt an irresistible desire to go out and join the gang of boys again. They had told him they met at the Vespucci bathing place early in the afternoon, to plan the day's adventures, and when he had got over his first fear and repugnance the company of those young hooligans began to exercise a mysterious attraction over him. He was lying on his bed with the shutters closed; it was warm and dark. He was playing as usual with the wooden switch of the electric light. Few sounds came to him from outside; the wheels of a solitary carriage, the clatter of plates and glasses through the open windows of the *pension* opposite. In contrast with the silence of the summer afternoon the sounds inside the house seemed to stand out more clearly, as if cut off from the rest. He heard mother go into the next room and her heels tapping on the tiled floor. She went to and fro, opening and shutting drawers, moving chairs about, touching this and that. "She's gone to lie down," he thought suddenly, shaking off the torpor which was gradually invading his senses; "and then I shan't be able to tell her I want to go on the beach." He sprang up in alarm at the thought, and went out on the landing. His room looked over the balcony facing the stairs, and his mother's room was next to his. He went to her door, but finding it ajar, instead of knocking as he generally did, he gently pushed the door half open, moved perhaps by an unconscious desire to spy upon his mother's intimacy. His mother's room was much bigger than his, and the bed was by the door; directly facing the door was a chest of drawers, with a large mirror above it. The first thing he saw was his mother standing in front of the chest of drawers. She was not naked, as he had pictured and almost hoped when he went in so quietly; but she was partly undressed and was just taking off her necklace and earrings in front of the glass. She had on a flimsy chiffon chemise which only came half-way down her loins. As she stood leaning languidly to one side, one hip was higher and more prominent than the other, and below her solid but graceful thighs her slender, well-shaped legs tapered to delicate ankles. Her arms were raised to unfasten the clasp of her necklace and, through the transparent chiffon, this movement was perceptible all down her back, curiously modifying the contours of her body. With her hands raised thus, her armpits looked like the jaws of two snakes and the long, soft hair darted out of them like thin black tongues, as if glad to escape from the pressure of her heavy limbs. All her splendid, massive body seemed to Agostino's fascinated eyes to lose its solidity and sway and palpitate in the twilight of the room, as if nudity acted on it as a leaven and endowed it with a strange faculty of expansion; so that at one moment it seemed to billow outwards in innumerable curves, at another to taper upwards to a giant height, and to fill the space between floor and ceiling.

Agostino's first impulse was to hurry away again, but suddenly that new thought, "It is a woman," rooted him to the spot, with wide-open eyes, holding fast to the door handle. He felt his filial soul rebel at this immobility and try to drag him back, but the new mind which was already strong in him, though still a little timid, forced his reluctant eyes to stare pitilessly at what yesterday he would not have dared to look upon. And during this conflict between repulsion and attraction, surprise and pleasure, all the details of the picture he was contemplating stood out more distinctly and forcibly: the movements of her legs, the indolent curve of her back, the profile of her armpits. And they seemed to correspond exactly to his new conception, which was awaiting these confirmations in order to take complete sway over his imagination. Precipitated in one moment from respect and reverence to their exact opposite, he would almost have liked to see the improprieties of her unconscious nudity develop before his eyes into conscious wantonness. The astonishment in his eyes changed to curiosity, the attention which riveted them and which he fancied to be scientific in reality owed its false objectivity to the cruelty of the sentiment controlling him. And while his blood surged up to his brain he kept saying to himself: "She is a woman, nothing but a woman," and he somehow felt these words to be lashes of insult and contempt on her back and legs.

When his mother had taken off her necklace and put it down on the marble top of the chest of drawers, she began with a graceful movement of both hands to remove her earrings. In order to do so she held her head slightly to one side, turning a little away from the glass. Agostino was afraid she might catch sight of him in the big standing mirror which was nearby in the bay window; for he could see himself in it, standing furtively there, just inside the folding door. He raised his hand with an effort, knocked at the doorpost and said: "May I come in?"

"One moment, darling," said his mother calmly. Agostino saw her disappear from sight and, after rummaging about for a while, reappear in a long blue silk dressing gown.

"Mamma," said Agostino, without lifting his eyes from the ground, "I am going down to the beach."

"Now?" said his mother, abstractedly. "But it's so hot. Hadn't you better sleep a little first?" She put out one hand and stroked his cheek, while with the other she rearranged a stray lock of her smooth black hair.

Agostino suddenly become a child again, said nothing but remained standing, as he always did when any request of his had been refused, obstinately dumb, and looking down, his chin glued to his chest. His mother knew that gesture so well that she interpreted it in the usual way. "Well, if you really want to very much," she said, "go to the kitchen first and get them to give you something to take with you. But don't eat it now . . . put it in the cabin . . . and mind you don't bathe before five o'clock. Besides, I shall be out by then and we'll swim together." They were the same instructions she always gave him.

Agostino made no reply, and ran barefooted down the stone stairs. He heard his mother's door close gently behind him. He put on his sandals in the hall and went out on to the road. The white blaze of the midday sun enveloped him in its silent furnace. At the end of the road the motionless sea sparkled in the remote, quivering atmosphere. In the opposite direction the red trunks of the pine trees bent under the weight of their heavy green cones.

He debated with himself whether to go to the Vespucci Baths by the beach or by the forest; but chose the former, for though he would be much more exposed to the sun he would be in no danger of passing the baths without seeing them. He followed the road as long as it ran by the sea, then hurried along as fast as he could, keeping close to the walls. Without his realizing it, what attracted him to the Vespucci, apart from the novel companionship of the boys, were their coarse comments on his mother and her supposed amours. He was conscious that his former disposition was changing into quite a different feeling, crueller and more objective, and he thought that their clumsy ironies, by the very fact that they hastened this change, ought to be sought out and cultivated. Why he so much wanted to stop loving his mother, why he even hated himself for loving her, he would have been unable to say. Perhaps because he felt he had been deceived and had thought her to be different from what she really was, or perhaps because, not being able to go on loving her simply and innocently as he had done before, he preferred to stop loving her altogether and to look on her merely as an ordinary woman. He was instinctively trying to free himself once for all from the encumbrance of his old, innocent love which he felt to have been shamefully betrayed; for now it seemed to him mere foolishness and ignorance. And so the same cruel attraction which a few minutes ago had kept his eyes fixed on his mother's back now drove him to seek out the humiliating and coarse companionship of those boys. Might not their scoffing remarks, like her half-revealed nakedness, help to destroy the old filial relationship which was now so hateful to him? When he came within sight of the baths he slowed down, and though his heart was beating violently so that he could hardly breathe, he assumed an air of indifference.

Saro was sitting as before at his rickety table, on which were a half-empty bottle of wine, a glass, and a bowl containing the remains of fish soup. But there seemed to be no one else about, though as he got nearer the curtain opened and he saw the black body of the Negro boy Homs lying on the white sand.

Saro took no notice at all of the Negro, but went on smoking meditatively, a dilapidated old straw hat rammed down over one eye. "Aren't they here?" asked Agostino in a tone of disappointment. Saro looked up and observed him for a moment, then said: "They've gone to Rio." Rio was a deserted part of the shore, a few kilometers further on, where a stream ran into the sea between sandbanks and reeds.

"Oh dear," said Agostino regretfully, "they've gone to Rio . . . what for?"

It was the Negro who replied. "They've gone to have a picnic there," and he put his hand to his mouth with an expressive gesture. But Saro shook his head and said: "You boys won't be happy till someone's put a bullet through you." It was clear that their picnic was only a pretext for stealing fruit in the orchards; at least, so it seemed to Agostino.

"I didn't go with them," put in the Negro obsequiously, as if to ingratiate himself with Saro.

"You didn't go because you didn't want to," said Saro calmly.

The Negro rolled in the sand, protesting: "I didn't go because I wanted to stay with you."

He spoke in a honeyed, singsong voice. Saro said contemptuously: "Who gave you permission to be so familiar, you little nigger? We're not brothers as far as I know."

"No, we're not brothers," said the other in an unruffled, even triumphant tone, as if the observation gave him profound satisfaction.

"You keep your place then," said Saro. Then, turning to Agostino: "They've gone to steal some corn. That's what their picnic'll be."

"Are they coming back?" asked Agostino anxiously. Saro said nothing but kept looking at Agostino and seemed to be turning something over in his mind. "They won't be back very soon," he replied slowly. "Not till late. But if you like we'll go after them."

"But how?"

"In the boat," said Saro.

"Oh yes, let's go in the boat," said the Negro. He sprang up, all eagerness, and approached Saro, but the latter did not give him a glance.

"I have a sailboat . . . in about half an hour we shall be at Rio, if the wind's favorable."

"Yes, let's go," said Agostino happily. "But if they're in the fields how shall we find them?"

"Never you fear," said Saro, getting up and giving a twist to the black sash round his stomach. "We shall find them all right." Then he turned to the Negro, who was watching him anxiously, and added: "Come on, nigger, help me carry down the sail and mast."

"I'm coming, Saro, I'm coming," reiterated the jubilant Negro, and he followed Saro down to the boat.

Left by himself Agostino stood up and looked round him. A light wind had sprung up from the northwest, and the sea, covered now with tiny wavelets, had changed to an almost violet blue. The shore was enveloped in a haze of sun and sand, as far as the eye could see. Agostino, who did not know where Rio was, followed with a nostalgic eye that capricious indentation of the lonely coast line. Where was Rio? Somewhere out there, he supposed, where earth, sky and sea were mingled in one confused blackness under the pitiless sun. He looked forward intensely to the expedition, and would not have missed it for worlds.

He was startled from these reflections by the voices of the two coming out of the hut. Saro was carrying on one arm a pile of ropes and sails, while in the other he hugged a bottle. Behind him walked the Negro, brandishing like a spear a tall mast partly painted green. "Well, let's be *off*," said Saro, starting down the beach without glancing at Agostino. His manner seemed to Agostino curiously hurried, quite different from his usual one. He also noticed that those repulsive red nostrils looked redder and more inflamed than usual, as if all their network of little branching veins had suddenly become swollen with an inrush of blood. "*Si va . . . si va . . .*" intoned the Negro behind Saro, improvising a sort of dance on the sand, with the mast under his arm. But Saro had nearly reached the huts and the Negro slackened his pace to wait for Agostino. When he was near, the Negro signaled him to stop. Agostino did so.

"Listen," said the Negro, with an air of familiarity. "I've got to talk something over with Saro . . . please oblige . . . please . . . by not coming. Go away, please!"

"Why?" asked Agostino, much surprised.

"I told you I've got to talk something over with him . . . just the two of us," said the other impatiently, stamping his foot on the ground.

"I *must* go to Rio," replied Agostino.

"You can go another time."

"No—I can't."

The Negro looked at him, and his eyes and trembling nostrils betrayed a passionate eagerness which revolted Agostino. "Listen, Pisa," he said, "if you'll stay behind I'll give you something you've never seen before." He dropped the mast and felt in his pocket and brought out a slingshot made of a fork of pinewood and two elastics bound together. "It's lovely, isn't it," and the Negro held it up.

But Agostino wanted to go to Rio. Besides, the Negro's insistence aroused his suspicions. "No, I can't," he said.

"Take it," the other said again, feeling for Agostino's hand and trying to force the slingshot into his palm. "Take it and go away."

"No," repeated Agostino, "I can't."

"I'll give you the slingshot and these cards, too," said the Negro, feeling in his pocket again; and he drew out a small pack of cards with pink backs and gilt edges. "Take them all and go away. You can kill birds with the slingshot . . . the cards are quite new."

"I told you I won't," said Agostino.

The Negro turned on him an eye of passionate entreaty. Great drops of sweat shone on his forehead, his whole face was contorted in an expression of utter misery. "But why won't you?" he whined.

"I don't want to," said Agostino, and he suddenly ran towards the bath man, who was now standing by the boat. As he reached Saro he heard the Negro call after him: "You'll be sorry for this." The boat was resting on two rollers of unplaned fir a short way up the beach. Saro had thrown the sails into the boat and seemed to be waiting impatiently. "What's he up to?" he asked Agostino, pointing to the Negro.

"He's just coming," said Agostino.

And in fact the Negro came running over the sand with great leaps, holding the mast under his arm. Saro took hold of the mast with the six fingers of his right hand, and with the six fingers of his left reared it up and planted it in a hole in the middle seat. Then he got into the boat, fastened the sail and loosened the sheet. Saro turned to the Negro and said: "Now let's shove off from underneath."

Saro stood beside the boat, grasping the edges of the prow, while the Negro made ready to push from behind. Agostino, not knowing what to do, looked on. The boat was of medium size, part white and part green. On the prow, in black lettering, was written *Amelia*. "Ah . . . issa," commanded Saro. The boat slid forward on its rollers over the sand. As soon as the keel passed over the hindmost roller the Negro bent down and took it in his arms, pressing it to his breast like a baby; then leaping over the sand as in a novel kind of ballet, he ran and placed it under the prow. "Ah . . . *issa*," repeated Saro.

The boat slid forward again quite a distance, and again the Negro gamboled and caracoled from stern to prow, with the roller in his arms; one last shove, and the prow of the boat dipped into the water and it was afloat. Saro got in and placed the oars in the rowlocks; then, grasping one in each hand, he motioned to Agostino to jump in, excluding the Negro as if by prearrangement. Agostino entered the water up to his knees and tried to climb in. He would never have succeeded had not the six fingers of Saro's right hand seized him firmly by one arm and pulled him up like a cat. He looked up. Saro was lifting him with one arm, without looking in his direction, for he was busy adjusting the left-hand oar. Agostino, in disgust at being grasped by those fingers, went off and sat in the stern. "Good," said Saro, "you stay there; now we are going to take her out."

"Wait for me, I'm coming too!" shouted the Negro from the shore. Exhausted by his efforts he sprang into the water and seized the edge of the boat. But Saro said: "No, you're not coming."

"What am I to do?" cried the boy, in an agony of disappointment. "What am I to do?"

"You can take the trolley," answered Saro, standing up in the boat and pulling hard. "You'll get there before us, see if you don't."

"But why, Saro?" wailed the Negro, thrashing along in the water beside the boat. "Why, Saro? I want to go too."

Without a word Saro dropped his oars, bent over and covered the Negro's face with his enormous hand. "I've told you you're not coming," he said quietly, and with one push sent the Negro over backward in the water. "Why, Saro?" he went on wailing. "Why, Saro?" and his melancholy voice, mingled with the splashing of the oars, made an unpleasant impression on Agostino and aroused in him an uneasy sense of pity. He looked at Saro, who smiled and said: "He's such a nuisance. What do we want with him?"

The boat was already some way from the shore. Agostino looked round and saw the Negro get out of the water and, as he thought, shake his fist threateningly at him.

Saro silently took out the oars and laid them down in the bottom of the boat. Then he went to the prow, undid the sail and fastened it to the mast. The sail fluttered uncertainly for a moment, as if the wind were blowing on both sides of it at once; then suddenly, with a violent shock swelled in the wind and leaned over to the left. The boat obediently settled down on its left side too, and began to skim over the waves, driven by the light breeze. "Good," said Saro, "now we can lie down and rest a bit." He settled down in the bottom of the boat and invited Agostino to lie beside him. "If we sit in the bottom," he explained, "the boat goes faster." Agostino obeyed, and lay down beside Saro.

The boat made swift progress in spite of its heavy build, rising and falling with the little waves and occasionally rearing up like a foal which feels the bit for the first time. Saro lay with his head resting against the seat, and one arm behind Agostino's neck, controlling the rudder. For a while he said nothing; then: "Do you go to school?" he asked at last.

Agostino looked up. Saro was half-lying and seemed to be exposing his wide, inflamed nostrils to the sea air, as if to refresh them. His mouth was open under his mustache, his eyes half-shut. His un-buttoned shirt revealed the dirty, grey, ruffled hair on his chest. "Yes," said Agostino, suddenly trembling with fear.

"What class are you in?"

"The third."

"Give me your hand," said Saro; and before Agostino could refuse he seized hold of it. To Agostino his grasp felt like a vice. The six short, stumpy fingers encircled his whole hand and met below it. "What do they teach you?" Saro went on, stretching himself out more comfortably and sinking into a kind of ecstasy.

"Latin . . . Italian . . . geography . . . history . . ." stammered Agostino.

"Do they teach you poetry . . . lovely poetry?" asked Saro, in a low voice.

"Yes," said Agostino, "poetry as well."

"Recite some to me."

The boat plunged, and Saro shifted the rudder without changing his beatific attitude. "I don't know what . . ." began Agostino, feeling more and more embarrassed and frightened. "I learn a lot of poetry . . . Carducci . . ."

"Ah yes, Carducci," repeated Saro mechanically. "Say a poem by Carducci."

"*Le fonti del Clitunno*," suggested Agostino, terrified by that hand which would not let him go, and trying little by little to escape from it.

"Yes, *Le fonti del Clitunno*," said Saro in a dreamy voice.

> *Ancor dal monte che di foschi ondeggia*
> *frassini al vento mormoranti e lunge*

began Agostino in a shaky voice.

The boat sped on, and Saro, still stretched at full length with closed eyes and his nose to the wind, began to move his head up and down as if scanning the lines. Agostino clung to poetry as the only means of escape from a conversation which he intuitively felt to be dangerous and compromising, and went on reciting slowly and clearly. Meanwhile, he kept trying to release his hand from those six imprisoning fingers; but they held him more tightly than ever. With terror he saw the end of the poem drawing near, and not knowing what to do he joined the first line of *Davanti a San Guido* on to the last line of *Fonti del Clitunno*. Here would be proof, if any were needed, that Saro didn't care a bit about the poetry but had something quite different in view; *what*, Agostino could not understand. The experiment succeeded. *"I cipressi che a Bolgheri alti e schietti"* suddenly began without Saro giving the faintest sign of noticing the change. Then Agostino broke off and said in an exasperated voice: "Let go, please," and tried at the same time to pull his hand quite away.

Saro started, and without letting go of him, opened his eyes and turned to look at him. He must have read such violent antipathy and such obvious terror on Agostino's face that he suddenly realized that his plan, for he certainly had a plan, was a complete failure. He slowly withdrew one finger after another from Agostino's aching hand and said in a low voice, as if speaking to himself: "What are you afraid of? We're going ashore now."

He dragged himself to his feet and pulled round the rudder. The boat turned its prow towards the shore.

Still rubbing his cramped fingers, Agostino got up from the bottom of the boat without a word and went to sit in the prow. By now the boat was not far from the shore. He could see the whole beach, the white stretch of sun-bleached sand which at that point was very wide, and beyond the beach the dense, brooding green of the pines. Rio was at a gap in the high dunes, overhung by a greenish-blue mass of reeds. But before they got to Rio, Agostino saw a group of people on the beach, and from the center of this group there rose a long thread of black smoke. He turned to Saro, who was sitting in the stern controlling the rudder with one hand. "Is this where we get out?"

"Yes, this is Rio," replied Saro indifferently.

As the boat drew nearer and nearer to the shore Agostino saw the group gathered round the fire suddenly break up and start running down to the water's edge, and he at once saw that it was the boys. He could see them waving and probably calling out, but the wind carried their voices away. "Is it them?" he asked nervously.

"Yes, it's them," said Saro.

The boat drew nearer still and Agostino could clearly distinguish the boys. They were all there: Tortima, Berto, Sandro, and the others. And there was the Negro Homs, leaping along the shore and shouting with the others, a discovery which for some reason gave him a very uncomfortable feeling.

The boat made straight for the shore where with a rapid turn of the rudder, Saro brought it in crosswise, and throwing himself upon the sail clasped it in both arms and lowered it to the deck. The boat swung motionless in the shallow water. Saro took a small anchor from the bottom and threw it into the water. "Let's go ashore," he said. He climbed over the edge of the boat and waded through the water to meet the boys who were waiting on the beach.

Agostino saw the boys crowding around him and apparently offering him congratulations, which Saro received with a shake of his head. Still louder applause greeted his own arrival, and for a moment he was deceived into thinking they were welcoming him cordially. But he soon realized he was mistaken. Their laughter was mocking and sarcastic. Berto called out: "Good old Pisa, he enjoys going out for a sail," while Tortima, putting his fingers into his mouth, gave a rude whistle. The others imitated him. Even Sandro, usually so reserved, looked at him with contempt. As for the Negro, he did nothing but jump about around Saro, who went on ahead towards the fire the boys had lit on the beach. Surprised and vaguely alarmed, Agostino went and sat down among the others around the fire.

The boys had made a sort of rough oven out of damp compressed sand. Inside was a fire of dried pine cones, pine needles and twigs. Heaped up in the mouth of the oven were about a dozen ears of corn, slowly roasting. Spread out on a newspaper near the fire were masses of fruit and a watermelon. "He's a fine one, is our Pisa," said Berto, when they had sat down. "You and Homs are buddies now, you ought to be sitting together . . . you're brothers, you two; he's black, you're white . . . that's all there is to it . . . and you both like going for a sail."

The Negro chuckled appreciatively. Saro was bending down to give the corncobs another turn in front of the fire. The others laughed derisively. Berto went so far as to give Agostino a push which sent him against Homs, so that for a moment their backs were touching;

one chuckling with depraved self-satisfaction, the other bewildered
and disgusted. "But I don't know what you mean," said Agostino
suddenly. "I went out in the boat; what harm is there in that?"

"Aha, what harm is there in that? He went out in the boat. What
harm is there in that?" repeated many scoffing voices. Some were
holding their sides with laughter.

"Yes, indeed, what harm?" repeated Berto, turning to him again.
"No harm at all! Why, Homs thinks it's grand, don't you Homs?"

The Negro assented ecstatically. And now the truth began dimly
to dawn on Agostino, for he couldn't help seeing some connection
between their taunts and Saro's odd behavior in the boat. "I don't
know what you mean," he declared. "I didn't do anything wrong in
that boat. Saro made me recite some poems, that's all."

"Ah, ah, those poems," was heard on all sides.

"Isn't it true what I say, Saro?" cried Agostino, red in the face.

Saro didn't say yes or no; he contented himself with smiling, watching him all the while with a certain curiosity. The boys interpreted
his air of pretended indifference, which was really a cloak for his
treachery and vanity, as giving the lie to Agostino. "Oh, of course,"
they all struck up together: "He asks the host if the wine is good,
eh, Saro? That's a good one! Oh, Pisa, Pisa!" The Negro was having
his revenge, and enjoying himself particularly. Agostino suddenly
turned on him, trembling with rage, and said: "What is there to
laugh at?"

"I'm not laughing," he replied, edging away.

"Now, don't you two quarrel," said Berto. "Saro will have to see
about making you friends again." But the boys lost all interest when
the issue seemed to be settling itself peacefully, and were already talking of other things. They were telling how they had crept into a
field and stolen corn and fruit; how they had seen the enraged farmer
coming towards them with a gun; how they had run away, and the
farmer had fired salt at them without hitting anyone. Meanwhile,
the ears were ready, beautifully toasted on the embers. Saro took
them out of the oven and with his usual fatherly air parceled out one
to each. Agostino took advantage of a moment when they were
busy eating, and sprang across to Sandro, who was sitting a little
apart, eating his corn grain by grain.

"I don't understand," he began. The other gave him a knowing
look and Agostino felt he need say no more. "The Moor came by
trolley," said Sandro slowly, "and he said you and Saro had gone
sailing."

"But what harm is there in that?"

"It's no business of mine," replied Sandro, casting down his eyes. "It's up to you . . . you and the Moor. But as for Saro," he stopped and looked at Agostino.

"Well?"

"Well, I wouldn't have gone out alone with Saro."

"But why?"

Sandro looked carefully round him, then in a low voice gave the explanation which Agostino somehow expected, without being able to say why. "Ah," he said . . . but he could say no more and went back to the others. Squatting in the middle of the boys, with his imperturbable, good-natured head on one side, Saro had the air of a kind paterfamilias surrounded by his sons. But Agostino felt a deep loathing when he looked at him, greater in fact than he felt for the Negro. What made Agostino hate him more was his silence when appealed to, as if he wanted the boys to believe that what they had accused him of had really taken place. Besides, he could not help noticing that their scorn and derision had set a wide gulf between him and his companions—the same gulf which he now realized separated them from the Negro; only the Negro, instead of being humiliated and offended, as he himself was, seemed somehow to relish it. He tried more than once to turn the conversation on to the subject which so tormented him, but was met with laughter and an insulting indifference. Moreover, in spite of Sandro's only too clear explanation, he still could not quite grasp what had really happened. Everything seemed dark around him and within him, as if instead of beach, sea and sky, there were only shadows and vague, menacing forms.

Meanwhile, the boys had finished eating their roasted corn and tossed the bare cobs away in the sand. "Let's go swim at Rio," suggested someone, and the proposal was immediately accepted. Saro went with them, for it was agreed that he should take them all back to Vespucci in the boat.

As they walked along the sand Sandro left the others and came over to Agostino. "If you're offended with the Moor," he said, "why don't you put the fear of God into him?"

"How?" asked Agostino, in a discouraged tone.

"Give him a good hiding."

"But he's stronger than me," said Agostino remembering the duel of the iron arm. "Unless you will help me."

"Why should I help you? It's your concern . . . yours and his." Sandro pronounced these words in such a way as to make it quite clear that he took the same view as the others as to the reason for Agostino's hatred of the Negro. A sense of terrible bitterness pierced Agostino to the heart. So Sandro, the only one who had shown him any kindness, believed that calumny too. After giving him this advice Sandro went off to rejoin the others, as if he were afraid of being seen with Agostino. From the beach they had passed through a forest of young pines; then they crossed a sandy path and entered the reed beds. The reeds grew thick and tall, and many had a white, plumy crest; the boys appeared and disappeared between their long green spears, slipping about on the damp earth and pushing the stiff, fibrous leaves aside with a dry, rustling sound. At last they came to a place where the reed bed widened around a low, muddy bank; at sight of them big frogs leaped from all sides into the opaque, glassy water; and there they began to undress, all together, under the eyes of Saro, who sat fully clothed on a rock overlooking the reeds, and appeared to be absorbed in his cigar, but was really watching them all the time through his half-closed eyelids. Agostino was ashamed to join them, but he was so afraid of being laughed at that he too began to unbutton his trousers, taking as long as he could about it and keeping an eye on the others. The rest seemed to be overjoyed at getting rid of their clothes, and bumped into each other shouting with glee. They looked very white against the background of green reeds, with an unpleasant, squalid whiteness from groin to belly, and this pallor only emphasized a sort of graceless and excessive muscularity which is especially to be found in manual workers. The graceful, well-proportioned Sandro, whose pubic hair was as fair as that on his head, was the only one who hardly seemed to be naked, perhaps because his skin was equally bronzed over his whole body; in any case his nakedness was quite different from that repulsive nakedness displayed in the public baths.

Before diving in the boys played all sorts of obscene pranks; opening their legs wide, poking and touching each other with a loose promiscuity which astounded Agostino, to whom this sort of thing was quite new. He was naked too, and his feet were black from the cold, filthy mud, but he would have liked to have hidden himself in the reeds, if only to escape the looks which Saro, who sat hunched up motionless like one of those huge frogs native to the reed bed, darted at him through half-closed eyes. But as usual his repugnance was less strong than the mysterious attraction which bound him to the gang; the two were so indissolubly mixed up together that it was impossible for him to distinguish between his horror and the pleasure which underlay it. The boys displayed themselves each in turn, boasting of their virility and bodily prowess. Tortima, the vainest of all, and in spite of his disproportionate strength the most squalid and plebeian looking, was so elated as to call out to Agostino: "Suppose I was to appear before your mother, one fine morning, naked like this, what would she say? Would she go along with me?"

"No," said Agostino.

"And I tell you that she'd come along at once," said Tortima. "She'd just give me one good look over, to see what I was good for, and then she'd say: 'Come along, Tortima, let's be off.'" The gross absurdity of his suggestion made them all laugh, and at his cry: 'Come, Tortima, let's be off!' they flung themselves one after another into the water, diving in head over heels, just like the frogs whom their coming had disturbed.

The shore was so entirely surrounded by reeds that only a short stretch of the river was visible. But when they got into the middle of the stream they could see the whole river which, with an imperceptible motion of its dark, dense waters, flowed toward the mouth further down among the sandbanks. Upstream the river continued between two lines of large silvery bushes which cast delightful reflections in the water; till one came to a little iron bridge, beyond which the reeds, pines and poplars were so dense as to prevent further passage. A red house, half-hidden among the trees, seemed to keep guard over this bridge.

For a moment Agostino felt happy, as he swam in that cold, powerful water which seemed to be trying to bear his legs away with it; he forgot for a moment all his wrongs and crosses. The boys swam about in all directions, their heads and arms emerging from the smooth green surface. Their voices resounded in the limpid, windless air; seen through the transparency of the water their bodies might have been the white shoots of plants blossoming out of the depths and moving hither and yon as the current drew them. Agostino swam up to Berto, who was not far off, and asked: "Are there many fish in this river?"

Berto looked at him and said: "What are you doing here? Why don't you keep Saro company?"

"I like swimming," replied Agostino, feeling miserable again; and he turned and swam away.

But he was not so strong or experienced a swimmer as the others; he soon got tired, and let the current carry him towards the mouth of the river. He had soon left the boys and their clamor behind him;

the reeds grew thinner; through the clear, colorless water he could see the sandy bottom over which grey eddies flowed continually. At last he came to a deeper green pool, the stream's transparent eye as it were; and when he had passed this his feet touched the sand, and after struggling a moment against the force of the water he climbed out on to the bank. Where the stream flowed into the sea it curled round itself and formed a knot of water. The stream then lost its compactness and spread out fanwise, growing thinner and thinner till it was no more than a liquid veil thrown over the smooth sands. The tide flowed up into the river with tiny foam-flecked wavelets. Here and there in the watery sand, pools forgotten by the stream reflected the bright sky. Agostino walked about for a little, naked on the soft, mirroring sand, and enjoyed stamping on it with his feet and seeing the water suddenly rise to the surface and flood his footprints. There arose in him a vague and desperate desire to ford the river and walk on and on down the coast, leaving far behind him the boys, Saro, his mother and all the old life. Who knows whether, if he were to go straight ahead and never turn back, walking, walking on that soft white sand, he might not at last come to a country where none of these horrible things existed; a country where he would be welcomed as he longed to be, and where it would be possible for him to forget all he had learned and then learn it again without all that shame and horror, gently and naturally as he dimly felt it might be possible. He gazed at the dark, remote horizon which enclosed the utmost boundaries of sea and shore and forest and felt drawn to that immensity as to something which might set him free from his bondage. The shouts of the boys racing across the shore to the boat roused him from his melancholy imaginings. One of them was waving his clothes in the air, and Berto was calling: "Pisa, we're off!" He shook himself and walked along at the edge of the sea to join the gang.

The boys were thronging together in the shallow water. Saro was warning them in fatherly tones that the boat was too small to hold them all, but he was clearly only teasing them. Screaming, the boys flung themselves like mad upon the boat; twenty hands at once clutched the sides, and in a twinkling the boat was filled with their gesticulating bodies. Some lay down on the bottom, others sat in a heap in the stern around the rudder, some in the prow, others on the seats; others again sat on the edge and let their feet dangle in the water. The boat really was too small for so many, and the water came almost to the top.

"We're all here then, are we?" said Saro in great good humor. He stood up, let out the sail, and the boat sped out to sea. The boys cheered its departure loudly.

But Agostino did not share their happy mood. He was looking out for a favorable opportunity to prove his innocence and remove the unjust stigma which oppressed him. He took advantage of a moment when the other boys were deep in some discussion, to scramble up to the Negro who was sitting alone in the bow and resembled in his blackness a new kind of figurehead. Squeezing one arm hard, Agostino demanded: "What did you go and say about me just now?"

It was a bad moment to choose, but it was Agostino's first opportunity of getting near the Negro who had taken good care to keep at a distance while they were on shore. "I spoke the truth," said Homs, without looking at him.

"What is the truth?"

The Negro's reply terrified Agostino. "It's no good your squeezing my arm like that. I only spoke the truth. But if you go on setting Saro against me I shall tell your mother everything. So look out, Pisa."

"What!" cried Agostino, seeing an abyss open beneath his feet. "What do you mean? Are you crazy? I . . . I . . ." He stammered, unable to follow up in words the frightful vision his imagination suddenly summoned up. But he had no time to continue. Shouts of derision broke out all over the boat.

"Look at them both side by side," laughed Berto. "Look at them! What a shame we haven't got a camera to take them both together." Agostino turned round, his face burning, and saw them all laughing. Even Saro was smiling under his mustache, as with half-closed eyes he puffed at his cigar. Agostino drew back from the Negro, as from the touch of a reptile, and with his arms around his knees sat watching the sea, his eyes full of tears.

On the horizon the sun was setting in clouds of fire above a violet sea, shot with pointed, glassy rays. The wind had risen and the boat made slow progress, listing heavily to one side under its load of boys. The prow of the boat was turned out to sea and seemed to be directed towards the dark profiles of far-off islands which rose among the red smoke of sunset like mountains at the end of a distant plateau. Saro, holding firmly between his knees the boys' stolen watermelon, split it open with his seaman's knife and cut off large slices which he distributed to them paternally. They passed the slices and bit into them greedily, spitting out the seeds and tearing off pieces of the flesh. Then one after another the sections of red, close-gnawed rind flew overboard into the sea. After the melon it was the turn of the wine flask, which Saro solemnly produced from under the stern. The bottle made the round of the boat, and even Agostino was obliged to swallow a mouthful. It was warm and strong and at once went to his head. When the empty bottle had returned to its place Tortima sang an indecent song, and they all joined in the refrain. Between verses they pressed Agostino to sing too, for they had noticed his black mood; but no one spoke to him except to tease him and incite him to sing. Agostino felt within him a heavy weight of pent-up grief which the windy sea and magnificent fires of sunset on the violet waters only made more bitter and unbearable. It seemed to him horribly unjust that it was on such a sea under such a sky that a boat like theirs should be sailing, so crowded with malice, cruelty, falsehood and corruption. That boat, overflowing with boys gesticulating like obscene monkeys, with the fat and blissful Saro at the helm, was to him an incredible and melancholy sight in the midst of all that beauty. At moments he wished it would sink; he would have liked to die himself, he thought, and no longer be infected and stained by all that impurity. How far away seemed the morning when he had for the first time looked upon the red awning of the Vespucci Baths; far away and belonging to an age already dead. Each time the boat rose on an unusually high wave they gave a yell which made him shudder; each time the Negro addressed him with his revolting and hypocritically slavish humility, he tried not to listen and drew back still further into the prow. He was dimly conscious of having on that fatal day entered upon an age of difficulties and miseries from which he could see no way of escape. The boat made a long trip, going as far as the port and then turning back again. When they at last touched land Agostino ran off without saying good-bye to anyone. But he had not gone far before he slackened his pace and looking back saw the boys helping Saro pull the boat up on the beach. It was already getting dark.

That day was the beginning of a dark and troubled time for Agostino. On that day his eyes had been opened for him by force, but what he had learned was too much for him, a burden greater than he could bear. It was not so much their novelty as the quality of the things he had learned which oppressed and poisoned him; they were too appalling and too portentous for him to assimilate. He thought, for example, that after that day's disclosures about his mother his relations with her would have become clarified; that the uneasiness, distaste and even disgust which, after Saro's revelations, her caresses awoke in him would somehow, as if by enchantment, be resolved and reconciled in a new and serene consciousness. But it was not so; the uneasiness, distaste and disgust remained, rising in the first instance from the shock and bewilderment to his filial love occasioned by his obscure realization of his mother's femininity, and after that morning in Saro's tent rising from a bitter sense of guilty curiosity which his traditional and abiding respect for his mother rendered intolerable to him. At first he had unconsciously tried to break loose from that affection by an unjustified dislike, but now it seemed to him a duty to separate his newly won reasoned knowledge from his sense of blood relationship with someone whom he wanted to consider only as a woman. He felt that if only he could see in his mother what Saro and the boys did—just a beautiful woman—then all his unhappiness would disappear; and he tried with all his might to seek out occasions which would confirm him in this belief. But the only result was that his former reverence and affection gave place to cruelty and sensuality.

At home his mother did not hide herself from him any more than she had before, and was unaware of any change in his attitude towards her. As his mother, she had no sense of shame; but to Agostino it seemed that she was wantonly provocative. He would hear her calling him, and would go to her room to find her at her toilet, in negligee and with her breasts half-uncovered. Or he would wake to find her bending over him to give him his morning kiss, with her dressing gown open so that he could clearly see the shape of her body through her fragile, crumpled nightgown. She would go to and fro in front of him as if he were not there; putting on or taking off her stockings, putting on her clothes, applying perfume or make-up; and all those acts which Agostino had once thought so natural now seemed to him the outward and visible signs of a much more embracing and more dangerous reality, so that his mind was torn between curiosity and pain. He kept saying to himself: "She's only a woman," with the objective indifference of a connoisseur. But a moment later, unable to endure either her maternal unselfconsciousness or his own watchfulness, he would have liked to shout: "Cover yourself up, go away, don't let me see you any more, I'm not the same as I used to be." But his hope of judging his mother as a woman and nothing more almost immediately suffered shipwreck. He soon saw that even if she had become a woman she remained in his eyes all the more his mother; and he realized that the cruel sense of shame which he had at first attributed to the novelty of his feelings would now never leave him. He saw in a flash that she would always remain for him the person he had loved with such a free and pure love; she would always mix with her most feminine gestures those purely affectionate ones which for so long had been the only ones he knew; never would he be able to separate his new conception of her from his now wounded memory of her former dignity. He did not for a moment doubt that the facts of her relationship with the young man really were as reported by the boys in Saro's tent. And he wondered secretly at the change which had taken place in him. At first he had only felt jealousy of his mother and antipathy towards the young man; both feelings being rather veiled and indefinite. But now, in his effort to remain objective and calm, he would have wished to feel sympathy for the young man and indifference towards his mother. But this sympathy seemed somehow to make him an accomplice, and his indifference to make him indiscreet. He very seldom went out with them now on the raft, for he generally contrived to avoid being invited. But whenever he went he was conscious of studying the young man's gestures and words almost as if he wanted him to overstep the limits of permitted social gallantry, and of studying his mother almost in the hope of having his suspicions confirmed. At the same time these sentiments were intolerable to him because they were the exact opposite of what he wanted to feel, and he would almost have liked to feel again the pity which his mother's foolish behavior had once aroused in him; it was more human and affectionate than his present merciless dissection.

Those days of inner conflict left him with a confused sense of impurity. He felt that he had exchanged his former state of innocence, not for the manly calm he had hoped for, but a dark, indeterminate state in which he found no compensating advantages, but only fresh perplexities in addition to the old. What was the good of seeing clearly, if this clarity only brought with it deeper shades of darkness? Sometimes he wondered how older boys than himself managed to go on loving their mother when they knew what he knew; and he concluded that such knowledge must at once destroy their filial affection, whereas in his own case the one did not banish the other, but they existed side by side in a dreary tangle.

As sometimes happens, the place which was the scene of these discoveries and conflicts—his home—became almost intolerable to him. The sea, the sun, the crowd of bathers, the presence of many other women at least distracted him and deadened his sensibilities. But here, between the four walls of his home, alone with his mother, he felt exposed to every kind of temptation, beset by every kind of contradiction. On the beach his mother was one among many other sun bathers; here she seemed overpowering and unique. Just as on a small stage the actors seem larger than life, so here every gesture and word of hers stood out with extraordinary definition. Agostino had a very lively and adventurous sensibility in regard to the familiar things of his home. When he was a child every passage, every nook and corner, every room had had for him a mysterious and incalculable character; they were places in which you might make the strangest discoveries and live through the most fantastic adventures. But now, after his meeting with those boys in the red tent, these adventures and discoveries were of a quite different kind, so that he did not know whether to be more attracted or frightened by them. Formerly he used to imagine ambushes, shadows, spirits, voices in the furniture and in the walls; but now his fancy, even more actively than in his exuberant childhood, attached itself to the new realities with which the walls, the furniture, the very air of the house seemed to him to be impregnated. And in place of his old innocent excitement which his mother's good-night kiss and dreamless sleep could always calm, he was tormented by a burning and shameful curiosity which at night grew to giant proportions and seemed to find in darkness more food for its impure fire.

Everywhere in the house he seemed to spy out traces of a woman's presence, the only woman whom he had ever known intimately; and that woman was his mother. When he was with her he felt as if he were somehow mounting guard over her; when he approached her door he felt he was spying on her; if he touched her clothes he felt as if it was herself he was touching, for she had worn these clothes, they had held her body. At night he dreamed with his eyes open, and had agonizing nightmares. He would sometimes imagine himself to be a child again, afraid of every sound, of every shadow, and would spring up to run and take refuge in his mother's bed; but as soon as his feet touched the ground he realized, sleepy and bewildered though he was, that his fear was only a cunning mask for curiosity and that directly he was in his mother's arms his nocturnal vision would reveal its true purpose. Or he would wake suddenly and wonder whether by chance the young man of the raft were there at that very moment in his mother's room on the other side of the wall. Certain sounds seemed to confirm this suspicion, others to contradict it; he would toss restlessly in bed for a while, and at last, without the smallest idea how he had got there, would find himself in the passage in his nightshirt, listening and spying outside his mother's room. Once he could not resist the temptation of going in without knocking, and he stood motionless in the middle of the room in the diffused moonlight which entered through the open window, his eyes fixed on the bed where he could distinguish his mother's black hair spread out over the pillow, and her long, softly rounded limbs. "Is that you, Agostino?" she asked, waking up. Without saying a word he turned and hurried back to his room.

His reluctance to remain alone with his mother drove him more and more to Vespucci. But here other torments awaited him, and made the place as odious to him as his home. The boys' attitude towards him after he had been out alone in the boat with Saro had not changed at all; it had in fact assumed a definite and final form, as if founded on an unshakable conviction. For he was the one who had accepted that signal and sinister favor from Saro; it was impossible to get that idea out of their mind. So that, in addition to the jealousy and contempt they had felt for him from the first on account of his being rich, was now added another source of contempt . . . his supposed depravity. And in the minds of those young savages the one seemed to justify the other, the one to grow out of the other. They seemed by their humiliating and cruel treatment of him to imply that he was rich and therefore naturally depraved. Agostino was quick to perceive the subtle relation between these two charges, and he dimly felt that they were making him pay for being different from them and superior to them. His social difference and superiority were expressed in his clothes and his talk about the luxury of his home, in his tastes and manner of speech; his moral difference and superiority impelled him to refute the charge of having had any such relations with Saro, and kept showing itself in open disgust at the boys' manners and habits. So at last, prompted by the humiliating position in which he found himself rather than exercising any definite choice of his own, he decided to be what they seemed to want him to be . . . that is, just like themselves. He began wearing his oldest and dirtiest clothes, to the great surprise of his mother, who noticed that he no longer took any pride in his appearance; he made a point of never mentioning his luxurious home, and he took as ostentatious pleasure in ways and habits which up to that time had disgusted him. But worst of all, and it needed a great effort to nerve himself to it, one day when they were making their usual jokes about his going out alone with Saro, he said that he was tired of denying it, and that what they accused him of had really happened, and that he didn't care whether they knew it or not. Saro was startled by these assertions, but perhaps from fear of exposing himself did not deny them. The boys were also very much surprised to hear him admitting the truth of gossip which had seemed to torment him so much before. He was so timid and shy that they would never have given him credit for so much courage, but they very soon began raining down questions on him as to what had really happened; and then he lost heart, got red in the face and refused to say another word. Naturally the boys interpreted his silence in their own way, as being due to shame and not, as it really was, to his ignorance and incapacity to invent. And the usual load of taunts and low jokes became heavier than ever.

But in spite of this breakdown he really had changed. Without being conscious of it himself, without really trying to, he had, by dint of spending so much time with the boys every day, ended by becoming very like them, and had lost his old tastes without really acquiring any new ones. More than once, in a mood of revolt against Vespucci, he had joined in the more innocent games at Speranza, seeking out his playmates of earlier in the summer. But how colorless and dull those nicely brought-up boys now seemed to him, how boring their regulation walks under the eye of parents or tutors, how insipid their school gossip, their stamp collections, books of adventure and such-like. The fact is that the company of the gang, their talk about women, their thieving expeditions in the orchards, even the acts of oppression and violence of which he had himself been a victim, had transformed him and made him intolerant of his former friendships. It was during this time that something happened which brought this home to him more strongly. One morning when he arrived late at Vespucci he found no one there. Saro was off on some business of his own, and there were no boys to be seen. He wandered gloomily to the water's edge and seated himself on a float. Suddenly, as he was watching the beach in the hope of seeing at least Saro come in sight, a man and a boy about two years younger than himself appeared. He was a small man, with short, fat legs under a protruding stomach, a round face and pointed nose confined by pince-nez. He looked like a civil servant or professor. The boy was thin and pale, in a suit too big for him, and was hugging a large and evidently new leather ball to his chest. Holding his son by the hand, the man came up to Agostino and looked at him doubtfully for some time. At last he asked if it was possible to go for a row.

"Of course," replied Agostino, without hesitation.

The man considered him rather suspiciously over the top of his glasses, then asked how much it would cost to go out for an hour on a bathing raft. Agostino knew the prices and told him. Then he realized that the man had mistaken him for the bath man's son or for one of his boys, and that somehow flattered him. "Very well," said the man, "we will go."

Agostino didn't need telling twice. He at once took the rough pine log which served as roller, and placed it under the prow of the boat. Then, grasping the ends of the two floats in both hands, his strength redoubled by this singular spur to his pride, he pushed the raft into the water. He helped the boy and his father to get on, sprang after them and seized the oars.

For a while Agostino rowed without speaking. At that early hour the sea was quite empty. The boy hugged his ball to his chest and kept his pale eyes fixed on Agostino. The man sat awkwardly, with knees apart to make room for his paunch. He kept turning his fat neck to look about him, and seemed to be enjoying the outing. At last he asked Agostino who he was, the bath man's son, or employed by him. Agostino replied that he was employed by him. "And how old are you?" asked the man.

"Thirteen," replied Agostino.

"There," said the man, turning to his son, "this boy is almost the same age as you, and he's already at work." Then to Agostino: "And do you go to school?"

"I should like to, but how can I, sir?" he answered, assuming the hypocritical tone which he had heard the boys put on when asked a question like that. "We've got to live, sir."

"There, you see," said the father to his son. "This boy can't go to school because he has to work, and you have the face to make a fuss about your lessons."

"There's a lot of us in the family," said Agostino, rowing vigorously, "and we all work."

"And how much can you earn a day?" asked the man.

"It depends," replied Agostino. "If many people come, about twenty or thirty lire."

"Which of course you give to your father," interposed the man.

"Of course," replied Agostino, without a moment's hesitation, "except what I make in tips."

This time the man didn't think it necessary to point him out as an example to his son, but he nodded his head approvingly. His son said nothing, but hugged his ball still closer and kept his pale, watery eyes fixed on Agostino. "Would you like to have a leather ball like that, boy?" the man suddenly asked Agostino. Now Agostino had two identical balls, which had been lying about for a long time in his room with his other toys. But he said: "Of course I should, but how am I to get one? We have to buy necessities first." The man turned to his son and said to him, probably half in fun: "There now, Peter, give your ball to this boy who hasn't got one." The boy looked first at his father and then at Agostino, and greedily hugged his ball tighter; but still he didn't say a word. "Don't you want to?" asked his father gently. "Don't you want to?"

"It's my ball," said the boy.

"Yes, it's yours, but if you like you may give it away," persisted the father. "This poor boy has never had one in all his life; now, don't you want to give it up to him?"

"No," said his son emphatically.

"Never mind," interposed Agostino at this point, with a sanctimonious smile, "I don't really want it. I shouldn't have time to play with it . . . it's different for him."

The father smiled at these words, pleased at having found such a useful object lesson for his son. "He's a better boy than you," he went on, stroking his son's head. "He's poor, but he doesn't want to take away your ball, he leaves it to you; but whenever you want to grumble and make a fuss, I hope you'll remember that there are lots of boys like this in the world, who have to work, and who have never had balls or any toys of their own."

"It's my ball," repeated the boy obstinately.

"Yes, it's yours," sighed his father, absent-mindedly. He looked at his watch and said in a tone of command: "It's time we went back; take us in, boy." Without a word Agostino turned the prow towards the beach.

As they approached the shore he saw Saro standing in the water watching his maneuvers attentively, and he was afraid the bath man would give him away. But Saro didn't say a word; perhaps he understood, perhaps he didn't care; he gravely helped Agostino pull the boat up the beach. "This is for you," said the man, giving Agostino the sum agreed on and something over. Agostino took the money and gave it to Saro. "But I'm going to keep the tip," he added, with an air of self-satisfied bravado. Saro said nothing; scarcely even smiling, he put the money inside the sash bound around his stomach and walked slowly across the beach to his hut.

This little incident gave Agostino a definite feeling of not belonging any more to the world in which boys of that sort existed, and by now he had got so used to living with the poor that the hypocrisy of any other kind of life bored him. At the same time he felt regretfully that he wasn't really like the boys of the gang. He was still much too sensitive. If he had really been one of them, he thought sometimes, he would not have suffered so much from their coarse and clumsy jokes. So it seemed that he had lost his first estate without having succeeded in winning another.

One day, towards the end of the summer, Agostino went with the boys to the pine woods to chase birds and look for mushrooms. This was what he enjoyed most of all their exploits. They entered the forest and walked for miles upon its soft soil along natural aisles, between the red pillars of the tree trunks, looking up in the sky to see if somewhere between those tall trunks there was anything moving among the pine needles. Then Berto or Tortima or Sandro, who was the most skillful of all, would stretch the elastic of his slingshot and aim a sharp stone in the direction they thought they had seen a movement. Sometimes a sparrow with a broken wing would come hurtling down, and go fluttering lamely along with pitiful little chirps till one of the boys seized it and twisted its neck between his fingers. But more often the chase was fruitless, and the boys would go wandering on deeper and deeper into the forest, their heads thrown back and their eyes fixed on some point far above them; going even farther and farther till at last the undergrowth began and a tangle of thorny bushes took the place of bare, soft soil covered with dry husks. And with the undergrowth began their hunt for fungi. It had been raining for a day or two and the leaves of the undergrowth were still glistening with wet, and the ground was damp and covered with fresh green shoots. In the thick of the bushes . . . there were the yellow fungi, glittering with moisture; sometimes magnificent single ones, sometimes families of little ones. The boys put their fingers through the brambles and picked them delicately, holding the head between two fingers and taking care to bring the stalk away too, with earth and moss still clinging to it. Then they threaded them on long, pointed sprigs of broom. Wandering thus from patch to patch of undergrowth, they would collect several kilos for Tortima's dinner, for he, being the strongest, confiscated their finds. That day their harvest had been a rich one, for after wandering about a good deal they had found some virgin undergrowth where the fungi were growing closely packed together in their bed of moss. It was getting late before they had even half-explored this undergrowth; so they began to tramp slowly homeward, with several long spits laden with fungi and two or three birds.

They generally followed a path which led straight down to the shore; but this evening they were led farther in pursuit of a teasing sparrow which kept fluttering along among the boughs and continually gave the illusion of being just within reach, so that they ended by walking the whole length of the forest, which to the east came to an end just behind the town. It was dusk as they emerged from the last pine trees on to the piazza of a remote suburb, with rubbish heaps and thistles and broom scattered about and a few ill-defined paths winding over it. Stunted oleanders grew at intervals around the edge; there were no pavements, and the dusty gardens of the few little villas which bordered it alternated with waste ground enclosed by bits of fencing. These little villas were placed at intervals all round the piazza and the wide expanse of sky over the great square added to the impression of loneliness and squalor.

The boys cut diagonally across the piazza, walking two and two like a religious order. At the end of the procession came Tortima and Agostino. Agostino was carrying two long spits of fungi and Tortima held a couple of sparrows in his great hands, their bloody heads dangling.

When they had reached the far end of the piazza Tortima nudged Agostino with his elbow and, pointing to one of the little villas, said cheerfully: "Do you see that? Do you know what that is?"

Agostino looked. The villa was very like all the others; a little bigger perhaps, with three stories and a sloping slate roof. Its façade was gloomy and smoke-grimed, with white shutters tightly closed; while the dense trees in the garden almost hid it from view. The garden did not look very big; the wall around it was covered with ivy, and through the gate one could see a short path with bushes on either side, and a double-paneled door under an old-fashioned porch. "There's no one there," said Agostino, stopping.

"No one, eh?" laughed the other; and he explained to Agostino in a few words who it was lived there. Agostino had several times heard the boys talking about houses where women lived alone, and how they shut themselves in all day, and at night were ready to welcome anyone who came, in return for money; but he had never seen one of these houses before. Tortima's words roused in him to the full the sense of strangeness and bewilderment which he had felt when first he heard them discussing it. And now as then he could hardly believe that there really existed a community so singular in its generosity as to dispense impartially to all that love which seemed to him so far away and so hard to come by; so he now looked with incredulous eyes on the little villa, as if he hoped to read on its walls some trace of the incredible life that went on inside it.

Compared with his imaginary picture of rooms on each of which a naked woman shed her radiance, the house looked singularly old and grimy. "Oh yes," he said, with pretended indifference, but his heart had already begun to beat faster.

"Yes," said Tortima, "it's the most expensive in the town." And he added a number of details about the place and the number of women, the people who went there and the time you were allowed to stay. This information was almost displeasing to Agostino, substituting as it did sordid details for the confused, barbaric image he had formed when he first heard tell of these forbidden places. But assuming a tone of idle curiosity he put a great many questions to his companion. For, after the first moment of surprise and disappointment, an idea had suddenly sprung up in his mind and ' laid fast hold of him. Tortima, who seemed to be well informed, gave him all the information he needed. Deep in conversation they crossed the piazza and joined the others on the esplanade. It was now almost dark and the party broke up. Agostino gave his fungi to Tortima and started home.

The idea which had come to him was clear and simple enough, however complicated and obscure its origin. He had made up his mind to go to that villa this very night and sleep with one of the women. This was not just a vague desire, it was an absolutely firm, almost desperate resolution. He felt that this was the only way he could escape from the obsession that had caused him such intense suffering all that summer. If he could only possess one of those women, he said to himself, it would forever prove the boys' calumny to have been ridiculous, and at the same time sever the thin thread of perverted and troubled sensuality which still bound him to his mother. Though he did not confess it to himself, his most urgent aim was to feel himself forever independent of his mother's love. A simple but significant fact had convinced him of this necessity, only that very day.

Up to now he and his mother had slept in separate rooms; but that night a friend of his mother's was arriving to spend a week with them. As the house was small it had been arranged that their guest should have Agostino's room, while a cot was to be made up for him in his mother's room. That very morning he had been disgusted to see the cot set up beside his mother's, which was still unmade and covered with bedclothes. His clothing and books and washing things had been carried in with the cot.

The fact of sleeping together only made Agostino hate still more that promiscuity with his mother which was already so hateful to him. He thought this new and still closer intimacy must suddenly reveal to him, without hope of escape, all that up to now he had only dimly suspected. Quickly, quickly he must find an antidote, and set up between his mother and himself the image of another woman to whom he could turn his thoughts if not his eyes. And the image which was to screen him from his mother's nakedness, and which would restore her dignity by removing her femininity . . . one of those women in the villa on the piazza was to supply that image.

How he was to get himself received in that house and how he would choose the woman and go off with her were matters to which Agostino did not give a thought—indeed, even if he had wanted to, he would never have been able to picture it. In spite of Tortima's information, the house and its inmates and everything belonging to it were surrounded by a dense atmosphere of improbability, as if one were not dealing with reality but with the most daring hypothesis which might at the last moment prove fallacious. The success of his undertaking depended on a logical calculation; if there was a house, then there were women too, and if there were women there was the possibility of meeting one of them. But it was not quite clear to him that the house and the women really were there; and this was not so much because he doubted Tortima's word as because he was totally lacking in terms of comparison. Nothing he had ever done or seen bore the faintest resemblance to what he was about to undertake. Like a poor savage who has heard about the palaces of Europe, and can only picture them as a slightly larger version of his own thatched hut, so he, in trying to picture those women and their caresses, could only think, with slight variations, of his mother; the love making could only be conjecture and vague desire.

But, as so often happens, his very inexperience led him to busy himself with practical aspects of the question, as if once these were settled he could also solve its complex unreality. He was particularly worried by the question of money. Tortima had explained to him in great detail exactly how much he would have to pay and to whom; and yet he could not quite grasp it. What was the relation between money, which is generally used for acquiring quite definite objects with recognizable qualities, and a woman's caresses, a woman's naked flesh? Was there really a price, and was that price really fixed, and not different in each particular case? The idea of giving money in exchange for that shameful and forbidden pleasure seemed to him cruel and strange, an insult which the giver might find pleasant but which must be painful for the one who received it. Was it really true that he would have to pay the money directly to the woman, and in her very presence? He somehow felt he ought to hide it and leave her with the illusion of a disinterested relationship. And then, wasn't the sum Tortima had mentioned too small? No money would be enough, he thought, to pay for such an experience . . . the end of one period of his life and the beginning of another.

Faced with these doubts he decided to keep strictly to what Tortima had told him, even if it turned out to be false, for he had nothing else on which to base his plan of action. He had found out from his friend how much it cost to visit the villa, and the figure did not seem higher than the amount he had been saving for a long time in his terra-cotta money box. With the small coins and paper money it contained he must surely be able to get the amount together, and it might even prove to be more. His plan was to take the money out of the money box, then wait till his mother had gone to the station to meet her friend, when he would go out in his turn, fetch Tortima and set off with him to the villa. He must have enough money for Tortima too, for he knew him to be poor and certainly not in the least disposed to do him a favor unless he was going to get something out of it himself.

This was his plan, and though it still seemed to him desperately remote and improbable he resolved to prepare for it with the same care and certainty as if it had only been an outing in a boat or some expedition into the pine woods.

Eager and excited, freed for the first time from the poison of remorse and impotence, he almost ran all the way home from the distant piazza. The front door was locked, but the French windows of the drawing room stood open, and through them came the sound of music. His mother was at the piano. He went in; the two subdued lights over the piano lit up her face while the rest of the room was in darkness. His mother was sitting on the piano stool, and beside her, on another, sat the young man of the raft. It was the first time that Agostino had seen him in their house, and a sudden presentiment took his breath away. His mother seemed to divine his presence, for she turned her head with a calm gesture of unconscious coquetry, a coquetry of which Agostino felt the young man to be the object rather than himself. She at once stopped playing when she saw him, and called him to her. "Agostino, what do you mean by coming in at this hour? Come here."

He went slowly up to the piano, full of revolt and embarrassment. His mother drew him to her and put her arm around him. He noticed that his mother's eyes were extraordinarily bright and young and sparkling. Laughter seemed to be on the brink of bubbling up through her lips, making her teeth glitter. She quite frightened him by the impetuosity, almost violence, with which she drew him to her, as if she were trembling with joy. He was sure that these manifestations had nothing to do with him personally. And they reminded him strangely of his own excitement of a few minutes before, as he ran through the streets in his eagerness to fetch his savings and go with Tortima to the villa and possess a woman.

"Where have you been?" his mother went on, in a voice which was at once tender, cruel and gay. "Where have you been all this time, you naughty boy?" Agostino made no reply; he did not feel his mother really expected one. That was just how she sometimes spoke to the cat. The young man was leaning forward, clasping his knees with both hands, his cigarette between two fingers, and gazing at his mother with eyes as sparkling and smiling as her own. "Where have you been?" repeated his mother. "How naughty of you to play truant like that." She rumpled up his hair on his forehead and then smoothed it again with her warm, slender hand, with a tender but irresistible violent caress. "Isn't he a handsome boy?" she said proudly, turning to the young man.

"As handsome as his mother," the young man replied. She smiled pathetically at this simple compliment. Full of shame and irritation, Agostino made an effort to free himself from her embrace. "Go and wash yourself," said his mother, "and make haste, because we are soon going in to supper." Agostino bowed slightly to the young man and left the room. Behind him, he immediately heard the music taken up again at the very point where he had interrupted it.

But once in the passage he stood still and listened to the sounds his mother's fingers were drawing from the keys. The passage was dark, and at the end of it he could see through the open door into the brightly lit kitchen, where the cook, dressed in white, was bustling about between the table and the kitchen range. His mother went on playing, and the music sounded to Agostino gay, tumultuous, sparkling, exactly like the expression in her eyes while she held him to her side. Perhaps that really was the character of the music, or perhaps his mother read into it some of her own fire and sparkle and vivacity. The whole house resounded to the music, and Agostino found himself thinking that out in the road lots of people must be stopping to listen, wondering at the scandalous wantonness which seemed to pour from every note.

Then, all at once, in the middle of a chord, the sounds stopped, and Agostino was convinced—he could not have told how—that the passion which had found expression in the music had suddenly found another outlet. He took two steps forward, and stood still on the threshold of the drawing room. What he saw did not much surprise him. The young man was standing up, and kissing his mother on the lips. She was bending backward over the low stool, which was too small to hold her body; one hand was still on the keyboard and the other was round the young man's neck. Even in the dim light he could see how her body was arched as it fell backward, with her chest thrust forward, one leg folded behind her, and the other stretched out toward the pedal. In contrast to her attitude of passionate surrender, the young man preserved his usual easy and graceful carriage. As he stood, he held one arm round the woman's neck, but apparently more from fear lest she might fall over than from any deep emotion. His other arm hung at his side and he still had a cigarette between his fingers. His white-trousered legs, planted far apart, expressed deliberation and complete mastery of the situation.

The kiss lasted a long time and it seemed to Agostino that whenever the young man wanted to interrupt it his mother clung to his lips more insatiably than ever. He really could not help feeling that she was hungry . . . famished for that kiss, like someone who has been starved too long. Then, at a casual movement of her hand two or three solemn, sweet notes sounded in the room. Suddenly they sprang apart. Agostino took a step forward and said: "Mamma." The young man wheeled about, and standing with his legs apart and his hands in his pockets, pretended to look out the window.

"Agostino!" said his mother.

Agostino went to her. She was breathing so violently that he could distinctly see her breasts rising and falling through her silk dress. Her eyes were brighter than ever, her mouth was half-open, her hair in disorder; and one soft, pointed lock, like a live snake, hung against her cheek.

"What is it, Agostino?" she repeated, in a low, broken voice, doing her best to arrange her hair. Agostino felt a sudden oppression of pity mingled with distaste. He would have liked to cry out to her: "Calm yourself, don't pant like that . . . don't speak to me in that voice." But instead, he put on a childish voice and said, with exaggerated eagerness: "Mamma, can I break open my money box? I want to buy a book."

"Yes, dear," she answered, putting out a hand to stroke his brow. At the touch of her hand Agostino could not help starting back. His movement was so slight as to be almost imperceptible, but to him it seemed so violent that he felt every one must notice it. "Very well then, I'll break it," he said. And he left the room quickly, without waiting for a reply. The sand on the stairs made a gritty sound as he ran up to his room. The idea of the money box had really only been a pretext; the fact was he didn't know what to say when he saw his mother looking like that. It was dark in his room; the money box was on a table at the far end. Through the open window a street lamp lit up its pink belly and great black smiling mouth. He turned on the light, picked up the money box and flung it on the ground with an almost hysterical violence. It broke at once and from the wide opening poured a quantity of money of every description. There were several notes mixed with the coins. He went down on hands and knees and frantically counted the money. His fingers were trembling and, while he counted, the image of those two down in the drawing room kept getting mixed up with the money that was lying scattered over the floor—his mother, hanging backwards over the piano stool, and the young man bending over her. But when he had finished counting he discovered that the money did not amount to the sum he needed.

What was he to do? It flashed through his mind that he might take it from his mother, for he knew where she kept it, and nothing would have been easier; but this idea revolted him and he decided simply to ask her for it. But what excuse could he make? He suddenly thought of one, but at that moment he heard the gong sounding for supper. He hastily hid his treasure in a drawer and went downstairs.

His mother was already at table. The window was wide open and great velvety moths flew in from the courtyard and beat their wings against the white lampshade. The young man had gone and his mother had again assumed her usual dignified serenity. Agostino, as he looked at her, wondered why her mouth bore no trace of the kisses which had been pressed on it a few minutes before, just as he had wondered that first time, when she went out on the raft with the young man. He could not have defined what feelings this thought awoke in him. A sense of pity for his mother, to whom that kiss seemed to be so disturbing and so precious; and at the same time a strong feeling of repulsion, not so much for what he had seen as for the memory which remained with him. He would have liked to expel that memory, to forget it altogether. How was it possible that such troublous and changing impressions could enter through one's eyes? He foresaw that the sight would be forever stamped on his memory.

When they had finished, his mother rose from the table and went upstairs. Agostino thought he would never find such an opportune moment to ask for the money. He followed her up and went into her room with her. His mother sat down at the dressing-table and silently studied her face in the glass.

"Mamma," said Agostino.

"What is it?" she asked absentmindedly.

"I want twenty lire."

"What for?"

"To buy a book."

"But didn't you say you were going to break open your money box?" asked his mother, gently passing the powder puff over her face.

Agostino purposely made a childish excuse.

"Yes, but if I break it I shan't have any money left. I want to buy a book without opening my money box."

His mother laughed fondly. "What a baby you are." She studied herself a moment more in the glass, then she said: "You'll find my purse in the bag on my bed. Take out twenty lire, and put the purse back again." Agostino went to the bed, opened the bag, took out the purse and took twenty lire from it. Then clutching the two notes in his hand he flung himself on the cot beside his mother's. She had finished her make-up and came over to him. "What are you going to do now?" "I'm going to read this book," he said, taking a book of adventures at random from the bed table, and opening it at an illustration.

"Very well, but remember before you go to sleep to put out the light." His mother was still moving about the room, doing one thing and another. Agostino lay watching her, with his head pillowed on his arm. He obscurely felt that she had never been so beautiful as on that evening. Her dress of glossy white silk showed off brilliantly her brown coloring and the rich rose of her complexion. By an unconscious reflowering of her former character she seemed to have recovered all the sweet, majestic serenity of bearing she used to have; but with an indefinable breath of happiness. She was tall, but Agostino had never seen her look so imposing before. Her presence seemed to fill the room. White in the shadow of the room, she moved majestically about, with head erect on her beautiful neck, her black eyes calm and concentrated under her smooth brow. Then she put out all the lights except the bed table, and bent down to kiss her son. Agostino drank in again the perfume he knew so well, and as he touched her neck with his lips he could not help wondering if those women . . . out there in the villa . . . would be as beautiful and smell as sweet.

Left alone, Agostino waited about ten minutes to give his mother time to have gone. Then he got up from the cot, put out the light, and tiptoed into the next room. He felt about in the dark for the table by the window, opened the drawer and filled his pockets with coins and notes. He felt with his hand in every corner of the drawer to see if it was really empty, and left the room.

When he was on the road he began to run. Tortima lived at the other end of the town, in the caulkers' and sailors' quarter, and though the town was small he had a long way to go. He chose the dark alleys bordering on the pine woods, and walking fast and occasionally running, he went straight ahead until he saw, appearing between the houses, the mast of the sailboats in the dry dock. Tortima's house was just above the dock, beyond the movable iron bridge which spanned the canal leading to the harbor. By day this was a forgotten, dilapidated spot with tumble-down warehouses and ships bordering its wide, deserted, sun-baked quays, pervaded by the smell of fish and tar, with green, oily water, motionless cranes and barges laden with shingle. But now the night made it like every other part of the town, and only a ship whose bulging sides and masts overhung the footpath, revealed the presence of the harbor water lying deep in between the houses. Agostino crossed the bridge and headed toward a row of houses on the opposite side of the canal. Here and there a street lamp irregularly lit the walls of these little houses. Agostino stopped in front of an open lighted window, from which came the sounds of voices and clatter of plates, as if they were having a meal. Putting his fingers to his mouth he gave one loud and two soft whistles, which was the signal agreed upon between the boys of the gang. Almost at once someone appeared at the window. "It's me, it's Pisa," said Agostino, in a low, timid voice. "I'm coming," answered Tortima. He came down, still eating his last mouthful, red in the face from the wine he had been drinking. "I've come to go to that villa," said Agostino. "I've got money here . . . enough for both of us." Tortima swallowed hard and looked at him. "That villa the other side of the piazza," Agostino repeated. "Where the women are."

"Ah," said Tortima, understanding at last. "You've been thinking it over. Bravo, Pisa. I'll be with you in a moment." He ran off and Agostino walked up and down, waiting for him, his eyes fixed on Tortima's window. He was kept waiting a long time, but at last Tortima reappeared. Agostino scarcely recognized him. He had always seen him as a big boy with trousers tucked up, or half-naked on the beach and in the sea. Now he saw before him a young working man in dark holiday clothes: long trousers, waistcoat, collar and tie. He looked older too, because of the brilliantine with which he had plastered down his usually unruly hair; and his spruce, ordinary clothes brought out for the first time something ridiculous and vulgar in his appearance.

"Shall we go now?" said Tortima as he joined him.

"But is it time yet?" asked Agostino, hurrying along beside him as they crossed the bridge.

"It's always time there," said Tortima with a laugh.

They took a different road than the one Agostino had come by. The piazza was not far away, only about two turnings further on. "But have you been there before?" asked Agostino again.

"Not to that one."

Tortima did not seem to be in any hurry and kept his usual pace. "They'll hardly have finished supper and there'll be no one there," he explained. "It's a good moment."

"Why?" asked Agostino.

"Why, don't you see, we can choose the one we like best."

"But how many are there?"

"Oh, about four or five."

Agostino longed to ask if they were pretty, but refrained. "What do we have to do?" he asked. Tortima had already told him, but the sense of unreality was so strong in him that he felt the need of hearing it reaffirmed.

"What does one do?" said Tortima. "Nothing simpler. You go in . . . they come and show themselves . . . you say: 'Good evening, ladies,' you pretend to talk for a bit, so as to give yourself the time to look them well over . . . then you choose one. It's your first time, eh?"

"Well," began Agostino rather shamefacedly. "Go along!" said Tortima brutally. "You're not going to tell me it isn't the first time. Tell that to the others, if you like, but not to me. But don't be afraid. She does it all for you. Leave it to her."

Agostino said nothing. The image evoked by Tortima of the woman initiating him into love pleased him . . . it had something maternal about it. But in spite of these facts he still remained incredulous. "But—but do you think they'll want *me*?" he asked, standing still suddenly and looking down at his bare legs.

The question seemed to embarrass Tortima for a moment. "Let's go on," he said, with feigned self-assurance. "Once there, we'll manage to get you in."

They came through a narrow lane to the piazza. The whole of it was in darkness, except for one corner where a street lamp shone peacefully down on a stretch of uneven sandy earth. In the sky above the piazza the crescent moon hung red and smoky, cut in two by a thin filament of mist. Where the darkness was thickest Agostino recognized the villa by its white shutters. They were closed, and no ray of light showed through them. Tortima, without hesitation, crossed over to the villa. But in the middle of the piazza, under the crescent moon, he said to Agostino: "Give me the money; I'd better keep it."

"But I . . ." began Agostino, who did not quite trust Tortima. "Are you going to give it me or not?" persisted Tortima harshly. Agostino was ashamed of all that small change, but he obeyed and emptied his pockets into Tortima's hands. "Now keep your mouth shut, and come along with me," said his companion.

As they came near to the villa, the darkness grew less dense, and they could see the two gateposts, the garden path and the front door under the porch. The gate was not locked, and Tortima pushed it open and entered the garden. The front door was ajar. Tortima climbed the steps and went in, motioning to Agostino not to make a sound. Agostino, looking curiously about him, saw a quite empty hall, at the end of which was a double door, with brightly lit panes of red and blue glass. Their entrance was the signal for a ringing of bells, and almost immediately the massive shadow of someone seated behind the glass door rose against the glass, and a woman appeared in the doorway. She was a kind of servant, middle-aged and very stout, with a capacious bosom, dressed in black with a white apron tied round her waist. She came forward, sticking out her stomach, and with her arms hanging down. She had a swollen face and sulky eyes which looked out suspiciously from under a mass of hair.

"Here we are," said Tortima. Agostino saw from his voice and manner that even he, who was usually so bold, felt intimidated.

The woman scrutinized them hostilely for a moment; then she made a sign, as if inviting Tortima to pass inside. Tortima smiled with renewed assurance, and hastened toward the glass door. Agostino made as if to follow him. "Not you," said the woman, putting her hand on his shoulder.

"What!" cried Agostino, at once losing all his fear. "Why him and not me?"

"You've really neither of you any business to be here," said the woman firmly; "but he will just pass, you won't."

"You're too little, Pisa," said Tortima mockingly. And he pushed the door open and disappeared. His stunted shadow stood out for a moment against the panes of glass; then it vanished in the brilliant light.

"But what about me?" insisted Agostino, exasperated by Tortima's treachery.

"You get off, boy, go away home," said the woman. She went to the front door, opened it wide, and found herself face to face with two men who were just coming in. "Good evening . . . good evening," said the first, who had a red, jolly face. "We're agreed, eh?" he added, turning to his companion, a pale, thin young man. "If Pina's free, I'm to have her . . . and no nonsense about it."

"Agreed," said the other.

"What's this little fellow doing here?" the jovial man asked the woman, pointing to Agostino.

"He wanted to come in," said the woman. A flattering smile framed itself on her lips.

"So you wanted to go in, did you?" cried the man, turning to Agostino. "At your age, home's the place at this hour. Home with you," he cried again, waving his arms.

"That's what I told him," the woman said.

"Suppose we let him come in?" remarked the young man. "At his age I was making love to the maid."

"Well, I'm blest! Get away home . . . home . . . *home*," shouted the other, scandalized. Followed by the fair man he entered the folding door, which banged-to behind him. Agostino, hardly knowing how he got there, found himself outside in the garden.

How badly it had all turned out; he had been betrayed by Tortima, who had taken his money, and he himself had been thrown out. Not knowing what to do, he went up the garden path, looking back all the time at the half-open door, the porch, the façade with its white shutters closed. He felt a burning sense of disappointment, especially on account of those two men who had treated him like a child. The laughter of the jovial man, the cold, experimental benevolence of his companion, seemed to him no less humiliating than the dull hostility of the woman. Still walking backward, and looking round at the trees and shrubs in the garden, he made his way to the gate. Then he noticed that the left side of the villa was illuminated by a strong light coming from an open window on the ground floor. It occurred to him that he might at least have a glimpse of the inside of the villa through that window; and making as little noise as possible he went towards the light.

It was a window open wide on the ground floor. The windowsill was not high; very quietly, and keeping to the corner where there was less chance of his being seen, he went up to the window and looked in.

The room was small and brilliantly lighted. The walls were papered with a handsome design of large green and black flowers. Facing the window a red curtain, hanging on wooden rings from a brass rod, seemed to conceal a door. There was no furniture visible, but someone was sitting in a corner by the window for he could see crossed legs with yellow shoes stretched out into the room. Agostino thought they must belong to someone lying in an armchair. Disappointed at not seeing more, he was going to leave his post when the curtain was raised and a woman appeared.

She had on a full gown of pale blue chiffon which reminded Agostino of his mother's nightgown. It was transparent and reached to her feet; looking at her long, pale limbs through that veil was almost like seeing them float indolently in clear sea water. By a vagary of design the neck of her gown was cut in an oval reaching almost to her waist; and from it her firm, full breasts seemed to be struggling to escape, so closely were they pressed together by the dress, which was gathered round them into the neck with many fine pleats. Her wavy brown hair hung loosely on her shoulders; she had a large flat, pale face, at once childish and vicious, and there was a whimsical expression in her tired eyes and mouth, with its full, painted lips. She came through the curtain with her hands behind her back and her bosom thrust forward, saying nothing and standing quietly, in an expectant attitude. She looked at the corner where the man with the crossed legs was lounging; then, silently as she had come, she turned and disappeared, leaving the curtain wide open. At the same time the man's legs vanished from the sight of Agostino. He heard someone get up and withdrew from the window in alarm.

He returned to the path, pushed the garden gate open, and came out on the piazza. He felt a keen sense of disappointment at the failure of his attempt, and at the same time a feeling almost of terror at what awaited him in days to come. Nothing had happened, he had not possessed any woman. Tortima had gone off with all his money, and tomorrow the same old jokes would begin again and the torment of his relations with his mother. Years and years of emptiness and frustration lay between him and that act of liberation. Meanwhile he had to go on living just as before, and his whole soul rebelled at the bitter thought that what he had hoped for had become a definite impossibility. When he got home, he went in without making any noise; he saw the visitor's luggage in the hall and heard voices in the sitting room. He went upstairs and flung himself on the cot in his mother's room. He tore off his clothes in the dark, and throwing them on the floor got into bed naked between the sheets. . . .

After a little he became drowsy and at last fell asleep. Suddenly he woke with a start. The lamp was lit and shone on his mother's back. She was in her nightgown and with one knee on the bed was just going to get in. "Mamma," he said suddenly, in a loud, almost violent voice.

His mother came over to him. "What is it?" she asked. "What is it, darling?" Her nightgown was transparent, like the woman's at the villa; the lines and vague shadows of her body were visible, like those of that other body. "I want to go away tomorrow," said Agostino, in the same loud, exasperated voice, trying to look not at his mother's body but at her face.

His mother sat down on the bed and looked at him in surprise. "But why? . . . What is the matter? Aren't you happy here?"

"I want to go away tomorrow," he repeated.

"Let us see," said his mother, passing her hand gently over his forehead, as if she were afraid he was feverish. "What is it? Aren't you well? Why do you want to go away?"

His mother's nightgown reminded him so much of the dress of that woman at the villa: the same transparency, the same pale, indolent, acquiescent flesh; only the nightgown was creased, which made this picture even more intimate and secret. And so, thought Agostino, not only did the image of that woman not interpose itself as a screen between him and his mother, as he had hoped, but it actually seemed to confirm the latter's femininity. "Why do you want to go away?" she asked again. "Don't you like being with me?"

"You always treat me like a child," said Agostino abruptly, without knowing why.

His mother laughed and stroked his cheek. "Very well, from now on I'll treat you like a man. . . . Will that be all right? But you must go to sleep now, it's very late." She stooped and kissed him. Then she put out the light and Agostino heard her get into bed.

"Like a man," he couldn't help thinking before he fell asleep. But he wasn't a man. What a long, unhappy time would have to pass before he could become one.

[Translated by Beryl de Zoete]

# NOW THAT YOU'VE READ MORAVIA'S AGOSTINO:

Perhaps at no other time in history have the agonies and anxieties of adolescence been so thoroughly explored as in our own. Numerous novelists have sought to penetrate in retrospect this separate, walled off world, but few of them have succeeded in creating a masterpiece like *Agostino*. A quiet book but not a gentle one, *Agostino* has become a little primer of adolescent hell, a hell recognized, endured, and, in utmost anguish and bewilderment of spirit, accepted by a sensitive boy of thirteen years.

The author, an Italian who calls himself Moravia, is among the most exciting writers in Europe today. Virtually unknown outside of Italy until 1949, he has since become popular abroad as well as at home (in the United States, for example, more than three million copies of his books have been sold in paper-bound editions alone, and three of his novels have made the best-seller lists). Despite his general popularity, however, Moravia can not be dismissed as merely a brutal realist of the boudoir. On the contrary, he is a substantial writer who deserves to be considered as the leader of the literary renaissance which bloomed in the rubble of post-Fascist Italy. Few novelists can equal his ability to interpret the mood which gripped his generation both before and after the second World War. As readily as he evokes the natural beauty of his native scene, he catches (and uses for contrast) the atmosphere of moral decay and despair which was poisoning his people. Moravia has been accused of dwelling to no purpose on the more squalid and sensational aspects of their lives, but the body of his work reveals that, like Thomas Mann in *Mario and the Magician,* Moravia recognized the sickness that was creeping into the Italian character and foresaw the loosening of the moral fibre of his people. For Mann the symptoms of this sickness were nationalism and negative will; for Moravia they were sexual amorality and resigned fatalism. His success as a writer is the outcome, not of exploitation of the lurid, but of a sensibility conjoined with honesty, a meticulous devotion to his craft, and a determination to make use of various personal adversities.

He was born Alberto Pincherle, in 1907, in Rome, to a prosperous, intellectual family. As did Conrad, he developed an early love of literature through the inspiration of his father, an architect who kept a library well-stocked with the classics, especially the works of Shakespeare and Molière. "I believe these books had a great influence upon my work," says Moravia. "They led me to regard men as individuals, possessing a destiny superior to their individual importance." The parents planned a diplomat's career for their son and had him educated by a succession of French, English, and German governesses. At the age of nine, he became gravely ill with tuberculosis of the leg bone. He was confined to bed for the next eight years, the last two of which he spent in a sanatorium at Cortina d'Ampezzo, in the Alps. There he studied very little, but to avoid boredom, read as many as seven books a week in French, English, and Italian. In the eighth year, the illness turned critical, and he was forced to take daily sunbaths on a terrace from dawn to dusk. The sanatorium experience was perhaps the most formative of his life. During the long solitary days of convalescence away from his family he learned the meaning of loneliness and developed the ambition to write. To relieve his loneliness, he pursued his ambition, and at the age of seventeen was embarked upon his first novel.

In 1925, he was able to leave the sanatorium, but because he needed exposure to a warm sun and a dry climate, his parents took him to live in

Bressanone, also in the Alps. There he continued work on his novel and also wrote several short stories in French, which by the late twenties began to appear in a review called 900. When his novel, *Gli Indifferenti*, was published in 1929, it created a sensation and brought Moravia an Italian reputation at the age of twenty-two (as *The Indifferent Ones*, in 1932, it was barely noticed in America, but a better translation in 1953, called *The Time of Indifference*, revealed its merits to critic and crowd alike). This early novel shows Moravia's preoccupation with the theme that was to recur in his work: the brutality and indifference with which the worldly deprive the young of their innocence and ideals.

In the following year, Moravia took up this theme again in "A Sick Boy's Winter," a fine short story similar to *Agostino* in tone and development. A boy in his early teens, suffering from tuberculosis of the leg bone in an Alpine sanatorium, is initiated into the ways of men by a cruel, crude room-mate whose vulgarity he instinctively despises but whose worldliness he helplessly envies. He tries to win his older friend's esteem by seducing a young female patient. The affair ends in disappointment and embarrassment, and gains him only the scorn of his room-mate. As the story concludes, the boy, sunbathing upon a terrace, reflects bitterly that "He was alone, and his recovery seemed a long, long way off." Other stories of this nature, sunny on the surface but dark and pessimistic beneath, and another novel, *Mistaken Ambitions* (translated in 1937), established Moravia as one of Italy's most promising writers—and also marked him as a man who would bear watching by Fascist authorities, suspicious of anyone who seemed critical of social or economic conditions.

About this period, Moravia was forced to turn increasingly towards writing of a journalistic nature in order to live. In the service of *Corriere della Sera*, a Milan paper, he travelled extensively and lived abroad in Paris, London, Athens, and Mexico, reporting his experiences and observations in a tone acceptable to educated readers. In 1935, he was in New York. When Americans asked him about his future as a writer in Fascist Italy, he explained that he intended to concentrate on his craft and to avoid politics. In 1940, *La Mascherata* (*The Fancy Dress Party*, 1950, in translation), a satire on an easily-recognizable dictator who is infatuated with an amorous widow, suggests how difficult that resolve was to keep. The manuscript had to be submitted, as required by law, to the Fascist Ministry of Popular Culture, where ultimately it was read by Mussolini himself. To Moravia's surprise, Mussolini permitted the book to be published; but shortly afterwards, he ordered it withdrawn from publication, no doubt alarmed by the scandal it caused even in circles that had no passion for clean living. The novel lacks real bite, but makes clear that Moravia, while reluctant to protest as openly as Thomas Mann was doing from exile, worked as he could against Fascist rule.

However, he found himself increasingly at odds with the government, until finally the sale of his books was banned and he was forced to sign magazine articles with a pseudonym. In 1941, he married Elsa Morante, a young writer, and retired to the island of Capri, where he began work on *Agostino*. Writing during the war so inured him to distraction that he can now, he says, "write in a hotel lobby with someone playing a bull-fiddle in the next chair." When the Fascist regime fell in 1943 and the Germans occupied Italy, Moravia fled with his wife into the mountains in order to escape impending arrest. Several times the couple tried to cross into Allied territory, but the heavy fighting prevented them. Until the area was liberated nine months later, they hid and lived in a pigsty. Moravia managed to save the manuscript of his work in progress but was unable to complete it because he lacked even a supply of ink.

After the liberation, he returned to Rome and finished *Agostino*. Published in 1944 under its present title, it won a national prize for literature three years later. However, the English translation of this volume was held back by his American publisher, who wished to re-introduce him to the American public with *The Woman of Rome*, a smashing success in Italy as *La Romana*. This harsh study of the moral disintegration of a beautiful girl who must learn to live without love in the jungle of sex excited the American public in 1949, and gave Moravia a reputation as Italy's liveliest novelist. But in 1951, *Agostino*, published as part of *Two Adolescents*, eclipsed this reputation to his greater fame.

Since then, his work in translation has appeared regularly in America. On the heels of *Conjugal Love* (1951) came *The Conformist* (1952), which many a critic considers, as does Moravia himself, his most accomplished work. In his typically deliberate manner, Moravia traces the moral and political development of a naïvely cruel youth who recognizes, when it is too late, that his false values and fascism were bred by conformity to bourgeois standards. For the excellence of his work, in 1952 he was made a Chevalier de la Légion d'Honneur.

That same year Moravia became a controversial figure as well as an honored one. Reprints of his books were banned on moral grounds in Chicago. He was invited to the United States by the Cultural Attaché in Rome, and three months later when ready to leave, was refused a visa by the State Department. Thirteen prominent American writers protested in an open letter against this action, pointing out that the Soviet Union had refused him a visa when *Corriere della Sera* wanted to send him there for a series of articles. Eventually reason prevailed, and in 1955, Moravia came to this country on State Department invitation. His fellow writers and critics (he does film reviews for the Italian journal, *L'Europeo*) found him to be a handsome man with greying temples, strong, brooding features, and a slight limp that neither restricted his constant movement nor prevented him from taking keen delight in the simple pleasures of life.

Since *The Conformist*, Moravia has written four collections of stories, a theatrical adaptation of *The Fancy Dress Party*, a perceptive report on life in Red China, and three novels. *A Ghost at Noon* (1954) is about the Roman film world which Moravia had observed while writing scripts for his own stories and novels. It is revealed as a world of base interests which undermine the novel's protagonist, who because of his spiritual nobility and aspirations, is destined, like Agostino, to failure in every concrete experience of practical life. *Two Women* (1957) is a profound and highly compassionate expression of a tragic period in the history of a people, much of it written in Ciociaria during the Allied invasion of Italy. Several critics hailed the novel as the great rebirth of the writer.

*The Empty Canvas* systematically and consciously deals with "automatism," a recurrent but minor theme of his previous work (c.f. Camus). The society of *The Empty Canvas* is founded on the idea of purchase and trade. In it even human energy is changed into something to be bought and sold and man himeslf is thus transformed into something which has no value except as a product.

His second collection of stories, *Roman Tales*, is interesting in terms of Moravia's development. His focus shifts from the weak-willed, acted upon, frustrated or indifferent middle-class intellectuals of his first collection called *Bitter Honeymoon* (1937) to members of the working class. The critic Sean O'Faolain has noted that Moravia appears to prefer the crude hams of these tales to his drooling bourgeois Hamlets, but to other readers, these occupants of subterranean Rome will seem hard and unfeeling in a life of trickery, deception, and dishonesty. Moved only by their appetites, they increasingly resemble automatons whose human vision is limited to the visible. His next collection, *New Roman Tales*, is a series of independent character sketches loosely linked by their common background of modern Rome and dreary working life. Authentic atmosphere is created by a few details and the characters have vitality, but the limitations of space (these sketches first appeared, like *Tales*, in two columns of *Corriere della Sera*) limit dramatic development.

Moravia's most recent collection of stories, *The Fetish*, returns to the bourgeois society of *Bitter Honeymoon*, but now we see his intellectuals trying to cope with the new dimensions of a neo-capitalist middle-class society.

These volumes leave no doubt that Moravia, if not a moralistic writer, is certainly a writer who is intensely interested in the moral problems of his time and their implications. Behind his grim view of life lies the suggestion of a possibility unrealized, a potential gone to waste. The tragedy of Moravia's characters develops out of the difference between their reach and their grasp. They have within them the capacity for aspiration, renunciation, and even selfless attachment, but often they lack the will or the way to overcome the corrupting influences around them. Moravia seems to be saying that until they can learn to assess their world and accept responsibility for the execution of their role in it, they can know no peace. His characters move in a Darwinian world, among forces which corrupt human nature and create the frustration and anguish that mark their lives.

*Agostino* is a characteristically lovely and repellent blend of sunshine and sensibility, cruelty and corruption. It is also a parable of the Fall, with an adolescent as Adam and with society as the serpent. Agostino lives in a garden of innocence, idolizing his beautiful mother, until he eats of the fruit of knowledge. With shattering suddenness, his sheltered little sphere is transformed into a melancholic world of anguish, aggression, and amorality, and his confused lyricism about his mother changes into painful awareness of her as a woman. From his experiences he emerges no longer a child but not yet a man, knowing for certain only that the road ahead will be dark and troubled. His mother? Her impulses are good, but they are swept away by the appetites of the flesh. His "friends"? They will continue to frequent the bordellos. Cheerfully insensitive, they can neither be hurt nor help those who are hurt. In the end, Agostino is alone, isolated in the adolescent agonies which will father his adult ills. *Agostino*, a fine example of Moravia's work, deserves to be called one of the minor masterpieces of our time.

Moravia's style, evolved under the Fascist prohibition against depicting poverty, immorality, and corruption, has a curious structure, combining a vagueness about the workaday life of his characters with a dispassionate, almost scientific exactitude about their intimate actions. Yet he explores the bourgeois milieu without turning its representatives into clinical cases and he handles sexual experience truthfully and tellingly without sacrificing discreetness or delicateness of tone.

## FOR FURTHER INFORMATION:

"The Art of Fiction," *Paris Review* (Summer 1954), 71-37 (an interview).

Thomas G. Bergin. "The Moravian Muse," *Virginia Quarterly Review*, XXIX (Spring 1953), 215-225.

Guiliano Dego. *Moravia*. Oliver and Boyd: Edinburgh and London, 1966.

Frances Keene. "Moravia, Moralist," *The Nation*, CLVI (May 23, 1953), 438-440.

P. M. Pasinetti. "The Incredible Italians," *Saturday Review* (March 29, 1952).

Charles Rolo. "Alberto Moravia," *The Atlantic* CXCV (February 1955), 69-74.